SONG FOR SOMEONE

*Popular Music History*
Series Editor: Alyn Shipton, Royal Academy of Music, London.

This series publishes books that extend the field of popular music studies, examine the lives and careers of key musicians, interrogate histories of genres, focus on previously neglected forms, or engage in the formative history of popular music styles.

## Published

*An Unholy Row:*
*Jazz in Britain and its Audience, 1945–1960*
  Dave Gelly

*Being Prez: The Life and Music of Lester Young*
  Dave Gelly

*Bill Russell and the New Orleans Jazz Revival*
  Ray Smith and Mike Pointon

*Chasin' the Bird:*
*The Life and Legacy of Charlie Parker*
  Brian Priestley

*Desperado: An Autobiography*
  Tomasz Stańko with Rafał Księżyk,
  translated by Halina Maria Boniszewska

*Eberhard Weber: A German Jazz Story*
  Eberhard Weber, translated by Heidi Kirk

*Formation: Building a Personal Canon, Part 1*
  Brad Mehldau

*Handful of Keys:*
*Conversations with Thirty Jazz Pianists*
  Alyn Shipton

*Hear My Train A Comin':*
*The Songs of Jimi Hendrix*
  Kevin Le Gendre

*Hidden Man: My Many Musical Lives*
  John Altman

*Ivor Cutler: A Life Outside the Sitting Room*
  Bruce Lindsay

*Jazz Me Blues:*
*The Autobiography of Chris Barber*
  Chris Barber with Alyn Shipton

*Jazz Visions: Lennie Tristano and His Legacy*
  Peter Ind

*Kansas City Jazz: A Little Evil Will Do You Good*
  Con Chapman

*Keith Jarrett: A Biography*
  Wolfgang Sandner, translated by Chris Jarrett

*Komeda: A Private Life in Jazz*
  Magdalena Grzebalkowska,
  translated by Halina Boniszewska

*Lee Morgan: His Life, Music and Culture*
  Tom Perchard

*Lionel Richie: Hello*
  Sharon Davis

*Long Agos and Worlds Apart:*
*The Definitive Small Faces Biography*
  Sean Egan

*Mosaics: The Life and Works of Graham Collier*
  Duncan Heining

*Mr P.C.: The Life and Music of Paul Chambers*
  Rob Palmer

*Out of the Long Dark: The Life of Ian Carr*
  Alyn Shipton

*Ray Brown: His Life and Music*
  Jay Sweet

*Rufus Wainwright*
  Katherine Williams

*Scouse Pop*
  Paul Skillen

*Soul Unsung:*
*Reflections on the Band in Black Popular Music*
  Kevin Le Gendre

*The Godfather of British Jazz:*
*The Life and Music of Stan Tracey*
  Clark Tracey

*The History of European Jazz:*
*The Music, Musicians and Audience in Context*
  Edited by Francesco Martinelli

*The Last Miles: The Music of Miles Davis,*
*1980–1991*
  George Cole

*The Long Shadow of the Little Giant*
*(second edition):*
*The Life, Work and Legacy of Tubby Hayes*
  Simon Spillett

*The Ultimate Guide to Great Reggae: The*
*Complete Story of Reggae Told through its*
*Greatest Songs, Famous and Forgotten*
  Michael Garnice

*This is Bop:*
*Jon Hendricks and the Art of Vocal Jazz*
  Peter Jones

*This is Hip: The Life of Mark Murphy*
  Peter Jones

*Trad Dads, Dirty Boppers and Free Fusioneers:*
*A History of British Jazz, 1960–1975*
  Duncan Heining

*Two Bold Singermen and the English Folk*
*Revival: The Lives, Song Traditions and Legacies*
*of Sam Larner and Harry Cox*
  Bruce Lindsay

*Vinyl Ventures:*
*My Fifty Years at Rounder Records*
  Bill Nowlin

# Song for Someone
## The Musical Life of Kenny Wheeler

Brian Shaw and Nick Smart

equinox

SHEFFIELD UK    BRISTOL CT

Published by Equinox Publishing Ltd.

UK: Office 415, The Workstation, 15 Paternoster Row, Sheffield, South Yorkshire S1 2BX
USA: ISD, 70 Enterprise Drive, Bristol, CT 06010
www.equinoxpub.com

First published 2025

**British Library Cataloguing-in-Publication Data**
A catalogue record for this book is available from the British Library.
ISBN-13   978 1 78179 219 3 (hardback)
          978 1 80050 607 7 (ePDF)
          978 1 80050 650 3 (ePub)

**Library of Congress Cataloging-in-Publication Data**
Names: Shaw, Brian, 1977- author. | Smart, Nick (Trumpet player) author.
Title: Song for someone : the musical life of Kenny Wheeler / Brian Shaw
    and Nick Smart ; foreword by Dave Holland.
Description: Sheffield, South Yorkshire ; Bristol, CT : Equinox Publishing
    Ltd, 2025. | Series: Popular music history | Includes bibliographical
    references and index. | Summary: "This book brings together over 130
    original interviews and new archival and biographical research on
    Wheeler's life and music, chronicling his journey from small town Canada
    to international acclaim. It is as much a perspective on the history and
    development of jazz in Britain and Europe as it is the extraordinary
    tale of this improbable pioneer"-- Provided by publisher.
Identifiers: LCCN 2024034074 (print) | LCCN 2024034075 (ebook) | ISBN
    9781781792193 (hardback) | ISBN 9781800506077 (pdf) | ISBN 9781800506503
    (epub)
Subjects: LCSH: Wheeler, Kenny. | Jazz musicians--Biography. | Trumpet
    players--Biography. | Composers--Biography.
Classification: LCC ML419.W466 S53 2025 (print) | LCC ML419.W466 (ebook)
    | DDC 788.9/2165092 [B]--dc23/eng/20240807
LC record available at https://lccn.loc.gov/2024034074
LC ebook record available at https://lccn.loc.gov/2024034075

Typeset by Witchwood Production House Ltd

This book is dedicated to the memory of
Doreen Wheeler (née Yeend) (1933–2022).
Without Doreen and the unendingly loving and
selfless support she gave her husband and family,
the world would never have known the musical
genius of Kenny Wheeler.

# Contents

*List of illustrations* .................................................................................... viii

*Acknowledgements* ...................................................................................... xi

*Foreword by Dave Holland* ........................................................................ xv

    Introduction ........................................................................................... 1

**1**   A Long Time Ago ................................................................................ 7

**2**   The Imminent Immigrant ................................................................ 35

**3**   Everybody's Song But My Own ....................................................... 56

**4**   Song for Someone ............................................................................ 100

**5**   Gnu High .......................................................................................... 162

**6**   Music for Large and Small Ensembles ........................................ 227

**7**   Angel Song ....................................................................................... 296

**8**   The Long Waiting ............................................................................ 355

*Epilogue. Present Past, Past Present: The Musical Legacy of Kenny Wheeler* ........... 414

*Sources* ......................................................................................................... 421

*Notes* ........................................................................................................... 429

*Index* ........................................................................................................... 497

# List of illustrations

Photo 1: Jack Reid, Kenny's maternal grandfather. ........... 9

Photo 2: Young Wilf Wheeler Sr. seated far right, holding his trombone, with Gilbert Watson's Orchestra. ........... 10

Photo 3: Wilf Wheeler Sr. with his children. Front, left to right: Wilf Jr., George, Wilf Sr., Mary; middle: Helen, Paul, Mabel; back: Kenny. ........... 11

Photo 4: Kenny's parents, Mabel and Wilf Wheeler Sr. ........... 15

Photo 5: The concert at the Collegiate: Left to right: Bill Jelley, Kenny, Boris Zenchuck, Paul Lindo. (Art Talbot is seated at the piano behind Lindo.) ........... 24

Photo 6: The Bruce Anthony band, Kenny third from right. ........... 27

Photo 7: The Wheeler family with their big prize. Left to right: Paul, Helen, George, Wilf Sr., Mabel Sr., unknown, Mary, Mabel Jr., unknown. ........... 32

Photo 8: Kenny and Doreen on their wedding day. ........... 41

Photo 9: Kenny and Doreen on their wedding day. ........... 41

Photo 10: Kenny with the Tommy Whittle Orchestra: Cafe Royal, Leicester Square, London, 1955. Left to right: Tommy Whittle, Eddie Taylor, Don Riddell, Kenny, Freddy Logan, Ronnie Baker, Keith Christie, and Joe Temperley. ........... 49

Photo 11: Kenny (left), with the Buddy Featherstonhaugh band. ........... 52

Photo 12: Kenny and siblings pictured with their parents, spouses, and children on his first return visit to Canada. Kenny is top row, second from left. Doreen, pregnant with Louann is middle row, second from left. Mark, front row alongside his cousins, third from left. ........... 53

Photo 13: Doreen with Mark, left, and young Louann, right. ........... 54

Photo 14: Kenny with the John Dankworth Big Band, c. 1959–60. ........... 57

Photo 15: Kenny with the Dankworth Orchestra, Marquee Club, Oxford Street, London, 1961. Left to right (back row): Alan Branscombe (p), Kenny Wheeler (t), Spike Heatley (b), Leon Calvert, Ron Simmonds (t), Ronnie Stephenson (d, hidden), Gus Galbraith (t); (front): Danny Moss, Art Ellefson (ts), Roy East (fl), John Dankworth (as), Eddie Harvey, Tony Russell (tb), Ron Snyder (tu). ........... 63

Photo 16: Kenny, Evan Parker, Dave Holland and Derek Bailey at the recording of *Karyōbin*. ........... 87

Photo 17: Kenny and Evan Parker at the recording of *Karyōbin*. ........... 89

Photo 18: Kenny and Alan Skidmore at Montreux Jazz Festival, as featured in *Coda* magazine in December 1969. ........... 103

Photo 19: Jon Hendricks looking on as Kenny plays in Ronnie Scott's quintet, Sunbury Jazz Festival, 1968. ........... 108

Photo 20: Kenny playing with Anthony Braxton's quartet, Montreux Jazz Festival. ....158

Photo 21: Kenny playing at with Montreux Jazz Festival as part of the Anthony Braxton Quartet. ................171

Photo 22: Kenny Wheeler being introduced as a new orchestra member in the James Last Appreciation Society fanzine. ................179

Photo 23: Kenny Wheeler playing piano at a post-gig jam session with James Last Orchestra bandmates, including Derek Watkins seated directly to Kenny's left. ................181

Photo 24: Kenny in "Uncle Bert" mode, with Alex and Leo Taylor (Leo on the right). ................200

Photo 25: Kenny playing lead trumpet with the Banff Big Band, next to Ingrid Jensen. ................219

Photo 26: Kenny, Don Thompson, and Dave Holland in concert at Banff. ................220

Photo 27: Azimuth pictured in Ethel's Place, Baltimore. Left to right: Kenny Wheeler, Norma Winstone, and John Taylor. ................237

Photo 28: Kenny in concert with the 1985 Banff Faculty, which included Dave Holland's Quintet. Left to right: Don Thompson (p), Steve Coleman (as), Dave Holland (b), John Abercrombie (g), Julian Priester (tb), Marvin "Smitty" Smith (d), Kenny (t). ................240

Photo 29: Kenny's *Flutter By, Butterfly* quintet on tour in 1987, pictured here at Pori Jazz Festival, Finland. Left to right: Dave Holland, John Taylor, Kenny, Bill Elgart, and Stan Sulzmann. ................245

Photo 30: Kenny at his surprise 60th birthday party, with his sisters Mabel (left) and Helen (right). ................264

Photo 31: The *Music for Large and Small Ensembles* band: Left to right: Duncan Lamont, Dave Holland, Evan Parker, Henry Lowther, Ian Hamer, Alan Downey, Derek Watkins, Stan Sulzmann, Dave Horler, John Abercrombie, Peter Erskine, Norma Winstone, Chris Pyne, Julian Argüelles, John Taylor, Ray Warleigh, Kenny, Hugh Fraser, Paul Rutherford. ................271

Photo 32: Kenny and Norma at the *Music for Large and Small Ensembles* recording session. ................273

Photo 33: The all-star *The Widow in the Window* quintet at a signing at Tower Records London. Left to right: John Taylor, Dave Holland, Peter Erskine, John Abercrombie, Kenny. ................278

Photo 34: The Kenny Wheeler Quintet outside Blues Alley, Washington DC. Left to right: John Taylor, Gary Peacock, Kenny, John Abercrombie, and Peter Erskine. ................281

Photo 35: "F---ING FINE!" from the last page of Kenny's manuscript score of the *Sweet Sister Suite*. ................304

Photo 36: Kenny and Dave Holland at the recording session for the ECM album *Angel Song*. ................319

Photo 37: Kenny recording *Angel Song*, Lee Konitz in the background. ................322

Photo 38: The *Angel Song* quartet. Left to right: Bill Frisell, Lee Konitz, Kenny, and Dave Holland. ................324

Photo 39: John Abercrombie warming up in the dressing room at Blues Alley while Kenny buzzes his mouthpiece. 337

Photo 40: Kenny's big band in soundcheck for the 75th birthday tour, Bristol. 358

Photo 41: Kenny and John Taylor. 366

Photo 42: Toronto Jazz FM studios for a live session. Left to right: Nikki Iles, Norma Winstone, Duncan Hopkins, Kenny, and Anthony Michelli. 372

Photo 43: Kenny at his 80th birthday concert, Royal Academy of Music. 376

Photo 44: Assembled performers at Kenny's 80th birthday concert, Royal Academy of Music. Left-to-right (back row): John Parricelli, Martin France, Andrew Bradley, Norma Winstone, Kenny, Derek Watkins, John Barclay, Julian Argüelles, Duncan Lamont, Martin Hathaway, Stan Sulzmann, Dave Holland, Dave Stewart, Mark Nightingale; (front row): Nick Smart, Pete Churchill, Nikki Iles, John Horler, Dave Horler, Chris Laurence, Evan Parker, John Taylor, Henry Lowther, Trevor Mires. 377

Photo 45: Dave Douglas, Kenny, and Nick Smart at New York University. 386

Photo 46: The final night of FONT. Left to right: Craig Taborn, Kenny, and Dave Holland. 389

Photo 47: Kenny recording in isolation for *The Long Waiting*. 391

Photo 48: Kenny and Derek Watkins at Derek's party, May 2012. 395

Photo 49: The opening reception of the Kenny Wheeler Exhibition. Left to right: John Taylor, Kenny, Chris Laurence, Martin France, Evan Parker, and Stan Sulzmann. 398

Photo 50: Doreen Wheeler making friends laugh, feigning exasperation next to the giant photo of her husband. 400

Photo 51: Nikki Iles and Kenny laughing between takes at the *Mirrors* recording session. 403

Photo 52: Kenny and Doreen at their 60th anniversary party. 408

Photo 53: Kenny at his most pensive, at the *Mirrors* recording session. 416

# Acknowledgements

As we have noted throughout this book, Kenny was incredibly generous with his time and resources. In turn, so many people have been wonderfully forthright in providing resources for this book. These pages contain the results of interviews with over 130 people who all gave their time freely, and many more shared private recordings, photos, and newspaper/magazine articles.

Kenny's family and his extended musical family have been tirelessly supportive and helpful with their time, recollections, and materials. The project would have been unthinkable without the blessing of the Wheelers. Kenny knew we were starting the project but passed only a month later; but, after that, Doreen Wheeler, Mark Wheeler, and Louann Newman were amazing in their encouragement of this work, as were other members of their family circle, including Andrew Bradley, Tracy Wheeler, his granddaughters Bethan, Rachel, and particularly Ruby, Phoebe and Sophie, who shared memories with us. In Canada, Kenny's sister, Mabel Ball, opened her home to Brian, talked to him about their family life for hours, and connected him with Kenny's old friends Bill Jelley, and Rod and Ann North, all of whom shared important details about Kenny's childhood. We also wish to thank his nieces and nephews Carri Driver, Pat Cadeau, Jayson and Michele Jelley, and many others in the extended Wheeler family for their assistance. (Special thanks to Pat Cadeau for making Brian a batch of butter tarts, Kenny's favourite dessert!)

Close friends and colleagues from all over the world were similarly big-hearted with their assistance. In particular, Dave Holland, Evan Parker, Norma Winstone and Stan Sulzmann have given wise counsel at every step. Christine Allen, Anthony Braxton, Taylor-Ho Bynum, Pete Churchill, Steve Coleman, Jack DeJohnette, Brian Dickinson, Dave Douglas, Art Ellefson, Peter Erskine, Robin Eubanks, Tony Fisher, Bill Frisell, Jan Garbarek, Mike Gibbs, Duncan Hopkins, Dave Horler, Nikki Iles, Ingrid Jensen, Larry Klein, Chris Laurence, Dave Lee, Dave Liebman, Henry Lowther, Vince Mendoza, Mark Miller, Adam Nussbaum, Ted O'Reilly, Chris Potter, Nick Purnell, Alex von Schlippenbach, Wadada Leo Smith, John Surman, Don Thompson, Ralph Towner, and Kenny Werner also shared memories, stories, personal archival photos, interviews, and recordings, helped to clarify details, names of supporting musicians, and any other crucial information and viewpoint imaginable. Huge thanks also to Manfred Eicher for his contribution and support, and to Steve Lake at ECM for his assistance.

We also thank and remember of all those who contributed to our work and sadly passed away during the decade we were working on this book, including: John Abercrombie, Stuart Brooks, Tony Coe, John Cumming, Palle Danielsson, Art Ellefson, Martin France, Hugh Fraser, Duncan Lamont, John Marshall, Rod North, Bobby Wellins, and especially John Taylor, who was so central to Kenny's life and music for so many years.

Special thanks must go to Naoyuki Kamiko who so generously shared with us an incredibly well-researched and detailed discography he assembled, having originally given it to Kenny as a gift. Other archival research has been key to the work behind the scenes, and we couldn't have done this without the help and support of Suzanne Rackover and Lianne Caron at the library of the Banff Centre for the Arts, Kate O'Brien, Samantha Blake, Felix Carey, James Codd, Jessica Hogg, and Julian Carr at the BBC Written Archives Centre in Caversham, and David Nathan at the National Jazz Archive in Loughton. Thanks also to Andy Linehan, Stephen Cleary, Rachel Garman, Steven Dryden, and Paul Wilson at the British Library, and from the Royal Academy of Music Library and Collections we wish to thank Adam Taylor, Kathy Adamson, and Joanna Tapp.

Private recordings of rare BBC broadcasts and other live tapes of Kenny's were shared with us by Simon Spillett, Pete Hurt, Stan Sulzmann, John Wickes, John Thurlow, Evan Parker, George Chisholm, Norma Winstone, and so many other online resources curated by fans and archivists of the music. Mark Micklethwaite at Jazz 91 FM in Toronto provided us with audio recordings of Ted O'Reilly's fantastic radio interviews with Kenny from the 1980s.

The wealth of photos used in this book were graciously provided by so many wonderful photographers, friends, family, and associates of Kenny's, including Caroline Forbes (whose work was used throughout this book and is especially featured on the cover), Mabel Ball, Luca D'Agostino, Carri Driver, Patrick Hinely, Chris Hughes, Derek Billy Lawton, Harry Monty, Rod North, Renee Rosnes, Peter Vacher, Wendy Watkins, and, of course, the Wheeler family archives.

Special thanks to Dr. Arnon Bentovim, who, through a chance encounter, provided us with the opportunity to discuss the likely effect Kenny's childhood may have had on the behaviour and personality traits that so shaped his life and music.

Thanks to senior colleagues at the Royal Academy of Music who have supported the writing of this book, including Principal Jonathan Freeman-Attwood, Deputy Principal Timothy Jones, and Head of Postgraduate Programmes (and Nick's PhD supervisor!) Neil Heyde. Thanks also to Matthew Herd for transcribing interviews at the British Library Sound Archive. Brian's former institution, Louisiana State University, provided him with a very productive sabbatical, generous travel support to conduct in-person research in Canada, and his former Graduate Assistants Shelby Lewis, Louie Eckhardt,

Pagean DiSalvio, Michael Hull, and Phil Shapiro contributed hours of their time transcribing interviews for use in the book.

Sincere thanks to the team at Equinox Publishing: to Janet Joyce, Val Hall and Sarah Lee for their ongoing commitment and patience, Dean Bargh for copyediting, and especially our series editor Alyn Shipton, who has worked tirelessly with us on this from day one. We would also like to thank Mark Lee for the cover design.

Nick would like to thank his wife Helen for her continued patience and support as one year spilled into ten while we worked on this – for the holidays never taken waiting for "well, when the book's finished"! And to my mum Anne Smart, and dad Richard Smart, who passed away while we were working on this – thanks for believing in me over the years and instilling the power and joy of music in me. Lastly, heartfelt thanks to Brian who has become a best friend for life during this process – I could no way have done this without him, nor frankly would have tried. In essence, I guess what I'm saying is it's *his* fault we did this . . . but I'm immensely proud we have, so thank you!

Brian would like to thank: my wife, Lana Van Boven, son Thomas, and stepson Elliot for their love and patience with the years-long process of researching, writing, and editing this book, and their pretending to be amused by my unending references to funny things Kenny might have said in any given situation. I would also like to thank my parents Garry and Mary Shaw and my parents-in-law Alan and Ginger Van Boven for their support over the years, and for hosting me and Nick at their respective homes during some of our summer writing sessions. Thanks especially to my friend and former teacher Mark Maegdlin, who first introduced me to Kenny Wheeler's music by playing *Gnu High* in a Keith Jarrett seminar when I was a freshman at Eastern Illinois University. Finally, thanks to my dear friend Nick for being gullible enough to tackle this enormous project with me and believing it could be done. This book would have never happened without you! Kenny, who always had a way of connecting people, introduced the two of us, and must have somehow known we would end up being the best of friends.

*Brian Shaw and Nick Smart, November 2024*

# Foreword
## Dave Holland

One of the wonderful things that happened to me in my life was meeting Kenny Wheeler when I was a young musician. He became a good friend, and I had the privilege of making music with him and playing many of his incredibly beautiful compositions. He was one of the composers in the 1960s that redefined the song form and its harmonic and melodic language. The first time I played his music was in 1968 when he invited me to take part in a recording of *Windmill Tilter*, his suite for big band commissioned by Sir John Dankworth. I still remember the impact that hearing his music for the first time had on me. There is an immediately identifiable sound to his playing and composing that has been a major source of inspiration to me and many other musicians around the world. Kenny's music is emotionally powerful and deeply personal; *Part One* of his masterpiece *The Sweet Time Suite* brought tears to my eyes when we first rehearsed it.

Kenny was a very disciplined musician and maintained a rigorous practice schedule throughout his life, resulting in a prodigious technique that gave him tremendous control of his instrument. We both were members of Anthony Braxton's quartet in the 1970s and Anthony wrote music for the group that was extremely creative and often technically challenging. Some of the trumpet parts he wrote for Kenny were very difficult to play, but Kenny had both the courage and the virtuosity to execute them.

He brought that same discipline to his composing. When we were on tour during the 1980s he was diligently doing exercises in counterpoint while we were travelling. This consisted of musical exercises that followed strict compositional rules and he would sit on the train or the tour bus writing them out in a manuscript book as we travelled. We both taught for several years at the summer workshop at the Banff Centre in Banff, Canada, where a wide range of his compositions were studied and performed. He often wrote new compositions for the trumpet players to play in his masterclasses as well as for the student ensembles that he tutored.

This biography of Kenny Wheeler, written by Nick Smart and Brian Shaw, traces in detail the many steps he took during his life's journey. Through interviews with family, friends, and colleagues as well as meticulous research into other sources of information, they paint a picture of the life behind the music along with the experiences that shaped Kenny's musical thinking. It's also a story of a musician's life in a certain time and place, lived through a period that saw major developments in music and the opening up of new creative possibilities for jazz and other forms of improvised music.

Kenny's interest in music began during his early years in Toronto, where he started listening to Jazz as a teenager and developed a lifelong love for it. In 1952 he moved to London, England, in search of playing and employment opportunities and there he lived the life of a working musician learning his craft. Over time, Kenny created his own musical voice, and this biography tells the story of how it developed and led to both the creation of a large number of his original compositions and arrangements and an archive of recordings that documents the significant contribution he made to music.

Kenny was a much-loved and respected member of the musical community and there are plenty of anecdotes about him that are shared by friends and colleagues. Although I had the honour and pleasure of spending countless hours talking with him about life and music over a period of about 45 years, this lovingly created biography by Nick and Brian revealed many details about Kenny's life that were unknown to me and gave me a new understanding of the man, the musician, and his lifelong commitment to more perfectly express himself through his music and share his great gift with us all.

# Introduction

> **Who he was, as a person, was embodied in the music in a certain way, which is the highest form of artistry.**
>
> *Dave Holland*

The history of jazz in America has been famously portrayed as a family tree, seen on many educational posters adorning music department walls.[1] The base of the trunk is represented by those at the source of the music, such as Scott Joplin, Jelly Roll Morton, and Buddy Bolden. The stylistic founders of jazz – such as Louis Armstrong, Duke Ellington, Charlie Parker – extend out of the branches of the tree, and so it goes on through the various evolutions within the music. If one were to think about the place of Kenny Wheeler within this metaphorical image, there is no doubt that he would appear as a large and significant part of several branches of European jazz. His place in that family tree would form connections with the very beginnings of an identifiably European jazz sound, continuing into the avant-garde. He represents the growth of a new harmonic sophistication, the birth of European free improvisation, a unique soloistic vocabulary, exceptional instrumental virtuosity, a revolutionary approach to composition and orchestration, and much more.

Shortly before Kenny's death in September 2014, we set about co-writing his biography. In the preceding years, the idea had already entered our minds. We were both leading more and more lectures, concerts, and teaching residencies on Wheeler's music, and would increasingly talk about his life and the circle of people intrinsically connected to the music we were playing. It felt necessary to explain to the student participants which *role* they were playing in the big band, because the solos or melody lines they had, even the character of their particular part, was there *because* Kenny had written it for a specific person. In other words, the saxophone part written for Ray Warleigh was different than the saxophone part intended for Duncan Lamont because of who they were, and most crucially, how Kenny related to them in his own musical life. Of course, the immediate comparison that comes to mind is with Duke Ellington, who famously wrote for the distinct members of his band; but, knowing these people personally, we were aware it was more than just how they *play* – to Kenny, it was about who they were as personalities and his history with them.

So, these ideas would increasingly be talked about in seminars and rehearsals, and colleagues began to ask leading questions about whether we had thought about writing his biography. In all honesty, it felt too daunting a task at that stage, especially with our own busy lives as performers and educators. But when we got to know one another (having been introduced to each other by Kenny), we also talked about the fact there was no biography and discussed whether we could – or even should – do it. On top of this, a few academic theses about his music were being written, and, however good or accurate the technical analysis may have been, none were able to address the other fundamental (and to us indelibly linked) question of *why* to begin with he had approached the elements of his music in the way he had. We felt that answering this question required a dedicated biography. We increasingly began to feel a responsibility, being people who could actually tell his story from within his musical and personal network. Nick, with his experience as a professional trumpeter, his closeness to Kenny during his last 15 years, and his position as Head of Jazz at the Royal Academy, has ties to many people associated with Kenny. Brian studied with Kenny (as much as studying with him was possible at all) at the Banff Centre for the Arts in Canada, and published a book of Kenny's solo transcriptions in 2000. He also remained in touch with Kenny through those same final years of his life. So, in late summer 2014, we decided we would tackle this task together.

In the last years of his life, Kenny's health was failing, and it became apparent to us that many of the relevant people around him – especially from his early days – were also in poor health or had already died. His wife of over 60 years, Doreen, was at some points in worse health than he was (even though she ultimately outlived him by nearly eight years). His sister Helen, with whom he was extremely close throughout his life, and who followed his career more closely than anyone else in his family, passed away in 2012. Kenny's close friend and musical colleague, pianist John Taylor, died suddenly following a heart attack he suffered during a performance at Saveurs Jazz Festival, France, in July 2015, less than a year after Kenny's own passing. We thought: if someone doesn't do this soon, so much of the Kenny Wheeler story – which is a part of *their* story, really – would be lost forever.

At first, our discrete locations seemed a disadvantage. But Brian's location in North America allowed for easier travel to Kenny's hometown of St. Catharines for interviews with childhood friends and his surviving family. Nick, in London, was able to conduct in-person interviews with many of Kenny's surviving musical associates. We were able to "divide and conquer," sharing the writing and research duties, with each of us heading up our own chapters of the book.

People within Kenny's circle were extremely generous with their time and energy. Kenny's family – in London and in Canada – gave many hours for interviews and provided precious old photos and letters. His musical colleagues and professional associates were also very forthcoming with interviews, helping us make contacts, and in some cases digging out old datebooks to nail down the exact chronology of events. All these people – including

Kenny's former students from Banff and elsewhere — were just as generous with us as he was with them. Just as Kenny brought people together from all parts of his life, this spirit of sharing and community made this daunting project seem a little more possible. It also encouraged us to keep working, even when our own lives as musicians and academics (and people with their own lives to live) became crowded.

The most common question that came from fellow musicians, friends, or especially the family members we interviewed was inevitably phrased something like: *Kenny never said anything. What the hell are you guys going to write about?* As this is a central issue of any biography (be the subject an introvert or extrovert), we started thinking seriously about this question. There was evidence that even Kenny himself seemed to be against the idea. In a 1991 feature in his hometown newspaper, the interviewer asked him about the possibility of a biographical film:

> "Of course," [Kenny] notes, tucking the last of the chicken salad into his mouth, "they wouldn't make a film about an ordinary jazz player who never did anything like drugs. It would be too boring."
> So, no bio? "Hmmm." Wheeler shakes his head. "Never."[2]

On one of the last occasions he visited Kenny in his care home, Nick told him we were undertaking the project. Kenny was pleased to know we were doing it, although, predictably, he questioned whether anyone would be interested. It may have been a self-deprecating quip on one level, as in his later years he would just *occasionally* acknowledge that he recognized his legacy to some extent. But having travelled internationally and having heard the passion with which he was discussed and the emotion felt when experiencing his music, we appreciated more than Kenny just how many people would be interested in his story all over the world: trumpeters, composers, educators, aficionados of British and European jazz – or just fans of jazz generally.

The consistent link between Kenny's personal relationships and his artistic development is in many respects the central and most substantial thread of his biography, and the most enlightening part of the story, through which a distinct perspective on British and European jazz history also starts to emerge. Kenny's choices and decisions are seen again and again to have been formed as much by the way he feels about the people he is with as by the music he is playing. He had no "master plan" for his career; instead, he was led by the encounters in which he felt most welcomed and at home. The music followed from this. What emerged from this process is a fascinating breadth of musical activity, underpinned and made possible only by an astonishing capability across this gamut of musical activity. If one starts to conceive of a "Kenny Wheeler network" within the context of British and European jazz, it is remarkable to note how comprehensive it is in covering all the major events of the period; from the early big-band stars to the giants of London bebop and the young innovators crafting a new British jazz sound, and on to the mavericks of the emerging free improvisation scene – not to mention all his commercial and session work.

Kenny was not only present, but frequently crucial, in a great deal of this. His musical "family tree" extends to practically every branch of jazz activity in that time. This was enabled by the sheer breadth and range of what he was capable of as an artist, as a jazz trumpeter, as a free improviser, and as a composer/arranger. His work spanned commercial session and freelance work, "conventional" jazz playing, and the free jazz scene. These elements go on to shape his unique compositional approach, and once again his story reveals that it was this massive set of skills that defined his musical evolution and set him apart from his peers.

Some of the most significant new research in this book is connected to Kenny's first BBC broadcasts as a bandleader. He frequently cited the importance of these occasions in providing an outlet for his own music, but prior to this biography these sessions have not been documented in a way that clearly shows his evolution as a composer after he began leading his own big band. It becomes very clear that his relationships with his musicians are at the heart of many of his choices: he chooses his brass colleagues from the commercial studio world for their reading and intonation, "conventional" jazz players for their harmonic language and connection to the tradition, and free jazz players to bring to life what he so frequently described as his blend of melancholy and chaos.

As part of this project, we wanted to underscore Kenny's significance directly and record a selection of principal voices that addressed this. So, we finished our key interviews with the most fundamental of questions, one that we ourselves had been pressed into considering: *Why is Kenny Wheeler important?*

The differing responses overwhelmingly highlighted his uniqueness and significance, as well as the love so many musicians felt for him and his music, and it further underlined the need to tell his story in all its complex detail: his personality, his instrumental strength, his original compositional voice, his connection to the jazz tradition. This one question inspired some remarkable responses from some of the most influential artists of this period:

> One of the reasons I have been able to stay in music is because I have met people like Kenny Wheeler . . . And so, this guy is one of the guys in my heart. I will always love Kenny Wheeler and my hope is that when the mature histories are written, Kenny Wheeler will be written about in a way that is correct. He was a virtuoso restructural innovator.[3]
>
> *Anthony Braxton*

Well, besides the fact he was a very skilful musician and had a great knowledge of how to write and arrange music, he is also such a soulful and solitary musician. It's a very lyrical approach, and at the same time very energetic, a vivid kind of musical partner. And he has a personal tone and a character, and this is what counts; so many people today that play technically very well, play all the lines, have all the knowledge, have a lot of information, but they can't tell a story. Kenny was a good storyteller as well.[4]

*Manfred Eicher*

To me, he's important to me in the same way Glenn Gould is. He is an example that you can do it your way, and that you don't have to do it the way everyone tells you to do it . . . He didn't seem like he was swayed to go along with any trends or to go along with what's fashionable or anything at all like that. And at the end of it all he wound up being a trend in himself . . . People like Kenny are important because, if the young guys pay attention, they'll realize it's possible to do your own thing.[5]

*Don Thompson*

Kenny Wheeler is important because he's the perfect balance of beautiful linear mastery and freestyle crazy![6]

*Ingrid Jensen*

Dave Holland, a lifelong colleague of Kenny's, noted his personal contribution to their generation:

Kenny was a true original, always in the music – as an instrumentalist, you can hear two notes and you'd know it was Kenny. For his generation, he contributed a harmonic language, which at that time was brand new. Who he was, as a person, was embodied in the music in a certain way, which is the highest form of artistry.[7]

*Dave Holland*

This was something saxophonist Chris Potter, a modern jazz master from a newer generation, expanded on further in his response:

He really brought a unique, beautiful, fresh voice to the music. There's no mistaking his music for anyone else's. I think he's someone that enough people knew about that he was an influence, but maybe a lot of people don't know just how much came from him.[8]

*Chris Potter*

Born in January 1930, Kenny was actually a generation older than many of his colleagues in the contemporary scene of the period in question. Vocalist Norma Winstone who, along with Dave Holland, was part of his close musical family, commented not only on his importance as an innovator but also his connection to the history and tradition of the music with which he grew up:

> It's an important music in the whole scheme of things, because everything about it has the tradition in it, and yet it's original. His playing and compositions are just very original – you can't exactly say you've heard anything like them – and yet behind them there's history and this love of the tradition.[9]

> *Norma Winstone*

In addition to his musical contributions, Kenny's humility, gentle wit and self-deprecating personality was also legendary among those who knew him. His character was central to the paths he chose in his musical journey and in many ways is encapsulated in a remark he made to the Canadian journalist Mark Miller for a *DownBeat* interview in 1975: "If I ever got to like my own playing I'd give up."[10]

*This* is what we have written about.

# 1 A Long Time Ago

I never really knew how deeply it affected him, but I really believe that is where the genius, or the deepness of what he did with his music, came from.

*Mabel (Wheeler) Ball*

By almost any measure, Kenny Wheeler possessed one of the most enigmatic personalities in modern jazz. He was a painfully shy and humble man who played the trumpet with fiery power; he wrote meticulously organized compositions but became an icon of the free scene; he was famously self-effacing but still felt overlooked; and despite his crippling nervousness and anxiety he became one of the music's most revered and original voices. But these paradoxes in Kenny's nature had deep roots within his family tree.

The Wheeler side was characterized by a long line of quietly skilful people who were unafraid to make great leaps of faith. His great-grandparents Robert and Susannah Wheeler moved to Canada from England in 1876, bringing along their three children: 14-year-old Edith, seven-year-old George, and three-year old Frances. The Wheelers made their new home in Toronto, where Robert worked as a gardener. The family remained members of their native Church of England, but after the two eldest children were in their twenties, they left their father's religion. Though they both still lived under the same roof as their parents, Edith identified herself as a Methodist in the 1891 census, and George became a Congregationalist, later converting to Christian Science, a relatively new organization at the time.[11] George became a printer and soon started his own family, marrying Kathleen Ryan, a Canadian woman of Irish Roman Catholic descent (and a year his senior) in Toronto in 1892.[12] They had seven children: George Jr., Ivy, Clifford, Wilfred (who would become Kenny's father), Olive, Vincent, and Kathleen Jr.[13]

Wilfred Robert Wheeler was born 10 November 1899. Wilf, as he was called, rode the streetcar as a youngster to attend Christian Science lessons with his father on Saturdays, but attended De La Salle, which was a Catholic school. A musician at heart, Wilf began working as a trombonist in the local dance bands that were becoming increasingly popular.[14] In the 1920s, when George Sr. moved his family west to California to open a print shop near Los Angeles, Wilf and his closest sister Ivy stayed in Toronto. The courage shown in Wilf's decision to remain behind – echoing both his father's rejection of the family faith and his grandfather's brave transatlantic move – demonstrates the independence and boldness in the Wheeler character.

The maternal line of Kenny's genealogy was less stable. Kenny's maternal grandfather, John Francis Reid, or Jack, as he was called, was born in 1873. He was the oldest of six siblings and the only one to retain the family name of his father, Francis Reid, a broom maker. Nine years after Francis's death from pneumonia in December 1883,[15] his widow Christina married Irish immigrant Thomas Feeney and the rest of Jack's siblings chose to adopt the name of their new stepfather.[16] Aged 25, Jack Reid married Mary Walsh, nine years his junior.[17,18]

Their third daughter, Mabel Agnes Reid (who would become Kenny's mother), was born in Toronto on 23 May 1904. Along with her parents and two older sisters, Mabel's Irish-born maternal grandparents also lived in the family home.[19] Mabel's early years were not pleasant. Her parents suffered from alcoholism, and it is thought she and her older sister Mary Christina even spent a period in an orphanage.[20] Sadly, Mary Christina died at the age of 22 after complications from an internal haemorrhage. Despite this painful childhood, the music that filled their home provided some happier times. In addition to his work as a baker, Jack Reid played music and led his own band.[21] A family photo shows him in full band uniform, holding a traditional Irish instrument tucked smartly under his arm.[22]

Jack's daughter Mabel found jobs in her teens. She worked as a switchboard operator and as a chocolate dipper for Diana Sweets in Toronto.[23] She also loved to go dancing and, on one such occasion, teenaged Mabel met a young trombonist named Wilf Wheeler. The petite, fun-loving Mabel must have been quite a contrast with the studious, disciplined, and bespectacled Wilf, who was nearly five years her senior. The couple soon fell in love and were married in Toronto at St. Michael's Cathedral on 8 June, 1922.[24]

Wilf continued to work steadily as a musician in those days, playing with Gilbert Watson's Orchestra around Toronto.[25] He also spent a brief period in New York, where he played gigs in the Catskills and eventually joined one of the road bands of the famed American bandleader, Paul Whiteman.[26] (The most popular dance bands of the time had several franchise ensembles that worked under the name – if not the direct baton – of the star.) Mabel came to visit Wilf during one of his extended periods in New York after they had been married for only a year. She soon made it clear that she didn't want the instability of a musician's lifestyle, so he began to restrict his gigs to those much closer to their Toronto home. The couple soon started a family and, eager to provide stability, Wilf began to work as an accountant for Watson Motors, a Ford dealership.[27] In June 1925, their first child, George, was born. Just over a year later, their second child, Wilfred, arrived. A daughter, Mary, was born in September 1928, and on 14 January 1930 their fourth child, Kenneth Vincent John Wheeler, was born.[28]

Photo 1: Jack Reid, Kenny's maternal grandfather.
Courtesy Mabel Ball

Wilf and Mabel's family grew rapidly; in fact, they had eight children in fewer than ten years. Just 11 months after Kenny's birth, Boniface, a boy, was born prematurely in December 1930 and died after just 12 hours. The year 1932 brought happier news, with the birth of another girl, Helen. Their last son, Paul, arrived in November 1933, and their final child, a daughter named Mabel, was born in December of the following year.

The two-storey Wheeler home was located at 81 Rushbrooke Avenue in a relatively poor section of Toronto. All nine of them lived in half of a large house that was divided into two residences. The family attended St. Joseph's Catholic Church, and the children attended its affiliated parish school.

Kenny first came into contact with music-making at home in Toronto, beginning to play the piano when he was seven or eight years old. Unlike his older brother Wilf, who became a fairly accomplished pianist, Kenny didn't stick to the instrument during his childhood. "The few friends I had would call you a 'sissy' if you played the piano, so I quickly got rid of that," he said. "I was always a loner. I never had many friends."[29] His naturally shy personality was likely to have been exacerbated by the fact that the family moved around a great deal during his early years. To support their large family, his father had to constantly seek new and better employment in Canada's struggling post-Depression economy.[30] As production efforts for the war intensified, Wilf Sr. secured a position in the office of an aircraft manufacturing company and moved his family to Owen Sound, Ontario. Some 120 miles northwest of Toronto, Owen Sound had a population of only around 14,000 when

Photo 2: Young Wilf Wheeler Sr. seated far right, holding his trombone, with Gilbert Watson's Orchestra.

Courtesy Mabel Ball

the Wheelers arrived there in 1941. Now aged 11, Kenny attended Catholic school at St. Mary's.[31]

It was in this Owen Sound house that Wilf Sr. first brought home a cornet for Kenny. "He didn't advise me or ask me to take lessons; he just gave it to me," Kenny said. "I looked at it for a few weeks before I started to do anything with it."[32] Soon, though, Kenny began teaching himself to play using method books and technical studies, which were "something kind of simple. My father showed me a couple of things, but it wasn't like he was my teacher on a regular basis. He just left me to do it."[33]

In July 1942, a tragedy shook Kenny's family when his maternal grandfather, Jack Reid, died suddenly under mysterious circumstances. The event was covered in the *Toronto Star*:

> The body of John Reid, 69, Eastern Ave., was found by P.C. Thomas Smith of Central garage in Ashbridge's Bay at the foot of Knox Ave. Monday. Police said the discovery resulted from a report that a man had found Reid's hat in the vicinity. Neighbors told police they had not seen the man around his home for several days.[34]

Jack Reid was a staunch Catholic and an alcoholic with a "fiery temper". With 12th July being Orangemen's Day (the Protestant celebration of William

Photo 3: Wilf Wheeler Sr. with his children. Front, left to right: Wilf Jr., George, Wilf Sr., Mary; middle: Helen, Paul, Mabel; back: Kenny.

Courtesy Mabel Ball

of Orange's 1690 victory over James II), some of his descendants believe that his death was no accident: perhaps the result of the combination of alcohol, Jack's quickness to anger, his Loyalist roots and heightened Nationalist sentiments on that day.[35]

In 1943, Wilf Wheeler moved the family once again, after finding work in the office of another wartime aircraft manufacturer in Windsor, Ontario. The Wheelers lived on Westcott Road, in the first of two homes they would rent there. Counter-intuitively, Windsor actually lies south of the American city of

Detroit, across the US–Canada border formed by the Michigan River. During this time, Kenny's mother Mabel, and occasionally his sister Mary, visited her uncle Ed Feeney in Detroit.[36] (Ed was the youngest son of Kenny's great-grandfather Francis Reid and one of the siblings who took his stepfather's name, Feeney.)

Music was ever-present in the Wheeler home and dance bands were Wilf Sr.'s favourite. Kenny recalled how his father "kind of liked jazz, but he was [interested in] more of the Tommy Dorsey/Glenn Miller big dance bands, and I guess he liked a lot of Dixieland."[37] During this period, his father took him to hear the Duke Ellington Orchestra play live. (At that time, theatres in Detroit included both a band and a film on the same show.[38]) It was a musical experience that would stay in Kenny's mind forever. "When I heard those notes in the flesh I couldn't believe it, you know."[39] "I can still hear [trombonist] Lawrence Brown's sound in my ear."[40] With the radio in the house nearly always playing, Kenny began to seek out the music that appealed to him. "Late at night, [if] you were allowed to stay up, and you fiddled with the radio dial, you could sometimes find jazz here and there," he said.[41] "By doing that, you'd hear Glenn Miller, and stumble on something a bit different, and you'd say *Wait a minute, what's that*? This was jazz, I guess. So I started to get a liking for that stuff."[42] As he listened more, he also started to pick out musicians he felt were different, or special. "I began to notice the other kind of players as well – who you wouldn't normally hear . . . The first was really Buck Clayton. At that time, he was on quite a lot of records – Billie Holiday records, Kansas City-type things."[43] It was around this time that Kenny first heard a piece of music that triggered a profoundly emotional reaction:

> . . . one of the first records I heard which really affected me was the Coleman Hawkins recording of "Body and Soul". I was fifteen at the time and the first time I heard it I immediately burst into tears. I think not so much with sadness – it just communicated to me . . .[44]

He concluded with an observation that would return in later years: ". . . I have always loved beautiful melodies. I must be a little twisted because beautiful sad melodies make me feel very happy."[45]

By the time he was 14, Kenny was already playing in public.[46] He played in a small jazz band with a group of kids in Windsor at the high school there. "It wasn't really a school band, just a few fellows who got together and played."[47] He soon joined the Royal Canadian Navy Reserve HMCS "Hunter" Band, led by a retired British Army musician named Phil Murphy.[48]

> In Windsor this guy had a Navy band. He was teaching kids from 13 to 18 or something. I remember I had my own actual real uniform. Navy whites and all that stuff. I was, I guess, 14, and looked about 7. I had one of those little faces, y'know. Marching up the street with my cornet and my uniform on, very proud.[49]

Kenny also took cornet lessons with Murphy in Windsor. Murphy was a teacher preoccupied with the formation of his students' embouchures: the shape a brass player holds their lips to make the sound. He even forbade other students from playing closely related instruments, such as the bugle. Murphy taught Kenny a questionable technique:

> He was a very good teacher; except in his method, you say the word "dimm" and then you play. I tried that and it didn't work. Eventually I kind of opened up my chops a bit and I ended up getting quite a big sound but only had a range of about an octave.[50,51]

The acceleration of Kenny's musical interests in Windsor coincided with his mother's increasing struggles with alcohol. During this period, it is probable that resentment and frustration took their toll on Mrs. Wheeler's mental health and she would occasionally disappear for days at a time.[52] At heart, she was a lively person who loved to sing and dance and play the piano; she was a social being. She was now living an exhausting domestic existence, raising seven children on very little money and moving to new cities every couple of years. Considering her own traumatic upbringing, it is understandable that she may have been ill-equipped to deal with the daily pressures of such a life. Kenny's elder brothers George and Wilf Jr. both left home at a fairly young age, ostensibly deciding that joining the military during wartime was preferable to the chaos and instability taking root at home.[53] In a situation in which other fathers might have given their young children up to foster care, Wilf Sr., strong in his Catholic faith, kept the Wheeler family together. The remaining older siblings looked after the younger ones as best they could while their father worked. Without a mother at home, though, certain household tasks and maternal oversights went unchecked: in one episode, Kenny was sent home from school because his clothes were dirty and he smelled.[54] Faced with such humiliation at school and loneliness from his mother's absence, Kenny found his greatest solace in the music that was quickly becoming the preoccupation of his inner world.[55]

The family remained in Windsor for just two years, until the wartime manufacturing plant closed in 1945 and they were forced to move yet again. In early December of that year they relocated 225 miles northeast to St. Catharines, where Wilf Sr. had been hired as shop manager of Murphy's Auto, a General Motors dealer. The owner, Frank J. Murphy, knew that the Wheelers were a large family, so he purchased the house at 21 Salina Street, next door to his own, and rented it to Wilf. The two-storey red-brick home with a pillared porch sits in a comfortably middle-class neighbourhood and was a significant step up from the smaller houses they had rented previously. Wilf could now walk to his new job on Ontario Street, just a few short blocks away from their home. (For a man who worked much of his life in the auto-mobile business, Wilf was yet to own a car himself.)

Kenny's sister Mabel called St. Catharines "a new beginning – the best move my dad ever made".[56] But only three weeks after they moved to St. Catharines, their mother disappeared again. She was away from the family periodically over the next two years, leaving her husband and the children to fend for themselves. Occasionally she would come home, "stir up things", and leave again. Young Mabel remembered hearing loud arguments between her parents. "As a kid, you just don't want to hear that kind of stuff," she said. Their mother eventually ended up staying in Detroit with her uncle, Ed Feeney. After an extended period of heavy drinking and not eating, she appeared so ill Feeney called her husband to bring her home. Wilf dutifully drove for hours on the bumpy 1940s Canadian roads, bringing their daughter Mabel with him. As arduous as the trip was for him, it was an even more traumatic experience for her, only 11 at the time. Mabel and her father must have been shocked when they reached Detroit. Mrs. Wheeler was so malnourished that she weighed a mere 66 pounds. On the drive home, she suffered severe and disturbing hallucinations caused by delirium tremens. By the time they arrived back in St. Catharines she was in such a vegetative state that Wilf, fearing the worst, asked a priest to administer last rites.[57] Fortunately, she survived.

Since there were no mental health or rehabilitation facilities in the local hospital, Mrs. Wheeler needed to go 35 miles away to Hamilton Ontario for treatment, but no beds were available there. So, while Wilf was away at work, Kenny and his remaining siblings, Helen, Paul, and Mabel, took turns caring for their mother at home. Once a bed finally opened up in Hamilton, Mrs. Wheeler went to receive the care she needed. Mabel remembers that Wilf rented a car on Sundays to make the drive so that she, Helen, and Paul could visit their mother, but she doesn't remember Kenny ever making that trip. Mabel says this period is a horrible memory for her even now, adding "you can imagine what it must have done to Kenny, who was an introvert anyway."[58]

---

As far back as anyone can remember, Kenny preferred to be alone. His sisters Mabel and Helen each recalled he would get so lost inside his own head that he would not even speak as he passed them on the street. "Right away jazz music appealed to me when I was a kid because I was a loner, coming from a broken home and all that," Kenny said.[59] (This, along with his brief mention to Brian Priestley that "we were a problem family, that's not a very pleasant story, so I won't go into it", counts for the only times the authors are aware of that Kenny ever publicly mentioned – even in passing – his difficult home life.[60]) "I was very alone inside my head, didn't have friends, but because my father was a semi-professional musician, there was music in the house. Through that

Photo 4: Kenny's parents, Mabel and Wilf Wheeler Sr.
Courtesy Mabel Ball

I got to jazz. I think jazz is attractive to lonely people."[61] Kenny's sister Mabel said nearly the same thing: "I really believe that his music – a lot of it, that's where it comes from – deep within him . . . that's probably how he dealt with it. *Music*. That's what kind of helped heal him, I think."[62]

Kenny's personality was developing a great deal during this time. His sister Mabel remembers he was sort of a "peacemaker" who brought his brothers and sisters together, never caused any trouble, and avoided conflict. He was extremely shy and quiet, to the point that others would hardly notice his presence at all. Even at this age, he seemed to possess a particular type of melancholy, which later came out in his music. Mabel said, "I never really knew how deeply it affected him but I really believe that is where the genius, or the deepness of what he did with his music, came from."[63]

Although Mrs. Wheeler's struggles caused a great deal of pain for the family, there were still many happy times at 21 Salina Street. Kenny remembered his mother playing piano by ear and singing some of her favourite tunes, including "A Shanty in Old Shanty Town" and "My Melancholy Baby". Kenny's older brother Wilf often played old standard tunes on the piano, and their sister Helen was a good singer. Paul became an accomplished woodwind player. Mrs. Wheeler sometimes sang from her perch atop the piano, or even danced an Irish jig while her husband and the kids gathered round her playing music in the small family parlour.[64]

Despite his shyness, Kenny's interest in music brought him new friends who eventually became regulars at the Wheelers'. Wilf Sr., although strict, loved the fact that his children and the local kids were making music in their home. He was still a very active musician himself, playing gigs on both trombone and baritone saxophone on weekends. Kenny's friend Bill Jelley called the Wheelers' home a "perfect outlet" because they were a musical family, they had a piano, and their dad didn't mind. Bill could even bring his drums there to play along with the guys.[65] This situation wasn't perfect for everyone, though. Kenny's youngest sister Mabel, who liked music, but "didn't understand jazz", wasn't really interested in having all that cacophony quite so close to her. The guys were there almost every night. In response, Mabel would close the large wooden sliding doors to shut out the music so she could listen to the radio in the corner of the living room. Other times, she would just leave the house altogether and seek refuge at the home of a friend with a far quieter family.[66]

---

When Kenny and his family moved to St. Catharines in December 1945, bebop was "just seeping up to Canada".[67] This new style of jazz, incorporating complex melodies and harmonies at fast tempos, had taken a while to reach almost anywhere outside of the cities where it could be heard live. A conflict between James Petrillo (head of the American Federation of Musicians) and the music industry resulted in a ban on recording lasting from August 1942 until, for most major labels, the end of 1944. So, even though bebop was occasionally broadcast over the radio, this musical prohibition effectively silenced a crucial period in its recorded development. Because of this, the new music seemed to many record buyers as if it had sprung up from the swing era without warning.

When Kenny moved to St. Catharines, he met a group of teenagers who were not only interested in bebop but were modernists in general, fascinated with the latest developments in classical music, art, fashion, and philosophy. In a small city like St. Catharines, the mainstream population tended to exclude young men with interests outside the accepted norms of sports and girls.[68] "I just wanted to play," Kenny said. "People accepted jazz, but where I lived, jazz musicians were regarded almost as social outcasts. There were only about five people interested in playing while I was at school and we were all looked on as 'characters'."[69] Bonded by their rejection from popular teenaged society, these "characters" changed Kenny's life. They brought him out of his melancholic inner world and provided him with the outlet he needed to balance the instability he endured at home.

The group revolved around its first three members: pianist Art Talbot (the "focal point" of their group and widely considered the most musically talented), Art's cousin, saxophonist and clarinetist Paul Lindo (the group's "intellectual"), and drummer Bill Jelley (the group's visual artist and philosopher). Bill had known Art since they were in elementary school together. Early on, the guys would get together in the garage at Art's house on North Street, with Art on guitar, Paul playing woodwinds and Bill keeping time with brushes on a garbage can. Kenny met Art and Paul at the local high school, St. Catharines Collegiate, where Paul and Kenny actually played together in the school band.[70] They later introduced Kenny to Bill. These were the guys who played Charlie Parker and Dizzy Gillespie records for Kenny for the first time. "I didn't like it in the first place – I thought, 'Well, this is Chinese music isn't it?' but because I had a group of friends, I quickly got to like it, you know. I wanted to keep them!"[71] This nucleus of "bebop friends" (as Kenny called them) soon expanded. In addition to Art, Paul, Bill, and Kenny, there was Stan Bigger (a "rather odd character") who played bass, and an alto saxophonist named Kenny Thompson.[72]

By the time Kenny arrived in St. Catharines, these young jazz enthusiasts were already listening to radio broadcasts coming from New York, including those by announcer "Symphony Sid" Torin on New York's WHOM. Once records became available again after the recording ban, they were also checking out the newest 78s created by the stars of the bebop movement, most notably Charlie Parker and Dizzy Gillespie. The boys would send money with anyone they knew who was headed to New York, so that person could bring back a stack of the latest records. Many times the guys would listen to music upstairs in Kenny's room at the Wheeler home on Salina Street, where he had discs by Lennie Tristano, Ella Fitzgerald's "How High the Moon", others by Charlie Parker, and some early Miles Davis. Bill Jelley's house was another hangout. Bill had a Victrola record player and recalled playing Charlie Parker's "Ko-Ko" at slower speed so they could better analyse the saxophonist's impossibly fast bebop lines.[73]

Kenny Thompson's father owned the Geneva Food Shop, a hamburger joint, at the corner of Geneva and Welland Streets where the guys hung out and listened to Duke Ellington's "Take the 'A' Train" and other "great pop music" (as Bill called it) on the jukebox. The Geneva Food Shop served as a central meeting place a couple blocks away from Art and Paul, who both lived on North Street and Bill, who lived on nearby Dacotah Street. It was much more of a hike for Kenny – who lived about a mile away – but agreed well with Kenny's lifelong love of long walks.[74] Just down the street was a fruit stand belonging to the family of another young drummer, John Meloni, who became part of their social circle. Other friends included Abe Anderson, who played baritone sax, and Gus Garriock, who didn't play an instrument but was a jazz fan.[75]

Both similarly shy, Kenny and Bill Jelley became close friends. Bebop brought the young men a "new life", which they probably both needed. Coming from difficult home lives, they had much in common. For years, they even thought they had the same January 13th birthday. (Kenny only discovered his was the day after when he finally saw a copy of his birth certificate much later in life.[76]) When Bill was only 14, his father left the family, forcing him to quit school in order to support his newly single mother. As "a working man" at such an early age, Bill had access to alcohol that he shared with his bebop friends when the guys were hanging out at his house. Bill joked, "If you could say I put Kenny on to bebop, I also put him on to booze." Although Kenny enjoyed a beer or glass of wine throughout his life, he never developed a problem with alcohol.

There were times when Bill and Kenny would stay up all night talking, sometimes discussing music, philosophy, or just trying to figure out exactly why "the kids were taking care of the parents".[77] Sometimes, Bill would have to cut their conversations short because they had stayed up all night talking and he needed to leave to go to work. "If Kenny hadn't had someone to talk with, he would have exploded," Bill said, adding that Kenny was the closest thing he ever had to a brother. He knew "when he was talking to Kenny, he was listening".[78] Close friendships like this would be the bedrock of Kenny's stability throughout his life. "It's well known that friendship circles are a tremendous counter to adversity," said Dr. Arnon Bentovim, a lifelong jazz fan and lover of Kenny's music who is also a renowned family psychiatrist. He continued:

> So it's interesting that there's a notion of *adverse* childhood experiences and *protective* childhood experiences, so networks of friendship, the groups that [Kenny] found the whole way through, obviously that was tremendously important because, for somebody who was really quite shy and not an extrovert sort of individual, to be with a group of people that he felt comfortable with would be absolutely essential.[79]

Kenny and Bill Jelley were matched musically as well. Bill, an intuitive musician who liked to listen carefully to the soloist he was accompanying, often played behind the beat (calling himself the "Lester Young of the drums"). Kenny also tried experimenting with his rhythmic feel: "I remember I was playing . . . and for some reason or other, one night I decided to change my whole style and I went into this laid-back thing . . . the whole band nearly collapsed. I just kept playing, but you know, I was dragging the beat and I wasn't playing da-de-dah-de-dah . . ."[80] Bill followed Kenny's lead to the point that the band ground to a complete halt. When pressed later as to why he tried that, Kenny's answer showed a prematurely wise instinct to want to challenge his musical comfort zone. "I don't know why I did that, I think I just wanted to change *something . . .*"[81]

Another of Kenny's early friends, named Tommy Fancy, had been recently discharged from the hospital for tuberculosis, and was on bed rest in his home. "Tommy was a big band freak," Kenny said.[82] It was at Tommy's house that Kenny first met Gene Lees, who was a fellow student two years his senior at St. Catharines Collegiate. Although Lees wasn't really a part of the bebop gang, he and Kenny forged a lifelong friendship that would prove to be very formative for his life and career.

———·———

Wilf Sr. supported his children's music-making and even paid for music lessons for all of them, regardless of whether the family could afford it. As Kenny's interest in music began to intensify, his father became eager to help him find more advanced instruction than he was getting at St. Catharines Collegiate. During the summer of 1946, Wilf wrote to the Broadway School of Music in Buffalo, seeking lessons for Kenny's interests in trumpet, music theory, and arranging. A reply came directly to Kenny from Arthur F. Welte, who had evidently thought "Wilfred" was a female name. Welte, the humble director of the Welte Music School, was oddly emphatic about certain details in his salesman-like pitch of his programme:

> Kenneth;
>
> The letter, written by your Mother, to the Broadway School of Music, has been turned over to me. The Broadway School of Music, instructs accordion only.
>
> I shall be glad to discuss your musical future with you AND your mother at any time. I note that you are interested in studying for advancement in technic at playing the trumpet AND Harmony and Arranging.
>
> I do not know what the laws regarding transportation of a musical instrument, across the border, however, if you should run into any difficulties in this regard, you may carry your mouthpiece in your pocket and use one of my trumpets during the time of taking your lesson.
>
> In studying the three courses mentioned above, you may take your trumpet lesson at one time and your Harmony and Arranging at another, OR to save you the time and transportation, you may take both lessons during the same afternoon, etc. This is entirely to your choice. You may advise me as to your preference.
>
> My School of Music is the only School that teaches EVERY branch and subject relating to Music, in, or around Buffalo and Western New York State:

We teach the playing of EVERY instrument, Orchestra and Band; also, Harmony, Arranging, Composition, Counterpoint, Theory, Conducting, and Pedagogy (the Art of Teaching).

The course in Harmony and Arranging will, undoubtedly, be a source of delight to you, in-as-much as it condensed to the point of your getting and showing RESULTS in a matter of WEEKS instead of the old method of YEARS.

You may be interested in KNOWING the details, which I will give you when we meet.

The School is available to you during every afternoon. You may write to me at the address shown below, or you may drop in to see me.

To save time, I will now consider an appointment and time which I will keep open for you. If you do not report at that time, I will consider that you do not wish to study with this Music School and no harm will be done. I take this method of setting an hour for you, so that it will not be necessary for you to contact me before the first lesson. Let us set the time for Thursday, August 15 at 2:00 P.M. Daylight time. (1:00 P.M. Standard time)

> musically yours,
> Arthur F. Welte
> Welte Music School,
> 74th Armory, Connecticut and
> Niagara Sts., Buffalo, N.Y.
> (2 blocks from Peace Bridge)

Wilf's reply came a bit later than Welte had arranged, and clarified his little misunderstanding:

> September 11, 1946

> Dear Mr. Welte,

> Ken. And I will call on you about 4.00 o'clock to-morrow afternoon (Thursday, 12th.) We will then discuss the matters referred to in your letter of August 9th.

> Yours truly,

> (Mr.) Wilfred R. Wheeler

> P.S. If this should not meet with your plans – wire me collect at 57 Ontario Street, St. Catharines, Ont.

We can assume from this correspondence that Kenny decided to begin lessons with Welte after their initial meeting on 12 September 1946. Like Kenny's teacher in Windsor, Welte also ran a military band. As suspected from the tone of his letter, Kenny said that Welte was indeed "a bit of a con man, in a way. He used to get me to do musical problems, you know, weird problems to do with theory. And I'd spend a long time doing that, and I enjoyed that, but

I used to think, 'What's this got to do with a trumpet lesson?'"[83] Welte didn't do much for Kenny's trumpet playing, but soon afforded him an unforgettable opportunity to meet his heroes:

> He wasn't really very good, but I liked him a lot, and he said to me one summer, "Do you want to come to New York with the army band?" I said, "I can't do that, I'm a Canadian." He said, "Don't worry about that." So I went to the Catskill Mountains with this army band, only because he said we'd get two days off at the weekend, and I knew I would get to 52nd Street, which seemed like a dream to me. When the weekend came, Friday night, a bunch of us got the train and I got off at Grand Central Station and practically flew up to 52nd Street. I was 17 and looked about 12, and I had this American army uniform on. People looked at me as much as to say "What's this kid doing with the army uniform on?" I went straight for, I think it was, the Three Deuces where Charlie Parker was playing with Miles . . . I remember, this is my great claim, I spoke to Charlie Parker. I went up to him at intermission and said, "Where's Miles?" And he said, "He's out back." And that was the extent of my talk with Charlie Parker. I couldn't find Miles.[84]

After this experience, Kenny and his friends were no longer content to merely hear their favourite players on records or over the radio. They often travelled by bus, streetcar, or hitched a ride with friends to hear live music. Many of the most interesting big bands of the era played the Niagara Falls Arena, including those led by Lionel Hampton, Stan Kenton, Dizzy Gillespie, and Claude Thornhill. Kenny was already a fan of Thornhill's star alto saxophonist Lee Konitz by the time he heard the band live in late 1947 or early 1948:

> I remember once I went to hear Claude Thornhill's band – and Lee was in it. Being young and stupid, I noticed that they played a thing that was "Anthropology" . . . [and] when he played the solo he didn't play anything in the middle eight at all. So I went up to him and said "Excuse me Mr. Konitz, but can you tell me why you didn't play anything in the middle eight of your solo?" and he said, "I couldn't think of anything."[85]

These enthusiastic young Canadians also crossed the border into the United States to hear the touring bands. Kenny specifically recalled hearing small groups led by Dizzy Gillespie and trombonist J.J. Johnson in Buffalo.[86] Although Bill and Kenny were white and Art and his cousin Paul were from a mixed-race family, the guys generally frequented the clubs owned by and featuring black musicians, because that was where their favourite music happened. (As Kenny recalled, blacks and whites had their own private clubs for music in Buffalo at the time.[87]) Venues including Kleinhan's Music Hall were often the destination for Kenny and his friends when they wanted to hear a headliner group such as Frank Sinatra or the Stan Kenton Orchestra.[88] The

Amity Hall and the Colored Musicians' Club also hosted jam sessions where the boys went to listen but didn't have the courage to sit in.[89]

In the 1940s, Buffalo was a stop for the best musicians from New York. On 20 March 1949, the guys heard Charlie Parker's quintet play at Amity Hall in Buffalo. With the leader on alto saxophone, they heard trumpeter Kenny Dorham, bassist Tommy Potter, drummer Max Roach, and pianist Al Haig.[90] Parker made a strong impression on Kenny: "He was our idol, all of us young guys. Charlie Parker was a god. And Kenny Dorham was magnificent."[91] After the gig, the guys pressured Art to get up on the stand to play for Haig, who urged the young pianist to move to New York. (At the time, Art's talent was considered comparable to that of Oscar Peterson, a fellow Canadian whose star was just beginning to rise in the United States.) A similar situation happened when Art was asked to sit in with Lionel Hampton's band. Unfortunately, Talbot never left the area, playing gigs in the region less and less frequently.[92]

Occasionally, the guys would take a longer trip. Bill Jelley and Kenny once hitchhiked to Toronto to hear Canadian-born tenor saxophonist Georgie Auld. They couldn't get anyone driving a car to pick them up, but a brick truck stopped for them. The driver didn't let the two teenagers in the cab, so they had to ride to Toronto in the back of the truck with the load of bricks. "We were bouncing all over the back of that truck all the way to Toronto. Kenny was thin as a rail in those days. I thought, *Jesus, Kenny's going to fall through those bricks!*"[93]

———·———

Outside of their jam sessions at 21 Salina Street or at Bill Jelley's place, the bebop gang didn't perform together much. But in late 1947, Gus Garriock, who had the requisite skills and "connections", organized a concert at the Collegiate.[94] At the time, St. Catharines Collegiate hosted concerts fairly regularly; one such event starred Manitoba native Gisele MacKenzie, who later became famous on the 1950s American television show *Your Hit Parade*.[95] Two bands were set to play: one with Kenny and his friends playing bebop, and another band playing more traditional swing music, led by alto saxophonist Mynie Sutton and featuring pianist Bill Bradley, his brother trumpeter Howard Bradley, and drummer Rod North. Bassist Boris Zenchuck played with both groups. This more straight-ahead group enjoyed a friendly rivalry with the modernist boppers. Howard Bradley "couldn't stand" bebop and there were ongoing arguments between the groups' members over the musical tastes of the other.[96] (This conflict, on a small scale, echoed the one taking place between boppers and the "mouldy figs" in the larger jazz community at the time.) Sometimes guys from both groups would congregate at Rod North's house to listen to his sizable collection of 78s, which included both big-band and bebop records. Initially, Rod shared Howard's dislike of bop, until someone explained the concept of *contrafact* to him. (Contrafact is a musical device, used often in bebop, in which a new melody was written over the chord changes from an existing tune.) When the friend explained that Dizzy Gillespie's bebop tune "Groovin' High" was based on the old standard "Whispering", Rod whistled the older tune's melody while a record of "Groovin' High" played: bebop suddenly made sense to him.[97]

Some time before the concert at the Collegiate, bass player Art Davis brought Kenny along to a jam session at the Bradley brothers' house. Rod remembers this first encounter with Kenny, who just sat in the corner, "and sat there, and sat there, and sat there, and finally someone said, 'Hey kid, stand up and take a chorus!'" When he did, Rod was knocked out by the sound coming from the seemingly reticent young trumpeter. "The first thing that hit my head was that, to me, he sounded an awful lot like Buck Clayton. Not an imitation, but there was just something about the way he played."[98] Not surprisingly, Clayton was one of Kenny's favourite trumpet players at the time.[99] Another of the trumpeters Kenny admired early on was Billy Butterfield. He had caught Kenny's ear as the soloist on the 1940 recording of "Stardust" with the Artie Shaw Orchestra. Kenny described him as someone who had a "milky tone" but, more importantly, could play wide intervals cleanly – a technique that later became a trademark of Kenny's playing. "He could do those octave leaps with nothing in between. That always impressed me a lot," Kenny said.[100]

At the Collegiate Concert (facetiously dubbed "Canada's First and Only Jazz Concert" by Jelley) the Sutton group took the stage first, playing mostly standards and jazz tunes from the swing era. They were followed by the beboppers, who played some remarkably current repertoire – including Charles Thompson and Illinois Jacquet's "Robbin's Nest" and Fats Navarro's "Fat Girl"[101] – two tunes that had just been recorded in the first half of that same year.

With disappointing ticket sales and production costs to be paid, Garriock lost his shirt on the venture. Garriock's wife gave Bill Jelley grief when she ran into him after the concert, joking that their young family hadn't eaten for the month following. Regardless of the apparent lack of local interest, the concert was important in the history of art in St. Catharines. Niagara-based writer Terrance Cox said that the event

> encapsulates the coming to Niagara of modern jazz; it reveals, in hindsight, the cultural dynamics involved. During the late 1940s, Niagara was prescient in its reception of musical change; it got the news early. Conflictedly, this region was both a hotbed for major talents and a stultifying backwater that failed to foster them and led them to leave.[102]

Around this time, Art, Paul, Bill, Kenny, and Kenny's sister Helen took the streetcar to Niagara Falls to record some of the music they'd been playing together in a studio there. (The "studio", probably a low-key operation normally used for fun by young musicians far less serious than this group,

Photo 5: The concert at the Collegiate: Left to right: Bill Jelley, Kenny, Boris Zenchuck, Paul Lindo. (Art Talbot is seated at the piano behind Lindo.)

Courtesy Rod North

unfortunately happened to be near a streetcar that could be heard in the room.) The group cut four tunes: "Lester Leaps In", "Fat Girl", "Robbin's Nest", and "Don't Blame Me" (a vocal feature for Helen). For a small Canadian city in 1947, this was a very forward-looking group of young musicians, playing new music by their heroes on the cutting edge of bebop. Even then, Bill had a feeling that the recording might someday be an important document for posterity. Since the 78 rpm records were cut "direct to disc", there was only one opportunity at a complete take. If there was anything the musicians didn't like about their performance, no edits or other fixes could be made. From the moment it was recorded, Bill felt that some of the participants were "hell-bent on destroying it". Helen didn't like her feature because she thought the key the guys chose was too high for her voice. Kenny, self-critical even then, didn't like his solo on the tune either, even though Bill thought it was a "masterpiece for its time". There were only a few copies made; sadly, none seem to have survived to the present day.[103]

Kenny sought any possible opportunity to perform. While at St. Catharines Collegiate, he played in the "dreadful"[104] orchestra, even serving as its assistant librarian during the 1946–47 school year.[105] The Orchestra performed during Wednesday morning assemblies, described later by Gene Lees:

> "I remember you in that high school orchestra," I said [to Kenny]. "I never could understand how you stood it. I think you were the only trumpet in it. It was a weird instrumentation, anything they could find. Lots of fiddles and no cellos. That orchestra was so out of tune all the time. But I guess you were getting some kind of experience."[106]

Kenny was unsatisfied with his trumpet playing. He said, "I just stumbled around in the dark trying to get better. I wanted to go – I heard you *should* go – to NY to study off of one of the 'big guys' but I never had the money or the nerve to do that."[107] Some of the greatest jazz trumpet players were primarily self-taught and found idiosyncratic ways to solve their technical problems: unconventional methods that could lead to lasting physical damage. One need look no further for evidence of this than the deep scarring of Louis Armstrong's upper lip[108] or Dizzy Gillespie's famously puffed cheeks, which compromised his technique in later years. Aware of his own limitations, Kenny reflected:

> I don't think I practised properly, whatever it was, because I was well into this period of open lip thing you know . . . I never had a range at all, but a good big sound . . . I used to play on the bottom lip, all curled over . . . It was a horrible way to play. I mean, I didn't get over that for many, quite a few years after that.[109]

Even if his practice habits weren't as effective as he'd wished, Kenny did spend hours and hours practising the trumpet. He played from Jean-Baptiste Arban's *Complete Conservatory Method*, which is often referred to as the "trumpet player's Bible", used a metronome, and buzzed his mouthpiece frequently.[110] (Mouthpiece buzzing is used by trumpeters to improve their tone, accuracy, and flexibility.) Rod North even remembered riding to a gig while Kenny buzzed his mouthpiece in the back seat of the car the entire trip.[111] Kenny also had access to a few of his father's books on jazz playing, which were quite rare in those days: "He had improvising books at the house and he bought me a book by Roy Eldridge . . . he was always bringing books, a Harry James book or that kind of [thing] . . . and they always had little bits about how to improvise."[112]

Although Kenny experienced frustrations with the instrument, they were not apparent to his classmates at the Collegiate. The 1948 issue of the school's annual, the *Vox Collegiensis*, dubbed him "Hot Lips Wheeler", adding "Boy, can he dish it out on the horn!"[113] One can only imagine how this moniker made the shy teenager cringe.

Once he finished high school, Kenny spent around six months studying in Toronto at the Royal Conservatory of Music. There, he took trumpet lessons with Ross McLanathan,[114] and, more significantly, studied composition with John Weinzweig, one of the leading figures in serialism in Canada. Weinzweig, whom Kenny called a "great teacher", used Paul Hindemith's 1943 *A Concentrated Course in Traditional Harmony* as his textbook.[115] "He probably wouldn't remember me. I was probably just one of a hundred students he had,"[116] Kenny said, adding, "that's about all the studying I did in Canada".[117]

Wilf Sr. did not encourage his children to pursue music as a full-time career.[118] His own worries about securing steady and better employment to support his large family led him to advise them to "make sure you have another profession handy, something to fall back on".[119] In an effort to please his father after he graduated high school, Kenny worked in and around Toronto, including a series of odd jobs as a bank clerk, at a printing works, in insurance offices, and at a paper factory.[120] At one point he even worked at a supermarket in Detroit, irritating the manager to the extent that he "just had to look at me and he turned blue with anger. I was one of those fumbly type people that keep knocking things over. I'm horrible with my hands. Eventually he just looked at me and said, 'Why don't you go back to Canada?' So I did."[121] None of these jobs – which only ever lasted for a few months – were a good fit for Kenny. "Whatever job they gave me to do, I could do it quick, but I'd have to spend the rest of the day pretending I was busy, you know, and I think they found me out after a while."[122] This period lasted from around mid-1948 (when Kenny finished his final year at St. Catharines Collegiate) until early 1952. It is not clear whether Kenny actually graduated from the Collegiate, because he never passed the school's English course.[123] It was a frustrating time for Kenny: struggling with a normal job in the day, struggling to find trumpet work at night, and then ultimately failing at both and having to return to St. Catharines. "I always went home with my tail between my legs saying, 'Well, I'm home again!'"[124]

———·———

At the time, the legal drinking age in Ontario was 21, the same as it still is across the border in the United States. Since most of the guys in Kenny's musical circle were not of age to work in the pubs around St. Catharines, they did their best to find other places to play. One outlet was a "hamburger joint" (as Bill Jelley called it) at the east end of Hartzel Road. Kenny, Bill, Art, and Paul all played in a group there, led by a tenor saxophonist from Welland named Joe Calarco. They also played at Club La Salle, a venue still in existence in Port Weller, on Lake Ontario. The guys developed a bit of an unexpected following in the area. Kenny said:

> Well, actually, funnily enough, we had a following from some of the rougher elements of the, well, you know, these slightly more hooligan

teenagers seemed to, somehow they found some attraction to us because in our way we were rebels, you know. I mean, not, we didn't do anything violent but just to look at us you could see we were different . . . from some of the harder elements we had some sort of respect. I never quite analysed why but [laughs] . . . we were certainly not something to get too close to I don't think.[125]

At nearby Port Dalhousie, there was a pavilion in Lakeside Park that was home to local big bands. During the summer months, these bands played the pavilion almost every night of the week.[126] These bands played "jitney dances" at the pavilion, for which dancers paid

a nickel each to crowd the floor. To hits of the day, sweet or hot, they did the foxtrot or the jitterbug, for two choruses at best. Then came the rope. Burly fellows encircled the youthful crowd, hauling a rope of nautical thickness to clear reluctant patrons off the polished hardwood and usher them out for another nickel's worth of repeat business.[127]

Bruce Anthony's band was the most significant of the bands that played the Lakeside Park pavilion regularly. It was in Anthony's band that Kenny got his

Photo 6: The Bruce Anthony band, Kenny third from right.
Courtesy Wheeler family

first real training as a section trumpet player. "It had nothing to do with jazz," Kenny said, "but it wasn't quite so commercial as the other bands."[128] Kenny was a standout even then; a newspaper feature on the Anthony band said that "during the best years the band included such soloists as Kenny Wheeler, Wilf Williams, and brothers Bill and Howard Bradley."[129] In addition to gigs at the pavilion in Port Dalhousie, the Anthony band played at hotel dances and high-school functions throughout the area. A photo of the ensemble from the period shows a rail-thin late-teenaged Kenny, in the back row, undoubtedly its youngest member (see Photo 6).

Kenny was already experimenting as an arranger during this time, contributing charts including "Bye Bye Blues" and "It's Wonderful" to the Anthony band's book. He was also starting to seek work outside of the area and, even more profoundly, demonstrating an awareness that he would have to leave Canada altogether to become a professional musician. An unusually direct and self-promoting letter to a prospective employer from 22 March 1949 reads:

> 21 Salina Street,
> St. Catharines, Ontario,
> Canada.
>
> Mr. Sidney Foster,
> Orchestra Leader,
> The Elbow Beach Surf Club,
> Bermuda.
>
> Dear Mr. Foster,
>
> I have been in touch with Mr. Clifford Orson of Toronto, who suggested that I write you about playing in your orchestra.
>
> I play dance trumpet and am nineteen years old, and of good appearance. I have played with the best bands around here and Niagara Falls and played at the Arena there with the stand-in band, and at Port Dalhousie in the summer. I have had the best of coaching at Buffalo and studied harmony and arranging.
>
> Just recently I had an offer to play with an established band in Toronto. However, I would like to leave Canada, as I intend to make music a carreer [sic]. I am a good sight reader and can improvise if required – but do so legitimately. I have a knowledge of other instruments including string bass and piano.
>
> I just graduated from high school and am free to travel as I have no attachments. Wm. Currie and George Pitchko will also be in touch with you and I would like to go with them, as we would make a good combination and know each other.
>
> My understanding is that the job would pay $60.00 per week in Canadian money – plus room and board; with return fare provided.

Although I'd be willing to stay for a longer period, I believe a six months' contract is usual.

Please write or wire me.

Yours truly,

(Kenneth Wheeler)

As he mentioned in the letter, he began playing with the "stand-in band" at the Niagara Falls Arena, where he had only recently been on the other side as a listener. He also worked in a local band led by Bob Wybrow, whose group was hired to play during the intermission of visiting headliners so there was no break in the dancing and musical entertainment.[130] In 1948, Kenny, Bill, Paul, and Art were asked by two World War II veterans to play at their new "open-air dance floor" in Haliburton, Ontario, over 200 miles northwest of St. Catharines. Kenny and his friends had been looking for steady work and this opportunity was perfect, even though the dance floor hadn't yet been built. The entrepreneurial World War II vets found work for the musicians in the nearby "big, posh" lodges while they waited for their venue to be finished. Kenny and the guys resided locally while they were playing, made steady money, and had a great time on the beach when they weren't working. It was a great experience for them, even though the dance hall never materialized.[131]

The following year, the guys went up to Haliburton on their own to play a separate gig at Edgewater Beach Lodge. At the beginning of the summer the guys stayed at the lodge, playing only a couple nights a week and taking excursions on the boats and playing games, etc. As the tourists arrived, they began playing up to five nights a week. No longer able to avail themselves of the lodge's amenities, they soaked up the sunshine on the sandy beaches instead.[132] Kenny, already a capable pianist, had recently purchased a used Deagan vibraphone back in St. Catharines and brought it north with him. This addition allowed the group of clarinet, piano, drums, and vibes to begin exploring some new repertoire, such as Lionel Hampton's small-group arrangement of "How High the Moon".[133]

As the summer ended, the situation became less fun. The lodge owed them money. After a few drinks one night, a couple of the guys, angry at their predicament, punched holes in the "paper thin" walls of the room where they were staying at the lodge. Bill Jelley continued:

> [Early the next morning] we decided we'd call a cab with whatever money we had and get out of there. The guy who ran it was a crippled-up guy who'd had a stroke who was a mean bastard and usually carried a jug of whiskey with him – somebody you didn't want to deal with, you know. He was steaming, and we thought "We've got to get out of here" – we'd wrecked the place! We've got this cab coming, and all of a sudden we see this guy coming out of the office – this guy's coming across the sand, and the cab comes, and we're trying to get in the cab, get our shit in the cab

before he gets to the cab – and the cab driver drops his keys in the sand. I turned around and this guy is coming – closer and closer – and we got the hell out of there just barely in time. It was Kenny and I, because he had vibes and I had that big ass set of drums. Art and Paul just took off; Art had his sheet music for piano and Paul just had his clarinet case. Those guys went into town, but we had luggage to contend with! So we get in the cab, we took off into town, went to the train station, put our stuff on the train, shipped it to St. Catharines – we put it on collect back to St. Catharines and got rid of it – and Kenny and I, with no money left to take the train ourselves, hitchhiked back from Haliburton.[134]

———·———

If Mrs. Wheeler caused the most chaos but had the most fun in the family, her husband was the opposite – a rock of stability and routine, and the "glue" that held everything together. Bill Jelley commented that, at the time, the guys in Kenny's circle of friends found Mr. Wheeler to be "stoic and sober . . . but later thought that he had to be that way because of how things were at home."[135] He was very strict with the way he lived – he had a strong work ethic and tremendous discipline. Kenny said that when his father came home from work every day, "he had his life sorted out so I think he had like 20 minutes for eating, 20-minute nap, 20 minutes' practice."[136]

Wilf Sr. was also firm in the way he ran the household. He made sure his children all went to mass every morning before school, and he attended church with them every Sunday. The Wheelers were members of the Cathedral of St. Catherine of Alexandria in downtown St. Catharines, at the corner of Church and Lyman Streets. Kenny avoided most of the people by entering through the side door of the church; many times his siblings, seated in the main part of the sanctuary, didn't even know he was there.[137] At home, their father dictated that the family have proper meals together – "that was the English [grandparents] part coming out . . . sitting down and eating properly," Mabel said.[138] He was not tolerant of bad manners, once rebuking his daughter Helen after she dared to pick up a pork chop and eat it off the bone. During October, the month of the Holy Rosary in the Catholic tradition, the family would kneel down after dinner and pray the Rosary. Mabel recalled that her teenaged siblings would sometimes snigger to themselves, not always taking this ritual as seriously as their dad would have liked.[139]

Wilf Sr. practised the trombone regularly. He had set aside their home's dingy, unfinished basement to be his music room, which he would later lock away from curious grandchildren. He continued to regularly work in dance bands on the weekends, sometimes riding his bike to gigs when he couldn't get a lift with anyone else. The kids teased him occasionally, calling him "Bicycle Pete".[140]

The Wheelers also observed the Catholic tradition of having fish on Fridays during Lent. On one such Friday, long after Kenny had left the house, Mabel's then-boyfriend (later husband) Bryon Ball joined the family for supper. Mabel remembered:

> My mom – God love her. She always had the haddock soaked in the old fashioned sink. We sat down at the table to have fish and chips. Bryon had gone into the kitchen to wash his hands before we went to sit down and eat. My dad sat down to eat – and he was eating soap! What happened was, when Bryon went to wash his hands, the soap fell in with the fish, and she fried it. Bryon never even admitted it. My dad was little but, oh, he had a powerful voice: *MABEL! WHAT DID YOU DO TO THE FISH?*

Being new to the family and not willing to embarrass himself, Bryon only identified himself as the culprit to Mabel in the car after dinner.[141]

Although their poor mother got the blame for the fish incident, she became the hero of one of the family's favourite stories when she was responsible for the Wheelers finally getting a set of wheels. She had entered a raffle at a carnival hosted by the St. Catharines Lions Club and, remarkably, won the top prize of a new blue Buick sedan. When the phone rang that evening with the news, the steady, routine-bound Mr. Wheeler, already in his pyjamas, asked if they could wait until the next morning to claim their prize. Unbound by formality when handed the keys the following day, Mrs. Wheeler remarked, "I was hoping I'd won a refrigerator!" to the perplexed officer of the Lions Club.[142] This event became family legend, not only for the great stroke of fortune it represented but also for the warm way it showed their true personalities. A photo (Photo 7) captures her big moment, surrounded her husband and five of their grown children. Kenny, who preferred to be anywhere but the centre of such attention, was notably absent, probably gigging in Toronto or toiling away at one of his doomed short-term day jobs.[143]

At this time, Wilf Sr. was working far more gigs as a professional musician than Kenny was and never wanted to miss one. After they won the car, when they were on vacation in Northern Ontario, Wilf would even drive several hours back to St. Catharines for his gigs. He played dances with society bands on Saturday nights, and played on Sunday afternoons at Montebello Park with the Lincoln and Welland Regiment Band, returning to the family vacation that night.[144] Kenny and his father admired each other greatly, especially as they grew older. Although he downplayed his forays into the freelance musician scene in Toronto, Kenny did get a few gigs. While he was living in Toronto pursuing one of his dreaded "day jobs", he played "Polish weddings" in the city and worked with some dance bands in the area:

> Polish weddings I used to do, which used to last for about two days and at the end of it my lip would be out here somewhere, but it was quite an experience playing those things . . . You'd start to play this music and every

Photo 7: The Wheeler family with their big prize. Left to right: Paul, Helen, George, Wilf Sr., Mabel Sr., unknown, Mary, Mabel Jr., unknown.

Courtesy Mabel Ball

time a new couple would come in you'd have to stop whatever tune you were playing and play "The Wedding March", then they'd come over and give the prizes and stuff some money down the bell of the horns and . . . so it went on for two days, those things.[145]

He even had a chance encounter with one of his heroes when Duke Ellington was in Toronto playing one of the city's prestigious venues. "I didn't say a word to him," Kenny said. "It was in Toronto when I lived over there when I was young and his band was playing at, I don't know, Massey Hall or somewhere, and I just went into this place for a cup of coffee and he was there. I didn't know what the hell to say, so I didn't say anything!"[146]

Eager for more musically fulfilling work, Kenny took a gig playing with some of his old friends, including Bill Jelley, at the Club Norman in Toronto. The establishment was a spacious supper club with a jazz lounge upstairs (where the precocious Art Talbot played) and a dance hall downstairs where Kenny, Paul Lindo, and Bill Jelley played. The guys had to wear uniforms, which they hated. (In fact, on a few occasions in his later career, Kenny was never less happy than when in a band uniform.) Paul was resistant to cut his hair to keep the gig, but was finally convinced to submit to the management's dictatorial demands by Bill Jelley, who cut Paul's rather unruly mane himself.[147] Although Kenny was probably very happy to have this gig with his old friends, there were three major problems with the situation: Kenny was underage (at the time, the drinking age in Ontario was 21), it was a non-union gig, and the club was located rather inconveniently across the street from the Toronto musicians' union office. According to Kenny's sister Helen, "One of his so-called friends, a part-time musician from St. Catharines, went there to see him and then squealed on him [to the union]."[148] As punishment, Kenny was expelled from the Niagara local 298 chapter of the American Federation of Musicians, of which his father was the sergeant-at-arms. It apparently took a good deal of behind-the-scenes negotiations – and money – for Mr. Wheeler to get his son reinstated. It was a very embarrassing episode for Kenny. For the rest of his life, he remained a fully paid-up member of AFM local 298.

———·———

Exasperated with his son's inability to maintain employment, Kenny's father found a course for him at McGill University. Kenny said, "if you went to this school and did this music course you could end up as a high school teacher who taught music, but you'd have to teach other subjects because there were no jazz schools in those days."[149] To prepare for the course in Music Education, Kenny worked diligently on his piano skills. He studied with Edward Hattey,[150] one of the best teachers in St. Catharines, and spent the next six months – most of early 1952 – practising several hours a day. "I made a determined effort to get up to standard," Kenny said.[151] When he arrived in Montreal, he got a room at the YMCA and went to visit McGill: ". . . so I went there with the first term's money in my pocket and I walked around, and then I just realized that that wasn't going to be me at all. I couldn't see myself in front of a group of bored teenagers trying to tell them about music," he said.[152] "I told myself, 'I can't be a high school teacher. I don't want to be one, and I don't know what to do."[153]

But, deep down, Kenny knew what to do. The necessity to leave Canada, expressed so prophetically in the letter to Sidney Foster from three years earlier, still held true. "Well, it seemed obvious to me . . . It was the only thing to do. I had decided I wasn't going back to St. Catharines, no matter what. I just couldn't go back anymore."[154] Though he could have gone to the United States, Gene Lees speculated that Kenny would have been unable to get a visa at that time, but the reason Kenny commonly gave is that "the Korean War was on. I would have been eligible for the draft, and, I thought, maybe I won't get in a band, but they'll give me a gun and send me over there. That's why I didn't go to the States."[155] This was more than mere speculation: he knew this first-hand. His friend Bill Jelley had moved to the States a couple years before, became a legal resident and, as such, was eligible for the draft. By 1951, Bill was on a ship bound for East Asia.[156]

Kenny also toyed with the idea of going to Paris to study with famed pedagogue Nadia Boulanger, probably the most celebrated composition teacher in the world at the time. Boulanger trained such diverse and successful students as Aaron Copland, Elliott Carter, Quincy Jones, and Astor Piazzolla. In typical fashion, he demurred, "I mean, she probably wouldn't have taken me, but [I wanted] to study with somebody and work up to be able to study with someone like her, you know."[157] He considered other, more exotic options, like Cuba or South America, but in the end he decided he should go somewhere English-speaking.[158] Even a few years before, when he was playing at the lodge in Haliburton, he wrote in a letter home that he "would like to go to school in England this year and then transfer to the Royal Academy next year".[159]

In the midst of this dilemma, Kenny sought out his old friend from St. Catharines, Gene Lees, who by then was working for the *Montreal Star*. Lees had also wanted to escape "puritanical Ontario".[160] He was enjoying the thriving jazz scene in Montreal, which had recently given rise to stars including Oscar Peterson and Maynard Ferguson. "Montreal was an unabashedly corrupt city whose nightlife was wide open and roaring," Gene said. "Prohibition had never been enforced in Quebec, and Montreal had plenty of what Gide, I think it was, called 'that leisure without which we can have neither vice nor art.'"[161]

Gene Lees recalled the most poignant of scenes that somehow embodied the obstacles Kenny would have to overcome due to his shy personality. Soon after Kenny arrived at McGill University in Montreal, the two of them went to the Café St. Michel where some musicians, including trombonist Butch Wantanabe, were playing. Gene sat with Kenny near the stage. He wanted desperately to sit in. Gene tried to persuade him to ask, but Kenny just couldn't bring himself to do it. He just sat there, and even though they could clearly see the trumpet on his lap, no one asked him to play. "My heart ached for him," Lees said.[162]

Kenny confided in Gene about his dilemma over whether or not to enrol at McGill. Gene told him that there were lots of big bands in England in need of brass players, and he encouraged him to head to London and try to make a go of it. In possibly the boldest and most out-of-character act of his life, Kenny took Gene's advice – and the money from his father for McGill – and booked his ticket for England.[163] In the days before he left, Kenny was playing piano accompanying Gene, a crooner "in the Frank Sinatra tradition" in some Montreal clubs.[164] In late September 1952, Gene saw Kenny off at the Port of Montreal, where he boarded the RMS *Scythia* to Southampton. Kenny Wheeler was 22 years old.

He appeared in the ship's registry simply as:

282 / Kenneth Wheeler / Musician / Canada[165]

# 2  The Imminent Immigrant

**He was a brain and a half, Ken. There was a lot going on there.**

*Bobby Wellins*

There is a long tradition of older, more established jazz musicians sharing their knowledge and resources with the younger generation. Joe "King" Oliver had this relationship with the young Louis Armstrong. In *Pops: A Life of Louis Armstrong*, Terry Teachout wrote: "Oliver took Armstrong under his wing, and Little Louis, who still longed for someone to take the place of his vagrant father, responded with a filial respect whose intensity was documented in the tributes he later paid to the playing of the man he called 'Papa Joe'."[166] Dizzy Gillespie showed kindness and encouragement by visiting a 20-year-old trumpet player named Clifford Brown in the hospital when he was very badly injured in a car accident.[167] "'You've got to keep it going,' preached Gillespie; his praise and encouragement stunned Brownie and gave him new confidence. It made him all the more determined to renew his jazz career."[168] After mentoring him as a youth in St. Louis, Clark Terry helped a junkie named Miles Davis get off the streets of New York – even at great cost to himself.[169]

Elder musicians tended to look out for Kenny Wheeler as well: the trumpet teacher in Buffalo who provided a way for him to get to New York for the first time; the guys in Bruce Anthony's dance orchestra who introduced him to the art of big-band trumpet section playing; and his St. Catharines friends Art Talbot and Paul Lindo, who took him into their group and gave him a sense of belonging, both socially and musically. When Kenny boarded the RMS *Scythia* in Montreal, similar generosity and good fortune followed him. A Canadian trio, including bassist Johnny Bell (who later changed his name to "Thick Wilson" and played bit parts in film and television) was entertaining the passengers on board.[170] They told Kenny where he could find affordable lodging once he arrived in London. "The guys in the trio on the boat said, 'Well, come with us'",[171] and suggested a bed and breakfast near Oxford Circus. This is exactly where Kenny went when the ship arrived in Southampton on 2 October 1952.[172]

Once in London, Kenny searched newspaper listings for local jazz clubs, finding one in particular that he visited several nights in a row. (Kenny has recalled this as "maybe the Mapleton", but was probably the Flamingo Club, which, in late 1952, was located in the basement of the Mapleton Restaurant, on Coventry Street. In other interviews, he said it could have been Club

Seven.[173]) "There were some good players, like Leon Calvert, and I think Dizzy Reece was playing there . . . It was a bit out of my league at that time . . . I took my trumpet along and asked to play one night, and they did let me sit in, but nobody said anything. They never said I was any good, or bad."[174] This lack of response was a profound knock to Kenny's confidence. He often referred to the effect it had on him, describing it as making him go into what he called a "shell", shattering what little youthful confidence he had. Maybe it hurt all the more because, at the time, even though Kenny thought he was "pretty good"– even imagining himself as a "distant Miles Davis" – these players took no notice of him. It must have been a different response to what he was expecting, or maybe the musicians were less welcoming than he'd imagined: "I found England rather odd, socially, at first," he recalled.[175]

Despite this initial indifference on the part of other musicians, Kenny managed to get a gig only three weeks after his arrival in London, apparently under his own leadership. The advertisement read:

ZAN-ZEBA, 39 Gerrard Street, W.1. 12 till 4 every Saturday
presents this week Ken Wheeler, Canada's Sensation
with Johnny Rogers, Dickie DeVere, Lennie Metcalfe, Archie Mack.[176]

The basement at 39 Gerrard Street was home to a club that only occasionally hosted jazz gigs, and provided an all-night refuge for taxi drivers, serving tea, coffee, and sandwiches. Ronnie Scott remembered that "Quite a few musicians used to use the place, either to hang out between gigs, or else to rehearse or play a jazz gig for a handful of fans."[177] The original owner was Soho entrepreneur Jack Fordham, who was unable to turn much of a profit from the location. Fordham would eventually rent it to Scott and his business partner Pete King where they first opened their jazz club, "Ronnie Scott's", on the site seven years later.[178] Whether or not he was aware of it, other musicians were quietly taking notice of Kenny and his idiosyncratic style. Another newly arrived Canadian expatriate remembered hearing the shy young trumpeter for the first time in November 1952 at the 100 Club on Oxford Street: "He was very different then as well, you know. His phrasing, everything was different than anyone else."[179] The musician listening was saxophonist Art Ellefson, who had just made a parallel move from Canada to England a couple of weeks after Kenny.[180]

Kenny's first letter home to Canada, sent shortly after his arrival, must have caused quite a stir in the Wheeler household.[181] While his family remained happily under the impression that he was dutifully preparing to be a music teacher at McGill, Kenny was in fact 3,000 miles away struggling to find his place in the London music scene. Having not heard from him for a few weeks, Wilf Sr. contacted the university, who replied by telegram that they had no record of a "Kenny Wheeler."[182] Despite their initial shock, Kenny's siblings were very proud of his decision. Mabel said, "When I think back that Kenny would have that kind of drive or nerve to get on a boat like that and just take off – that was so against what he was really like. He really was a quiet, shy person. For him to be so adventuresome was amazing. It was the best thing he could ever have done."[183] Helen saw it the same way: "The whole family was in shock for two weeks. It was unbelievable. Not Kenny! I don't know about the rest of them, but I was glad. Because I knew it was really important for Kenny, and I was glad to see him do something different."[184] His friend Gene Lees agreed: "It was an incredible act of courage for someone so reticent. I couldn't believe it myself."[185] Even Wilf Sr., initially taken aback at his shy son's uncharacteristic boldness – and likely slightly annoyed that he'd spent the tuition money he'd given him on a transatlantic ticket – was proud of his son's adventurous spirit. Kenny had set off for the musician's life his father had always wanted for himself.[186]

"They were glad to hear from me, I think," Kenny said.[187] "Although my father always had little ways of never letting me forget what I did."[188]

———·———

Two positive results came from Kenny's traumatic experience sitting in at that English jazz club. First, he met a young Scotsman there who had a job checking coats, to whom Kenny casually mentioned he was running out of money. "Being the age I was, 22, I guess somehow things like that don't bother you so much."[189] But he needed to find a new place to live – and soon. The young Scotsman said that he was staying at a rooming house, and that Kenny could come stay with him there. He took him up on the offer and remained there for a few weeks.

The second fortuitous event to come from this experience was a direct result of living at the boarding house. Within just a few weeks of arriving in London, Kenny serendipitously met a young woman named Doreen Yeend over the telephone:

> The young Scottish guy had a girlfriend, who was a girlfriend of Doreen's. And I think [Doreen] rang up one day, and said his girlfriend couldn't meet him at this time they'd set. So for some reason or another, I got talking to Doreen . . . And being cocky and confident, I made a few jokes, and I said, "Why don't you write me a letter?" or something, and I think we corresponded a little bit, and decided to meet up . . .[190]

The daughter of Robert and Violet Yeend, Doreen was just 19 years old at the time.[191] She had a job polishing pens in a factory that manufactured upscale writing utensils in Hackney, not far from her parents' Bethnal Green home. She also remembered meeting Kenny on the phone:

> It used to be every Thursday, my friend [and her] boyfriend used to phone one another, and see one another perhaps weekends. That's how I came

to talk to him. Cocky me, I'd say "give me the phone . . ." [when] Ken answered, I said, "I'll come to talk to him" . . .[192]

The pair exchanged photographs, and Kenny eventually asked her to meet in person and go on a date. "I wore a zoot suit and all, because it was still my Canadian influence," he said. "With big shoulders and draped trousers! . . . I must have looked weird in London! But for some reason she liked me."[193] Kenny took her to the 100 Club. "She'd never been to a jazz club in her life. She didn't know what jazz was all about, even."[194] However, old traits die hard and the ever-shy Kenny was barely able to speak a word to Doreen on their first date. "She must have thought, 'What the hell is this?'" he said.[195] His impressions were correct: Doreen found Kenny's shyness disconcerting at the club that night, to the point of being a bit unsettling. Sixty years later, she said, laughing, ". . . sitting there like a dummy, I was thinking, 'What's happening now? What's next? Will he murder me? He might be a strangler!'"[196] When Doreen grew tired of listening to music she wasn't exactly interested in while sitting with a date who couldn't find the courage to speak to her, she understandably decided it was time to go home. "He took me back to the tube station, bought the ticket and that was it."[197] Kenny, on the other hand, ever-focused on music, went back to the club to hear the last set.

Obviously, Kenny didn't have much romantic experience before he met Doreen. Even though he was the older of the young pair, he was likely just as naïve as his date. "I was quite hopeless with ladies in Canada. I had known a couple of girls, but nothing . . . I was completely hopeless."[198] Kenny explained that young men were ignored by girls in St. Catharines, "unless you're an ice hockey player or a football player or something". He said that back in Canada they thought he was a "strange bebop musician . . . Some of us used to walk around with big shoulders and great trousers. We played the part, you know? I'm sure people either thought we were homosexual or took dope or something!"[199] His sister Mabel remembered that there were some girls he had crushes on in high school, but that was about all. One girl Kenny really liked in high school in St. Catharines was Barbara McMann, a beautiful and popular young woman who he probably thought was out of his league.[200] One can only speculate as to whether or not he had any romantic success in the months in Toronto before moving to London.

Despite their semi-disastrous first date, Doreen was still interested in Kenny. "I used to ring him up every so often, then we got together," she said.[201] Before long, Kenny overcame his shyness and the couple started dating. Although it had led him to meeting his new girlfriend and had saved him in a time of poverty, Kenny's living situation at the rooming house became increasingly uncomfortable. The manager of the rooming house who supported the helpful Scotsman was constantly bringing home new young men, and his public displays of affection in the shared space of the house were embarrassing to Kenny. "I remember one night I came in . . . [He] was hugging a young ballet dancer still in his tights . . . and I thought 'I'd better start thinking about getting out of here.'"[202] This said, the rooming house manager never made any advances on Kenny – he was apparently more interested in the Scotsman.[203]

It was now late 1952. Still not completely supporting himself as a professional trumpeter, Kenny read in the newspapers that there was a need for extra assistance at the post office for the Christmas rush. He got a job there for a few weeks and as a result could finally afford his own flat.[204] During the first week of that December, there was a dense "pea soup"-like fog choking the city. "The Great Smog of 1952" was dangerous indeed. Recent studies have estimated that around 12,000 people may have died from the effects of the suffocating combination of air pollution and London's notorious fog.[205] The air was apparently so thick that parents were advised to not let their children attend school for fear they would get lost on their way. People had to cover their nose and mouth when going outdoors.[206] This public health crisis, which lasted between 5 and 8 December, motivated the British government to legislate and led to the Clean Air Acts. Living in the East End of London at the time, Kenny and Doreen both remembered this time vividly, although the experience didn't seem to faze Kenny. "Being that age, you didn't think about it. You're just young and stupid!"[207]

———·———

When the Christmas season ended, Kenny needed to find other work. The plentiful dance band gigs promised to him back in Canada had so far seemed to be a product of Gene Lees's imagination. Just as he was becoming frustrated with his inability to find sustained work as a musician, he found out about Archer Street. Archer Street was just a short, paved lane between Rupert Street and Great Windmill Street in Soho. But in an era before domestic telephones were common, it served as a hub for freelance musicians to connect with bandleaders needing extra players.[208] On Monday afternoons, when the nearby pubs closed, musicians near the top of the pecking order and newcomers alike gathered there to find gigs, to get paid for previous work, and to meet socially.[209] The stage doors of several nearby theatres, including the Apollo and the Lyric, also opened out onto the narrow street, so it was a natural place for musicians to congregate.[210]

Bassist Dave Holland, who would seek out Archer Street nearly a decade later as a 17-year-old, recalled that musicians used their instrument cases as props:

> If you were a bass player you had a bow case, and if you were a drummer you had a stick bag so they could identify what you played . . . So I went down with my bow case because everybody was doing it. And somebody would come up to you, you'd be standing around the street chatting, and say, "Are you free on so and so for this?"[211]

Archer Street was also a centre of social activity. Even local stars at the top of the London jazz scene including Joe Harriott, Ronnie Scott, and Tubby Hayes came to Archer Street to spend social time with their musician friends. Art Ellefson recalled:

> Well, the idea was that everyone went there to get work, but I never got any gigs there! I just went for the social side. It was a small street, and it was full of musicians. There was a small café there as well – the Melody Inn it was called – that had a football machine, so I used to spend a lot of time on that . . . And then we'd end up in the Red Lion on the corner with guaranteed results. It was a pub, and we sat in there and would talk a load of rubbish, which got more rubbishy as the evening went on. I don't recall seeing [Kenny]. I spent a lot of time there with Bobby Wellins and a lot of other people who were in the jazz scene at the time. It was a great social day I always found, but I can't recall getting too many gigs there. Well, your face gets known, anyhow. Maybe something could come out of it later.[212]

Kenny remembered his own experience with Archer Street:

> Well, the dance band was still in full flight when I arrived, you know, so there were all kinds of big bands on the road, and they all had three or four trumpets so there was plenty of work around. And they had this street where they used to collect every Monday afternoon, all the musicians would just go and stand there – it was like a marketplace . . . And there was a lot of wheeling and dealing and hustling going on – but even if you didn't push yourself or didn't say anything – eventually somebody would say, "Hey, I need four trumpets – do you know anybody?" And somebody would say, "I think that guy plays the trumpet."[213]

Archer Street's popularity and usefulness slowed fairly quickly in the mid-1960s as it became more common for musicians to own a telephone, and declined into oblivion with the advent of the home answering machine.[214]

Soon, Kenny made an important decision. He had been offered a gig with a band that was about to travel to Ireland. Kenny wanted Doreen to come with him, but her father wouldn't allow such a trip.[215] "So eventually I said, 'I suppose we'd better get married,'" Kenny explained years later in a faux-romantic tone.[216] At this point in their budding relationship, one wonders if Doreen understood Kenny's droll sense of humour, but she seemed not to be bothered by the practicality of the situation. "We got married," she said, citing the bottom line: "It only took five months!"[217] Kenny's pragmatism also showed itself in his choice of his best man, Art Ellefson. "He phoned me one day in 1953 when we hadn't seen much of each other since the time I first heard him play, and asked me to be his best man at his wedding." Kenny told him that he chose him because he didn't know anyone else.[218] "Our relationship was kind of strange," Ellefson said.

Photos 8 and 9: Kenny and Doreen on their wedding day.
Courtesy Wheeler family

Kenny Wheeler and Doreen Yeend married on the 28th of March 1953 in the Roman Catholic Church of St. Anne on Underwood Road in London. Doreen's older sister Joyce was maid of honour. Their wedding portrait, taken on the steps of the church (Photo 8), shows a smiling young Doreen, beautiful in her long white dress, one arm clutching a newly moustachioed Kenny (decked out in a suit and tie) and the other cradling a bouquet of white calla lilies. A photo from their reception (Photo 9) shows Kenny holding Doreen tightly while kissing her in front of their three-tiered wedding cake. After the wedding, Doreen moved into Kenny's flat.[219] A few days later, he was off with the Roy Fox band – the first gig he had picked up on Archer Street.

The American cornet player Roy Fox was known for playing extremely softly – so softly that he could serenade audience members without interfering with their conversations. This skill earned him the nickname "The Whispering Cornetist". Fox came to London in 1930 to play at the Café de Paris and stayed, forming a new band after his original group returned to the United States. By the time Kenny got his first work with the band, Fox had largely moved away from leading the band under his name to operating a booking agency.[220] "It was the old kind of standards type big band. But I enjoyed it, you know,"[221] Kenny said. "Fox was quite famous in England as a commercial bandleader. He liked jazz, and you'd get to play jazz solos in his band."[222] A feature in the *New Musical Express* titled "Roy Fox Launches His New Band" included a photo of Kenny in the trumpet section. When he joined the band in early April 1953, the group (which the features author called "... rough, but has the makings of a good dance band because it has a beat") began several days of rehearsals before departing on a tour of the north of England and Scotland. Kenny's North American background must have been considered a bit of a novelty at the time, as the article goes out of its way to mention "Ken Wheeler, who hails from Canada ..."[223]

By the summer of 1953, Kenny left the Fox band and was on the road again, this time with his new bride, playing with tenor saxophonist Freddie Courtenay's band for an engagement on the Isle of Wight. The resort at Yarmouth, called the Savoy Summer Camp, hosted the band for the summer season. Kenny joined Courtenay, alto saxophonist Colin Moore, and trombonist Ken Wood on the group's front line. The group's drummer had a set of vibes which Kenny practised at lunchtime, carrying on an interest he'd begun back in Canada with his bebop friends. As with his piano playing, Kenny was actually quite an accomplished vibraphonist and, much to his embarrassment, people who had heard him practising at lunch would request him – not the drummer – to play the vibes for them at night.[224]

That autumn, Kenny began playing with a group led by Derek New at the Celebrite restaurant.[225] Kenny said, "I think the Celebrite was the first one I got where I had to play with a cup mute all night", because the band, decked out in coats and bow ties, was playing for talkative diners and needed to control their volume.[226] By going a bit more "commercial", he was starting to make some money. Kenny had mixed emotions about his improving economic situation: "I got £18 a week, and because I was still living just up the street from my wife's parents – who were real Bethnal Green cockneys – I felt so guilty because her father was making £12 a week at that time and then here I come along with £18 a week. It seemed like a fortune to me."[227]

In February 1954, Kenny joined some of his former summer bandmates from the Isle of Wight with trombonist Ronnie Rand's Blue Rockets at the Tottenham Palais.[228] "Saturday afternoon would be the ballroom dances. It was kind of a schizophrenic existence there. I can't remember, people like Colin Wright was on first alto, Ken Wood, who I still see his name occasionally was on trombone, Freddie Courtenay was a saxophone player but no real big names that ever got up into the jazz world were there."[229] Kenny was still dissatisfied with his trumpet playing and was suffering from some bad habits; after every night, his mouthpiece left a white mark on his lip. Playing fourth trumpet in dance bands like the Blue Rockets provided Kenny with an opportunity to work on his limitations with endurance and range – at that point due to what he called a "terrible embouchure" – without risking his employability:

> I realized that I wasn't going to make too many years as a trumpet player if I went on like that, so I got a job in another commercial band which was pretty horrible ... I had to make sure I had a regular wage coming in and

it also enabled me to play fourth trumpet, so I just stuck my lip and made sure that it stayed inside the mouthpiece . . . [T]he first few months were pretty horrible because I could hardly play but I managed to play enough to keep the job. After about six months things started to get a bit better.[230]

For a trumpet player to take themselves through an embouchure change without guidance, while holding down a full-time gig, remains an extraordinary feat. It demonstrates what a fundamental understanding of the instrument he must have developed, and this experience may explain his lifelong commitment to a diligent practice regime. These dance gigs were not only good for his trumpet technique but also for his development as a jazz musician. "You got to improvise more because you had to play for a bit of dancing but you got to play standard tunes and play solos on them – which was great for me," Kenny said.[231]

Kenny also played in various nightclubs at the time, which also helped his musical growth. "You could learn a lot of tunes in a job like that, either a quintet or a quartet. You had to come up with new standards . . ." He did "a couple of nightclub jobs in London, from 10 at night till 4 in the morning. I got an all-night bus back to Bethnal Green. That's when they still had the ladies on the street in London . . . *Like a good time, Dearie*?" he mimicked.[232] While not exactly the type of music he desired to play artistically, playing in the nightclubs had the additional benefit of helping Kenny gain better control over his nerves: "I've always had trouble with nerves and the fear of playing badly," he said. "I used to use too much pressure and my lip tires easily when I'm nervous. It's one of my problems that there is an audience there. When I feel someone is actually listening to me, I get worried, and I only play well when I can be calm and relaxed. Though I feel less tense in a big band, where I am among friends, it is still a very annoying problem for me."[233]

Over the next twenty-odd years, Kenny would play many gigs that may not have been the most musically fulfilling because he had a family to support. Once they became parents, Doreen took care of the children and their home, allowing Kenny to take any work that came his way. Throughout his life, Doreen was the rock who held their family together and made it possible for Kenny to pursue his career, which increasingly became aligned with his artistic vision. Reflecting on it later, he seemed unfazed by the frequent changes of bandleaders and relative musical obscurity that was central to this period after he moved from Canada:

> . . . there was no shortage of work, because it was the end of the big band era, so you could get a job on fourth trumpet even if you couldn't blow your nose on it. Now it's different, of course – much harder . . . I was a late starter. I mean, some of the young musicians worry at 22 that they're not going to get an LP, that they're not getting recognition.[234]

In addition to his commercial work in the dance bands, he saw more of his friend Art Ellefson. "We got to like each other right away," Kenny said.[235] The two had much in common. Like Kenny, Art was Canadian and had played in and around Toronto while still in his late teens.[236] Soon after his arrival in London, Ellefson began playing in dance bands, including the Vic Lewis Orchestra. Another organization Art was associated with at the time was led by the Trinidadian clarinetist Carl Barriteau. He was a formidable technician of the Artie Shaw school with great power and an extremely wide dynamic range, especially remarkable for the clarinet. He was voted best clarinetist in England by *Melody Maker* magazine seven years in a row.[237] When Barriteau's trumpet player left, Art recommended that Kenny replace him: "I arranged for Ken to do an audition for Carl. I was in the band and Carl needed a trumpet player, and I said 'I know this guy.' A couple [other] guys showed up. One guy did the audition. I looked around for Ken, and he had disappeared, so he didn't get the job!" Art continued, "Later on, we needed a trumpet player again and he got the job then."[238] However, Wheeler was reticent to join Barriteau's five-piece front line, saying "I really shouldn't have taken the job, because I didn't have the chops for it. It was a really hard book." Nevertheless, Kenny enjoyed the band a great deal. Kenny said the band "was a little more adventurous, but it was still based on old standards and things like that".[239] Unfortunately, his anxiety in performance led him to reject any live radio dates that Barriteau offered. "I told Carl, 'I'll be in the band', but I just couldn't do the broadcasts."[240] Kenny's perfectionism was a source of unease not only for himself, but also occasionally caused problems for his bandmates.[241] Ellefson explained:

> He never made a mistake – ever. He was a flawless player. It was a hard book – apparently it was very difficult for trumpet. We used to do Sunday concerts, and one night – well, this happened a couple times – the bass player came up to me, who was a friend of mine, and said "Kenny is so nervous he can't go on." I would go up to Ken and get him to play. He'd go up front for a solo and you could see his knees shaking – he was just absolutely terrified – and yet he would play wonderfully. It was really embarrassing to watch – a guy who was as great as him being so frightened of playing in public. We never talked about it – I didn't want to embarrass him about it. I just knew he was very nervous in concerts. Dances not so bad, but Sunday concerts, a lot of them at that time really made him nervous.[242]

During this time, Kenny's old friend Gene Lees was dealing with his own performance issues back in Canada. One of Gene's friends recommended him for an appearance on an amateur variety show called *Opportunity Knocks* on the CBC. After being accepted onto the programme and realizing that he would be accompanied live by a large studio orchestra, he became very nervous and was thrown off during the broadcast by a new arrangement of his chosen tune, entering the bridge of the song prematurely. According to his own account, although he recovered quickly, the humiliation of the experience jarred him for a number of years. Among other consequences, the blow to his confidence meant he never followed through on his promise to join Kenny in London.[243] Unaware of all this, Kenny continued to wait for his friend. "Even after three or four months I still expected [Gene] to come. Suffering away I was in England, and I kept thinking 'Gene'll be here any day, and save me.' [He] seemed so much stronger than I," Kenny said. "I thought, 'We'll form this nice trio, and Gene will be singing, and it will be all right.' And then after three or four months, it dawned on me: he's not coming." It wasn't until some 30 years later that Gene had the courage to tell Kenny about the devastating performance on *Opportunity Knocks* and confess why he didn't move to England after all.[244]

In 1954, long after Kenny had become "a little bit annoyed" with him, Gene was finally able to pay him and his new bride a visit.[245] He was still working as a writer for the *Montreal Star* when he was asked to cover the Royal Canadian Air Force's operations with NATO in Europe. Without telling them in advance, Gene flew to England, made his way to London, found the Wheelers' address in Bethnal Green, and knocked on their door. Doreen was preparing to go out for the 21st birthday of one of her friends: "Someone walked down the top of the street and I knew right away it was for me. And I just thought, 'Oh my God. Look at me!'" When Doreen answered the door, her hair fully adorned in curlers, she explained that Kenny was in Manchester, on tour with the Barriteau band. "It didn't bother him. He came in and introduced himself, and he said, 'Let's take a walk up to the market', so I had curlers in my hair walking up to the market! . . . then he said, 'Let's go to Manchester.'" Doreen cancelled her party plans with her friends and the two boarded the train. On the trip, he talked to her about music. She made the mistake of politely saying, "Don't think I know that one, try singing it to me." But Gene Lees wasn't exactly a subtle vocalist: "He wasn't the type of person to sing soft," she said, having been made uncomfortable by his musical exhibitionism on the train.[246] As if this weren't enough unwelcome entertainment, Gene also whistled Charlie Parker tunes on the train. "She thought [he was] mad," Kenny said. "But she liked [him]. Just for her to go out of Bethnal Green at that time was an experience . . . She'd never been anywhere at that time. She enjoyed the whole adventure. It was something completely new for her."[247] Since Doreen had phoned Kenny in advance of leaving London, he met her and Gene at the train station in Manchester.

Gene recalled hearing Barriteau's band that night:

> I remember the musicians laughing during the breaks. They said Carl Barriteau had such powerful chops that he could play clarinet louder than a whole brass section . . . What I remember is the extraordinary power of

his playing; the fact that the musicians liked him; and that he seemed to have a higher opinion of Kenny's playing than Kenny did.[248]

———·———

Doreen and Kenny moved from his flat into Doreen's parents' house at 14 Gales Gardens in 1954.[249] Gales Gardens was a very short, narrow street just west of the Bethnal Green Underground station that hosted a row of small houses which were shared by two and sometimes three families, each of whom would occupy a single floor. Kenny and Doreen shared a single bedroom and an outdoor bathroom. On 25 September 1955, Kenny and Doreen's first child, Mark, was born at the East London Maternity Ward.[250] Doreen originally wanted him to be named Kenneth, after her family's tradition of naming first-born boys after their fathers, but when Kenny protested, she compromised and give Mark his father's middle name instead, Vincent. They asked Art Ellefson to be his godfather and named a woman who lived on Gales Gardens named Kitty Bell (a practising Catholic) his godmother. Although Kenny and Doreen weren't particularly religious, they brought their children up Catholic out of respect for the deeply held faith of Kenny's father.[251]

In 1956, they moved down the street to number 22, where they stayed for several years. Crammed into three small rooms, the Wheelers shared this house with two other families. Mark recalled:

> We had no central heating or bathroom and an outside toilet (bearable in the summer but crap – if you'll excuse the pun – in winter). We had a small kitchen (with a door to the outside loo) and front room on the ground floor with our only bedroom being on the first floor . . . At the end [of the street] where we lived, we did not have houses opposite but we did have a wood yard opposite behind which was a railway line. My Mum's Mum and Dad lived in the same street, as did one of my Mum's brothers (Ronnie) and her sister (Joyce) and their families. Her other brother Bobby was a 20-minute walk away with most of my Mum's cousins and aunts/uncles also within easy walking distance.[252]

Although she had the benefit of family nearby, Doreen's early years as a young mother were difficult. Kenny took every gig he could to make ends meet; many of these night-time club jobs left Doreen at home alone with baby Mark, who suffered from eczema from infancy until his late teens.[253] Kenny was attentive to his young son and was eager to ease his misery; he even accompanied Mark on some of his doctor visits for treatment. Doreen chose not to work, preferring to stay home with Mark. Money was tight in the early days. "We just managed," she said. When gigs were scarce, Kenny occasionally helped make ends meet by working as a deliveryman for her brother's business. "He hated it," she said.[254]

Mark recalled Kenny being away often but always making time for family during the holidays:

> He was always around from Christmas Eve through to the New Year and I know he regularly turned down work over that period so that he could be at home. We did get used to him being away and accepted it as part of family life. We had the rest of the family close by, so we did a lot with them when my dad was away . . . I really think that people could not figure out what my Dad actually did and why he was away so much.[255]

When he was home, many times Kenny was in his room practising. Sometimes little Mark would be allowed in the room with him, pretending to play the trumpet with him. But, most of the time, Kenny was alone. "It was normal . . . he would just be in there, just practising in the little room . . ." Doreen did most of the child rearing, since Kenny was gone so frequently. He wasn't a disciplinarian, but Mark remembers once when he stuck his tongue out at his mother, his dad smacked him. "It didn't hurt," he said, but "it was a shock because he did it."[256]

———  ·  ———

After leaving Barriteau's band, Kenny joined another ensemble, this time a leading jazz group fronted by saxophone star Tommy Whittle. Strongly influenced by Lester Young and Don Byas, Whittle won top honours in polls by *New Musical Express* and *Melody Maker*. Like Kenny, Tommy Whittle had also played in Carl Barriteau's band. Whittle's manager at the time urged him to form his own band, which he did, including Kenny on trumpet, trombonist Keith Christie, Ronnie Baker on alto saxophone, Joe Temperley on baritone saxophone, pianist Don Riddell, Freddy Logan on bass, and drummer Eddie Taylor.[257] Kenny said Whittle "appeared at my door one day and said, 'Would you like to play in my band?' I guess that was the first real jazz band I played in . . . a very enjoyable situation."[258]

The Tommy Whittle Orchestra recorded two albums for Esquire in November 1955 and March 1956 comprising mostly jazz standards. These are the earliest known commercial recordings of Kenny's trumpet playing and writing. Although he was considered a late bloomer by jazz trumpet standards – Bix Beiderbecke, Fats Navarro, Clifford Brown, and Booker Little never saw the age of 30 – few musicians can match the level of development that 26-year-old Kenny Wheeler displayed on this recording, especially on his arrangement of "Autumn in New York". Much of his mature and instantly recognizable musical persona is already in place: the "fat" trumpet tone, harmonically explorative lines, and unorthodox approach to rhythm and phrasing were coming into focus. This is not to mention the mature voice Kenny showed as an arranger here, already displaying a predilection towards lush orchestration, unconventional chord progressions, and contrapuntal interplay.

Five years later, Kitty Grime wrote that this association was possibly Kenny's "most interesting assignment" during this era of his career.[259] Kenny said, "They were still dance gigs but it was far more jazzy than anything I'd ever done, and naturally, being Tommy it would be. He had his little commercial things for the audience, but if you've got people like Keith Christie and Joe Temperley, you know . . ."[260] As a bandleader, Whittle was less tolerant than Barriteau of Kenny's idiosyncrasies, which forced him to address his issues with his chops and nerves: "He had no sympathy for me when I used to say, 'Tom, my lip's tired.' He would say 'shake it!' [*laughs*] But it was good for me because I really got pushed, you know."[261]

Despite the encouragement he mostly received, Kenny would continue to fight self-doubt. A lukewarm feature on the Whittle band from October 1955 by Tony Brown couldn't have helped matters:

> At the Samson and Hercules at Norwich last week another band joined the bulging ranks of one-night-stand attractions. It should not be gathered, however, that the Tommy Whittle Orchestra is just another band. The Whittle band reflects to some extent the virtues that have made Tommy a widely respected musician. It is orderly, conscientious, and musically interesting. It is vigorous, too, even if it doesn't match the fire of the old Ronnie Scott band whose instrumentation (less a tenor) it duplicates. The Whittle band certainly has a solo strength comparable to the original Scott band. Tommy himself is a fluent and lucid player; Joe Temperly [*sic*] on baritone manifests a refreshingly coherent style; Keith Christie plays, as he always does with a great appreciation of dynamics; alto saxist Ronnie Baker and trumpeter Kenny Wheeler both show great promise as exponents of the Modern.[262]

Although the reviewer is kind enough to the Whittle band up to this point, he saves a few jabs for Kenny:

> It was, perhaps, too much to expect that they would knit immediately into a well-balanced ensemble. Individual volumes too frequently spoke for themselves. Temperly's beefy tone protruded most of the time; Baker's alto too often was lost; and the lead voice of the trumpet lacked the fullness and conviction that is essential in this particular line-up.

and:

> Kenny Wheeler I regard as a trumpet player as yet a long way from his potential. But his work deserves attention, despite the fact that he lacks the confidence at present to express himself fully and pungently.

Kenny would have to suffer reviewers like this one throughout his career: those who praised him in one sentence and criticized him with the next.

Photo 10: Kenny with the Tommy Whittle Orchestra: Cafe Royal, Leicester Square, London, 1955. Left to right: Tommy Whittle, Eddie Taylor, Don Riddell, Kenny, Freddy Logan, Ronnie Baker, Keith Christie, and Joe Temperley.

Courtesy the Peter Vacher Collection

Even though the group featured such a great deal of emerging talent, it was unable to survive the harsh economics of the London jazz scene. After just over a year together, Tommy Whittle disbanded the group. It has also been suggested that Kenny's continued refusal to perform on live broadcasts with Whittle's band due to his nerves might have contributed to a lack of understanding by listeners of how the band truly sounded, thus limiting their potential appeal and popularity, ultimately accelerating their demise.[263]

As mentioned, Kenny was developing not only as a trumpet player but also as a composer/arranger. He began to analyse the writing on recordings he liked, including the 1953 recording "A Ballad" by the Gerry Mulligan Tentet, which he "took to pieces and learned a lot about jazz harmony especially".[264] Later in 1956, Kenny began playing with Buddy Featherstonhaugh, who was putting together a brand-new band. On 3 December 1956, he recorded four tunes (including one of Kenny's originals called "Goldfish Blues") with Featherstonhaugh's "New Quintet", with the leader on clarinet and baritone saxophone, Bobby Wellins on tenor, bassist Bill Stark, and drummer Jackie Dougan. The liner notes cite Kenny's contribution, calling him "a charming and introspective jazz player with a great deal of talent both on trumpet and piano".[265] Featherstonhaugh had been very active as a tenor saxophonist and clarinetist throughout the late 1930s and '40s (he played with Louis Armstrong's British band and Spike Hughes's Decca band), but took a ten-year hiatus from music after World War II, ostensibly to return to race car driving, in which he had been active in the '30s.[266,267] Bobby Wellins joked that there were rumours Featherstonhaugh was "born on the wrong side of the blanket", meaning that there was "some kind of hint that he was related to the then Queen Mother!"[268]

Kenny played both trumpet and piano with Featherstonhaugh's band. "The first thing we ever did was a summer session at Butlin's [seaside resort] where we were supposed to play rock 'n' roll, and I was the piano player – I was supposed to stand up [and play] *à la* Fats Domino or one of those people," he said. (It is simultaneously difficult and hilarious to imagine the shy young Kenny doing his best to ham it up at the piano in this way.) "But we ended up just playing jazz, which was surprising. I think we lasted the summer, but I kept expecting for us to get sacked," he said.[269] "I think a lot of customers didn't like what we were doing."[270] At least this summer gig had one important perk: Kenny could bring Doreen and little Mark along.

With Featherstonhaugh, Kenny got to see a good bit more of the world than just the Butlin's camp at Clacton. During this period of "the troubles" with Cyprus, the British Army sent the band on a tour of the Middle East to entertain the troops stationed around the Mediterranean. Travelling with the band were two comedians who had a routine, with gags and songs that Kenny accompanied on the piano. Bobby Wellins recounted one night the band got their hands on some ouzo after the concert:

> Of course there was a bit of hilarity after that. A bit of this and a bit of that, and the next thing, Ken and I were drunk and dancing on the tables. I think we thought we were Gene Kelly or Fred Astaire, somebody. He was fun, Ken. When we were on these gigs, the gigs were fantastic. That was a fantastic tour. Jackie Dougan, Ken, and I, we had a lovely time there.[271]

The band also travelled to Malta, Benghazi, Tripoli, and up the North African coast. Wellins remembered how one of the "jolly padres" who was on hand to welcome them insisted that they stop for tea at a site in Libya that was home to some well-preserved ancient ruins:

> We stopped at a place called Khoms that was famous because of a Roman theatre. We couldn't walk on the desert during the day – it was far too hot – but at night it was freezing cold. So one of these jolly padres says,

"I'll show you around . . . Oh no, won't take long . . ." and all of a sudden he's circling back, he's moved round into the back you know, "Careful" [*in a very blasé tone*]: "Just be careful, there's a nest of scorpions . . . Some snakes here, just be careful." Well, when you see these things on television, that's one thing, but when you see them in the flesh – they move much quicker than you imagine . . . VROOM! Bloody hell![272]

Later that night, much to their irritation, the guys discovered there was no room for them in the brick building intended to house the officers (and Featherstonhaugh), so they were forced to spend that night in a large tent outside with their beds pushed together. The band members slept in shifts with one bandmate always on the lookout for the unwelcome creatures they had encountered earlier that day at Khoms.

Despite all the fun and adventures Kenny was having on tour, he maintained his musical work ethic. "Wherever we were in the hotels, there was usually a piano somewhere in the basement. We'd go down there in the mornings after breakfast and do our practising," Bobby Wellins said. ". . . we had to pick a tune, I remember the tune was 'Once In A While'. He soloed first – it was just him and I – and when he was soloing, that's when it dawned on me that I would have to grow some to be able to solo at that standard. It was just absolutely brilliant!" He was also disciplined with his study of composition. When they returned from their tour, Kenny told Bobby that he had registered for a postal course in advanced algebra to sharpen his mind for writing. "He was a brain and a half, Ken," said Wellins. "There was a lot going on there."[273]

---

The next year brought yet another musical association: this time with tenor saxophonist Don Rendell's Jazz Six. Kenny made one album with them, *Don Rendell Presents the Jazz Six*, in late January 1957.[274] The group, (including Rendell on tenor, Ronnie Ross on alto and bari, Arthur Watts on bass, Don Lawson on drums, and Ken Moule on piano, with whom Kenny would later record the *Adam's Rib Suite*), recorded several tunes over a period of four dates. One of these, "Out of Nowhere", was an arrangement that Kenny created for the occasion.[275] His treatment of the standard is upbeat, with a rhythmically quirky introduction and coda and lots of counterpoint between the horns. In a departure from most small-group repertoire of the period, Kenny's arrangement sends off each of the soloists with written ensemble material. Possibly reflecting his discomfort with bebop, Kenny's trumpet solo is a bit nervous and more on top of the beat than much of his work, but it is still interesting and refreshing in its melodic contours and unpredictability.

In 1958, Kenny joined Vic Lewis's Orchestra. Lewis, an ambitious bandleader and devotee of Stan Kenton, organized several tours of the United States beginning in 1956. These tours were part of the Musicians' Union exchange agreement, which basically dictated that the United States had to

Photo 11: Kenny (left), with the Buddy Featherstonhaugh band.
Courtesy Wheeler family

provide a British band an opportunity to play in exchange for every American band that played in the UK. In 1958, Lewis's Orchestra was reciprocating a UK tour of Glenn Miller's ghost band, led by drummer Ray McKinley. Lewis's tour was to be two weeks long. The guys in Lewis's band discovered, however, that McKinley's tour was to be three weeks, so they would have to stay overseas another week with no work. The young Scottish saxophonist Duncan Lamont, who would become Kenny's long-time friend and musical collaborator, but was a reluctant member of the Lewis band at the time, saw to it (with the British Musicians' Union) that they were paid for a third week.[276] Probably the most glaring issue with this arrangement, though, was that, while UK audiences were generally familiar with and eager to hear the American bands (McKinley's revival band was capitalizing on the success of the recent 1954 film *The Glenn Miller Story*), the deal did not work quite so well in reverse. Vic Lewis's talent-rich ensemble – which included future film star Dudley Moore on piano – played mostly universities and military bases and went largely unnoticed on the 1958 and 1959 tours on which Kenny performed.[277]

Photo 12: Kenny and siblings pictured with their parents, spouses, and children on his first return visit to Canada. Kenny is top row, second from left. Doreen, pregnant with Louann is middle row, second from left. Mark, front row alongside his cousins, third from left.

Courtesy Carri Driver

The March 1958 Vic Lewis American tour, with its unexpected extra week of paid vacation, was significant to Kenny personally, however; it provided him an opportunity to get home to see his family in St. Catharines. Six years had passed since Kenny left Canada, and when he returned home for the first time, he brought his English wife (pregnant with their second child) and three-year-old Mark with him. A group family portrait from the visit shows all seven happily reunited Wheeler siblings, with husbands, wives, and 13 children, their parents smiling in the second row (see Photo 12). (Poor little Mark's hands, bandaged from his eczema, are also visible.) For the Canadian Wheelers, who had been through so much pain, this was clearly a joyous reunion. Kenny's sister Mabel said that his visits to Canada always brought the family together. "It was so nice to have him there. It was just like he made it cheerful – and you'd never think that of Kenny! . . . [W]e always got together whenever he came home, and it was so much fun."[278]

Photo 13: Doreen with Mark, left, and young Louann, right.
Courtesy Wheeler family

Later that summer, on 6 August 1958, the Wheelers' second child, a girl named Louise Ann, was born in Bethnal Green Hospital. Louann, as she is called, was a "tiny child".[279] Doreen and Kenny chose her aunt Joyce and her uncle Ronnie to be Louann's godparents. They also moved further down the street to 35 Gales Gardens, into another shared home, this time with Doreen's aunt and uncle, Maud and Steve Asser.

Kenny was back on another fairly unremarkable tour of the US with the Vic Lewis band early the next year. A memorable exception was the final concert, presented "in front of a glitterati of celebrities and jazz musicians" at the legendary New York jazz club Birdland.[280] Unfortunately, the performance didn't go well. Kenny remembered: "We had one disastrous night in Birdland when the band . . . we all fell apart, or something! People like . . . Nat Adderley was sitting in the audience and the band just went [*cracking sound*] . . . It was horrible!"[281]

In April of 1959, Kenny joined a special edition of Woody Herman's "Anglo-American Herd" for a UK tour. Herman could only bring a certain number of musicians with him, owing to the terms of the MU exchange agreement under which the band had come.[282] He brought with him seven Americans similarly destined for future stardom, namely Nat Adderley, Zoot Sims and pianist Vince Guaraldi, best known for his music for the *Peanuts* television specials. The ensemble was completed with several prominent British players, including Kenny's former bandleader Don Rendell and his old friend Art Ellefson, among others. Even with their considerable experience, it took the Brits a while to adjust to the intensity of the American bandleader's approach. "We thought things were going quite well and then Woody really hammered us," recalled Don Rendell. Herman thought they were being too tentative; Eddie Harvey remembered, "the British had not grasped that Woody wanted them to play with about four times their usual volume".[283] But Jim Godbolt put a more positive spin on the collaboration: "This was not a publicity stunt," he remarked in *A History of Jazz In Britain*: "It was a genuine musical association, a mark of respect to those local musicians who had made such progress, mostly by listening to records, that they could take their places in a crack American orchestra."[284] The band played 15 cities throughout England and Scotland during most of the month of April 1959, performing at impressive venues, including London's Royal Festival Hall. Nat Adderley had clearly moved past any memory of hearing the "disastrous" Vic Lewis performance at Birdland earlier that year. Following the Herman tour, Adderley observed, "Kenny Wheeler was just formulating his style. He was very good, obviously."[285]

The live record of this band (from the performance in Manchester on 18 April 1959) includes an interesting solo by Kenny on Horace Silver's blues in C called "Opus de Funk", a seven-minute blowing vehicle which gives ample room for several soloists. Playing in a harmon mute (a choice now perhaps most closely associated with the sound of Miles Davis), Kenny played the last solo of the tune, creating lines that are at once rhythmically quirky, ducking and jabbing in and out of time, expanding the harmonic vocabulary well beyond his fellow soloists, even playing a bit "outside" here and there. At the end of the tune, an exuberant Woody Herman acknowledges Kenny twice by name to the enthusiastic audience. The fact that Herman selected Kenny to take part in this all-star ensemble shows his increasing reputation not only in England but also among some important international artists.

Not long after the tour with Herman, Kenny Wheeler received a call that changed the course of his life. John Dankworth, the leader of one of the most successful and innovative bands in England, was scheduled to play the famous Newport Jazz Festival later that summer – and he needed a new trumpet player.

# 3 Everybody's Song But My Own

Ken Wheeler has long been the musician whom I most admire in this country. Indeed, I think he is one of the finest jazz musicians that Europe or even the world has yet produced.

*John Dankworth*

Although professional big bands remained common in 1959, being offered a chair with the famous John Dankworth band was still a significant break for Kenny. This would become one of the defining musical relationships of his early career, propelling the 29-year-old to wider recognition and ultimately providing the vehicle for his first album as featured composer and soloist, *Windmill Tilter*.[286]

Dankworth's band was one of the busiest in Britain, and in the summer of 1959 they were to tour the United States as part of the ongoing Musicians' Union exchange agreement, just as Vic Lewis had done. Although it was Kenny's third trip to the States in two years, touring with Dankworth was a much higher-profile affair. Whereas the Lewis band had mostly performed low-key concerts at universities and air bases, the Dankworth tour was to include concerts opposite icons like Duke Ellington and Louis Armstrong, as well as a performance at the prestigious Newport Jazz Festival. The Dankworth tour would also include a performance at Birdland; Kenny must have hoped that it would put to bed the uncomfortable memories of their more recent concert there with Lewis's band.

Towards the end of May 1959, just a few weeks before the American tour,[287] Kenny was invited to join the Dankworth band to replace trumpeter Colin Wright.[288] While the famous Newport appearance is thought of as being one of his first gigs with the band, Kenny had in fact played domestic engagements with them before that tour. Dave Lee, the pianist and Dankworth's band manager at the time, remembered Kenny first coming into the band for a concert in Harrogate prior to the US departure.[289] Describing how he was invited into the band, Kenny was self-deprecating as usual: "I guess John Dankworth must have found [out] about me from somewhere from somebody. I think it was him who got in touch with me and asked if I wanted to join the band to go specifically to Newport in the States – the Newport Jazz Festival. But, as I said, I don't know how he found out about me."[290] He later conceded,

Photo 14: Kenny with the John Dankworth Big Band, c. 1959–60.
Courtesy the Peter Vacher Collection

"Obviously he must've checked me out quite good because he wouldn't have hire[d] somebody to take the band to Newport which was, at that time, quite a big deal for an English band . . . so he must have heard something in what I did that he wanted . . ."[291]

For someone with Kenny's nervous disposition, landing this job must have been a scary yet exciting prospect. "I was a bit frightened to join the band, but I was also looking forward to it."[292] He said, "I think [Dankworth] liked the fact that I didn't play straightforward bebop. A lot of young trumpeters wanted to sound like Dizzy Gillespie or Miles Davis back then."[293] Dave Lee recalled Dankworth saying to him, "Listen, have you heard of Kenny Wheeler? He's very, very fine and I'm going to get him in the band."[294] Whatever the reason, Dankworth would continue to hold Kenny in the highest regard; less than 20 years later he would describe him as "the most brilliant, original and inventive jazz trumpet player in the world".[295]

Being a trumpeter in such a busy working band was physically demanding, and Kenny had already expressed anxiety at being up to the job. He recalled trying to ascertain just how challenging it would be on the trumpet:

> I was so frightened in the [first] band, I remember in the rehearsals – Bob Carson was the third trumpet player – I said "How high do the parts go?" He said, "They only go up to D or E♭. You can get those notes, can't you?" I said, *Oh, sure* but I couldn't – at that time C was about my limit![296]

So, with Kenny on board, the band set out for the States. Although his position dictated that he had a somewhat limited role at first ("I was playing the fourth trumpet chair . . . I had a couple of solos"), he admitted that this level of anticipation was felt by more than just himself. "I think the whole band was frightened to death of Newport."[297]

If the band was apprehensive about Newport, it was nothing compared to the ordeal Dave Lee was about to experience. "Newport was disastrous. I could have died," he said, without a hint of irony.[298] As manager, Dave had helped book the tour under the Musicians' Union exchange rules, so he arrived in America ahead of the band to prepare for the tour. He was greeted straight off the flight with a limousine parked under the tail of the plane and whisked away immediately to see the legendary manager and promoter Joe Glaser, manager of arguably the two greatest jazz musicians: Louis Armstrong and Duke Ellington. More importantly, Glaser was also the head of the American Booking Corporation, which was responsible for this trip.

Dave found himself in the heavy company of one of America's most intimidating businessmen. On this first meeting with Glaser (with a visible gun holster and huge piles of cash on the table) Dave was greeted bluntly: "I don't like your goddamned band. It sounds as if you're copying Ellington or Basie or someone. If I want Basie and Ellington, I'll hire Basie and Ellington – so I want something very interesting while you're here!"[299] Although Glaser would warm to him later in the trip, Dave was in a state of abject terror as he awaited the arrival of Kenny and the rest of the band.

When the Dankworth band arrived, their photo was captured on the aeroplane steps and was later used for the *Bundle from Britain: Live at Newport* album cover.[300] Almost immediately, there were more surprises in store. The band was taken straight from the airport and, to their surprise, driven to a rehearsal studio.[301] Dave Lee explained: "What they do at Newport is this – the big band plays, has its own 45 minutes . . ." This is what they were expecting, but Dave continued: ". . . then there are certain new singers that [the record companies] want to launch, as it's marvellous that their first recording is [live] at Newport Jazz Festival, it's a big plus [and] it's normal actually – Duke Ellington's done it, Count Basie's done it, everybody's done it."[302] The band would play their set, then the leader of the band would walk off and the singer would come on and perform their set, which would be recorded for their album. This seemed simple enough, except for the fact that the band – apparently even including Dankworth himself – had no idea this was going to be the case.

Dankworth did not want his band to accompany another singer. His wife, vocalist Cleo Laine, had been asked in advance if she would be singing at any point on the tour, and had confirmed that she would not. So without the need for a work permit, she was travelling without one. Dankworth made it quite clear that "There would only be one singer sharing with us at Newport had they asked for one – and that's Cleo. But they haven't asked, so there's not going to be one, and that's the end of it."[303] But the Top Rank record company which Dankworth shared with Debby Moore (the singer in question) must have insisted, since the band was taken straight to the rehearsal studio and the plan to back her for the recording went ahead. Dave Lee remembered: "in fact Quincy Jones did the arrangements . . . marvellous arrangements I can tell you, and the band was knocked out . . ."[304] Quite how this situation had come as such a surprise to Dankworth remains a bit of a mystery – in June 1959's *New Musical Express*, the planned collaboration with Moore was actually mentioned in Nat Hentoff's weekly US column "American Airmail",[305] so one can only assume Dankworth must have been told at some point.

With that eventful first day behind them, the band bus made the journey from New York up to Newport on Friday July 3rd. Following a request from Glaser's office, they agreed to pick up another musician who needed a ride to the festival. ". . . it was Dizzy Gillespie!" Kenny remembered.[306] This encounter would set the tone for a day surrounded by legendary jazz players. "[Newport] was quite an honour for an English band,"[307] Kenny said. "Nothing like that had ever happened before, seeing all the big names around."[308] It was also a chance for him to reunite with his old friend Gene Lees, who had by then been working at *DownBeat* magazine for about eight weeks and caught up with Kenny at the festival.[309] The band stepped off the bus just in time to hear the roar of the crowd reacting to Johnny Griffin burning through

"Cherokee".[310] The programme for that day was remarkable; the afternoon sets alone had included Griffin, Horace Silver's Quintet, Roy Eldridge and Coleman Hawkins, as well as the Maynard Ferguson Orchestra. Dankworth's band was to play on the Freebody Park stage as the first act of the evening segment.[311] They kicked off the evening at 8:30.[312] The band was due to perform their 40-minute set, and then stay on another 40 minutes to play the material they'd rehearsed with Debby Moore. The rest of the night included Thelonious Monk's Quartet, Oscar Peterson's trio and, of course, Dizzy Gillespie's Quintet.

In such rich company, one can only imagine the nervous excitement Kenny and the rest of the musicians must have felt as they prepared to take the stage. As Dankworth planned the programme, Dave Lee reminded the musicians, "Whatever John calls up for us to play, don't forget to put at the back the Quincy Jones numbers because we don't get off the stage, we stay on as the band to accompany this girl."[313] Dave went into the bandleaders' tent to get the set list from Dankworth. As he was leaving, he noticed the inclusion of five numbers for Cleo Laine to sing at the end of the set. Dave turned back to the tent and explained to John that without a work visa, Cleo couldn't sing, as it would be illegal. Dankworth replied, "You're the manager, fix it. I want Cleo to sing and that's final." Dave, only too aware of the mob-like presence hanging over their trip, was now in a panic. He went off to find Jackie Greene, his liaison with the Glaser office, and Newport founder George Wein. They both told Dave in no uncertain terms that Cleo was not going to be performing: "Tell Dankworth if she walks out on stage, I'm switching off the microphones and lights, everything." Dave replied, "I've got a better idea: *you* tell him!" The message was delivered by Wein himself. "If you don't want to play you can go back to Britain as far as I'm concerned, but she [Cleo] does not sing."[314] With that resolved, the band took to the stage – though Dankworth had a plan.

The musicians lined up offstage, ready for the performance. Kenny, no doubt apprehensive about his solo duties on at least one of the pieces, stood alongside his trumpet-section mates Stan Palmer, Bob Carson, and lead trumpeter Derrick Abbot. The way the set opened was that Dave Lee would walk onstage alone and begin playing two choruses of a 12-bar blues at the piano. Then, bassist Eric Dawson would walk on and join him for two more, followed by drummer Kenny Clare for two additional choruses. Gradually, the full band would come onstage and they would begin. Dave Lee began his solo piano introduction, but this time two choruses went by and no sign of Eric Dawson. Eventually he appeared, joined in, looked at Dave and just shrugged his shoulders. Again, several more choruses than usual went by before Kenny Clare finally appeared, then yet another extended gap before Danny Moss finally appeared for his tenor solo. Eventually, the full band came on in, presumably also a little confused at the delay. And so it continued for the whole set: Dankworth had extended each song to the point that by about the fourth tune they had used up their entire allotted time! Two tough-looking guys from the record company appeared at the side of the stage, with Debby Moore ready to sing. "Hey Dave, she's on now," one of them called out. But Dankworth resolutely ignored their demands to finish and Dave was helpless to do anything. The band, playing their newly extended tunes, took up her whole set time as well as their own and she never got to perform. Moore verified this story, saying "That is true. [Dankworth's] wife was a singer so he wanted her to sing, so I was left out. I was a little disappointed, but I figured everything happens for a reason."[315]

Despite all the drama behind the scenes, the band's set was a success and Dankworth recalled a praiseworthy mention by John S. Wilson of the *New York Times*, calling the band ". . . masters in the art of making the music swing."[316] Kenny takes his only solo (on the album at least) on the tune "Royal Ascot". He plays in a cool, almost West Coast way, but there are charming traces of his idiosyncratic style forming: the searching melodic lines and the sometimes unusual, almost back-to-front articulation. It is possible Kenny took other solos in the set, given the way Dankworth opened up each tune, but Dave Lee confirmed that these extended versions on the live album were edited to their usual length for the record. He said, "I do know that the numbers we played were much longer than the ones that came out on the record. We took much longer – we took [up] two whole programmes."[317]

It must have been with relief and euphoria that Kenny and the band stepped off the stage following their successful Newport debut. Not so for Dave Lee. He was just beginning his reluctant involvement in that murky world where the mob and the music industry met. While Kenny and the rest of the band enjoyed a beer, Dave was greeted from the stage by the record company heavies with guns bulging in their jackets, who told him simply, "Now listen, we've paid Quincy Jones for eight arrangements, there's the recording van which needs to be paid for, etc., etc." They went on: "That comes to thirty-five thousand dollars. So tomorrow morning you're going to bring me thirty-five thousand dollars in cash. If you don't have thirty-five thousand dollars, you ain't leaving this country."[318]

In a panic, Dave went running back to the bandleaders' tent to find Dankworth. But he was nowhere to be seen: he and Cleo had gone straight from the stage into Jimmy Rushing's car and departed. In desperation, Dave called Harold Davison, the legendary British impresario and agent for this tour. He was in luck. Davison was home. To this day, Dave maintains that if Harold hadn't been home, he would have been a dead man. Harold, a powerful figure himself, spoke with Jackie Greene and promised to have the money wired over first thing. His word was good enough.

But, with all the drama, Dave quit the band then and there while they were still in the States. He completed the tour but the fear and stress he had experienced was just not worth it for him.[319] Dave did, however, continue to work with Kenny from time to time and later used him on a jingle recording session, bizarrely as part of a Dixieland band. (Dave said Kenny also played beautifully in that style.) Dave also featured Kenny on his own album, *Jazz Improvisation of Our Man Crichton*, in 1965.[320]

The remaining American engagements, although less well documented than the famous Newport concert, were no less extraordinary at the time for the Dankworth band. They would again bring Kenny into close contact with the musical heroes of the day, including a concert at New Jersey's Palisades Park at which Benny Goodman and George Shearing were in the audience.[321] (These two jazz stars were in no danger of being mobbed; Cleo Laine recalled "almost nobody turned up".)[322]

The day after Newport was Saturday, 4 July. The Dankworth band was booked to play a concert supporting Louis Armstrong's All Stars at Lewisohn Stadium, a grand amphitheatre in Harlem on the campus of the City College of New York. The date had added significance: as well as being American Independence Day, the 4th of July also happened to be the birthday celebrated by Armstrong. (Incidentally, it was also the 26th birthday of Doreen Wheeler, who was spending it back in the UK with toddler Mark and baby Louann.) On that day, Louis Armstrong was still recovering from a heart attack he had suffered in Italy only a couple of weeks earlier, but he was present in the stadium that evening for his birthday festivities. (Cornetist Wild Bill Davison covered Armstrong's role in the All Stars.) Following the Dankworth set, the All Stars came on to play while the Dankworth band remained on stage, with the idea that they would finish the concert by playing the last few tunes together. Though Armstrong had not been performing, before the finale it was announced that he was present and he was coming on to the stage. Dave Lee recalled "the whole audience stood up and lit a match or a lighter and with the light to their face, their faces just visible, they all sang 'Happy Birthday'."[323] Dankworth also remembered the tremendous audience reaction. Armstrong was overcome and spontaneously decided he would play after all, against his doctor's orders. With a mouthpiece in his pocket, he borrowed a trumpet from Stan Palmer, who was on the far end of the trumpet section.[324] Although it must have been a beautiful moment, Louis's impromptu involvement had unintended ramifications. The concert promoter had agreed on a reduced fee on the basis that Armstrong was *not* going to play. Once Louis decided to sit in, the unfortunate promoter then immediately owed the regular, much higher, fee to Joe Glaser! (Dave Lee, already traumatized from the gangster-related drama of the day before, would also accidentally witness further mob aggression as he stumbled in on some "persuasively firm" negotiations with the poor promoter later that evening.[325])

The penultimate booking of the tour was at the famous Birdland club, and to conclude the trip they played a week opposite Duke Ellington's band in New Jersey. The concerts were in a "big top" marquee and ran from Tuesday 7 to Sunday 12 July, 1959.[326] In fact, Ellington's diaries suggest the week was originally supposed to be Armstrong's All Stars instead of the Ellington band, but they agreed to step in due to Louis's health problems – after all, both were

Photo 15: Kenny with the Dankworth Orchestra, Marquee Club, Oxford Street, London, 1961. Left to right (back row): Alan Branscombe (p), Kenny Wheeler (t), Spike Heatley (b), Leon Calvert, Ron Simmonds (t), Ronnie Stephenson (d, hidden), Gus Galbraith (t); (front): Danny Moss, Art Ellefson (ts), Roy East (fl), John Dankworth (as), Eddie Harvey, Tony Russell (tb), Ron Snyder (tu).
Courtesy the Peter Vacher Collection

managed by Glaser. One can only imagine Kenny's thrill at seeing Ellington's band up close every night. By all accounts the two groups of musicians got along well; Dave Lee recalled seeing Kenny and Johnny Hodges having a laugh over a drink one night.[327]

Following the success of this tour, Kenny finally had his two-week vacation back home in Canada. It was his third return visit since he had left almost seven years before, and he was particularly grateful to be returning so soon after the Vic Lewis tour.[328] It must have been quite a homecoming for Kenny; he was now a member of the most famous band in the UK, returning triumphantly off the back of an extraordinary star-studded US tour. It would have been quite in character, though, if he never even mentioned it!

Following his Canadian vacation, Kenny returned to London in time to appear at the 1959 Beaulieu Jazz Festival on Saturday, August 1st.[329] He played with the Dankworth band at this event, but probably not with Vic Lewis, despite appearing on the Vic Lewis album titled *At the Beaulieu Festival*.[330]

Throughout the first half of the 1960s, the vast majority of Kenny's playing career was taken up with his job in the Dankworth band. On returning from the US, the band was busier than ever. Despite his success, John Dankworth was not a musician to stand still: he was about to disband the big band and re-form it with a new generation of musicians. Kenny pondered the difference between the Dankworth ensembles in his typically candid interview style: "The old band was more consistently exciting, but then when this [new] band does get good, it's spectacular, but it isn't so often."[331]

The line-up of *The Criminal* soundtrack, recorded by this fresh incarnation of the Dankworth band in July 1960,[332] shows that saxophonists Pete King and Kenny's old friend Art Ellefson were among the new players added to the band. Lead player Gus Galbraith joined the trumpet section alongside regulars Kenny and Dickie Hawdon; other newcomers included trombonists Eddie Harvey and Ian McDougall, a third fellow Canadian expatriate. Young pianist (and later Hollywood star) Dudley Moore also played on the record. Kenny took occasional harmony lessons from Moore, who had been an Oxford organ scholar and studied composition at Magdalen College. Chorale writing was second nature to Moore, so playing the role of dutiful teacher, he would sit at the back of the band bus and mark Kenny's exercises.[333]

This was an exciting new era for the Dankworth band; one that would herald new explorations for Kenny as a composer, and ultimately towards his first recording as co-leader. Before that could happen, though, he and Doreen would have to overcome their most difficult personal tragedy. Settled into their Bethnal Green home at 35 Gales Gardens, the young Wheeler family were expecting their third child in early 1961. But after Doreen went into labour on the 17th of February, their baby daughter, Alice, died at birth.[334] Alice was laid to rest in Manor Park Cemetery. (In keeping with common practice of the time for stillborn babies, Alice was buried sharing the grave of a recently deceased woman.[335]) It was, of course, devastating for the family. Mark, who was not quite six years old and eagerly expecting news of a younger brother or sister, was called out of class and taken to the headmistress's office where he found his dad waiting for him. Kenny told him what had happened and explained to Mark that his mum was not well.[336]

Indeed, Doreen had a very difficult time in the years following the loss of her baby. Due to a heart murmur acquired after a childhood episode of scarlet fever, she was advised not to have any more children after this loss; another pregnancy could have been dangerous.[337] She later recalled how she just could not overcome the sadness. People would say to her, "You've got to get over it, you've got two children," to which she replied simply, "But that's not the point, is it. You can't."[338] Kenny described their struggles in various letters home to his parents over the next few years. In that summer of 1961, he wrote to his parents that Doreen was doing better. Although she could sometimes still get out of breath quite easily, she had learned to take it easier.[339] In a letter two years later, he described how she was more cheerful these days, and that "up until a few months ago she seemed to get depressed very easily, but she's much more stable now".[340] There were some moments of respite in the early '60s too, including when the four Wheelers took their first family holiday to North Wales together in September 1961 during a break from Dankworth's schedule. (Kenny remarked how they were all looking forward to it as the band had been so busy.[341]) Nevertheless, the Wheelers felt the sadness of their loss for decades. Presumably in baby Alice's memory, Kenny included compositions on his 1998 album *A Long Time Ago*[342] titled "Ballad for a Dead Child" and "Alice My Dear".

Following Kenny's own passing decades later, Louann found a funeral director's card among his belongings. It gave the information about the location of baby Alice's grave, and Louann was able to track it down and visit for the first time. When she mentioned this to her mum, Doreen surprised her by recalling details of the cemetery and revealed that she had actually visited the site with her own mother. Although rarely mentioned directly within the immediate family, every year Doreen would remember Alice's birthday. Mark recalled one year she said, "the baby would have been 40 today".

Despite the demands of his young family and the personal difficulties of the early '60s, there is no doubt that Kenny's musical career was starting to attract attention. An increasing number of magazine features and reviews attested to the impression he was beginning to make. In her November 1960 review of *The Criminal*, Kitty Grime singled Kenny out as "perhaps the most absorbing soloist there".[343] She expressed her admiration even more assertively later in a 1961 *Jazz News* feature: "These days more and more people, especially musicians, are naming him among their favourite trumpet players. Ken has something of his own to offer as a soloist, and his distinctive scores, too, are played with respect by the Dankworth band." Grime finishes with this particularly telling statement: "Also significant is the appearance of 'Wheelerisms' in the solos of his section-mates."[344] For the rest of his life, these trademark gestures would betray the effect he had had on younger players whom he had influenced. Section-mate Dickie Hawdon confirmed the awareness of Kenny's individuality in his own 1961 *Jazz News* feature: "You name any British musician who doesn't copy records . . . I'll name you one — Kenny Wheeler."[345]

Curiously, when asked about his playing during this period, Kenny replied,

> I'm not consciously working on a style of my own, but I suppose it's there at the back of my mind. Sometimes, of course, you find yourself falling back on clichés, even if they're your own. Everyone does – Harry Edison has a little phrase he always plays, but it always sounds good to me. I try not to be influenced by anyone, and I like to listen to as many different

people as I can . . . I like Miles' "time", Art Farmer's sound, Dizzy's jazz technique, Clifford Brown's endless flow of ideas, Maynard Ferguson's and Harry James's trumpet playing, and many others.[346]

What also emerges in these early interviews and features is Kenny's honesty about his struggles with nerves and performance anxiety. It was understandably not commonplace to speak openly about this, especially in magazine pieces where the conventional wisdom may have led most people to think it was an opportunity to "sell" the best side of themselves as the unruffled, cool professional. Not Kenny. His candour would occasionally draw him into potentially sensitive waters in later interviews: his general feelings about critics, the politics of the UK jazz scene, and the difficulty he later found in getting gigs at home.[347] But in these early interviews his honesty is endearing, and may have been of some comfort to fellow musicians who had quietly suffered with the same problems. There were repeated mentions of his nerves in the Kitty Grime's 1961 piece, and in a 1962 *Coda* magazine feature he went as far as to describe himself feeling that his music was at a dead end. Though he was not worried about it, he said: "If I could learn to control myself I think I could go a lot further. A big problem is getting over worrying about what people think of your playing."[348] Art Ellefson remembered this being such an issue for Kenny that he explored possible avenues for help:

> When he was with Dankworth's band, he went into some sort of psychological interlude with one of the trombone players in the band – and they went to this study in psychology. I think that helped him a bit. I never did find out what it was that they were doing. He went to some fellow, I know nothing about it, but I remember him and Tony [Russell] talking about it a little bit. Ken never talked about himself. Ever.[349]

Even though Ellefson's last statement is at odds with the openness Kenny sometimes demonstrated in interviews, this issue with nerves was obviously something he did try to address. His son Mark also remembered Kenny going to meditation sessions to try to deal with his nerves in the early '60s.[350] It remained a problem throughout his life. Kenny's friend and regular bassist Chris Laurence remembered that as late as around 2005 he suggested a lady he could go and see about performance nerves, using a kind of hypnotherapy-based approach.[351] Up until his final few concerts, he would sometimes even take a beta blocker to settle his performance anxiety.

Another curious theme from the articles in this period is that, as Kenny's personality seeps into the consciousness of jazz fans and writers, a distinctive identity emerges that would stay with him for life. The 1961 Kitty Grime piece actually finishes by saying "Ken Wheeler seems shy and silent, but he shows an impish sense of humour when least expected. 'I'm sure I'm exuberant underneath, but when I show it at all, people look at me as if I'm mad. But that's the real me. I've always found it difficult to express.'"[352] This curious mix of shyness and humorous self-deprecation, coupled with his massive talent, meant that close friends often felt the need to fight in his corner for him. Not that it was in any way a manipulative strategy on his part, but maybe more like Kenny subconsciously projected a particular kind of helplessness that inspired a protective reaction in those around him. Sometimes this would result in him getting the support and assistance he needed but was unable to ask for directly. This idiosyncratic cocktail of characteristics would be a feature throughout his life, shaping his relationships with future musical allies.

Another example of Kenny's personality taking centre stage in a written profile comes from the aforementioned 1962 *Coda* magazine feature, "Canadians in London". Pam Bevin finishes the article by explaining that

> Kenny Wheeler is a very serious-looking, shy person. For example, when I phoned him to ask if he would give me an interview, he was reluctant, as he didn't think anyone would be interested in reading about him. I told him it was because there was insufficient awareness of Canadian musicians that I wanted to write this series, and also that his two fellow countrymen in the Dankworth band, Ian McDougall and Art Ellefson, had praised him very highly and felt that recognition of his talent should be recorded in some way, in the hope that it might open the eyes (and ears) of the public and promoters generally.[353]

This seems a slightly odd piece of behind-the-scenes information to have included in the actual printed article, so Bevin must have felt it was in the reader's interest to understand this side of Kenny's personality. It is not the first account of people speaking up on his behalf – some of them with humorous consequences; trumpeter Ian Carr remembered that he and his brother Mike went up to Dankworth at a 1960 concert and told him that they should give Kenny more solos. Dutifully, Dankworth later gave Kenny a solo, only for him to finish it too early and for the bandleader to have to call over to him, "*No, no, keep going!*"[354]

Kenny later became friends with Ian Carr. Ian had moved down from Newcastle to London in 1962 to join Harold McNair's band after Harold had heard him on the northeast-based Emcee Five recording *Let's Take Five*.[355] Ian already knew of Kenny through his brother, who had been in the RAF in Cyprus. Mike had been based at one of the airbases on which Kenny had performed with the Buddy Featherstonhaugh group during their mid-1950s Far East tour. Ian remembered his brother saying to him, "you should listen to Kenny Wheeler, he plays really weird but it's great, it's very different, you know!" Ian and Kenny had also briefly met when the Dankworth band went up to play in Newcastle and later sat in with the Emcee Five. When Ian finally moved to London he looked Kenny up for a specific reason: although Ian had landed the job with Harold McNair, Ian could not read a note of music! McNair had paid a sergeant in the American Army to write some arrangements and, when he sent out the parts, Ian paid Kenny to meet him at a studio and teach him how to play them. Ian offered to pay Kenny a pound, which he refused to take, but Ian insisted "you must take it 'cause I might want to ask you again!"[356] He did exactly that: later in 1965 when Ian was preparing for a New Jazz Orchestra recording session, he sought further reading help from Kenny.[357]

Regardless of the performance anxieties he struggled with, this was a busy and successful period for Kenny. He was regularly recording as a member of the Dankworth band and being increasingly featured as a soloist. On one occasion, in November 1962, the band recorded a television special for the BBC show *Just Jazz*.[358] In what must be some of the earliest video footage of Kenny playing, they performed an arrangement of the standard "Just in Time" with Kenny playing the mellophonium on the section parts in the opening theme before the solos. When he moves to trumpet to take a 16-bar solo following Dankworth, he sounds strong and secure on the horn but his nerves are apparent in the way he occasionally rushes – which is in itself quite unusual for him – but, as we have discussed, he really doesn't sound like anyone else. There were three stand-out albums from this period which also illustrate what a productive era it was for Dankworth. Significantly, these included two new programmatic albums, *What the Dickens!*[359] and *The Zodiac Variations*,[360] which would sow the conceptual seeds for Kenny's own first release as a leader at the end of the decade.

A couple of years before those albums were recorded, a more light-hearted collection of Dankworth sessions took place, which also demonstrated Dankworth's increasingly broad avenues of employment. The band provided the music and soundtrack for an animated children's cartoon, *Hamilton the Elephant*, with Kenny's trumpet taking the starring role of musically portraying Hamilton (Dankworth's suggestion[361]). Kenny's involvement in the lead role of this venture captured the imagination of the *St. Catharines Standard* feature writer sufficiently for it to be included in a September 1962 edition. The headline reads "In Jazz Band, on Cartoon Show. City Trumpeter: Two Strings to his Bow"! The article goes on to list some details about Kenny's earlier life, the move to England and his early work there, as well as the Dankworth invitation that came prior to Newport. It then explains the concept of the cartoon: Hamilton could twist up his trunk to make it play just like a trumpet. Kenny would play the written parts and improvise around Hamilton's movements and the programme would be cut together. There is some great playing: in one episode, Hamilton saves the day after a TV studio orchestra goes on strike by covering all the parts. Hamilton literally blows the roof off the concert hall, with Kenny playing some exciting high notes in the finale.

———·———

Dankworth's album *What the Dickens!*, recorded on four separate dates through the latter half of 1963, is a suite based on characters and scenarios from Charles Dickens's work. Owing to the presence of several famous guest soloists, Kenny largely plays just his section parts, although he does make solo contributions on the track "Demdest Little Fascinator". He shows an already very distinctive playing approach characterized by his highly personal articulation and behind-the-beat time feel, with sometimes quirky and unexpected phrase endings. He also solos on the more uptempo "Sergeant Buzfuz", where again he is free with the time, giving an elasticity to the phrases which sounds modernistic in hindsight. On "The Pickwick Club", trumpeter Jimmy Deuchar takes an impressive solo showing just what a magnificent command he had of the bebop vocabulary of the time. When Kenny would later speak about the development of his own playing, he would often refer to his own struggle to get to grips with what he called "conventional" bebop, citing Deuchar as an example of someone who had mastered it a way in which he had never been able.[362]

*The Zodiac Variations* was recorded on two separate sessions in October and November 1964. The first was in New York with a host of famous American guest soloists, including Zoot Sims, Phil Woods, Clark Terry and someone who would later become Kenny's friend, valve trombonist Bob Brookmeyer. Bob and Kenny were not to meet on this occasion, however, as the regular Dankworth band members had not been present on the New York session, instead recording their parts separately on the November date in London. This necessitated a feat of reel-to-reel editing; Dankworth had to splice together the two sessions, trying to match the different studio sounds and variations in tempo from New York to London, even at one point overlapping the two drummers.[363] Despite the star-studded line-up, Dankworth again makes space for some of his regular band members to contribute solos, such as Ronnie Scott ("Aquarius"), Danny Moss ("Leo"), and Art Ellefson ("Aries"), as well as all the other trumpeters: Gus Galbraith ("Aries"), Leon Calvert ("Cancer") and the new Dankworth trumpeter from Wales, Greg Bowen, who provides a beautifully laid-back muted solo on "Taurus". (Greg would become one of Kenny's favourite lead trumpeters.) Kenny himself contributes a solo on the album's final track, "Capricorn and Coda". Making a rare appearance improvising on the mellophonium, his style is still clear; his tone, articulation and phrase structure are definitely present, but he is a little less technically fluent on this instrument and uses a narrower range than he might have on the trumpet. *The Zodiac Variations* was also performed live for the second series of the BBC television show *Jazz 625*, in June 1965. Here Clark Terry and Bob Brookmeyer were featured live with the band, so it is probable that Kenny would have met Brookmeyer in person at this point.[364]

Kenny makes perhaps his first significant contribution as a featured soloist on the album *Shakespeare and All That Jazz*.[365] Released in 1964, it was officially Cleo's album as leader, credited to "Cleo Laine featuring the music of John Dankworth". There is a lot of close harmony and textural writing involving plenty of section playing from Kenny, but he is featured as a soloist at least as much as Dankworth, if not more. His approach certainly contributes to the uniqueness of the album and is part of what defines it as a landmark British jazz record. Kenny takes a muted solo on the first tune "If Music Be the Food of Love", and he plays weaving lines behind Cleo on "Duet of Sonnets". But the most recognizable Kenny first appears on the fourth track, "Winter". His characteristic time feel is immediately apparent and, although it might feel like the solo never quite gets into a flow, it is typical Kenny: explorative improvising that occasionally plays off the upper extensions of the harmony and gives his lines a floating, unresolved quality. He also plays the mellophonium (mistakenly listed as tenor horn) on some band parts of this album.[366]

There is some more rare video footage of Kenny from 10 May 1964, when the Dankworth band were filmed for the BBC's *Jazz 625* series. As well as a couple of pieces from the recent *What the Dickens!* LP and one from the earlier *The Criminal*, they also perform a Dankworth original called "Mark 1" which features Kenny in the soloist role out the front of the band with J.D. himself.[367] The song is a regular blues where both Kenny and Art Ellefson take three-chorus solos with a background riff on the third. While Art's solo comes right out of the great swing masters such as Ben Webster or Coleman Hawkins, Kenny's solo sounds completely contemporary over this otherwise very straight-ahead swing backing. The lack of a chordal "comping" instrument (no piano/guitar) makes it sound even more modern. The phrasing is unpredictable, varied in length, and he picks up closing ideas as the new motif for the next phrase. His time feel is also particularly elastic, adding to the contemporary, even slightly unsettled feeling; he sometimes gets behind the beat and other times rushes to catch up. It is a clear example of him in his middle period of his development; there is an enormously individual artistic voice emerging but, at the same time, a kind of frustration at not yet having found the right context in which his approach fully makes sense. Regardless, he is paving the way for what would soon become his musical direction.

---

In the fall of 1964, Kenny's parents visited him in London for the first time.[368] The St. Catharines-based Lincoln and Welland Regimental Band undertook a foreign tour and both of Kenny's parents, along with his brother Paul and wife Nora, made the trip. Following the band's performance in Amsterdam, they flew to London. Mark recalls meeting them off the plane and bringing them into London after being given a toy KLM badge by his grandfather. Kenny would have been particularly happy to see them because, earlier in 1963, he had written to his parents expressing disappointment that another Dankworth tour of the US that would have enabled him to visit them had been cancelled unexpectedly.[369] Mark remembered Kenny was excited but nervous before they arrived. It was the first visit his parents had made and the first time they were to meet the English side of his family. There was also a problem: their home at 35 Gales Gardens was too small to host this many visitors and, in fact, all four Wheelers shared a single bedroom in that flat.[370] To fit everyone in, the whole family swapped houses with Doreen's brother Bobby. Before their four- or five-day visit, Bobby was instructed to repaint the entire house to smarten the place up to get ready.[371] The effort to which Kenny and his English family went to host his Canadian family shows the closeness they felt despite the long distance that separated them. Over the years, they kept in touch not only by letter but also by sending cassette tapes to one another. Forty years before Skype or FaceTime, it was a fun and perhaps more intimate way for the families to stay connected, hear the kids sing songs and tell stories to one another with the latest news.[372]

Throughout the early '60s, Kenny wrote new big-band charts and arrangements in addition to his playing career. Indeed, he worked on his writing skills just as diligently as the upkeep of his trumpet technique. His early talent in this area had been shown with his "Autumn in New York" arrangement back in Tommy Whittle's group, but he found more outlets for full big-band writing as the 1960s progressed. As a teenager, Kenny was already drawn towards the orchestration of the music. He remembered that when the big bands came through Canada he would try to speak to the guy who did the arrangements, frequently the pianist, and they would often say, "Well, if you really want to study music you should go to Paris", often mentioning the name Nadia Boulanger in the same breath. This was what had initially planted the idea in his mind to try to head for Paris back when he initially left Canada and headed for Europe.[373] But Kenny worked persistently through his own study; as early as the 1961 Kitty Grime feature he talks about how "playing the piano is essential for me, though I try to arrange as much as possible away from the piano". Even at this stage, he describes writing arrangements for John Dankworth's band, where his idiosyncratic writing style was emerging somewhat ahead of its time. He said, "I like to do arrangements for the Dankworth band, but they don't often come off. The ballads I've done seem to go all right, but the band has trouble with the faster originals. To me they're simple, but I can't explain them to the others sometimes." What is interesting about this is his reaction to these problems; he acknowledges the embarrassment when a chart doesn't work, but at the same time shows a conviction about his approach and a determination to persevere: "You shouldn't have to explain about music, really, but sometimes the band might play one of them down and it will sound chaotic, and everyone gets embarrassed. This is something I'm trying to tackle, by doing more writing all the time." He closes with the most profound of compositional insights: "I think I must be lacking in the right kind of simplicity, somehow."[374]

In his typically modest way, he refers to fitting in his regular writing practice around the busy Dankworth schedule. "I usually try to write something on Monday, but seldom succeed in writing anything worthwhile," he said – but that can't have been entirely true.[375] His writing was already gaining attention from an international audience: in 1963 he was commissioned to write five arrangements for the Canadian Broadcasting Company's *Jazz Club* broadcast in Vancouver – certainly demonstrative of his growing reputation as a writer.[376]

Despite his own hard work and output, Kenny maintained, "I always had it in my mind that I wanted to study and learn . . ."[377] and so, from mid-1962 through to around 1964, he undertook two periods of more formal study with two leading London-based composers.[378] The first was with the composer Richard Rodney Bennett, with whom he focused mainly on serialist techniques; Bennett himself had spent two years in Paris studying serialism with Pierre Boulez. Kenny described his first lesson with Bennett to Gene Lees: "The first thing he did when I walked in was to say, 'Sit down, I'm going to play a lot of different musics for you. You don't have to tell me what composer it is, just tell me what you like and what you don't like.' I thought that was a great way to start. We got into serial writing."[379] Kenny ended up composing some atonal pieces for flute, oboe, and clarinet which were based on a three-note series. These compositions were passed onto the Society for the Promotion of New Music (SPNM) where they were accepted and performed, although Kenny, in typical fashion, never heard them himself.[380]

In early 1963, Kenny asked Bennett, "Do you think a musician needs counterpoint?" to which he replied, "Yes, but I would be too bored to teach it to you!" Kenny in turn moved his studies over to American composer William (Bill) Russo, who was then teaching in London and running a big band on Saturday mornings at Morley College. That band was the basis of the group that became the original London Jazz Orchestra. Russo, who had achieved recognition for his work in the 1950s with the Stan Kenton Orchestra, had moved to England in 1962 to work for the BBC. Several prominent musicians in London began to study with him, and the significance of being in his rehearsal band was noted by many players. "You had guys who worked round the clock, like Don Lusher, who would still be in the [Bill Russo] band because it was a prestigious thing to be a part of," Duncan Lamont recalled.[381] But for all of Russo's wider influence on the scene at the time, it was the disciplined study of counterpoint with him that would prove most useful for Kenny. "Oh really it was the, you know, very fruitful period for me. Studying counterpoint, baroque counterpoint, was great for me. It loosened me up as a player and a writer I think, just to see the way melodies work against each other and stuff like that, you know . . ."[382] Kenny added, "that's why my writing chops were getting so good . . . it was great."[383] He continued writing new big-band pieces around that time, including some for Russo as part of his studies and one for a 1964 BBC broadcast by the Cliff Hardie Big Band, in which they played his composition "The Troublemaker."[384]

There were other profound lessons for Kenny embedded in Russo's methodology that would shape Kenny's own expectations of written music from then on. He recalled to Gene Lees that sometimes for Russo's lessons you didn't even have to pay in cash; you could offer to do some editing instead. "That's when I realized how important it was to be neat," Kenny said.

He would give you scores to edit. If the dynamic wasn't just under the note, you put a tick beside it. All the little things like that. If the crescendo didn't go right to where it was supposed to. It spoiled me. Because music after that, I realized, is so messy. Most people didn't take care in sessions that things were right. With him, what was there was perfect.[385]

And indeed, from then on, Kenny was also impeccably detailed in his scores, despite his trademark scratchy handwriting.

Even though he was shy, Kenny was quite proactive, even bordering on entrepreneurial in creating opportunities to perform his music and keep up his small-group jazz playing alongside his busy schedule with Dankworth. In a letter home to his parents, Kenny described the shape of a typical working week: "We usually work from Thursday to Sunday with the big band, and on Tuesday I play in a quintet with Art Ellefson." He continues, "Also on Wednesday John Dankworth and I have a quintet", before adding a rare note of business acumen: "It pays to keep in with the bandleader."

The Tuesday-night session he ran with Art which he mentioned in his letter home was at The Plough pub in Ilford. There, Kenny did more than just play; he and Art shared the organization of the gig. Later, along with some other members of the Dankworth band, Kenny was involved in the creation of a rehearsal band that could play their newly written big-band music.[386] This was a productive time which gave him opportunities to implement the techniques he had worked on with Russo and Bennett's guidance. Even then, he was quite prolific in his output: Kenny remembered one aspect of Russo's pedagogical approach that motivated this work ethic: "He got very angry if you didn't come with a lot of work done!"[387]

While he was keeping up a studious schedule of practising and composing, life in London's East End went on around Kenny and his family. Doreen continued to take care of all the domestic duties and the day-to-day business of looking after the kids. This was not a duty she objected to; Doreen was proud of her role. In fact, when one of the nuns at Mark's school made a remark to him about his ongoing eczema problems, Doreen went to the school to confront her. (What had irritated Doreen was not so much the unfairness of reprimanding a child over his eczema, but rather the insinuation that his clothes weren't clean.) Doreen took pride in running the house well. The family was used to Kenny's comings and goings and she was surrounded by family when he wasn't there, though Kenny would phone her every day when he was on tour.[388] Louann remembered him always calling two or three times each day when he was away, not even for long conversations or about anything in particular; she thought it was probably just that Kenny wanted to hear his wife's voice.[389] Doreen described how Kenny's schedule meant he was ". . . not a 'football in the park' kind of [dad], and he couldn't go to many school plays and things like that because he was working".[390] He would go whenever he could, of course. Louann was a good dancer and remembered seeing him appear at the back of the school hall during dance recitals with his trumpet case in hand, just in time to watch her perform.[391] Doreen admitted that she used to get annoyed at times: not exactly at Kenny, but rather at the fact there were other fathers whose more conventional jobs meant they were able to attend school occasions that Kenny could not. Doreen was sometimes concerned about what other people might think about the fact that Kenny wasn't there, and if they might be judged for it.[392] As with any family, there were of course times she could have done with more hands-on support. At one stage, Doreen had a dispute with the Bethnal Green council about which school Louann would attend. She wanted to go to Morpeth School but lived outside the catchment area, so Doreen locked horns with the council and withdrew Louann from school while they fought about it. Unfortunately, in the end it was in vain, and Louann had to attend the closer Robert Montefiori School. Doreen wanted the best education for her children so they could have the option of attending university if they chose.[393]

During their time in east London, there was one occasion when Kenny had a closer encounter than he would have liked with some of Bethnal Green's more infamous residents. Having moved from 35 Gales Gardens in 1965, the family settled at 72 Ramsey Street, one of a row of maisonettes that overlooked Valance Road in which they'd all finally have their own bedrooms. (Amusingly, young Mark had gone over to Canada for the summer to spend time with his grandparents and cousins, and returned home to find his family had relocated without his knowledge![394]) Their new abode overlooked the house owned by Violet Kray – mother of the notorious Kray twins. Mark Wheeler remembered how his Auntie Joycie (Doreen's sister) lived in MacDougal House very close to Ramsey Street. Joycie's husband Jonny had been doing some work for the Krays, and occasionally brought home the odd carriage clock or other domestic item to give to Kenny and Doreen, which were almost certainly of dubious provenance. Mark recalled being at his auntie's with his mum and cousin Nikki when the police raided the house. Doreen ushered the family into the lounge and sent the two kids home to Ramsey Street with the instruction that they should hide the questionable items with her brother Ronnie, in case the police continued the raid into their home for any reason. Mark said he arrived home to find his dad practising the trumpet and told him what happened. Kenny immediately dropped the horn and flew into a panic of rushing randomly to and fro, drawing all the curtains and peeking anxiously out of the windows. They gathered the potentially suspect belongings and moved them up to Uncle Ronnie's, who promptly launched them into the canal in a series of bin bags. In the end, the police never came, so it was all for nothing. (Kenny had just as fragile a nerve for a life in crime as he did for music performance.[395]) 1960s society meant this was not the only interaction between the world of the Krays and Kenny's extended musical family; many of the musicians from that period, including Bobby Wellins and Norma Winstone, performed regularly in nightclubs owned by the Kray twins. Norma recalled a weekly residency at the Regency Club, a seemingly normal gig, until "later into the evening when the men in overcoats would appear again". Eventually – instinctively or by a nod – the band knew that their services were no longer required, and they'd pack up for the night.[396]

---

By the mid-1960s, Kenny's involvement with the London jazz scene and the music profession in general exploded with a wide variety of work opportunities and artistic innovations. There was a creative outpouring of contemporary jazz centred around Ronnie Scott's club on Gerrard Street, and the commercial recording scene became busier than ever.

Kenny already had a musical relationship with Ronnie Scott from the early '60s. Among other live appearances, in May 1963 they played together for a BBC "Network 3" broadcast in a group performing under the name The Seven Souls.[397] But it was the scene at the Gerrard Street club (which became known as "The Old Place" after Ronnie vacated the venue and relocated to his new venue on Frith Street[398]) that was transformative for the young musicians at the time. After Benny Golson played the final set in the original Ronnie Scott club on 27 November 1965, there was some time left on the lease of the Old Place, and Ronnie famously handed it over to the younger musicians as a venue to play and develop their new music. A community of like-minded musicians that embraced all the new innovations in jazz formed around it, and many of the leading musicians who would go on to be stars of the movement found opportunities to rehearse and perform there. Bassist Dave Holland recalled the scene around the Old Place and the generosity of Ronnie and co-owner Pete King: "It transformed the scene in London for the young players. It had a powerful effect: not only could we play seven nights a week but we had a place to rehearse in the afternoons; we could stay on all night until the sun came up and jam, things like that."[399] Ronnie and Pete continued to run the Old Place, even sometimes at a financial loss, until the lease finally expired in 1967.[400] For Kenny, involved in much of this new music, this was also a period during which several key musicians and lifelong friends would first enter his life.

The first of these was indeed Dave Holland, who was born in Wolverhampton in 1946 and had grown up in the Midlands. His father deserted the family when he was an infant, so he was raised by his mother, his uncle, and his maternal grandparents.[401] Like the Canadian Wheelers, Dave's family moved several times during his childhood, which was unsettling for the shy boy. When they eventually settled in Walsall he was able to have some stability and began to explore his new-found interest in music. Having started on ukulele and piano, Dave eventually joined a youth "guitar club". Some of his friends from the club formed a band but, with no bassist to fill the chair,

Dave volunteered to take on the challenge. He immediately fell in love with the bass and everything about the role it played; by the age of 15 and with a few years' experience of performing in youth clubs around the area, Dave became committed to a life playing music. Following the end of his mother's second marriage the family had some financial difficulties, so Dave made the decision to leave school and start work. There were no professional musicians in the family so that seemed like an unrealistic option to him. Instead, he interviewed to join the police force, but quickly realized it was not what he wanted. He was already earning a bit of money playing gigs, so he decided "why not just keep doing that?" Following a summer season in Scarborough (where he learned to read music fluently), Dave was given the gig on a UK tour with American singer Johnnie Ray. Ray's band was made up professional players from London including saxophonist Bobby Wellins, Kenny's old bandmate from his Lewis and Featherstonhaugh days. This tour and the contacts he made ultimately led to Dave's move to London in the September of 1964, just before his 18th birthday. Following early gigs at a Greek restaurant and his enrolment at the Guildhall School, Dave became increasingly busy across the capital playing a wide range of music. He took everything he could and was often working six nights a week, at one point having three steady gigs on Sundays. All of this was while he was studying at the Guildhall, and even playing principal bass in their first symphony orchestra.[402] In London, Dave lived in various houses with other jazz musicians of the time, including drummer John Marshall. In another house, he lived with pianist John Taylor, perhaps the colleague who would become most closely associated with Kenny throughout his life.

John Taylor, or "J.T.", as he would become affectionately known – in part to distinguish him from Johns Marshall and Surman – was born in Manchester in 1942. He spent most of his school years in Hastings after the family had moved there in 1953 via a two-year period in Kidderminster. Theirs wasn't an overtly musical household as Kenny's had been; J.T.'s father worked for the Post Office while his mother looked after the home, but crucially he did have a sister 15 years his senior who was learning classical piano by the time he was born. This was his first experience with music and, following in his sister's footsteps, he began teaching himself the piano at about the age of six.[403] Initially learning by ear, and then with his self-taught father's help, the young J.T. later began more formal lessons before discovering jazz in his early teens. While still living in Hastings, J.T. was getting more and more gigs in the local area alongside his day job as a civil servant – the same job he'd had since leaving school at 16.[404] His work eventually transferred him to London in 1964, when his involvement in music really took hold. While he had the best of intentions to focus on his career and gain promotion, he soon found himself at jazz clubs like the Bull's Head and Ronnie's Old Place as he became more and more immersed in the scene.

Astonishingly, Kenny first crossed paths with both these younger musicians on the exact same night in the mid-'60s. Kenny recounted this in various interviews: "I went to a rehearsal band of Alan Cohen at Ronnie Scott's Old Place – and I heard this piano player playing and I thought '*Who the hell is that?*' and then I heard this bass player and I thought '*What's going on?*' It was John Taylor and Dave Holland."[405] It is possible that fading memories may have blurred the exact chronology; J.T. remembered that he also had a residency with Tommy Whittle in The Hopbine pub in Wembley; Tommy would invite a different guest each week and on one occasion Kenny was the guest.[406] J.T. could not recall which of these events happened first, but it doesn't matter. That night in Alan Cohen's band left an indelible impression on Kenny, and both Dave Holland and John Taylor became among his closest friends and musical allies for the rest of his life.

As the mid-'60s jazz scene buzzed with new creative energy, Dankworth, who became increasingly busy with other activities such as film scoring, temporarily stopped working with his big band. But thanks to the exposure received through the years with Dankworth's group, Kenny had established quite a reputation as a trumpet player. In addition to his involvement in the innovations that were developing around the Old Place, Kenny's break from the busy schedule with Dankworth also meant he was free to take on more studio work than ever before. On one such session, a young tenor saxophonist in the two-piece horn section was in awe of the (then unknown to him) older professional trumpet player who crept into the studio and read and played everything perfectly, although the shy trumpeter hardly said a word to him. The 16-year-old saxophonist was Stan Sulzmann, then playing with a Wimbledon 'Palais' band that had been booked for the session. Stan was another player who would go on to be a lifelong friend and collaborator of Kenny's, and their paths would soon cross again more formally soon.[407]

Kenny would also frequently appear in the many stellar trumpet sections of ad hoc big bands formed for jazz sessions around the time, and he made close connections with many of the studio musicians from this era of his career. A 1964 album from a more established big band, William Russo and the London Jazz Orchestra's *Stonehenge*,[408] marked the culmination of Kenny's time studying with the visiting American composer. It is an extraordinary and ambitious recording, and the nuanced attention to detail in the musicians' interpretation of the music certainly supports the many anecdotal accounts of how thoroughly Russo rehearsed the band. On 5 August 1965, Kenny also participated in the one and only live performance of The Animals big band at the Fifth Annual Jazz and Blues Festival in Richmond, Surrey.[409] The Emcee Five and The Animals had once shared a manager in Mike Jeffreys. Lead singer Eric Burdon had also known Ian Carr from his Newcastle days, so when the idea for the big band occurred it was Ian who was charged with putting the band together. Kenny played trumpet and contributed the arrangements for the occasion. He transcribed some Ray Charles pieces from the recordings and added a few original arrangements of other numbers The Animals wanted to perform.[410]

There was so much work going on and so many different things Kenny was involved in that it is only possible here to give an indication of just how busy and productive this period was for him. Focusing on the year 1966 as an example, Kenny appeared on Stan Tracey's album *Alice in Jazz Land*,[411] Kenny Clare and Ronnie Stephenson's *Drum Spectacular*[412] and the Tubby Hayes Orchestra's *100% Proof*.[413] (There were several BBC broadcasts with Tubby's big band as well). In the same year, Kenny also played on Georgie Fame's album *Sound Venture*[414] as a member of the Harry South Big Band. Kenny admired Harry and liked him personally and would later dedicate a piece to him in his *Sweet Time Suite*.[415] The trumpet section for Fame's *Sound Venture* album included Ian Hamer, Greg Bowen and Tony Fisher, all trumpeters with whom he would have lifelong musical friendships. Also on the session were saxophonists Ray Warleigh and Tony Coe, whom Kenny knew from the Old Place and with whom he would also enjoy a life of music-making. The same year, Kenny and old friend Art Ellefson also appeared on the album *Brave New World* by Jack Hammer,[416] who had found fame (and presumably no small fortune) as co-writer of the Jerry Lee Lewis hit "Great Balls of Fire".

---

Word of Kenny's talent soon reached Europe. The NDR (North German Broadcasting) was running a "Jazz Workshop" series which regularly included British musicians. As early as October 1962, Kenny was invited to perform as part of a swinging group along with many of his regular colleagues at the time, including Les Condon, Ronnie Ross, Ray Premru, Alan Ganley, and Art Ellefson. The programme also included two of Kenny's compositions, "Huck" and "Yogi".[417] In 1965, the Austrian pianist Friedrich Gulda enlisted him into an extraordinary ensemble to record his album *Music for Four Soloists and Band No. 1.*[418] It was a stellar line-up: alongside fellow Londoners Tubby Hayes, Stan Roderick, and Alfie Reece were American rhythm-section stars Ron Carter and Mel Lewis, while the soloists included J.J. Johnson and fellow trumpeter Freddie Hubbard, whom Kenny greatly admired. Hearing Freddie on the Herbie Hancock album *Empyrean Isles*[419] had blown Kenny away, and he once said that the way Freddie played on that record was how he had imagined he'd always wanted to play the trumpet but couldn't.[420] For Kenny, hearing Freddie firsthand was perhaps cause for further self-doubt and dissatisfaction with his own playing – but he would soon do something radical to address that situation.

Kenny recorded two more albums with Friedrich Gulda in 1966, the first of which was a performance as part of the International Competition for Modern Jazz in Vienna. Both recordings once more featured stellar musicians like Miroslav Vitous and Joe Zawinul, as well as Ron Carter and Mel Lewis again. (In fact, a few years later, Kenny would deputize in the Thad Jones/Mel Lewis band at their Ronnie Scott's residency, so it is possible Lewis would have remembered him from these Gulda sessions and knew he was up to the job.) Also in 1966, Kenny also took part in his second broadcast for the NDR Jazz Workshop in a quintet formed around Stan Tracey's *Under Milk Wood*[421] group of Bobby Wellins, Jeff Clyne, and Jackie Dougan.[422] These early European appearances were just a first foray into the Continent for Kenny. There was much more to come.

---

Kenny took part in several other significant jazz albums and projects throughout this period, and the pioneering music created is still recognized as an important development in British jazz. One such collaboration was with Jamaican saxophonist Joe Harriott. Harriott had teamed up with the Indian violinist John Mayer to produce the "Indo-Jazz Fusions" concept which resulted in three albums between 1966 and 1968. The first incarnation of the project was called the Joe Harriott Double Quintet, and two further volumes also included Mayer's name. It was literally a double quintet: five Indian classical musicians and five jazz musicians. Kenny was inspired by Joe Harriott's playing; he said, "I loved playing with Joe Harriott. When he played a solo it was so amazing that it gave you the feeling you couldn't wait to solo yourself, rather than feeling intimidated by it. He set you on fire."[423] Interestingly, the Indo-Jazz groups also featured pianist Pat Smythe, someone Kenny would work with often and who also had a friendship with famous US pianist Bill Evans. Pat later passed Kenny's composition "Sweet Dulcinea Blue" to Bill Evans in a pile of tunes, and Evans went on to record it for Fantasy Records on his 1978 album *Quintessence*.[424],[425]

Another colleague of Kenny's who has taken his place in British jazz history is composer and bassist Graham Collier. Graham enjoyed an intensely productive period during the late '60s and Kenny recorded with him for his debut album *Deep Dark Blue Centre*[426] in January 1967, as well as on *Workpoints*, recorded live in March 1968.[427] Graham was a prolific figure who attracted the great young players of the time to perform his music; his ensembles included many of the musicians Kenny worked with in other settings, including John Surman, Mike Gibbs, Karl Jenkins, and Harry Beckett, as well as Henry Lowther and the slightly younger Stan Sulzmann. Both the latter musicians recalled the personal significance of working with Kenny for the first time in a more open jazz setting as part of Graham's 12-piece band, as opposed to the sessions and sideman work they had done with him before.[428] Throughout these projects with Graham, though, Henry was already working alongside Kenny in Dankworth's new big band, re-formed for the second time in 1967 with yet another personnel change.

This new Dankworth band was assembled to record his *The $1,000,000 Collection* album in May 1967.[429] Among others, it included trombonists Chris Pyne and Mike Gibbs, tuba player Dick Hart, saxophonist Tony Coe, pianist Alan Branscombe, bassist Kenny Napper, and drummer John Spooner.

In addition to Henry Lowther, the band also included another very important trumpeter in Kenny's future life: the phenomenal young lead player Derek Watkins.[430]

At the time he first worked with Chris Pyne, Kenny was immersed in composing and exploring his expansive harmonic vocabulary. Kenny recalled meeting him through the trumpeter Gus Galbraith, who was also running a rehearsal band. Gus asked Kenny to include some of his music one week, and anxious of issues that must have previously occurred he asked Gus, "Do you have a trombone player who can play my kind of chords?" Gus replied, "Oh yeah, I have got a guy now." Kenny recalled, "he meant Chris Pyne – and he was right, Chris could play it." Chris Pyne would play a role in Kenny's music until Chris's death in 1995. "I think that's what gave me courage to maybe write a bit more adventurous," Kenny said.[431] This second new Dankworth line-up was meaningful for Kenny in many ways, but most importantly, they would soon record Kenny's own album.

---

Even more significant than the prolific creativity and plentiful commercial work, the most life-changing event of this period for Kenny was his involvement in the burgeoning "free jazz" movement. Kenny's engagement with free jazz is so important because it represents the conscious and decisive action he took as his own musical frustrations reached their peak.

His dissatisfaction had been growing for some time, both with his own playing and with the professional and musical balance of his career. For all the accolades he would later receive as part of the free jazz movement, it is his initial spark of motivation to seek out the "free" scene that is most profoundly revealing and would fuel his tenure in the genre. This was a quietly resolute action which in its own way was as tenacious as his dramatic move to London a decade-and-a-half earlier. It is crucial to understand the big-picture context in which Kenny found this new wave of music, and the smaller occurrences that represent his character so accurately. There are two such features that stand out as definable personality traits in this way, and they are characteristics that would resonate throughout his life's decisions.

The first is shown in his decision to explore free music in response to his own playing frustrations. It shows a deeply insightful ability to examine his processes, and then understand instinctively what he needed to do to move forward. This self-awareness is clearly an indicator of a great artist, but it did not come out of the blue. As early as 1962, he described feeling that his music "is at a dead end"[432] and in later interviews he consistently referred to the frustrations of feeling he had not mastered "conventional" bebop and was not getting enough work playing "jazz gigs" in the scene: "I wasn't a great bebopper, although that was my roots; I never could really play it and there were great people around who could: Tubby Hayes, Jimmy Deuchar. But I was determined, I wanted to play with somebody . . ."[433] This was echoed on a separate occasion, when he said, "I went along to [John Stevens's] club because I was really quite frustrated. I wasn't getting any jazz playing in the then current jazz world."[434]

The second trait of Kenny's personality is equally critical and just as revealing. In addition to his insight that it might help develop his own playing, a big part of the reason he persevered with free music was that the people he was playing it with made him feel welcome and wanted. He liked them and felt comfortable playing with them; they made him feel accepted. And, for Kenny, that alone was enough to build the basic conceptual foundation for all his future collaborations. Indeed, choosing musicians he liked personally would be central to all the big bands he would later form, and would remain at the heart of his choice of personnel for all future projects, whenever the decision was his to make.

These features are important to remember as they demonstrate his motivations for staying involved in the free scene – because, in the end, despite all the success and recognition he later found through it, free music was not Kenny's principal choice for an outlet of self-expression. Was he good at it? Yes. Did he enjoy it? Certainly, as long as it was with the right people. But one only has to listen to his own performances to quickly understand that, while he often incorporated elements of free improvisation into his music, even significant moments as introductions or segues, it was not primarily what he chose to focus on at any length as a bandleader. This observation was backed up by Evan Parker himself when talking to Kenny about his free playing many years later, saying to him:

> The great thing is that you've done playing in that context as well and you're a leading figure in that, and it's almost like a sort of *side issue* for you, in a way . . . Not that you approach it casually or anything like that, but it's something you've managed to do *as well* as keep all the other stuff happening, which is amazing.[435]

This is interesting because, for Kenny, although free playing held great value to him, it also served as a tool for his own development. It was a workout: a detox (or retox perhaps), something to redress the balance of his own playing, his own internal need for both melancholy *and* chaos. He said

> . . . free jazz, whatever you want to call it, has had the same thing on me, you know, when it's been off it's been really bad, but you just feel as if you've got something out of your system, which I never think of when I play on a normal jazz gig, for want of a better word. I always think afterwards, if it was really good you feel a bit peaceful for a while but free jazz I always felt like I got rid of something . . .[436]

Playing free jazz was also a source of employment, of course: a way through which his reputation in Europe grew immeasurably larger, providing a means of meeting other like-minded musicians. So Kenny's involvement with the free scene has such significance in this story because of *why* he did it, *what* it led to, *who* the friends were he made playing it, and *how* it affected his own style of jazz playing. Its importance lies in the story behind the music just as much as – or maybe even more than – the music itself.

There are two clearly defined aspects of interest within his personal recollections of this period. Since he almost always uses the word "frustration" to describe both, it is easy to get these distinctions confused, so they are worth clarifying. Kenny articulates two perspectives on his motivation for seeking out the free scene. First, there is his frustration with his own self-perceived struggle and ultimate failure to master bebop to a satisfactory level as a trumpeter. "I was very frustrated, because I spent about 20 years trying to play straight bebop. Although I love it, it's my roots, but I could never do it . . . I mean, I love Miles and Dizzy and all them, but then trying to play in that [way] . . . I couldn't do it, so I wasn't getting many jazz gigs . . ."[437] Second, there is his frustration with the balance of professional work he is doing: the contrast between the abundance of (what he called) "commercial music", versus the lack of what he felt was "jazz music". "I was making a living playing commercial music but I was frustrated because I couldn't play jazz [gigs] . . ."[438] This might appear to be a contradiction given the playing he was doing at that time; recordings with Tubby Hayes, Stan Tracey, and others. These repeated references to not getting "jazz gigs" are telling because they indicate how Kenny clearly demarcated in his own mind the work he *was* getting at that time, as opposed to what he felt he wanted to be doing as a jazz artist. Even when the work involved sitting in a big band playing jazz arrangements and taking the occasional solo, it was still not exactly what he would describe as a "jazz gig".

Curiously, there is no obvious anecdotal evidence to suggest that other musicians felt dissatisfied or underwhelmed with Kenny's playing themselves. There are no quotes saying, "I guess Wheeler was OK on the section parts but he couldn't really solo!" Kenny later reflected on it himself:

> If I had been like as good as Jimmy [Deuchar] or Dizzy Reece at what they were doing they probably would have asked me to do gigs but I think they could see there was something lacking in me, I don't know. I would dread getting up if someone counted off a real fast "I Got Rhythm" or "Cherokee", I would probably go into a shell and crumble.[439]

There are no accounts to suggest who the "they" might be that felt this way, so we must assume that this was a perception of his playing that existed principally in his own mind. Incidentally, he was indeed called upon to solo on a burning tempo alongside one of the great exponents of that type of playing. An out-take from Tubby Hayes's big-band broadcast in May 1966 includes a terrific solo from Kenny on "Seven Steps to Heaven", at a fearsome 320 bpm.[440]

He still sounds very idiosyncratic but it comes over as something unique and intentional; it is much too strong in concept and instrumental command to be just a "lesser" version of uptempo bebop playing. But, of course, when Tubby plays after him, one can immediately hear the difference in approach and time feel, so it is understandable why Kenny might have been making this comparison between his way of playing and a so-called "them" who had mastered bebop in the way Tubby had.

The real explanation behind Kenny's self-deprecating reflections is probably simpler, and again particular to his personality. It was the result of an often naturally inclined pessimism; however busy things were career-wise, it was not doing quite what he wanted, so he still felt somehow unlucky. *Down-Beat* magazine later described this poetically in a comparison to Eeyore from *Winnie the Pooh*: "Wheeler has a tendency to be hard on himself, expect the worst and be slightly suspicious when things turn out better than hoped."[441] After that article appeared, there was a toy Eeyore stuck to the window of Kenny's music room for the rest of his life.

------·------

At the end of 1965, a group of like-minded musicians, led by the drummer John Stevens, found premises in Central London in which to regularly experiment with improvisation.[442] This new movement in music, which Kenny referred to as "avant-garde" (though he didn't like the label[443]) was already proving a little too challenging for established venues.[444] They had begun playing this music at The Sun pub on Drury Lane, in a group including saxophonist Trevor Watts and trombonist Paul Rutherford – both of whom were musicians Stevens had known through their shared time in the Royal Air Force band – as well as bassist Harry Miller.[445] John Stevens found a place they could play through Veryan Weston's vocalist sister, Armorel.[446] It was called the Little Theatre Club, and this original group of musicians from The Sun became the first incarnation of what would become known as the Spontaneous Music Ensemble (SME).

The Little Theatre Club would open up to these musicians on Friday and Saturday nights, after the small theatre productions had finished and it transformed into an after-hours hangout for actors,[447] and the musicians would perform on the stage among whatever theatrical sets the current production happened to be using.[448] The venue was just a small room up four flights of steep stairs in Garrick's Yard, toward the back of the Garrick Club in the heart of Covent Garden.[449]

In early 1966, Kenny went to seek out this new music. In recollections, he consistently stuck to the story that he knew this avant-garde music was being played at the Little Theatre Club, so he went down to hear it. He said he hated listening to it at first but went along for a few more nights and then eventually he was invited to sit in.[450] Although he sometimes described it as though he didn't know the performers, he already knew all the musicians through the regular jazz scene and Ronnie Scott's Old Place.[451] Henry Lowther even recalled that the first time he properly heard Kenny play jazz it had been with John Stevens; Henry also said it was the first time he really understood why all the musicians were raving about Kenny. (In late 1965, Henry played opposite them for a BBC broadcast at the Paris Theatre, and Kenny was in a septet led by John Stevens that was still playing very much conventional swing.[452]) In recollections from John Stevens and Paul Rutherford themselves, it seems they had been actively encouraging Kenny to come down to the Little Theatre Club and sit in with them all along; the truth is probably somewhere in the middle. Nevertheless, it is most significant that Kenny finally chose to attend, and what happened that first night was equally profound for him. It is another story he recalls with consistency in interviews – amusingly and revealingly – almost all of which include the word *berserk*! He described it to Ian Carr:

> I just started to go up and listen and, I hated it on sight, completely hated it . . . but after, I dunno wasn't very long, three or four days, John Stevens says, "Well, do you want to play?" and I said, "Well, why not?" So I went up and played and, I dunno I think for about 10 minutes I just went completely berserk on the trumpet playing anything at all you know [*chuckles*], and I couldn't say if it was good or bad but I, it was, I found it very therapeutic, I got something out of my system and, for many years after and still probably, I feel the same about free jazz is that, I find it therapeutic, you know.[453]

An astute reflection indeed, and that specific notion of not knowing whether "it was good or bad" but always finding it "therapeutic" was a description he often repeated. Typically private, Kenny chose to keep these thoughts inside at the time; he never mentioned any of this to the other musicians. Evan Parker said, "that [only] came out later by reading interviews".[454] Dave Holland, who also became a regular at the club, recalled hearing Kenny there. Though he was not specifically describing the first night, it shows the impression Kenny made in this setting: "I was just astounded at what he could do – I mean, I'd never heard a trumpet player – sound-wise, playing-wise, ability, originality . . ."[455]

There are two other noteworthy details regarding Kenny's feelings about his (self-perceived) failure with bebop that ultimately led him to the free jazz movement. The first thing to note is that it was specifically the 'time feel' of bebop he thought he could not master; it wasn't the harmonic aspect or the technical demands of executing the vocabulary on the trumpet: it was about the rhythmic placement particularly. "Well, I never could play straight-ahead bebop on the beat – I thought you had to play da-DEE-da-DEE [referring to the articulation on the trumpet] – and I couldn't do it, because I always liked to play around with the beat, you know . . ." He explained, "I think it comes from one of the first players I really liked, Dexter Gordon, who played a lot behind the beat – and I liked that kind of thing that he did. I think that influenced me a lot. But I never knew many trumpet players who played like that."[456] The second point is that these feelings never once crossed over into a dislike of straight-ahead players or their music: "I was never disappointed with bebop – I never criticized it . . ."[457] On another occasion he expanded further:

> I always had problems with bebop: I never really could play, I mean, I loved it, it's my roots and that's what I always listen to but, I mean they had people around London who were absolutely magic at bebop: I mean Tubby and Joe Harriott, Dizzy Reece, Jimmy Deuchar, all those people, Hank Shaw. I couldn't, I just could not see myself leading the life they led booked in pubs as a jazz soloist because I just didn't feel I could play it.

Revealing a bit more inner confidence, he continued: "I thought I had something, but I was very reticent about getting up with those kind of people. I used to be frightened out of my life about playing with those people."[458] His feelings about this demonstrate a seemingly contradictory mix of quite conservative musical tastes alongside his innovative approach to the music and the instrument. In the context of all the elements he describes struggling with, the psychological release he finally felt in discovering free jazz was enormous. When remembering the feeling after he had played that first night at the Little Theatre Club, he joked, "Oh, *freedom*! Is that what it means?!"[459]

We can't be sure which musicians were there that first night, but it is almost certain it would have included the core team of Stevens, Rutherford and Watts, and probably at least one of the regular bass players. Kenny's memory of it frequently presumed that Evan Parker would have been there as Evan went on to play such a huge part in his life, but Evan arrived on that scene a few months later.

As his involvement with the SME intensified, Kenny took part in the first recording with the group only a couple of months after the Little Theatre Club residencies had begun. In March 1966 they recorded the album *Challenge* for the Eyemark label,[460] in a group including the core regulars of Stevens, Watts and Rutherford, plus bassists Bruce Cale and Jeff Clyne. At this time, the music still had composed elements (usually introductions and endings) framing the group improvisations, with the writing being done by either Stevens, Watts, or Rutherford. Stevens later described how *Challenge* was a good representation of where the SME was at the time: "it was all on the cards – waiting to find a way of developing whatever that music turned out to be".[461]

In mid-1966, Evan Parker finally joined the group. The saxophonist was much younger than Kenny and already in awe of him. He recalled how, via John Stevens, "I knew Kenny as a soloist and I loved his music. He was a star to me. I remember seeing him on the Central Line [tube] sometimes, obviously on his way to Bethnal Green – [though] I didn't know that at the time, I just thought, 'What's a star like that doing on the tube?!'"[462]

Evan Parker was born on 5 April 1944 in Bristol, before moving up to London at the age of nine after the family relocated to Stanwell, near Heathrow

Airport. He started playing the saxophone in school and emulated the usual role models, particularly Paul Desmond, before discovering John Coltrane. He attended university in Birmingham to study botany, but his passion for music and philosophy soon took over from his plant studies and he spent his second-year grant on a Selmer Mark VI saxophone. Through some friends at the Royal College of Art, he was asked to record some "futuristic" music for a film soundtrack and, when the film was shown in London, Evan met John Stevens for the first time, introduced through a mutual friend that knew they would share similar musical interests. Not surprisingly, the friendship developed and, in that summer of 1966, when Trevor Watts was away on holiday, John Stevens invited Evan down to the Little Theatre Club to play with the group, and with that one simple invitation one of the great voices of European free jazz entered the story.[463]

With Evan now on board, the final important figure to come along and complete the cast was guitarist Derek Bailey. He had been invited down by Watts during a brief period when John Stevens and Evan Parker were living abroad in Copenhagen.[464] This collective of players was hugely active throughout the late '60s, with Kenny also now firmly established as an accidental pioneer of the movement. The SME performed frequently in various combinations and in 1967 recorded some music initially intended to be a soundtrack for a film. (That version of the group included the bass player Barry Guy, by then also a regular.) They added further recordings to the soundtracks they'd already documented, intended for release under the album name *Withdrawal*, but these recordings did not actually surface until some 30 years later.

Throughout this period, many other musicians were attending the late-night sessions at the Little Theatre Club. Dave Holland had started going down to explore the new scene and recalled how interested visiting musicians would also get involved; Dave remembered the first time he'd ever seen a solo bass set was when Barre Phillips first came over to London and played there.[465] Even a number of curious players from the straight-ahead scene would go to check it out, including the likes of Tubby Hayes and Phil Seamen, who performed there.[466] Kenny even brought his friend Art Ellefson along a few times, although Art didn't really claim to understand what was going on. On one occasion, Art showed up even later than usual into the night and one of the musicians said, "Hey Art, you're late," to which he replied, "Yeah, about 20 years late!"[467]

On 20 March 1967, the SME recorded a broadcast for the BBC Light Programme's *The Jazz Scene* in their weekly "Jazz Club" slot. They called the music "Springboard" and recorded it live at the Paris Cinema in London with the same core group of seven musicians: Kenny, Evan Parker, Trevor Watts, Paul Rutherford, Derek Bailey, Barry Guy, and John Stevens. When the programme was broadcast a week later, presenter Humphrey Lyttelton openly addressed the controversial and challenging nature of this music with his announcement, "Now, let's face it, this first half hour by the Spontaneous

Music Ensemble is not going to be everyone's cup of tea!" But armed with his admirable BBC Reithian values, he continues, "but if Jazz Club is going to reflect accurately what's going on on the British jazz scene, and we feel that that's our job, well, we're going to have music both ultra-traditional, and ultra-modern, which arouses controversy."[468] Though it seems amusing now, this shows the very open suspicion and resistance free music faced in some camps right from the beginning; kudos to the producers who took it on so readily.

Photo 16: Kenny, Evan Parker, Dave Holland and Derek Bailey at the recording of *Karyōbin*.
Courtesy Evan Parker/Wheeler Family archive

Perhaps the most iconic SME recording from that period is 1968's *Karyōbin*,[469] not least of all because of its unique personnel – a quintet consisting of Kenny, Evan Parker, Derek Bailey, Dave Holland and John Stevens – but also because it was the only time these five musicians ever played together in that exact configuration.[470] It is indeed fortunate that it happened to be captured on a recording session rather than lost to the night in the Little Theatre Club, as must have happened with so many other one-off occurrences. Evan calls this his first album ever, because it was released at the time, unlike the earlier 1967 recordings that did not appear until decades later. By the time of *Karyōbin*, the group approach had moved away from even the smallest bits of written material like those used on *Challenge*. "That's a key moment, when John suddenly started to think, 'Well, we don't need these written things, we can just play,'" Evan said.[471] John Stevens described what he thought about influencing the music:

> Now, again, I couldn't resist the temptation to organize something in rela-
> tionship to it [the session], to get us as quickly as we could to the point
> of interaction. Maybe that was because we weren't regularly playing as a
> quintet anyway, and improvising together. So all it was, was a count of
> two beats: one [*snaps fingers simultaneously*] . . . two . . . play . . . nothing
> . . . play . . . nothing . . . improvise . . . – so in those single-beat clusters of
> sound I was hoping, gradually, the group to come right in and connect
> – and you can actually hear it on the beginning of *Karyōbin* – the way it
> opens.[472]

The full title of the record is *Karyōbin: Are the Imaginary Birds Said to Live in Paradise*.[473] It was recorded by Eddie Kramer at the renowned Olympic Sound Studios, on 18 February 1968, originally for Island (UK) Records and later reissued on the Chronoscope label.[474] John Stevens was friendly with Eddie Kramer, the engineer already famous for having recorded The Beatles, The Rolling Stones, and Jimi Hendrix at Olympic. Kramer had the opportunity to record projects of his own interest if it was done through the night, so he approached John and Evan who were currently playing as a duo. They both agreed to add the remaining three players. Stevens pointed out that to some people at the time, Kenny was an odd choice, "but we always loved Kenny's playing . . . Kenny's involvement with free music was very much me, not forcing him, but saying 'Come on Ken, you've gotta come and do this . . .' so it wasn't his choice, but more and more as he did it I suppose it has become more of his general language of music-making now."[475]

Olympic still had some musicians from the rock world coming and going, and on one of the original *Karyōbin* tapes there was a faintly audible electrical buzz where the old doorbell was rung and interfered with the wiring: it was Yoko Ono arriving at the studio to see Eddie Kramer. Evan recalled "she came and listened for a bit and she said, 'What you're doing is much more interest-ing than Ornette' . . . And then she invited John [Stevens], Derek and me to do a couple of gigs with her, which we did. This was before the relationship with John Lennon was public."[476] Jimi Hendrix also made an appearance at one of the late-night recording sessions at Olympic. Memories fail as to whether that was the *Karyōbin* sessions or a separate occasion, but Hendrix was also fascinated by what they were doing.

The individual playing and chemistry between the musicians on *Karyōbin* is a remarkable representation of the free music they were developing at the time. On this album, Kenny is certainly making a defining contribution to a new instrumental vocabulary for free improvisation on the trumpet that remains influential and timeless. As Evan observed: "Everybody loved Kenny's imagination – well, technique and imagination – in a free context. He was

Photo 17: Kenny and Evan Parker at the recording of *Karyōbin*.
Courtesy Evan Parker/Wheeler Family archive

the only trumpet player with that kind of technique that was interested also in playing free."[477]

A year or so later, after he had been spotted by Miles Davis and moved to New York, Dave Holland took a cassette of *Karyōbin* over to Miles's house one night:

> I played it for Miles . . . I thought, "Oh, I'll take *Karyōbin* over" – because I was wanting the band to play freer . . . I was hoping he would say, "Oh, man, that's really good, let's do something like that", which is completely ridiculous now, I know. And what he said [was], "Wow, that trumpet player really plays well. If you want to play that way, you'd better get your own band." Which actually was good advice, you know. Again – it wasn't him saying anything smarmy – it was, *If you've got a direction you want to go you should do it yourself.* It wasn't like a put-down. It wasn't, *Aw, get your own band – I'm not going to play that way.* I can appreciate what he said.[478]

Kenny looked back on just what a happy and productive time the late '60s was for him as these complementarily opposing musical worlds co-existed: "That was a great period, I mean, there was so much going on; Mike Gibbs was active and John Surman and the Little Theatre Club and Mike Westbrook and the Brotherhood of Breath and the Old Place, it was just a fantastic period.

I thought that last half of the '60s in London and people [were] much more mobile."[479] It is important to note that all this new activity in the free scene was not in place of any of his other playing – it was *in addition to* everything else he was already doing. "I was leading a schizophrenic life," Kenny said. "I was doing studio work and free jazz and everything and I just loved it, it was great." Explaining his busyness, he said, "I suppose I was moving around more than most people because by that time I was finally beginning to play [the trumpet] well enough so I could play in studios and different things . . . and that I guess was why I got asked so much to so many different things."[480] He summed up this separate but parallel musical life, saying, "You know, it was a long time before anybody knew I could play a chord symbol!"[481] But he always acknowledged the importance of finding his place in the free scene: "I don't know what would have happened if I hadn't met them, I can't imagine . . . I'm glad I did meet them, and I'm glad of the influence they had on me . . . ," he said, before musing, "I became one of those people who was too far in for some and too far out for others!"[482]

---

In this same period, Kenny first heard the trumpeter who would be the single biggest influence on him as a player: one who would help him finally synthesize this "schizophrenic" musical existence into one coherent, unique, recognizable and personal style.

Following an SME gig at Edinburgh Art College around 1966, Kenny went back to stay at the flat of Jackie Docherty, a keen follower of the jazz scene who was working in the record department of a local bookstore.[483] Jackie was leaving to stay at his girlfriend's so Kenny could have his room, but before he left they listened to some music. Jackie recalled playing Kenny the Eric Dolphy album *Outward Bound*[484] and how Kenny was struck by Freddie Hubbard's playing on the track "G.W.": he felt it was different and he hadn't heard Freddie play quite like that before.[485] Jackie then held up an LP and said, "Have you heard this?" Kenny said no, and Jackie proceeded to play him the Booker Little album *Out Front*.[486] Kenny was enraptured. When Jackie finally left for his girlfriend's place, Kenny was still listening over and over to the LP that would change his life.[487] Kenny consistently repeated the significance of this evening in later interviews, reiterating what a profound discovery it was for him.

It should be noted that Evan Parker also recalls playing *Out Front* for Kenny at a student house in Birmingham following a gig with John Stevens: he remembered Kenny quietly listening and turning gradually whiter as the profundity of what he was hearing set in.[488] We will probably never know for sure in what order these events occurred – it is probable that both happened but were rolled into one recollection in Kenny's mind.[489] Placed chronologically, a sample of Kenny's own memories of this are:

And the first person who really gave me . . . opened the door for me was when I heard Booker Little. I think it was John Stevens, some night, we were at a town somewhere, we went to somebody's flat after and I think it was John Stevens who said, "listen to this trumpet player". I just breathed a complete sigh of relief you know, when I heard him play, 'cause I thought, "my God, there is another way!"[490]

and:

I think it was again with John Stevens somewhere after the gig somewhere, somebody said, "you should hear this guy play" and they put on a record of Booker Little and then, a door opened for me right away, automatically, I thought "oh, there's another way."[491]

and also:

But then I remember one night when I was playing in the – I don't know if it was with Globe Unity or who it was with – we went to somebody's house one night and they played me a Booker Little record – and I thought *My God!* That opened a whole new door for me, you know. You can do other things, but you can still be in the tradition. Because he was so different, but still somehow a bebop player, you know. And that gave me the courage to go my own way, I think.[492]

That last sentiment is, of course, the crucial feature of this revelatory encounter. He told Gene Lees: "That gave me courage to search out and have faith in my own thing and not feel guilty because I couldn't play strict bebop."[493] It was as though Booker Little embodied a kind of validation of the inner conflicts Kenny felt, somehow granting him permission to finally just be himself.

Kenny clarified this effect on a number of occasions and made an important distinction as to exactly how he, as an artist, internalized the influence. "I didn't want to copy him necessarily, I just saw he was showing me that you could do jazz, as I knew it, in a different way and still be part of the tradition. And so I began to listen to him a lot and I admired his writing and his playing a lot."[494] He went on:

I never tried to analyse what it was about him that was different, but I thought his tunes were different and his playing was different . . . [*pauses*] . . . I'm sorry he died so young 'cause I never got to meet him, but he definitely gave me a sort of a purpose in my jazz life. Soon as I heard him I could see the light at the end of the tunnel somehow, you know what I mean, and it was after that that I began to get a sense of direction in what I was doing that, I found the benefit from free playing and conventional playing at the same time.[495]

That last statement is also a recurring theme. Kenny often said he had felt most happy with his playing during the period he was very busy with both "free" and "conventional" jazz gigs once he had found the way to consolidate the two.

> I found that the one helped the other. If I did get a normal sort of jazz gig, with tunes, I felt the free jazz helped that, and also that helped the free jazz gigs. Somehow the free jazz helped loosen me up on changes, and those gigs brought my playing in free jazz in a bit, where it was more controlled.[496]

An important question arising from all this is whether there is a definitive example following this event where the influence and effect of Booker Little became apparent in Kenny's own playing: where this new-found confidence and coherence manifest themselves musically. The most obvious and categorical *yes* to that question would be in his album *Windmill Tilter*,[497] and the timing could not have been better. Recorded in March 1968 – only 18 months or so after that evening in Edinburgh – one hears a fully formed Kenny in extraordinary form, with more than a small trace of Booker Little in his approach. This is not to say Kenny didn't sound like himself, rather that this influence is more clearly woven into the individual style already apparent on his previous Whittle and Dankworth recordings.

On 11 and 12 March 1968, the Dankworth band, which had re-formed the year before for *The $1,000,000 Collection*, recorded a new LP at the CTS studios in Bayswater.[498] For the first time, the music was not Dankworth's own, but rather a whole record dedicated to someone else's writing. Although titled *Windmill Tilter: The Story of Don Quixote Told by Ken Wheeler and the John Dankworth Orchestra*, it was without question a Kenny Wheeler album, and in that respect, his first. Dankworth agreed: "One other very important LP, issued under my name, I consider very much the property of the man who wrote and arranged all the music and was the featured soloist – Kenny Wheeler."[499] Dankworth made his feelings clear at the time, writing on the back sleeve "I am most proud to be associated with this record, as I think it is one of the most exciting to involve my own orchestra in recent years."

The situation that led up to this recording is shrouded in half-remembered truths: an act of generosity by John Dankworth mixed with a marketing concept combined with a story repeated often enough that even the teller thought it true. The received wisdom behind this album is that it is about Don Quixote and that it was entirely written while Kenny was recovering from a wisdom tooth operation. Neither of these facts are quite accurate, nor are they that simple.

Before embarking on a dismantling of the chronology of what actually happened for the sake of accuracy, let us first focus on the most important thing about *Windmill Tilter*: that it is an astonishingly conceived and executed, original and fresh work of beautiful European large-ensemble writing. It is still revered to this day. The number of musicians who remarked that they had never heard (or played) music quite like it before Kenny came along would make for too repetitive a list of quotes here, but it was obviously influential and marked Kenny's arrival as both composer and soloist in his own right.

But was it written about Don Quixote? Not at all. The fact is that all the big-band pieces were written well before *Windmill Tilter* became a concept album, and all were performed by the Dankworth band before the recording sessions under their original titles which were different than those listed on the album. There was one piece, originally called "In Passing", which Kenny had written for the Morley College Big Band which became "The Cave of Montesinos" on *Windmill Tilter*. Kenny said it was actually written as an exercise; given Bill Russo's connection to Morley, it might have been composed while Kenny was still studying with him.[500] And one can believe that; there is a sense of "exercise" about it: the passing of almost canonic phrases from section to section and the exploration of different metric modulations necessitating a fresh treatment of the material two or three times over. But, as ever with Kenny's composing, the technique is beautifully hidden behind the seamless logic of its construction. This clarity of process and the effortless beauty of its execution would later make his writing a model for study in jazz schools across the world.

Another piece being performed by Graham Collier's 12-piece group called "Blue 25" was renamed to appear on *Windmill Tilter* as "Don No More". And the other four charts were all in the Dankworth book under their original titles: "Poochurbreenz'beenz" became "Don the Dreamer", "Bossapop" became "Altisidora", and "Marko" became "Bachelor Sam". (Mark Wheeler believed that "Marko" was originally named after him; if so, it is one of the first examples of Kenny's tradition of dedicating compositions to family members.)

The final big band piece, "Sancho", was first called "Zebbidee". This last working title particularly reveals the true origins behind Kenny's two initial concepts for the music: "I had an idea. I wanted to do an album of losers – because I've always loved losers . . . But I think eventually I wanted to do an album of characters from . . . that cartoon thing that was on . . ."[501] Here, he was trying to recall the children's television show *The Magic Roundabout*, on which Zebedee (as it is correctly spelt) was a character. Kenny expanded on that original idea of losers: "I've always warmed to losers. A lot of jazz musicians have been a mixture of great talent and uncertainty about how to get through life."[502] When asked which famous losers didn't make it to the final "losers package", he laughed. "Oh, I think I had in mind famous losers, like you know, people who I thought were losers, like Arthur Miller [*sic* – he probably meant Miller's *Death of a Salesman* character Willy Loman here] and people like that . . . [*laughs*]."[503]

Kenny's thinking returned to the cartoon: "I wanted to base it on *The Magic Roundabout* children's TV show – I liked the characters and its humour . . ."[504] but he acknowledged, "John [Dankworth] kind of, a little bit talked me out of what I wanted to do with it."[505] Kenny got the impression that "John might have thought that wasn't quite the right image for jazz!"[506] He continued: "I don't think Dankworth thought that was a great idea, so I think I went to the local library in Bethnal Green and I asked a lady there who looked after things if she had any ideas of what I could do."[507] He said, "I wanted to know who some of the great losers were,"[508] and she eventually guided him: "'Well, try this book called *Don Quixote* by the famous writer [Cervantes] . . .', so I didn't read the book, but I skimmed through it . . . so Dankworth seemed OK about that."[509] So with the Don Quixote concept now fixed, apparently at the random suggestion of a Bethnal Green librarian, the scene was set to pull it all together as an album. Kenny confirmed that this was essentially a marketing idea with which to package the album: "It does help to have some sort of literary thing put on, rather than just calling the songs Joe or John or Jane, or whatever. It makes the public take a little more notice."[510] He also verified that the compositions ". . . all had different titles and then when we did the record, and got this idea of the Don Quixote thing, I had to change all the titles to suit the book."[511] The final step would be to compose the small-group interludes that would bind the concept together and make more of a suite out of the works. On *The $1,000,000 Collection*, Dankworth had explored the same device himself, inspired by works like Mussorgsky's *Pictures at an Exhibition*, in which the opening "Promenade" music connects the larger pieces.[512]

From the available memories and records, it seems that the true chronology of events is at least close to the received narrative. In late 1966, Kenny was struck down with impacted wisdom teeth on the bottom jaw. He needed an operation and was to be in hospital for a few days, plus weeks of recovery time before he could play.

> A lump came up in my mouth, and I thought, "That's it, it's cancer." But it was an impacted wisdom tooth and it set up a pouch of poison. I was in the hospital two or three days, but they said, "You won't be able to blow a trumpet for about three months." There was a big hole, and they put this packing in, which was okay, except when they had to put a new one in and pulled the old one out. It was like they were pulling out something from the bottom of your toes.[513]

Mark Wheeler said: "He gleefully reminded us every time they [changed the gauze] how painful it was!"[514] Mark also recalled visiting his dad in the hospital following the operation. "He was probably the world's most miserable patient . . . ! It was either the London Hospital or the Bethnal Green Hospital, so close to where we lived . . . he just kept moaning about the fact he couldn't play . . ."[515] But, despite the ordeal, Kenny remembered that time positively.

> In some ways it was the best three months of my life . . . 'cause Johnny Dankworth had then said to me, "Well, would you like to write an album for the band?" And that's when I wrote, well I did have some music which I'd already written but not much, so that's when I got all the music ready for that album . . .[516]

The last statement he makes is probably where the confusion has arisen as to when the *Windmill Tilter* music was originally written. It seems likely that when he said, "I did have some music which I'd already written but not much," he was referring to the older tunes "In Passing" and "Blue 25" which already existed, while the rest of the big-band pieces were written at the later stage. They were not, however, written about Don Quixote – as we now know, that came later: these were individual compositions, not designed as a suite.[517]

These new pieces were to be orchestrated (and the two existing compositions would have needed rearranging) for the latest instrumentation of the re-formed Dankworth band. Kenny described the actual offer of recording the album at all as being "on the condition that I use his band . . ."[518] The orchestra was now made up of two groups of mixed instruments: one with Kenny himself, trombonist Mike Gibbs, and saxophonists Tony Roberts and John Dankworth; the second group included saxophonists Ray Swinfield and Tony Coe, trombonist Chris Pyne, and tuba player Dick Hart (or Alfie Reece), augmented by the trumpet section of Derek Watkins, Henry Lowther, and Les Condon, plus the rhythm section including drummer John Spooner and pianist Alan Branscombe, as well as the percussionist and vibes player Tristan Fry.[519] The big-band rhythm section did not include guitar, as Henry pointed out: "J.D. never included a guitar in any of the various big bands he had had over the years and there wasn't one in the *Million Dollar Collection* band."[520]

This line-up was convened in May 1967 for the recording of *The $1,000,000 Collection* album, followed by a three-week residency at Ronnie Scott's.[521] Henry Lowther, who was working for the Automobile Association at the time, initially turned down the offer of the gig as he didn't see how he could fit it in around his day job. He almost immediately regretted his decision; luckily for Henry, after the band's first performance in Brighton didn't go so well due to some personal issues with the trumpeter they used instead, the fixer called Henry back to ask him to reconsider. Thankfully he did, and thus began a friendship and collaboration that would last from Kenny's first big-band album until his last.[522] (The same was also true for lead trumpeter Derek Watkins.)

The band was a close-knit group with long friendships and musical collaborations being established. Bassist Kenny Napper used to joke that the band was like something from *Snow White* – with Dankworth being the title character and all the members given a dwarf nickname ending in a "y": Derek Watkins was "Wily", Kenny was, of course, "Shyly", and tuba player Dick Hart was, for obvious reasons, "Moby".[523] Despite the excitement and humour surrounding the launch of the re-formed band, reviews of the Ronnie Scott's residency and the first outing of *The $1,000,000 Collection* music were mixed. Amidst certain compliments about Dankworth's standing and pedigree, as well as the soloists ("men of the calibre of Kenny Wheeler, Chris Pyne and Tony Coe"), Ronald Atkins of the UK *Guardian* concluded that

> the band's ultimate impression is of plain liquorice [*sic*] encased in brightly-coloured wrapping. On a primary level it just does not swing, the drummer being perhaps too involved with the written note to produce anything beyond the most perfunctory rhythmic backing. The compositions themselves, though bristling with accomplishment, boil down to a kind of jazz-influenced programme music . . .[524]

Though they were received more warmly in *The Times* and the *Sunday Times*, this review demonstrates something of the changing times into which the new Dankworth band was entering: that is, a new jazz world where free music was gaining momentum and bold newcomers were drawing attention at Ronnie Scott's Old Place, including South African musicians like Chris McGregor and Dudu Pukwana, whose recent arrival had injected an exciting new energy into the scene.

With the Ronnie Scott residency and *The $1,000,000 Collection* recording behind them, the band convened in March 1968 to record *Windmill Tilter*. There were some small changes in personnel from the activities of 1967: pianist Bob Cornford came in to replace Laurie Holloway and trumpeter Henry (Hank) Shaw was added to the section.[525]

Perhaps the most significant personnel change to the Dankworth band for the recording of *Windmill Tilter* was the last-minute bass substitution. Dave Holland came in to replace Kenny Napper, who had cut his finger on a bread knife the day before the recording.[526] Dave said, "by that time I'm living in an apartment with [drummer] John Marshall – and my phone rings one day . . . they said there's a recording session tomorrow . . ." As Dave was a strong reader, he remembered

> . . . at this time I was doing a lot of studio work . . . it was kind of my goal, well that and play jazz on the side, because I didn't know I was going to be able to make a living playing jazz so I thought "well, I'll make my money playing in the studios" and then do the gigs on the side.

So the call came from the fixer: "We've got a session tomorrow, our bass player has injured his finger, not tremendously badly, but bad enough he can't play – and we need a bass player. Kenny said he'd heard you play, and he thought I should give you a call."[527]

Of course, Kenny and Dave knew each other by this point. *Karyōbin* had been recorded the month before and the encounter in Alan Cohen's band was even earlier, but Dave says he knew nothing of Kenny's abilities as a writer before the *Windmill Tilter* session. So it was still a tremendous show of faith that they placed the responsibility (literally) in Dave's relatively young hands; and it is an astonishing performance to have sight-read the music with that depth of musical insight. Dave offered further reflections of the session:

> I'd been listening to the Thad Jones big band – particularly to Richard Davis's approach to big band. It was really different [from] the other players I'd heard. He was much freer with the band, a lot more active . . . I realized that you can play in a big band but still play in a really modern way with it. So when I got that offer to do that, I came in with that point of view . . . I'd been practising with Tony Oxley a lot and trying to play with the new feels that had come out of Tony Williams's thing. Tony [Oxley] and I would practise playing those uptempos and trying to get on top of the beat to keep it moving forward, so I was into that way of thinking about the bass . . . then I had this music to play that Kenny had written and of course the first thing was that it wasn't the classic big-band brass, saxes, sound, with big hits and stuff – they were there, but it was in such a unique way . . . and then the mixed voicing thing – which I hadn't really known anything about much, so the whole context of the music . . . and then what he'd written harmonically for me . . . the way he'd integrated bass parts with the band was fantastic and wonderful to do. But then the harmonic movements were like the kind of things I'd been listening to that Joe Henderson had written, or Wayne Shorter – so I suddenly found that I'm in a big band that's using that type of language – so it was really stimulating for me to play.[528]

These sessions were physically demanding for Kenny, who had written himself a huge amount to play. The stress on Kenny's stamina was exacerbated by the fact he was also in the middle of a Ronnie Scott's residency at the time with the American vocalist Jon Hendricks, who was in the UK with his pianist Larry Bucovitz. Hendricks added Ronnie Scott and Kenny to form the front line along with himself, as well as Johnny Griffin guesting for some of the engagement.[529] On the *Windmill Tilter* sessions Kenny was taking substantial solos on virtually every tune, as well as playing long stretches of the lead melodies and writing himself into the accompanying figures of section parts. This is possibly a more subtle indicator that this music was not conceived as a suite but as a series of individual pieces. Although it may be conjecture, when one looks at his other extended works that were *conceived of* as suites, Kenny tends to take a busy ensemble role but be much more democratic with the solo duties. This theory was echoed in a memory of Henry Lowther's from the sessions: Les Condon was moved over to act as Kenny's "bumper" (a kind of assistant role when the music is especially demanding) and cover some of his written parts if necessary, hence trumpeter Hank Shaw was brought in as third trumpet. It is doubtful Kenny would have needed such support, given his legendary stamina, but it is demonstrative of how much of a test of endurance it was to record all that music back-to-back. When Kenny tried to give away one of the trumpet solos (probably "Sancho", as the solo is actually in the trumpet 2 part rather than the solo flugelhorn part) to one of the others in the section, Derek Watkins set him straight with blunt but affectionate humour: "It's *your* fucking album, *you* play it!"[530]

The response to *Windmill Tilter* from the band was enthusiastic, even in the recording sessions. Mike Gibbs remembered after one successful take, ". . . as the last note was cut off, Chris Pyne let out a yelp of delight!" Dankworth was furious: in this pre-digital age when it was difficult to edit out noises, Chris had ruined the take. Mike Gibbs was himself already a respected composer and later commented on the effect *Windmill Tilter* had on him: "When I think about it, it was high up there. It was music that on a first listen always tantalized my ear to know there was more in it. It wasn't just, 'Oh that was nice', it needed more listening to get to the musical gems." Mike also offered a curious observation about Kenny's own character and presence; he had no memory of Kenny himself at the recording sessions: "Not because he wasn't there," Mike said, "but because he always took up less space than his physical body."[531]

Once the recording sessions were complete and the Don Quixote concept had been established, the interludes that would bind the music into a suite needed to be recorded. These were done on a later session by a small group that included guitarist John McLaughlin. Henry Lowther confirmed this series of events and offered an explanation as to how Kenny may have known McLaughlin:

> The quintet tracks were recorded at a later date, maybe even as much as a year later.[532] I don't know whether it was Kenny's idea or J.D.'s to include them as links but J.D. had used the same idea on the *Million Dollar Collection* album . . . so I suspect it was him. Around this time Kenny had been doing gigs with a quintet led by a drummer called Mike Scott. This was an eclectic band that included Sandy Brown on clarinet and a guitarist called Rick Hewson. (Rick Hewson was a composer who went on to make a lot of money producing modern "dance" albums and also for writing for films.) Kenny had probably got to know John McLaughlin at this time in this band because John used to dep a lot for Rick Hewson, and I used to dep for Kenny.[533]

With the *Windmill Tilter* album complete, the contract was signed on 29 August 1968. John Dankworth expressed his enthusiasm about the LP, writing on the back sleeve: "I am most proud to be associated with this record, as I think it is one of the most exciting to involve my own orchestra in recent years."[534] *Melody Maker* also captured something of the excitement surrounding its release which clearly articulates the reverence in which Kenny was held at the time. The wholly positive review begins: "The grapevine has buzzed for months with reports of this album, and after a brief heart-stopping rumour that Fontana had swallowed it, Kenny Wheeler's musical score woven 'round the Don Quixote theme has been issued."[535] Despite their enthusiasm for the album's release, *Melody Maker* still led with the headline: "The loser comes up with a musical winner". After the pressing, and shortly before its release, the family went up to the Fontana offices in London to collect their two free copies. They went back to their favourite Lyons Corner House to celebrate the occasion and sat down as a family in Hyde Park, as young Mark clutched both LPs. Years later he said, "I just thought *that* was the bloody bee's knees!"[536]

This entire period was a creative boom for Kenny and marked the beginning of an era of even greater growth into his mature style. Just five months before the release of *Windmill Tilter,* a new opportunity emerged through which Kenny would gain wider exposure as a writer and bandleader: his first broadcast as a bandleader for the BBC.

# 4  Song for Someone

**The idea behind this band was to try to get special musicians from and into different areas of jazz to play together and to try to write music especially for them. That is, the thought of the musicians came first and then the music.**

*Kenny Wheeler*

On the morning of 23 May 1969, Kenny went into the familiar BBC studios in a new role: as the leader of his own group. He was about to record for the *Jazz Workshop* programme on Radio 1, to be broadcast a couple of weeks later on 11 June.[537] This was the first in a series of mostly annual broadcasts which would serve as Kenny's principal outlet as a big-band composer and the catalyst for much of his prolific output; later, he even became the subject of a BBC television documentary filmed during one of these sessions. In interviews over the next 30 years, Kenny would cite the importance of these occasions as a viable means of getting his own big band together when the finances of a regular gig would simply not permit it. "I usually get a yearly broadcast from the BBC," he said. "It's a good opportunity . . . you have something to write for."[538] He seized this chance to compose new music for each broadcast and would often vary the size and makeup of each ensemble, occasionally rearranging his music as necessary. But Kenny was well aware of the amount of unacknowledged work involved: "It's a bit of a labour of love – because you have to write everything yourself for basically nothing, and copy it, and ring up all the musicians. But it's still worth it in the end, I think."[539]

On this first occasion the recording was listed as "The Kenny Wheeler Group", with his contract specifying "yourself plus eleven musicians".[540] A *Melody Maker* article just prior to the broadcast explained: "He used three different pianists and eight others including John Surman, Ronnie Scott, and the possibly surprising choice of Duncan Lamont."[541] Whatever "surprise" Duncan provoked at the time subsided over the next 45 years, as Kenny chose him to play in practically every one of his bands, engaging him right up until his final big-band recording. Duncan is a good example of the loyalty Kenny showed to several key musicians he faithfully employed in his bands. It is another demonstration of how important it was for him to have the players around that he liked as friends as well as musicians. The rest of the personnel is not known, but careful listeners agree that he was also joined by Ray Warleigh on alto and Tony Roberts on bass clarinet.[542] One thing is certain:

this first broadcast is not a regular big-band session, not even a reduced or unconventional line-up he sometimes used – just a smaller group of mixed front line with a rhythm section. And whoever the three (!) pianists were, they don't sound like they're playing at the same time. The group performed six original Wheeler pieces on the programme: "T.A.S.W.", "Dallab", "D.G.S.", and "W.S.I.M.C.", and two reworkings of pieces from *Windmill Tilter*: "Sweet Dulcinea Blue" and "Don No More". His playful titles are in evidence here with "Dallab" (*Ballad* reversed) and "W.S.I.M.C.", an abbreviation of "Who's Standing in My Corner". (This a reference to his preferred standing place in Ronnie Scott's club where he could watch the music from a quiet corner without being bothered by anyone, until one night – much to his irritation – he found it occupied.[543]) "W.S.I.M.C." is a wonderful composition with some early use of mixed-metre writing woven into the phrasing of the melody. Otherwise, it is a quite standard head/solos/head chart, with the solo sequences not including the shifts of metre. Kenny sounds very relaxed and authoritative leading the front-line section on the tune, and his improvising has all the usual strength of presence and character from this era of his career.

———·——

Kenny's BBC broadcasts not only propelled him to wider recognition as a bandleader/composer, they also cemented lifelong musical friendships. One such crucial relationship was highlighted on his second big-band broadcast as a leader, in June 1970, when Kenny engaged vocalist Norma Winstone for the first time in his own band.

Norma was born in Bow in London's East End, in September 1941. Her parents loved the music of Frank Sinatra and Fats Waller, and at the age of seven she began taking piano lessons. She loved to sing, and was encouraged by her parents who took her to see musical films or occasionally to the opera. At the age of ten, she and her family moved to Dagenham in Essex. After being encouraged to apply for a place at Trinity College of Music as a Junior Exhibitioner, Norma was accepted and began to attend weekly classes. Although she knew and liked classical music, she chose not to study classical singing, already aware that she didn't want to sing in that way. Too afraid to do the public performances that were expected at the school, Norma eventually stopped her piano lessons and took up organ lessons instead. But this had an entirely non-musical motive: she had developed a crush on a charming older pupil who also happened to be studying the organ and was in his final year: Dudley Moore! Through her voice teacher, Norma began to pick up some work as a singer, although it wasn't the type of singing she wanted to be doing. She was already experimenting with singing standards and beginning to paraphrase the melodies or play around with the rhythm. Unfortunately, this approach didn't agree with the "background" type of function gigs she was singing at the time.

One day, a friend at her office job suggested that Norma go with her to The Black Lion pub in East Ham, which hosted a resident jazz trio. Norma agreed and went along to sit in. Fortunately for Norma, the group's male singer was about to leave, so she was invited to take up the residency for two nights a week. This was the start of her career. Gaining more confidence through these vocal "guest spot" nights on the circuit, she eventually met John Taylor at a gig at the Prince Albert pub in Chingford. John gave her his telephone number in case she ever needed a pianist, and they began to perform together regularly when she secured the Friday-night gig at The Lilliput in Bermondsey. Soon, John and Norma also became romantically involved and eventually moved in together in September 1967. They were married in 1972.

Norma was active in the same burgeoning jazz scene that was springing up around the Old Place and the Little Theatre Club, and she knew many of the musicians who were frequenting those venues. She remembered seeing Kenny there one night, aware of him by reputation only. As she was also involved in the new improvised music scene, they actually recorded together for the first time on an early Spontaneous Music Ensemble session just a few months after *Karyōbin*. Captured on 14 July 1968, this was an all front-line improvisation with Kenny, Norma, Trevor Watts, and Paul Rutherford.[544] As Norma became more involved in the plethora of new music being made in that era, she began to sing more contemporary "wordless" front-line parts with groups led by Michael Garrick and Mike Westbrook, and she slowly got to know Kenny better as he invariably cropped up in many of the same circles.[545] Given their increasingly close association, it is not surprising that Kenny called Norma to take part in his second big-band broadcast for the BBC that summer of 1970. What was a bit of a surprise for Norma, however, was that for much of the music he had written her into the ensemble as another instrumental part, and had done so with no apparent warning or asking whether she would, or even could, do it: "Kenny never ever asked me if I could read, he just wrote the stuff out . . . I could read, luckily! I suppose he knew I could, because [of] other things I had done."[546] Kenny described how he had come to that decision: "I wanted Norma in the band, but you can't have a . . . I don't want her, you know, 'Here's our lady vocalist, will now sing . . .', I wanted to have her actually in the band, so I thought 'well, why not?'"[547] The broadcast went out on 20 July 1970 and included the new pieces "Some Days Are Better" and "Sweet Yakity Waltz". The results of that orchestrational experiment stuck; Norma's pure vocal sound would be an integral part of Kenny's music for the rest of his life.[548]

As with so much of this period, it was a truly prolific time for Kenny. He played many broadcasts with other bands, including two more with the Tubby Hayes Big Band[549] and another broadcast in April 1969 with the Mike Gibbs Orchestra featuring bassist Jack Bruce, fresh from the recently disbanded supergroup Cream. Mark Wheeler recalled going with his dad to a Gibbs recording because he had been so star-struck by the famous bassist: "*Dad,*

*Dad, it's Jack Bruce!*" Mike would graciously calm him down, addressing him as "Junior".[550] This wasn't the only time that year Kenny's rock 'n' roll credentials would impress his son; in October 1969 Kenny performed with Keith Emerson's prog-rock band The Nice (a favourite of Mark's friends) when he appeared on their live recording of the *Five Bridges* suite.[551]

Photo 18: Kenny and Alan Skidmore at Montreux Jazz Festival, as featured in *Coda* magazine in December 1969.
Photo by Jean Waldis; courtesy Colin Harpur

At the end of the 1960s Kenny was also a member of Alan Skidmore's quintet. The group took part in a couple of broadcasts in 1969 and was selected by the BBC to represent Britain at the Montreux Jazz Festival that year in a jazz competition run by the European Broadcasting Union.[552] Notably, Skidmore's quintet also featured John Taylor, playing with Kenny for the first time in a small-group jazz setting and on what would be their first official recording together. J.T. recalled:

> I [had] met Alan Skidmore with John Surman's Octet . . . and [Skidmore] formed this quintet with Kenny, Harry Miller, Tony Oxley, and me . . . We went to [Montreux] and we played, and you know, you get a prize . . . and we didn't win the first spot, we got the second spot which enabled us to

play twice there which was good. I remember that because that was my first flight, and I sat next to Kenny![553]

Interestingly, there were two juries involved in the competition: the official one, which as J.T. described, selected Finland's Eero Koivistoinen Quartet as first-place prize winners. There was also a second jury made up of some 20 members of the jazz press, and they selected the British group as the best ensemble that year.[554] Skidmore described that band, and that trip, as a turning point for him:

> It really was a fantastic quintet, so together and sharp for that time. If anything, it was a bit on the lines of Miles Davis' *Four and More* period with Tony Williams and Ron Carter, but there was a certain amount of freedom as well. We were playing original compositions; some free shit balanced with frantically fast tunes on structured changes.[555]

The quintet also recorded Skidmore's *Once Upon a Time . . .* album in that year for the Deram label.[556] The musicians are in rare form on that mix of composed and open-form sections, and it is a fine example of a remarkable group from the time with bassist Harry Miller and the *tour de force* drumming of Tony Oxley at its core. Tony was someone Kenny had also grown close to through their connections with both the improvised music scene and other regular jazz gigs. Earlier that same year, in January 1969, Tony had recorded his own first album as a leader, *The Baptised Traveller*.[557] It is yet another defining classic from the period, which featured Kenny with Evan Parker, Derek Bailey, and bassist Jeff Clyne. Kenny and Oxley would work together much more over the next few years. Though Kenny would frequently complain about the coverage he received from various journalists, he had his fair share of fans and supporters. Not least of these was BBC presenter Charles Fox, who described Kenny as "undoubtedly *the* musician of 1969" in his review of Oxley's *Baptised Traveller*.[558]

In addition to his astonishingly busy career as a sideman, Kenny's BBC broadcasts also gave rise to a group he would co-lead. Fronting the band with his old Dankworth colleague saxophonist Tony Coe, they called the group Coe, Wheeler & Co. The band featured Pat Smythe on piano, Ron Mathewson on bass, and usually drummer Spike Wells, occasionally becoming a sextet with the addition of trombonist Chris Pyne. Active for at least five years, the band performed at Ronnie's many times and did a number of broadcasts through those years.[559] On their first broadcast in June 1970, they played mostly Kenny's tunes, including "Some Doors Are Better Opened", "Don't Go Short", "Don't Bother", and once again, "Don No More" from *Windmill Tilter*. They also included the bossa nova "Reza" by Brazilian guitarist Edu Lobo. The band's repertoire later expanded to include pieces by Smythe and Coe, as well as some more surprising contemporary choices like "Poppa, Daddy and Me" by Jack DeJohnette and "Vision" by Keith Jarrett. Kenny added other originals, titled with his now trademark wordplay ("Noo Wan" and "Shake a Spear", for example). The line-up of the group also varied depending on availability, and on at least one occasion they played without Tony Coe present at all. The 1972 broadcast recorded on May 8th had the regular rhythm section of Pat Smythe, Spike Wells, and bassist Daryl Runswick, but with Tubby Hayes in place of Tony, who was ill. On this occasion the group, now "Coe-less", was simply called "Wheeler & Co." and included Chris Pyne. They performed mostly Kenny's originals "Tokyo Pete", "Fasteetoo", and "Life Cycle", and the set also included a Grant Green tune and an original by Runswick.[560] The group built up quite a reputation but, sadly, never recorded an official studio LP. This may well have had something to do with the organizational skills – or lack thereof – at the helm of Coe, Wheeler & Co. Stan Sulzmann recalled seeing them perform at Ronnie Scott's on more than one occasion:

> They'd finish a number and we're sitting in the audience watching, and nothing would happen . . . All their heads would go down, like a rugby scrum, a huddle going on . . . and nothing. Nobody would say anything. They couldn't decide anything, so the pauses in between pieces were longer than the tunes. It was fantastic, you just had to watch it . . . but that was Kenny being a bandleader![561]

Indeed, if there was one musician capable of matching Kenny's endearing inability to make a decision, Tony Coe was probably that person – so, when the two of them got together to lead a band the results were predictably shambolic. To keep what little order there was, Pat Smythe would often step up to act as the bandleader. In fact, Tony Coe recalled that he thought it was actually Pat's idea to get the group together.[562] (When asked later what it was like to co-lead a band with Kenny, Tony just laughed.[563])

This character trait of Kenny's was most exacerbated when he was paired with someone of a similar disposition, regardless of whether they were a fellow musician, friend, or even family. His sister Mabel recalled her brother's legendary decision-making skills:

> That got to be a family joke, because whenever [Kenny] would come home, and my brother Wilf and Bill Jelley, they'd get together and go out for an evening. My older son Brian, he liked to go with them . . . and, he said, they would all stand around with their hands in their pockets and no one could make a decision about where they were going![564]

Despite Kenny's shyness, he began to get more significant attention in the press during this time, and his personality was still a point of focus in many articles. Just as in some of the magazine features in the early '60s, he remained an enigma to interviewers and readers alike. The aforementioned *Melody Maker* piece from 1969 was no exception, opening like this:

> "Well I don't like to have too much written about me." Not a great start to an interview, you may say, but Kenny Wheeler's modesty is no secret. In fact, it's the cause of much head-shaking among fellow musicians. For instance, when the recent Tubby Hayes Big Band broadcast seemed to require a cut in one of the numbers, Ken volunteered "I've already got one solo so . . ." Needless to say, his offer was not accepted, for he is probably the soloist most admired by colleagues on the British Jazz Scene.[565]

Jazz writer Benny Green went a step further. In 1970, Kenny had recorded for Ken Moule (an old band colleague from the Don Rendell days) on an LP called *Adam's Rib Suite*,[566] which was an ambitious project of orchestral sophistication that was also performed live for a BBC broadcast. In a glowing review of the album Green wrote in *The Observer*: "The 11 tracks . . . are graced with the brilliance of Kenny Wheeler, perhaps the world's most underrated jazz musician, whose trumpet and flugelhorn playing here are faultless."[567] Truly, his playing here is impeccable – as powerfully as Kenny could play, his tone, dynamic approach, and intonation are perfectly matched to the lighter character of the strings and flute.

So, as the word spread, it was somewhat timely that 1970 was the year Kenny tied for first place in the *DownBeat* critics poll for "Talent Deserving of Wider Recognition" on trumpet, sharing the honour with none other than Woody Shaw.[568] Some years later, in 1978, their joint recognition would be the subject of a *Washington Post* feature on the two trumpeters, focusing on their role in the "re-emergence" of the trumpet. It described them as ". . . the most important trumpeters . . . they use the trumpet as an expert compositional tool . . ."[569] Not long after they shared the award, Woody Shaw performed at Ronnie Scott's, and Kenny's good friend and fellow trumpeter Ian Hamer took Kenny along to see him. Ian was quite a character and, like Duncan Lamont, another musician to whom Kenny showed tremendous loyalty over the years in his large ensembles. Ian also had a habit of proudly introducing Kenny to famous musicians when he would probably have preferred to stay in the background. On this occasion at Ronnie's, Ian rushed up to Woody Shaw with Kenny in tow and said, "Hey Woody, this is Kenny Wheeler who tied first place with you in the *DownBeat* poll!" Woody looked over to Kenny and said, "Oh yeah, are you really that good?" With his tongue no doubt planted firmly in his cheek, Kenny replied, "Yeah Woody, I am!"[570]

The *DownBeat* honour was an accolade that reflected just what an innovator Kenny had become on his instrument. Leaving aside his extraordinary work as a composer, his trumpet playing alone was getting noticed far and wide. There was a creative diversity and intensity to the jazz scene at the time, and it fuelled the development of Kenny's artistic voice. The speed at which he was progressing is captured particularly well on a live LP from Ronnie

Scott's in October 1968.[571] It is with Ronnie's own group at the time, which he facetiously called his "Nine-Piece Aggravation".[572] Alongside Ronnie on tenor saxophone the line-up included Ray Warleigh, John Surman, Chris Pyne, and Kenny, plus pianist Gordon Beck, bassist Ron Mathewson, and two drummers: Tony Oxley and Kenny Clare.[573] It was an important group for the time: a sign of Ronnie embracing the younger players and newer innovations as well as offering opportunities for them to write for the band. Kenny and Gordon Beck both contributed compositions for this recording, including Kenny's "Sweet Dulcinea Blue" and "Second Question". American saxophonist Joe Henderson also provided some arrangements for the band while he was in town working at the club.[574]

But the different generations and stylistic leanings in the band were not always headed in the same direction. John Surman described the feeling in the band: "It was a kind of uneasy alliance, as any band that had, you know, the likes of say at some point Tony Crombie and Tony Oxley both playing in it, I mean you can imagine those two is chalk and cheese, and so there was a sort of underlying undertone of irritation there!"[575] Kenny also recalled the dynamic:

> It was great to play in Ronnie's band, yeah. Although Ronnie . . . had a fantastic sense of humour, he could be a bit abrasive to you. He wanted to play his own [music] – which is fine, it was his band – but he wanted to play his "on the beat" music. But us young guys, people like John Surman, Ray Warleigh, Chris Pyne, and myself, we were kind of young and itching to play new things, you know. So we kept pestering Ronnie to maybe branch out a bit – but he was determined to stay in that Zoot Sims sort of swing thing. And he was great at it, Ronnie.[576]

The group was extremely busy at that time. Alongside several broadcasts, national tours, and residencies at Ronnie's club – sometimes joined by vocalist Jon Hendricks – they also recorded two episodes of BBC 2 TV's *Jazz at the Maltings* concert series.[577] On another occasion, in the two weeks directly before the October live recording back at the club, they were engaged as the backing band for a Scott Walker tour.[578] John Surman recalled that tour, saying, "It was an attempt to keep the band together by Pete King and Ronnie, and understandable for all that, and I suppose we did get reasonably well paid for it and that would be welcome. But you know, it was a side issue and I don't think it did anything, really, to consolidate the band."[579] On the day of the first gig with Scott Walker in London, Kenny and John Surman were on a session for the film *All Neat in Black Stockings*, a light comedy about an amorous window cleaner on the soundtrack of which, written by Bob Cornford, Kenny and Tony Coe were featured soloists. When the session finished, Kenny and Surman "high-tailed it" to the Scott Walker gig at Finsbury Park Astoria, to be greeted by large crowds in their tour merchandise T-shirts and so on.[580] They took to the stage in front of screaming fans, and a deafeningly loud

Photo 19: Jon Hendricks looking on as Kenny plays in Ronnie Scott's quintet, Sunbury Jazz Festival, 1968.

Courtesy Harry Monty

accompaniment. Surman recalled, "Kenny takes it all in his stride doesn't he, but I think he might have drifted off and put a sub [replacement] in for a few of the performances!", also noting, "I do remember doing at least one gig without a reed in, as my kind of protest, because you were completely inaudible!"[581] (Incidentally, the association with Walker did some good for at least one of the group; Walker produced Ray Warleigh's *First Album* for Philips[582] in 1968.[583]) Despite the work they were getting, those underlying differences gradually set in. Kenny remembered: "Well, eventually John Surman left the band because Ronnie wouldn't branch out, I think, and Karl Jenkins came in to the band."[584] Surman confirmed his feelings of frustration and his role in departing the band:

> I was certainly one of those guilty parties. I think I got tired of playing the blues in A minor, you know, when there was nobody in [the audience] late at night and all that kind of stuff. And I kind of drifted off and got tired of the niggling, and also yeah, there were other things I wanted to do so yeah, I would have been one of the ones who was beginning to lose interest. I think Ronnie accepted that, and I kind of disappeared in my childlike, stupid way without saying anything. I just didn't show up for a couple of gigs . . . you know, because I was afraid to say "I'm sorry guys, I've had enough." I didn't know how to say that, I was young and naïve.[585]

Nevertheless, besides the drama and ultimate demise surrounding Ronnie's "Nine-Piece Aggravation" (a nickname perhaps now understood more fully), the live album from October 1968 captures the band wonderfully. To put it in context, the album was made only seven months after he recorded *Windmill Tilter*, yet the way Kenny plays – especially on the Donovan ballad "Lord of the Reedy River" – is another step forward toward his fully formed artistry. There is a new-found rhythmic freedom and fluency in his improvising, and his wide intervallic ideas are more adventurous and assured. His command of the harmonic tension and release is more advanced, and the sheer intensity of it is palpable. The Kenny Wheeler on that recording could be the same mature player as on the later ECM albums, whereas the same cannot be said for his playing in the period just before this.

In this short span from 1969 and into the early 1970s, there was an outpouring of significant recordings and performances taking place in the booming British jazz scene. Without wishing to diminish the importance of each of those albums, it is only possible here to give an overview of just how many Kenny was involved in, all albums that helped define British jazz in that era. When one looks at the landmark British jazz albums of the time and holds that list next to Kenny's own discography as sideman, the amount of overlap illustrates just how central he was to the music of that period. It is also noteworthy to highlight that this was not the case for too many other musicians at the time, if any. Despite it being a profoundly busy period for the pool of players who frequently appeared on many of these records, none of their discographies covered quite the same professional, stylistic, or generational scope that Kenny's did.

———·———

Kenny worked with John Surman often and the two appeared together on countless occasions in myriad ensembles. In addition to their work in Ronnie Scott's band, they also played in concerts and recordings with the Graham Collier and Mike Westbrook groups, as well as many recording sessions. Surman's description of the influence Kenny had on him strikes a curious parallel with the way Kenny described hearing Booker Little for the first time:

> He appeared to me, as it were, completely formed. He had his way of playing that was, you know, *there*. The way that I remember him sounding then, and the last time I heard him play, you wouldn't have made any mistake about who it was. He was distinctively Kenny from the very beginning . . . such a personal way of playing. And that did have an enormous influence on me. He and Albert Mangelsdorff, oddly enough two brass players, were two musicians with whom I heard that you could play the kind of harmonic stuff that came from bop, and so on and so forth, but with personal patterns [and a] personal approach to the harmony, and yet still be within those structures. And their way of playing I think was very influential to me in some kind of way that I couldn't put my finger on, but I've always thought that.[586]

In August 1968, Surman recorded his self-titled debut album for the Deram label,[587] having become quite a star in his own right. It was recorded across two sessions, the second of which featured Kenny. The concept for the LP was based on the successful group Surman had at the time with Trinidadian pianist and steel pan player Russ Henderson. He explained how it was a natural extension of the scene at the time:

> The pretence of the album was based on the calypso jazz group . . . which was quite popular . . . and then I was able to extend it, because basically it was a similar rhythm-section with Russ and the West Indian percussionists and so on. But also at the time, I'd started the trio with Dave [Holland] and Alan Jackson, so that was the format. And then naturally, Paul Rutherford [and Kenny, etc.] – these were guys who obviously I was jamming with at the Little Theatre Club from time to time and down at the Old Place. So it was constructed to be an album in the two halves, but featuring the calypso jazz which was popular, and that was the selling point.[588]

On that second session with Kenny was Dave Holland, who, unbeknownst to him, was making one of his last jazz recordings in the UK before his life would be changed forever. Miles Davis had heard Dave performing at Ronnie Scott's in July of that year with vocalist Elaine Delmar, and the legendary trumpeter was impressed enough to invite Dave to join his quintet in New York the next month.[589]

Kenny's work with pianist and composer Mike Westbrook's "Concert Band", again with Surman, first appears on the LP recordings *Marching Song Vols. 1 and 2*,[590] both from April 1969. Westbrook was extremely busy with broadcasts and live engagements throughout the period, and Kenny was a frequent member of the trumpet section. He was involved in the premiere of Westbrook's *Metropolis*, a piece written with support from the Arts Council. It was premiered in May 1969 and later recorded for an album of the same name in August 1971.[591] Incidentally, *Metropolis* is one of the few times on record one can hear Kenny freely improvise on mellophonium, an instrument he had played occasionally (and somewhat reluctantly) with Dankworth's band. It is also noteworthy historically as the first commercial recording session on which J.T., Kenny, and Norma all appeared together. But with so many different concerts and broadcasts during this period and long before Azimuth's existence, it would hardly have struck them as significant at the time.

Kenny was so ever-present in these new big bands that his involvement was practically expected by the other musicians. John Taylor recalled, "it seemed that Kenny was on most of these sorts of things",[592] though Kenny responded to the observation in a typically self-deprecating interview, quipping "all the best trumpeters are busy with studio work!"[593] But J.T.'s point was echoed by trombonist and composer Mike Gibbs, who was with Kenny on many session dates as well as using him in his own band. He explained why Kenny was used so much on these projects:

> Because he was so extraordinary both as an improviser and as a section player, but also because he was one of the lads. I mean, in those days . . . in my generation, Kenny was one of the guys *automatically*, because he was so reliable. Actually, Kenny's soloing was like a bonus, even if he didn't solo like he did, he would have been one of the first calls . . . it was automatic that he would be on.[594]

Mike also saw him on other big band sessions, whether they were jazz or not, and recalled a peculiar habit: "Kenny was always early. He would immediately go to the fourth [trumpet] chair and put his gear there. He didn't wait to be told where to sit, he just chose the fourth chair."[595] Trumpeter Tony Fisher was also with Kenny on many of these sessions and confirmed Kenny's dash to the end of the section:

> Oh always, always, Kenny would plonk himself on the end! Much to my annoyance really with him, I used to say, "For God's sake!" I mean, you know Kenny, despite his reputation as a jazz player which is fine, he also had *really* good chops. He could play something quite heavy going you know, and without too much trouble at all. And often, it maybe, particularly on a commercial recording, you'd be playing something and I'd say,

"Kenny, do you want to do [lead on] this one?" . . . "Oh no, that's not me, I don't want to do that kind of thing," you know, and he could have walked through it blindfolded easily! That was him.[596]

As a result of where he would seat himself and the way the bands set up, Mike Gibbs was often positioned directly in front of Kenny when they played. This had an unexpected and lasting effect on Mike:

> Kenny's time [feel] was so *right*, you know how when you sit in the band, the moment you hear something your ear automatically makes a judgement to do with balance, etc. . . . Kenny's thing was, he played the written part with such rhythmic accuracy that it meant my ear, instead of going to the drums for the time, automatically went to the strongest rhythm, and that was Kenny! This amazed me because it was an education – I found myself doing it not out of choice . . . it was always Kenny who shone through. He did this unconsciously. He wasn't trying to do it, he was just playing it properly.[597]

Gibbs recorded his own self-titled big band debut for the Deram label in 1970.[598] The large band included many of Kenny's regular colleagues, including his familiar trumpet-section mates Derek Watkins and Henry Lowther, but also trombonists Bobby Lamb and Ray Premru. Lamb and Premru also ran their own big band, an ensemble comprising many of the leading musicians of the day who found themselves increasingly occupied with studio work. One otherwise very positive review of that band highlighted this aspect of the personnel with the headline "Refugees from the studios". It described how "Its members include the cream of the capital's session musicians, men raised in the 1950s at the end of the Ted Heath–Stan Kenton big band era, who now play mostly among the glass screens, baffle-boards and microphonic tendrils of the recording studios."[599] This evocative description certainly shows what a professional transition some of Kenny's colleagues were going through at the time studio work was increasing exponentially. Of course, Kenny was equally involved in that world, too; the difference for him, though, was that it didn't come at the expense of his full immersion in the creative outpourings of the day. This set him apart from many colleagues his own age, allying him instead with the musical generation that was at least a decade younger.

By the start of the 1970s, Kenny had finished his involvement with the Dankworth orchestra; his friend Henry Lowther took over his role as principal soloist in the small group. The band still performed some of Kenny's music in concerts, though, and Kenny even came back for one final recording session in 1972 when they made the album *Full Circle*.[600,601] His work with the crown jewels of British jazz did not end with Dankworth, however. Kenny played on many broadcasts and recordings with the Tubby Hayes big band in that era, including the studio album *200% Proof*[602] and the saxophonist's BBC *Jazz Club* broadcast as leader in March 1973, which would be his last.[603]

The sheer volume of activity in the London scene and the change in the Musicians' Union rules meant that some prominent American jazz musicians recorded in the city. Kenny took part in album sessions with several of these greats: most significantly, the small-group recordings on which he takes a prominent role as soloist and front-line member. The first of these was with drummer Philly Joe Jones, on his *Trailways Express* album, recorded in London in October 1968. The band includes saxophonists Pete King and Harold McNair and trombonist Chris Pyne, with Ron Mathewson and Mick Pyne joining the great drummer in the rhythm section. *Trailways Express* is a great album of straight-ahead jazz playing but one can hear again that Kenny's approach is markedly different from that of his bandmates. It is most evident on Jones's uptempo composition "Mo Jo", and their version of Tadd Dameron's "Ladybird". On both tracks, Kenny's solos demonstrate his elastic approach to the time feel, and the content and articulation of his lines come from a completely different vocabulary. His playing is its usual idiosyncratic and personal self, but in this context one can especially appreciate why Kenny felt the way he did about bebop. What he was unable to recognize himself, though, was the freshness and originality that everyone else heard in him. (In later years of modern pop psychology, he might have been described as having "imposter syndrome" – a classic symptom of which is the inability to recognize the value in something you seem to do quite naturally.) The other interesting small-group album from the period led by a famous American guest is the album *Humming Bird*,[604] recorded in early 1970 in London by Duke Ellington's famous tenor saxophonist, Paul Gonsalves. Kenny plays beautifully on the gently lolloping bossa nova title track composed by drummer Tony Faulkner. Compared to the *Trailways Express* session, here the playing approach is generally a bit looser, meaning Kenny's individuality suddenly fits right into context – especially because it is paired with Paul Gonsalves, another characterful player. This scenario illustrates how important musical combinations were for Kenny. How the way others played around him could either make sense of his individuality, or highlight its unusualness, depending on the context and situation. In this case, it works beautifully.

The recording of that album was not entirely straightforward, however. The record happened because the saxophonist was going to be in London and the album's producer Jack Sharpe wanted to get him into the studio with some local musicians.[605] Gonsalves, a prolific heroin user, knew the British saxophonist and promoter Jack Sharpe through Sharpe's work promoting gigs with visiting American artists; but Sharpe had also run a Soho club and allegedly had the underworld connections necessary to hook up musicians like Gonsalves who needed to "manage their condition".[606] Tony Faulkner became involved because the album's drummer, Benny Goodman (not to be confused with the famous American clarinetist and bandleader), lived in Cardiff near Tony and Goodman knew Tony was a writer, so he asked him to contribute two tunes for the album. The session itself didn't start until one o'clock in the morning because Gonsalves was coming to the studio straight after finishing two concerts earlier that night. Trombonist Dave Horler recalled the session clearly (which documented his first-ever valve trombone solo on record) and he remembered collecting Kenny and taking him to the studio in Stoke Newington for what followed:

> I drove Kenny to the studio, and [there was] no Paul Gonsalves of course because he was well late, and when he did finally arrive, erm, he was totally bladdered! Totally out of his head, couldn't even see the music stand! And they brought out these arrangements . . . 'course he couldn't read anything . . . We played and the night went on and slowly, slowly he sobered up, or whatever it was he was on, and then started to play his magic stuff. But then he started to get a bit, wanting a drink, so they sent a taxi to Ronnie Scott's club to pick up a bottle of whisky for him![607]

There were several other appearances with visiting American artists, but these tended to be big-band sessions on which Kenny just had a section role rather than the intimate small-group settings on the albums mentioned previously. Coincidentally, two were led (or co-led) by famous jazz drummers, the first of which was Louie Bellson. His *Louie in London* album[608] was recorded in May 1970 and featured trumpeters in the section from the musical generation before Kenny, including Stan Roderick, Stan Reynolds, and Eddie Blair. Although not that much older than him, they were certainly not players engaged with the new jazz scene in which Kenny was so immersed: another testament to his cross-generational versatility. The second was Kenny's involvement with the Kenny Clarke/Francy Boland Big Band, a fine big band with a truly international membership. Drummer Kenny Clarke, one of bebop's founding fathers, co-led the band, and Kenny (Wheeler) was invited to perform as part of a British contingent that joined the band for a four-date European tour in 1969. The format was a "Battle of the Bands" with the Clarke–Boland ensemble joining the Kurt Edelhagen Orchestra, and none other than the Thad Jones/Mel Lewis big band: both groups Kenny would get to perform with in the next couple of years. He was joined on the tour by UK musicians including Derek Watkins, Tony Coe, Ronnie Scott, and Derek Humble, and trombonist Nat Peck.[609] Joining Kenny and Derek in the trumpet section for this Clarke–Boland tour was the American trumpeter Benny Bailey, someone whose playing Kenny admired enormously – once describing him to Henry Lowther as "the most exciting lead player he'd ever worked with".[610] The band also included saxophonists Johnny Griffin and Sahib Shihab, and ex-Ellington bassist Jimmy Woode, who had actually also helped establish the band along with Clarke and Boland.

The trip started with the recording of the album *At Her Majesty's Pleasure . . .*,[611] with its various prison-themed tracks, in Cologne on 5 September 1969. They then began the Battle of the Bands tour which took place in Cologne, Rotterdam, Basel, and Frankfurt, concerts which were also broadcast on the radio, and for television in Rotterdam.[612] For the televised concert, Kenny takes a solo on the 12-bar blues introduced as Kenny Clarke's "Rue Chaptal" (although, confusingly, the melody is actually Sonny Rollins's "Tenor Madness"). The tune is a "down the line" trumpet feature where each player solos one after the other. This sort of thing would no doubt have been a scenario terrifying enough for Kenny as it was, but add to that the television cameras and the entire Thad Jones–Mel Lewis band looking on, and one can only imagine the state he must have been in. But Kenny performs marvellously as usual, having mastered the instrument to such a high degree by this point the one thing that never let him down, even when nervous, was his totally full-bodied and commanding sound: always so centred in its pitch and resonance, it was almost impossible for him to ever sound "bad" during this period. For it was all Kenny's traits as a musician – the harmonic originality, his unusual phrasing and articulation, that tumbling and flexible time feel, the unique mix of free elements mixed in with descriptive harmonic vocabulary (never mind his compositional output, his extraordinary *sound* on the instrument) – that made him recognizable in a single note. His mastery of the trumpet and his peculiar brand of virtuosity was the result of a deep understanding of how to play efficiently. The trumpet is an unforgiving instrument, and Kenny had somehow worked out how to play right at the centre "slot" of each note: the target area where the tone takes on the fullest resonance possible for the least amount of work. Kenny's grasp of that detail is what enabled him to show such remarkable stamina when improvising at high intensity, kept him in such impeccably good pitch, and gave him his legendary sonic breadth and projection. That projection was actually commented on in a review following a gig with Karl Jenkins in February 1972, at which Jenkins had unveiled his new ten-piece jazz-rock ensemble at the 100 Club. In his review for the *Guardian*, Ronald Atkins described how in such a group the horns can tend to be swamped by the amplification, before adding: "All the horn soloists played well enough, but only Kenny Wheeler managed to project himself completely free from the amplified background."[613] This story was echoed in later years in a 1984 big-band concert at the Music Gallery in Toronto, which had been organized (and also conducted) by Tim Brady. The highly regarded Canadian musician Don Thompson, with whom Kenny would later be close, recalled the rehearsal for the big band:

> When we rehearsed, we played about the first three tunes without Kenny, he just sort of sat there. And I think Arnie [Chycoski] and Al Stanwyk may have both been in the trumpet section, it was really a powerful band . . . and it was a big band. And Kenny would just sit there [saying], "Sounds great, guys" and all that kind of stuff, and then on about the third tune Kenny says "Maybe I'll play this one." Well he got out his horn – and it was flugel too – and the band started to play. And then when he came in, he drowned out the whole band! And Arnie Chycoski couldn't believe it

> . . . he couldn't believe anybody could play flugelhorn and drown out the whole trumpet section![614]

It wasn't actually about just about the volume, either. Kenny never "blasted" to the point where his tone became forced or unattractive. It was just that the core of the sound was so resonant and full of overtones that it seemed loud in the way that it could fill a room. The other benefit of this, of course, was that it was a tone that recorded beautifully.

It is no surprise, then, that Kenny was in increasing demand as a studio player throughout the period. It also happened to be a time when there was still a lot of commercial session work so, on top of everything else he was involved in, he kept incredibly busy in the studios. Many of these sessions are not individual things that need to be listed here; they were "bread and butter" dates of inconsequential music and probably occurred on most days, or at least several per week. Kenny also played on many sessions that were booked through the BBC's light entertainment manager, where he was often hired as an "extra/deputy" for the radio orchestra. They would record the themes and incidental music for shows such as *Late Night Extra*, *Night Ride*, *Open House*, and *The Saturday Show*, as well as "light music" sorts of programmes where the music was featured a little more centrally, including *Softly Sentimental*, *Sweet and Swing*, *Dancing to Midnight*, and *Brass and Strings*.[615]

This busy period in the studios and beyond coincided with the Wheeler family moving from 72 Ramsey Street to 141 Wallwood Road in Leytonstone. That change of address is documented in Kenny's BBC contracts from September and October 1972, when his home address changes from one session to the next. But, this is amusingly followed a year later by an administrative blunder in the lead-up to his 1973 broadcast as a big-band leader; the contract was wrongly issued to their old address and so had to be rewritten and submitted to Wallwood Road just in the nick of time to make sure the session went ahead.[616]

The broadcast came after the recording of one of his most significant works, *Song for Someone*,[617] and used the same brass-heavy line-up that Kenny had settled on in this period. In addition to the mixed section of himself, Norma, and three saxophones, the band for this broadcast also had four trumpets, five trombones and tuba, two pianists (on acoustic and electric pianos), plus bass and drums. This was a similar instrumentation to that used on the previous year's BBC outing, but for this broadcast he had the additional support of Bob Cornford conducting. The addition of a conductor had as much to do with Kenny's shyness as it was the musical requirements of the job, as John Taylor observed:

> He generally chose somebody that he would trust and knew would do the job he wanted . . . That's always been the case. He always found somebody that was able to, not necessarily know what he wanted, but how to deal

with the musicians . . . Which of course Kenny was always, erm, unlikely to really take that . . . [*chuckles*] . . . He found that very difficult, didn't he, all the way through his life.[618]

Norma Winstone had a similar view on the subject:

Well, I mean, *bits* of the music needed conducting, but I think it was a way of devolving responsibility. You know, sort of telling a section, *Can we go over that again?* He'd never have done that. He'd have just left them to figure out how to play it. He never gave any instruction that I remember.[619]

Kenny elaborated on this a couple of years later when asked directly, "Why don't you lead your band?" He explained that, apart from the obvious focus he needed to play his own solo parts, there were other reasons:

I did try it once [directing] but I don't have any personal magnetism or authority, you know . . . this one record, I ended up actually shouting at them and nobody took a blind bit of notice, they just all carried on talking so I thought, "To hell with this! I am going to get somebody in to conduct!"[620]

It may not have been the only way in which his sensitive personality affected the musical and personnel decisions for these broadcasts. As seen earlier, Kenny experimented with unconventional line-ups for these broadcasts: whether it was unusual numbers of forces like five trombones, or doubling up on pianists or guitarists – these were things that frankly would have made the session more challenging to compose for and the music more difficult to reuse in any other (more conventional) context. John Taylor speculated:

I often had the idea that the reason he used, on certain times, two piano players or extra soloists in the saxophone section or whatever, he'd have two simply because he didn't want to tell one not to come and do it! [*laughs*] He didn't find it easy to say "Oh, I've got John Taylor doing this rather than you, Alan" or whatever, so instead of that he'd have two. I'm not sure that was always brought on by musical reasons![621]

———·———

Despite not always representing the kind of music he wanted to play, the commercial sessions during this period were still significant for Kenny. There he made many close friendships, especially with his brass colleagues. These musicians would become a significant part of his creative output, and he would continue to choose to play with them on his own musical projects whenever possible for the rest of his life. In addition to his commercial work for the BBC, there was a great number of other sessions contracted through independent fixers and filed with the Musicians' Union. These MU records show just how many mainstream television shows he played on in the period, including popular classics like *Top of the Pops*, *Morecambe and Wise*, and TV specials hosted by the likes of Cilla, Lulu, or Tom Jones.

Kenny's proximity to these sorts of celebrities was of occasional interest to his family, and his sister Mary even once asked him to try to get a signed photo of Tom Jones. He wrote back to her at the time apologizing, "I'm sorry about not getting you that picture of Tom Jones. I know it's silly, and I have actually been on a recording session of his, but I just feel too embarrassed to ask for one . . . But I know a couple of people who work with him, so I'll ask one of them to get me one."[622] Kenny and Doreen were close to Mary, who had even been over to London to visit them once. Since she was suffering with health issues at the time, she was especially on Kenny's mind, and the entire Wheeler family was increasingly concerned for her.[623]

Another famous television show Kenny played for intermittently over a few years was Bruce Forsyth's *The Generation Game*. Kenny principally played on it in 1971 and 1973: a stark contrast, coinciding as it does with one of his boldest periods of creative jazz. The TV show's musical director was Ronnie Hazlehurst, who wrote instrumental music for the band to play while the characters got up to their hijinks on the screen. Fellow trumpeter Tony Fisher said, "Ronnie would write background music that was always extremely good quality, and the band was a lovely small band with one trombone, three saxes, two trumpets, rhythm section. And the two trumpets were *often* me and Kenny Wheeler." Kenny continued to share trumpet duties on the show over a few years with Tony and Eddie Blair.[624] Tony explained, "Eddie was the first call on that [show] really to be honest . . . when Jud [Proctor] was asked to contract it he was asked to get Eddie and me, and often with it being such a busy time, [occasionally] one of us wouldn't be there. And whoever it was that wasn't there, then Kenny would be there."[625] How surreal it would have seemed to modern jazz fans of the time to know that one of their icons was also playing background music on such a beloved British family entertainment show!

Though Kenny seemed to avoid the "pigeonholes" that could often exist within the jazz scene, he could not always avoid it with some of the studio fixers of the day. Tony Fisher recalled a shocking reaction from one fixer to the suggestion that they might book Kenny for a session:

> I can't remember who [the contractor] was – but there were a few of them around who really didn't know much about what was going on. And I got this call one day, and the guy said to me, "Oh, I've got this session coming up; four trumpets, I've got you and two other guys and I cannot get a fourth trumpet player." And this was a big-time fixer, and he said, "I've gone right through the book, and I thought maybe you might know somebody . . ." And I said, "Well not really, I think I'll know the people you know. However, a person who doesn't do very many sessions, but should

do, is Kenny Wheeler." And do you know what this clown's reaction was? He said, "Kenny Wheeler? He's a jazz player, I can't have him – he can't read!"[626]

Aside from how shockingly ill-informed that response was, it is interesting to note that Tony – as a musician who really did almost nothing but studio work through this period – had the perception of Kenny not doing *that* many sessions. Henry Lowther also described just how busy it was possible to be at the height of the studio era:

> In those days when we used to go and do studio work, you know, we'd do three sessions a day, five or six days a week. And you don't really know who you're working for, often the artist isn't there – it's just you and a producer. After years of [it], you know, you don't ask – you just do it.[627]

Even though the amount of sessions Kenny played appears to be a lot of work to modern eyes, he maintained that he "... was never one of the top calls. Those guys were working three sessions a day ... My limit was about six or seven a week, which still gave you a good wage to live on, much better than the average man."[628] At least part of that reflection may be through Kenny's naturally inclined humility, because, as Henry recalled, Kenny did indeed have his heyday. "In that kind of world, often it's 'flavours of the month'. And Kenny and I were, for a little while, flavours of the month, the two of us – it [was] very fashionable!"[629] But, overall, he was not quite as busy as the main studio guys, and Tony Fisher recalled Kenny joking with him about this on one of the *Generation Game* episodes they did together. Tony said to Kenny, "I wish I did a quarter of the work you do jazz-wise." Kenny came back right with: "I wish I did a tenth of the work you do commercial-wise"! Tony continued more seriously: "And it was true, because he deserved to ... he was really a very, very good trumpet player, and *should* have done a lot more work than he did ... As much as he would have hated it – I'm sure he would have hated it!"[630] Tony was probably right about that, but Kenny did acknowledge that some extra money would have been useful. In the same letter home to his sister Mary mentioned earlier, he described their situation:

> Doreen and I are both okay. I don't know where we'll go on our holiday yet, but I hope we can find somewhere nice and quiet. I've been very busy lately and need a rest. But I don't seem to get much further ahead with money. The more I make, the more the cost of living seems to go up.[631]

Indeed, at one stage in 1972 they even received a "rent in arrears" letter from the housing department, so perhaps the extra commercial work would have helped. That said, the family was never *really* in trouble where money was concerned, and as Mark Wheeler has acknowledged, the kids never went without what they needed.[632]

Not all the session work Kenny did was anonymous and in the background. Much of it was great-quality, popular instrumental music of the time and, in fact, in Tony Fisher's recollection of it, just seeing Kenny there in the studio was a positive omen: "A lot of the work we were doing in those days was not all that musical you know, but if you see Kenny there you'd think, 'Hello, who-ever's booked this has maybe got an idea there might be a bit of jazz to play', in which case, naturally, that would be Kenny's . . ."[633] These commercial big-band recording sessions represent an interesting juxtaposition of perception between the regular studio players and Kenny. For someone like him, who was playing a lot of very serious jazz all the time, doing a big-band record-ing session with bands like the Bob Leaper Big Band or the CCS big band would still have been at the very commercial end of his work. For the players doing almost exclusively session work, however, these types of recordings would have been at the "jazzier" end of their work spectrum – with Kenny's presence perhaps even further reinforcing that feeling. The 1970s album *Try This on for Size* by the Bob Leaper Big Band[634] is a great example. The tracks are all very good big-band arrangements of songs by Tony Hatch and Jackie Trent, including hits like *Downtown, Don't Sleep in the Subway*, and *Who Am I?*, the latter having a fantastic harmon mute solo by Kenny. Kenny also played on other recordings on which big bands played the pop hits of the day, including the first two albums, both self-titled, by the rock infused big-band group CCS (the "Collective Consciousness Society") in 1970[635] and 1972.[636] The band featured well-known British blues man Alexis Korner, and both albums showcased arrangements of tunes from bands such as the Rolling Stones and Led Zeppelin: notably their famous instrumental of "Whole Lotta Love", which after making it onto the charts became the theme tune for the BBC's *Top of the Pops* for many years. The album also included another hit single, "Tap Turns on the Water", released in 1971. Kenny's daughter Louann remembered being particularly proud of her dad being on this one: "I was so excited about that, I took the little 45 [rpm] into school and I was playing it, going 'That's my dad on the trumpet'! I don't think he was proud of it . . . but I was . . . I wanted everyone to hear it!"[637]

There were other similar records like Pete Moore's *Solid Rockin' Brass* (1973) for the Gold Star label,[638] *Latin Vibrations* (1972) for Polydor,[639] *The Very Original Brasso Band* (1971) album for EMI,[640] and the strangely experi-mental 1973 album *The Gentle Rain*, released by Moody,[641] which was a col-lection of arrangements of pop tunes by composer and keyboardist Nick Ingman. The latter is not a big-band record; Kenny was more like a soloist on this '70s jazz fusion-meets-synth-meets-funk kind of album. He takes some unusual featured solos, particularly on the Ingman original "Lonely Jelly". He also plays the melody and improvises in full rock-out mode on the Beatles' "Fool on the Hill". Admirably, Kenny must have been told to just be himself, as he really doesn't hold back in terms of his approach on this whole album.

It is as committed improvising – with all his trademark free vocabulary – as anything he'd later play with groups like the United Jazz + Rock Ensemble.

In 1970, Kenny also appeared on studio sessions as varied as Blossom Dearie's *That's Just the Way I Want to Be*,[642] Chaquito's *The Great Chaquito Revolution*,[643] the original cast recording of *Jesus Christ Superstar*,[644] and the Memphis Slim album *Blue Memphis*.[645] The latter was recorded on June 18th, one of Kenny's last bits of commercial work before a family summer trip. He had just enough time to fit in his own 1970 big-band broadcast on June 21st and the Coe, Wheeler & Co. broadcast on June 29th; then he was off to Canada for the summer with Doreen and the kids. Mark remembered that being one of the only times they could afford for all four of them to visit together, so it was a meaningful trip for the family. While they were away, they received the sad word that Doreen's father had died. Unable to afford four new plane tickets to fly back early, Kenny's father lent them the money for just Doreen and Louann to return home and attend the funeral.[646] Louann, still not into her teens, didn't want to stay in Canada and be apart from her mum.

———·———

In addition to Kenny's work as a trumpet player in "semi-commercial" big bands at the time, artists were commissioning him as a composer and arranger. In one particularly interesting case, he was asked to write a series of originals and arrangements for fellow Canadian trumpeter Maynard Ferguson. Kenny had played a couple of gigs in bands backing Maynard in the '60s, including one performance with the Dankworth band for BBC television's *Jazz 625* in 1965, and a BBC Radio 1 *Jazz Club* in 1968 presented by Humphrey Lyttelton. (The latter was recorded at a time of high confidence for Kenny, just after *Windmill Tilter* and *Karyōbin*; he takes a single solo on the broadcast behind which Maynard can be heard clearly exclaiming his positive encouragement).[647] When Kenny was invited to do some arrangements for Maynard, he described the commission as "semi-commercial", writing in a letter back home to his sister Mary.[648] Though the arrangements had broad appeal – and are still of great interest to Maynard fans who might not otherwise know Kenny's work – they are interesting as examples of Kenny writing for a specific soloist other than himself, and a trumpeter at that. On the 1970 *M.F. Horn* album,[649] recorded with Maynard's new British band, Kenny contributes the original composition "Ballad to Max". It is a distinctly Kenny Wheeler chart, from the introductory chord voicings and harmonic language to the opening leaping interval in the melody which snakes motivically back downwards, before more wide intervals and harmonic U-turns. He even uses an unaccompanied tenor saxophone cadenza to get back from the double-time section to the ballad feel in order to finish the tune: a device he would later often use in writing for his own big band. Indeed, Kenny confirmed Maynard's brief instructions: "He didn't restrict me in any way – he just said, 'Write something for the band.'"[650]

There is also a short example of him recycling his own material in "Ballad to Max". The third melodic phrase (bars 5 and 6) of Maynard's opening melody is repeated exactly in the middle of a composition by Kenny for a broadcast with Ronnie Scott, from January 1970. This latter tune of Kenny's is actually a fiercely uptempo burner, but has a half-tempo release section in the middle of the theme that uses the exact same phrase in the fourth and fifth bars. This example bears out the old composer's adage "Never throw anything away".

For Maynard's 1971 album *Alive and Well in London*,[651] Kenny provided more commercial arrangements of pop songs from the day: "Fire and Rain" by James Taylor, "My Sweet Lord" by George Harrison, and Elton John's "Your Song". Kenny once said that it was easier for him to arrange his own compositions since "you conceive the whole thing rather than have to go with somebody else's melody and harmonies,"[652] but he still manages to write some sophisticated harmonic passages. In moments where the nature of these pop tunes necessitates a bit of repetition, he is able to draw on all his skills with counterpoint to create a sense of build and development towards the inevitable musical climax. He sometimes also re-presents the same figures (riffs, really) using different octaves or orchestrations to get more mileage out of the same musical content. He would use this technique in his original big-band writing on many occasions, expanding lead-sheet melodies into large ensemble masterpieces. On "Fire and Rain", Maynard presents the melody with broken phrases and half-valve smears, oddly (given the improbable comparison) not unlike Lester Bowie would later do in his own ventures into pop songs with his Brass Fantasy band. That passing similarity doesn't last long, as Maynard proceeds to drive the piece home with a typically screaming yet impressive *tour de force*. He is in peak form on all these records. It must have helped that, as a trumpeter himself, Kenny knew how to place the big melodic moments in the most effective register of the instrument. This was not lost on the great lead and commercial trumpet player (and veteran of Maynard's bands) Wayne Bergeron, who said, "Of all the great writers on Maynard's English albums, Kenny Wheeler's charts were the best. He knew how to write Maynard in a way that was adventurous and harmonically interesting but still suited him perfectly as a soloist."[653] The most interesting reworking is the opening part of "Your Song", where Kenny used a subtle change of time signature and a complete reimagining of the opening harmonic movements with the displaced theme before it releases into a more conventional pop groove. Even then, there are chords and rhythmic phrasings that betray the fact that the arranger is rooted in a different type of music entirely.

Kenny's final work for Maynard was on the 1972 album *M.F. Horn 2*,[654] on which he contributed a stunning arrangement of Michel Legrand's "Theme from 'Summer of '42'", and an original composition titled "Free Wheeler". On the Legrand chart, Kenny is back in the hands of a great jazz composer, and you can hear his increased comfort arranging strong material; with a good melody to work with, he is able to construct beautiful counterlines and orchestrate some densely balanced voicings for the brass without obviously repeating himself. Some of the introduction and climax is reminiscent of his later writing for brass ensembles in the 1990s: pedal points with broken accompanying chords and soaring trumpet melodies. "Free Wheeler" is positively dramatic in the opening themes after the piano introduction. It is a completely convincing Wheeler original composition without any apparent consideration for the "semi-commercial" context; there's even a free-ish improvisation between the piano and drums that wouldn't have been entirely out of place at the Little Theatre Club – no doubt a play on the word "free" in the title. *Free Wheeler* is actually a track of great variety, practically a condensed version of one of his later suites.

Around the same time as his first commissions for Maynard, Kenny also contributed some pieces for one of the titans of the library music companies, KPM. Alongside some of the giants of the TV/light music writing scene, composers such as Keith Mansfield wrote for KPM and were behind iconic, household theme tunes like the BBC's *Wimbledon* and *Grandstand* shows. A lot of great writers provided work for KPM, including Duncan Lamont, Stan Tracey, and John Dankworth from the jazz scene, as well as commercial writers such as Mansfield, Johnny Pearson and David Lindup. But there was also a deluge of bland, incidental background sort of music in the catalogues of these companies, and Kenny, unable to shake off the depth of his jazz sensibilities, sounds almost *too* jazzy alongside the library music of the others. He contributed some little gems to the KPM 1000 series' *Impact & Action: Vol. 2*,[655] and quite a few tunes on *Underscore: Volume 2*.[656] They all had typically bland titles such as "Safe Landings" and "City Sequence", or "Progress Report" from *Flamboyant Themes: Volume 4*.[657] But Kenny's attempts to write the sort of background-type music more normally associated with library music are oddly fascinating. One can clearly hear his compositional voice, but some of it sounds almost like whole pieces of the sort of "connecting material" he might include between the main sections in his own pieces, like a Kenny Wheeler composition with none of the strong themes he'd normally write. (It is very curious to hear which bits of his own compositional voice he thought were too clearly jazzy, and which bits *he* thought might be mainstream enough for this purpose.) Needless to say, his jazz pedigree and authenticity prove to be too deeply internalized to ever be completely disguisable.

Among the massive variety of work Kenny was doing in the early '70s, there is another particularly charming recording session that has stood the test of time. In late 1970, his old friend Duncan Lamont was approached to compose the music for a children's animation for BBC TV, an adaptation of the children's books written by Duncan's friend David McKee. The show, called *The Adventures of Mr. Benn*, became something of a British classic, watched by generations of children in the 1970s. When McKee ("Mac") brought the book over to his house to show him the stories, the first ideas for the theme sprung immediately into Duncan's mind. Mac asked him to compose the music and offered the advice, "Although it's for children, don't write down to them. Just write as good as you can."[658] They agreed on the size of the group and Duncan arranged for the musicians to receive triple the regular session rate, which would include the buyout of any future rights. The week before the session Duncan phoned Kenny: "Are you free next Wednesday? . . . I'm doing this television thing." Kenny replied, "Er, yeah." There was little more to it than that, but it would be a very well-paid afternoon's work.

In his typically laid-back fashion, Duncan was still composing the last few bits of music before heading off to the studio on the day of the session. "I turned up at two o'clock," Duncan said, "and there was no Kenny. So I said, 'Oh, never mind, just start without him.'" Despite their efforts, his absence affected the music. Duncan explained, "In *Mr. Benn* there's things like cadenzas that are [only] two saxophones; I mean, it should have been Kenny leading the thing!" He continued, "So about 2:15 I said, 'I'd better go and phone Kenny' . . . He was at home! I said, 'Kenny, aren't you supposed to be working today?' He said, 'Oh, Duncan, you were so casual about it, I thought you were kidding!'"[659] Kenny left for the studio immediately while the others carried on recording, arriving an hour later. They proceeded to record all 13 episodes that afternoon and, according to Duncan, allegedly broke the Olympic Studios record for doing the most music in the least amount of time. They sped through the pieces, often recording just the very first run-through before moving on to the next, a feat that required great skill from the players. Duncan said,

> On *Mr. Benn*, I think a lot of the mystique . . . was something about the way Kenny played on that that was so *serious*. I mean, he was a very *serious* player, [and] seriously good . . . There was a cadenza on *Mr. Benn*, which was Mr. Benn going to see the King you know, [*sings complicated fanfare*] and I thought, that poor guy, I can't write this for him. And Kenny came in played it right away, like, [as] if it had been the most satisfying classical trumpet player.

Duncan had also written some charming instrumental interludes to be played while the bowler-hatted Mr. Benn got up to his adventures. The music is a big part of the legacy of *Mr. Benn*, and Duncan commented further on Kenny's role: "There really was something about the seriousness and the integrity of Kenny's playing that actually enhanced the group . . . It never even occurred to me until about 40, 50 years later. I suddenly thought about it and thought, 'I think Kenny really made it.'"[660] Years later, in 2011, Duncan would re-book Kenny to play on one of his last recording dates on a big-band album of the *Mr. Benn* music. He once again highlighted the special qualities Kenny brought to a situation:

> If it had been someone else playing the trumpet, if it had [just] been *a* studio player playing the trumpet, it wouldn't have had that mystique

that he adds to everything he does. He's just [an] astounding musician. I hate to use the word *genius* because it's so overused, but if genius means something that you can't figure out why somebody can do it, then I think maybe the word genius is quite applicable.[661]

---

Kenny had played plenty of other sessions with Duncan. Back in November 1968, they recorded on a particularly unusual couple of dates that ended up being released as two volumes on Esquire some 20 years after the recording, under the title Alan Branscombe & Friends, *Swingin' on the Sound Stage*.[662] These albums came about by chance, as the musicians had actually been booked into Shepperton Studios to record music for a film by the famous Hammer Productions. They were hired by the experimental composer Basil Kirchin, with whom Kenny would record three avant-garde albums over the next few years in groups that included Evan Parker. But on this occasion in 1968, Kirchin had hired a mixture of studio and free players for the session. Duncan recalled ". . . it was quite a big orchestra, maybe seven celli or whatever, and a selection of avant-garde players and other people playing these rapid, little motifs that happened all the time . . . Derek [Bailey] was there, Evan was there."[663] They set up and began recording the first piece with these gnarly repeated figures played by the strings, with Evan Parker roaring away over the top, but it was not what they wanted. "Immediately the director came out screaming his head off, he said 'This is rubbish' . . . 'I can't hear a theme' . . . and Basil said, '*There's dozens of themes!*'" Kirchin and the director had a screaming argument and Basil walked out on the production. With no music to play, but still gainfully employed, the musicians continued to show up each day and whiled away the hours sitting around the studio or going to the pub. Various composers, known or otherwise, would occasionally appear with various bits of music, but the director didn't like any of it. In the end, cinematographer Peter Newbrook, who had been behind the camera in several famous films including the recent *Lawrence of Arabia*, but who was also a serious jazz enthusiast, recognized the quality of the jazzmen in his midst and allowed them two days' recording on the famous Shepperton soundstage. They played mostly busking standards and a handful of originals, but in Duncan's memory, this was never supposed to be a record. It was only after multi-instrumentalist Alan Branscombe's passing that Newbrook issued the sessions as a tribute to him on Esquire Records, the label Newbrook had set up with Carlo Krahmer. Kenny plays some outstanding swinging trumpet on the track "For Pete's Sake", and fellow trumpeter Eddie Blair demonstrated just what a tremendous soloist he was capable of being when he was allowed free from the constraints of his more regular studio work.[664] Not all the Hammer film sessions were quite that dramatic; Kenny and Ronnie Scott are prominently featured on the soundtrack to a 1972 Hammer film called *Straight on Till Morning*, which also had a cameo and theme song by Annie Ross.[665]

Kenny also had a seemingly unlikely quintet with the highly regarded mainstream clarinetist from Scotland, Sandy Brown. They had played in London clubs like Ronnie Scott's Old Place, and in December 1968 Kenny played on Brown's album featuring arrangements of the music from the popular stage show *Hair,* called *Hair at Its Hairiest.*[666] Along with the swinging bass and drums of Lennie Bush and Bobby Orr and mainstream trombonist George Chisholm, the band also featured guitarist John McLaughlin as the only chordal instrument, just months before he moved to the United States to join drummer Tony Williams's new band Lifetime. There is an interesting solo that Kenny takes on the track "Manchester England", which is a blues in a major key. As Kenny didn't like to solo on the major blues form, this is a particularly rare and good example of him doing so at a point in his career when his style had already reached maturity. It demonstrates some specific, subtle developments in his playing when contrasted with the earlier Dankworth blues "Mark 1" from 1964. Aside from the increased strength and conviction on the horn, Kenny displays a more comfortable, organic consolidation of some conventional bluesy language and his more idiosyncratic vocabulary. He sounds very much at ease and in control, which somehow gives the solo a more assured feel than the more searching quality from earlier years. Much later he tried to articulate to Ian Carr exactly what it was he'd always found so challenging about the blues:

> I find it hard to play to play a . . . [*laughs*] . . . a major blues because I feel that if I play these funky blue notes, I'm trying to sound like I *can* play the blues, you know what I mean . . . ? Whereas I don't mind a minor blues because they're all there already! . . . [*both laugh a lot*] . . . I've always dreaded it when somebody says "Let's play a blues" and I think, "Oh God, how will I get away from trying to play those blue notes which, um, how can I make them sound like I'm not deliberately trying to play them, [but] make them sound natural . . . ?"[667]

For most people, though, far more memorable than Kenny's discerning deconstruction of the blues is the sleeve of the LP, picturing a rather "*Hair*-y" Sandy Brown clutching his bass clarinet, otherwise completely naked (front and back respectively on each side), his blushes spared only by a rather fetching sporran.

---

Occasionally, it was possible for Kenny's work to create an opportunity for a family holiday. The family had a few holidays on the Channel Islands when the kids were young, and one of these was in early 1971 when Kenny accepted an invitation to play on a new album for Scottish saxophonist Jack Duff, now resident on the island of Jersey.[668] Kenny arranged to take the family on the trip and booked the accommodation, though perhaps without paying quite enough attention to the details. As Mark Wheeler recalled, his dad got quite a surprise on the plane: "The only time I ever saw him panic a little bit [was when] he'd booked us into this hotel, and on the plane he looked at the room rate and went a funny colour. He said, 'Oh, oh I didn't realize it was *that* much!'"[669] At that point, of course, it was too late, and the family took their holiday in what turned out to be one of the finest five-star hotels on the island.

The album Kenny would record on this trip was *The Enchanted Isle*,[670] Jack Duff's musical tribute to Jersey, and another peculiarly striking example of the effect Kenny's approach could have at the time. It being quite a conventional hard-bop sort of record, the other players kept their approaches fairly straight-ahead, but Kenny's playing transformed it into something completely different. He mixes the usual strong, soaring melodic phrases with some quite angular and dissonant resolutions. Rhythmically, he moves between precise statements to completely fluid tumbles – at times within a single phrase – and breaks off into completely free, wild forays. These are as "out" as anything he might play in a totally free setting, but here over a swinging rhythm section accompaniment. In fact, it is likely that he was trying to provoke a response from the rhythm section that would take the music somewhere outside the straight-ahead *ting-ting-ta-ting* behind him, since it was really not where his head was at that time. Kenny is utterly assured on the instrument, with his huge sound and commanding stamina in some high-octane solos. Years later, on hearing this relatively unknown recording, Evan Parker commented, "Nowhere is the affinity with Booker Little more clear."[671] Although on the surface it may not evoke Little's exact vocabulary on the trumpet, it certainly shows the new-found freedom that Booker's influence afforded him.

---

For all the sessions and sideman appearances he took part in, it was within the London jazz scene that Kenny did his most significant and lasting work of the time. This was a period in which a remarkable amount of ground-breaking music was being made and, thankfully, recorded. John Surman summed up the creative energy:

> Let's remember that at the time . . . the avant-garde was actually the popular form of jazz. Actually, in all kinds of movements in the arts; if you think about painting, [i.e.] Rauschenberg . . . and you think about modern dance and everything, that was a very exciting time period . . . so there was this kind of explosion of energy, and almost gave young players like us the permission, as it were, to just be ourselves within this music. Which up until that point, if you think about it, from its original origins as a kind of World music in New Orleans with all those influences – Spanish marching bands, African percussion and all that stuff – it got very stylized up until bebop if you know what I mean . . . The whole discussion about what was

jazz and what wasn't jazz, but [in] the late '60s that was exploded . . . and London was a big centre.[672]

With the music scene in London more diverse than ever, it was inevitable that these new influences would be absorbed by the jazz musicians. There was a further foray into Indian and jazz fusions with a new band called the Indo-British Ensemble in which Kenny took part. The music was composed, arranged, and conducted by Victor Graham. It is actually a very respectful and authentic collaboration that acknowledges the previous work of John Mayer and Joe Harriott on the sleeve, so it is let down slightly by the unfortunate lack of imagination that led to the album being titled, rather artlessly, *Curried Jazz*.[673]

The new jazz-rock fusion movement was also taking hold, and Kenny's old friend Ian Carr had helped spearhead it with his band Nucleus. Having won first prize at the 1970 Montreux Jazz Festival (where Skidmore's quintet had been placed second the previous year) the success of Nucleus grew. The size of the band's line-up responded in kind: Kenny joined the expanded version of the group, called Nucleus Plus, with others including Tony Coe and Norma Winstone. He appeared on Ian's *Labyrinth*[674] suite, recorded in 1973 and performed live the following year at Camden's Roundhouse,[675] and on the earlier recording of *Solar Plexus*[676] in 1971. Ian explained:

> It was [a commission] from the Arts Council. I got a grant to do it, and with that grant I was able to buy my first keyboard. I didn't have a piano, and I didn't have much money either, but I bought a keyboard . . . For the first time, I could work on harmonies and really compose properly, you know . . . And it's a pretty basic thing, *Solar Plexus*, but having said that, the actual playing on it [is at] a very high standard . . . Kenny Wheeler's solo on "Changing Times" is a wonderful solo . . . Everybody gave fantastically to that [recording]. I was pleased.[677]

It was also a very productive time for the jazz composers who welcomed the musical breadth of the era with a number of heavily conceptual projects and recordings; Mike Gibbs was one of the key pioneering musicians embracing the jazz-rock movement.[678] On his own eponymous debut album for Deram in 1970, he uses a large line-up, again featuring bassist Jack Bruce and Kenny's trumpet colleagues Derek Watkins, Henry Lowther, and Ian Hamer. Although Kenny was always an admirer of Mike's writing, he readily admitted that he wasn't a big fan of much of the jazz-rock music at the time. Kenny believed, however, that Mike's was among the most successful integration of the two,[679] adding, "I always enjoyed the Mike Gibbs band very much."[680] Mike recalled another habit of Kenny's which expressed not only his respect for Mike, but also showed how curious Kenny remained as a writer:

I was very flattered occasionally . . . when we were at a rehearsal doing my music, and Kenny would run over, not say anything to anybody . . . but just to look at the score. I mean maybe he was checking a note, but I also think [it was] for musical reasons. That pleased me immensely because already I knew his ear was up there with the gods![681]

Kenny also recorded on Mike's 1970 album *Tanglewood 63*,[682] and *Just Ahead* in 1972.[683] And in 1974 he participated in the performance that became Mike's live record with vibraphonist Gary Burton, *In the Public Interest*.[684] The concert was at the Rainbow Theatre in Finsbury Park on March 21st, and it stuck in Mark Wheeler's memory as perhaps the best he ever heard his dad play: "I remember sitting there thinking *'fucking hell, where did that come from?!'* . . . 'cause he was always just doing his scales and arpeggios [practice] at home, and then all of a sudden he's up there just roaring away!"[685]

There were other broadcasts with Gibbs's band, both at the BBC and in Europe such as 1973's NDR Jazz Workshop, where Kenny was becoming increasingly engaged as one of the star guests of the time. In 1975 he recorded the last album he would play on with Gibbs for the next fifteen years: an LP called *Mike Gibbs Directs the Only Chrome Waterfall Orchestra*.[686] This was written after Gibbs had accepted a teaching position at Berklee College of Music in Boston in 1974. Each year he would get a new concert's worth of material together, and in that first year the music he wrote would be the material that formed the *Only Chrome Waterfall*. (The peculiar name was coined by student writer Richard Niles, after Mike said he thought the music sounded metallic and wet.[687]) The ensuing album featured a rhythm section of Steve Swallow and Bob Moses, as well as saxophonist Charlie Mariano.

After playing on Mike Westbrook's *Metropolis* in 1971,[688] Kenny appeared on record with Westbrook for the last time on the 1975 album, *Citadel/Room 315* on the Novus label.[689] There are some rock-infused grooves on this album too, among a broad array of styles and influences. The trumpets have some demanding section parts, led by Derek Healey, a wonderful trumpet player from the earlier generation who was not often found on the contemporary jazz records of this period even though Kenny played with him regularly in commercial sessions and big bands. Kenny himself doesn't have any solo contributions – just a lovely written flugel solo on one track – but his friend Henry Lowther is featured on a couple of the pieces, showing just what an individual and wonderful musician he is.

John Surman teamed up with Kenny and another Canadian in London, saxophonist and composer John Warren, for the 1971 album *Tales of the Algonquin*, which was also on the popular Deram label.[690] "It was a fantastic event [and] an amazing band for its time", Surman said, although the reason for doing it was that it was the final commitment of his three-album contract with Decca (Deram's owner). Also, with a slight shift in public popularity of jazz and the departure of a supportive executive at the company, Surman saw it as a great opportunity to get something of John Warren's down on tape.[691] The album has become widely regarded as a classic of the period, but there were a few issues to overcome on the recording dates. It took place in Decca's own Broadhurst Gardens Studios in London, but what was annoying for the musicians was that the larger upstairs studio had been booked out for the week by the Moody Blues and was sitting empty, so the *Algonquin* sessions had to be crammed into the smaller studio downstairs. Added to this tension, the tape machine was beset with technical glitches and it took a long time to get the material for the second side on tape.[692] The music they recorded is wide-ranging, from hard-swinging jazz solos to more open, reflective passages. Kenny's strength is evident throughout, and his is the dominant voice in the trumpet section on the tricky ensemble passages (in addition to his strong soloing such as on "We'll Make It"). The album also features John Taylor in fine form, and with no guitarist to share the comping duties it is an example of just what an inspiring and provocative accompanist John Taylor was, with an approach steeped in all the American jazz influences of the time but a European harmonic sensibility and his own contemporary rhythmic language.

The years J.T. spent backing vocalists and guest horn players as "house pianist" on gigs like the Lilliput were instrumental in his learning the art of accompaniment. He played not only with Norma Winstone but also with singers Marion Montgomery and Cleo Laine, and he always valued the experience of the time he'd spent in these accompanist roles.[693] J.T. also joined Kenny to appear as one of three great pianists (with Gordon Beck and Stan Tracey) in a Southwark Cathedral concert on 27 April 1974, which resulted in the recording of a double live LP called *Will Power (A Shakespeare Birthday Celebration in Music)*. The concert, which commemorated the Bard's 410th birthday, was released on the Argo label in 1975.[694] In addition to the three pianists, the rhythm section included Ron Mathewson on bass, Tony Levin on drums, Trevor Tomkins on percussion, and two cellists. These forces joined vocalists Norma Winstone and Pepi Lemer, who had some tricky two-part melodies to deliver: some almost kitschy pop, with others pieces quite angular in nature. Kenny and Tony Coe made up the front line and the playing is stunningly tight for a live recording. Kenny's sound is so huge in the acoustics of the cathedral that the soaring unison lines with Tony sound far bigger than just two players – especially on the '70s fusion grooves underpinning Ian Carr's *Will's Birthday Suite*, where the electric keyboards provide a very '70s Miles Davis sort of sound. The album also featured original contributions from Mike Gibbs, Stan Tracey and Ian Carr (who produced the album), as well as Neil Ardley, who had been directing the newly formed New Jazz Orchestra in the late '60s.

Despite all this varied and creative work at the time, Kenny played with more bands than just those based in London or Europe. On one very special occasion, in late March 1972, he was invited to sub in the trumpet section of one of the most revered big bands of all time, the Thad Jones/Mel Lewis Jazz Orchestra. Having just returned from a five-week tour of Russia, they undertook a ten-day residency at Ronnie Scott's club, with a trumpet section including Cecil Bridgewater and the eighteen-year-old lead prodigy Jon Faddis; also on this occasion bassist George Mraz replaced Richard Davis.[695] Even though it had been only three years since Kenny had played opposite this group as part of the Battle of the Bands European tour, and he had also recorded twice with Mel Lewis back in the mid-'60s as part of Friedrich Gulda's projects, it is unclear exactly who recommended Kenny to sub for these gigs. It may have been at Ronnie Scott's suggestion, or possibly the guys in the band remembered him from those previous encounters. Either way, it was a considerable honour to appear with that group, and Stan Sulzmann recalled that it was a privilege of which Kenny's friends at the time were especially in awe. (Stan also recalled some typically domestic kerfuffle over the money as the club apparently wanted to pay Kenny the "local player" rate, rather than the higher "visiting American" rate that the rest of the band received.[696]) The Jones/Lewis band members were also impressed with their last-minute trumpet sub. Jon Faddis recalled the impression Kenny made, especially on Pepper Adams, the band's legendary baritone saxophonist:

> Kenny was very quiet and very professional in the way he interacted with the musicians before the music began. Then Kenny played a solo on "The Second Race" (number 4 in the book), and everybody was amazed at the fluidity and creativity of his solo, especially Pepper Adams, who kept asking, *Did you hear that? Did you hear that?!* Kenny came in and read the parts and played great. The solo Kenny played that night was extraordinary; it was really special. Pepper was really quiet and not necessarily outgoing, so for him to say something about another musician and what he was playing, you knew Pepper was moved and that he was impressed by the uniqueness of what he was hearing. That also impressed me. I felt the same way about how Kenny played.[697]

Drummer Tony Faulkner also remembered the significance of that band's visits to London, and his surprise at seeing Kenny there in the ranks: "I went to Ronnie's whenever I was able to hear the Thad Jones/Mel Lewis band . . . anyway, so I was in Ronnie's, the first time I went there on that particular visit, and bugger me, there's Ken Wheeler in the trumpets!" Tony also asked Kenny what it had been like to be a part of it:

> I do recall talking to him about it. I said, "What was it like playing in the Thad Jones/Mel Lewis band?" – because, again, it was my favourite band at that time of just about any – and he said, "It was very different, they

just play differently to the way we play." . . . He was talking about the time feel, and also the phrasing feel.[698]

Trumpeter Jon Faddis speculated about what Kenny might have meant by that observation:

> I don't know what he [Kenny] was used to . . . but Thad was about the groove . . . there were a lot of spontaneous things going on too, Thad would conduct the rhythm section in solos and Mel would catch it right away . . . things like, "bam", stop-time, and then Roland Hanna would play by himself . . . so I think part of it was [free], not the floaty ethereal type of thing, but it was like hardcore groove, which was Thad coming out of Basie's band, because it was always *dance*. You've got to be able to dance to it [and] it's got to make you feel something . . . but during solos, things could go *out*.[699]

The legacy of these early encounters with that famous ensemble would echo years later in the musical association and mutual admiration Kenny would share with Pepper Adams.

———·———

With the London scene being as busy as it was, and much of the work involving the same core team of players, conflicts of availability were inevitable. In some cases, it led to the bandleaders themselves extolling the virtues of their own creative validity – and sometimes questioning that of others. For instance, Mike Gibbs recalled how his early associations with Dankworth would occasionally clash with Graham Collier's dates: "I remember how upset Graham was, you know, if I got a gig with Dankworth and it clashed with Graham [then] I took the Dankworth gig. Graham was sort of bewildered that I would take the 'commercial' gig, instead of his serious jazz. That was his attitude . . ." But Mike acknowledged, "I sort of see where he was coming from, because he was so deeply devoted to his ambitions as a composer."[700] One wonderful snapshot that captures the extent of Kenny's busyness with the key musical happenings of the period came in a three-day recording of concerts, televised as part of the *Jazz Scene at the Ronnie Scott Club* series, in which Kenny participated every night with different bands. This was the end of August 1969, around the same time Kenny and his family would have been collecting their two free copies of the newly released *Windmill Tilter* LP. He appeared on consecutive nights with Ronnie Scott's group, Mike Westbrook's Concert Band, and Alan Skidmore's Quintet, respectively.[701] No recordings of these concerts appear to exist but it would be wonderful to hear an example of what must have been these intensely different performances taken so close together.

In the midst of this relentless activity, two of Kenny's closest colleagues also launched their solo careers. In 1972 (in addition to marrying Norma Winstone), John Taylor began to compose for and record his new sextet, and Norma released her own debut album. In 1970, the producer Peter Eden established Turtle Records, and, having worked closely with John Surman on his Deram albums, Eden asked Surman to recommend projects he could record for his new label. J.T. had already made his first recorded appearance on Surman's second album, *How Many Clouds Can You See?*[702] for Deram.[703] So, around the end of 1970, Surman approached J.T. to record for Eden's new label. This was the end of a prolific period of musical development for J.T., who was 29 years old when he started the band. (This is perhaps late by today's standards, but he had only quit his office job four years earlier.) The advent of J.T.'s sextet was also the first time he had seriously done any composing of his own, which seems remarkable when one hears the sophistication and maturity of his writing.[704] That clarity as a leader was confirmed in Surman's self-effacing account of his role as producer: "Peter Eden had asked me to produce that album . . . but I don't think I had to do anything because, you know, J.T. always knew what it was he wanted to do – so I just popped along and smiled sweetly from the control room!"[705] The album became *Pause, and Think Again*,[706] recorded in February of 1971 by J.T.'s new sextet: a group that would be quietly legendary for its powerful and exploratory performances. The group featured Chris Laurence and Tony Levin in the rhythm section, with Stan Sulzmann, Chris Pyne, and Kenny in the front line. In addition to producing the album, John Surman also appears as a guest soprano saxophonist. J.T.'s writing for the group is sophisticated and way ahead of its time. There are rhythmic ostinatos that sound fresh even to contemporary ears, with a varied and rich harmonic vocabulary and adventurous open forms. He skilfully orchestrated for the front line, with the three horns dipping in and out of rhythm-section parts and with figures that typically avoid the soli as one would hear in a conventional horn section. Norma Winstone also joins the core sextet for the final track, "Interlude/Soft Winds", a J.T. piece for which she composed lyrics. This is yet another fiendishly intervallic melody which she delivers with seemingly effortless accuracy.

Kenny was an influence on John Taylor's development as a composer. J.T. said:

> Certainly Kenny's always been a big influence for me. [It's] fantastic to have been so closely involved with him over the years, and I know I've learned an awful lot from him – particularly about this area of how it all fits together – his wonderful skills of melodic improvising . . . and the depth of his harmonic understanding . . . [It's] unbelievably clever.[707]

But the admiration was very much a mutual one, as Kenny was very open about the influence J.T. had on him as well. In masterclasses and workshops in later years, Kenny would frequently cite the pianist as his favourite musician.[708] More specifically, Kenny described the influence that J.T.'s sextet had on him: "It was great – John's writing was so hard; that was the opening to me that you could write stuff like that."[709]

The group made their second recorded appearance in the early summer of 1971 at the Wavendon Festival, in a series of concerts curated by John Dankworth and Cleo Laine at their new Buckinghamshire home and venue, created from a converted stable block. In addition to appearing with J.T.'s sextet at that year's festival, Kenny led a quintet with altoist Mike Osborne. The group appears to have been formed as a one-off for the occasion, as there are no other examples of it being mentioned.[710] The BBC recorded both these groups anyway, with the J.T. sextet being subtitled *My Lady in Autumn.* The sextet existed and performed intermittently for almost the next decade. They often played at the Phoenix in Cavendish Square, along with other venues that promoted and sustained similar original projects.[711]

Although the band had a unique chemistry and played often, even recording for a handful of BBC broadcasts, there are only two official releases by the group. After *Pause, and Think Again*, the second album is 1975's *Fragment,*[712] which was released on cassette only, for Gordon Beck's Jaguar label.[713] *Fragment* was recorded live for Capital Radio in January 1975, the same month Kenny turned 45. On the recordings that exist, J.T.'s sextet captures some of the finest playing on record by all the members. The rhythm section explores the boundaries between groove and freedom with a playful harmonic and metric counterpoint. The front-line solos are also consistently stunning. Chris Laurence remembered well not only that "[Kenny] would make your hair stand on end", but that "everybody would be really pushing the boundaries of things . . . and trying to play the parts right . . . It was extremely exciting."[714] When Kenny recalled the challenges of the music, it was particularly Stan's affinity with J.T. that shone out: "I remember in the band, Chris [Pyne] and I were never actually lost, but we could never play it the way Stan could. Even then, Stan could go through everything."[715] Stan and J.T. were close at that time, playing and working together in many different situations, and in the sextet, Stan was entrusted to give the musical cues from his front-line position wherever necessary.[716]

There could be some edgy moments in a band that took that many musical risks. Chris Laurence recalled:

> There'd be hardly any formal rehearsals, no, you'd just turn up there and do it, not work on things for weeks and weeks . . . none of that . . . [it was] *let's do it and see what comes out.* And Tony Levin wasn't a great reader, but he was great, he always put a lot into things and would pick up quickly on how things could work – we'd all do that . . . We never discussed sort of dynamics and things like that . . . he didn't lecture us . . . it was [all] written into John's music.[717]

Despite the musical success of the band, J.T. eventually wound down the sextet as his focus shifted to developing the evolving musical relationships he had with Kenny and Norma, which would become one of the most significant groups of their careers by the end of the decade.[718] But there was one final performance of the J.T. sextet decades later in the summer of 1991 at the 100 Club, a place they had played back during the group's original reign. This was a charity concert for Action Aid, organized by Henry Lowther to celebrate his 50th birthday. Henry had always loved the band, and J.T. reassembled the ensemble as a gift for him. It was a stellar evening which also included John Surman's Brass Project, Stan Tracey's Octet, a small group led by Julian Argüelles, and a selection of free players including Paul Rutherford and Evan Parker. Sadly, by that time, trombonist Chris Pyne was suffering badly in his battle with alcoholism and addiction and was not in good shape for the sextet performance. As the set progressed, Kenny, ever averse to any negative drama and especially this particular condition, kept edging further and further to the side, leaving Stan to manage Chris alone, trying to keep him in place just to get through the gig.[719] Although it must have been particularly upsetting for Kenny to see his old friend like that – considering the devastating toll that illness had taken on his own family – it was difficult for all the musicians. At one point that night, Derek Watkins took Chris aside and talked to him at length, trying to counsel him through it.[720] The situation was tragic for Stan, too, who had so loved playing with Chris in the sextet the first time around:

> Chris was a great player, really lovely, he was a real jazz player. He was a bloody good trombone player with that fiery, bright, happy sound. He was a very happy sort of player, you know, he was like he was as a guy, joyful. He was just roaring you know . . . but very tight, [the front line] would really play together so it had a *sound*.[721]

This sad end to what had been such a formidable group was further coloured by the surprisingly recurrent conflict of whether a "charity" gig should be reviewed in the press. On this occasion it was, and some of the musicians were unhappy as they had all given their time for nothing, and in some cases – like Stan's – under very difficult circumstances.[722] The more lasting and positive legacy of that group is, of course, in the handful of recordings they left behind. Stan said, "The best band of all that period was John's sextet . . . because of the music, the writing, the way he wrote for sextet. Nobody's written like that since or before. It sounded huge . . . a really orchestrated band. It was a great band . . . not like anything else at all."[723] He added that these were "golden years for Wheeler, of course; he had everything then: magnificent sound, time, experience, imagination, individuality, and age was on his side. He was like a god to me at that time, as was John Taylor. I only learned they were human with all the same frailties much later on."[724]

Norma Winstone made her debut recording as a leader with *Edge of Time*, released on the Argo Record Company label in 1972.[725] Having recorded for the Decca-owned label in January 1970 as part of Michael Garrick's *The Heart is a Lotus* album[726] and topped the *Melody Maker* poll for best vocalist in both 1970 and 1971, the label approached Norma for a project as leader.[727] As she began thinking about what to do for the project, she decided on a core ensemble including most of the players from J.T.'s sextet, including, of course, Kenny. Norma said:

> It seemed I had, more or less, carte blanche to do what I wanted. So I thought, well why don't I have different line-ups, you know, have a core bigger line-up which was about ten musicians, and then do some smaller things, which I did – trios, a duo. I got Neil Ardley to organize something – they were all people that I'd been working with . . . I obviously knew Neil [from the New Jazz Orchestra] because I got him to do a Mike Taylor song, and also John Warren – I [wrote some words for] one of his pieces, "Perkins Landing" . . . There was so much happening at that time, it's difficult to remember![728]

In addition to the two pieces contributed by Surman, Norma co-wrote three of the seven tracks with J.T.: the title track, "Songs for a Child", and the longest cut on the album, "Enjoy This Day". The latter includes some fantastic early examples of the chemistry between Norma and Kenny improvising together, with J.T.'s fully formed rhythmic vocabulary accompanying them. Her technical virtuosity and the freedom with which she moves between regular melodic improvising and a freer textural approach is like nothing else of the time. "Enjoy This Day" is also the only track on which Kenny is featured, with a long and powerful trumpet solo that demonstrates his melodic clarity alongside wild and free flurries – and a less common device in his playing of the time: repeated and displaced rhythmic phrases and sequences. It is evident here how comfortable that familiar rhythm section was in providing the accompaniment to Kenny; they are also able to fluctuate organically between the compound groove and looser, free implications of the time.

Several members of the *Edge of Time* band were old friends of Kenny's. Once again, Henry Lowther is in the trumpet section, and other regulars of the time – Art Themen, Mike Osborne, and Alan Skidmore – are among the saxophones. Bassist Chris Laurence remembered the sessions and the musical risks they took. "It was very exciting. It was a very free record – warts and all – whereas now you can chop and change things round a bit, in those days it was more difficult because you'd end up with little bits of tape everywhere, and then go, *Where was that last take?!*" Chris continued: "There was never the time or money to do that [much editing], so you just did the record, and that was what came out . . . like doing a broadcast, but it was kept."[729,730]

Kenny also continued his involvement in the free improvisation scene of the period. His musical relationships with two of the most significant drummers of the day developed further, with the groups of Tony Oxley and John Stevens (the latter usually as part of the Spontaneous Music Ensemble), often including similar personnel. Kenny appeared on two further albums (and the usual broadcasts of the time) with Tony Oxley's sextet, which included SME regulars Evan Parker, Paul Rutherford, and Derek Bailey: *4 Compositions for Sextet* for CBS in 1970,[731] and *Ichnos* for RCA the following year.[732] The Spontaneous Music Ensemble also had further releases in this period which included Kenny among their changeable line-up: two records with larger groups included *The Source: From and Towards,* recorded in November 1970,[733] and a live LP recorded in London's Notre Dame Hall in May 1971 but not released until 1979.[734] Side 1, subtitled "Let's Sing for Him", features four vocalists, including Norma, and is dedicated to saxophonist Albert Ayler, who had died in November 1970. Ray Warleigh also appeared on both these albums: another of the players who, like Kenny moved regularly between studio work, modern British jazz, and the free scene. The other curious SME recording of the time is *So, What Do You Think?*[735] This album is noteworthy because of the return of bassist Dave Holland and, interestingly, it features almost the same band as on *Karyōbin* but with saxophonist Trevor Watts in place of Evan Parker. *So, What Do You Think?* was recorded in January 1971 for the Tangent label and released in 1973. Trombonist Paul Rutherford was also leading his variously sized "Iskra" bands at that time, and Kenny appeared in a 12-piece incarnation for the album Paul Rutherford and Iskra 1912, *Sequences 72 & 73*, recorded over three sessions in from 1972 to 1974.[736] This ensemble included Kenny's free colleagues Evan Parker, Derek Bailey, Trevor Watts, Tony Oxley, Malcolm Griffiths, and Norma Winstone.

It was not, however, always the predictable faces making up the personnel of the experimental ensembles of the early 1970s. There was one notably unique configuration of players that remains an almost bizarre exception to the rule. "Splinters" was the brainchild of John Stevens, who had the idea of forming a cross-generational "free jam band".[737] It was a fascinating ensemble featuring Kenny, Trevor Watts and John Stevens, all of whom one could say represented the younger free scene. They were joined by three of the most iconic figures from the older, straight-ahead bebop-influenced jazz period: Tubby Hayes, Stan Tracey, and the second drum kit of Phil Seamen. The band was underpinned by the wonderful bassist Jeff Clyne, who, much like Kenny, frequently oscillated between the two scenes. The intention of the group was to explore improvisational common ground; such was the musical prowess of each member that the results are, perhaps surprisingly, quite engaging and successful. (When one considers the changing landscape of the jazz scene and the amount of attention journalists were giving to the new avant-garde pioneers, it was also quite an understandable PR move on the part of these bebop titans to be willing to engage with some of this new activity.) With the explosion of the R&B scene in London as well as the new movements in jazz in Britain, much of the regular work had dried up for the older musicians, to the point that Stan Tracey even considered employment as a postman.[738] Splinters' first performance was Monday, 22 May 1972 at the 100 Club and, thankfully it was well recorded by Trevor Watts.[739] The result was finally released some 37 years later in 2009 as an album titled *Split the Difference* on the Canadian label Reel Recordings.[740,741] John Stevens described the opening moments of the evening's music: "We were gonna go out and play free music, whatever shape that took. However that went, that's what the music would be", but he recalled his nerves at taking to the stage alongside Phil Seamen for the first time: "I looked at Tubby and I looked at Phil, and one of them said, '*Go on then! Start!*' I felt quite tentative. It was *free* playing."[742] On hearing the music years later, bassist Jeff Clyne noted, "I think there's more time/no [chord] changes playing than actual free textural playing . . . I suppose looking back at it now it might seem almost mainstream, but at the time it was quite daring."[743] Kenny agreed with that assessment when he was asked about that group. "It was more conventional than what Tony Oxley was doing, for instance," he said, adding, "I play differently but, I don't know, I don't analyse things like that very much. I just try and do it without thinking about it too much."[744]

Despite this last statement, there was some evidence to suggest Kenny was still thinking about new ways to develop and explore his options on the trumpet. Henry Lowther recalled a curious observation Kenny made when they were at Ronnie's together listening to Joe Henderson around this period:

> It was a time when saxophone players started doing this kind of loose thing, like [*sings a flurry of notes*] sort of stuff, which was never a part of the vocabulary of previous tenor players . . . not so much playing "defined" notes, but kind of like waving your fingers about. And I remember Kenny saying to me, "It would be great if we could do that on the trumpet." And he went through a period of [experimenting] . . .[745]

Henry described how Kenny would hold the trumpet with his left hand but place his thumb up through the gap to hold down the first valve with his left thumb, and then execute the "flurry" of notes with his right-hand fingers on just the remaining second and third valves. He recalled seeing him trying out this idea on a Mike Gibbs tour: "I remember Ian Hamer and I watching Kenny doing that and saying, 'Look, see what he does, puts his thumb up on the first valve' . . ."[746] Perhaps the most interesting thing about it is the fact he was still searching for physical and technical things he could tweak on the instrument to refine his concept within the free, textural language of his improvisation.

As a group, Splinters would only undertake one further performance with the original personnel on 12 September, a few months after the group's debut, which thankfully was also captured on a private tape. It was part of a new series of weekly gigs at the Swan pub in Stockwell called "Grass Roots", set up by Stan Tracey's wife Jackie, and Harry Miller's wife, Hazel.[747] The Swan gig would be the last time that extraordinary line-up played together: Phil Seamen died suddenly that October. After the loss of Seamen, the band continued intermittently for the rest of 1972, including a further Stockwell gig in October and a concert in Notre Dame Hall in November, as well as a BBC *Jazz Workshop* broadcast in December to finish the year.[748] But following Tubby Hayes's death in June 1973, and despite a handful of appearances with alto saxophonist Pete King in place of Hayes, the group itself, as Stevens described, "began to splinter".[749]

Sadder times were still to come for Kenny. On 23 August 1973, his sister Mary tragically died at the age of 44, having battled for years with alcoholism and addiction. Mary was the sibling who seemed to have borne the Wheeler children's traumatic upbringing most overtly, perhaps compounded by entering an abusive relationship in her youth rather than finding the stability and love that Kenny had been so fortunate to find with Doreen. Whatever the nature or reasons for her decline, it was a devastating blow to the entire family. With Kenny being so far away from Canada, times like this were always particularly tough on him. Before this tragedy, his youngest sister Mabel had already scheduled her first trip over to London to see them, and despite the heartbreaking events that unfolded, she came to visit just a week after Mary's death. It meant a great deal to Kenny to have that family connection so soon after the loss of their oldest sister.[750]

---

Despite his grief – or perhaps as a way of avoiding it – Kenny kept up his relentless schedule and the music he was called upon to play became more varied than ever. The experimentation of the time meant players from entirely different scenes occasionally overlapped, with jazz musicians being brought into more contemporary classical contexts. Such was the case with one notable performance at the Proms from 1974, with a piece by composer and pianist Frederic Rzewski. Prom 11 from that year was a live BBC Radio 3 broadcast from the Roundhouse in Camden on 29 July at 9:30 pm. The programme featured a world premiere of Tim Souster's "Zorna", and Proms or UK premieres of Roger Smalley's "Monody", Karlheinz Stockhausen's "Across the Boundary" (the fourth piece from his *Für kommende Zeiten* collection), and the piece Kenny was involved in, Rzewski's "Les Moutons de Panurge".[751] The performers in the concert were centred around Intermodulation, Roger Smalley and Tim Souster's live electronic group.[752]

Intermodulation's performance of the Smalley and Stockhausen compositions comprised the first half of the concert. For the second half, which included the Souster and Rzewski pieces, a group of "soloists" augmented the Intermodulation group: Kenny on trumpet, Evan Parker and Tony Coe on soprano saxophones, Alan Hacker on piccolo clarinet, trombonist

Paul Rutherford, John White on euphonium, Barry Guy on bass, and John Marshall on drums.[753] Rzewski's "Les Moutons de Panurge" has an interesting mathematical structure. Evan Parker described the additive (and subtractive) nature of the piece as "A 65 note melody played in the form 1, 1 2, 1 2 3, 1 2 3 4 [and so on until you get to] . . . 65", at which point the players play the whole line, then repeat the process in reverse playing from "2 . . . 65, 3 . . . 65 . . . [and so on to the last note]."[754] Once that cycle is complete, the players are to hold the last note until everybody has caught up, and then begin a spontaneous improvisation together, hence the use of these leading free players in the performance. The angular nature of the melody and the complexity of the counting means it is deliberately very difficult for the players to maintain the unison throughout, so Rzewski gives a very "jazz-like" instruction: "If you get lost, stay lost!" Kenny later recalled playing the piece himself: " . . . the problems he posed were really absorbing, like the piece where you had to play 100 bars [actually 65 notes] straight, and then play them backwards. But I don't compose music like that . . ."[755]

This last statement may not be strictly true. Kenny does, in fact, in at least two very notable compositions, utilize exactly this kind of additive, or "developing variation" technique. On the ending of his *Heyoke* suite the following year, and the "Opening" chorale of *The Sweet Time Suite* a few years later, he uses a modified version of this device to wonderful effect. Whether or not it was as a direct result of this encounter with Rzewski's music, or more broadly as a result of his formal composition lessons (possibly dating as far back as his study in Canada with serialist John Weinzweig), we don't know – but he certainly embraced the technique and made it his own on more than one occasion.

However profound or significant this meeting of musical genres, the jazz musicians were never above poking a little fun. As they worked their way through the piece Evan paraphrased Marshall McLuhan, quipping, "The *tedium* is the message!"[756]

The early '70s represented a new-found period of belonging for Kenny. He had assembled his musical family and his sense of place in the jazz community. Even though many of the older (at least musically speaking) generation had welcomed and admired him, his own dissatisfaction with his music and his playing had rendered him unable to feel at home in any one of those scenes. He even described it as such some years later: "I was going through a bad mental period . . . I mean, I was quite happy in some ways 'cause I was studying and writing . . . but I still couldn't find my place, you know?"[757] By this time, all the turbulence of his frustrations with pure bebop had settled; he had engaged with free jazz and managed to consolidate his parallel musical worlds through the discovery and considerable influence of Booker Little. He still experienced ongoing battles with nerves and self-confidence, but those issues were never really at the heart of what had dogged him throughout the '60s. The fact was that, through the Old Place, the Little Theatre Club, his

BBC and European broadcasts, the commercial recording sessions, and his own writing and arranging, he had found himself; doing all these different things actually *was* what made him who he was. So with everything settling in place, the time was right for him to commit to documenting his newly formed artistic self, and that was exactly what he did in January 1973. Such was the role and presence of Dankworth in the story of *Windmill Tilter* that it was his next project, *Song for Someone*, that was truly his first album as a leader.

———·———

John Taylor compared Kenny's approach to writing *Song for Someone* with Duke Ellington's well-known aesthetic of composing for specific people rather than a prescribed instrumentation. He described the project as "the first time Kenny had written for an ensemble made up of individual soloists with whom he had a close musical connection, rather than a conventional big band . . ." or for that matter, somebody else's big band – as had been the case with the Dankworth orchestra.[758] Kenny stated this intention on the back sleeve of *Song for Someone*:

> The idea behind this band was to try to get special musicians from and into different areas of jazz to play together and to try to write music especially for them. That is, the thought of the musicians came first and then the music.[759]

In many ways that statement alone is emblematic of Kenny's lifelong methodology and shows the importance he placed on the personalities behind the instruments. Kenny's old friend Ian Carr quite rightly summarized his concept, saying, "So it comes down to relationships *again*, that's really interesting, that's good!"[760] That *Song for Someone* is regarded as such a singularly defining moment of Kenny's artistic development is absolutely correct. With so little other material from the time available, this LP represents the culmination of his musical vision up to that point.

It is also important to note that history tends to hold aloft isolated milestones rather than frame them within the context of the artist's output at the time. Such is the case with the intensity of Kenny's work and growth over that period, as *Song for Someone* was in fact preceded by years of preparation and refinement. But what this LP encapsulates is unquestionably of great importance; it is Kenny's first hand-picked big band, embodying his concept of carefully balancing combinations of studio, conventional jazz, and free players.

> I thought I would like to have all my people I work with, and favourite people, in the band no matter what – whether they're Dixieland, free players or what they are . . . I mean I had Keith Christie and Derek Bailey, and I thought I better have some of the studio guys just for intonation and playing things right . . . so that's how that funny band [came to be] . . .[761]

It is noteworthy that these "combinations" are not only present at a personnel level. The same three elements – studio, jazz, and free – are also equally in balance within his compositions. They are also fully coalesced within his own playing, represented by the precision of his instrumental technique, the eloquence of his harmonic vocabulary, and the wails, squeals, and tumbles that come from his more recent explorations into the world of improvisation.

By delving a little deeper into his first BBC broadcasts, a clear picture emerges of how the conceptual groundwork for *Song for Someone* was laid in the preceding years. As we have established, the album is important because of the incorporation of free elements into his conventional big-band writing (absent from *Windmill Tilter*, aside from the single cadenza that sets up "Propheticape"), but these free intros were actually a device Kenny had begun to weave into his music as early as his first BBC broadcast back in May 1969. On that session, he added an improvised piano intro to start "Don No More", and on "D.G.S." he used a long, free duet introduction between John Surman's baritone saxophone and Tony Roberts's bass clarinet. On both those tunes he also used another idea where a certain soloist breaks down the time to morph into a completely free improvisation before the composition and rhythmic structures re-establish themselves for the next section of ensemble writing. Kenny used his improvisers as another compositional technique, adding variety and flow to navigate from one section of written material to the next and bringing in the vulnerable human element of risk into the music. As he described: "So I thought, well to write for [this new band] I can't write *all* conventional or *all* free, so I started to write this funny mixture . . ."[762] He expands on this even further on his second BBC broadcast in June 1970 where the *Some Days Are Better* suite includes free trombone solos that break up the form between regular groove and harmony sections, as well as an extended Mike Osborne alto solo which breaks out of nowhere into an almost free, burning "time-but-no-changes" section. There is also a substantial and virtuosic free interlude by bassist Ron Mathewson to segue between "Dallab" and the *Some Days Are Better* suite. This latter composition is also noteworthy because it is another early example of mixed-metre writing from Kenny. While the solo section stays in 4/4 with a tumbling "tag" section at the end of the sequence in 3/4 (a device he would more famously use on the *Gnu High* composition "Smatter" a few years later), the main theme is actually in mixed-metre groups of four and three. It is not simple writing. Given the short amount of rehearsal time they were given, it shows how ambitious and trusting Kenny was of the players in his new band. On that same 1970 broadcast, "Don No More" is revisited. Here, Norma Winstone, on what was her first broadcast as part of Kenny's big band, also provides a free solo interlude to segue from the ending of the previous "Sweet Yakity Waltz" and goes into a wordless version of the "Don No More" melody. It is also significant that Norma had written her own lyric to the melody which she sings on the tune at the end. This was her very first setting of words to Kenny's music and was the beginning of a special pairing – Kenny's melodies with Norma's lyrics – that would become intertwined from then on.[763]

These broadcasts also show Kenny beginning to revise and reuse his own material, experimenting by adding elements not present on the original versions in order to loosen things up. "I wanted to get the music to the stage where we could do a whole continuous set with no interruptions, so I decided to have free interludes between pieces," he explained, adding: "For me this worked very well, but I think that at the time audiences were a little confused by this."[764] This is an interesting development from the composed, small-group interludes he used between pieces on *Windmill Tilter*. The master tapes for *Song for Someone* reveal that they actually recorded a third tape (labelled "free links for use between tracks") but, following a few issues with the mix early on, Kenny decided not to use these on the final album.[765]

As his band performed more and he found himself increasingly in the role of reluctant bandleader, one cannot help but speculate as to whether this "continuous set" idea was for Kenny as much a mechanism to prevent him having to speak to the audience between pieces as it was a musical concept. The Irish bassist Ronan Guilfoyle, who would later know Kenny through his teaching at the Banff Centre in Canada, recalled a story from exactly this period that supports this theory. In the early '70s, Ronan was in the audience for an engagement Kenny played with a top local trio in a crowded and enthusiastic Dublin venue. After the gig, a member of the rhythm section told Ronan that:

> . . . after three tunes the piano player Noel [Kelehan], suggested to Kenny that he should maybe say something to the audience, 'cause he hadn't said anything and they were playing all [Kenny's] original music. So Kenny turned to the mic, as if to say something, stood looking at the mic for about 20 seconds and then turned back to the rhythm section and said, "I think I'm gonna get sick!"[766]

In addition to the musical techniques and concepts he used before, the *Song for Someone* tunes themselves also began to appear in his BBC broadcasts leading up to the album recording, albeit under different original titles – a habit he retained from the *Windmill Tilter* era.

Throughout this entire period, Kenny usually had one BBC broadcast per year, but in 1971 he was given two broadcasts with his big band. On the first of these, recorded 21 February for Humphrey Lyttelton's *Jazz Club*, Kenny performs the piece "Causes Are Events", which would appear on *Song for Someone*. (That composition had also already been used for a German radio broadcast in November 1970.) Interestingly, alongside the increased use of free jazz elements in Kenny's writing, and at the opposite end of the jazz spectrum, he featured the vocalist Bobby Breen on a few broadcasts, here singing an arrangement of "God Bless the Child". On the second broadcast that year, recorded on 13 May for Charles Fox's *Jazz in Britain*, the composition and soon-to-be title track of his new LP "Song for Someone" first appeared.[767] It is a haunting, searching ballad, with his trademark soaring melody line and consummate control of harmonic tension. But this first broadcast version has an extended swing section at the end of the main ballad form (which is otherwise the same as the LP) not included on the album version. On that broadcast they also performed a tune listed as "Micka" (or "Mickay"[768]), which appears on *Song for Someone* under the new title "Toot Toot".

Two further *Song for Someone* tunes got their initial outing on Kenny's next broadcast in 1972 for the BBC's *Jazz in Britain*:[769] "Ballad Two" and "The Good Doctor", under their original titles "Owt Dallab" (more typical wordplay) and "Council Sweet", respectively.[770] The only other composition to appear on the *Song for Someone* LP is "Nothing Changes". Since there is no record of it prior to the session itself, it may indeed have been written just for the recording. Norma recalls that when Kenny first asked her to write the lyrics, the piece was originally called "Eventually Yours",[771] but it is listed on the master tapes simply as "Song". Indeed, "Nothing Changes" is the only piece on the album that is more conventionally song-like. It is also another wonderful early example of Norma writing lyrics for Kenny's music – only her second setting of lyrics to his melodies after 1970's "Don No More".[772]

"Nothing Changes" has another interesting and rare quality in that he uses mutes in the brass to create different textural effects. Whilst there are momentary sections of straight mute in *Windmill Tilter* and a few pencilled instructions in the parts to play "in stand" or bucket mute, Kenny rarely wrote for muted brass. Neither did he use woodwind doubles in the saxophones the way so many other writers do. He later clarified the reasons for this, saying, "In my big band music, I don't use woodwind doubles or brass mutes mainly because I do few gigs, and when I do a gig, we don't have sound systems sophisticated enough to pick up these items." That last statement would have been certainly untrue in his later years when he was playing the best theatres and touring with his own sound-engineer, so it is more likely to have been motivated by what he reveals in his concluding statement: "Besides, I have always liked the full ensemble sound."[773]

Throughout these early 1970s broadcasts, not only the compositions for *Song for Someone* became increasingly fixed, but the personnel he uses also coalesces into a more consistent line-up. Another of the legacies from the Dankworth days shows itself in him sticking with a trumpet section of three, which from 1970 forms around the final *Song for Someone* section of Greg Bowen, Ian Hamer, and Dave Hancock.[774] The trombone section in these BBC years also forms around a core team comprising the final *Song for Someone* players Keith Christie, Bobby Lamb, and Jim Wilson on bass trombone, although Chris Pyne is also added to the section and Malcolm Griffiths plays bass trombone on one track on the album. Alfie Reece is the regular tuba player throughout this period. The use of tuba in the band is another interesting continuation from his Dankworth instrumentation days, but it is something Kenny persisted with throughout the '70s. Not until his early 1980s broadcasts did Kenny dispense with the tuba and settle on a more conventional trombone section, probably in response to an increasing amount of work as a guest with European groups where a typical big-band instrumentation was easier for them to accommodate. Mark Wheeler remembered how much his dad liked Alfie Reece, and how Kenny and Doreen would often have Alfie and his wife over for dinner. So it is possible Kenny wanted Alfie there in the band as much because he was a friend as it was a wish for that particular sonority; once again, *the thought of the musicians came first and then the music.*[775]

Strong echoes of Dankworth remained in Kenny's writing with his use of the "band within a band" approach. On these broadcasts there is a smaller group of soloists embedded into the larger band in place of a conventional saxophone section. The players vary occasionally on each date but by and large became a settled line-up that, on *Song for Someone*, included Kenny and Norma, Dave Horler on trombone, and saxophonists Mike Osborne and Duncan Lamont.[776] The rhythm section had become a more stable team made up of both John Taylor and Alan Branscombe on piano and/or electric piano. Although J.T. had speculated whether this use of two pianists was more a personal decision than a musical one, Kenny said that it was both:

> I wanted to have two piano players, and I thought, "Well, you can have." I mean, in those days I'd never heard of anybody who'd used two pianos before, ever. So why not have two piano players? Who says you can't have two? I wanted Alan Branscombe and John Taylor. I said, "Well, have both of them." This is me talking to myself, so I did but I'd never heard of anybody do it before that.[777]

In addition to the two pianists, bassist Ron Mathewson was a regular fixture. Kenny's musical intention behind the choice of drummer was always clear. Though he used another colleague from the free scene, Paul Lytton, in 1970, and Spike Wells once in 1973, it was Tony Oxley who was the primary sound in Kenny's mind and the drummer who would record on *Song for Someone*: "I wanted a very loose sound, good-quality music but . . . a very loose rhythm section, hence Tony Oxley."[778]

The free jazz personality within Kenny's small group of soloists – who instigated the whole project and made the recording possible – was Evan Parker. Kenny first used Evan in his big-band broadcasts as a guest improviser in 1971; in his recording from May of that year there is a piece featuring and dedicated to Chris Pyne and Evan called "CPEP".[779] Again, the inclusion of this piece and the use of Evan within the ensemble shows how much Kenny was embracing his new idea of bringing together the different musical areas of his life in the years preceding *Song for Someone*. It also shows in what high personal and musical regard he held Evan – a sentiment Kenny felt his entire life. "CPEP" has some distinctive compositional devices that Kenny didn't use very often in his later works. The piece is in two halves, the "CP" part being quite an uptempo tune on typical "Kenny" changes, culminating in a big pause chord at the end of Chris Pyne's trombone solo. Chris then sets off a curious little rising triplet figure, which is repeated among the band at the players' own discretion. (It's a rare example of Kenny including free or improvised elements in the actual ensemble parts, a device a composer like Graham Collier more commonly used.) Out of that transition the improvising focus shifts from Chris to Evan, who undertakes an intense and completely free duet with Oxley for almost two minutes (remember that all of this is in the middle of Humphrey Lyttelton's Radio 2 *Jazz Club*) before foreboding brass chords cut across the texture to a screaming climax. The end of this astonishing and uncompromising musical drama is met with a roaring cheer from the assembled studio audience.[780]

At the time, it was clear to listeners that Kenny was presenting bold and exciting new music, embracing a big-band concept encompassing the full scope of modern jazz of the era. It was from this point of view that Evan Parker instigated the recording of the *Song for Someone* album. Evan, along with Derek Bailey and Tony Oxley had founded the Incus Records label in 1970. Having successfully secured Arts Council funding for one project already (*Ode* by Barry Guy's London Jazz Composers Orchestra[781]), and with a shared love for Kenny's music, they obtained a grant for him to record. (How typical of Kenny's lifelong passive approach to his career that others were responsible for nearly every element in making one of his most important recordings.) Since the musicians had a connection with Olympic Studios and it was familiar to all of them, it was decided to record there.[782]

In later life Kenny would sometimes describe his music as being a balance of a "pretty" or "melancholy" tune, mixed in with an element of "chaos".[783] And occasionally, with this number of big personalities involved with him throughout his life, these chaotic elements would extend beyond the music and into life itself. The recording of *Song for Someone* included its fair share of those times. The first of two days of recording, 10 January 1973, got off to a rocky start when bassist Ron Mathewson failed to appear. Dave Horler said, ". . . that was a madhouse . . . Ron was late; they found him eating a can of cold beans on his bed at ten o'clock when we were supposed to start!"[784] Once they had actually started, the band opted for an unusual set-up in the room, with Tony Oxley's drums right in the middle, making it very hard to get any sort of separation on the recording. Adding to this difficulty was the engineers' early experiments with eight-track recording, as Evan explained:

> Well, nobody had much experience in the box – I mean, I knew where the box was and I knew what a desk was and I knew what faders were, but beyond that . . . Also, the engineer, he was the boss of Olympic, Keith

Grant, well Keith was a player himself, like a sort of semi-pro, rehearsal big band kind of guy, and he had certain fixed ideas about how to [record] . . . eight-track was state of the art at that point, and nobody really knew quite how to use eight tracks – in one sense, it wasn't enough, and in another sense, it was more than anybody was used to.[785]

The physical set-up in the room created its own challenges, in terms of being able to hear each other and in terms of the "spill" into each other's microphones. The volume of sound in the room coupled with the inability to isolate individual sections of instruments led to some loss of detail in Kenny's contrapuntal writing. Norma remembered that "Tony [Oxley] didn't want to be behind [acoustic] screens, you see; he said he just couldn't play like that. He wanted to be out in the middle of the room, so of course he was [heard] in everybody's microphones."[786] J.T. recalled the effect it had, too, saying, "That original recording suffered because of that, because I think the set-up made it impossible to get the clarity that was necessary, simply because they'd bunged us rhythm section [players] right in the middle of the band."[787] The difficulties of the set-up were compounded by the way the engineer decided to group the channels on the eight-track recording, as Evan described:

> So you've got some quite strange decisions being made to do with assumptions about phrasing. For example, "put the lead trumpet on the same track as the bass drum channel, because they always hit the accents together", that was the kind of thinking – which is reasonable enough if it was that kind of big band, but . . . when it came to [the mix], a lot of Kenny's inner voices weren't really there.[788]

There was another consequence of Kenny's decision to bring these different players together from such dissimilar scenes: although it was conceptually exciting, it also meant that the band would sometimes disagree with each other's musical approaches. Tony Oxley's much looser style was a departure from the conventional way of drumming that most of the brass players were accustomed to; he also had an unorthodox drum kit which included various "pots and pans".[789] Oxley's inclusion was a very conscious choice by Kenny, though, and exactly what he wanted in the music. He explained:

> The drummer I had was Tony Oxley . . . he's a great drummer, but he doesn't conform at all, he's very loose . . . I loved the effect of it, the whole looseness of this big band . . . having more like a quartet rhythm [section] feel than a tight feel. I couldn't stand that tight big-band feeling. I liked the idea of good-quality big-band music played very loosely – I guess getting more towards Ellington, a bit.[790]

It just so happened that, at least to begin with, the looseness reached a point where the brass players found it nearly impossible to feel the "time" at all. Kenny explained further: "For these session guys, it was very difficult, playing in a band like this, a combination of inside and a lot of outside playing. The drummer never gave you 'one'. It used to be really funny to look at all their feet going in different places. *I've got 'one'! I've got 'one'!*"[791]

During the session, these differences of approach eventually boiled over into a row when tuba player Alfie Reece finally spoke up. Evan paraphrased the exchange going something like this:

> *Alfie*: Tony, you couldn't give us a little bit more "two and four" or a clearer "one" or something, just so we know where we are? It's quite tricky, this music.
>
> *Tony*: What?! I'm not here to be your fucking metronome! If you can't count you shouldn't fucking be here![792]

Even though this reads like a heated exchange, everyone's recollections were relayed with a sense of humour rather than implying conflict. With a vast amount of big-band experience himself, Dave Horler had an interesting take on Tony's retort: "He was wrong there: he *is* supposed to be the time-keeper." He nonetheless conceded, as he recollected this mix of worlds: "I didn't like the free stuff much in those days, [although] I got to like it a bit better later on. But I was wrong, you know. Kenny *was* right – it's very exciting."[793] Lead trumpet player Greg Bowen observed: "The thing is, with all his pots and pans and things, Tony [Oxley] also had fantastic 'time' [feel]. That's what I liked, you know – all of a sudden, he'd play some time and everybody would go, *Oh, wow!*"[794]

Tony was a great musician, of course, so he wasn't oblivious to the phrasing. The piece "Causes Are Events" is a particularly clear-cut mix of free and conventional big-band writing. There are different instrumental combinations in the improvised sections, interspersed with almost straight-ahead swing writing at times – including an angular bebop-ish line which Norma sings with incredible ease and accuracy. In the midst of all this exchange between "improv and reading", there are occasional moments where Tony's drum fills cut right across a big brass entry, at the one moment they could have used a conventional set-up – but, again, without these moments it wouldn't be the same record. This is the combination Kenny wanted and it was simply different from what some of the players expected. In a last word on the matter, Dave Horler further explained the challenges that Tony's style of playing created for the other musicians:

> . . . It's very exciting; the free stuff and the mad drumming and all that – it *can* be very good, but it's very difficult to play . . . because [the] drummer hasn't got any idea of how difficult it is, as a brass player, to hit a high B♭ in the right place if [he's] hitting fucking saucepans![795]

Far more important than these momentary conflicts – and the amusing exchanges that came as a result of Kenny's concept – is the extraordinarily fresh music that the musicians committed to tape. This of course is what really matters when telling the story of Kenny's musical achievements. He was always more comfortable speaking positively about his writing than he ever was about his playing, but, even so, it is striking just how confident and enthusiastic he was when describing this period and his first proper big band. Kenny said, "I loved the general effect. I thought it was great: much different from anything I'd heard from anybody else anywhere."[796] Recognizing his own innovative concept, he said, "I never thought, 'Well, I'm doing something new here.' But I guess it was new . . ."[797] There was, however, one final practical hurdle to overcome, and that was to mix it.

With the complications already described in the way the channels were grouped on the eight-track, and the amount of audio spill across all the microphones, Kenny wasn't satisfied with the first mixes. Evan recalled:

> . . . [these were] the kind of problems we had; sometimes it was awkward to separate the drums out from the trumpets – [maybe] one needed to be louder and the other quieter, or it was sometimes the other way around – we needed separation . . . it took quite a lot of work to rescue it to a standard that Kenny was happy with.[798]

To do that they sought help from Bob Cornford, a person Kenny respected and was pleased to have on board, since he normally didn't involve himself much in the post-production. Evan said: ". . . there was no question that we had to find some time somewhere to do another mix. And that's where Bob Cornford's experience came in, and Bob's ear. Bob's ability to read a score, you know, [was] in a different league from anything I could do."[799] Through Bob they secured some time at another studio to remix the album. Evan continued:

> We couldn't do it [again] at Olympic; it would have been too embarrassing for somebody. So we took them to a studio called Advision, where they also had eight-tracks very early on. So there were limitations on our room for manoeuvre, if you like, but Bob sorted all that . . . Basically he took over . . . I just sat there and watched and tried to pick up a few tips. So we scraped by, and it's the record it is.[800]

That wouldn't be the end of Bob Cornford's involvement with the band; having saved the mix, he later conducted Kenny's next BBC broadcast for *Sounds of Jazz* in October 1973. Incidentally, both that broadcast and the one a year later in November 1974 included Kenny's uptempo swing piece "Ticketeeboo" – a composition that would feature again some years later on his 60th birthday tour.[801]

With all Kenny's confidence in his big band of the early '70s, and given how highly regarded both the group and the bandleader were at the time, it is both surprising and perhaps indicative of Kenny's inability to promote his career that they did hardly any live performances outside of the BBC broadcasts. In fact, in the nearly ten years from when he first recorded his big-band music with *Windmill Tilter* until he finally undertook an Arts Council tour with his own band in 1978, the Kenny Wheeler Big Band did a total of three live performances – all in London. As a result, by the time his unique band and music were properly heard outside the capital or on the BBC, Kenny was almost 50 years old.

The first two of those three live gigs were around the time of the *Song for Someone* recording. On 8 January 1973 the band played as part of a series called *Fanfare for Europe* at the Cockpit Theatre, just two days before recording *Song for Someone*. The next time they played a concert was nearly two years later in December 1974 at the Seven Dials, a pub venue in Soho run by the Jazz Centre Society.[802] Given just how few gigs Kenny ever did with his band, the Seven Dials evening has its own typically "Kenny-ish" twist, as described by Ronald Atkins in his *Guardian* review: "It is so typical of Kenny Wheeler to be given a concert of his own and then to feature himself only in the second half." Atkins goes on to explain how Kenny had given over the first set to two small groups led by Norma Winstone and Ian Hamer:

> The band he led at the Seven Dials, Shelton Street, made its debut two years ago. Since then, a record (Incus 10) and a couple of broadcasts (one to be relayed in a week or so) is about all we have heard under the name of one of the most gifted and undoubtedly self-effacing of our jazzmen.[803]

The review goes on to praise the playing of some of the other band members, including Mike Osborne, Malcolm Griffiths, and Stan Sulzmann, the latter by now a regular fixture in Kenny's bands. They had become colleagues through their various sideman and studio work as well as in J.T.'s sextet, in which Kenny had already expressed his admiration for Stan's playing and musicianship.[804] At this period in his big band, Kenny was still sticking with the inherited configuration from the Dankworth days – the group of mixed instruments comprising Kenny, Norma, and usually Dave Horler or Malcolm Griffiths on trombone, plus two saxophones – instead of the usual saxophone section. Mike Osborne was being increasingly replaced on alto by Ray Warleigh, and Duncan Lamont's tenor role was turned over to Stan Sulzmann and became a soprano and baritone chair. The use of additional featured players such as Evan would continue as needed, but was not part of the default orchestration concept.[805] It was only later on, when Kenny began to get commissions from European big bands, that his line-up morphed into the conventional five-piece saxophone section – but he always retained himself and Norma as an augmentation to the standard big-band instrumentation: the final iteration of Dankworth's "band within a band" concept.

It must have been a challenge and even a disappointment for Kenny that his big band was sometimes perceived to fall in the crack between two categories. He often referred to it being "slightly in the middle . . . again, to put labels on it, the 'free jazz' people would say it's 'too far in' and then 'in' people would say it's 'too far out'."[806] It was a sentiment he elaborated on further in a conversation with Evan Parker some years later:

> I suppose I always considered myself *really* a "jazz" person, and then I started to break some of the boundaries I suppose when I met all you guys with that first big band – [but] I never felt I could go *too* far because I wanted to still keep known as a sort of a jazz player you know? To go the way, for instance, and write like Barry [Guy] – or try and write like Barry which I probably couldn't anyway – wouldn't have been, for me, right in my head, you know what I mean?[807]

One particularly harsh criticism appeared in *Crescendo* magazine and described the Arts Council support of *Song for Someone* as a "waste of taxpayers' money" – which made Kenny laugh at first but later made him angry.[808] As often when reviewing Kenny, critics would give with one hand and take away with the other. In the aforementioned *Guardian* review of the 1974 Seven Dials gig, Atkins explained that the earlier 1973 performance at the Cockpit Theatre had combined the freer elements much more, whereas on this occasion the band "never strayed far from the orthodox". He finishes with a compliment, though, writing that Kenny's solos "showed yet again why we rave about him".[809]

For Kenny, all this punditry led to a complicated and not altogether trusting relationship with critics for the rest of his life. Ultimately, he also felt like his concept of combining his two musical identities wasn't totally embraced by listeners: "I'd probably be still writing to this day that kind of music if it had been accepted, but it tended to be noticed more for the free playing than for the melancholic melodies." Kenny also acknowledged a secondary factor: "I started to go abroad and work a little bit at the radio stations, and they wanted more, not conventional music, but stuff that their band could play . . . so that's why that kind of thing has petered off."[810] So, it is parodoxical that, while the European big bands provided valuable work, they also dictated something of a dilution of his original concept and the need for a more conventional instrumentation. This is yet another reason why those early BBC broadcasts and the *Song for Someone* LP are so important in understanding the evolution of his big-band writing.

In fact, the details from this period are crucial to an understanding of Kenny's later and more well-known big-band composing. One needs to contextualize it within the framework of his original, straightforward intentions: to include both the free and conventional sides of his music, and to do so in a band of his closest friends and colleagues. This was, after all, something he arrived at full of conviction at the coalescence of one his most profound periods of development. He later said: "To me jazz has always been a medium through which to express yourself, and in my own playing and composing, I try not to deviate from my own idea of what jazz is."[811] In an interview with Mark Miller shortly after the release of *Song for Someone*, he was asked if he was happy with the result: "Yeah, I'm often pleased with things I write but never with anything I play. I don't know what's behind all that. I suppose if I ever got to like my own playing I'd give up." When asked if he was writing for the individuals, he responded, "I try to, yeah, I wouldn't put myself in that class [referring to Ellington] but I try to do that . . . and it does work . . . with the big band I write for, it's got to be now that I don't think I could find many different players to make the music sound the same."[812] In a later interview, Miller also pressed Kenny about this mix of the two musical worlds, asking, "Which is the real you?" He replied, "I don't know. I like mixing them up, I really do."[813]

Throughout this time, the creativity and experimentation that was going on in London – to which Kenny was central – was gaining notoriety in Europe. Some of the European radio stations, especially Hamburg's NDR, were engaging more British players in their *Jazz Workshop* series, creating cross-continental collaborations of like-minded musicians. There was also a particularly burgeoning free improvisation scene in Germany, and it was within that movement that Kenny would receive increasing recognition and employment over the next chapters of his life.

<hr>

As far back as 1969, in the early years of the Spontaneous Music Ensemble and the British free jazz movement, Kenny was getting invited to Germany for various radio sessions alongside some other well-known English players from the contemporary scene. Admittedly, he had been invited to Europe even earlier than this for the Friedrich Gulda projects, but that was still very much in a sideman/section player capacity; now, he was a fully fledged soloist at the forefront of the new musical vanguard. The NDR Jazz Workshops led the way in inviting players from the London scene to perform and collaborate in their Hamburg studios. Originally the inspiration of NDR's Hans Gertberg and the Swiss composer Rolf Liebermann, the Jazz Workshops were established in 1958 and designed to bring musicians together who might otherwise not have collaborated, giving them a platform to "develop their art free of commercial pressure" over a generous seven days of rehearsal.[814] The resulting concerts were recorded for broadcast, and later also filmed for German television. One of the first of these workshops to feature Kenny as a principal soloist was the Jazz Workshop led by John Surman in 1969.[815] The session was filmed in black and white in the NDR's Studio 10 on 18 April 1969 and released decades later on DVD by Cuneiform. That (released) recording features mostly Surman's compositions, plus one each by two Austrian musicians who had been invited to join the workshop; but Kenny also contributed his ballad "Dallab". John Surman explained:

> The process was: you went there for a week and you worked in the big studio. Somebody was the leader, sometimes they brought the bulk of the material, but other people brought compositions as well; you'd be invited to bring a piece for whatever the line-up was. I know from the session that's on Cuneiform Records that I was consulted – Gertberg pulled me to one side after one of the other ones I'd done and said, "We'll do one around you, who would you like?" And I made some suggestions, it *certainly* would have been Kenny and Skid [Alan Skidmore] and Ozzie [Mike Osborne] and my rhythm section. I think Gertberg thought that Ronnie [Scott] would be a good addition and I felt that would be fine, too, and then of course he brought in the two guys from Austria, who I didn't know about, Erich Kleinschuster [trombone] and Fritz Pauer [piano]. So you know, the leader would be consulted and then I brought the material, but others [did too] and Kenny brought this beautiful ballad, God, he plays on that and it's just astonishing.[816]

The video is a wonderful document of some of the significant forces in the British scene playing at the height of their powers, and Kenny showing all his breadth, immaculate as ever on the written material and on his blistering improvisations.

Kenny was back at the NDR Jazz Workshop studios with Surman on 7–12 December 1969, but this time to be reunited with Austrian pianist Friedrich Gulda in a sextet with bassist Barre Phillips, guitarist Pierre Cavalli and drummer Klaus Weiss. The sextet performed Gulda's compositions: all dedications to other musicians, including "To John Coltrane", "To Albert Heath", and "To João Gilberto". At some point in the months between the April '69 session and this one in December the studio equipment must have been updated, as this session (as well as being superbly recorded) is also filmed beautifully in colour – resulting in what must certainly be one of the earliest examples of quality colour footage showing Kenny playing in a small-group setting: a fascinating bit of film as he approaches the peak of his artistic development. He also looks unbelievably youthful in his buttoned-up blue shirt and brown corduroy suit, especially when you remember he is actually five months older than the far more aged-looking Gulda. To put this event in full context, December 1969 is actually just weeks before Kenny's 40th birthday, a mere 18 months since he recorded *Windmill Tilter/Karyōbin* and only six months after his own debut BBC broadcast as a leader – so it is a critically significant time for him. Despite all the self-confessional accounts of his struggle with performance nerves, one is immediately struck by how at ease he looks. He is so poised in his playing: a weirdly cool, still and balanced stance with his left foot slightly forward, totally relaxed in his delivery on trumpet and flugelhorn. There are lots of great close-ups on his chops showing the security of his embouchure, and how the simple efficiency of breathing and blowing freely created this enormous tone with no visible force or apparent effort. Even in his forays into the upper register, Kenny's quiet confidence and authority abounds, and there's hardly any movement of his chops at all in his now trademark fluid octave slurs: a textbook-worthy level of efficiency on the instrument that is the gold standard for trumpet players in any style.

The music is also a curious mix of styles. "To John Coltrane" has a very "tripletey" swing feel, "Gilberto" is, unsurprisingly, in a Latin-ish groove, "Heath" an uptempo swing, and they finish with a flat-out rock 'n' roll blues called "To the New People". This last is a slightly disconnected mix of straight-ahead conventional jazz and wild free moments in the solo or group improvisations, but without anything in the compositional structures that particularly helps prepare or contextualize the duality. This must have been something Kenny was aware of as he more successfully balanced these elements in his own writing during the *Song for Someone* period, carefully crafting the framework for this duality within the music. Nevertheless, the footage presents a great opportunity to hear Kenny take on these different styles as a soloist, and the uptempo "To Albert Heath" is particularly interesting when you compare it with the Dankworth "Mark 1" footage from *Jazz 625* five years earlier. In 1969 his more developed, refined approach sits confidently alongside the otherwise straight-ahead swing accompaniment. What had previously felt occasionally incongruous or out of step with the context now bristles with so much conviction and flow that it just *works*, in spite of his detachment from the bebop vocabulary one might expect to hear.

After the Friedrich Gulda session finished, Kenny, John Surman, and Barre Phillips headed to the southwest of Germany. They began a three-day workshop from 12–14 December 1969 at the Baden-Baden Free Jazz workshop, led by the great American avant-garde trumpeter Lester Bowie. The group was quite a historic gathering of influential improvisers from the European and American scenes. Bowie, himself leading the large ensemble, was joined by colleagues from the Association for the Advancement of Creative Musicians (AACM) and the Art Ensemble of Chicago, including saxophonists Joseph Jarman and Roscoe Mitchell and drummer Steve McCall. Kenny and Surman were joined by fellow Brits Alan Skidmore and Tony Oxley, and esteemed European colleagues including Albert Mangelsdorff, Gerd Dudek, and Palle Danielsson, who were all musicians with whom Kenny would do much more work in the coming years. Soon after Baden-Baden there was another noteworthy NDR session: in January 1970, he was back with Howard Riley and Tony Oxley for "Convolution", named after a Riley composition. That group featured fellow trumpeter Manfred Schoof and Evan Parker, Derek Bailey, and the double double-bass team of Jeff Clyne and Barry Guy.[817]

As it happens, Lester Bowie was not the only celebrated American avant-garde trumpeter Kenny was invited to work with around this time. Two years after the project with Bowie, Kenny would again head to Europe for a different project with a big band led by Don Cherry (the trumpeter who had risen to fame as part of the Ornette Coleman quartet) and the noted Polish composer and conductor Krzysztof Penderecki. The piece had originally been written for the Globe Unity Orchestra with the intention that they would perform it in Berlin the year before, but Penderecki failed to deliver the scores in time for the rehearsals.[818] So, in the end, the double album was recorded live by Southwestern German Radio (Südwestfunk) at the Donaueschingen Music Festival on 17 October 1971.[819] The first set of the concert features music by Don Cherry, and the second includes the work *Actions for Free Jazz Orchestra* by Penderecki. This ensemble showcases yet another stellar line-up of European jazz names, including trumpeters Manfred Schoof from Germany, the Polish trumpeter Tomasz Stańko, as well as iconic figures like Peter Brötzmann, Han Bennink, and Kenny's fellow Londoner Paul Rutherford.

These opportunities on the Continent and the general recognition of the developments in London's jazz scene were by no means unique to Kenny. For example, on the opening day of the Berlin Jazz Festival on 1 November 1972, the programme was turned over to an event called *London Music Now*, celebrating a snapshot of the contemporary British jazz scene. The concert opened with the Tony Oxley Sextet followed by a duo with Evan Parker and Paul Lytton, a trio version of Paul Rutherford's ISKRA 1903, the Howard Riley Trio, a solo set from Derek Bailey, and then all the performers brought back together in the form of the London Jazz Composers Orchestra to close out the concert. The opening and closing bands featured Kenny, the latter including his composition "What's Parker Beckett to Me Mr. Riley". (The title is another piece of wordplay dedicated to and named for the featured soloists, Trevor Watts, Evan Parker, Harry Beckett, and Howard Riley.) An interesting and unusual piece for Kenny, it was clearly written for that ensemble specifically. Unlike anything else he wrote around this time, it opens with free improvisation followed by pause chords that come in and out on cue, before a militaristic snare drum rhythm sets up written brass hits that launch the next free improvisation. Only halfway through does some regular "time" emerge to set up some more typical writing for the band. Even then, the music is free and disjointed, but it is all still clearly Kenny. It is a fascinating, episodic piece which serves as a great example of just how nuanced and considered his own compositional balance was when it came to integrating free music in his own big band, as this is far freer than anything he did for his own group in this period.[820] The whole event must have posed its own challenges, as many years later Barry Guy wrote to Kenny recalling the "intensely difficult rehearsals but rather fine concerts".[821]

Large-ensemble improvised music provided Kenny with the majority of his work on the Continent and beyond, and gave him even more exposure as a free player. Without question, the group through which Kenny received the most sustained attention in Europe was the only other improvising large ensemble at the time, led by pianist Alex von Schlippenbach. Schlippenbach had been commissioned to write a piece for the 1966 Berlin Jazz Festival combining Manfred Schoof's quintet, Gunter Hampel's quartet, and Peter Brötzmann's trio. "Globe Unity" was the name of the Schlippenbach composition for the occasion, and it became the working name for this core group of musicians that would later be enhanced with other European and American players.[822]

Kenny first joined the Globe Unity Orchestra in November 1970 for a performance at the Kongresshalle in Berlin, also recorded and released as the second part of the *Globe Unity 67 & 70* LP.[823] It was Manfred Schoof who had first told his old friend Schlippenbach about Kenny years before; they'd worked together in January of that year for "Convolution" and Kenny must have been fresh in their minds. Schlippenbach also recalled how some of the players from the Wuppertal scene, such as Peter Brötzmann, had more of a familiarity with the London players at the time than he himself did. However it came about, Kenny joined Globe Unity alongside trumpeters Schoof, Tomasz Stańko, and Bernard Vitet in an incarnation of the band that also included his SME colleagues Evan Parker, Derek Bailey, Paul Rutherford, and others. Alex von Schlippenbach remembered his first impressions of Kenny when he came into the group:

> Kenny, for me, was always a very modest, quiet guy. I admired him a lot because I'd already heard about his fantastic musicianship, but he did not speak so much. I was happy to have him in the band and everybody respected him a lot of course, but he was a very modest character – you could *feel* he knows everything about what was going on. And I was a bit surprised that he was so interested in this all-improvised music, because I knew he had this background in all this big-band business in England and had already played with very famous musicians, plus he was kind of a generation before me – even though he wasn't so much [old] already, he was already somehow established.[824]

Indeed, Kenny was very happy to be there. He frequently spoke about the way his involvement with the group further opened up his career beyond the UK, as well as being vaguely amused that it was via free jazz he was becoming so well known, often joking: "After many years of that, somebody said to me, 'Oh, I didn't know you played changes!'"[825] But the thing that stuck with him most throughout this period of playing free jazz was the same sense of "getting something out his system" that he'd felt in his Little Theatre Club days. He continued to be very open about how free music helped liberate his regular jazz playing, but also spoke directly about the experience in Globe Unity having a mixture of results:

> Sometimes it can be very good and other times it can be – nothing at all happens because we don't have any music, any key or anything, we just walk up to the stand and start playing which sounds horribly chaotic. And

that is what it can be sometimes, but on the odd time something good can happen, I find it a therapy for myself.[826]

Although playing with Globe Unity was an unquestionably a positive experience for him overall, he explained the group's somewhat chaotic approach to the material: "I enjoyed some of it, [but] I could have enjoyed it a lot more, I think. Often too many people played all the time and, you know what I mean, there wasn't enough space left for anything. That was my only main complaint, but I generally enjoyed the whole period of living at that time."[827]

However mixed his feelings could be about it, Globe Unity remained a steady source of employment for Kenny throughout the next decade and beyond. As well as regular concerts and broadcasts, he recorded six more albums with them before the end of 1975, including the acclaimed *Live in Wuppertal* in 1973,[828] and an ambitious larger-scale event in 1974 with the Globe Unity Orchestra and a full choir from the NDR.

There were two other German big-band leaders that Kenny was working with quite regularly throughout the early '70s: Kurt Edelhagen and trombonist Peter Herbolzheimer. He participated in a number of broadcasts, recordings, and concerts with both of their groups, including one broadcast with Edelhagen in March 1974 on which they included Kenny's composition "Owt Dallab". On one occasion, Kenny's new European career intersected with his London stomping grounds when Herbolzheimer's "Rhythm Combination & Brass" made a live recording[829] at Ronnie Scott's in May 1974.[830]

There is no doubt, however, that, among all the different European engagements of the time, one stands out for its significance with regard to Kenny's future. In November 1970, John Surman was invited back to the NDR to lead a "John Surman and Friends" project, which became known as "Conflagration" after the composition Barre Phillips contributed. They performed pieces by a few of the musicians, including a version of Kenny's "Causes Are Events".[831] The full line-up for this occasion was based around Surman's group "The Trio", with Surman, Phillips, and drummer Stu Martin. That core unit was enhanced by front-line players including Kenny, Alan Skidmore, and Mike Osborne from the UK, and European trombonists Albert Mangelsdorff and Eje Thelin.

The group was completed with the addition of an American band which Dave Holland had established with Chick Corea, initially as a trio with Barry Altschul. When that trio added saxophonist and composer Anthony Braxton, it became established as "Circle" in a quartet formation, and it was the full four-piece group that participated in this NDR project. Braxton and Kenny's first meeting during this "Conflagration" project led to a working relationship over the next six years that brought Kenny to an even more international audience, especially in North America.

With his Circle rhythm section of Dave Holland and Barry Altschul, Braxton first formed his quartet with Kenny just three months after their

Photo 20: Kenny playing with Anthony Braxton's quartet, Montreux Jazz Festival.
Courtesy Harry Monty

first meeting. They convened for a recording in London's Polydor studios on 4 February 1971. Four of the compositions they recorded on this occasion would form part of the LP *The Complete Braxton*.[832] It was an experience he would look back on with fondness and gratitude, and even perhaps a bit of rare self-satisfaction. "Playing with Anthony Braxton was for me a great experience," Kenny said. "Dave Holland and Barry Altschul were in the band . . . [so] you could do whatever you wanted, but in a sense, you weren't completely free – you had to follow a bit – [Anthony's] conception."[833] As well as being highly conceptual, Braxton's music featured long, angular lines which were unbelievably difficult to play on the trumpet and provided Kenny with some of the most technically challenging repertoire of his career. As usual, Kenny played down how he coped with the challenge, saying, "I think he was impressed at the attempt I made to play it, anyway!" while acknowledging, "I did practise a lot, yeah."[834] Dave Holland confirmed the truth of this when recounting how far Kenny went in order to master that music:

> [Kenny] worked hard . . . He put so much time into learning it. I mean the time he spent on Braxton's music – because Braxton wrote these absolutely unforgiving lines for the trumpet – and Kenny, you know, Kenny just did it! I think even Braxton was surprised . . . I mean we were all . . .

because he would just write what[ever] he felt . . . but then Kenny would actually play the whole thing.[835]

Braxton's decision to use Kenny had not come out the blue. He recalled how he had first heard Kenny when Dave had played *Karyōbin* for him:

> It was a recording of John Stevens, an LP with Dave Holland, Evan Parker, and Kenny Wheeler . . . it was my first opportunity to hear Kenny, and I was struck immediately by his sound – which is such an incredibly beautiful sound – and how unique his rhythmic logics were. And there were two or three recordings, I think, that Dave turned me on to.[836]

The other recording he is referring to was *Windmill Tilter*, something Dave Holland was so proud to have recorded before leaving the UK that he would play it for friends. Saxophonist Dave Liebman also recalled Dave playing *Windmill Tilter* for him in New York in 1969: "On one of our hangouts he said, 'Oh, do you know this Kenny Wheeler?' and he put that on . . . I never heard big-band [writing] like that in my life . . . I was like, you know, *Who is this guy?*"[837]

Following their first meeting in Hamburg, Braxton described how he felt a "kindred connection" with Kenny and they became friends:

> Kenny Wheeler was a wonderful man – an incredible musician. As a person, he was as sensitive with depth as his actual playing. He really *was* his music . . . I was blown away with [him] and I came to understand that this would be a person that I would like to have considered play into a group that I wanted to form after Circle . . . [Kenny] had been on my mind from the beginning, as far as asking whether he would be interested or not, in coming into a quartet situation with me, Dave Holland, Barry Altschul and himself – and that the quartet would be a quartet that would be my quartet, playing my music. I made that clear to everyone. And I was very fortunate and lucky that Kenny was open to doing it.[838]

When Braxton was in London for the 1971 recording, he visited Kenny at the Wheelers' Ramsey Street home to discuss his group, and music in general. Mark Wheeler remembered the visit and how Braxton was "a lovely guy, very gently spoken". He was so gentle, in fact, that despite being invited he was anxious not to disturb the family at home, and so tentatively waited at the door trying to more subtly get their attention. Mark recalled:

> I remember that, yeah, because it was almost like an animal scratching at the door, and it kind of went away, and it started again . . . it was like a two-glass panel . . . I said, "Oh look, there's a man – that must be him!" and Anthony Braxton came in! . . . [Kenny and Braxton] just sat there chatting, and I thought I had some sort of grasp of music until I heard them two talking – and I thought, *Oh my God!*

The two Wheeler kids had become accustomed to strange and eccentric visitors to their family home by now. Kenny's daughter Lou remembered playing outside with friends once as they noticed a strange, bearded, bohemian-looking man approaching the block (recall that this was London's working-class East End) and she somehow knew deep down, *I bet he's visiting my dad* . . . Sure enough, the man ambled by them and marched straight up to their front door. (This time, the man in question was Evan Parker.) She recalled that it was nothing unusual anymore, and indeed the whole neighbourhood had become used to these comings and goings. Lou remembered the general feeling among her friends: "I think the kids took it as 'that's what they do, that's the Wheelers . . .'!"[839]

Despite the new Braxton quartet getting established at this point, there was something of a lull in activity before they became very busy later in the '70s. There were some live performances in France with two different configurations in 1973; in the summer of that year, a Braxton quartet with Kenny performed at the Châteauvallon Jazz Festival, but with Jean-François ("J.-F.") Jenny-Clark on bass, and Charles "Bobo" Shaw on drums. A review from this night described the concert:

> They played a suite especially written for this occasion. A piece that showed some of the aspects in the music of the multidirectional Anthony Braxton. Wheeler and Braxton matched each other beautifully, Wheeler is a musician who has much in common with Braxton, an intellectual player with a cool sound and a good ear for Braxton's intricate written lines . . .[840]

At the end of 1973, on 7 December, there was another French concert in Salle Paul Fort, Nantes, with yet another duo joining Kenny and Braxton: this time pianist Antoine Duhamel and bassist François Mechali. Some of that music would later appear on the *News From the 70s* album,[841] but it would be another couple of years before this relationship with Braxton became a more consistent and busy touring group.

—————·—————

There is a very good case to be made that 1970 was the most consequential year of Kenny's musical life: his meeting Braxton in Hamburg, the *DownBeat* poll, the first broadcast with Norma, joining Globe Unity, among other things. As remarkable an encounter as it was – when Kenny first met Braxton – there was in fact someone else present in the Hamburg studios that day who would have an even greater influence on Kenny's future. Dave Holland explained:

> Barre [Phillips] and I already knew each other, so on this break we just started something going, just improvising, free improvisation with each other. It was fun, and when we got to the end of the piece we were playing, a young man came up out of the audience. He was the same age as me, and introduced himself – he said, "I'm Manfred Eicher. I'm just starting

a new record label called ECM, and I really enjoyed what you guys just did. Would you have any interest in making a recording?" And Barre and I just looked at each other, you know, *He wants to record two bass players improvising – what is this?!* And of course we said, "Yeah – of course we would, that'd be great!"[842]

It was not only the beginning of a long and fruitful relationship for Dave and Manfred; Chick Corea had also urged the fledgling producer to "check out the soulful trumpeter" on the Hamburg project.[843]

# 5 Gnu High

**I mean, we all knew he was good, but I've never heard him sound quite as masterful as he does here.**

*Steve Lake,* Melody Maker

In June 1974, Kenny resumed playing with ensembles led by Anthony Braxton, beginning at the Moers Festival in Germany with the quartet including Dave Holland and Barry Altschul. That September, Braxton went into Generation Sound Studios in New York to record four compositions that would become part of the Arista LP *New York, Fall 1974.* In the liner notes for the album, critic Bill Smith calls Kenny "one of the most interesting of the current brass players, a Canadian musician now resident in England, where he is acknowledged as the leading exponent of new music, as well as being the most sought after session man in London, an unusual combination in this world of almost totally commercial music."[844] Although Kenny would argue with this description of his status at the "top" of the London studio scene, this quote acknowledges his versatility in a way that many other writers missed.

Later that fall, Kenny and Dave joined Braxton in Toronto at Burton Auditorium with a group including, among others, baritone saxophonist Roscoe Mitchell and trumpeter Leo Smith (now Wadada Leo Smith). This is the first time Kenny met Smith, a soft-spoken American trumpeter who would join him later for more Braxton projects, and invite Kenny to be part of his own ECM album in 1978. Smith recalled that Braxton had assimilated two different ensembles in Toronto, with himself in one group and Kenny in the other. They sat and talked, and Smith said that Kenny was "shy but not someone who wouldn't connect. We talked about music – Kenny liked orchestration and things like that. It's hard on the road to get to more serious or in-depth stuff . . . Our respect for each other was just based on being in the same environment."[845]

More work with Braxton's ensembles followed in California the following year, and then a longer period of rehearsals and performing in Europe during May of 1975, which included another appearance by the quartet at the Moers Festival. Being associated with these leading lights of the New York avant-garde meant Kenny was getting more attention than ever. One reviewer at Moers was particularly impressed with Kenny and drew an interesting comparison with his old London friend and bandmate:

Canadian trumpeter Wheeler was in super-form. He has excellent technique, creative imagination and fine taste. In a way he resembles Dave Holland: both are quiet, reflective on the outside, so that their sudden bursts of passion have breath-taking impact. Braxton has found the perfect companions and the festival could not have been brought to a better finish.[846]

Having completed one of the final Coe, Wheeler & Co. broadcasts for the BBC *Jazz Club* programme,[847] Kenny rejoined the Braxton quartet in June 1975 to rehearse for about two weeks at the Creative Music Studio near Woodstock, NY, in preparation for a concert at Studio Rivbea.[848] Rehearsals with Braxton were intense. In addition to the long hours he kept the ensemble together during that particularly hot summer, the music was conceptually challenging and technically difficult.[849] Smith described rehearsals with Braxton: "When you're doing rehearsals before the tour, you'd rehearse all day – you go in the morning like 9:00, go to lunch, come back, go all the way through, it's evening now . . ."[850]

The day after these rehearsals with Braxton finished, Dave Holland drove Kenny from his home in Woodstock to downtown Manhattan. As Dave and Kenny were headed to New York, pianist Keith Jarrett was also travelling to the city from New Jersey with ECM founder and producer Manfred Eicher. (The producer had just been helping Jarrett, who was his friend – and top-selling ECM artist – paint his house.[851]) Considering how physically and mentally exhausting those Braxton rehearsals must have been for Kenny, it is simply extraordinary that later that day he would make his first album for ECM, which became one of the most significant milestones of his career: *Gnu High*.[852,853]

———·———

There was a certain inevitability in the way Kenny's association with Manfred Eicher materialized into his own ECM album, since he was already working with many of the new ECM artists. Dave Holland and Barre Phillips had recorded their duo for the label following their introduction in Hamburg, and Evan Parker also recorded the fifth ever ECM release in August 1970 with the Music Improvisation Company, three months before Manfred Eicher had heard Kenny play. "I heard of him through the English musicians, through John Stevens, and others. I talked with Evan Parker, of course, I mean everybody was talking about the name. [So] I knew about Kenny, but the first time I'd heard him in the context of an ensemble was in Hamburg," Eicher said.[854] He was immediately struck by Kenny: "His phrasing, his tone, and his sound were really special . . ."[855] When Eicher heard more of Kenny on recordings, he was equally impressed by him as a composer:

> What I liked about Kenny was especially his writing. He had a different way of writing . . . I mean, his touch – it was different . . . he was not in any kind of neighbourhood of any of the favourite players I had around. I really liked that.[856]

Once they began to discuss making a recording, Kenny and Manfred had to choose a band for the album. They quickly agreed on Dave Holland and drummer Jack DeJohnette, whose playing Kenny loved. The issue of a pianist was more complicated, though. Manfred and Kenny had discussed using Chick Corea or even Herbie Hancock for the session, although Kenny had already thought to ask his friend John Taylor to play. According to Kenny, however, Eicher ultimately wanted Keith Jarrett to do the session.[857] Eicher remembers this slightly differently:

> I don't remember that he wanted to have John Taylor, but I remember that we talked about a few piano players. I had recommended – and it was very welcomed – that he would have Jack DeJohnette and Dave Holland. And I thought, since this is already kind of an American rhythm section . . . I asked Keith, because Keith was working with a different kind of thing and so we put this band together. It was not a band that Kenny was playing with in London with people such as John Taylor, this was something else. So I thought let's ask Keith, and Keith asked to send the music, and then he said to me, "Yes, I'll do it."[858]

Kenny eventually agreed, and accordingly had to phone John Taylor to let him know he was off the date: "Sorry John, but do you mind if I have Keith Jarrett on this one?"[859] There was a logic to Eicher's thinking: the rhythm section had a shared experience in Miles Davis's band, and Jarrett's own star was on swift upward trajectory at that time, having recorded the legendary *The Köln Concert* album for ECM[860] – the best-selling solo jazz album of all time – just a few months prior.

It is worth pausing at this point in the *Gnu High* story to acknowledge the influential album it became. It has attained an almost mythic or cult status over the years, not only as Kenny's ECM debut and for his own breathtaking playing and composing, but also for the presence of Keith Jarrett. A musician who became more enigmatic over the years, Jarrett withdrew from the wider jazz scene and mainly spent the last 30 years of his career playing either solo or with just two other musicians.[861] Even before the birth of his "Standards Trio", the opportunities to hear Jarrett as a sideman were very limited. Since *Gnu High* is one of the last times he would appear in this role, the prospect of him appearing in a (post-Miles Davis) trio alongside Dave and Jack, playing original music by Kenny, was truly compelling.[862]

With the personnel fixed, Kenny's recording was set for June 1975, at New York's Generation Sound Studios. Dave Holland received his parts in advance, as he did for all of Kenny's recordings, because he said he needed time to "decode" his difficult harmonies and also Kenny's somewhat spidery manuscript.[863] There is some disagreement, however, whether Jarrett received his music ahead of time or not. In agreement with Manfred, Dave Holland said, "I know [Kenny] at least sent Keith and I some music, and I think that he sent Jack music, too."[864] But Ian Carr, in his biography *Keith Jarrett: The Man and His Music* says that "Jarrett saw the music only a few hours before the session."[865] Jack DeJohnette also shared the recollection that Jarrett hadn't seen, or at least looked at, the music ahead of time: "Keith came in and read everything," he said.[866,867] Kenny agreed: "Manfred said he'd given him the parts but I've got a sneaking suspicion that he only looked at them, glanced at them, half an hour before the thing, you know, he just came in and ran straight through them."[868] Jarrett also seemed to imply that he had not received the music before the recording date:

> People may wonder how responsible I am to music when I get it – whether I just glance at it . . . this incredibly talented person who just glances at it and relates to it! But when I get music from somebody, even if it's a lead sheet, I'm doing a lot of work with it, and I'm very happy if people send me the music ahead of time. To me, that's the difference between possible disaster and at least an amicable scene . . . I felt very uncomfortable all during that session . . .[869]

Though professional, Keith Jarrett's demeanour during the session was cold. When Kenny arrived at the studio, the pianist was already seated, warming up. Although Kenny was the leader of the record date and roughly 15 years senior to his bandmates, he was hesitant to speak to Keith. He faced his nerves and walked over to the piano. Reaching out for a handshake, he said, "Hi, I'm Ken Wheeler." Jarrett barely looked up, silently raised a hand in a dismissive half-hearted greeting, and continued to play.[870]

Jack DeJohnette matter-of-factly confirmed Jarrett's lack of communication: "Keith came in, played the music, didn't say a word to Kenny, and when it was over, he left."[871] Dave Holland concurred: "Not much conversation went down with Kenny and Keith, as far as I remember. Keith was a little aloof, I would say."[872] Manfred Eicher supported this, saying, "There was not much talking, there was almost no talking," adding, "the response and the interaction happened inside the music, no matter what was talked about around it."[873] Kenny agreed: "Musically it was fantastic, socially, maybe not the warmest of occasions."[874] The session was chilly that day not just in terms of the vibe in the room but literally, as it was the middle of the heatwave and the studio's air conditioning had been on full blast: "It was kind of cool in there . . . and also the atmosphere!" Eicher joked.[875] Jarrett's attitude during the recording of *Gnu High* is no surprise to many of his fellow musicians. Fellow pianist Richie Beirach, himself a significant and influential force in the music of the time, commented: "It was staggering how great *Gnu High* was. I loved the music. And [Kenny] brought the best out of Keith," before joking, "Keith was a sideman, so he couldn't be an asshole, right? . . . I mean, he was *less* of an asshole . . . !"[876]

As if Kenny wasn't tense enough, Jarrett further increased the anxiety when he looked through the music and returned one of the pieces Kenny wanted to record. "I can't do anything with that one," he said, adding, "I've played tunes like that before and I can't play them."[877] "So I skipped that tune," Kenny said.[878] Based on Jarrett's demeanour and his own chronic self-doubt, Kenny assumed Keith's response meant he didn't like any of the music.[879] But Jarrett's reaction probably showed his own lack of comfort with the material more than it did his taste for or against it. Ian Carr made the pianist's thoughts clearer:

> . . . Jarrett was ill at ease himself partly because the music was not exactly his bag, and also because he was not too familiar with it. Kenny Wheeler's music is harmonically extremely rich and full of "vertical" chord changes – in other words, successive chords which imply very different scales – and to make sense of such music the chords and the improvisations need to be clearly related.[880]

Jarrett explained further:

> I had a lot of trouble trying to deal with playing those kinds of changes. That wasn't where I was at at the time . . . That album, *on paper*, didn't provoke my interest . . . It wasn't that I couldn't do them [the chord changes]: sometimes the structures were so inorganic and fully described that I wanted to make them something with round sides . . . and they would have these vertical messages every beat or two . . .[881]

This is an interesting – and accurate – observation of Jarrett's: Kenny's compositions during this time are indeed very harmonically specific and he often wrote more fully notated piano parts than was common in small-group jazz. This places the emphasis on the soloist to interpret and improvise on the specific harmonic landscape dictated by the composition, rather than imposing more open choices (Jarrett's "round sides") on a looser "sound-world" with traditional chord symbols. The magic would come from the players who could somehow find a way to do both – perhaps most notably John Taylor – and of course Jarrett himself once he started playing. Eicher agreed with Jarrett's observations, explaining that

> the music was maybe not exactly what Keith would have written himself, but he was immediately inside this music and really adding to and opening up the concepts in the music. Kenny is known as a writer who has a lot of [harmonic] ideas . . . so Keith was showing respect for the structure of the music but also introducing different ideas about phrasing, melodic flavour, and flow.[882]

It is perhaps too easy to criticize Jarrett for his behaviour on that session, especially when directed at someone as beloved, gentle, and seemingly vulnerable as Kenny. DeJohnette gets to the heart of the matter:

> I mean, to be fair, Keith agreed to do it. So there must have been something in Kenny's music that made him agree to do it, you know what I mean? Keith is not somebody who would accept something if he didn't like it. It's like him playing electric keyboards with Miles. Miles knew [Keith] didn't like electric instruments; he didn't like electric instruments but he played the shit out of them. Because he didn't like them, that's why he sounded so great on them, if you get what I'm saying. So, you know, Keith can be like that sometimes. But he came in and was respectful to the music.[883]

There was really no rehearsal prior to the *Gnu High* recording. "I guess Kenny had an idea of what the rundown was," Dave Holland said. "Kenny was a little shy in the studio . . . My impression was that he had a hard time telling Keith what he wanted, although decisions were made about how it would go, who would solo where, and things like that. He would say 'Is it OK?' He wouldn't be like 'Now, you do this, and you do that.'"[884] Jarrett said, "I wanted to kind of blend more and it was hard because [Kenny would say] 'Would you do a solo introduction on this?' – you know, 'Well . . . OK.' And I tried to deliver that music – not deliver where I was at at the time."[885] Eicher didn't intervene much, other than to occasionally give suggestions as to the overall shape of the music.[886] During the session, when asked by Eicher how he felt, Jarrett said, "I don't know . . . this is not my thing, you know."[887] Kenny admitted: "It was a little bit difficult, although I had allies because I knew Dave and Jack DeJohnette already."[888] Dave was aware of Kenny's nervousness and watched out for him throughout the session. "I wouldn't say I helped him get through it, but I definitely kept an eye on him, as we do," he said.[889]

Tensions eased once the tape began to roll. "The music had that feeling of discovery in the takes, because everybody's searching for things to do," Jack said. "What you hear is the spontaneity of the moment."[890] Dave described their approach, which might also have been a way to open up the music for Keith:

> What was interesting was that Jack and I always liked to mess with the time – and Keith liked to, too – so when we started improvising . . . it was fascinating how it developed, because the forms were still there, but rhythmically we were playing them in a really free way – so that the speed at which you were going through the form would remain the same, but we weren't dividing it up into beats. We were dividing it up into *spaces* – with kind of the underlying beat still being felt – but not necessarily being played explicitly. So it had this wonderful combination of the form and the shape and the harmony of the tunes, but then this really free kind of way of interpreting them.[891]

The first track, a 22-minute, three-part suite called *Heyoke*, brings together the best of Kenny's writing and playing styles of the time. The title of the work comes from the *Heyoka*: a character in Lakota Native American mythology, who uses the wind "to beat the drum of thunder. His emotions are portrayed opposite the norm; he laughs when he is sad and cries when he is happy, cold makes him sweat and heat makes him shiver."[892] It can't be a coincidence that this resonates with some of Kenny's own paradoxical sayings, most obviously *sad songs make me happy* – although when asked about the title he simply said that he was reading American Western novels during the period he was composing the piece.[893] Continuing this programmatic theme, Kenny said that he intended the opening phrases of the second part of *Heyoke* to evoke the foreboding sound of a bugle call from an approaching cavalry, coming to attack the Native Americans.[894] This section is likely an example of the music that Jarrett found so vertically oriented and specific. The harmonic structures here are difficult to describe within the confines of common jazz chord nomenclature. In fact, in his handwritten manuscript, Kenny doesn't even attempt to use conventional chord symbols for most of the movement, instead writing very specific harmonic voicings in a three-lined stave (solo line plus a grand staff), and indicating "Out of tempo" at the top of the page.[895] This part of the suite fuses seemingly disparate elements of Kenny's musical background in a remarkable way: marrying free jazz with strict harmonic structures. Jack DeJohnette emerges in the foreground to form a bridge into the third part of the suite, a very brief canonic movement employing a compositional method in which each cell – starting with two notes – is repeated and added to. As mentioned earlier, this technique may also have been inspired by Rzewski's "Les Moutons de Panurge" which he had played at the Proms the year before recording *Gnu High*.

The second composition on the album, alternately called "Smatter" (on the original ECM jacket) and "'Smatta" (in printed scores and in Kenny's manuscript) is a classic in the Wheeler catalogue. (The title comes from a colloquialism Kenny remembered from Canada, where "What's the matter?" became "S'matta?"[896]) Following a stunning statement of the melody and the first solo, Kenny's sparse final chorus – perhaps a result of confusion about whether or not he was finished – generates an extraordinarily imitative and beautiful conversation with Jarrett, who seems to complete Kenny's musical thoughts as they are formed. Another highlight of this track is Jarrett's astonishing contrapuntal elaboration of the melody, stated out of time after his solo.

Like *Heyoke*, the final selection on the album, *Gnu Suite*, is a set of different tunes. The first was originally labelled "Slobal" (an abbreviation of "Slow Ballad") and, like *Heyoke* (part 2) and "'Smatta", had appeared on BBC broadcasts the previous year.[897] The melody of the second part, originally called "Sip a Little Gnu", is technically very difficult to play on the flugelhorn. The rapid wide intervals, covering over two-and-a-half octaves, are challenging for even the most accomplished trumpet player. If nothing else, Kenny's stunningly beautiful (not to mention pitch-perfect) interpretation of the melody on this track alone should render the entire album worthy of a careful listen.

The legend is that *Gnu High* was made using only first takes, although Dave remembered it being recorded in "first or second takes".[898] During part two of the *Heyoke* suite, Kenny got lost during his solo and wanted another chance – especially after Jarrett had walked over to him to explain where he had gotten lost in his own tune.[899] But the rest of the band and Manfred, who liked the spirit of the take, convinced him to keep what he'd played anyway, which is what ended up on the recording. The entire record was completed in under six hours.

Written by Steve Lake (who would go on to work as a producer for ECM, including Kenny's final album), the *Melody Maker* review of *Gnu High* was glowing:

> Put simply, this is a breathtakingly beautiful album. These guys don't seem to touch the ground at all, but sail serenely overhead . . . there's not one lick here that one could describe as merely perfunctory, the consistency of invention dazzling. Kenny himself is the biggest surprise. I mean, we all knew he was good, but I've never heard him sound quite as masterful as he does here, gently nudging Jarrett aside to deliver lines of searing melancholy that would leave Miles at the starting post.[900]

Other critical reactions to *Gnu High* at the time were mixed. While universally enamoured with Jarrett's reluctant contributions to the recording, some critics found fault with Kenny's performance. *DownBeat's* Mikal Gilmore gave the record a positive rating (a substantial four stars); but while heaping praise on Kenny's substantial technique, he complains that "cleanliness, in this case, is too close to sterility. Wheeler's attack and dynamics are monotonously dispassionate, his colouring and sonority undilutedly dull. He has confused the virtue of facility with the vice of frigidity and consequently his presence in the ensemble proceedings inspires little more than tenuous support."[901] Gilmore offers a hopeful (if backhandedly complimentary) bit of counsel for Kenny's future outings, although seemingly unaware of his close connection to Dave: "Certainly Wheeler's talents deserve better than recording with musicians who are virtual strangers, regardless of their high-profile talent. He is a musician who performs best in larger, more familiar ensembles, and who badly needs the resonant foil of other horns."[902] Other reviews were similarly congratulatory to Jarrett and nonplussed by Kenny. The *New York Times*, in a review of several of Jarrett's recent recordings, gave mention of the record, referring to it with an amusing typo:

> Listeners who fancy Jarrett's more melodious moments may prefer "Gun High" by Kenny Wheeler, the trumpeter. The pianist is featured in a rare appearance as a sideman and he dominates the record rather decisively with his rhapsodic solos and lambent accomplishments. Even at

its prettiest, his playing here has the sort of intensity and substance one finds in his solo recordings . . .[903]

Despite its initially lukewarm reception by critics, *Gnu High* has garnered a great deal of praise in the years since its 1976 release. A 1989 ECM profile in the *Philadelphia Inquirer* called the album "a shining summation of the ECM sound . . . filled with intelligent, lyrical compositions that suggested an uncluttered approach to jazz improvisation".[904] *Billboard*, in a feature on Wheeler written over 20 years later, re-examined the album in an inset piece called "ReDISCussion". In his appraisal, Bradley Bambarger calls the album a "touchstone in modern jazz; a testimony to the artistic efficacy of thoroughness in conception and spontaneity in execution".[905] In a 2007 survey titled "1000 Albums to Hear Before You Die", the *Guardian* includes *Gnu High* (alphabetically between records by Kanye West and Barry White), praising Wheeler's "captivating, dolorous writing, pristine sound, and unique phrasing".[906] Perhaps even more significantly than the critical reaction has been how *Gnu High* affected young musicians in the years following its release. The album had a lasting impression on guitarist Bill Frisell and his colleagues at Berklee in Boston, where he'd also heard Kenny with Braxton's quartet a few years earlier. "I remember so clearly that *Gnu High* record . . . it became part of what school was about! Everybody was flipping out about this record, and we were all trying to play those songs, and it really had a huge impact . . ." He added, "it was rare to hear someone with that scope, or that imagination. There was no one like that, there never was or has been anyway . . ."[907] Seattle-based tenor saxophonist Steve Treseler has said that a friend once recommended *Gnu High* as a sort of "gateway drug" into Wheeler's output, hailing it as "the *Kind of Blue* of the '70s".[908]

Of course, Kenny could never accept such accolades. When asked about *Gnu High* by fans, he would say, "Oh, you mean *Old Low*?"[909] In fact, the album title itself was a self-deprecating parody of the style of album titles like Ornette Coleman's *The Shape of Jazz to Come*. "It was kind of a joke," Kenny said. "I mean, Americans probably would say, 'This is a *new high* in music.' But I've always liked animals, like goats and gnus, so I thought I would call it *Gnu High*."[910] He was, as always, dissatisfied with his own playing on the album and never forgot about where he claimed to have gotten lost in the *Heyoke* suite. He maintained that when his records were finished, though, "I never think about them. Sometimes I listen to them and think, 'Oh, I could have done that better' . . . [but] I still find it very hard to listen to a lot of my playing. I still cringe when I hear it."[911] Somehow Kenny was able to keep his self-criticism in better check when hearing his compositions. "The tunes I write I can hear a bit more often and think, 'Oh, that sounds like quite a nice tune.'"[912] Dave Holland recounted a final Kenny comment as the band was leaving the recording studio:

At the end of the whole thing, we were all packed up and ready to go – "So how are you doing, Kenny?" . . . he said [*sounding disappointed*] "I'm OK . . ." I said, "I thought it went really well!" Kenny replied, "Yeah, well, it would have been OK if I could have got a good rhythm section . . ."[913]

Photo 21: Kenny playing at the Montreux Jazz Festival as part of the Anthony Braxton Quartet.
Courtesy Harry Monty

During mid to late 1975, Kenny squeezed in one further BBC broadcast with his big band and was busy touring Europe and North America with the Anthony Braxton quartet.[914] Having toured Germany and Holland in May, and rehearsed extensively in New York in June, Braxton's quartet played at jazz festivals in Montreux and Antibes in July, did a week in October at the Five Spot in New York, and performed in Toronto in November. On 2 July, the group recorded an album for the Arista label called *Five Pieces 1975* in New York,[915] in the same studio where Kenny had previously recorded *New York, Fall 1974* with Braxton, and *Gnu High* a few weeks before.

Works such as the sombre "Opus 23E", the awkwardly swinging "Opus 23G", and "Opus 23H" (with Kenny's muted trumpet and Braxton on flute) exemplify the mature Braxton/Wheeler association. Although the language is angular and often unwieldy (especially in the ensemble portions of "Composition 23G"), the technical demands of the composed material on *Five Pieces 1975* are not nearly as unidiomatic for the trumpet as *New York, Fall 1974*, especially the fiendishly difficult, uptempo "Cut One"/"Opus 23B", with its thorny cascades of twisting chromatic lines. A video of the band at Montreux shows Kenny playing Braxton's trumpet parts from *Five Pieces 1975* confidently and calmly, with little movement in his embouchure or face except an eyebrow raised here and there for the high point of a phrase. Although Braxton admired Kenny greatly, his reaction to the trumpeter's technical mastery was less astonished and more a matter of course:

> He was a hard-working musician. You don't get to be a super-virtuoso on the level of a Kenny Wheeler unless you're not frightened of hard work. And this was a great master who was disciplined and always wanted to turn in a performance that was on the highest level. In that way he reminded me of Paul Desmond. He was really super-critical of himself, and totally wanted to do his best because he was very particular about his work.[916]

Braxton was also aware of Kenny's chronic dissatisfaction with his own playing:

> [Kenny] would play one of the most fantastic solos that I've ever heard in my whole life – and then later, after the concert, he would say, [*imitating Kenny's soft accent*] "Oh, Anthony, I'm sorry. I tried to do the best that I could do and I'm going to work harder" and I'm thinking, *How could someone possibly play better than what this guy just played?!* But he likes to erase himself out of the space, because he's a very sensitive guy, and he's not coming from an ego place. He's coming from a place of love and respect.[917]

The quintet's Arista recordings were very successful: sales reached 20,000, considered a major feat for a non-mainstream jazz artist. Radio stations played the records frequently, ranking them five times in the "Top Ten" playlists published by *Radio Free Jazz* between 1975 and 1977.[918] The ensemble was also praised by critics, even those who had reacted negatively to Braxton's earlier efforts. But Braxton became restless during this period. Michael Cuscana explained: "After six years, he felt that this group had reached its peak as a vehicle for his music and as an integrated performing quartet."[919] There were challenges with Dave Holland's and Barry Altschul's increasingly busy schedules, but perhaps the quintet's clearest obstacle was geography: Kenny lived in London while the rest of the group was located in the US. Kenny said:

When he went back to the States he still asked me to come over there and play, which I did for a period . . . He did want me to move over there to the States and he kept hinting at it. He didn't really have anything definite and I didn't feel like breaking into the New York music scene – it sounded too hard to me.[920]

Kenny's reasons went beyond his fears of making it in New York: "I was married and had kids, and was making a bit of a living over here, so I thought to go over there to the deep end [*trails off*] . . ."[921] Later, he explained further: "I felt I'd broken my roots already once when I left Canada; I didn't want to do it twice."[922] Braxton tried hard to convince Kenny to move to New York. He described his increasingly desperate efforts in absurdist terms:

Every other day, I either put a Magnum 357 to his head [or] I sometimes brought in, like, eight tons of dynamite! I tried to persuade him gently, too . . . You know that movie *The Pit and the Pendulum* with Vincent Price? [*laughs*] It started cutting into his shirt – but then the power went out. It wasn't like I changed my mind and got soft – the electricity went off – and so Kenny survived that day! [*laughter*] Yeah, well, I mean, you know. I said, "Kenny, look. Move to New York. Or I'm hiring 50 people to take you out. It's that clear." The only problem is that I ran out of money on the 49th person – so I couldn't finish the job![923]

In more serious language, Braxton acknowledged that Kenny's location made it difficult to rehearse and pursue new music with the quartet. Kenny looked back on this choice and another significant opportunity that arose around the same time:

In some ways I think back and wonder what would have happened if I had [moved to New York]. Especially in later years, because I did this period with Stan Getz over there – I played a week with him in Boston, I think. And I think he was moving on to Chicago to play, and he said, "Do you want to come with us to Chicago?" but at that time I had a few gigs with Braxton in New York, I think, so I said "Well, I can't, because I've already got a few gigs with Braxton." But I often wonder what would have happened if I had gone to Chicago with Stan Getz . . . I don't think that would have worked out somehow.[924]

One day, Braxton's friend, pianist and composer Muhal Richard Abrams called him to tell him about a trombonist named George Lewis.[925] Lewis joined the group for a week in Boston. "It was very clear to me after that experience that George and I had telepathy," Braxton said. "Kenny and I had telepathy [too] – but it was just different. And Kenny was doing so many different things – everybody wanted him."[926] Braxton continued:

I've always loved Kenny, but he was working with many different people, and it became easier to keep George and work with George. And then George was ready to move to New York. After Boston it was pretty clear to me that this would be the next progression for me, as far as redesigning the quartet.

Kenny held no resentment toward Braxton – or Lewis – for the change. "George Lewis came along and I couldn't blame him for going with George, who I think is a tremendous player," he said.[927]

Kenny would work with Braxton a few more times: he returned to New York in February 1976 to record once more under Braxton's name – this time for his Creative Music Orchestra, an ambitious big-band project for Arista Records released on the heels of the previous two Braxton albums.[928] This project received even greater acclaim, winning *DownBeat's* critics' award for best album in 1977.[929] Producer Michael Cuscana commented that the album "was not only the realization of a dream for Braxton, but also an easy avoidance of developing a new permanent working ensemble".[930] They also played together with the Globe Unity Orchestra, with ensembles led by Roscoe Mitchell and Wadada Leo Smith, and again with the Creative Music Orchestra in Cologne and Paris in 1978. But their productive association was essentially over. "It was great. The best period of my life – for me," Kenny said. Braxton's influence was difficult for Kenny to quantify, but he felt that Braxton had "made me very aware of space and not playing a lot of notes, things like that. The things I learned from that are not tangible."[931] Braxton acknowledged Kenny's influence on him as well:

> Kenny Wheeler's music affected the evolution of my syntax – and we were both lyrical and romantic players when we wanted to be. We had that overlap in our music. And that for me was appealing, because I've never given up anything; I've just tried to add to it. And I felt that was also true of Kenny. Kenny could function in the traditional big-band context, he could play with Duke Ellington, he could go with Count Basie, or with George Lewis! No problem for Kenny.[932]

In late 1975 and early 1976, Kenny recorded albums again in Germany with two very different ensembles: Globe Unity's *Pearls*[933] which also included Braxton, and a series of three LPs with the Francy Boland Orchestra.[934] Also in Germany, Kenny and saxophonist Jan Garbarek joined forces for a broadcast some 18 months before they would be paired on Kenny's next ECM album, *Deer Wan*.[935] On 23 January 1976, back at the NDR studios in Hamburg, they formed a quintet including bassist Palle Danielsson and drummer Jon Christensen (both members of Jarrett's European Quartet along with Garbarek), and completed with pianist Bobo Stenson.[936]

After these European outings, Kenny returned to North America where he had secured a contract to record an album for the Canadian Broadcasting Corporation.[937] He decided to record some of his tunes with saxophonist Art Ellefson, his old friend who had been best man at his wedding and was godfather to his son Mark. Kenny asked Art to put together the rhythm section for the date.[938] Ellefson chose pianist Gary Williamson, bassist Dave Young, and drummer Marty Morell. The album contains four cryptically titled Wheeler originals, including "Hi-Yo", "Slofa" (an amalgamation of "Slow-Fast" and one of the tunes he had just performed with Garbarek), "Quiso" ("Quintet Song"), and "Kitts" (likely dedicated to his hometown of St. Catharines, known as "St. Kitts", and also played on the Garbarek session). The two remaining tunes on the album are by Kenny's other bandmates: "Blues News" by Marty Morell and "H.S." by Art Ellefson. Ellefson remembered: "The place where we recorded – it was a rehearsal hall, and the piano wasn't the best. Gary Williamson brought along a Fender Rhodes. Kenny told me after that he hated Fender Rhodes! I had no idea of this – I just was trying to make sure he had a piano that was in tune!"[939] Although this album, released again much later in the digital age as *1976*,[940] possesses neither the recording quality or star power of *Gnu High*, it is an important document of several of Kenny's compositions during the period, playing music – some not recorded elsewhere – at the height of his trumpet powers with a long-time musical partner in his native country. Later in August the same year, Kenny had another broadcast for the BBC's *Jazz in Britain*. For this, he chose a reduced instrumentation of five saxophones, himself only on trumpet, with two trombones, horn, and tuba as his fellow brass players. This is the first time he had modified his large ensemble since it had coalesced during the *Song for Someone* period. On this broadcast, the group played a version of the composition "Slofa" from his recent trip to Toronto, in an arrangement expanded for the larger band.[941]

During this fertile period, while Kenny was finally recording small-group albums under his own leadership and touring with one of the most creatively challenging quartets in modern jazz, he continued working as a trumpet player in the studios. While commercial studio work helped Kenny maintain a good standard of living, it became increasingly draining of his energy. He enjoyed the camaraderie of the other studio players and the challenge of keeping his trumpet technique at the highest level, but his comments about the industry reflect his increasing desire to play his own music. Although a certain amount of his studio appearances were jazz-related and provided some musical reward, many of the more commercial sessions remained mind-numbingly mundane. There were definitely highlights, including two recordings with Phil Woods: the first for the saxophonist's *Floresta Canto* LP[942] in April 1976, and the second for the *I Remember* LP[943] in March 1978. There was a new and ambitious orchestral album for Tony Coe as well, titled *Zeitgeist*,[944] recorded in July 1976. Kenny also recorded with the Ted Heath Band in a live concert in 1977, one of his only appearances with this important British swing band. There was a memorable session with the great Clark Terry in September 1977, too: *Clark After Dark*,[945] a beautiful orchestral album of ballads with luscious string and big-band orchestrations. Many of the musicians involved in that recording have the fondest memories of both the music and of the guest star, a famously generous-spirited and warm man. Dave Horler recalled that Clark was over an hour late for the session due to some confusion. "The first tune was 'Misty', and he walked in and they put the red light on . . . he hadn't even seen it, and he just sight-read it and played it. Unbelievable."[946]

For Kenny, these sorts of sessions were great musically; it was the others he dreaded. In 1975, he told Mark Miller, "I go when the phone rings. I don't like it. I mean, I like the musicians; I think they're very high-quality, but 90 per cent of the music is kind of soul-destroying."[947] Happily, Kenny's growing popularity as a jazz artist meant that he had less availability for commercial studio work. But he remained steadily in demand and gave this example of a busy period in an interview at the time:

> This morning, I did a commercial for Chrysler, I think it was Chrysler cars. And tomorrow, I'm doing a Val Doonican television show. Earlier in the week, I did some radio jingles, I think for the States, I'm not sure. I mean I don't usually ask questions . . . I think I have a Johnny Mathis television show next week.[948]

What Kenny describes of the studio players he worked with and so admired could have been said of himself:

> They have to be very good players naturally because most of the time there is not very much to tax their capabilities, but you never know when you are going to walk into something which will over-tax it so you have to try and be prepared all the time to play the most difficult music, and the standard is very high amongst the studio musicians.[949]

For a trumpet player, this level of preparation is essential. Maintenance of the embouchure requires constant practice and dedication. The demands of playing in the studios certainly helped Kenny sustain the technique needed to play some of the most challenging parts that he had become known for, and control the agility his improvisational impulses required. As mentioned, merely executing the large intervals in the melody of *Gnu Suite* from *Gnu High* is a feat many jazz trumpet players would find nearly impossible. To do it with the consistent sound and accuracy with which Kenny did it is even more impressive on a technical level, not to mention the individualism and depth of feeling – that "soulful" quality Chick Corea had noticed – he brought to everything he played.

Whether or not it was vital to his longevity as a trumpet player, Kenny treated playing in the studios as a necessity. "Often I can't remember [a session] because it is like going to the dentist – I forget about them as soon as

I leave," he said.[950] Sometimes, young people who may have been unfamiliar with Kenny's own music would ask him about various sessions with famous pop groups he recorded for, only to get a blank look or an "I did?" in response. One recording he was asked about frequently was a 1977 date with drummer Bill Bruford of Yes and King Crimson fame. The album, *Feels Good to Me*,[951] includes a track called "Either End of August", on which Kenny improvised. He remembered the session:

> It was just another studio date to me. I didn't even know the name until afterwards and I asked. Someone said, "Oh, they're a big deal in the pop or the rock world." To me it was just another studio date. I was recommended by Allan Holdsworth . . . I wasn't really free to do exactly what I wanted, which is what a lot of studio work is now – you get a solo to play and they say, "Well, the first bar was nice, but could you do something different in the second" . . . all that kind of thing. I'm not really putting them down – it's just the way they work. I know teenagers say their only interest in me is the fact that I played on Bill Bruford's record. And I'm not particularly knocked out about my playing at all – mostly because I wasn't completely free to play the way I wanted.[952]

Kenny's nephew, Jayson Jelley (son of his sister Helen and her ex-husband, Kenny's long-time friend Bill Jelley), was awestruck when he discovered that his uncle had played on the Bruford album:

> I remember talking to him when I was a teenager and getting into rock 'n' roll music and stuff . . . He did a lot of those studio gigs and I'd always pick his brain about "What was it like to meet Bill Bruford?" and these rock stars that he worked with. To him it was just a day at the office . . . He would ask me questions about some of these people he worked with, like "This Bill Bruford, is he good?" and I said, "Yeah, he's in a couple of really big bands" and then he'd ask "Is he rich?" and I'm like, "Umm, yeah, probably" and he's like, "Well, then he should have paid me a little more!"[953]

Although intended in jest (especially concerning Bruford, who frequently collaborated with jazz musicians), Kenny's last comment to his nephew revealed his increasing resentment at the level of economic inequality that he and his fellow sidemen suffered when recording for pop artists. He was also frustrated with the lack of general musical knowledge that highly produced pop acts possessed – who were many times calling the shots and collecting the biggest cheques for their recordings, while trained, studied, and often-times far more talented musicians like himself were subjected to low status and even lower wages. Kenny explained:

> [I]n those days we used to call them "earn while you learn". A lot of them would come into the studio and they didn't really know an awful lot about actual [music] – they knew what they wanted in their head, but often we

would have to write out the parts and stuff. Of course, we wouldn't get any extra money, and if you complained, well, you're out.[954]

In a later interview he added: "Pop musicians, particularly in those days, knew nothing about music. They only knew two chords. When they'd go home in their Rolls Royces and I went home on the Underground, I did start to get a little bitter."[955] But this situation was simply a fact of life for the English studio musician.

Kenny could also be a victim of his own competence, asked to play things because he could. Bassist Chris Laurence recalled a session in which Kenny was suddenly put under a great deal of pressure to record on mellophonium:

> The fixer was a guy called David Katz, and we were all working for Elton John and people like that at the time, in the early '70s, and I remember David says, "well, I got this Kenny Wheeler, and he plays this fantastic instrument called the mellophonium." And Kenny turned up . . . and they were trying to sell Kenny, and Kenny wouldn't sell himself! And they'd sort of say, "Well, go on there, Ken, give us a blast of the old [horn] . . . !" And it was this awkward instrument, you know . . . it was a half trumpet, half French horn . . . I remember Kenny trying to play something . . . it was all a bit pressured and all that, but he managed to do it, of course . . .[956]

Although Kenny had played mellophonium with Dankworth, he barely played it beyond that period – only on occasion for Braxton and a bit for Mike Westbrook – otherwise it had mostly been consigned to the attic.

If Kenny occasionally felt some resentment towards the pop acts he recorded for, his emotions could be magnified when put in a situation that made him even more uncomfortable. Henry Lowther remembered a television special that he and Kenny played on with the pop star Leo Sayer, who had hits in the 1970s with songs like "When I Need You" and "You Make Me Feel Like Dancing":

> They only [needed] one trumpet – so [booking agent] David Katz decided to split it up, and give Kenny three and me three. Well, Kenny drew the short straw, because they had this idea that the musicians would dress up in these military uniforms and have to dance around Leo Sayer! This is *Kenny Wheeler*! White suit, with the scrambled egg on the lapel . . . [*laughter*] And it's often shy and awkward people like Kenny who often perform the worst *faux pas* . . . He was standing in the studio next to a couple of people, and he said, "It's bad enough having to play this music without having to do *this* as well!" But what he didn't know is that the woman standing next to him was Leo Sayer's wife![957]

For fans who revere Kenny Wheeler the jazz musician, it is indeed difficult to imagine him in these situations, playing in the orchestra for an episode of *Top of the Pops* just weeks before recording *Gnu High*, or in uniform

## ** THE BEST OF JAMES LAST

Readers Digest have recently issued here in the U.K., a six record set 'The Best Of James Last', to those who purchase in the near future, they throw in a seventh album entitled 'Cap'n James'. Apart from ordering by post, this set is available from the Readers Digest shop in Selfridges, Oxford Street, London.

The best, comprises six albums compiled as follows:-

1. Greatest Hits.
2. Love Must Be The Reason.
3. Classics.
4. Beach Party.
5. Non Stop Dancing.
6. Hammond.

Track titles of these six records can be found on the back page of this magazine. The seventh album in this set is a special compilation from the Kapt'n James series. The titles are as follows:-

Side A: Take Us With You Captain, Sail Again To Bombay, The Boy At The Rail, La Paloma, My Bonnie, Kari Waits For Me, The Banks Of Sacramento, What Shall We Do With The Drunken Sailor, Madagascar, Bound For The Rio Grande, Sailing Sailing, Tobacco And Rum, Love In Harbour, Gale Force 12.

Side B: Good Morning, Sailor Boy, Rule Britannia, A Sea Journey Is Fun, Today We Sail Away, The Way With Every Sailor, Aloha Oe, John Kenaka, Up She Goes, John B, Yellow Rose Of Texas, Good Night Ladies, In My Homeland, Must I Go.

**ETIENNE CAP**

**KENNY WHEELER**

5

Photo 22: Kenny Wheeler being introduced as a new orchestra member in the James Last Appreciation Society fanzine.

Courtesy JLAS

dancing around Leo Sayer a few years later, with considerably less strut than he'd marched as a young teen in the cadet band.[958] No wonder, then, that the serious, shy Kenny would cope by treating sessions much as his father likely treated his work as an accountant: to be done well and forgotten.

One association Kenny might have liked to forget was his time with the James Last Orchestra. It is mind-boggling to think of Kenny playing the part he did in this most "light" of party music orchestras. There is no polite way to describe this music that doesn't begin to smack of musical snobbery, so we must first acknowledge that James Last was one of the most popular touring bandleaders of his time, or ever. Having started out as a very successful jazz bassist, he is estimated to have sold in excess of 100 million albums and played to sell-out crowds in large concert halls worldwide for a period of over four decades.[959] As such, he was a notoriously generous employer who paid very high salaries to the musicians and treated them well, often creating a convivial, party atmosphere on the tours, with the players' wives even sometimes travelling with them.[960] The *Guardian* described how "the so-called *Gentleman of Music* tried to transform his concerts into a good-natured party, for which he, as conductor, provided the slick, cheerful and upbeat soundtrack."[961]

But there is no escaping the fact that the music, especially viewed through the prism of Kenny's musical life at the time, is terribly banal. Their non-stop medleys of reels, polkas, waltzes, and a smattering of pop hits was described as being "all blended together into a seamless, jaunty fusion. It was a formula that led him to be derided as the Emperor of Elevator Music."[962] Not least because of the financial remuneration, there were nonetheless many outstanding musicians willing to play in the orchestra, including Kenny's friend Derek Watkins, so the playing itself was always of high quality. Derek had become a fixture in the band (often a featured lead trumpet soloist on a Maynard Ferguson-style arrangement of a popular tune such as "MacArthur Park" or "My Way") and, for him at least, there was more in the way of musical reward from the concerts. No doubt in response to a passing conversation about money or difficult financial times and their unquestionable mutual admiration, Derek offered to get Kenny onto the gig.[963] And so it was that in November 1977, dressed in a silver lamé jumpsuit and with the promise of enough money to build their kitchen extension, Kenny undertook a tour with the James Last Orchestra. It is probably safe to say that, aside from the additional money it would have generated, it was unfortunate for Kenny but amusing for us that the tour also included a televised performance: episode 40 of the successful *Starparade* show.[964] To witness this giant of contemporary European jazz hacking his way through the "Chicken Reel" and other vapid medleys, just months either side of a BBC *Omnibus* feature, the recording of his next ECM album, and an upcoming British Arts Council tour, is as surprising as it is surreal. Kenny took the gig seriously, though. One of the pieces in the band's book was a feature arrangement of Rimsky-Korsakov's virtuoso showpiece "Flight of the Bumblebee", harmonized for four trumpets. Bob Lanese, who was part of the band at the time, remembered that Kenny took the music home to practise his part and "nailing it" the next day at the concert.[965]

In addition to the technical abilities demanded by the music, the gig also required certain bits of choreography and dancing. To call Kenny's efforts in this area half-hearted is a generous assessment: he is frequently the only motionless figure in a line of otherwise gently jiggling horn players. They did have some fun social times on tour, though. Doreen accompanied him for at least a part of it, spending some enjoyable times with Derek and Wendy Watkins, at one time having an impromptu late-night jam session with Kenny at the piano.[966]

Photo 23: Kenny Wheeler playing piano at a post-gig jam session with James Last Orchestra bandmates, including Derek Watkins seated directly to Kenny's left.
Courtesy Wendy Watkins

Painful as it was for Kenny, this short-lived James Last experience did pay for an extension on the kitchen of his Wallwood Road home. Although he surely parted company most willingly, Kenny's family teased him, saying he was fired because he couldn't do the dance moves. It was enough of a long-standing anecdote for Mark Wheeler to joke years later, "If he'd only danced a bit more, we could have had two storeys!"[967]

Occasionally, after a particularly difficult day in the studio, the musicians would celebrate its success and unwind at the pub. Kenny remembered, "You were so glad to be out of there that you went to the pub, because sessions were a pressure, you know."[968] These pressures could generate a fair amount of tension, which Kenny would break up with his sense of humour. John Surman remembered that, occasionally, just as the red light came on signalling the beginning of a take, Kenny would joke, "OK, tense up, studio!" which helped his colleagues – and maybe himself – relax.[969] One might imagine that such pressures might have affected someone who suffered with nerves as much as Kenny did, but trumpeter Tony Fisher recalled that Kenny

> . . . was a very nervous sort of guy, but at the same time, as soon as he got the trumpet in his hand, the nerves, to me, disappeared. And he would *never* foul anything up or come in in the wrong place and do stupid things like that, which some nervous people might do; he'd sail through things without any problem.[970]

Mark Wheeler speculated that, nonetheless, the pressure and financial necessity of being a session musician may have affected Kenny: when he was frustrated in the studios, he would occasionally do more drinking then than he normally did in those long two-plus-hour gaps between recordings. Although she wasn't a teetotaller, Doreen didn't approve of this, which may have caused some occasional friction between the otherwise close and loving couple.[971]

As Kenny began to perform more in Europe, commercial sessions became less frequent. In a 1979 interview for *Cadence*, Kenny said, "I haven't done hardly any [studio work] this year. It's only because I've been away from London, 'cause when they can't get you on the phone they just don't call you anymore."[972] He was indeed away from London more and more throughout this time, and increasingly involved with ensembles that would provide much more interesting musical opportunities and better pay. Before long, he would happily be able to decrease his amount of studio work even further.

Organized in 1975 for a television programme and intended by its founder, producer Werner Schretzmeier to fuse jazz and rock "for a younger generation", the United Jazz+Rock Ensemble (UJRE) was "an extraordinary mix of people" and considered a "band of bandleaders" for its well-known members, including Germans Wolfgang Dauner, Eberhard Weber, Volker Kriegel, and Albert Mangelsdorff, American saxophonist Charlie Mariano, and UK trumpeter Ian Carr.[973] The television show's band was so distinctive that it developed a passionate following, with letters pouring in demanding live concert appearances. Consequently, the band's first set of performances were recorded and the resulting live album cut from the first concert, *Live im Schützenhaus*,[974] sold over 60,000 copies. This unexpected success allowed them to start Mood Records, the label on which the group recorded themselves (and other ensembles) thereafter.[975] "It was not uncommon for 1,000 people to be turned away from one of our concerts," Ian Carr said.[976] The ensemble was a good musical experience for Ian, who was often showcased as a trumpet soloist and writer, but he was also admittedly attracted to the high pay provided by German recording sessions.[977]

Four years after the founding of the UJRE in 1979, Ian was apparently responsible for helping get Kenny into the group. When Kenny joined, the ensemble was in "a bit of a slump towards the end of the decade". Ian noted that, soon after, "it came up again in the '80s to a very high musical level".[978] Although Kenny had plenty of writing, performing, and recording outlets by this time, it was still a pleasurable experience for him to have his music performed and appreciated more widely in Europe with an ensemble with such an enthusiastic following. Good pay, elusive to English jazz musicians of any stature, must have enhanced his motivation to be in the group. An examination of Kenny's accounts from 1979 shows that Kenny's largest pay cheques came from the Continent. Aside from sessions and the occasional payment from the UK's PRS and MCPS collection agencies,[979] the bulk of his earnings come from his recording work for ECM and his gigs in Germany, including the Goethe-Institut, the organization that supported the Globe Unity Orchestra, and UJRE/Mood Records.[980] It is clear that these last two groups in particular provided some of the financial security that Kenny's studio work had previously. In an interview with Roger Cotterrell (the same year he first recorded for UJRE), he observed the increasing strain on his schedule between the domestic studio work and his performances on the Continent. He said of the sessions:

> There's no other way. You have to do it for money. I've heard a lot of jazz musicians put sessions down; but when the phone rings, they go, if they can get session work. It's a lot of people's aim to get into session playing. I just do it for money because I certainly couldn't live on jazz in England . . . In December, I got about four days with Globe Unity and then some more with Globe Unity in January. And in between all that was the usual lousy studio work. That's the way my diary tends to look.[981]

This dour attitude regarding his inability to fully break free from commercial ties and focus solely on jazz is expressed more and more candidly in interviews around this time, and coincides with his relative bitterness about the value of jazz in UK society, and towards bad pop music:

> There's a lot of pop music I like, particularly Brazilian things, Milton Nascimento – I love that. And things that Flora Purim has done. Stevie Wonder I like too. But punk rock and that kind of pop I absolutely hate. I

can't stand it. They dance around as though they are so aggressive. If they ever saw Evan Parker and heard him with a good amplification system like theirs, he would shatter them. I hate the whole commercial pop system.[982]

Even as far back as 1969, Kenny noticed the different levels of discrepancy between cultural value and artists' pay in Germany versus England. In the *Melody Maker* profile on him covering the release of *Windmill Tilter,* Kenny laments to Brian Priestley that "There seems to be more work on the Continent at the moment. I did a thing for Hamburg radio with John Surman recently, which is much better paid than radio work here."[983]

Whether his motivations for joining UJRE were purely aesthetic, financial, or perhaps a combination of both, Kenny became an important contributor to the group. *The Break Even Point,*[984] the first album he recorded with UJRE, includes two pieces that feature him as a soloist. The first, Eberhard Weber's "Alfred Schmack", is almost entirely a solo flugelhorn feature for Kenny. Very much of its time, "Alfred Schmack" offers a glimpse of Kenny trying to fit in to the lighter rock context, playing music that would almost work as a TV theme, with harmonic and rhythmic aspects very much influenced by the pop world of the mid–late 1970s. (Indeed, seldom elsewhere can you ever hear Kenny play *Do* – the root note – so often and deliberately.) Equally of its time, but perhaps more rhythmically interesting is "Song with No Name" by Barbara Thompson. Here, all three trumpeters (Kenny, Ian, and Ack Van Rooyen) spar during the opening section, trading stereo-separated cadenzas over long chords, followed by a Spanish-influenced/Phrygian theme which goes into a straight-ahead rock groove, and features a trumpet-dominated 7/8 melodic section. The album also includes one of Kenny's original compositions, punningly titled "One Sin a While": a darkly rich ballad full of Kenny's unmistakable harmonic language and beautifully orchestrated using Barbara Thompson's flute as a lead voice. A solo vehicle for alto saxophonist Charlie Mariano, "One Sin a While" begins with a long and very slow ballad tempo introduction and goes into a rock feeling which is somewhat reminiscent of some of his writing earlier in the decade for Maynard Ferguson.

Kenny seemed to take pleasure in playing with UJRE, telling Mark Miller in 1980 that "I quite enjoy it – they're all great players and [we] get treated well . . . They play to crowds of a thousand, I would think, which is probably a lot more than Globe Unity or a jazz band would get."[985] In an interview ten years later, however, he was a bit less generous about this segment of his career. When asked by interviewer Chris Parker if he felt that "jazz-rock was a fertile area", Kenny replied, "The way Mike Gibbs does it, yes. I love his music. As a horn player, you've got all that stuff going on in the rhythm section behind you and it takes away your exposure – with a trio, playing standards, you're exposed." He continued: "But it's not generally for me. The United Jazz and Rock Ensemble plays to big audiences – it's a good, commercial band."[986] By this time, even though he continued to play occasionally in the studios for nearly another decade, his attentions were being more devoted to ensembles led by two of his closest musical collaborators and, even more happily, his own music.

---

On 8 July 1977, as part of the celebrations for the Queen's Silver Jubilee year, Kenny's big band (billed as "The Kenny Wheeler Orchestra") shared a concert called "A Celebration of Jazz" with Stan Tracey's *Under Milk Wood* Quartet at the Queen Elizabeth Hall. This was a significant and rare event for Kenny: a live appearance for his 22-piece ensemble, which was a group as strong and musically diverse as anything he had presented for broadcast in the BBC studios. His confidence in this project was noted by a reviewer for *Jazz Journal International*, who called it ". . . magnificent . . . quite the bravest amalgam of session musicians and free jazz players that anyone has ever dared to put together. Only Kenny, drawing the respect that he does from all sections of the music spectrum could possibly put it together."[987]

With his career as a leader going as well as ever, Kenny travelled to Oslo later that same July to record his second album for ECM to be titled (once again with an animal-based pun) *Deer Wan*. For the personnel, he retained the powerful *Gnu High* bass and drum combination of Dave Holland and Jack DeJohnette, whose chemistry was heightened by the addition of guitarist John Abercrombie. They comprised the *Gateway* trio,[988] which was scheduled to record their second LP for ECM right after Kenny's recording. Though Abercrombie recalled that Manfred Eicher had recommended him to Kenny, it seems that the decision to harness the *Gateway* trio as the rhythm section would have made so much sense musically and economically that an additional recommendation would hardly have been necessary.[989] For Dave Holland particularly, it was an even more hectic yet productive time; later that same week, in addition to *Deer Wan* and *Gateway 2*,[990] he would also record his own solo bass record, *Emerald Tears*.[991] He remembered:

> That was the week at the studios in Norway. I think it was my first time there, and we had three sessions scheduled in that week – three recordings . . . [T]hey were all done back to back in six days or something like that in the same studio . . . It was nice because the *Gateway* trio was in its prime in a sense – we'd formed it relatively recently and the band was touring . . . It was such an intense week with these three records that I was really nervous about doing the solo album, so a lot of my mind was on when we'll be all finished and I'd be back at the hotel practising to get ready for that.[992]

To complete the *Deer Wan* quintet, Manfred Eicher contacted saxophonist Jan Garbarek, who lived in Oslo and was an obvious choice to partner with Kenny following the success of their NDR quintet broadcast the previous year. Eicher said that "from the very beginning Jan and I were talking about new kinds of groups and possibilities for getting musicians together . . . I thought Jan would also like to join this [recording] because he and Kenny Wheeler would just be a fantastic blend, because they both had such a magnificent sound concept."⁹⁹³ Garbarek had become known throughout the early '70s for his own ECM albums, including the acclaimed 1972 release *Witchi-Tai-To*.⁹⁹⁴ He was also a significant collaborator with Keith Jarrett in the pianist's European Quartet. By the time Jan recorded *Deer Wan* with Kenny, he had already contributed his stark, soaring sound to two of Jarrett's ECM albums: *Belonging*⁹⁹⁵ and *Luminessence*.⁹⁹⁶ Garbarek said: "Obviously, I was most flattered [to be asked to play on *Deer Wan*] because it's a stellar set-up, you know, with the musicians taking part in the session . . . The whole crew at that session were just musicians I looked up to – my heroes."⁹⁹⁷

The day before the first *Deer Wan* recording session, the musicians got together in Kenny's Oslo hotel room to review the tunes.⁹⁹⁸ John Abercrombie described their impromptu "rehearsal":

> . . . we all sat around and listened to a recording that Kenny had. [He had] recorded of a lot of this music with a big band in London, so . . . he had the music, he had the parts for us, and what he wanted each one of us to do – our separate individual parts – and he played the recording so we could follow along, and . . . he would explain what was happening, you know, and that was our rehearsal. We didn't really rehearse for the recording – in a real fashion – we didn't get together and play until we hit the studio, and then what we did was to, you know, just take each piece individually, and we would rehearse there, and then once we felt comfortable then we would record and then we would move on to the next piece. And we did that record, I think, in a day – which was kind of remarkable . . . it was just so relaxed, and just matter-of-fact, you know [*imitating Kenny's voice*], *Well, we're doing this record and here's the music I want you to play.*⁹⁹⁹

Abercrombie also recalled his reaction when engaging with the compositions for the first time: a markedly more positive response to Kenny's harmonic language than Jarrett's during the *Gnu High* sessions:

> That was when I became aware of what Kenny was about – from not only a playing standpoint, but the things he would write – which, to me on paper, looked like they were going to be hard, and kind of confusing, especially from a harmonic standpoint, but when I actually got into the studio and started to play some of this music, it felt very natural to me. There's something so natural about the music. It's very ironic, because I was kind of worried about it, like, "Am I going to be able to do this? It looks kind of tricky to me", but, like I said, it played itself. I didn't have to think much. If I had a question about a certain chord change or what I was supposed to do, he would say, "Just do what ever you feel there, John", or "Sounds great" – he would leave it very open – but if I had a specific [harmonic] question, he would answer it . . .¹⁰⁰⁰

ECM star acoustic guitarist Ralph Towner would make a cameo appearance on a single track, "3/4 in the Afternoon". Like Abercrombie, Towner also remembered working out Kenny's harmonic structures during their meeting in the Oslo hotel room. "We would go through the chords and the scales – and I would notate them maybe just a little bit differently than he would. But we would go over them, and he would change some of what they were called – at what scale point he would enter on."[1001]

The actual recording date was far less intense than the session for *Gnu High*. Jack DeJohnette remembered that "It was pretty relaxed . . . Kenny's a very shy person, anyway. He didn't talk too much, but he was explaining how he wanted the pieces to go. It was a nice, relaxed atmosphere." Kenny's nerves weren't as apparent during the recording of *Deer Wan*, either; or, at least, in Garbarek's eyes, his manner fitted in with the typical European demeanour. Garbarek said:

> There are musicians who are very confident and very brash about what they're doing of course, but the way [Kenny] was is a very normal behaviour for a musician here in Norway, or Europe in general, so that's exactly how I would have dealt with it myself. So, I didn't really think much about it. The only important thing is that he had authority when he was actually playing: no shyness when it came to making a statement musically. That was certainly the case – so his personality can be whatever! We need all kinds, and there are all kinds of musicians and leaders and arrangers. So if Kenny could appear to be shy, he was still clear about his decisions when it came to what he wanted with the pieces he had – they were all well thought-out and he wasn't afraid of presenting them to us.[1002]

Garbarek also recalled that "Kenny was well prepared", so there was "no time wasted in the session".[1003] Ralph Towner explained more about the process of recording for ECM during that time:

> [Talent Studios in Oslo] was wonderful. Jan Erik Kongshaug was always the engineer, and they had a great reign . . . There was not a lot of talk going on between Manfred or the engineer or us. In between takes was very silent. All the recordings were done in two days or less. So you really weren't doing a lot of out-takes. So the kind of playing that you do in that situation has to be affected quite a bit, knowing that you're not going to . . . let's say you become *very decisive* in the way that you play. Because you can't think "Oh, I'll just do another take of this." You can't have that mentality with ECM, because you just don't have that many dates of recording and basically your first takes are always the best anyway – the most fresh. So that's kind of the situation that's done with almost all ECM records, and I think that's one reason the players have to be of a certain calibre, a certain kind of player, who can be accepting of what they're playing.[1004]

John Abercrombie had a strong reaction to hearing Kenny for the first time while recording the album:

> I got to hear him play, you know, and that was a revelation, because I had never really played with anyone who played trumpet the way Kenny played . . . I was just so taken with his music and his playing, and it felt very natural to play his music and to play with him, even though he had a very distinct way of playing and phrasing. I mean, it wasn't like . . . when you play very even kind of groupings of patterns and eighth notes . . . he doesn't play that way of course . . . he just kind of plays over the time, and plays all these gorgeous phrases, so you'd have to be a little careful when you're playing with him. It's very open, but you also have to be strong in yourself and know where you are because . . . it's not going to be musically as obvious where he is when he improvises because he is so free when he plays. He's playing everything from completely within the harmony. I mean, he's such a harmonic whiz, but you don't get that feeling when you hear the music somehow.[1005]

The album contains four tracks: opening with the substantial *Peace for Five* (actually a suite in three continuous parts), then "3/4 in the Afternoon", "Sumother Song", and finishing with the title tune. *Peace for Five* begins with a symmetrical two-part waltz (originally titled "Watzle"[1006]) featuring Garbarek playing the melody on soprano saxophone, backed by rhythm section and seven flugelhorns multitracked by Kenny. *Deer Wan*'s use of overdubbing like this represented a departure from the acoustic immediacy of *Gnu High*. Garbarek recalled: "We were trying out all these new possibilities with multi-track recording. We would go back and add a little bit here and there." Toward the end of the 16-minute track there is an even more powerful use of these overdubs, and a further reminder of what exceptional command Kenny had over the highest, most intense range of the instrument. It is such an extraordinary bit of trumpet playing that Ian Carr was even compelled to ask him about that section of the suite in an interview years later: "I could only do it once a month – I'd have to rest for a week after it!" Kenny laughed, humble as ever about his talent.[1007] The closing melody is presented rubato over Jack's forceful yet free soloing on the drums, with the bass and guitar filling in the harmony while Kenny and Jan soar over the top. This technique – a melody played in free time over a chattering, interactive rhythm section – is a classic device of Kenny's, used to great effect in other works.

Kenny's improvised solo on *Peace for Five* is one of his masterpieces. In fact, the solos from this album are some of the few from his career to which he could bear listening. Some 20 years later, he told Ian Carr ". . . I suppose the solos from *Deer Wan* I can live with."[1008] Considering his generally critical view of his improvising, the fact that this is one of the only on-the-record (albeit backhanded) compliments he ever gave to his own playing is not surprising. It also provides some perspective about the relative quality of his solos on this album compared against his other recordings – many of them acclaimed by musicians, critics, and jazz fans alike, regardless of his own opinion of his playing.

The title of the second track, "3/4 in the Afternoon", is a play on the tune's time signature and features both guitarists, Towner and Abercrombie. They were able to avoid the potential pitfalls of a two-guitar recording: "Kenny left it up to John and I to play together even when accompanying," Towner said. Having played together live on multiple occasions and recorded as a duo the previous year on ECM's *Sargasso Sea*,[1009] Towner said, "John and I were an experienced team as a duo and managed to improvise in a way to avoid too much conflict between the two guitars."[1010] Kenny's solo on this track is another textbook example of his mature style, covering the entire practical range of the instrument with a floating ease and clarity of execution that has earned two published transcriptions, including a substantial analysis in the *Jazz Educators Journal* by Barry Long.[1011]

Kenny's uptempo solo on the second half of "Sumother Song" delivers chaotic cascades of notes in the upper register of the instrument, showing again how the language he developed in his free improvisations had coalesced into his overall voice, even when soloing on harmonic changes. Writing about this composition in preparation for a lecture a few years later in an amusing bit of rambling, Kenny explained the tune's title:

> . . . is a play on words. The song is what I call a "Mother Song". "Mother songs" are kind of sweet, sad, romantic songs. They usually date from the first 20 years of the century. I guess examples of other "Mother Songs" would be "You Are My Heart's Delight", "Pale Hands . . .", "Deep Purple", "Chloe", "Melancholy Baby". You probably haven't heard of most of these songs but they are probably songs you could sing to your mother as well as a girlfriend. And so I could have called this song "Some Kind of Mother Song". Or another meaning could be "Sum of Other Songs" or another meaning could be something to do with the way especially black musicians like to use the word "MOTHER". I know what they mean when they use this word but I can't explain it. It is a little bit derogatory but I think it can also be slightly humorous. It can also mean "Some Other Song" which is a little bit flippant or light perhaps meaning it is only another song.[1012]

It may be no accident that Kenny mentions his own mother's favourite song "My Melancholy Baby" in this list of "mother songs". Calling it "probably the sweetest and maybe saddest song I have written", Kenny might unconsciously be laying bare his own complicated feelings about his mother – loving her as a dutiful son while also recalling the sadness she both endured – and caused – during his childhood.[1013]

After Garbarek's solo on the title track, "Deer Wan", Kenny takes an incredibly active, energetic solo in which he presents some of his most fertile melodic playing on the record. (A delightful moment occurs at around

5:15, when he sets up a series of upward leaps, each higher than the last, and Abercrombie, before Kenny can finish his phrase, completes it for him.)

Just as with the *Gnu High* group, the band assembled for *Deer Wan* unfortunately never toured or performed live. "Somehow we lived in different spheres," Garbarek said. "We played with a different set of musicians and it just wasn't that easy or natural to get together."[1014] A striking contrast between *Deer Wan* and *Gnu High*, however, is the difference in critical response. Immediately following the release of *Deer Wan* reviews were uniformly positive. For example, *DownBeat* gave the record 4½ stars, and declared that "Wheeler's latest for ECM should confirm his place as one of today's most interesting and versatile trumpeters . . . Wheeler emerges a romanticist in the grand heroic mode. His compositions and trumpeting suggest an Olympian majesty. There is grace and eloquence, as well as a purity of sound and purpose."[1015] Perhaps the strongest contrast between these first two ECM albums, however, is the difference in Kenny's feelings about them. For once, he was pleased with the final product. In addition to his relative satisfaction with his solos, he also said that *Deer Wan* was

> my own favourite of my small band records. Most people, or musicians anyway, like *Gnu High* better, but I like *Deer Wan*. I like the songs, and I think the record is well-balanced. *Gnu High* is to me a little like a collection of songs, whereas *Deer Wan* I think has more of an identity, at least as far as the songs go.[1016]

Manfred Eicher agreed, saying "When I listen to this record . . . it is such a wonderful musical concept, great pieces, and very good sound . . . that was something that was unheard of from that time."[1017]

———·———

In 1977, the Contemporary Music Network of the Arts Council of Great Britain commissioned Kenny to write a suite which would be performed on a tour of the country. The busy tour of one-nighters lasted from 12–22 January 1978, stopping in Grimsby, Leeds, York, Leicester, Nottingham, Huddersfield, Liverpool, Manchester, Sheffield, and Birmingham. This would have been an important tour, because, up to this point, despite his global reputation and soon approaching the tender age of 48, Kenny had amazingly only done three live concerts with his own big band. The centrepiece of the Arts Council tour performances was a new work called *The Little Suite*, not named for its size – a substantial 25 minutes – but rather the trumpeter who had influenced Kenny more than any other, Booker Little. Titling the work *The Little Suite* "was the kind of joke that Kenny liked," Evan Parker said.[1018] In addition to the suite, Kenny rearranged music from *Gnu High*, *Deer Wan*, and *Song for Someone* for the tour.[1019]

He put together an ensemble featuring several soloists from the *Song for Someone* album, including Norma Winstone, Evan Parker, and Derek Bailey. Kenny also included American saxophonist Steve Lacy, who was a veteran of Thelonious Monk's and Gil Evans's bands. The other band members included a section of four trombones: Malcolm Griffiths, Paul Rutherford, Chris Pyne, and Dave Horler; and four saxophones: Tony Coe and Ray Warleigh, augmenting Parker and Lacy. He again used two pianists: J.T. played acoustic piano and synthesizer while Pat Smythe played electric piano. The rhythm section was completed with regular colleagues Chris Laurence on bass and Tony Oxley on drums. In another departure from his usual big-band instrumentation, Kenny was the only trumpeter – something he had experimented with once before in his 1976 BBC broadcast.[1020] On the *Little Suite* tour, Kenny's compositions would again be linked by improvised "Free Interludes", performed by a designated soloist or a combination of musicians. This had become a well-established device in his big-band broadcasts, which he would use to join sections of future large-scale works.

Just as on *Song for Someone*, Kenny was inspired by the disparate musical backgrounds he'd brought together: "Kenny loved all that . . . [He] was like a little bee going from flower to flower," Chris Laurence said. He also remembered that the band was "full of characters" – and that drummer Oxley, true to form when it came to playing the parts, "would do whatever he wanted to do".[1021] Kenny was not only sly with his song titles, he could manoeuvre equally deftly around the idiosyncrasies of various personnel. Though well established as a brilliant improviser, Evan Parker was quite inexperienced at the time when it came to reading music. Keen to provide some written material for him to play, Kenny slowly tricked him into learning to read music. Evan explained:

> He said, "I could just write you out a few long notes, that would be all right?" and then I said, "Well yeah, that would be all right", and then each year there would be one or two shorter notes. So basically, to the extent I can read at all, it's because Kenny just wouldn't accept that, you know . . . It was a kind of encouragement.[1022]

Reviewers found the programme for the *Little Suite* tour musically intriguing, often remarking on the interplay of improvised and written material. *Times* reviewer Richard Williams noted of the crowded Imperial Hotel performance in Nottingham that "at its best, it achieves an absorbing juxtaposition which emphasizes the unity and continuity of jazz".[1023] The *Guardian's* Ronald Atkins wrote "a strong case could be made for developing this particular type of media mixing". Atkins saved his highest praise for the *Little Suite* itself, which he called "a worthy tribute from one supreme lyricist to another".[1024]

This was also a fruitful time for Kenny's closest friends and collaborators. In early 1977, John Taylor wanted to make a full album of the duo he had been developing with Norma Winstone, his wife since 1972 with whom he had two young sons. Frustrated with the lack of recording opportunities and in need of audio examples of the duo to play for potential labels, John decided that he and Norma should create a studio demo. He told Norma, "I think I'll see if there's any interest in Europe."[1025] J.T. made a list of record companies that he thought might be interested, or in which he was interested. For his first stop, John saw Manfred Eicher at ECM in Munich. Before approaching Eicher, J.T. asked his close friend John Surman, who had worked for the producer previously, for suggestions about recording with Manfred and how best to make the approach. Surman remembered that "he brought me a tape with Norma and said – one of them was a [standard Clifford Brown] piece that Norma had written the lyrics to called 'Joy Spring', and I liked that. But, I said, 'I would take these three pieces of yours, I wouldn't take that one, because ['Joy Spring' is] kind of a traditional format for Manfred.'"[1026] J.T. agreed, and took his original material to pitch instead of the standards. "I liked John," Eicher said. "I also knew John from the English musicians, and I listened to the BBC."[1027] During this period, just before he left for Munich, John had been experimenting with a new synthesizer. Norma remembered that "the night before he went [to Germany], he was messing around with it, and he came up with a loop, and stuck a microphone [in front of me], and he said to me 'Just improvise over that.'" On hearing this track, Manfred loved it, replying, "I can hear a flugelhorn with this."[1028] He meant, of course, that he could hear *Kenny's* flugel with the voice and piano, and, since they were already working closely with him, they felt he was a natural choice. Manfred recalled that "I thought, a duo is fine, but maybe . . . could we add Kenny? And John welcomed this idea immediately."[1029] It was a very lucky break for J.T. "I don't know if he ever got around to the other [record labels]," Norma said.[1030]

J.T. wrote all the compositions for the trio's early recordings himself, with Norma contributing lyrics to some of the pieces. Kenny was more than happy to be in this chamber trio, initially contributing just as a sideman. He admired J.T. greatly as both a player and composer, going back to the first time he heard him and Dave Holland together at the Old Place. "[J.T.] was always different. That's what I liked, the unexpected, always."[1031] And, of course, Kenny also loved working with Norma, whose voice had become a fundamental part of his music. Plus, the three were already close friends; they had assembled at Kenny's house on Wallwood Road a few times, but these "rehearsals" were basically informal visits to play through the tunes and, as Norma put it, to "have a cup of tea". She also commented on how Kenny was comfortable in the sideman role, when he wasn't musically in charge:

Kenny, I think, quite liked instruction, you know. He liked to know what you were supposed to do, and then, you know, if it was a free bit, it was a free bit. He tended not to really instigate, which John would. I mean, John was very adventurous. Kenny – if you put him in that situation – would be adventurous, but I don't think he really ever sort of took off on his own . . . John would say to him, "You just play – you start this off on your own" and he'd know what we were going into . . . But I think he was quite, in a lot of ways, quite organized really, in his thinking, his preparation. He might sort of throw it all out the window if the situation was right, but I think . . . all the freedom and everything that he had was in his playing, incorporating everything he knew, and everything he had to say was in his solos . . . I don't know that he was ever trying to do anything particular, but he was just responding to the music. It was there, and "this is what I play on this" – and what he played was always astounding!

To back up Norma's observation, Kenny complained openly about the burdens of group leadership to Toronto jazz radio host and long-time friend Ted O'Reilly, slightly putting his foot in his mouth on-air:

Yeah, I usually play better . . . not better, maybe, but I usually end up playing for other people, because, to tell the truth, it's too much bother to be the leader . . . You have to make sure everybody gets paid, make sure everybody's on time, air tickets, phone calls, interviews – not that I mind interviews, Ted – sorry![1032]

There was no title for the trio's first album, nor even a name for the group when they travelled to Oslo's Talent Studios in March 1977 to record for ECM, some four months before Kenny recorded *Deer Wan*. Although they had performed and recorded together in various combinations, they had not toured or even performed live as just a trio. The recording date was really the first time they had tried this music out in a real way. Norma remembered:

I suppose we didn't really know how it would work, because you can have some things in a recording but maybe they won't work with a live group. Because we did things with the synthesizer that you'd have to set up. You *could* do it live, and we did do it live, but for instance . . . John had got these compositions [like] "Sirens' Song" which needed overdubbing – there were things we were going to use the recording techniques [on, like] overdubbed voices and overdubbed piano.[1033]

The first piece they recorded that day was "O". Norma said that the idea was that, after playing the theme, they intended to improvise on the 9/8 form of the final melody section. "We got there and we did it a bit, and then Manfred said, 'Why don't you just play free at this point [instead]?'" With that idea in mind, they recorded a take with Manfred's suggestion, and that approach made the album. When they moved on to "Sirens' Song" they were also trying it for the first time and experimenting as they went. This freshness was captured in the recording: "We got to the piece with the synthesizer, so John just set up that loop . . . I don't think we ever rehearsed that [either]."[1034]

"The first day was a bit tense," Kenny said. "The first few hours, everybody was very tense because John was worried that [Manfred] wouldn't like the music. But as everything got more and more relaxed, it just got better and better and John grew in confidence . . ."[1035] Just having the opportunity to hear themselves filtered through the famous "ECM sound" (engineered by Jan Erik Kongshaug) was inspiring enough to help the trio – even Kenny – shake off any nervousness. He said:

> It couldn't be more than five or six [tracks on the record] but the sound they got, I mean within five minutes you got back into the studio [control room] to hear something played back and you have never heard a sound like it, you know, and that cheers you up for a start when you hear your instruments sounding like that.[1036]

"Greek Triangle" consists solely of Kenny's trumpet overdubbed in several parts: one of the first examples of him doing this. The track starts with a kind of fanfare for trumpets (presumably written by J.T.) followed by an extraordinary improvisation for the multiple "Kennys", still engaging in all the interactive dialogue and explosive flair one had come to expect from him. Norma remembered one of the other tunes didn't have a title, setting off a fortuitous set of exchanges between John and Manfred:

> So we played that and me and Kenny just improvised over it. And the end of the session Manfred said, "Oh, let me know when you find a title for that piece . . . to me, it's like a journey – it feels like a journey, that piece." So, when we got back home, John looked in the thesaurus. And under "journey" he got "direction", and he looked under "direction" and he got the word "azimuth". And he looked it up, and "azimuth" meant the arc from the zenith to the horizon. And he thought, "Well, that's a nice name." And it also is an instrument on ships – an azimuth ring, which determines direction. So he just wrote Manfred, and said "We'll call that piece 'Azimuth'" and Manfred said, "Let's call the album *Azimuth* – let's call the *group* 'Azimuth!'"[1037]

Towards the end of the session, there was a palpable sense of relief among the trio and a change in demeanour. Kenny remembered how J.T. overcame his early nerves, joking that "by the end, John was very cocky, actually strutting around the studio!"[1038] Norma told a touching story about the final take of the recording, as John overdubbed his piano solo on "Sirens' Song":

> When I hear John's solo, I just remember that thrill, because we'd recorded everything, and he put the solo on afterwards. And Manfred had liked it, you know, what we did . . . So it was quite fraught – scary, really – but

then, at that point, all the anxiety had gone because he'd liked the stuff. John was putting on his solo – and it was *so beautiful*. I remember just – there's bits of it – when I hear that I am back in there sitting down in that studio listening in the sound box, to this solo going on. It was so lovely.[1039]

It is understandable that this would be a memorable moment for Norma. The situation was already tense enough for her: Kenny already knew Eicher from recording *Gnu High* just two years before and John knew him from making the arrangements to record this album, but she was meeting him for the first time. This was also the first time that Norma felt that she liked the sound of her own voice. Like Kenny, she had been persuaded by the luminous ECM sound:

> For a long time, I was so interested in improvising I tended to ignore the sound I made, which I think was a mistake. Most times when I listened to playbacks, I didn't really like my voice. But the ECM recordings convinced me I could actually make a pleasant sound and that influenced the way I sang. I've thought a lot more about my sound since then.[1040]

This recording marked the birth of the Azimuth trio.[1041] Although John was the impetus and de facto leader for the group, Manfred Eicher had basically created Azimuth. Norma concurred: "It would be lovely to say, 'Yeah, it was our idea', but really it was Manfred Eicher's idea. He could just hear it somehow, with the voice and the flugel and the keyboard. So that's how Azimuth was born." Eicher summarized: "I think the result was a wonderful record, which became a very influential and important kind of chamber music band of its own . . . and something that was entirely new to that time."[1042]

Adding to the pressure was a BBC film crew, there to record footage for a television special about Kenny for the *Omnibus* series. The special, filmed over several days in March and May 1977, was a feature on Kenny's life and work. Preceded by a story on the Count Basie Orchestra, it originally aired on BBC 1 on 27 October 1977. The first part of the special offers a rare glimpse into one of Kenny's live BBC broadcasts, filmed in Maida Vale Studio 3 with a live audience in attendance. The full big band plays an arrangement of the second part of the *Heyoke* suite, and continues with excerpts from two new compositions, "Hotel Le Hot" and "Branetu" (more word play, putting together the beginnings of the words "Brand New Tune" for the title). Later, the camera shows Kenny carrying his trumpet and flugelhorn in leather gig bags, walking from the Leytonstone Underground station to his home.[1043] Kenny, seated at the piano in his music room, discusses his work in recording sessions, and even complains a bit about the conditions under which his annual broadcasts took place – somehow oblivious to the fact that he's moaning about the BBC in an interview *to the BBC* – that he has to copy all the music and book all the musicians himself for nothing. The last part of the programme contains the sequence that features Kenny and the as-yet-unnamed Azimuth trio in their

Oslo recording session. The cameras caught moments of the trio recording "O", and even documented them departing on the aeroplane, holding back other passengers so that they could film Kenny, John, and Norma as they boarded the British Airways jet.[1044]

The *Omnibus* production shows Kenny fairly accurately, capturing his soft-spoken, shy personality (with a dash of his sense of humour) and balancing his creative jazz ambitions with a portrayal of the practical aspects of his "day job" as a working studio musician. But the original concept for this episode planned to show Kenny in a less favourable way. The producers had planned to compare Kenny's life – depicting him in almost comically pathetic terms as near-poverty and sickly – with that of famed 1930s English bandleader Nat Gonella, shown as a once ubiquitous musical star but now living a life of reticence, stuck in the past and reduced to feline companionship. An early pitch for the special was summarized in this internal BBC memo, showing how they aimed to contrast these two trumpeters whose heydays were separated by nearly four decades in a wholly negative light, showing neither to their best advantage:

> In 1937, Nat Gonella was voted No. 1 trumpet-player in the Melody Maker's poll of jazz musicians. He topped the bill at the Palladium, hosted a weekly radio show, had a huge fan club, lived in Mayfair, knew the Prince of Wales.
>
> In 1977, Kenny Wheeler was voted No. 1 trumpet-player in Jazz Monthly's poll. (Melody Maker have discontinued their jazz poll). For most of his working life, he plays as a "session musician" in ad hoc bands, theatre orchestras, backing groups. Twice a week, he plays his *own* music in the upstairs room of a pub in Barnes, to a tiny audience of enthusiasts. Occasionally he flies to Germany, to play at jazz concerts, where he is acclaimed as a star. He lives on the breadline in Kilburn [*sic*], has no car, is often ill.
>
> The plan is, to make a film which contrasts these two lives in music, 40 years apart. Cine-verite coverage of Kenny Wheeler's frantic working week would be intercut with Nat Gonella reliving his lost youth in his miserable retirement bungalow in Lancashire, surrounded by scrapbooks, souvenirs, 78s, and cats.[1045]

Thankfully, the producers kept the Gonella profile separate, and showed Kenny to be both the straightforward working musician and creative artist that he truly was at the time.

———•———

From the outset, Azimuth had limited performing opportunities and a mixed reception. They appeared at the Band on the Wall club in Manchester in October 1977, a performance that was given an encouraging review in *DownBeat* by Chris Sheridan: "Their ECM recording should at last afford these musicians deserved recognition in America. That is vital, because their talents are too large to be confined by British insularity . . . Music as vividly poetic as made by this trio demands to be heard."[1046] Interestingly, this gig occurred on the same night that Kenny's BBC *Omnibus* feature was first broadcast.[1047] Sheridan's review briefly recounted the comic story of Kenny's mortified reaction when someone in the club brought out a television to watch the special which happened to be airing during Azimuth's break between sets, saying he "had almost to be physically prevented from hiding in the john".[1048]

Called "gentle, ethereal, and elusive" by Canadian jazz critic and historian Mark Miller, Azimuth's music – representative in many ways of the ECM "house sound" – didn't appeal to everyone. The label already had its detractors. The most notable of these early on was German jazz authority Joachim-Ernst Berendt, who accused Manfred Eicher of "promoting a 'new jazz fascism' where only 'pretty sounds' were allowed".[1049] English critics, whom Kenny found generally willing to sacrifice their own, "really put down ECM for a long time".[1050] (If only he had known how the BBC had originally intended to portray him in the *Omnibus* feature!) Kenny was also perplexed – and openly frustrated – by the lack of interest tour promoters and festival organizers showed in Azimuth. Often referring to it as "the band everybody loves to hate", he expressed his confusion about why the band wasn't in greater demand in a 1979 interview with *Cadence* magazine:

> . . . it's another band that I really like but that nobody seems to want for dates . . . And it's strange, because, to me, on paper people should be *jumping* on that band, because it's only three people, so economically it's not bad, and it's so different because we're piano, voice, and trumpet, and you'd think they'd go, "Oh, let's try *that*." But there seems to be no interest in that band whatsoever, and I can't understand why not. You know, Norma is great, and John is . . . and I'm lousy [*laughter*].[1051]

A few months later, speaking to Mark Miller, Kenny was less self-effacing and more openly bitter about the situation: ". . . in England the response has been totally negative . . . We don't look good. A lot of people go to *look* at jazz, don't they? We're not jumping about or wearing funny clothes; we're just interested in music. Sometimes people mistake your apparent shyness for the idea that you can't play if you look like that."[1052]

As ever-present as the negative reviews of Azimuth seemed to be, Kenny would have done well to focus on the increasing amount of positive coverage he himself was receiving during this time. In a short period between 1978 and 1980, he had a very positive run of reviews published:

> a lyrical power which is the envy of many of his colleagues
>
> *DownBeat*, 9 February 1978

a trumpeter of mellow fruitfulness and absolute integrity

*The Guardian*, 11 April 1978

Kenny Wheeler is one of the few trumpeters who can impart the speed of a number with one note; he can place it like a straight left to the point of the jaw or pull it en route, hobbling the velocity. He can also bring you to the brink of tears with a species of tremolo and gulp in brass . . . his solo seemed to call all the shots in every department lifting the group neck-and-crop into a passionate clarity.

*Melody Maker*, 1 September 1979

Oh my, how he can play.

*Toronto Globe & Mail*, 27 August 1980

He also had a charming feature published in his hometown newspaper, the *St. Catharines Standard*, calling him "one of the world's jazz giants".[1053] In addition, the *Washington Post* ran a 1978 article called "Trumpet Reemergent" crediting both him and Woody Shaw with being the most important trumpeters in modern jazz at that time.[1054]

His compositions – not just his arrangements – were also beginning to be recorded by major American jazz stars. In addition to the 1976 Bill Evans recording of Kenny's "Sweet Dulcinea Blue" on the album *Quintessence*,[1055] saxophonist Stan Getz recorded his "Quiso", and played his "The Cry of the Wild Goose" on gigs, the second of which was released on a posthumous live recording from San Francisco's Keystone Korner jazz club.[1056] Kenny remembered his time playing with Getz in the US in the mid-70s: ". . . it was great, the week with Stan Getz, because I admired him in a way, because I'd sent six tunes of my tunes to him and he took the time out to practise them and play them – and he could play them good."[1057] He also recalled getting a glimpse of Getz's darker side:

Although he was quite kind to me during that week, I'd heard stories that he could be nasty later on. Because even when I was there that week, the drummer was Billy Hart, I think, and [Stan] got Billy Hart into the band room and complained about the way he was playing. So I didn't want that to happen [to me]. Billy Hart later said to me, "Is it OK the way I'm playing behind you?" and I said, "No, I love it!" The more the better I like, the more busy the better.[1058]

As always, Kenny was more able to be positive about his compositions than his trumpet playing. When discussing these two artists recording his works, he told the BBC he was "flattered", adding that it was "a real ego booster to have something like that happen".[1059] Kenny would have his chance to repay Bill Evans's honour, playing on a 1979 album recorded in tribute to the pianist titled *Seven Steps to Evans*[1060] led by Gordon Beck, with Stan Sulzmann, Ron Mathewson, and Tony Oxley.

Kenny's performance associations were moving upwards, too. In addition to the aforementioned deputizing in the Thad Jones/Mel Lewis band in 1972 and his work with Stan Getz, he was being called on to play with increasingly higher-profile artists, or as a star guest himself. In July 1977, just days before he recorded *Deer Wan*, Kenny was called to deputize in Horace Silver's band at Ronnie Scott's for trumpeter Tom Harrell, who was ill. Kenny joined the quintet front line alongside saxophonist Larry Schneider, who recalled that "Kenny played great under difficult circumstances."[1061] In his review for *The Times*, journalist Richard Williams wrote: "Kenny Wheeler was deputizing for the ailing Tom Harrell, but the seam was barely visible . . ." before adding the sort of backhanded jab Kenny had grown to expect from reviews at home: "Wheeler's trumpet appeared, as always, to be in a controlled skid, technically breathtaking but emotionally detached."[1062]

Another last-minute opportunity arose the following year, when Kenny was asked to deputize with the Gil Evans band in a performance in Italy, the only time these fellow Torontonian masters shared the stage.[1063] Kenny remembered:

> I only played for him one gig, just a four front line, that's all . . . I don't know who the trumpet player was, but something happened and he couldn't make it, so I got called either the day before or the morning of the day to come over . . . it was a really good experience, to do it, but that was my only real contact with him except I heard the band a few times, you know.[1064]

Later in the same year Kenny was invited to be a guest soloist (along with Tony Coe) at a festival in Chichester in a retrospective concert with Woody Herman and His Orchestra. There were new opportunities abroad, too: in March 1979 he was the featured soloist in Zurich for the Swiss Radio Days Jazz Series, playing with pianist Klaus Koenig, bassist Peter Frei and drummer Pierre Favre. Two of the tracks from this session are available and Kenny is again in exceptional form. One is a first recorded outing for Kenny's composition "A Simple Toon", and the other is Duke Ellington's "Come Sunday": a surprising choice to some, perhaps because Kenny so rarely recorded standards, and more surprising still because he played trumpet instead of flugelhorn on this ballad.[1065]

---

Azimuth returned to Oslo to record their second album, *The Touchstone*,[1066] in June 1978. The music for the record (once again, all composed by John Taylor) was more difficult to learn and record than the previous album, especially

Photo 24: Kenny in "Uncle Bert" mode, with Alex and Leo Taylor (Leo on the right).
Photo by Roberto Masotti, courtesy Norma Winstone

in terms of the rhythmic structures. Norma remembered that "Mayday" was especially challenging, with its alternating bars of four and five:

> That's one I remember finding quite difficult. Because we had more synthesizer stuff on the first thing with [tunes like] "The Tunnel" . . . but that was just . . . a thing set up on the synthesizer and I just had some words that I'd written, and I improvised using those words, and Kenny just improvised. So there's nothing really to rehearse there – we just did it.[1067]

In early 1978, soon after recording *The Touchstone*, Azimuth undertook their first tour on the Continent. Their trip included seven gigs and two live radio broadcasts within days of one another: the first back at the NDR studios on 3 February and the second at Sendesaal Bremen on 6 February. The music that was captured provides a rare example of the energy the group could generate live, all of them interacting at the very height of their powers. The improvisations are fearless, with different combinations of solos, duos, and the full trio punctuating the composed material. In the duo with Norma that follows, it is very interesting to hear Kenny start to touch on and explore an intervallic idea that would go on to yield much more significant material on his next ECM album, in one of the finest solo improvisations of his career.

The Azimuth tours – though rare – were memorable. Kenny and Doreen travelled with the whole Taylor family in John's Volvo Estate, with various keyboards, sound equipment, and sometimes an organ (!) strapped to the top. They named the car "SYD" because of the letters on its licence plate, and Kenny dubbed the crew the "Jazz Gypsies". Norma recalled an amusing scene on the road in Germany:

> Kenny used to sit in the front in the passenger seat. And he'd be reading – he'd always have a newspaper or something. And it was so funny, because in Germany, that's where the driver would have been sitting normally, and you'd just see people overtake [us], and this person's sitting there reading the newspaper![1068]

This story is even funnier if we recall that Kenny never learned to drive a car. Kenny would even tease John and Norma's children with the threat "If you kids don't behave, *I'm* gonna drive!" – to which they'd reply with fake horror, *Oh, no!*

While on the road with Azimuth, Kenny used a portable tape recorder to record himself practising. He gave a couple of his tapes to the kids, containing recorded messages for them while taking a rest from the trumpet. "He was so lovely with children," Norma said. Kenny would put on various silly accents and voices on the tapes, like a fake big-city American "tough guy" character, like one might hear on a radio comedy like *The Goon Show*. He also invented alter egos for himself and Doreen: "Uncle Bert" and "Auntie Madge". Norma re-enacted the tapes: "He just did it while he was practising – one time he was practising [a particularly tricky tune of John's] and he suddenly said: "OK, yoose kids, you Joe, Fred, that's a tune by your daddy, Jack, called 'Jake and Bob'. I play it often, but I don't often play it . . . Anyway – just one piece of advice for you kids – stay away from that jazz music – t'won't do you no good!" Another was:

> [*Kenny*] Joe and Fred – this is your old Uncle Bert speaking. You be good boys for your mommy Doris and your daddy Jack. No running around the table . . . Anyway, here's your Aunt Madge to say a few words to you kids. Come over here, Madgie!
>
> [*Doreen*:] Hello Joe and Fred! Take no notice of your Uncle Bert. You are good boys!
>
> [*Kenny*] They ain't good boys! . . . I suppose you are . . . I suppose you are when you get enough Coke and crisps![1069]

In between these touching and hilarious comedy routines on the "Uncle Bert" tape is some of the most extraordinary insights into his trumpet practice: playing into a harmon mute to keep quiet in the hotel rooms, he ran two-octave arpeggios with varying articulation and repeated excerpts from demanding pieces he was working on at the time. At one point, following some outrageous technical passage of playing, he adopted yet another funny voice and said to the boys: "You just heard the greatest trumpet player in the country . . . In the city he's not so good, but in the country he's the best!"[1070]

Kenny's comic timing was legendary among his colleagues. He could be quiet for long stretches of time, even hours; one of his classic lines about himself was "I don't say much – but when I do, I don't say much."[1071] Norma remembered one of her favourite Kenny stories from the *Azimuth* tour:

> We were talking in an airport . . . again, he'd sat there for ages and had said nothing at all. And John and I were talking about different sort of areas of music, classical, romantic, neo-romantic, and I said, "Well, OK, what would you call Debussy then?" And this voice suddenly came: "I'd just call him 'Claude'!"[1072]

Kenny was also famously averse to conflict, generally avoiding confrontation at all costs. Another story from the tour of Germany, again told by Norma, illustrates both these points:

> I can remember one time when we were driving in Germany somewhere with Azimuth, and Kenny was in the back and I was in the front. John was driving. And we couldn't find where we were supposed to go. And John wouldn't ask, you know. He was just driving: "No, I'll find it, I'll find it." So we started having this altercation in the front and Ken said *nothing*. He was sitting in the back seat . . . I said, "How do you manage when you're on your own?" and he said "Well, I'm worse than this when I'm on my own." And this little voice from the back seat came, "I'd sure hate to be

with him when he's on his own!" So that completely broke up the whole thing. We burst out laughing.[1073]

In December 1979, Azimuth recorded *Départ*.[1074] This, their third album, again included compositions written solely by John Taylor, but set itself apart from the previous recordings by including a fourth musician, guitarist Ralph Towner. Manfred Eicher, constantly searching for new sound combinations, had suggested that the trio invite a guest to join them.[1075] Towner liked their music and had become interested in the group after he happened to have been in the studio during the mixing session of the first Azimuth album. Towner's duo with John Abercrombie had also toured opposite Azimuth, so it was natural for J.T. to invite Towner to play the session. He fitted in with the trio, with whom he felt a kinship, easily, sensing they occupied the "same musical sphere". Towner said, "they were so . . . in tune with each other . . . They had such an aesthetic that was so fully developed – there was no bickering." Towner also enjoyed the freedom and mutual respect he encountered when recording with them:

> You weren't put into sort of a musical straitjacket; you were there because of how you played and you understood how *they* played. It wasn't necessary to write a part that anyone could have been flown in to play or overdub a solo or something. You were there because of your musical concept and how you played.[1076]

Similar to the sessions for the two previous Azimuth albums, Norma remembered that there wasn't a lot of discussion or rehearsal before recording *Départ*: "Ralph just played – we didn't rehearse – we just got to the studio. There almost wasn't any point because it was all about what happened at the time – because sometimes the music would just be the chord progressions for Ralph." Kenny also felt the collaboration had been successful, and a month later described *Départ* to Mark Miller as "the best of the three" records that Azimuth had made up to that point.[1077]

---

After Kenny had recorded *Gnu High* and *Deer Wan* as a leader, Manfred Eicher began asking him to contribute to projects under the leadership of other emerging ECM artists. Eicher said that Kenny was "a wonderful musician when he came into the sessions of others. I think Kenny was one of the most important soloists and creators at that time for ECM . . . I can remember all of the albums that he contributed to in a very special way."[1078] After his initial recordings with Azimuth and a 1977 recording, by Globe Unity called *Improvisations*,[1079] the first of the label's albums on which Kenny recorded in a small-group sideman role was Wadada Leo Smith's *Divine Love*[1080] in September 1978. Smith had first met Kenny at York College in Toronto when he was with Anthony Braxton. The two played together again in Braxton's Creative Music Orchestra in February 1976 and May 1978, and also in Creative Orchestras led by Leo himself and Roscoe Mitchell for Moers Music in 1979. For *Divine Love,* Leo and Kenny appear alongside fellow trumpeter Lester Bowie, all three playing with harmon mutes. Incidentally, they had only recently appeared on the same festival at Moers in May 1978, although not as a trio – each was a part of his own group.[1081]

The three trumpeters play together only on one six-and-a-half-minute composition on *Divine Love,* called "Tastalun". Smith explained how the piece was constructed:

> The main reason I chose him was for his sound and the way he executed harmonic progressions. In that piece . . . it had chord symbols [for Kenny's part] but not chord progressions . . . it would go from whatever chord I wanted to go to but it never recurred as a progression . . . [Kenny] would play that line, and then Lester's line had a ratio of different kinds of velocity units which was measured in certain kinds of ways – but not metrical, just that these symbols were hooked up in a way where it was best geared for his kind of musical technology. And my line was all velocity units, which meant that it was kind of best for me. So we had these three lines that move across, that each person has a particular connection with the score, and it worked wonderful. We made one take.[1082]

In addition to being invited to collaborate with the leading African American trumpeters in improvised music, Kenny was partnered alongside the most notable European trumpeters of the day. It is testament to the range of his career (and probably in no small part due to his Braxton connection) that he was recognized in both scenes in this way. One impressive gathering of European trumpet talent came at the Baden-Baden New Jazz Meeting in 1978 and accompanying performances in Mainz. The band included the five trumpets of Manfred Schoof, Ack Van Rooyen, Tomasz Stańko, Enrico Rava, and Kenny, plus bass clarinetist Michel Pilz and vibraphonist Tom van der Geld joining a double rhythm section. One of Kenny's compositions, "Ba-Ba", was played at the concerts, the title presumably a tribute to Baden-Baden.[1083] In August 1979, Manfred Schoof led a further gathering of four trumpets and rhythm section for a broadcast of his own, including Kenny and Tomasz Stańko. For this broadcast Danish trumpeter Palle Mikkelborg joined them to complete the all-trumpet front line.[1084]

Another ECM album to which Kenny contributed more extensively was tenor saxophonist George Adams's *Sound Suggestions,*[1085] recorded in May of 1979. A veteran of ensembles led by McCoy Tyner, Gil Evans, and Charles Mingus, Adams played in a style that combined his American roots of rhythm and blues, funk, and bebop with a modern approach inspired by John Coltrane and Rahsaan Roland Kirk. The group assembled for this recording included another tenor saxophonist, the German musician Heinz Sauer, plus the rhythm section of Dave Holland, Jack DeJohnette, and pianist Richie Beirach.

Beirach remembered the recording session for *Sound Suggestions* well. He said that "Manfred hired Kenny to ensure that the sextet record would not be chaotic or crazy. He was right. Kenny wrote really interesting arrangements, very fresh, and not big-band." Given his personality, it is interesting that Eicher would choose Kenny to be the "hired enforcer" for much of anything, but Beirach noted that "Kenny was able to lead them without being the leader, by the force of his personality and his musical sound . . ." Beirach continued:

> We talked about the music, and he was so quiet but very strong. He would let everybody talk first, and then he would say, "Well, since *I* wrote the song, or did the arrangement . . ." [*laughs*] He had a lot of authority but never asserted it . . . very modest and powerful . . . He was the extremely sure hand on that record.[1086]

One telling story about the session for *Sound Suggestions* involves a small a surprise regarding the repertoire. George Adams usually sang a blues or two on his gigs – even with Mingus – and one of the tunes he wanted to include on the album was a hard-swinging Chicago-style blues titled "Got Somethin' Good for You", complete with roaring free horn solos on the 12-bar form and Jack's cymbals crashing every bar in a groove so wide that it's almost a shuffle. It is hard to imagine anything further from the ethereal, melancholic refinement of much of ECM's typical output at the time (especially when compared to a group like Azimuth), so "Got Somethin' Good for You" is almost shocking to hear. It did come as a surprise to one person in particular, as Beirach recalled:

> Manfred didn't know about the blues. And Kenny didn't feel any need to tell him; it was just another tune. [Kenny] arranged it with the three horns, it sounded big, like a Blakey sextet, with Freddie Hubbard, and Curtis Fuller, and Joe Henderson, like [*sings the melody*] and we played it. It was so swinging, one take, and I was looking at Jack, thinking, "Manfred's not gonna like this!" Kenny was completely cool, deadpan, nothing. Very unemotional on the surface, Kenny. So, we finished the tune and everybody's going "Yeah!" And we go in [to the recording booth], and Manfred's head was on the mixing desk – like somebody died. He didn't like it. George, you know, it didn't bother him, nothing. So Manfred turns to Kenny . . . "Kenny, what are you doing, why didn't you tell me? I didn't know about this song." George said, "Yeah, I always sing a blues." And that was it.[1087]

Since the tune ended up on the final album, Manfred must have known they'd captured something amazing and unique. He continued to make his influence felt in other ways during the session. Two of the tunes Adams recorded for the album were Kenny's original compositions. One of these was "A Spire", a piece Kenny had first aired in a septet BBC broadcast he led two months earlier.[1088] A more complicated bit of wordplay than his usual pun-craft, "A Spire" is Kenny's tribute to Rahsaan Roland Kirk, who had died in December 1977; Kenny said, "He was aspiring to play again because he had a stroke and I really liked him a lot."[1089] Also, he continued, "Kirk" was similar to the German word *Kirche*, church, and churches have a spire.[1090] The tune is a very slow ballad in two parts, the second of which (like several of Kenny's tunes) modulates, restating the original melody up a semitone. Beirach noted that much of the day had required them to be "a real sideman, like a Blue Note [session], just reading music, playing the charts . . ." So when it came to "A Spire", Jack DeJohnette too was basically playing time, as he had been for everything else. After the first take, Richie remembered:

> Manfred came out of the studio – brilliant the way he really made a difference – and said, "Jack, don't play the time. Play free." Which meant that he was playing all around it, and me and Dave Holland had to keep the time together, which was really hard. But we did it, and it was fantastic. It built up and became something more than a ballad.[1091]

The second tune of Kenny's they recorded demonstrated his ability to lead those rubato unisons with the sort of authority that had so impressed Richie Beirach: it was his piece "Baba", from the recent Baden-Baden concerts, the title slightly rewritten.

———·———

Just a month after recording *Sound Suggestions*, Kenny returned to Talent Studios in Oslo to record on an album for Ralph Towner. The two musicians seemed to share a unique chemistry, and these special sessions became Towner's 1979 ECM recording *Old Friends, New Friends*.[1092] As with all ECM albums, Manfred Eicher was very involved in the recording process and was crucial to the record's sound. Towner said:

> Manfred would make a lot of suggestions . . . there'd be pieces that . . . he'd sort of motion to keep it going to continue a certain section. And of course the sound is really [great] – the engineer is brilliant – but [Manfred] really was the ultimate expert on the sound – getting the sound exactly the way he wanted it. And he could make it finally materialize before your ears in the mixing. All of a sudden it would leap into this kind of clarity and beauty . . .[1093]

Occasionally, though, there were moments when the artists would find Manfred's "hands-on" approach more difficult to accept. On the *Old Friends, New Friends* sessions, Towner had everyone in the studio and had recorded one of his tunes which he was especially fond of and had planned to play piano – not guitar. But Manfred rejected it, which infuriated Towner in the moment:

I was sitting stewing, and I remember my hands landing on the piano and I said, "Ooh – what's this?" so I said, "Everybody out!" so everybody went in the control room while I wrote another ballad. And that took about five minutes – and I said, "OK – let's try it!" Everyone came back in, and we did one take – and not only was it the first time it had ever been played, but that was the recorded version. *The first take*. Kenny just sounded great.[1094]

The tune Towner wrote in a five-minute a burst of creative rage? "Celeste", a mini-masterpiece of a ballad, named for his daughter, and now one of his most well-known compositions. Also worthy of mention is "Special Delivery", on which Kenny executes an exceptionally tricky melody in unison with Towner; the piece is so unidiomatic for a brass player that it is virtually inconceivable that it could have been written for any other improvising trumpeter in the world working in 1979. Even more impressive is the fact that this impeccable, almost classical, trumpet technique is exhibited by the same musician who played such an affecting solo on "Celeste" on the same album.

In July 1980 Kenny returned once again to Oslo to record on an album led by bassist Arild Andersen, with Steve Dobrogosz on piano and drummer Paul Motian. The tune "A Song I Used to Play" is a favourite of Kenny's son Mark Wheeler. Capturing a particularly soulful Kenny in his prime, a careful listener might just hear a touch of Lee Morgan's influence popping out in the middle of his solo. Not surprisingly, Kenny admired Morgan. London-based pianist and educator Simon Purcell remembered a masterclass with Kenny and J.T. in the late 1980s where a student asked what they thought about transcribing solos. J.T. shuffled uncomfortably and dismissively in his chair as a form of answer, but Kenny said categorically, "I tried for years to play like Lee Morgan but I couldn't do it, so I had to try to find another way."[1095]

One of Manfred Eicher's favourite ECM albums on which Kenny contributed as a guest was Rainer Brüninghaus's *Freigeweht*,[1096] recorded in August 1980. Manfred said Kenny "was fantastic . . . [the album is] really beautiful . . ."[1097] The album uses the overdubbing technique Kenny had begun to explore on *Deer Wan*. Brüninghaus's compositions employ mixed metres and, notably, the album is missing a bass player, making the piano and synthesizer responsible for holding down the rhythmic structures and underlying harmony. Overall, the music is trance-like, and on the title track the keyboards' ostinato contrasts beautifully with the melodic lines of Brynjar Hoff's oboe. With no bass to anchor their dialogue, the interaction between Kenny and Jon Christensen is even more rhythmic and exciting, with Kenny's flugelhorn sometimes soaring, other times jabbing.

Shortly after the release of *Départ* (and the recording of *Freigeweht*), Azimuth made their North American debut in Canada at the Edmonton Jazz Festival, on 22 August 1980. In another interview with Mark Miller, Kenny confessed to being anxious about the gig: "I'm always worried – I'd be worried if I wasn't worried."[1098] In this case, his customary nerves were probably amplified when he became the de facto Canadian headliner of the festival after Oscar Peterson cancelled his performance. As a perhaps unconscious response, Kenny seemed to retreat from the limelight even more than usual. In his review, Miller observed that "Norma Winstone took centre stage. Taylor sat amid a conclave of keyboards to her right, and Wheeler stood out of the spotlight altogether." He continued, reporting that Norma told the audience that she had to "do all the talking, because Kenny's too shy". Ralph Towner was also on hand for the concert, playing some pieces alone and joining Azimuth for two selections. Kenny was pleased with the turnout and the audience's reception of the group: "I was surprised that it was as known here as it seems to be. Quite a few people know our records, but I was ready for, and expecting, absolutely no recognition at all, so what I got was a pleasant surprise."[1099] Despite Kenny's reticence, the group's performance in Edmonton was an overall success, giving Azimuth encouragement and providing direction for the future. "I think from Edmonton we learned a lot about the group, things we have to do now," Kenny said.[1100]

———

Throughout the late 1970s and early '80s, Kenny worked frequently with Alex von Schlippenbach's Globe Unity Orchestra. The group continued to develop an enthusiastic audience on the Continent, and the group brought Kenny back to the Moers Festival in early June 1979.[1101] In addition to the 1977 album *Improvisations*, Globe Unity recorded the follow-up LP *Compositions* in 1979, also for ECM.[1102] *Compositions* begins with one of Kenny's originals for Globe Unity, called "Nodagoo", the title a typically Wheelerian wordplay on "No damn good".[1103] Although Kenny sensed that interest in free jazz was dwindling at the time ("I get the feeling that it's gone down a little bit in Europe. I don't think it's a fad, I just think the interest has dropped a little bit,"[1104]), the popularity of the ensemble – possibly due to its novelty and strong contrast with the increasingly ubiquitous jazz fusion of the time – was still sufficient to provide them with a five-week tour of the Far East in 1980.

Supported by the Goethe-Institut, the tour was the brainchild of producer, writer, and frequent ECM critic Joachim-Ernst Berendt, who wished to put a spotlight on what he called "new developments in European music".[1105] The ensemble was to play in Japan, Korea, India, Indonesia, and Malaysia over a period of around five weeks in February and March. This tour was certainly a high point of Kenny's association with Globe Unity. It was not only a major opportunity to see parts of the world he'd not yet experienced: in a gesture rarely afforded musicians of any time, the Goethe-Institut funded Doreen's travel so she could accompany Kenny on the tour.

It did not begin well for her. Nervous about all their upcoming travel, and perhaps not knowing that her expenses would be covered, the couple had set aside a pile of money for the tour – which Doreen left behind in their Frankfurt hotel room immediately before heading east. She said:

> We didn't have much money then and we thought we'd have to pay for the airfares for me. And they paid for everything . . . We didn't know this, so we were worried about the money . . . I wish I could do it again so I could see everything, because I was so worried about money . . .[1106]

Evan Parker also fell victim to this cloud of bad luck, leaving his soprano saxophone in a taxi early on during the tour. (Fortunately, he recovered the instrument soon after.) They began with a week in Japan, with dates in Hiroshima, Kyoto, Osaka, Nagoya, Tokyo, and Sapporo.[1107] Shortly following the band's arrival in South Korea, another mishap occurred. As he and Doreen were leaving their hotel, Kenny was in a foul mood, already anxious about the upcoming gig. Doreen remembered: "He said, 'I don't want to go tonight', and I said, 'You've got to go tonight – you've got to play with all these musicians and you know you've got to play tonight'. '*Oh all right*', he said in a temper."[1108] As they exited, Kenny somehow got his trumpet stuck in the hotel's revolving door, smashing the instrument (unprotected in a soft case) and rendering it unplayable. "He walked into the door with a perfect trumpet and came out the other side with a battered trumpet!" Evan remembered, calling the situation "Ken in his Stan Laurel mode".[1109] Luckily, they were able to find someone who could get the instrument repaired before the next day's concert: ". . . A Korean fella took us to Seoul and then we had to walk around while they were doing it," Doreen said.[1110]

Although less stressful, the rest of the tour was also quite memorable. Evan recalled performing in Jakarta:

> We were supposed to play sort of early evening in the open air. And during the soundcheck, the call to evening prayers came, and there were bats flying over the bandstand, and the sun was setting slowly in the west. Ken played the opening bars of "Some Enchanted Evening". [*laughs*] I can still hear that. It was so appropriate, you know? That was the way we felt a lot of the time, was "Wait a minute. We've seen films with stuff like this in it, and here we are . . ." It was a poignant [thing] . . .[1111]

Alex von Schlippenbach remembered the concert later that night:

> The Indonesian public liked [the music] even without knowing what it was about. They loved to see people enjoying what they were doing – so if the band had fun, they had fun . . . It was the Chinese New Year, and it's good luck when it rains, so half of the population was praying for rain but we had to play open-air. So, by divine command, the first set was played, and for the second set it started to rain![1112]

Audience reaction in India to the Globe Unity Orchestra's approach was mixed. In Bombay, the band played on a shared bill following Art Blakey's Jazz Messengers and preceding Stan Getz's group. Schlippenbach said that most of the audience "didn't understand" their music, but that young people liked it. He was also moved when a member of the Greek Orthodox faith approached the band and presented them with a religious text.[1113] Others were not as easily swayed. Schlippenbach remembered that when the band finished, even Stan Getz had a joke at the band's expense: "When we finished, [Getz] came on stage and the first thing he played was some very weird [incoherent noise] on his saxophone, and then . . . the organizer of the festival said to the audience, 'Yeah! This is now Stan Getz playing the Globe Unity ending!'"[1114] A review published the next morning was no gentler, with the headline dubbing the band "INTOLERABLE CACOPHONY".[1115] The accompanying article even took a shot at the Goethe-Institut itself, resentfully labelling the performance "cultural imperialism". At one of the concerts – perhaps in Jakarta when the rains came – the wind came on so suddenly that the music, including one of Kenny's charts, was blown off of the band's music stands. "We had to improvise," Schlippenbach remembered. "It was no problem for us!" he joked.[1116] It was true: free improvisation was clearly in the band's comfort zone. Although the Globe Unity Orchestra had some charts, including Kenny's "Nodagoo", and various other written material, almost everything they played was improvised. Kenny explained, "We often rehearsed those pieces where you just have diagrams, you don't have any notes . . . graphic pieces. Sometimes we had no pieces at all; we just walked along and improvised. But in that situation, you almost had to fight if you really wanted to solo!"[1117] Kenny was amused by many of his bandmates' lack of awareness of his abilities as a "straight-ahead" improviser. "They never knew I could play jazz at all!" he laughed.[1118]

When Kenny returned from the Far East trip, there was little time to rest, as he embarked on a busy, seven-city tour of England with the London Jazz Composers Orchestra. SME members and other personalities from the free scene, including Evan Parker, Trevor Watts, John Stevens, Paul Rutherford, Tony Oxley, and Barry Guy, made up this ensemble, which played in Leeds, Sheffield, London, Manchester, Birmingham, Bristol, and Liverpool in mid-March 1980.[1119] The ensemble also made an appearance at the Bracknell Jazz Festival in July of that summer.[1120]

---

The lead up to Kenny's third album as a leader for ECM, *Around 6*,[1121] was fraught with personnel issues. Recorded in August 1979, the same month as George Adams's *Sound Suggestions*, early discussions regarding the line-up for *Around 6* initially went through a number of different revisions. Evan Parker recalled, "at a certain point, it was going to be Dave Holland on bass, Paul Motian on drums, John Surman on saxophone, me, [and] Ken."[1122] Scheduling issues also caused problems. A year after the session, Kenny explained:

It started out like the first two records I did with Jack DeJohnette and Dave, naturally I would have liked them, but they were both so busy now, that they couldn't make it, and then a horn player that was suggested first was John Surman, and we tried to set up about four different dates, and each one fell through. And Paul Motian was suggested, which I would like to have done it with – and who else . . . Eddie Gomez was [proposed], again, but nobody seemed available at the time that the record could be done . . . Suddenly I thought of, "Oh yeah, J.-F." Jenny-Clark . . . and Edward I'd played with, so I suggested him to Manfred, and Eje I suggested, and Manfred liked all the suggestions – and Evan I suggested. Of course Manfred's known Evan for years.[1123]

Quick to not have anyone feel like second-choice, Kenny explained, "I mean, the idea that these guys were last doesn't mean that they were [last] on the list, and we said 'OK, we'll take him' – It wasn't anything like that." So, the personnel settled as Kenny, Evan Parker, Eje Thelin on trombone, Tom van der Geld on vibes, J.-F. Jenny-Clark on bass, and Edward Vesala on drums. The time it took to finalize the personnel and instrumentation made it difficult for Kenny, who, in keeping with the tendencies he had now established as an experienced leader, preferred to write for specific players' musical personalities: "I like to write for the band, you know, any band that I write for. So I couldn't really settle down to get the writing started until the line-up was settled."[1124] He added, "There are a couple of ideas which are old ideas, but the rest was written specifically for that with those people in mind."[1125]

But there were issues with the some of the players chosen. Eje Thelin, brilliant improviser as he was, was not experienced in reading music. This, combined with the fact that Kenny's arrangements, with intricate – and not necessarily idiomatic – inner lines for the trombonist to negotiate, were virtually impossible to memorize given the time constraints of a typical ECM recording session.[1126] Despite being a leading drummer on the avant-garde scene, issues with the combination of Vesala and J.-F. Jenny-Clark meant that the stability of the rhythmic feel was not always consistent. And further contributing to the chaos of the session was a disagreement between Manfred and Tom van der Geld over the tuning of the vibraphone. Evan summarized:

Edward Vesala couldn't really play time. Eje Thelin can't read. And those two essential problems meant a lot of the material that Kenny had brought couldn't get used, because Eje Thelin found it hard to memorize – well, you can imagine, the inside parts of Kenny's things; they're not going to fall under the slide . . . So, it was J.-F. who saved the date actually, because there were moments where Ken was a little bit, you know, unsure how to proceed, because everything was taking so long.[1127]

One solution Kenny likely found for the reading issue was for himself to overdub the other two counterpoint parts on "Mai We Go Round". All these challenges were in stark contrast to the straightforward recording process of *Deer Wan* or the one-take immediacy of *Gnu High*.[1128]

The clouds hanging over the recording date for *Around 6* might have produced at least one significant musical silver lining. "Solo One", the second cut on the record, is simply solo flugelhorn. Exquisitely structured yet spontaneous, "Solo One" is a unique entry in the Wheeler catalogue, with essential aspects of his playing and compositional style represented throughout. The burnished sound, unexpected leaps into the extreme registers of the instrument, formal and intervallic symmetry, soaring melodies, and a touch of chaos are all present in this virtuosic, lyrical, and emotionally charged performance. Kenny explained the origins of "Solo One":

> It just happened very quick because the producer Manfred Eicher said, "Why don't you try a solo on it?" I had this little phrase which I'd been fooling around with and had been practising so I had a starting point. And to me, it just came off. If it hadn't have happened in that first take, I would have never got it. It's the only thing of mine that for some reason I could listen to and not cringe . . . I would say, the only really good thing I've liked that I've ever played![1129]

(The intervallic "little phrase" he refers to is the same one that appeared earlier in his duo with Norma on "O", back in Bremen with Azimuth.) Since time for the session was running short due to the previously mentioned difficulties, this improvisation might have been suggested by Eicher for the purpose of filling out the album length. Regardless of its impetus, "Solo One" is one of the few recordings of his playing with which Kenny was satisfied.[1130] In fact, he felt happier with this record in general, not just "Solo One". He told Mark Miller:

> Probably my playing on that third album I'm generally more happy with than most I've done, but I still cringe a bit when I hear it. It's the same thing I've been doing for ten years with the big band in a mixture of free playing and conventional playing . . . I play a little bit more of an example of my screech, free style of playing, which might shock a few people who've come to think of me as more of the soft melancholy and tend to think that's all I do and don't know the other schizophrenic style, whatever you call it . . . I like mixing them up. I really do. I'd like to be able to play a little bit more "inside" than I can – I never could play completely inside with just a straight rhythm section playing chords. I always got nervous if it's going well and I start screeching around and going "outside". I don't suppose I'll ever change that.[1131]

Critics mostly shared Kenny's satisfaction with *Around 6*. *DownBeat's* John Diliberto was the most effusive, proclaiming in his four-out-of-five-star review: "Wheeler's solos are almost perfectly honed executions", closing with: "The shadow of Miles Davis looms ominously over any contemporary trumpeter. At least in the art of choosing and shaping the perfect note, Wheeler has no reason to look backwards."[1132] Peter Goddard in the *Toronto Star* was similarly raving: "This album is as substantial as any I've come across this year."[1133]

Shortly after the recording sessions for *Around 6*, Kenny recorded much of the same music for BBC's *Sounds of Jazz* on 28 August, retaining only Evan Parker from the original ECM line-up. Saxophonist Alan Skidmore played in place of trombone, J.T. played piano instead of vibes, and bassist Chris Laurence and drummer Tony Oxley completed the band. One can sense the synergy Kenny has with this strong and familiar rhythm section; this is especially evident on the broadcast version of "May Ride", with J.T. and Oxley's interaction with Kenny lifting his solo in a way that the album version never quite did. It embodies what he often said about his preference for active drummers: "The more busy the better."[1134]

———·—

Nearly 30 years after Kenny rejected his father's idea of attending McGill to become a teacher in Canada, disdainful of the thought of standing "in front of a group of bored teenagers trying to tell them about music", he told Doreen "perhaps by now I may know enough to teach".[1135] His first major opportunity to do this – and at a very high level – came from his native country.

The Banff Centre is in the eastern Canadian Rockies, about 80 miles west of Calgary, Alberta. A beautiful, relaxing, and nurturing setting for musicians and creative people in general, the Banff Centre provides an outlet for students and professionals pursuing diligent study and sabbatical research, as well as hosting international festivals, conferences, and workshops. The Banff Jazz Workshop has hosted some of the most prolific and accomplished young musicians from Canada, the US, and around the globe. Current jazz luminaries who are Banff alumni are too numerous to mention, but they can be found across the globe as top performers, music educators, and arts leaders.

Banff's jazz programme began as an experiment conceived by David Leighton in 1972. He approached Canadian jazz stars pianist Oscar Peterson and clarinetist/composer Phil Nimmons and asked them to consider teaching in the summer at Banff. July 1974 was the first summer jazz workshop, headed by Peterson and Nimmons.[1136] After Nimmons led the workshop from 1975–80, the Banff jazz programme asked Karl Berger and his Woodstock, NY-based Creative Music Studio (CMS) to collaborate. Dave Holland recalled that the CMS was:

> . . . a school of improvisation, but improvising of all genres you know – so he had shakuhachi players, Indian musicians, African, from all over the world. And all the NY people, like the Art Ensemble, Ornette Coleman, by that time Jack [DeJohnette] was living up here too, so it was quite an active thing. So Karl was trying to get satellite programmes for the Creative Music Studio, partly because the CMS was struggling financially

– it always did. So, he was contacted by Banff . . . or he contacted Banff, perhaps, I think, to do the programme, and that was the first programme. It had Eddie Blackwell, I think [Lee] Konitz was on that, Kenny I think.[1137]

The following year, 1981, was the first year that Berger brought Dave and Kenny as part of the CMS to Banff. Dave, Kenny, and Don Thompson took over in 1982 and expanded it to a three-week course. It soon grew to four weeks, the first of which had a core group of faculty including Dave, Kenny, and Abraham Adzenyah. Adzenyah, a master drummer from Ghana, led the first week of the workshop, teaching rhythm and dance and giving instruction on original African drumming techniques. After Dave Holland's tenure, the Banff jazz workshop was led by saxophonist Steve Coleman from 1989–90, and Canadian trombonist/composer Hugh Fraser headed the workshop from 1991–98.

Kenny was an important member of the Banff jazz faculty. His 18 years there made up the majority of the teaching he ever did. Summers at Banff also provided important personal time for him, as Doreen accompanied him several of those years. They would often stay in a rented house in the town together with Dave Holland, enjoying the crisp mountain air and stunning scenery. Kenny also always made time to spend in St. Catharines with his Canadian family, either before or after his residency.

The schedule of the daily jazz workshop developed over the years into a fairly set routine. The first session of the morning was generally reserved for instrumental masterclasses led by corresponding faculty; naturally, Kenny taught all the trumpet players. Some mornings he would lead the trumpet students in a warm-up – often times having them read a chorale he had arranged of works by Bach, Gesualdo, and others. (Hugh Fraser fondly remembered hearing a Bach chorale floating across a field on a Banff summer morning, played by six or more trumpets.[1138]) Occasionally, he would even compose an original trumpet chorale for that morning's class. Once the students were appropriately warmed up, Kenny sometimes would have the trumpet players read a multi-trumpet piece he had composed for them. Many of these were densely contrapuntal and included chord changes; Kenny played piano to accompany the students while they took turns improvising on the piece's form. He also set up challenging games for the trumpeters. As an exercise in self-control, Kenny challenged each student to play a solo without using a single grace note while he accompanied at the piano. When they played a grace note, they were "out", and the next trumpeter had their chance.[1139] Don Thompson also remembers another game in which Kenny asked the students to "see if you can hear a note in your head, and find the note [with your trumpet], and see if you're right . . ." Characteristically, when it came his turn, Kenny, trumpet in hand, hesitated. "I'd better not try it – *I* might be wrong!"[1140] Ingrid Jensen remembered her trumpet sessions with Kenny at Banff:

For me it was incredible teaching, but I felt I couldn't keep up with what he was bringing in. He was never condescending. He would explain modes and how to manifest an idea over top of it. I think that some of the other [trumpet players] didn't show up when Steve Coleman and Dave Holland pulled out, [so] I sometimes got a one-on-one [lesson] with Kenny.[1141]

During the late mornings, there was usually a small group rehearsal. The students were organized into chamber jazz ensembles (usually four to six players) and coached by a faculty member on a rotating basis. Each faculty member generally brought their own material for the students to play through, or worked with them on the students' original music. Dave Holland explained "that was the principle of the course – to give a platform for each of the teachers to come in and individualize their music with the students, so they could get insight into how it was put together, and how to transform it".[1142] The close contact and attention the students received from the faculty also inspired students, many of whom had travelled to the workshop to be in the presence of and learn from their musical heroes. Banff alumnus and Irish-born bassist Ronan Guilfoyle remembers the first small-group rehearsal that Kenny came to coach: "What do you guys want to do?" he asked. "We want to play your music, Kenny!" came the response. "You must be crazy!" he said, producing four of his tunes from a suitcase full of his music he'd been carrying around. Kenny was very generous with the students at Banff, giving them many of his tunes – often in manuscript form – to take and play back home with their own groups.[1143] Later in the rehearsal, Kenny asked them if they had brought their own music. He played with them on one of Guilfoyle's tunes (which was dedicated to Pepper Adams). Kenny told Guilfoyle how much he liked the tune, going so far as to say he "wished he could write like that", and that it sounded like something Pepper Adams would have written. "To hear him play one of my tunes was a ridiculous thrill for me at the time," Guilfoyle said.[1144] The faculty also used the workshop as a laboratory for their own work.[1145] For many students, it was a point of pride and a rare privilege to have played a Kenny Wheeler composition with him before it appeared on an upcoming recording. Pianist Tania Gill remembers playing Kenny's "Present Past" with her group at Banff the year before he recorded it for ECM's *Angel Song*.[1146]

Not surprisingly, Kenny was not an overbearing presence as a teacher. He led by example, inspiring the students with his own playing while being very straightforward and honest. Pianist Richie Beirach, on the Banff jazz faculty with Kenny, admired him and called him "a great teacher" even if he occasionally wished Kenny displayed more confidence with students. Beirach said that Kenny "hated to sound, not even arrogant, just he hated to sound intellectual or authoritative", recalling that he would preface instruction with disclaimers like "this is just my opinion – I might be wrong". Beirach said he "just wanted to say, 'Man, *you're* the teacher, tell them what *you* think . . .' But he [Kenny] didn't want to hurt any young talent, because you could destroy talent . . ." Composer Darcy James Argue remembered Kenny revealing feelings of his own shortcomings while helping a trumpet player in his group:

> . . . [he] asked Kenny for advice on negotiating the altered scale. He looked at the floor and said, sheepishly, "The altered scale is the only thing I play." Then he added, *sotto voce*, " . . . and I only really know six of them." When you saw it close-up like this, it was obvious there was nothing false or affected about Kenny's chronic self-effacement . . . He genuinely did not want to think of himself as A Big Deal.[1147]

In a session dedicated to his suite *Heyoke* from *Gnu High*, Kenny provided another striking example of his modesty, pointing out, "I'm completely lost here", as a recording of the second part of the suite played over the speakers.[1148] Compositionally, however, Kenny had much more to say to students, even if his comments were still full of self-doubt. Richie Beirach observed:

> Kenny would hear a student's composition and would always begin by complimenting the good things, always. He wouldn't say "this chord sucks. What are you doing here? This is what *I* would do." He would say, "What is your rationale for that chord? How do you justify the chord?" A very good question, right?! Because of course they couldn't, because that was the weak point, and the chord was either a repetition of something earlier . . . he was very much, like me, very much aware of having too much of the same chord close together compositionally, because that makes the music sound like it's going to the same place. Especially if you have, let's say you have a climactic chord that's Dmin maj7. If you use that chord, like four, five bars before it, you've blocked out the possibility of a climax, which is architecture, right, even if it's a different melody.[1149]

After lunch, the faculty took turns leading "Common Sessions" in which all the students gathered and often one faculty member would speak about a topic of their choice. Kenny usually gave a class about his compositional process, using one of his tunes – sometimes in big-band score form – as an example. Although he often said in interviews "I must have a system but really don't want to know what it is", it is wrong to assume that Kenny wasn't methodical in his compositional process. Dave Holland remembered these classes:

> It was fascinating, because he would just take a tune and go through the song as how he wrote it. He would say, "I got to this point, and I couldn't really think about what to do next. So I tried something and, no, that doesn't really work. And I tried something else, and oh, *that* works . . ." But he went very honestly into what his creative process was: how each step of the composition evolved and the choices he was making.[1150]

Kenny was so paralysed by nerves at having to speak in front of large groups – Banff common sessions sometimes had 50–60 attendees – that he would write his entire presentation out longhand the night before and read it verbatim to the audience. (In this case, we are the beneficiaries of Kenny's suffering, as many of these manuscripts survive as a record of a process he would never have discussed otherwise.) His notes for these Common Sessions – and other composition lectures he gave when in residency at educational institutions around the world – show a great deal of thoughtful harmonic, melodic, and structural consideration. They also occasionally reveal his thoughts about the origin of the tune's title or something else on his mind at the moment. He also humorously described how the jazz students were perceived by the other participants when he began teaching at Banff:

> The other members of the Centre used to be very distrustful of the jazz students and used to hide all their belongings at night and if possible, hide indoors. But over the years they realized how serious all the jazz people were even though they are fun-loving, and they have come to like the jazz students very much and look forward to their coming. Sometimes we mix in with the other courses and some jazz student or teacher will write a piece using classical musicians, singers, dancers, or whatever. So the people in the other courses have realized that we are not just drug-taking, drink-taking hooligans but that we are good musicians who are quite capable of being on their level.[1151]

The days were quite long at Banff. Kenny said that "by the end of three weeks, boy, you're exhausted, from 9:30 in the morning to midnight, music all day. It's great but it's tiring."[1152] While the Banff faculty and students certainly did take their work seriously, there was always time for fun. Don Thompson recalls having a laugh at Kenny's expense one year with Norma: "One time Norma and I, for fun, wrote lyrics to 'Kayak'. They were really silly lyrics. I said, 'I've got some lyrics for the first couple lines of "Kayak"' and asked Norma if she could finish them for me:

> I hear the river callin'
> I got my Kayak happ'nin', baby,
> Don't ya want to come along,
> Come and sing a Kayak song with me,
> You know you won't regret it!

Don continued: "I wrote a lead sheet, on a piece of manuscript with big notes with tails on every eighth note, and I put the lyrics on it in with block letters. Just that much of it. And Norma wrote a little note on the bottom of the page:

Dear Mr. Wheeler,

I'm such a fan of your music. I've been working on these lyrics a long time. And that's as far as I've gotten, but I wanted to send them to you. When I finish it, I'll send you the rest."

Holding back laughter, Thompson told the rest of the story:

And she scrawled a name on the bottom you couldn't read, it was just a scribble of a signature, and she faxed it to Kenny, knowing that his fax machine wasn't set up to have an ID on it . . . So, we kind of forgot about it, and then I got a phone call from Norma. She said he was rehearsing with her and he'd seemed kind of grouchy. Then all a sudden on a break, Kenny came over and said, "You know, people are always writing words for my songs – now look at what somebody's sent me this time!" And he shows her the fax – and she just broke up! But she realizes that he doesn't have a clue where it's from. About a month later, I get an envelope from Kenny. "Don – thought you might get a laugh out of this. Somebody's written words for 'Kayak'!"

Kenny had some good-natured amusement at the students' expense, too. Pianist and composer Ellen Rowe remembered the first rehearsal with her combo:

Alto saxophonist Carol Chaikin was also in our combo, and the first day we were to meet we walked into our rehearsal room, where Kenny was quietly sitting in the back of the room. Carol didn't recognize him and in her forthright way said, "Who are you?" Without missing a beat, he said, "I'm *Barry Banff*. I own this place!"[1153]

Canadian bassist Duncan Hopkins recounted another Banff story when Kenny – who was known as someone to rarely make a negative comment about anyone, let alone a student – nearly committed an enormous and regrettable *faux pas* concerning a struggling young bassist in a group he'd coached that day:

At the end of the day, Ken went for a beer with a few of the faculty. Don Thompson and maybe a couple of the better students were hanging around, and they asked Ken how his ensemble was. And Ken said, "Oh, you know, I've got *the bass player*. He can't read, his time's bad, he can't play in tune . . ." And at this point the other guys are [*making motions for Kenny to stop talking*], realizing that this guy is just walking in behind him – and he's standing behind Ken just as he says " . . . *and* he has a terrible feel!" Ken, realizing what is happening, says, "He sounds great, though!"[1154]

In the years that there was a Banff Big Band, the students often played Kenny's music, as he was one of the few faculty with his own massive library of large-ensemble repertoire. The big band also played compositions and arrangements by other faculty and the students. Occasionally, there weren't enough students to make a full trumpet section for the band — or, at least, none of the players there were able to fulfil the strenuous technical demands of playing the lead trumpet part. In these cases, as Ingrid Jensen experienced, Kenny played lead. "Everything was there: no missed notes, killer time, great sound and total control of the horn," she said.[1155] She continued:

> It was special — it was mind-blowing. There was this other guy there who was playing pocket trumpet [in the section] and he kind of had an ego, trying to play higher than Kenny and Kenny would just say, "Why don't *you* play the bloody lead then . . . ?" Once [Kenny] found his footing and got all of us in balance with him, though, you could hear him just having a ball . . . He had no choice — he had to play lead — and he played the *shit* out of it . . .[1156]

Photo 25: Kenny playing lead trumpet with the Banff Big Band, next to Ingrid Jensen.
Courtesy Banff Centre Library Archive

Don Thompson also remembered witnessing Kenny's phenomenal abilities at Banff. "When Braxton was at Banff, I just couldn't believe it. Kenny was one of those guys, he could read anything," Don said. He also remembered hearing Kenny's powerful trumpet playing live for the first time. In rehearsal for an end-of-the-week faculty trio concert with Dave Holland and Kenny, Don said that "when Kenny played his first notes, he almost blew me out of the room with his sound."[1157] Ellen Rowe had a lovely memory of playing Kenny's music:

> The opportunity to play *The Sweet Time Suite* with him at Banff was possibly the single most important musical experience of my life. To be enveloped in those sounds and to have him standing next to me soloing over some of the movements was just such an incredibly emotional experience. The beauty of the music, coupled inextricably with his complete soloistic brilliance, was almost overwhelming.[1158]

Kenny's ongoing presence at Banff would continue to inspire students and faculty alike for some time to come.

Photo 26: Kenny, Don Thompson, and Dave Holland in concert at Banff.
Courtesy Banff Centre Library Archive

In the spring of 1982, Kenny and Paul Motian were finally reunited to play again after their Arild Andersen session together from two years previous. Thomas Stöwsand (of the Austrian booking company Saudades)[1159] organized a substantial tour for a "fascinating line-up" made up of players of Kenny's choosing, including Motian, Evan Parker, J.T., and J.-F. Jenny-Clark.[1160] Evan said that the tour was "quite a marathon . . . I think we had 29 concerts in 31 days." The group played in England in late March (Maidstone, London, Southampton, Nottingham),[1161] Scotland in early April (Dundee, Glasgow, Edinburgh),[1162] and moved on to Europe for several more dates. Although the music must have doubtlessly been extraordinary with those musicians, what Evan remembers most vividly happened offstage: "That tour, for me, was a sequence of illnesses. Each person in the band was ill in succession . . . it might even have been that Ken was quite ill to start with. And then, in Paris, J.T. was ill . . ." Once J.-F. got sick as well, they hired Riccardo Del Fra to play in his place. "And the irony of that is that [J.-F.] had spent a good hour saying [wistfully] 'Oh, the food in Italy . . .' But he had to stay at home, bed-ridden."[1163]

Kenny was also reunited with his old friend Bobby Wellins for two very fine, and very different, recordings in 1982. One was a Stan Tracey-led tribute to Thelonious Monk, and the other was Bobby's own record – quite unlike any of his others – titled *Birds of Brazil*. Bobby had originally intended to write a record about the birds of his own country, but someone from the World Wildlife Fund intervened and asked that he do it about the steady loss of the birds from the disappearing Brazilian rainforests. So Bobby said, "Yes we'll do that, and I got Tony Coe in, he did all the writing. And then we did a tour, and I thought it would be great to have Ken on it, because Ken and I were still seeing a bit of each other then . . ."[1164]

In June 1982, Kenny and Doreen returned to St. Catharines for his parents' 60th wedding anniversary celebration. It was a happy affair, with a banner with silhouette-style caricatures of Kenny's father and mother on the wall, and an appearance by the Wheeler family band, including Kenny on trumpet, Wilf Sr. playing trombone, Kenny's brother Paul on clarinet, and his brother Wilf Jr. playing piano. "There was a quality about Kenny – whenever he came home, he brought the family together . . . It just seemed that if he was coming home, there'd be some reason why we'd have to have a get together here," his younger sister Mabel said.[1165]

Despite the joyous occasion, at 82 years old, Kenny's father was in declining health. He continued to play the trombone in local bands, including keeping up his position with the Lincoln and Welland Regiment band in St. Catharines, but his glaucoma caused him to have to stop driving and sell the family car. Wilf Sr., who maintained his position as sergeant-at-arms with the Niagara Musicians Union (AFM local 298), was especially proud of his famous son. Local musician Warren Stirtzinger recalled him bragging about him, showing off Kenny's latest records at union meetings.[1166] Mabel said, "Kenny was living my dad's dream – because he would have loved to have been a full-time musician", adding that her father was proud of Kenny, "and yet I bet he never told him."[1167]

Wilfred Wheeler Sr. died on 12 January 1983. Kenny's sister Mabel and his brother Wilf Jr. made the arrangements, and the funeral was to be only two days later. The siblings disagreed about whether Kenny should be told immediately or not. His sister Helen, generally the more assertive of the other mild-mannered Wheeler siblings (and more involved in Kenny's music), was especially reluctant to tell Kenny about their father's death, concerned about the expense to Kenny both in terms of his career and his bank account. Since he was in London, he was bound to have engagements on the books, and, she argued – albeit without his consultation – the transatlantic flight would be too costly.[1168] Ultimately, Mabel made the decision to call Kenny and he decided he would come home for the funeral. "I thought he should know," she said.[1169]

Kenny did have at least one important gig in his diary on 15 January. Azimuth was in the midst of a British Arts Council Contemporary Music Network tour. Fortunately for Kenny, his musical family in London compensated so he could be with his actual family in Canada, and John Surman made himself available to cover the Azimuth date for him.[1170] Kenny arrived back in St. Catharines just in time. Before leaving for the funeral home, the Wheeler family waited for Kenny to arrive at the house on Blain Place. It happened to be 14 January, Kenny's 53rd birthday. "As soon as he came through the door, instead of being sad, we all started to sing 'Happy Birthday' to him," Mabel said, laughing. "It was like a party."[1171] But ultimately, of course, it was a profoundly sad event for the whole family, especially Kenny. His father was his first musical influence, who brought home the cornet that changed his life, held the family together as their mother struggled with alcoholism, and provided an example to Kenny of the kind of rigorous discipline that he brought to his own work.

All these things must have been on Kenny's mind when he paid his respects to his father. His sister Helen remembered that Kenny had "such deep feelings about things".[1172] Mabel agreed, saying their father's death was "very, very hard on him".[1173] "Kenny went to the funeral parlour all on his own," Helen said. "I remember walking in and seeing Kenny sitting all by himself by the coffin, just staring. It was such a sad picture, to see him. Kenny was so upset by Dad's dying."[1174] The officiating priest – who knew Wilf Sr. and his musical family well – wanted Kenny to play trumpet at the funeral mass. "That was not something that he was about to do," Mabel said.[1175] The Lincoln and Welland band, so near and dear to Mr. Wheeler, played several hymns instead.

1983 was a difficult year for Kenny and those close to him. Not only did he lose his father but the marriage between his close friends John Taylor and Norma Winstone ended later that year. John remained the leader of Azimuth and continued to perform with the trio, but Kenny and Norma noticed that J.T.'s energies had changed with the group. Kenny asked Norma, "When's he going to come up with some new music for us? He writes new music for other people and other things he's in, but he doesn't seem to come up with new music for us."[1176] If they were called for a gig, they did it, but, perhaps understandably, John was not chasing work for the trio as he had before.

Negative reviews also took their toll on the group's momentum. One concert at the Queen Elizabeth Hall, in a shared bill with the Gary Burton Quartet, generated a confluence of cutting criticism. Reviewers contrasted the energy of Burton's group – who opened the concert – with the relative serene quality of Azimuth, who played the second half. Richard Williams, writing for *The Times*, called them "a British trio which acts as a vehicle for the limpid compositions of its pianist John Taylor . . .", saying "they made a coolly seductive noise: the occasional dissonance jarred like an onion in a blancmange."[1177] This was the kindest of the reviews. Derek Jewell, writing for the *Sunday Times*, said, "The noise is almost relentlessly soothing, verging on soporific. Wheeler deserves a better setting, and an aura of dozey pretentiousness arises if the group is exposed long. They were, and hunks of the audience voted with their feet."[1178] But the harshest – and the one that especially stuck with them for years – dubbed Norma, Kenny, and John respectively as "Wordless, Doom-Laden, and Just Plain Dull".[1179] "I don't mind bad reviews but why get vicious?" he asked.[1180] It was so savage that it was almost comical, and Bob Cornford immortalized the epithets by leaving a card for the band backstage at their next gig addressed to *WL, DL, and JPD*.[1181]

Despite their separation and although Azimuth began to work less and less frequently, J.T. was still Kenny and Norma's favourite pianist. She said, "I would still ask John, if I had anything, and he'd still do everything. And we were great friends really; we would travel places together." John expected her to stop wanting to work with him. "He said to me, 'I know you say, "I'll always book you," but there'll come a time when you won't.' But I said, 'No, there'll never come a time when I wouldn't. You're the person I want to play with.'"[1182]

———··———

Following the death of his father, Kenny recorded his fourth album as a leader for ECM. The record's title, *Double, Double You*,[1183] is a tribute to Wilf Wheeler Sr. and a play on his initials. The titles of the tunes for the record are almost entirely named after members of his family: "W.W." for his father, "Ma Bel" for his mother Mabel (which might also be a play on her early job as a telephone operator[1184]), "Three for D'reen" for Doreen, "Blue for Lou" for his daughter Louann, and "Mark Time" for his son. Kenny's large family provided him a blessing and a curse when naming his tunes: "When you begin writing pieces for members of your family, you find that you then have to write pieces for everyone in the family, or some members of your family will be angry with you," he said.[1185]

Drummer Jack DeJohnette and bassist Dave Holland, veterans of Kenny's first two ECM records, joined him once more to record *Double, Double You* at New York's Power Station Studios on 5 and 6 May 1983. John Taylor completed the rhythm section on piano, finally making his way onto Kenny's ECM bandleader discography. Before the recording sessions, John and Kenny went to Dave's upstate New York home to rehearse for a few days. Saxophonist Michael Brecker joined Kenny for the record as well, rounding off the quintet personnel. He was already well known as a soloist in his own right and for his collaborations with his brother Randy in the Brecker Brothers, with a host of jazz and pop stars, and as a part of American television's *Saturday Night Live* band. Dave Holland had actually met Michael very early on in his career, when the 18-year-old saxophonist first moved to New York:

> Clare and I had a loft at that point, and there was a roof behind the loft that connected with the building on the other side of the block . . . and Mike's loft was on the other side, and he was living on his own. He'd climb out of his window at the back, walk across the roof, and climb in the kitchen window, and Clare would feed him . . .[1186]

Dave said that despite his revered status in the jazz world, Brecker was "a sweet guy", who "was always open and wanted to learn, you know . . . I think he loved Kenny's music . . . I know that he had a lot of respect for it." Comparing Brecker to Jarrett, Holland observed that "it wasn't like with Keith, where Keith had these reservations, just in terms of how it related to what he wanted to do. Mike jumped into it."[1187]

*Double, Double You* was well received by critics. *DownBeat*'s Kevin Whitehead gave the album 4½ stars, and was especially taken with Michael Brecker: "Brecker fans take note: his long solo in the middle of the 23-minute medley is one of his smokingest outings on record. And Dave Holland gets to dance around a couple of irresistibly shapely bass riffs on 'Foxy Trot.'"[1188] The *Washington Post* said, "Holland's digressive bass lines and Jack DeJohnette's nuanced cymbal work provide an insistent momentum under Wheeler's patient, poignant melodies. Wheeler's unhurried, crystal-clear trumpet tone gives his compositions an enchanting, seductive quality."[1189] Mark Miller called the album "the most aggressive of Wheeler's four ECM albums to date", observing that "Wheeler's compositions, like his playing, soar over the wide melodic intervals and sob quietly over the small ones, giving his music a compelling happy/sad, bittersweet character." Miller continued his praise of Kenny's personal sound: "It's a quality not to be mistaken for anyone but Wheeler, and this at a time when too few musicians these days are identifiable quickly, if at all."[1190]

---

In August 1983, Kenny was back in New York after baritone saxophonist Pepper Adams invited him to play with his quintet at Fat Tuesday's club. One of the leading soloists on his instrument and an original member of the Thad

Jones/Mel Lewis Jazz Orchestra, Adams was an admirer of Kenny's, going as far back as his 1968 recording *Windmill Tilter*. "Pepper loved that album," Kenny said.[1191] They had met at least twice before, on the European Battle of the Bands tour as well as when Kenny deputized in the Thad/Mel band at Ronnie Scott's in 1972.

Almost a decade after their meeting at Ronnie's, Kenny again had the opportunity to play with Pepper; the two joined Per Husby's trio for a short tour of Norway in May 1981. Two years later, from 16–20 August 1983 – just after Kenny finished teaching at Banff – Pepper brought him to New York for his residency at Fat Tuesday's club, located on Third Avenue in Manhattan's Gramercy Park neighbourhood. "I was overjoyed," Kenny said. "I got along with him right away."[1192] He joined Hank Jones on piano, Clint Houston on bass, and drummer Louis Hayes. They played several of Adams's original tunes, some standards, and even some of Kenny's own tunes, including "Old Ballad". Adams was encouraging of Kenny and supported him in playing in his own way: "In the middle of the week, I was playing not too far out, but my style, which was a bit out there. At the end of the week he said, 'Just play the way you play. I like it.'"[1193]

The last two nights of the residency were recorded and released on LP as *Pepper Adams Live at Fat Tuesday's*.[1194] Reviewers and listeners were puzzled by Adams's choice of personnel, especially Kenny, for the record. Mark Miller wrote that the collaboration had listeners "scratching their heads", calling their partnership "unlikely": "The trumpeter defers uncertainly to Adams' more secure lead, and the disparities are more apparent than the blend," he wrote. Miller is also critical of the audio quality of the recording, remarking that it sounded as if it were recorded in a shoebox.[1195] Other listeners agreed with Miller's assessment of the recorded sound. In a conversation about the recording with alto saxophonist Phil Woods, author Ben Sidran remarked that "the stage [at Fat Tuesday's] is so narrow. There's not much depth, so the band has to line up in a row." "It's like recording in a bowling alley," Woods replied.[1196] Regardless of issues of sound quality, members of the Recording Academy in 1985 seemed to have a higher opinion of the album: *Live at Fat Tuesday's* earned Kenny his first nomination for a Grammy award, nominated jointly with Pepper for "Best Jazz Instrumental Performance, Soloist".[1197] They didn't win; instead, young trumpet sensation Wynton Marsalis was awarded Grammys as a soloist in both the Jazz and Classical categories for the second year in a row.

Tragically, immediately before receiving his Grammy nomination, Adams was seriously injured in a freak accident. His car's parking brake failed, causing it to roll down his driveway, pinning him against his garage and crushing his leg. This event must have affected Kenny deeply, as he was still telling the story to some of his students at Banff years later.[1198] After months spent recovering from his injury, Adams was diagnosed with lung cancer and died on 10 September 1986.

Phil Woods appreciated Adams's uncompromising approach: "He always played full out. Pepper would never skate. He always had that intense passion from his big horn."[1199] The same could easily be said about Kenny. Perhaps this is the quality that Adams heard in him and recognized so ecstatically way back at Ronnie Scott's when Kenny subbed with the Jones/Lewis band; the shy baritone saxophonist recognized a kindred spirit in Kenny's musical – and social – personality. Their respect and admiration was mutual. "He was very encouraging. He was a very intelligent man and very funny. I was sorry that his end wasn't all that pleasant," Kenny lamented.[1200]

As the 1980s progressed and Kenny approached his 60th birthday, he showed no signs of slowing down. Indeed, several of his most significant projects were yet to come.

# 6 Music for Large and Small Ensembles

**People always used to tell me I sounded like Miles Davis, but there's one difference. Miles sounds sad and rich, and I sound sad and poor.**

*Kenny Wheeler*

In the early 1980s, Kenny began to reach a wider audience as a member of a new quintet led by his old friend Dave Holland. Although Dave had enjoyed a long and fruitful association with saxophonist Sam Rivers throughout the previous decade, he decided to leave the band in 1981 to focus on establishing a group of his own.[1201] In March 1982, however, Dave developed a serious infection that resulted in open-heart surgery. "When they were doing the operation, they found that the valve didn't need replacing and that they could repair it . . . So I don't have an artificial valve, I don't have to take all that medication and I do have a perfectly normal heart. I can jog, I can run, I can bike-ride, whatever I want. I can play the bass till the morning hours!" he later told the *New York Times*.[1202] "It was a close call, you know . . ."[1203] By July of that year, Dave was driving a van on his way west to teach once more at the Banff Centre in Alberta with his children and bass in tow.

This health scare gave a new urgency to Dave's life and music. The quintet he would form – which would become an important group of the era – came at a time when there was significant division in the jazz community about what it meant to follow "the tradition" – with the "young lions" in the US leading the charge to turn to a more literal interpretation of the tradition, playing standards, etc., versus the more abstract model, which meant continuing the tradition of innovation. The Dave Holland Quintet was certainly a proponent of the latter philosophy, but still had a strong conceptual connection to the roots of the music, especially in the group-improvisation approach of the horns: "I've always enjoyed New Orleans music, the traditional music, and there was something about the sound of that three-horn front line that I really liked."[1204] Incidentally, Kenny's abilities on the trumpet were not lost on one of the aforementioned young lions at the time. When asked at a workshop in the late 1980s what he thought of Kenny, one attendee recalled Wynton Marsalis replying unequivocally, "He's a *bad motherfucker*."[1205]

Just as with Kenny's ensembles, personal connections were at the heart of Dave's choice of musicians for his new group, and he made use of two of the relationships from the Sam Rivers band: his rhythm-section partner, drummer Steve Ellington, and the young saxophonist Steve Coleman.[1206] One way in which Dave's quintet was unique was its lack of a chordal instrument, such as piano or guitar. "I find that not having a chordal instrument gives a certain kind of freedom to the sound of the band, and I wanted to develop the three-horn front line," he said. Dave had also worked with trombonist Julian Priester during a trip to Seattle:

> I could really hear Julian Priester's trombone sound and Kenny's flugel and trumpet sound going together beautifully. And I had gone out to Seattle to do something at the school where Julian was teaching and we did a concert where I put together some music that included Julian in there, and when we played together I loved it . . . so Julian was the trombone player I thought about using because of his historical experience with Max [Roach] . . . Sun Ra, and all the [other] things he'd done.[1207]

Dave chose Kenny to complete the front line, which was an easy decision:

> Because – who else?! It's a simple answer. Tell me somebody else. I wanted a band who could do the full range of music – and I couldn't think of anybody who had that capability as well as Kenny did – to be able to go from a beautiful ballad to free improvisation . . . so that was the main thing. And, of course, my relationship with Kenny was an important part of it. But it was totally about music, of course. And then the other part was I've always wanted people who can write music in the band, so I thought it would be lovely to have Kenny write a couple of things for the band so we could feature those in the group.[1208]

Kenny did contribute a few titles to the band's book, including the new piece "5 Four Six" and a reworking of "The Good Doctor" from *Song for Someone*. As a player, Kenny favoured a cornet with this band on several tunes. Dave speculated that the cornet might have somehow brought Kenny closer to the feeling of New Orleans-style improvisation on tunes like "Homecoming".[1209] Kenny was also likely attracted to the dual characteristics of the cornet, blowing a little more freely like the flugelhorn he often preferred but projecting more like a trumpet.[1210]

Being part of this band provided many new challenges for Kenny. Steve Coleman, still in his mid-twenties compared with Kenny in his early fifties, was exploring complex rhythmic ideas in his pieces, as was Dave. Rhythm was an aspect of music that Kenny had not spent as much time consciously exploring as he had done with harmony and counterpoint, and it presented a different musical challenge to the one he had faced with Braxton. There, the difficulty lay in executing written lines on the trumpet, but the soloing was open. This was now a conceptual challenge in learning the language needed to improvise in the group. Steve Coleman described the early days of rehearsals at Dave's house in upstate New York:

> When we first started playing together, [Kenny] told me that he'd never thought about rhythm that much. At least not from that perspective. And that he hadn't done a lot of work in rhythm and that it was hard for him, you know, it was hard for him to kind of figure out what was going on because he had done most of his work in harmony and melody and stuff like that. And I told him that makes sense, living in Europe, it makes sense from that standpoint . . . and that's natural. There's nothing wrong with any of this; it's natural to grow up doing what everybody else around you is doing. I grew up differently, so that's why I'm doing it differently.[1211]

But it was a challenge Kenny loved. "That was a great experience for me, even though I felt that I wasn't playing the music as well as the others in the band. To be playing that music with Dave, Steve Coleman and Julian Priester – that was a great period for me."[1212] Speaking about the rhythmic nature of the music, he said: "I was just floating along, I don't think I was contributing to it too much . . . [Steve Coleman] brought these very difficult pieces – which were along the same lines as Dave's music. They were difficult to play and the rhythmic side of it was really difficult."[1213] He continued:

> The rhythmic side has always been my weak point. As long as I can hear the harmony, I know where I am and I can float around. But you couldn't float around in Steve's music. You had to know where you were rhythmically at every point. Even though I got a little better at it over the period of being with the band, I always felt a bit behind. But I enjoyed my experience in the band very much.[1214]

Kenny later shared these frustrations with Ronan Guilfoyle at Banff, saying that he "would have quit Dave's band because it was so hard, but stayed because everyone was so good".[1215]

These rhythmically complex pieces were only one element of the music, however. Dave wanted the individual personalities in the music as well as their skills: "Everybody had that ability to go through the whole range of music and have the historical reference in their playing, too."[1216] Steve also made it clear: "[Kenny] was a fantastic musician. He wouldn't have been there if he couldn't play the music . . . [but] he always did [give himself a hard time]; that's just his personality. He did that even on stuff I thought he was killing on."[1217] Steve continued: "What you try to do is have some things that are maybe one person's strong suit, and you try to have some things that are another person's strong suit – Duke Ellington was very good at this . . . so you're [always] using the strong elements of your band, and Dave did that too."[1218] Certainly, Kenny's writing was one of those strong elements, and, even though he didn't contribute as many pieces as some of the others, they certainly had an effect. "There were certain compositions that Kenny wrote that were fantastic," Coleman said. "He was definitely the best writer in the band . . . to me he was the most advanced cat in that area . . . I learned a lot from listening to his harmonic stuff and everything, because he was really, really strong . . ."[1219] Perhaps because he held him in such high regard, Steve was puzzled by Kenny's constant self-effacement, at first even a bit unsure of its sincerity. Steve even once tried to counter Kenny's self-criticism with some perspective, saying, "But, you're like *the god* of harmony!"[1220]

Following their first run of rehearsals at Dave's place, the band played two nights in New York City's Public Theater in April 1983. Performances in New York were always daunting for Kenny. Remembering a night with trumpet stars Randy Brecker and Jon Faddis in the audience, Dave said that Kenny "always saw NY as being a place where all these great trumpet players lived, and when he would play with me in New York I know he was always a little anxious. I didn't talk a lot with him about it, because he was dealing with it."[1221]

In the fall of 1983, the quintet met to rehearse for a few days in Switzerland for their upcoming ECM recording date. They met in an old farmhouse occasionally used to host concerts that was owned by two friends of the Hollands, pianist Six Trutt and his wife Renate.[1222] After the rehearsals, they went to Tonstudio Bauer in Ludwigsburg, Germany to record the album, which became *Jumpin' In*.[1223] After the record was released in the spring of 1984, the group toured the US, playing at Sweet Basil in New York, among other stops. By this point, drummer Steve Ellington had been replaced by Marvin "Smitty" Smith, a decision made largely because of the difficulties of geography: "I loved playing with [Steve Ellington] – but the only reason I stopped was because he lived in Atlanta, and I already had Julian in Seattle and Kenny in London, and it's completely impractical," Dave said. "I needed to have a drummer in New York so that he and Steve [Coleman] and I could rehearse separately and then when we got together with Kenny and Julian we'd have some of the stuff together and we could just add them to it."[1224]

The album was generally praised by critics, especially in the United States. The *New York Times* called *Jumpin' In* "one of this year's definitive jazz records", and the *Washington Post* dubbed Dave "one of the best acoustic bassists in jazz". John Fordham's review for the *Guardian* was more mixed:

> Holland's writing through much of this set oddly resembles Ken Wheeler's own, which often has a rather inconclusive, plush, radio big-band conservatism about it, and the compositions don't quite meet the challenge of Holland's dedication of the record to the memory of Mingus. But as sharers of the spirit of improvisation, Holland's musicians are superb. Their visit here in the winter will be eagerly awaited.[1225]

Fordham's expectations were likely exceeded when the quintet played London that November of 1984. In response, the critic dubbed them "a band of the highest class, vibrant and emotional but as logical as a game of chess".[1226] Kenny especially appreciated the reactions of his fellow musicians to the quintet: "I have played in bands which received the compliment from many musicians they did not know, of what we were playing, what was written and what was improvised. This happened several times while I was in Dave Holland's quintet, and to me this is about as high a compliment as you can get."[1227]

While on the road with the quintet, Kenny enjoyed taking long walks whenever he could, balancing solitude and social time. "We were all friends," Dave said, "so we would talk about life and what was happening in our lives a lot, as you do with old friends. We were doing a lot of train travel . . . so we were sitting in compartments talking to each other." All the while, Kenny maintained his focused discipline in his composing and trumpet playing. Dave was impressed with Kenny's work ethic, which he had witnessed previously in Braxton's quartet. Kenny would even do composition exercises on the train: "He would say he was going to study formal counterpoint, with the *cantus firmus* and all that, and he would sit on the train for hours working that stuff out," Dave said. "It was just a sign of that thing that Kenny had, which was to constantly be reaching for the next thing and trying to improve."[1228]

But Kenny continued to feel his imperfections profoundly. While no longer quite as hindered by the nervousness that affected him in his earlier years, he still experienced performance anxiety. Ever watchful, Dave was aware of it, too, recalling a scene at a small club in Brussels:

> It was one of those places where there is this stage – it wasn't a big stage – but towards the side of the stage there was this pillar here – and Kenny would always play on this side, Steve was in the middle and Julian here – and Kenny spent every minute that he wasn't playing a solo or doing the ensemble behind the pillar! . . . I didn't say anything. I just thought, "Man, that is just such a weird thing to do!" It was like he didn't want to be there, but he *did* want to be there . . . like this contradiction.[1229]

Even though Dave didn't understand Kenny's trepidation, he admired him for facing it:

> I mean, he never backed down. I told Kenny once, I used to think about St. George and the dragon, and I said, "You're like St. George – you face down the dragon every time you get on stage." And, to me, that's even more admirable than the ones who just get up and are, "OK, I've got it all together." To overcome that and then play the way he played . . . to me it was such an act of willpower and courage that he combined in doing that all the time.

After developing the band for the year with live appearances throughout 1984, including an Italian summer festival appearance in South Tyrol,[1230] two nights at Sweet Basil in New York in September, and an eight-date UK tour, the quintet returned to Tonstudio Bauer in November 1984 to record their second album, *Seeds of Time*.[1231] Again featuring compositions by all the members, including Kenny's "The Good Doctor", the album captures the ever-evolving nature of this band at its best.

———··———

Kenny's reputation continued to grow throughout the United States, where he would play with some of the most innovative young stars in jazz. In August 1984, he recorded for guitarist Bill Frisell's second ECM album as a leader.[1232] Bill's recollections of hearing Kenny back in the '70s show just what an impact the trumpeter was starting to have on that scene of like-minded and explorative young players. As a 20-year-old student in Boston in 1971, Bill went to the Jazz Workshop to hear Braxton's quartet: "That music for me at the time was the very edge of what was brand new . . . And to hear [Kenny], I never heard of him or knew anything about him at that point, but it was so startling, the whole thing. To hear his absolute clarity, well, everything I knew to be there later was there obviously at that point . . ."[1233] Bill took a break from his studies and left Boston for a few years, returning to the Berklee College of Music in 1975. At this point *Gnu High* had just been released: "[Kenny] was becoming kind of a larger-than-life [figure] . . . one of the people I was looking up to – Thelonious Monk, Sonny Rollins – he was amongst those larger-than-life role models for me."[1234] Another London-based musician made an impression on Bill and his friends: Mike Gibbs, who was teaching at Berklee at the time. Bill played in his student ensemble, having already become aware of and inspired by Mike's music. "Back when I first started listening to jazz, one of the first concerts I went to was to hear Gary Burton's band and I realized, *Wait a minute, why does this music sound this way?* They were playing a lot of Mike Gibbs's music – so he was so much a part of what my DNA was starting to become."[1235]

Bill's relationships with Mike Gibbs and Kenny would soon intersect. Following a couple of years in college, Bill moved to Belgium with a band in 1978. Gibbs had scheduled a tour of the UK and the band's usual guitarist, Philip Catherine, was unavailable. Remembering that Bill was in Belgium and that he knew a lot of the music from his Berklee days, Mike quickly hired him to play on the tour. "That was the first, *wow*, there's Charlie Mariano and Eberhard Weber . . . and John Marshall playing drums, and all those British guys, and Kenny – I was like, *Oh my God, Kenny Wheeler!*"[1236] As a result of that Contemporary Music Network tour with Gibbs, Bill was invited to play on an upcoming ECM recording date with Eberhard Weber, where he met Manfred Eicher for the first time. Frisell said, "I was so scared, I don't think I made much of a [impression]. I was so timid in the studio and . . . I didn't *ruin* the record but I just sort of got through it . . . but the connection was made."[1237] Bill eventually recorded his own debut, *In Line*,[1238] for ECM, and the following year began preparations for a follow-up album, *Rambler.*[1239]

> I can't remember if Manfred mentioned Kenny, or if it was in my mind, but Kenny was the first, sort of the catalyst for the whole thing. It might have been that Manfred said "Would you like to do something with Kenny?" and I was like, *wow* . . . and, again, I didn't know him well enough but I felt like because I had met him I could at least ask him and see what he says.[1240]

Bill wrote Kenny a letter: "I've been talking with Manfred about doing a record and would like to ask if you'd be interested to do it . . ." He explained further and mentioned some of the other musicians, finishing, ". . . I really would love to get to play with you again and sure hope you might like to do this project."[1241] Kenny gladly accepted and the plans for the record progressed. Bill said:

> I just put together what was for me sort of a dream [line-up], and I'd never recorded with my own [group] . . . So it was after this that I actually put together my own band . . . Everybody that was in there I was in awe of. I wrote a lot of music and then we had one rehearsal, but everybody was there, they were all people that were supporting me, no one was looking at their watch . . . Everybody, and Kenny for sure, gave me the confidence to be able.[1242]

In another recollection, Bill said:

> I still remember that going into the studio – I was just terrified. I was in some sort of altered state just trying to connect the wires to my guitar and I was like, *What is going to happen?!* But then we start playing . . . That's always the way it is with me, I'm always more nervous before and then the music will take over. It must be like that with him too because you can hear when he plays it just goes off like that.[1243]

Indeed, Kenny is in fantastic form throughout the record, and a surprising amount of his conventional studio technique is called upon for the quirky fanfare-type figures at the end of "Music I Heard", through to the exquisite beauty of his melodic playing on the title track, "Rambler". He is perhaps at his most strikingly effective on the folk-inflected simplicity of compositions such as "Strange Meeting", showing the harmonic invention and range he first demonstrated on the pop-ish "Lord of the Reedy River" back in Ronnie Scott's band in 1968. Bill explained:

> There's a couple songs on there that are *so* simple, like a folk song: very, very [simple]. He might have even made a comment about that, where it was more [like] maybe he wasn't accustomed to playing in such a triadic [way] . . . I just remembered the way he just put so much more in it than what was actually there . . . I guess he spoiled me, because that's what I expect from everybody when I play![1244]

While he was forging new collaborations with brilliant young artists like Bill Frisell, Kenny maintained ties with his ongoing associations. Both the United Jazz+Rock Ensemble and Globe Unity Orchestra continued to perform live and record new albums. The UJ+RE toured the UK for the first time in late 1984 in a highly anticipated debut appearance and a substantial 11-date tour, just preceding Kenny's tour with Dave Holland, even overlapping a few of the same venues. Kenny was singled out in a *Guardian* preview as one of "Europe's most celebrated improvisers", and was mentioned a few more times in their review of the London concert. His work also continued with Globe Unity; the group marked its 20th anniversary in 1986 with a recording of the same name.[1245] Globe Unity also made a notable appearance the following year at the Chicago Jazz Festival, where some members of the audience rejected the music. The *Chicago Tribune* reviewer wrote that they "seemed to regard Globe Unity's dense, spontaneous abstractions as the sonic equivalent of sauerkraut juice". The reviewer quickly added that he "couldn't have disagreed more, finding himself fascinated by the solos of trombonist George Lewis, tenor saxophonist Evan Parker and trumpeter Kenny Wheeler".[1246] There were also regular sessions for NDR with both these bands around this period, but the greater proportion of his work by this point had swung away from free jazz with only occasional forays back into that world.[1247] His many experiences there had clearly set him apart, however, affording him the reputation of an extremely adaptable musician.

In Europe, new connections resulted in sideman appearances on records with Dutch avant-garde bassist and composer Maarten Altena in 1982 and 1984, and with Danish guitarist Karsten Houmark in 1985. Azimuth also continued to work together as a trio and in extended forms. In May 1984, they played a week at Ronnie Scott's opposite the Monty Alexander Trio, where the group was expanded to include bassist Chris Laurence and the young drummer Steve Argüelles.[1248] In September 1984, the original Azimuth trio, augmented by drummer Tony Oxley, headed to southern Italy to perform with bassist Paolo Damiani and the Sardinian trumpeter Paolo Fresu. The live performance was captured for an album, *Live at Roccella Jonica*,[1249] where the leaderless band played a programme split between Kenny's and Damiani's compositions. The synergy between the three Azimuth bandmates is evident, especially in Norma Winstone's delivery of the beautiful "The Widow in the Window" melody leading into Kenny's solo, and on the collective free improvisation in Damiani's "Esablu". John Taylor is extraordinary throughout, showing just what an original force he had become.

Another vocalist was present at this gathering. The Italian singer Tiziana Simona and Kenny became friends around this time and the pair recorded an album not long afterward.[1250] The title track, "Gigolo", is a composition of Kenny's that had appeared in 1982 under the name "Sly Eyes". In addition to setting Italian lyrics to some of Kenny's compositions, Simona was also responsible for commissioning him to set to music some poetry by writers including Lewis Carroll and W.B. Yeats. (This was the music that would later become Kenny's suite of songs, *Mirrors*.) Kenny established further Italian connections during the mid-'80s, including a new relationship with the Soul Note label, contributing to a diversification of the labels on which he released his albums. The first of these Soul Note appearances was a quartet date led by Italian saxophonist Claudio Fasoli, for the album *Welcome*, recorded in March 1986 with bassist J.-F. Jenny-Clark and drummer Daniel Humair. Kenny's playing on this album is spectacularly assured, and he would soon be back on Soul Note for one of his finest non-ECM recordings as leader.

Not long after their trip to Roccella Jonica, Azimuth returned to Oslo to record their fourth ECM album, *Azimuth '85*.[1251] Recorded in March of that year, the album captures them at their best, but came at a challenging time for the band; although they were getting more and more recognition for their work, it was getting harder to secure gigs, with some reviewers still very critical of the trio. The tunes on *Azimuth '85* are nearly all John Taylor originals and show the range of harmonic and rhythmic influences he continued to absorb. There is also more use of overdubbing, both improvised and written. The opening track, "Adios Iony", is a great example, culminating in a classic J.T. two-handed rhythmic ostinato underneath multiple overdubbed voices. That tune was also a turning point in the session for Manfred. Norma remembered:

> We'd done a whole day and [Manfred] seemed not to really respond much to anything, and then suddenly Kenny and I just went, *What are we going to do!?* And we went in and started the beginning of "Adios Iony". We just improvised on about three notes and made these sort of . . . He likes that kind of thing, you know, just that sort of choral-sounding thing. And then, after that had gone on for a while, Manfred had recorded that bit which he liked, and then he played it, and John went in and at some point came in with [*sings rhythmic bassline figure*] and he *really* loved that. It was a happening. *Whoa, now we have something*. . . And it was alright from then on – but you have to grab [Manfred] with something, you know . . .[1252]

*Azimuth '85* features just one of Kenny's tunes: another melodic gem in 3/4 time titled "Who Are You?". The lyric for this is by Jane White, a rare departure from those penned by Norma. (White also set a wonderful lyric to Kenny's "Everybody's Song But My Own".)

Following the recording of *Azimuth '85*, the trio performed a set at the Bass Clef club in London. It was something of a Wheeler double bill, with Azimuth playing opposite his own quartet, which featured J.T., Chris Laurence, and John Marshall. Unfortunately, the night fuelled his negative feelings towards critics. He later told Brian Priestley, "I didn't want critics in . . . but the lady who runs it said, 'Oh yeah, John Fordham and Derek Jewell's coming in' and

I said, 'But I didn't want any critics because I know what they're like!'"[1253] The reviews were not glowing. John Fordham in the *Guardian* said that Azimuth "has found itself cast somewhat in the ECM Records house-style of slightly fey and indecisive romanticism". While complimenting "the increasingly mature and attractive voice of Norma Winstone" and pointing out that John Taylor "exhibits much of the flair and fluency of Herbie Hancock and Bill Evans", Fordham added: "while Wheeler displays a similar sure-footedness but expressed though a brittle anxious tone, the two are ideal partners."[1254] Derek Jewell was much more critical in the *Sunday Times*: "It's all untaxing, certainly different, but the voice quality veers towards blandness and, at times, uneasy strain. It's the lack of colour which ultimately makes Azimuth interesting rather than compulsive, but at least they had the sense to include 'Out Of This World' from the majestic treasure house of popular song, which is more than Wheeler's quartet later did."[1255] The last statement was actually not even correct, but Jewell continued, apparently speaking on behalf of all audiences' ability to listen to original music: "Why in six pieces can they not improvise upon one known song? The ear cannot absorb *all* new work *all* the time; and genuinely popular music, even at the art end, ignores the astonishing 20th-century repertoire completely at its peril."[1256] The reviews from that night left an impression on Kenny and obviously added to a feeling in him that must have been steadily growing. He referred to them in two different interviews at the time, first to Brian Priestley:

> . . . in one he said, "but why, oh why didn't he play a standard?" meaning me. I did a set with a quartet, then we did Azimuth as a trio. But obviously he'd never heard of "Soul Eyes" which has been recorded by John Coltrane and we played that. And that was his main, well, he didn't say much, that's about all he said, "didn't play a standard!" . . . So now if I play in London I'll say "I'll play there but I don't want any critics in." [*long pause*] Sounds a bit bitter I suppose, I'm not really bitter, I mean, I know nine times out of ten they're going to give you a strange review, anybody who's got anything to do with ECM.[1257]

He expanded further on his feelings about this in a conversation with Ted O'Reilly for Toronto's Jazz FM:

> The place was packed . . . you couldn't move in the place! So, I must have some attraction . . . I don't know, just . . . I was annoyed, I didn't want any critics in there. I have a thing to do with English critics, you know. I didn't even think about it . . . I don't feel that way in every country about critics. It's mostly England . . . they do tend to knock the local talent a lot. And there's an awful lot of good local talent there, in London. Like there is everywhere, I guess. And there have been campaigns everywhere, I think, against ECM. And, for me that was the worst city. They really put down ECM for a long [time] – now it's not so bad, it's gotten a bit better,

but . . . they tend to like to call everything "soft" and "romantic", which it wasn't, I don't think, there.[1258]

As with most artists, the bad reviews stuck in Kenny's mind more than the positive ones. Just the year before their Ronnie Scott's appearance, *The Times* had described Azimuth as ". . . one of the most imaginatively conceived and delicately balanced of all contemporary chamber-jazz groups . . ."[1259] But the critical jabs began to chip away at the band's momentum. Priestley asked Kenny if he thought these reviews had a negative effect on audiences: "Yeah, you can't help but think that it probably does . . . I think they do have a lot of influence, yeah . . ."[1260] Norma agreed, commenting that it had been "a bit daunting sometimes, some of the reviews: 'Just plain dull,' things like that. When you get reviews like that, nobody wants to book you. It was hard, so I think gradually we did less and less."[1261]

As hostile as some critics were, the trio also faced substantial challenges from within. Norma believed that her separation from John might have dampened his energy to develop the trio further. She described how after the separation, "We [still] went on, and it was like nothing had changed, [but] maybe he did lose the impetus with Azimuth . . ."[1262] Indeed, it wasn't quite the end for the band. There would be a final album following another long

Photo 27: Azimuth pictured in Ethel's Place, Baltimore. Left to right: Kenny Wheeler, Norma Winstone, and John Taylor.

© Patrick Hinely, Work/Play®

hiatus, and they were also being celebrated locally with an invitation to the Guildhall School of Music in London. That relationship with the Guildhall deepened further, enabled in part through his friendship with Ian Carr, who was also teaching there. The director of the Jazz Orchestra, Scott Stroman, had also sought Kenny out for the project and found him generous as always with his music. This led to some concerts with Kenny and the Guildhall Jazz Orchestra and a recording in March 1987.[1263] Scott described the effect Kenny had on the band: "He could just play along with the band and immediately you could feel how the thing was supposed to work . . . he really got people to play in a way that very many other artists who talk a lot [more] never could, you know. Somehow, he could just pull the music out of people – especially students."[1264]

Azimuth made two rare club performances in the US in 1987, playing at Fat Tuesday's in New York opposite John Abercrombie, Marc Johnson, and Peter Erskine. Steve Getz (Stan's son and an Azimuth fan) had booked both groups there and at Ethel's Place in Baltimore. In the sweltering August heat, jazz writer and photographer Patrick Hinely snapped photos of the trio between the soundcheck and performance. Taken in the courtyard of the Baltimore club, Hinely joked it was "hot and humid enough that we kept moving for fear that we'd mildew if we didn't".[1265] Norma remembered a funny incident from the trip:

> Kenny got locked in his hotel room because the door handle came off as he tried to get out. John and I were downstairs in the hotel waiting for him to go to the soundcheck and Kenny called reception to say that he was locked in. Luckily, there was a door to an adjoining room so they were able to get him out. As he used to say, "I have a problem with mechanical things . . ." But doorknobs?![1266]

Kenny continued to work with long-standing London colleague saxophonist John Surman, with whom he had a particularly busy period in the middle of the decade. 1984 began with a UK tour for Surman's Brass Project, a new venture that partnered Surman with arranger John Warren.[1267] The group featured Surman with the unique instrumentation of a brass ensemble, bass, and drums. This all-brass orchestration required a lot of stamina, and Kenny's strength is evident throughout. In a lukewarm *Guardian* review of the London date, he was praised in spite of some of the reservations: "There were decided longueurs in many of the open passages, solos that could have been half their length from most but Kenny Wheeler on trumpet and Surman himself . . ."[1268] The two Johns' (Surman and Warren) Brass Project would continue with some celebrated recordings, but none of them included Kenny. In fact, given how much they had done together, it is remarkable that Kenny and

Surman would never appear on record together again.[1269] Asked about why they never recorded again, Surman had some thoughts and regrets about the passing of time:

> I have pondered that for a long, long time, and I wonder if Kenny ever thought about it. It was almost as if . . . for things like the Brass Project, I was afraid to call Kenny. I mean, Kenny was Kenny! And I have a feeling he may have thought *Surman has got his own things* . . . I think we both kind of thought we were on parallel paths if you like. And then Kenny was working a lot with Evan and everything, and I didn't feel like kind of muscling in on his territory, I don't know what – I can't explain it really, perhaps our mutual respect got in the way or something, I'm not sure . . . He had his own things going with ECM, and so did I . . . I suppose it would have been natural in a way to put us together, but aren't we a bit like peas in a pod?!![1270]

Thankfully, there were two more notable collaborations together that were captured on tape, even if not formally released. On 19 March 1984, two months after the Brass Project tour, Kenny joined a quintet led by Surman for a concert as part of the Camden Jazz Festival, recorded and broadcast by BBC Radio London. The group once again included regular colleagues John Taylor, Chris Laurence, and John Marshall. They played mostly Surman's compositions, plus the wonderful J.T. tune "Windfall". The recording also demonstrated what was denied to the wider listening public: the audience's applause, which showed how enthralled they were. Jazz writer Barry McRae said, "It was a sublime trumpet solo by Wheeler near the end that finally separated the audience from their seats. Jazz does not get much better than this."[1271] There must have been an appetite for this group, as a year later the same band undertook a full UK tour in mid-April 1985.[1272] Surman recalled the tour, saying "It was great. The only aggravation was the state of the pianos in those days, which were driving J.T. round the bend: twangy, untuned, all that kind of thing! But that's to gloss over the fact that of course the music was great. What a knockout . . ."[1273]

Perhaps the most extraordinary concert with Surman was on 4 July 1985 in Ravenna, Italy. This was a band that was surely a candidate for an album, but all that was captured is some poorly recorded audio from this performance. While Doreen celebrated her 52nd birthday back home in London, Kenny took to the stage with Surman, J.T., Dave Holland, and Tony Oxley. Surman took charge of the announcements (as one would expect if the choice were between Kenny and, well, anyone else). The outdoor concert was billed under the heading "Composers Pool", but in his introduction to the already rapturous audience, Surman says, "We don't actually call ourselves the 'Composers Pool'; we call the band 'The Big Reunion' . . . We hope that the skies keep clear, and that the music keeps clear too." What ensues is nearly an hour of sheer intensity and improvisation from a British group that had accumulated

Photo 28: Kenny in concert with the 1985 Banff Faculty, which included Dave Holland's Quintet. Left to right: Don Thompson (p), Steve Coleman (as), Dave Holland (b), John Abercrombie (g), Julian Priester (tb), Marvin "Smitty" Smith (d), Kenny (t).

Courtesy Banff Centre Library archive

an overwhelming amount of shared musical history and individual experience. The chemistry is evident from the start of John Taylor's introduction which quickly sets up the blistering opening tune, with Dave Holland and Oxley exploding into the music from a standing start. There was almost no more talking; each tune was intertwined with improvised segues, into J.T.'s "Windfall", a new composition of Dave's and a new song of Kenny's called "Miold Man" – another tribute to his recently deceased father (the title a play on *my old man* and *mild man*) – before finishing with another burningly intricate theme.

Dave Holland's tune – introduced as "New One" – eventually became retitled "The Razor's Edge". This became the title track of the final album he would make with his quintet,[1274] which continued to work throughout the middle of the decade and increasingly became part of the core faculty under his leadership at Banff. Indeed, not long after this Ravenna trip, Dave and Kenny were at Banff, where Dave's entire quintet was present together for the first time as part of the faculty in the summer of 1985. This opportunity provided additional chances to get together and play on the workshop's faculty concerts and no doubt helped the development and longevity of the band.

They also provided a living model of an evolving and working professional ensemble for the students.[1275]

Although he remained a Banff faculty regular for a few more years, Julian Priester decided to leave Dave's group amicably in 1986. To take Priester's place, Dave bought in young trombonist Robin Eubanks. Robin is one of three brothers who would all work with Dave: not only Robin's younger brother, guitarist Kevin Eubanks (who went on to eventually front the band of *The Tonight Show with Jay Leno*), but also their youngest brother, trumpeter Dwayne Eubanks, who would later play in Dave's big band. Robin was also brought on to the Banff faculty by Dave and recalled an early encounter with Kenny:

> The night that I got there they had a performance with the group of the students and everything there, and they were playing some of Kenny's music. So, I said 'OK, I'm going to check it out', and they played that *Music for Large and Small Ensembles* whole suite, and I was *drop-jaw*, I couldn't *believe* what I was hearing. I was like, *Kenny, that's unbelievable*, and he says [*puts on the textbook Kenny voice*], "Oh, you know, this was just a little thing I threw together!" [*laughs*] It was some of the best stuff I ever heard . . .[1276]

Dave's quintet, now including Robin, performed a set at Freiburg Zelt-Musik-Festival on 31 May 1986.[1277] Video of the gig captured the band in extraordinary form, performing much of the music that would be featured on *The Razor's Edge*. Kenny appears relaxed but focused and, for a change –and after years of what Ted O'Reilly described as that "Wheeler baby-face" – at 56, he finally looks more like one of the band's more senior figures when juxtaposed against his younger colleagues.[1278] But he sounds incredible, playing much of the set on his silver Bach cornet. The opening of the gig showcased Kenny at his very best, blowing on the open modal sequence of Dave's tune "The Razor's Edge", including a long duo with drummer "Smitty" Smith. His stamina and power are undeniable in this outpouring of contemporary jazz trumpet playing, incorporating his free techniques with his characteristic melodic development.

In February 1987, the band returned once more to the Ludwigsburg recording studio to record *The Razor's Edge*. The album featured the same band as in Freiburg and included Kenny's composition "5 Four Six". It was very well received critically – jazz writer Kevin Whitehead summed it up in his review: "Kenny Wheeler's solo [on 'Brother Ty'] makes the case that he's one of the most deeply expressive brass players in jazz. He has an oddly satisfying mix of melancholy tone, eerie vocalizations and bop chops . . ." He continued, "For all Holland's instrumental prowess and structural ambition, there's nothing clinical about this music. He's one conceptualist who's not afraid to feel, a feeling musician who's not afraid to explore. So, if you like your jazz pretty but find

Wynton Marsalis just a little too tame, Dave Holland's quintet may be exactly what you're looking for."[1279]

Sadly, *The Razor's Edge* would effectively mark the end of this landmark quintet. Dave explained:

> It was my decision. It was a difficult decision, but I just couldn't sustain it anymore, was the honest truth. We'd hit a ceiling in terms of what kinds of fees we could get. I was coming home with hardly any money at all from the tours we were doing, after paying everybody and all the expenses – I had taken out a second mortgage on my house, in fact. I got frustrated with where the business was at, because I felt like the band was really doing good work and the fees weren't able to sustain it. I couldn't keep it going.[1280]

Dave Holland's quintet leaves a remarkable legacy of music and there is no doubt that this band became a highlight of Kenny's career. It also left him in even greater awe of Dave – not only a peerless bassist and composer but also a bandleader unafraid to present and promote his music in a way that Kenny never could. He said, "Dave Holland is very strong. I admire him so much. He can just do all that stuff and it doesn't seem to bother him."[1281]

———·———

Kenny remained busy as ever as a composer throughout the mid-1980s preparing his annual broadcasts. He would also occasionally premiere new tunes on broadcasts led by friends, and a song that would become one of his classics first appeared on one such occasion. Back in 1979, Kenny had agreed to play with trumpeter George Chisholm's 11-piece ensemble and to provide a chart or two for the broadcast. George recalled:

> He said, and I quote, "nobody ever asks me to do any arranging for them". You can imagine my shock . . . he went on to explain that all the writing he did was either for his own Big Band or for things which he was personally involved with overseas. Needless to say, I was like a "rat up a drainpipe" and asked if he would consider doing a tune for me . . . Kenny said that he had a tune which he could adapt for the line-up. . . . "Mal Function" . . . He also said that he was halfway through working on a new tune and if he got it finished in time he would do an arrangement of that . . . he obviously did, and the new tune was called "Everybody's Song But My Own".[1282]

Not long after this, two of Kenny's other new 3/4 compositions, "Who Are You?" and "The Mouse in the Dairy", first appeared in his own broadcast for the BBC's *Sounds of Jazz*, along with a second performance of the newly penned "Everybody's Song But My Own". Recorded 8 December 1981 and broadcast 10 January 1982, the programme featured a 12-piece band with Frank Ricotti on vibes, along with regular colleagues such as Henry Lowther,

J.T., Stan Sulzmann, Duncan Lamont, and Chris Laurence.[1283] Stan recalled more vividly a performance of "Everybody's Song . . ." the following year when Kenny played a quintet slot for Scottish television's *Jazz at the Gateway*. It was a memorable trip, as they had to fly up to and back from Edinburgh in a single day. The repertoire, also including "Foxy Trot" and "The Mouse in the Dairy", had particularly stuck in Stan's memory because the producer instructed them to memorize all the music.[1284] The normal structure for the show was to incorporate an American guest soloist with the house band of Gordon Beck, Philip Catherine, Niels-Henning Ørsted Pedersen, and Jon Christensen. (Michael Brecker was the special guest on the same episode as Kenny's quintet, but not recorded at the same time.) Kenny's group was invited up as the featured band for their segment, and along with Stan he was joined by J.T., Chris Laurence, and John Marshall.[1285] Marshall prioritized any opportunity to play with any group of Kenny's – he had even instructed his wife: "If Kenny Wheeler calls, then say yes. He takes precedence over everything!"[1286]

Kenny had begun to occasionally use smaller and unconventional line-ups in the early '80s as BBC budgets tightened, and perhaps the pressure of copying out all his own big-band music by hand alongside his ever-busier playing schedule became more challenging. In many ways, the 1980s really were the end of his big-band iteration from the previous decade; he moved towards a more standardized instrumentation (with the addition of Norma and himself) so that his music would be more readily playable by conventional big bands in Europe and educational big bands at universities. For example, he was the featured soloist and composer with the European Broadcasting Union (EBU) Big Band in a concert in London in May 1982. The ensemble was made up of musicians from 14 different countries, including Arild Andersen on bass, and fellow Brits Derek Watkins and Stan Sulzmann, with Bob Cornford conducting.[1287]

In a sign of the times, there was no BBC broadcast for Kenny's big band in 1983, but 1984 was much busier at the company's studios. That February, he had a big-band session back with his original extended line-up, where they played big-band arrangements of the *Double Double-You* tunes: "Foxy Trot", "W.W." and "Three for D'reen". In May there was a drummerless octet performance of the tunes "5 4 6", "Old Ballad", "Gentle Piece", and "Kayak". There was even one other live broadcast from his big band which includes the latter two pieces once more plus "The Widow in the Window" and "Ticketeeboo".[1288]

On 26 and 27 May 1987, Kenny went into Milan's Barigozzi Studio with his own quintet to record *Flutter by, Butterfly* for Soul Note.[1289] He had not recorded as a leader in four years, not since ECM's *Double, Double You*. The quintet, including Stan Sulzmann, John Taylor, and Dave Holland, completed by German-based American drummer Bill Elgart convened at Thomas Stöwsand's house in the Tyrolean town of Schwaz. Elgart was part of a trio with bassist Wayne Darling and Australian guitarist Pete O'Mara, and the trio had invited Kenny to join them as a guest for some live concerts in

Germany.[1290] The successful collaboration created a band that led to an excellent quartet recording in 1990 and further European tours throughout the early '90s. Bill described the impression Kenny had made on him when they first played together: "The thing that knocked me out most of all, I guess, he had such good time for someone who never really played time, you know . . . his phrasing was so free, the amount of music he could put in a space was just incredible to me. He was just a very special being."[1291] Kenny must have been equally impressed with Bill's playing; despite having only recently met, he was invited to join the quintet for the upcoming dates.

This new incarnation of the Kenny Wheeler Quintet was to undertake a substantial tour of Europe by train. They'd chosen Stöwsand's house as a central meeting point at which to have their initial rehearsals for the tour, and Stan recalled that saxophonist Tim Berne was also staying at the Stöwsand house the night they arrived, ready to depart on tour into Europe, just as they were. The next day the quintet boarded the first of many trains, heading into southern Germany for their first gig.[1292] The tour was made complicated by a lot of travel and a patchy schedule with odd gaps in the itinerary after some gigs fell through. Stan remembered that there may have been some personnel changes and issues in the weeks before the tour. He himself had been booked "quite late on" for it and remembered that at one stage there was talk of a "big-name drummer" being involved, recalling that even Roy Haynes or Elvin Jones had been discussed, and that at one point after that Tony Oxley was actually booked to do it.[1293] Stan was also unsure exactly who he had been brought in to replace, but assumed he was a later addition, given the timing of his booking. Unfortunately, once Stan and Bill Elgart were confirmed to complete the line-up, some of the promoters who expected bigger names cancelled their performances.

Once the tour got under way, the day-to-day job of managing the tour and the travel fell to Kenny, their reluctant leader. Elgart, who didn't know Kenny as well as the other players, was struck by the paradoxical nature of their bandleader's character: "Kenny was the most 'non-trumpet-player' personality I ever met. He was so introverted and so gentle . . . if you met him, you wouldn't think that music could be what came out of him."[1294] Stan, who knew him much better, remembered Kenny's self-induced anxieties while overseeing the tour logistics:

> He did a remarkable job, but you know what he's like when he gets into his "efficient mode" . . . He had all these bits of paper all carefully documented . . . he ran it incredibly well, but at a price to him, I could see . . . He's running around with this big pile of paper [*muttering*] "Right, we need to do this now" . . . like a military operation, not because that's the way to do it, but out of sheer terror. It was the only way he could do it. He was hating it, the actual job of having to sort of organize everything.[1295]

Photo 29: Kenny's *Flutter By, Butterfly* quintet on tour in 1987, pictured here at Pori Jazz Festival, Finland. Left to right: Dave Holland, John Taylor, Kenny, Bill Elgart, and Stan Sulzmann.
Courtesy Renee Rosnes

Although the music developed beautifully with such a great band, there were some gruelling journeys that added to the stress of the tour. One particularly stuck out in Stan's memory:

> The all-night one was an absolute killer . . . I remember it, three trains we got . . . We were in Italy and it was boiling hot . . . on the east coast somewhere in a seaside town, and the only way to get to Munich [was] we had to do three trains and we had to travel all night, changing at certain intervals, and Ken overseeing with his watch and watching . . . "Right, everyone, up and ready, we've got to get off here and change" . . .[1296]

They arrived with only an hour to spare to have a shower and get dressed before the gig. They had hardly slept. "When we got to Munich, we were completely done in, you know!"[1297]

Some hilarious close calls can often happen under this level of duress. Once while travelling between gigs, the whole band (except Dave Holland) had gone to the train's buffet car to get some food. The train pulled into a station and, while they were seated in the buffet car, eating and chatting, they looked back to see the back half of their train (which held all their bags, instruments, and Dave) uncoupling from their half and heading away down the tracks, destination unknown! In a panic they jumped up to look out the window, in disbelief about what had happened, when they suddenly noticed Dave on the platform standing among a huge pile of all their bags and instrument cases: he had noticed what was happening just in the nick of time and saved the day. "Once we knew we were all safe we were screaming with laughter," Stan said.[1298]

The lasting musical product of this tour is *Flutter By, Butterfly*, the album they recorded over two days near the beginning of their journey.[1299] It was released in 1988 and captures the musicians in exceptional form. *Flutter By, Butterfly* includes six tracks, three on each side of the original vinyl: "Everybody's Song But My Own", "We Salute the Night" and "Miold Man" on Side A, and the title song, "Gigolo", and "The Little Fella" opposite. The tunes were all relatively recent compositions of Kenny's, four of which were already in circulation: "The Little Fella" first appeared in an April 1981 broadcast with a curious nine-piece ensemble he called his "Ninentity". On the sleeve notes Kenny revealed the tune was written a decade earlier and was dedicated to an Irish leprechaun. He said it was "a cross between an Irish folk song and a McCoy Tyner piece".[1300] The album's opener, "Everybody's Song But My Own", is described by Kenny in the liner notes as having been written "about ten years ago" and the tango-inspired "Gigolo" had first appeared on his EBU Big Band broadcast in May 1982, but under its original name of "Sly Eyes".[1301] "Miold Man" had first been played by the quintet with Surman in Ravenna in 1985, but was first recorded in the studio a couple of months before *Flutter By, Butterfly* in March 1987, with Swedish band Rena Rama, on a recording released in 1998 called *The Lost Tapes*.[1302] The only two tracks that seem to make their very first appearance on this Milan session are "We Salute the Night" and the album's title track, "Flutter By, Butterfly", the latter a particularly curious case of a tune that doesn't seem to crop up anywhere other than on this single album. The liner notes say that "Flutter By, Butterfly" was "so-called because Stan Sulzmann's flute reminded Kenny of a butterfly in flight", adding that it is "the most recent composition on the album".[1303]

All of Kenny's albums have their own special qualities, but there is something about these recordings made by a working, touring band that give a clearer insight into how they sounded live. The special energy and interaction of a group that plays together regularly deepens musical connections; although shared history among the players can make up for this to a point, the communication becomes deeper still when those musicians have really played the music on tour. Although the greatest example of this was to come in a couple of years with *The Widow in the Window*, *Flutter By, Butterfly* is one of the only other instances of a band led by Kenny that also recorded mid-tour. The chemistry was further deepened as Stan and J.T. had just recorded a duo LP record (called *Everybody's Song But My Own?*[1304]) of Kenny's tunes, including four of the selections they play again on *Flutter By, Butterfly*.[1305] The other musicians on the tour revered Kenny as a writer. "When we came to make this album, I was more than ready to include other writers' compositions," Kenny said, "but the guys wanted to do my music."[1306] Acknowledging this, Mike Hennessey also wrote in his liner notes that "the high esteem in which so many musicians hold Kenny does compensate to some extent for the inadequacy of the public recognition he is accorded. But, unhappily, peer prestige doesn't pay the rent."[1307] Stan summed it up years later: "It's not an ECM-sounding record, but I think it sounds like a JAZZ album, and Kenny sounds wonderful."[1308]

Perhaps the most notable tune on the album is "Everybody's Song But My Own", especially because of the fame it would garner as a composition, becoming part of the modern jazz standard repertoire. Kenny contributed this detail (another example of Pat Smythe championing his music) to the liner notes:

> It is a called "Everybody's Song But My Own" because it is a piece that a lot of jazz musicians could have written. It was among a number of tunes that Pat Smythe gave to Victor Feldman. Victor liked it and used to play it from time to time – so I have dedicated this performance to Victor.[1309]

What a performance it is. Again, on this track the flugel and tenor unison on the melody is so entwined it morphs into a sound of its own. Kenny's solo on this tune is an absolute *tour de force*; he commences the solo with one of his most memorably melodic opening phrases and powers through a virtuosic display of musical and motivic development across four choruses of improvisation – as if the solo sets a statement of intent for the record.

*Flutter By, Butterfly* is also noteworthy in establishing of one of Kenny's longest-standing and most consistent front-line partners in Stan Sulzmann. For an album that came just three years after *Double, Double-You* with Michael Brecker – one of the greatest saxophonists of all time – the temptation to compare the two is inevitable. Yet Stan is formidable on this recording by any standard and shows why he is considered a godfather of the modern British saxophone. His personal sound and style, coupled with his peerless simpatico with Kenny, formed a musical bond that would remain until the end of Kenny's life.

---

That same year, 1987, Kenny and Doreen's daughter Louann married her long-time partner Mark Newman. For Kenny, this happy news was met with some trepidation, as he was suddenly pushed into the role of "father of the bride", the ceremonial duties for which he was amusingly ill-prepared. Mark Wheeler helped advise his dad prepare for the big event in the most basic of ways, since Kenny had no idea. Mark began by pointing out the obvious (to everyone but his dad): "It's your daughter's wedding – you've got to get a new fucking suit!"[1310]

On the day of the wedding, Louann remembers riding in the car with her dad. Even though it was *her* wedding day, she was comforting *him* because he was so nervous about having to give the customary speech at the reception. "He was petrified," Louann laughed. "Don't worry, Dad, it'll all be over soon," she said, trying to quell her dad's nerves while dealing with her own. "He just wanted to get it over with," she said. But Kenny overcame his fears. When it came time to raise a glass, he gave a brief but charming toast to the bride and groom. Louann recalled that it was "emotional and moving, and I was quite touched by it because he said some lovely things about me."[1311]

---

1988 would spark a decade of creativity and international recognition that would be the highlight of Kenny's career. His year began, however, with a serious medical issue in Canada. Kenny was there in early January to play a concert at Mohawk College in Hamilton and, of course, to visit family in nearby St. Catharines.[1312] When his sister Mabel arrived at their sister Helen's house (where he was staying) to drive him to the concert, she heard Kenny's voice calling out to her in an alarmingly weak monotone: "*Mabel . . . Mabel . . .*" She found him in the bathroom, bent over the sink, stricken with vertigo, unable to move.[1313] She called an ambulance and he was rushed to hospital where he was diagnosed with and treated for Ménière's disease, an inner-ear disorder which can result not only in dizziness but also hearing loss – which could have been devastating for him as a musician.[1314] Unable to travel or perform, Kenny spent the next several days recovering in hospital, forcing him to cancel other concerts in Toronto, Ottawa, Montreal, and Quebec City, ultimately delaying his trip home.[1315] This understandably worried Doreen greatly; she flew to Canada to stay with him while he recuperated and accompanied him back to London a week later. Mabel, who was a nurse, was convinced that this episode was caused by relentless air travel, but he had big upcoming plans the following month that would only allow him a brief period of rest and recovery in one place.[1316]

The upcoming tour had been in the works for quite some time, and was the brainchild of Nick Purnell, an energetic promoter and long-time admirer of Kenny. Purnell first worked with Kenny during his time with Birmingham Jazz, booking the trumpeter for several projects. When Purnell, a composer himself, was offered a broadcast of his own music on BBC Radio 3, he asked Kenny to be a part of his 10-piece ensemble.[1317] This personal association, along with an awareness of Kenny's infrequent touring, led Purnell to champion Kenny and his music with larger venues, promoters of festivals, and audiences alike.[1318] He was no doubt quite aware of Kenny's lack of interest in promoting himself, and, loving his music, saw a need for someone with access to and experience with promoters, and the diligence to follow through on it all. Like others in Kenny's life who made things happen for him, Purnell "simply decided to put [a tour] together".[1319] "Ken was always someone that promoters loved as a musician and composer but was not known for attracting an audience to recoup fees," Purnell said. "I knew that in order to generate promoter and audience interest, a Ken tour would have to be with a strong line-up."[1320] Purnell also realized that Kenny had not toured with a band with which he had actually recorded for ECM, so he initially proposed an all-star band the personnel of which would encompass his ECM albums up to that point, including Jan Garbarek, John Taylor, Dave Holland, and Jack DeJohnette, which was "sort of a combination of *Gnu High*, *Deer Wan*, and *Double Double You*. Ken was happy with the proposed group, so I started making phone calls," Purnell said.[1321]

J.T. and Dave agreed right away, but after Garbarek declined, they went back to the drawing board. Purnell then asked guitarist John Abercrombie (who had appeared on *Deer Wan*); drummer Paul Motian was also brought in to the proposed line-up. Unfortunately, Motian, who had been touring in the meantime, had grown tired of the road and backed out of the tour. At Kenny's request, Purnell then contacted American drummer Peter Erskine, who agreed to the tour, and the band was finally set.[1322] A veteran of big bands led by Stan Kenton and Maynard Ferguson, small groups fronted by Freddie Hubbard and myriad others, not to mention supergroups Weather Report and Steps Ahead, Erskine had also quickly become a much sought-after soloist in his own right. Nick Purnell felt that Peter might have lent a cachet of star power to the quintet in the eyes of some, but added that "perhaps the overall combination" of those five musicians might have been the real draw.[1323]

Without a doubt, Purnell's plan brought new exposure for Kenny. John Taylor said, "[Nick] did a great deal to promote the music, to put it together . . . he really made it possible for Kenny and that quintet to start off . . ."[1324] The eight-day tour began in Birmingham on 15 February and continued on to Liverpool, Nottingham, Manchester, Colchester, culminating in a performance in London at the 100 Club on Monday the 22nd and a concert the next night in Sheffield. Richard Cook penned a glowing preview in the *Sunday Times*. The piece, "Gracenotes with a Steel Lining", began by praising Kenny's playing, saying that it displayed "a kind of mastery [that] is hard-won and envied", and proclaimed that he was "probably playing the most absorbing music of his career".[1325] A second preview piece published the next day by Clive Davis (definitely not always a Wheeler fan) also set up the tour and highlighted its personnel. Davis later reviewed the Colchester performance and gave it an uncommonly warm reception, writing that "after just a handful of performances, Kenny Wheeler's all-star group . . . already looks and sounds like a fully-fledged working band."[1326]

In addition to Purnell's admirable business and promotional skills and the obvious drawing power of the quintet's stars, such glowing reviews – so rare in the British jazz press of the time – generated substantial interest in the tour. Purnell said that he thought all the dates of the tour had sold out, remembering that especially in Manchester, there were "so many people, we literally had to clear a way through to the stage for the musicians".[1327] This momentum became most evident at the 100 Club in London the following Monday night. Purnell, who had been working to set up for the band inside the club, left momentarily. When he walked outside, he was surprised by a "queue snaking down the street, only to realize they were there for Ken's gig".[1328] Purnell continued, "The gig itself was stupidly crazy. So many people . . . You couldn't move for [all the] people and it felt more like a rock gig", adding that the energy reminded him of a Rolling Stones concert.[1329] Dave Holland shared Nick Purnell's memory of the concert: "Kenny was a bit over-whelmed . . . I think it took him by surprise completely," he said. "It was just wonderful to see so many people turning out for Kenny and the band . . . I'm sure he thought, 'We'll be lucky if we get 50 people' or something. It was shoulder to shoulder — it was amazing."[1330]

A surviving bootleg recording of the 100 Club gig shows these memories of the lively audience to be accurate, and their excitement to be well founded. On "Aspire", the crowd reacted to each solo with enthusiastic applause, cheers, and whistles: not exactly par for the course on such an otherwise introspective modern jazz performance. Kenny interrupted the adulation with a three-minute cadenza introducing a medium uptempo version of the Jerome Kern standard "Yesterdays". In addition to the aforementioned tunes, the band played J.T.'s "Til Bakeblikk" (first recorded on *Azimuth '85*), and finished the first set with Kenny's "Everybody's Song But My Own" and "'Smatta". On the second set, the band began with Kenny's "Deer Wan" and continued with Dave Holland's "Jumpin' In". Purnell recalled his surprise at the crowd's explosive reaction to Dave's arco bass solo to his own tune, saying, "the audience just started screaming, clapping, etc. I'd never seen that."[1331]

At 58, Kenny had finally become successful enough as a jazz artist to be free from having to play commercial sessions. He continued, however, to work as a musician who was not really in control of the trajectory of his career. He was happy with many of the projects on which he was invited to play, but wanted to play his own music even more than he was. This, of course, meant being a bandleader, which Kenny found challenging to say the least. Tour booking, asking for money, liaising with promoters, and organizing travel plans comprised virtually everything other than writing and playing the music: in other words, crucial details that he just didn't care about. Accordingly, Kenny would continue throughout this period to rely on the opportunities that came to him: the next ECM album, upcoming tours with the United Jazz+Rock Ensemble, another Azimuth recording, work in Europe as a sideman, and other gigs. This would be unremarkable for many who only intended to be "working" musicians, but for someone writing such personal and intricate music of their own and actively voicing frustrations at the lack of opportunities to perform their own music, this friction becomes more relevant. But this situation was beginning to change. This success of this 1988 quintet tour, surrounded by an incredible band of stars who not only loved playing his music but admired and understood him, supported by the managerial advocacy he needed, marked the beginning of what would truly be a new high point in Kenny's career. Nick Purnell's foresight in showing that such a group could play Kenny's music at the highest artistic level *and* generate tangible audience excitement proved to concert promoters that such a venture could be economically compelling. Soon, Purnell would turn his energies to a follow-up tour of much larger proportions, just in time for Kenny's 60th birthday.

———··———

After his father died, Kenny continued to visit his Canadian family in St. Catharines as much as he could. In 1984, his mother dealt with problems with her vision and had corrective surgery. His sister Helen wrote him often with updates:

> She complains now and then that she can't see too well but she has been really calm lately and really enjoyable to be with. I think she has suffered enough now and now God is going to give her peace for the years she has left. Anyway, you will enjoy her company now. She even doesn't drink hardly at all.[1332]

During this time, Wilf Jr. (himself recently having become a widower) moved into the house at 12 Blain Place with their mum. As soon as he would go out to work, Mrs. Wheeler would call a cab and go to the bar and get some beers, even though she wasn't supposed to be drinking anymore. Their watchful neighbour would tell on her, but it was unnecessary; the evidence she left behind spoke for itself. Her daughter Mabel and grandson Jayson laughed years later, remembering when the family was moving her from her house into the nursing home: every time they'd move a piece of furniture, they'd hear, "*ding, ding, ding* – all these empty beer bottles would roll out!"[1333] After a period of declining health, and two years after going into the nursing home, Kenny's mother died on 25 March 1988. As had been the case when their father died, the daughters discussed whether to tell Kenny right away, because of how far he was away and his busy schedule. Mabel said, "Helen kind of called the shots that time, and didn't tell [Kenny] until it was too late for him to come home; so, he didn't get home for her funeral."[1334] Despite her difficult life, Kenny's mother had lived to be 83.

In May 1988, Kenny and Doreen began a new chapter in their lives by becoming grandparents. Their daughter Louann had a baby girl with her husband Mark Newman, whom they named Sophie. Although Kenny would soon warm up to his new role (the grandchildren affectionately called him "Poppa"), "it took him a little while," Louann said. When the baby was around five weeks old, Kenny was still too nervous to hold her. Finally, Louann said, "Dad, can you hold Sophie for me?" She didn't give him the chance to say no;

she just put her on his lap, "and he got used to it," she said, laughing. "We had to sort of dump her on him!"[1335]

Moderating the joy of their first grandchild's birth was some worrying health news for Doreen. Not long after Sophie's birth, Doreen was told by her doctor that her heart valve was going to need replacement in around ten years, and "if you want to see your grandchildren grow up, then you need to stop smoking now". She had tried to quit in the past, but framing this news in this way finally gave her the incentive, and she did. Her physician had been right – nearly ten years to the day afterwards, she entered Barnes Hospital in London and had a successful heart valve replacement.[1336]

While Sophie would be the first of Kenny and Doreen's grandchildren, four more arrived over the next decade. Mark and Jan Wheeler's first child, named Bethan, was born nearly three years later, in 1991. Not long after this joyous news, however, came some heartache for the Wheeler family when Mark and Jan divorced. Though difficult for everyone, Kenny was particularly devastated, as he had developed a close relationship with Jan.[1337] The two had developed nicknames for each other; Kenny called Jan "Dil", and she called him "Fil" ("daughter-in-law" and "father-in-law", respectively), and he had written one of his most popular tunes for her. Around this time, in a rare moment of candour, father and son had a heart-to-heart conversation about the breakup of their marriage, with Kenny advising Mark to "think seriously about what you're doing". According to Mark, his dad wasn't being judgemental, but rather framed things as "I can't tell you what to do, but this is my view . . ." Mark elaborated:

> I was sort of living in 141 [Wallwood Road] with my dad at that time. We had quite a lot of chats about lots of different things . . . He was really quite wise; there was a lot of wisdom hidden under that quiet exterior. We spoke about passion. He said, "Passion's not everything. You have to have friendship as well." It was just real, sensible, down-to-earth, proper stuff.[1338]

Mark remarried after his divorce, and soon he and his new wife Tracy gave Kenny and Doreen their third grandchild, Rachel, in 1993. The final two grandchildren soon followed; Phoebe, born to Louann and Mark Newman in 1994, and Ruby, born to Mark and Tracy in 1998. Ruby remembers how her grandfather reacted to the news of her birth: "I think Poppa's response to me being born sums up how he felt being surrounded by so many girls . . . My Nan [Doreen] called to him, 'Ken, you have a granddaughter!' and he simply replied, 'Another one!?'"[1339]

After Phoebe arrived, Louann and Mark Newman drifted apart, ultimately leading to the end of their marriage. Following the sadness of Mark and Jan's divorce, the end of Louann's marriage was frankly a little less painful for Kenny to accept, as he and Mark Newman never quite hit it off. They got along fine enough, but Kenny would occasionally get irritated with his son-in-law, who, according to Louann, "was too *bolshy* for him. He would come in [to the Wheeler home] and take over," she said. "Mark [Newman] would come in and turn the telly [channel]," while Kenny was watching. Characteristically, however, Kenny "wouldn't say anything, he'd just walk out of the room". This boiled over soon enough. Louann remembered, "There was point where he was so, so angry, that he went and wrote a tune. I never knew what that tune was . . . I'd love to know!"[1340] Just as he had since childhood, Kenny had once again avoided conflict by channelling his emotions into music.

Like those with his son, Kenny's deeper conversations with Louann were infrequent but meaningful. With both father and daughter being equally shy, these moments were probably even more precious and rare. Louann recalled a time, later in his life, when just the two of them stayed up late one night after Doreen had gone to bed. He opened up to her about his childhood. Louann recalled her dad recounting "how troublesome it was for him . . . the stuff he had to put up with his mum, which I was quite shocked about". Louann was profoundly moved by what her dad had revealed to her. "It almost made me cry," she remembered, comforting him, she said, "Oh my God, I'm so sorry for what you had to go through."[1341]

———·———

Starting in the late 1980s, Kenny played occasionally with George Gruntz's all-star international "Concert Jazz Band", including a fall 1987 tour of the United States. Gruntz, a Swiss pianist, composer, and arranger, usually took his ensemble on two tours sponsored by arts funding from the Swiss financial industry.[1342] Video of a concert from the tour – quite possibly from an appearance in Fort Worth, Texas – shows Kenny playing Joe Henderson's "Inner Urge" with the band alongside the composer, likely the only time Kenny ever played with the legendary saxophonist. This band placed Kenny alongside other jazz stars including trumpeters Marvin Stamm, Franco Ambrosetti, Enrico Rava, and Manfred Schoof, alto saxophonist Lee Konitz, horn player Tom Varner, trombonist Dave Taylor, and vocalist Sheila Jordan.[1343] For this and the next year's tours, Gruntz had hired Marvin Stamm to play lead trumpet. "I was so happy to have Kenny in this 'section of soloists,'" Stamm said, "Thank goodness for Kenny!"[1344] Having known Kenny's recordings but not having met him until the tour with Gruntz, Stamm (already well known as a veteran of big bands led by Thad Jones and Stan Kenton and groups under his own name) was thrilled to play next to someone he admired so much. He said:

> Kenny was *pure music*. So many musicians have become taken with technique, range, and all of that – probably due to the influence of Maynard [Ferguson] – but Kenny had none of that. Kenny had all the ability to play on the trumpet and flugelhorn through four-plus octaves, which was just amazing, but you didn't get into feeling any of that because everything that

Kenny used in his music had to do with the expression of an idea and the development of a line . . . It was all part of the song.[1345]

On that tour of the US, the band was scheduled to perform in Houston, Texas. One of Stamm's college classmates at North Texas was Bob Morgan, a Wheeler fan who happened to be the director of jazz at Houston's High School for the Performing and Visual Arts. After getting his phone number from Stamm, Morgan called Kenny to gauge his interest in working with his students. After politely declining the offer several times, Kenny finally relented and agreed to do the masterclass. To prepare the students in the days leading up to his visit, Morgan played some of Kenny's albums for them, and once they arrived, the student ensembles played for Kenny and Marvin Stamm. As it was early in the school year, the big band hadn't prepared much material but was rehearsing Sammy Nestico's arrangement of Ellington's "Satin Doll". Morgan admitted to being apprehensive to ask this master of modern music to play with them on such a well-worn standard, but Kenny surprised him by responding, "I'm always honoured to play on any Ellington song, and it's a lovely tune." Kenny also reminded the students how lucky they were to play in what he called a "dance band". Morgan remembered Kenny's explanation: "I grew up playing in dance bands, and to this day I still play in a dance band in London. It's not one you've ever heard of, and it doesn't pay much, but that doesn't matter. To me, to play surrounded by great musicians, there is nothing like it."[1346] Marvin Stamm said that Kenny "blew everyone away just by being who he was. He was so honest. He didn't seem to be stuck with any answers when students asked questions. These were the kinds of students who weren't worried with all that stuff; they just wanted to be in the presence of some-body like Kenny." Stamm loved watching Kenny in that situation. "You absorb the lessons yourself – probably me more than any of the kids!" he said, hav-ing done many such masterclasses himself over the years, probably far more than Kenny ever gave. "You put Kenny in a situation like that where people are really open and want what he has to give – he would deliver every time . . . I'm sure for Bob and for many of the students there who went on to play music, it was a pretty thrilling moment, something they'll never forget."[1347]

The following year, Gruntz took his Concert Jazz Band (although with dif-ferent personnel) on a tour of the Far East, including stops in Japan, Hong Kong, and Singapore. Trumpeter Arturo Sandoval, at this point famous for playing in the Cuban band Irakere, joined the trumpet section alongside Kenny, Marvin, and Manfred Schoof.[1348] According to Stamm, each member of the band got two solos a night. One piece that was used to feature Kenny was a tune from a Gruntz opera, which was also a feature for Sheila Jordan, called "Guinevere's Garden", on which Kenny took an extended solo.[1349]

Interested in him for not only his trumpet playing but also his compo-sitions, Gruntz wanted to arrange Kenny's tune "Everybody's Song But My Own" for the 1988 Japan tour as a flugelhorn feature, which he agreed to.

A contract was drawn up by EuroMusic, the Swiss music publisher, which Kenny signed on 30 June 1988. At the time, Kenny thought he was merely granting Gruntz the right to arrange his song, but in fact he was actually signing over the publishing of the tune (mistitled on the contract) to EuroMusic. It read:

> The composer hereby transfers to the publisher the original music written and composed by Mr. Ken Wheeler entitled: E.B.S.B.M.O. "EVERYBODY'S SOMETHING BUT MY OWN" [sic][1350]

This important distinction must have gone unnoticed for years until Kenny somehow realized he had actually sold the tune, not just the arranging rights. He wrote EuroMusic on 22 December 1992:

> Dear Sirs,
>
> Euromusic has publishing on one of my songs. This song is called "Everybody's Song But My Own." I would like to know how long Euromusic will hold this publishing. Also, when I agreed with Mr. George Gruntz to publish the song with "Euromusic" I understood that the publishing only concerned the big band record of Mr. Gruntz on which the song was performed. Could you please let me know about this.
>
> Sincerely,
>
> Ken Wheeler

The reply came a month later, with the company enclosing a copy of the contract. They were apparently mystified as to Kenny's question, since they seemed to think they were doing him a great service:

> Therwil/Basel
>
> January 20, 1993
>
> Dear Ken
>
> Thank you very much for your letter of December 22, referring to our publishing agreement of your song "E.S.B.M.O." (copy of contract enclosed).
>
> As you can see on the contract there is no restrictions marked on whether a fixed duration nor on the format, in which this your song should be published by EUROMUSIC (you say "Big Band Only". As a matter of fact, we – until today – have send out many copies of lead sheets prepared by George Gruntz, such to enable all kind of groups to perform your piece. In this way also Marvin Stamm got to play and record your song with one of his outfits.

Also did we send out copies of the full band chart to quite a number of interested bands around.

We think that we have done a quite good job so far and hope to continue for a long time. We also hope that you are with us and happy about the situation.

Very sincerely yours

EUROMUSIC ASSOCIATION
Gérard Lüll, president

Just like self-promotion and tour organizing, the publishing of his tunes had not been something Kenny wished to deal with. Dave Holland spent years trying to get him set up with his own publishing company to protect his compositions and generate more income:

> I'd started my publishing company right before *Conference of the Birds* – that was a big point of conversation amongst musicians [at the time], you know: *You've got to get your own publishing company* – otherwise, you won't have control over your music, you'll have to share half the mechanical royalties which come from the pressing and reproduction of the album – not the sales of the album. That's the best part of the money that comes in from a composition – the mechanicals – whether it's on DVD, CD, whatever . . . So I kept saying to Kenny, "Look, you've got to get your own publishing company – I'll show you, it's really easy. Just a few steps you've got to take. You know, you've got all this music starting to come out, and I'll help you out with it, no problem." For years and years and years, nothing happened with it, off into the '80s, I kept going with that, because I was recording some of his songs on the quintet album, and still, he wouldn't do it – so it all ended up in ECM's publishing, and then my daughter [Louise], who took a law degree and started working as a lawyer at an entertainment law firm in the late '80s, you know – I was talking to her about it, and she said, "Just tell him to call me and I'll set it up for him." And I told Kenny about this – I said, "Louise is ready to go – just tell her what you want." She wasn't going to charge him anything for it – because he's an old friend of the family – and he just never picked up on it. And you know, he'd say, "It's all right – I'm in the PRS system." And I'd say, "It's not the same – this is a different thing." . . . I'd back off at a certain point. I wouldn't push him too hard.[1351]

Although we do not know for sure what happened between the written contract and the exchange between Kenny and EuroMusic, we can piece together the following: Gruntz wanted to arrange the tune to feature Kenny with his band. He needed permission to do this, and offered to buy the tune from him. Kenny mistakenly assumed that Gruntz was just buying the right to arrange the tune and publish the arrangement, but what actually happened was that Kenny sold Gruntz (through EuroMusic) the sole rights to the tune itself, which allowed Gruntz to do whatever he wished with it (*including* arranging it), with Kenny receiving 50% (as per the contract) in royalties. This was also likely the standard issue contract between Gruntz and members of the band whose tunes the leader wanted to arrange to feature them on the tours.[1352] Stamm also described Gruntz's personality, which may be relevant. With Gruntz, "there's business, and there's friendship," Stamm said. "and they can exist side by side, but one doesn't necessarily have to reflect on the other."[1353] From the other perspective, Stamm speculated that "I can see Kenny not questioning it, in the initiation of whatever the talks were about it – he probably thought, like most of us, 'I've known George for a long time, and he's just another player like me, and whatever it is, he's going to be cool.'" It is important, too, to note that most of the players on the band, like Stamm admitted about himself, were not as dedicated to – or dependent on – composition as Kenny was, so this situation probably wouldn't generally have presented the problems that it did in Kenny's case.[1354]

It is not clear if the situation with "Everybody's Song But My Own" was ever resolved, but what *is* clear is that Kenny continued to play his tune – one of his best known compositions – as a regular part of his repertoire while holding a thinly veiled grudge about the matter for years. A couple of years later, at a concert in London's Purcell Room, it even came up in his announcements from the stage. Chris Parker, writing for *The Times*, said that "after beginning his concert by performing, with regular pianist John Taylor, an understated and genuinely affecting duo version of his famous composition 'Everybody's Song But My Own', he merely murmured something about the difficulty of establishing ownership of tunes . . ."[1355] (Predictably, he joked about the whole situation: "I've retitled it 'Everybody Owns My Song But Me'!") Even though Kenny didn't like to discuss such things too much, his friends and colleagues were aware of the situation, too. Fred Hersch (who released a 2011 album including the song and using its title as the name of the record) said, "He didn't really talk about his business, but I do remember him saying he'd given away the rights to 'Everybody's Song But My Own.'"[1356]

Back in late November 1985, Canadian composer and guitarist Tim Brady led the Composers' Cooperative Jazz Orchestra in a programme of Kenny's music in the Great Hall of Toronto's Music Gallery. Brady had just organized a concert of Gil Evans's music led by the composer the previous year. Even though Evans was born in Toronto too, Kenny certainly lived much more of his life in Canada than Evans had, and maintained stronger ties to the country throughout his life. Simply put, in identity and personality, Kenny was a much more "Canadian" musician and quite probably the most significant jazz composer to claim Canadian roots.

Usually grateful to have others do the talking, Kenny was uncharacteristically bold on his home turf during this visit. Mark Miller's glowing review of the concert noted that he was "in remarkably assertive form all around, to the point, quite out of character, of handling some of the introductions, complete with a few quips".[1357] He must have been quite comfortable in this setting, having his big-band music played by people who grew up looking up to him and respecting him as a quiet star who had left their country for Europe and done good. Some of the greatest musicians in Canada played the concert, including Don Thompson, drummer Claude Ranger, and trombonist Ian McDougall. The next generation of Canadian talent was well represented too, including bassist Jim Vivian, saxophonist Mike Murley, and trumpeters Arnie Chycoski and John MacLeod, the last of whom had become a Wheeler devotee and one of the first Canadian trumpeters to absorb Kenny's unique influence into his own sound. Even surrounded by all this talent, Kenny's voice as a soloist stood out. Miller observed:

> Only Wheeler, however, consistently offered improvisations of a freshness and power to match the qualities of his own writing. He is a changeable soloist emotionally, with a gift for making the unpredictable seem both logical and natural . . . Each solo is unique, and yet each with its rich, syrupy tone is identifiably a Wheeler creation.[1358]

Although the music-making was fantastic, the audience was, according to Miller, "disappointingly small", perhaps because the heat had gone out in the building that morning.[1359] Regardless, Miller rightly pointed out that "this hometown concert was Wheeler's personal triumph, and as balanced a display of his musical accomplishments as Toronto, or any other city for that matter, could wish."[1360]

Rare as this concert was (and it was certainly unusual that Kenny's big-band music would be heard anywhere with a sufficiently rehearsed ensemble and himself as soloist), an even rarer event occurred during this trip to Canada. Tim Brady had recently written a piece for 11 strings and solo improvisor. Having secured funding to record the work for the Justin Time label, Brady organized a recording of the strings in Montreal. With the tapes of the orchestra in hand, Brady recorded Kenny playing over the string tracks in a church in Toronto. Instead of having him listen through headphones, the engineers played the string recording through two speakers in the church, with the generous acoustic warming Kenny's sound and giving more life and ambience to the strings. Kenny's part for the piece, titled *Visions*, was entirely freely improvised: no written lines or chords. (Brady only provided him with cues for beginning and ending his solos.) "It wasn't a jazz piece – it was a piece with improvisation," Brady explained. He also recalled the beautiful moment of Kenny closing his eyes and ignoring the written directives while he recorded his solo for the 14-minute final movement of the piece. "I was standing beside him because I was turning pages so they didn't make noise . . . and I'm pretty sure that the last movement is a single take, and I'm pretty sure it's the first take," Brady said. "He closed his eyes and he was just playing. He was coming up to a section where he was supposed to stop. He just played through the places where he was supposed to stop, and I didn't care. Tapping him on the shoulder to stop would have been missing the point of improvising . . ." When it was done, Brady and the producers briefly considered recording another take. "We all kind of looked at each other and went . . . 'What's the point!?'" Brady laughed.[1361] In addition to providing a wonderful recording of his piece, Kenny also unknowingly gave Tim Brady a great gift at a crucial moment in his musical life:

> I was 28 years old, just out of graduate school, and you're writing stuff, and you're going *Is it good?* or *Is it bad?* . . . At one point when we were recording *Visions*, I think it was that one-take last movement, and I'm sitting there and I'm going, *it sounds phenomenal* . . . And I remember all of a sudden, I had this thought: *Holy shit, this music sounds great!* And then I had the realization, *Holy shit, I wrote this music that sounds great!* And no small part of that was Kenny's playing. So literally from that moment working with Kenny in the studio where he played my music so well that I [thought], "OK, if I'm really given the right players and the right circumstances, I'm not insane. I can actually write good music" . . . it was one of the most important musical experiences of my life, when I heard someone who plays that well play my music. I just went, *Wow*. He gave me that moment that no one else had ever given me, and I'm eternally grateful.[1362]

As he approached the age of 60, Kenny's career was beginning to flourish. 1989 continued to be exceptionally busy for him, and he was finally fulfilling the long-time goal of playing his own music as the majority of his work. In February of that year, he undertook one of his first North American teaching residencies (apart from his Banff visits) at the prestigious Eastman School of Music in Rochester, New York. The Eastman Jazz Ensemble, directed by Rayburn Wright, performed a set of Kenny's music (including "Kayak", "Sumother Song", "Gentle Piece", "Sophie" and "Foxy Trot") along with works by others.

On his return from Eastman, Kenny undertook another short UK tour as leader of his own quintet, this time with an all-star English band rather than with his more recent UK/US quintet. John Taylor remained, but the rest of the group was made up of old friends Stan Sulzmann, Chris Laurence, and John Marshall. Just after this tour, Kenny played another Azimuth performance in June, this time at London's Jazz Cafe in Camden. Just a couple of months later, Kenny and J.T. were playing in yet another formation at September's Outside In festival in Crawley, West Sussex. This festival grew out of the aesthetically ambitious template set out by John Cumming in his work at the Bracknell Jazz Festival, which had ended the year before. It included a lot of adventurous programming, which Kenny and J.T. complemented, as was noted in the *Guardian's* review of the event: "Jazz does have to renew itself and occasionally shock, but a festival audience also needs to be soothed emotionally. The lustrous sound of Kenny Wheeler's trumpet, backed at the piano by another leading romantic in John Taylor, certainly did this."[1363]

A significant visit to Europe also took place that year. In May 1989, Kenny and his long-time friend and colleague Henry Lowther went to Berlin for a week of rehearsals culminating in a radio broadcast with the Berlin Contemporary Jazz Orchestra. Like the Globe Unity Orchestra, this ensemble was the brainchild of German pianist and composer Alex von Schlippenbach, and that week presented music by Carla Bley, Misha Mengelberg, and Kenny, among others. Kenny had written his epic 23-minute composition *Ana* (which stands for *Another Arrangement*) for the band the year before and this piece remained on the programme for their 1989 residency.[1364]

During rehearsals for the broadcast, von Schlippenbach told the band that ECM founder and producer Manfred Eicher was coming to Berlin to record their concert. For the band (which had just been formed the year before) this was an exciting development. But for Kenny this was upsetting. He and Eicher had recently had a heated phone conversation which escalated to the point that Kenny slammed the phone down, hanging up on the producer. Still upset by the exchange, Kenny was now even more furious at Eicher. Henry Lowther explained:

> [Kenny] always wanted Manfred Eicher to come to England to record his British band, because of all the [European] radio bands and everything he ever worked with, the one he was most pleased about, most proud about, was the British band. And he wanted Manfred to record it and Manfred always refused, saying he was never interested in big bands. And so now, all of a sudden, he's coming to Berlin to record . . . in all honesty – an inferior band.[1365]

Kenny's frustration at Eicher's lack of interest in recording him – *especially* his big-band music – had been simmering for some time. In Kenny's defence, at this point it had been six years since his last ECM album was recorded, and he had begun to record under his name for other, smaller labels. And although he'd been writing new music for big bands nearly every year for various projects (most significantly his broadcasts for the BBC), his big-band music hadn't been commercially released since 1973's *Song for Someone*, which by this time was an out-of-print collectors' item. One-off engagements like this one in Berlin took time and energy away from his own projects and demanded additional time and energy for travel. A quote from the liner notes to *Flutter By, Butterfly* shows Kenny's aspirations: "I spend so much time on the road that I don't get enough opportunities to write new music. Maybe I'll just have to take some time off." Such comments were a frequent theme in interviews around this time, and this 1986 quote from an interview with Brian Priestley is even more revealing:

... I'd like somebody to commission me because I'd like to do an extended work ... I'd like to somehow do something where the improvisation is more involved in the composition, rather than just do the theme and maybe have a band chorus and then "OK, it's time for a saxophone solo" ... but I haven't got the time to do it for nothing.[1366]

And there was the rub. Kenny was once again caught – as artists often are – between doing the playing work that paid the bills and the work that satisfied himself musically. That friction must have become even more acute when he found out that Manfred was now coming to Berlin to record a lesser band playing one of his compositions. Henry put it this way:

I mean, the Germans had great problems playing his music. They could never play long crotchets [*quarter notes*]. When you get off-beat crotchets, you know, *dah-doo-dah-doo-doo-dee-duh-dah*, that thing coming from Gil Evans and that sort of West Coast music, that way of phrasing. The Germans would play *doo-dut, dut, dut, dut, dee-doo-dut* ... I was the one that always used to say stuff in the rehearsals, because Kenny would never say anything. I used to say, "Can we play those longer?" And then they'd do it longer, and then the next day, when you'd play it, they'd go back to *doo-dut, dut, dut, dut, dee-doo-dut* ... And a lot of those guys were free players who didn't read properly – they didn't have big-band discipline, you know.[1367]

Conversely, the musicians who had grown up with Kenny and his music in England on the free scene, in the studios, and in more mainstream jazz clubs were so familiar with Kenny's writing: they knew its harmonic idiosyncrasies, his humour, its fundamental *sound* – inside and out. Not only that, but many of them, especially the studio stalwarts, were expert readers and had precisely what Henry called "big-band discipline". As Derek Watkins often said, "*We know how to play Kenny's music.*"[1368]

So Kenny certainly missed his English friends during that week in Germany when the Berlin Contemporary Jazz Orchestra was playing his *Ana*, even though it was a band of European and American jazz stars. Kenny complained quietly under his breath in rehearsals, so only Henry, who was seated next to him, could hear. "He just moaned all the time," Henry said. "'That's not right! No! Can you speed it up a bit?! *Argh!*' [All week] he moaned about that ... he moaned about everything ... In his British band, he didn't have to [say anything]."[1369] In addition to his anger at Manfred, he was even more unhappy that week because he was having problems with his chops, to the point that he would sit out of playing his own solos in rehearsals, just sitting there silently watching the chords go by as the band played on. "Only in the concert did he play a solo, and he played a *blinding* solo!" Henry remembered.[1370]

The week was difficult for Henry, too. The American expatriate Benny Bailey had been hired to play first trumpet for the band. With Bailey unable to be at the first rehearsal, Henry had to play the lead parts. When Bailey arrived the next day, Henry handed him the lead book and said, "this is for you, Benny", to which he replied, "No, man, you play it. I haven't done that for 14 years."[1371] So, even though Bailey was the veteran first trumpet player of the Clarke/Boland Big Band (and someone whom Kenny had once described as the most exciting lead trumpet player he'd ever worked with), he let Henry (who was strong but didn't consider himself a lead player) cover all the top parts.

The day of the concert, Manfred Eicher arrived at the radio studio in Berlin to produce the recording. Kenny, while still angry, was also terrified to see Manfred in person after their unfortunate telephone exchange. Eicher could see the look on Kenny's face when he arrived in the studio: "Kenny was bold and very spontaneous but he didn't show it," Eicher said. "He was very kind and noble, very humble, and sometimes reserved, but I could see in his eyes when things were different."[1372] To his credit, Eicher immediately walked right up to Kenny and said, "In January, I'm coming to England to record your big band."[1373] Kenny must have been stunned by this sudden shift of tone in their relationship and Eicher's clever diffusing of what could have been a much more tense situation. Eicher "took the wind right out of Kenny by saying that," Henry said.[1374]

After the concert, the band had a performance at the newly founded INNtöne Jazz Festival, known as *Jazz am Bauernhof*, or "Jazz on the Farm". The venue, outside of the village of Diersbach, Austria (just across the border from the German city of Passau), is a modified old barn that had been turned into a concert hall. The Germans in the band mostly drove themselves there, but Kenny, Henry, and the band's American drummer Ed Thigpen (former member of the famous Oscar Peterson Trio) took a train to the festival. When they arrived, they realized that everyone in the band had brought their music, but they had left theirs on the music stands in the radio hall in Berlin, assuming a librarian or band manager would pick it up for them, as was customary in England. So, right before the concert, the trumpet section hurriedly copied their parts from Kenny's score so they had music to read.[1375] As if all this wasn't stressful enough, the trip back to England afterwards was fraught with difficulty. To begin with, Alex von Schlippenbach, who'd promised Kenny and Henry a ride to the airport in Munich, got into an argument with his wife (the pianist Aki Takase, who was also a member of the band) after the concert and the distracted couple sped away in a fury, leaving the trumpeters behind. Henry said, "there was some doubt whether we were ever going to catch the plane. Somebody got us a taxi ride over the border to the station in Passau to the train to Munich. I thought Kenny was going to have a heart attack. I've never seen anyone in my life as stressed as that."[1376]

Kenny and Henry made their flight back to London after all, and the Wheeler family met them at Heathrow to welcome them home. To cap off an incredibly stressful trip, they made the unusual decision to enjoy a well-earned drink at the airport before heading home. "How was it, Ken?" Doreen asked. Kenny just replied, "Henry played great lead trumpet, and I moaned all the time!"[1377]

———·——

Encouraged by the success of the 1988 quintet tour, the ever-resourceful Nick Purnell secured funding for a British Arts Council tour that would take place in January 1990, centred around Kenny's 60th birthday.[1378] This Arts Council funding not only supported the big-band tour but also allowed Kenny the time to write the extended suite he had been thinking about for years. Once Manfred Eicher told him back in Berlin that he was coming to England to record the band, Kenny had the extra incentive of knowing his new work was going to be recorded beautifully by ECM. This in itself is significant, as it was his first recording for the label in seven years and his first big-band recording since *Song for Someone*, released over 15 years previously.

Guided by Kenny's input, Purnell enlisted the all-star rhythm section from the 1988 tour (Abercrombie, J.T., Holland, and Erskine) as the nucleus of the band. The horn players were all Kenny's long-time associates and members of his annual BBC broadcast ensembles. Just as on *Song for Someone,* they represented every aspect of Kenny's musical life. From the inner circle of jazz musicians who played his music most came vocalist Norma Winstone, saxophonists Stan Sulzmann and Ray Warleigh, trombonist Chris Pyne, and the rhythm section; from the studios came trumpeters Derek Watkins, Henry Lowther, and Alan Downey, along with trombonist Dave Horler; from the free scene there was saxophonist Evan Parker and trombonist Paul Rutherford. Younger colleagues, including saxophonist Julian Argüelles and trombonist Hugh Fraser, were present, too, alongside old friends to whom Kenny was deeply loyal. Trumpeter Ian Hamer and saxophonist Duncan Lamont often told others of Kenny's faithfulness to them, acknowledging he could have hired anyone he wanted for his high-profile tour.

The members of the band returned Kenny's loyalty. The studio players could have easily made much more money by staying in London to record music for film, television, and commercials; Dave Horler even took two weeks off his job with the WDR Big Band in Germany to tour with Kenny. Norma, Evan, and Stan spent time and energy promoting Kenny's music with their connections in the music world in a way that he himself never would. And, of course, Nick Purnell spent so many unpaid hours doing work behind the scenes to make these tours possible: writing grant proposals, organizing tours, booking transportation and hotels, hiring personnel, promoting, arranging interviews, and even loading equipment in and out of venues – all to bring the world a bit closer to the music of this quiet genius.

On 13 January 1990, there was a surprise party at a pub to celebrate Kenny's 60th.[1379] (He had been told that they were just stopping for a quick drink before dinner.) Most of the band, plus Kenny's family and many of his

Photo 30: Kenny at his surprise 60th birthday party, with his sisters Mabel (left) and Helen (right).
Courtesy Wheeler family

friends, including bassist Ron Mathewson, BBC presenter Charles Fox, and others were there. As Kenny went to get his first drink, his sisters Mabel and Helen surprised him by popping up from where they were hiding behind the bar, having just flown over from Canada to serve their brother a birthday beverage and celebrate with him. Evan Parker remembered the party as lots of "big smiles and happy people, and [trumpeter] Ian Hamer being given a hard time . . ." by trombonist Chris Pyne, who was quite funny but was struggling with alcohol at the time. ("Chris usually started things," Evan said.) He also remembered another guest who was similarly overindulgent:

> Ken came in [to the pub] to settle up. He said, "How much do I owe you for last night?" Although it was his party, he had to pay for it . . . So, he'd come to settle up, and the landlord said – because he was somehow a friend of the family . . . he said, "What a lovely bunch of people, Ken. Those friends of yours? That's the nicest evening I've ever spent. Lovely. Except that one geezer with the dodgy eye." [Ron Mathewson.] Ken said, "Oh? What happened?" He said, "Every time he came to the bar, it was, 'Triple vodka.' 'Triple vodka.' 'Triple vodka.' 'Triple vodka.' Ken said, "Oh, that's OK, that's his regular drink!"[1380]

A few days later, on 17 January, there was a rehearsal of the new music for the tour, which would start the following day. The imported American musicians, including John Abercrombie, Peter Erskine, and Dave Holland, came directly from the airport to the rehearsal space. From the moment the players walked into the room, it became obvious that this would be something special. Kenny had composed and arranged well more than an album's worth of music for big band for this tour and recording, including the aforementioned seven-movement suite and several other new pieces. On the day of the rehearsal for the tour, 23-year-old saxophonist Julian Argüelles arrived at a time that he thought was plenty early. When he walked into the rehearsal room, however, he saw that nearly the entire band was already there, warming up and greeting each other. The experience made a deep impression on him. It was "powerful and scary," he said, adding, "the vibe was brilliant – there was a lot of love in the band."[1381] Peter Erskine recalled that the players were "dazzled by Kenny's writing, and I think everyone realized immediately the musical enormity and significance of this, and what a rare gift and opportunity it was to be a part of that . . . We all knew that it was something special."[1382] Hugh Fraser remembered showing up for the rehearsal, thinking he'd be playing a section trombone part like he'd played on the previous BBC broadcasts. "I was jetlagged . . . and he passes me the fourth trombone [part] and I said, 'Kenny, this is the *bass* trombone part' and he said, 'You can do it!' I said, 'I don't have a bass trombone . . .' So I ran down to the music store and got one!"[1383]

Some of the music from this new suite had appeared previously in various forms: a version of the first part of the suite originated in music from a nine-piece broadcast Kenny had written for the BBC in 1981, which then served as the introduction for a tune called "Le Grand Bill Evans", honouring both the American pianist in the title as well as French composer Michel Legrand.[1384] The second part of the suite, titled "For H." (dedicated to English pianist, composer, and arranger Harry South),[1385] had begun its life as "B Minor Get Out", but went on to have a life later in Kenny's repertoire as "Kind Folk".[1386] But some of the music for the tour was brand new, including "Sophie", which was written for his granddaughter who'd just been born in 1988, and "For Jan", which he had written for his daughter-in-law. Part four of the suite, "For P.A.", was written for Pepper Adams, with whom Kenny had recorded the Grammy-nominated *Live at Fat Tuesday's*, and with whom he had played when he subbed with in the Thad Jones/Mel Lewis band at Ronnie Scott's years before. Kenny said the title for Part 5, "Know Where You Are" was "just a twist on words, like 'you came to me out of nowhere' or "you're nowhere'". Part six, "Consolation: A Folk Song" is one of the most beautiful melodies that Kenny ever penned: a seemingly simple tune with the most beautiful – and difficult-to-play – harmonization. He called it "a gift from somewhere. I had it in my mind for about three years I think before I started writing it. I had this melody and I thought one day I'm going to write this for the big band, and I did." Part seven, titled "Freddy C", was written for trumpeter Freddy Clayton, and features some of the most intricate ensemble writing of the entire suite, of which it was the final movement.[1387]

The concert was also the premiere of some new lyrics written by Norma to Kenny's music. On "For Jan", the title and dedication were already set by the time he sent it to Norma asking for her to add words.[1388] Here, Norma's lyric depicted the inner world of a young wife and mother, and included the evocative phrase "the turning of wheels within wheels". Kenny had sent "For Jan" to Norma well beforehand, but she only received "Consolation" when she was reading it with the rest of the band at the rehearsal.[1389] Afterwards, contemplating the beauty of that melody, Norma had some lyrics come to mind and quickly wrote them down. No one, including Kenny and the rest of the band, would hear these lyrics until she sang them in her unaccompanied open solo, at the premiere of the suite, right before the band began Part 6.

On the 18 January 1990, the band took the stage at London's Queen Elizabeth Hall. This night was to be the fulfilment of a long-time dream of Kenny's: the world premiere of his new suite for big band. The gravity of the occasion, however, was slightly undermined by the casual behaviour of some of the band – for example, when trumpeter Ian Hamer walked onstage wearing an old sweater, holding a glass of scotch and a lit cigarette.[1390] But this mild levity was quickly swept away by the power of the music. Canadian classical trumpeter John Thiessen, then a Masters student at King's College in Cambridge, was in the audience to hear his fellow countryman's important premiere. He remembered:

> There was virtuosity and variety, but just as importantly, unity of purpose. Norma Winstone was astounding and the juxtaposition of her voice with the other instruments, most notably Kenny's, took us to another plane. We were listening to entirely new music, and as each piece unfolded, the amazement level in the audience seemed to grow ever greater, Kenny's seamless lines matched by the tightness of the ensemble, and thoughtful, inventive soloing. At the end of the concert, after a lengthy standing ovation, the audience simply stood there and no one wanted to leave. In true Canadian fashion, Wheeler said, "Sorry, that's all the music we have" and so, reluctantly, we all slowly headed for the exit doors. But the previous two hours had been as close to musical heaven as I can remember, and those fortunate to have been there probably felt the same.[1391]

The audience got it. They had just heard the first performance of a new work by one of the most important jazz composers in Europe, or anywhere for that matter. Several of Kenny's friends were in the audience, alongside many of his fans; these admirers had likely heard his BBC broadcasts on the radio for years but rarely – or never – had the opportunity to hear a band of this calibre play his music live in concert, so they must have sensed the significance of the night as well. "It was momentous . . . a big deal," Peter Erskine said, observing that members of the band spoke glowingly about *Windmill Tilter* (long out-of-print by this point) and that this tour had brought them full circle.[1392] With so many key members of the band (including Derek Watkins, Henry Lowther, Dave Holland, and Chris Pyne) having played on both *Windmill Tilter* and these 60th-birthday concerts, it is understandable why this sentiment would be in the air. When the perceptive veteran BBC personality Charles Fox introduced a broadcast of one of the tour dates – just six months after the premiere – he showed not only great awareness and understanding of the music's importance but also a larger appreciation for the composer himself:

> A concert by a Kenny Wheeler Big Band is always something of an event. After all, Kenny is without doubt one of the most talented jazz musicians to be found anywhere in the world. Since that lucky day back in the 1950s when he decided to leave Canada and settle in our midst, he's adorned the British jazz scene: the virtuoso soloist on both trumpet and flugelhorn, a composer, too, who can imprint his identity on both small and large groups, but who especially enjoys writing for a big band whenever he gets the chance. His standing among fellow musicians is reflected in the way that they will frequently give up better-paid gigs in order to play his music, the ultimate accolade. In January, Kenny celebrated his 60th birthday and in the most practical of ways: by taking a big band touring on the Arts Council's Contemporary Music Network. It's one of those concerts you'll be hearing. But just as Kenny is always delighted in appearing in all kinds of contexts, so his bands usually possess a piquancy brought about by Kenny's preference for mixing musicians from different periods and with differing approaches: selecting performers for their individual strengths rather than for any narrow allegiances . . .[1393]

The only people who seemed to question the substance and impact of this music, as usual, were members of the English print press, who took nearly every opportunity to pan the concert and the composer himself. In his review that came out in the next morning's *Times*, Clive Davis said that "the big band charts fell short of Wheeler's usual standards". He even took a shot at the audience: "Few musicians arouse as much affection – and protectiveness – as the Canadian-born trumpeter", adding that the "audience seemed more than willing to forgive him".[1394]

In addition to the press, there was another negative response to come, this one more personal. Diana Taylor, J.T.'s second wife, had been in the Queen Elizabeth Hall audience and had become quite upset on hearing Norma's lyrics for "Consolation". After the premiere, John confronted Norma, saying, "Those words are about us, aren't they?" Norma said, "I hadn't intended to write them about us. The whole idea of the song was that the 'Consolation' was the fact that two people may not be together anymore, but they're still part of each other . . . So, yeah, I suppose it *was*, obviously, about us . . ." John told Norma that "I'd rather you didn't sing them again because Di was really upset." Respecting their wishes, Norma destroyed the lyrics and never sang them again, explaining simply, ". . . they seemed to upset people". After the next night's concert in Manchester, Kenny noticed that she hadn't used the lyrics, saying to her in disappointment, "You didn't sing your lovely words – they were beautiful."[1395]

Following the lead of Clive Davis's pan of the concert (". . . below Wheeler's usual standards . . ."), *The Times*'s listings for the remainder of the tour delivered a progression of increasingly harsh digs at the music. At first, the tone was neutral:

> 13 January: "Opening dates of an Arts Council tour by the trumpeter, celebrating his 60th birthday."

> 19 January: "The trumpeter celebrates his sixtieth birthday with the help of a big band built around his own quintet, plus the likes of Evan Parker and Stan Sulzmann."

So far, so neutral. But, as the tour went on, the listings became more disapproving:

> 24 January: His sixtieth birthday big band boasts famous improvising names but lukewarm charts. The quintet, featured in the second half, provides more engaging listening.

They continued, finishing on 29 January in near comic despondency at the quality of the music:

> The trumpeter's 60th birthday big band makes the best of some disappointing charts.

Bear in mind that the above are merely the listings, the function of which is not to offer a critical comment but simply to inform about who is playing, when and where. It is truly amazing that whoever was writing these little ads could go out of their way to miss the mark with such gusto. What would any living composer in the big-band medium give to have written such similarly "disappointing charts" of their own?

In hindsight, the suite is now one of the most revered works of Kenny's entire output, cherished by jazz fans, musicians, and fellow jazz composers. Fellow Canadian and leader of his own ensemble, Darcy James Argue, wrote of the suite: "I guess it must have felt to everyone like Kenny Wheeler music and not big band music . . . though of course it *is* big band music, brilliantly constructed, a milestone of large ensemble jazz . . . the themes threaded throughout the 50-minute, 8-movement work . . . are some of his very finest . . ."[1396] Kenny once told the story of meeting a young Maria Schneider, who, at this writing, is the winner of seven Grammy awards and considered to have been at the very pinnacle of modern jazz composers for over two decades. When she was introduced to him, she took Kenny's hand and kissed it, saying "That was for 'Consolation.'"[1397]

Despite the almost laughably mean-spirited previews, the tour itself was joyous and memorable. The trumpet section took charge of the band's social activities, armed with a guide of all the top pubs in England, and, as Dave Holland remembered:

> . . . would go and check the beer out in the pub when we were stopping for lunch. We'd all stay on the bus and the trumpet section would go into the pub just to make sure it was of an appropriate standard, and if it wasn't, they'd get back on the bus and we'd go to the next one! . . . We had so much fun on that tour.[1398]

Abercrombie agreed, saying that touring with the English band was "hysterically fun . . . With Kenny, there was always a great sense of humour floating around the band."[1399]

The tour also saw some minor mishaps. The driver, a rather large fellow, somehow fell on Dave Holland's bass, where it had been placed at the back of the bus. "I remember the guys being mortified . . . They all thought I was going to freak out or something, and I just said, 'Oh well,' [because] the bass was playable."[1400] In Birmingham, the drummer Tony Levin, who was a friend of the band but not playing the tour, accompanied them on the bus to the pub for a drink after the Birmingham concert. Levin suddenly "went a terrible colour and just keeled over, lying there," Norma Winstone recalled. "We thought he was dead. John [Taylor] came and gave him the 'kiss of life'. I don't know whether his heart stopped or not, but John just blew into his mouth, and he came around."[1401] Possibly the most musically consequential setback anyone in the band experienced was a cold sore on the lip of the band's legendary lead trumpet player, Derek Watkins, a few concerts into the tour. The trumpeter must have felt absolute agony while continuing to play with his mouthpiece sitting on such a painful blister. "He was so distraught," Peter Erskine remembered, adding that he thought "it was kind of a superhuman performance" by Derek to have played Kenny's demanding music in that condition. Peter was a great fan of Derek's. Explaining the qualities he admires in a great lead trumpeter, he said, "There's that wonderful, ineffable, magical quality that comes into play, and just that spine-tingling, mind-blowing, hair-raising excitement that they bring to something, and it just electrifies the whole room. Derek had that in spades."[1402]

The morning after the band had played their Liverpool concert, they returned to London to record at CTS Studios in Wembley.[1403] Unfortunately, the session coincided with the worst of Derek Watkins's cold sore outbreak. Peter remembered that Derek "was dabbing alcohol feverishly [on his lip] during the two concerts before we went into the studio . . ." but that "he still sounded great on the recording". Nearly every member of the band interviewed for this book remembers this, with Stan Sulzmann adding that Derek "was suffering . . . It really was horrendous . . ."[1404] The unfortunate sore cost Derek the ability to play at his best on some of the charts, notably the climactic high shout chorus in "Consolation". (Alan Downey, a formidable lead trumpet player in his own right, had been sharing first-trumpet duties with Derek and covered that one for him, among others.) Kenny himself also overdubbed some of the lead parts that had eluded Derek after the rest of the band left the studio.[1405]

In typical ECM fashion, the recording was made quickly. They only did second takes on the first two movements of the suite; after that, it was all basically first takes. In live performances, the band had been treating the end of Part 7 ("Freddy C") as the end of the suite, as Kenny had written it. It was here that Manfred Eicher made a brilliant musical suggestion as a producer. Suspecting that it would help the piece feel more complete, Eicher proposed that Kenny play a cadenza and then have the band repeat the "Opening" chorale at the end of the suite as a "Closing", but this time with Kenny continuing to improvise over top of it.[1406] The suggestion was so fitting that the band continued to repeat the chorale at the end in later concerts, and anyone who knows the suite well now can hardly imagine it without this addition at the close of the piece, complete with Kenny's stunning fill on the final chord.[1407]

In addition to the suite, the band recorded Kenny's compositions "Sophie", "Sea Lady", and "Gentle Piece" for disc two of the album. They also recorded his "Ticketeeboo". Evan Parker remembered that "People were saying, 'Go on, Ken. Tell [Manfred] you want to record it.' And he says, 'OK, record it.'" Evan continued, saying Manfred replied, "'You can do that if you want.' He goes upstairs, switches the tape on, reads the paper. He knows it's not going to be on the record." "We recorded it – where is it?" Evan asked, replying to his own question: "I don't know, probably somewhere in a rubbish bin in Wembley."[1408] Although Eicher didn't recall exactly what happened to "Ticketeeboo", he hinted that the tune didn't fit in with the rest of the album: "Maybe it was decided that the concept and flavour of the album is concluded by the material . . . It was not a question of time, but a question of concept."[1409]

Because of the set-up of the band in the studio, Eicher had chosen to have Norma record in an isolation booth to be able to better control her sound and balance. This meant she had to sing on the recording session while listening to the band through headphones, not live in the room as she was used to. She explained:

> It's hard to sing all those things in isolation . . . so in the end I had to go into a box and then it came through the headphones and it's not the same . . . The idea was to put those lines [I had left out] on the next day, but we got back there and there was no time, so there are things left out [on the recording] that I should've been singing on.[1410]

Photo 31: The *Music for Large and Small Ensembles* band: Left to right: Duncan Lamont, Dave Holland, Evan Parker, Henry Lowther, Ian Hamer, Alan Downey, Derek Watkins, Stan Sulzmann, Dave Horler, John Abercrombie, Peter Erskine, Norma Winstone, Chris Pyne, Julian Argüelles, John Taylor, Ray Warleigh, Kenny, Hugh Fraser, Paul Rutherford.

Courtesy Caroline Forbes

As often happens, several members of the band expressed that they wished they could have done it at the end of the tour after the music had more opportunity to grow, since the playing became more and more together and exciting as they performed it night after night. Hugh Fraser remembered that many members of the band, especially Erskine and Abercrombie, played much more intensely during live performances more than they did on the album. Hugh even remembered times on the tour where things got so boisterous in concert that he thought to himself, *How the hell are we going to come in?!* and just then, "Peter would just hit one quarter-note on his snare drum and we would just know where we were." Hugh pointed out that "the music gets a lot better and evolves as it goes along [on the road] . . . so none of us were happy" about recording in the middle of the tour.[1411] Dave Holland agreed: "We were just thinking: man, we should be doing this at the *end* of tour."[1412] Peter Erskine explained further, "You leave the studio, you start playing this stuff more and more live, and it *really* comes to life. We were all sorely wishing that we could get one more chance to record the music. Be all that as it may, the album is quite outstanding."[1413] Manfred Eicher agreed. Even while still in the studio booth, he became convinced he had made the right decision to come to London to record Kenny's English band. He could hear the band's dedication to Kenny and his music:

> I liked the concentration and awareness of the musicians. There was this feeling, *We play Kenny's music for Kenny.* I think there was such a great unspoken solidarity. You felt it; everyone was painstakingly listening to what Kenny wanted to do . . . Everybody dedicated their way of playing to him . . . The English [musicians] had an ear for [his music], and a great respect and love for him.[1414]

Even with the regrets from some about the recording process, the album (released on ECM as *Music for Large and Small Ensembles*[1415]) is a masterpiece, and a jewel in Kenny's recorded output. Nick Purnell, who had put so much time and energy into organizing the tour and recording, remains in awe of their collective achievement. "I still get goosebumps listening to *Music for Large and Small Ensembles*, especially in the sections where I used to make sure I was at the side of the stage to listen: Dave Horler's solo [on 'For Jan'] and 'Consolation', for instance," he said. "Maybe it was more about this group and the big-band tour helping Ken finally achieve the credit he deserved?"[1416] And Peter Erskine, who had by that time (and since) played with so many celebrated groups, said simply, "That recording stands as one of the highlights of my musical life."[1417] Interestingly, Peter told Duncan Lamont that one of his favourite parts of every concert night was playing the straight-ahead time with the rhythm section behind Duncan's saxophone solo on "Freddy C". Duncan was apprehensive about playing a solo on one of Kenny's records surrounded by all the modern jazz stars in the band ("I should have given the

Photo 32: Kenny and Norma at the *Music for Large and Small Ensembles* recording session.
Courtesy Caroline Forbes

solo to someone else, but I didn't have the heart to refuse Kenny," he said[1418]),
but he remembered Peter enjoying it so much while they were listening to
a playback of Duncan's solo on the day of the session that he was dancing
around the control room, which put him at ease.[1419] (For listeners seeking an
excellent play-by-play, Steve Lake's original liner notes are incredibly descriptive and provide a helpful listening guide to this double album.)

The album release also finally cemented the new (and characteristically
punning) title of Kenny's large-scale work: *The Sweet Time Suite*, probably a
reflection of the fond memories he held of the people its movements were
named after, including Harry South, Pepper Adams, his daughter-in-law
Jan, Freddy Clayton, and other "kind folk". In its review, *The Wire* admon-
ished the label for its cover art, which is even more austere than ECM's usual
minimalist fare, and the album's seemingly bland title, even though it might
actually have been a clever take-off on composer Steve Reich's 1980 classic
ECM recording *Music for a Large Ensemble*. More importantly, however, the

review captured the quality of the music, saying *The Sweet Time Suite* was an "ambitious, magisterial conception which begins and ends with a heart-warming glow of unfolding chords . . ."[1420] The *Guardian*'s Ronald Atkins also gave the recording a rave review, calling the chorale that opens and closes the suite a "haunting theme, unwound by the brass at a pace that perhaps evokes the wide-open countryside of Wheeler's Canadian past . . ."[1421] With a laugh, though, Kenny was quick to remind anyone projecting such observations that he was "from the big city . . . *Toronto!*"[1422]

On 1 February, the day after finishing the 1990 big-band tour in Winchester, Kenny and his quintet (the rhythm section of John Abercrombie, John Taylor, Dave Holland, and Peter Erskine) immediately departed London for an intense 11-stop tour of Europe, playing a different city every night. The tight proximity of these two tours was probably chosen to make it more economically viable, since Abercrombie, Erskine, and Holland had already flown over from the US.[1423] The quintet first travelled to Rive-de-Gier in France (near Lyon) for their first concert on 2 February, then went on to play Le Havre, Paris, Ludwigsburg, Aversa, Bari, Palermo, Padova, Vienna, and Imola. They finished the tour on 12 February in Hamburg before flying to Oslo to record at Rainbow Studios for ECM the next day.[1424]

By this point, these men were not strangers. They had already toured England together as a quintet in 1988 and had worked together in various other formats, in some cases for decades before. Add this simpatico and mutual respect to the organizational discipline brought to all of them from the big-band tour of Kenny's music they had just completed, and you have the recipe for a working band of jazz stars on a level apart from any other group Kenny ever assembled, before or after. They all truly loved Kenny as a person and as a musician and brought him a comfort that allowed him to play his best; this long period together also provided Kenny an incredibly fertile environment to stretch out musically, and get physically even stronger night after night on the trumpet and flugelhorn. As long as their underlying technique is secure, brass players can benefit greatly from having their chops pushed to the limits by the challenge of playing long sets with exceptionally strong rhythm sections. Kenny's musical experience up to this point had certainly ensured that his playing fundamentals were intact: think of all the time he had spent keeping his tone and intonation in check in the studios, plus the relentless challenges of playing free music that would have mashed a lesser trumpeter's embouchure into mincemeat. Considering all this, one can understand how amazingly strong this must have made Kenny, and how remarkable he sounded during this entire tour and its resulting recording, even at the age of 60.

But as the oldest member of the band by a dozen years, Kenny needed more than brass-playing endurance. Every member of the quintet required a great deal of physical stamina and tenacity just to maintain the tour's gruelling schedule and, in some cases, to overcome what Peter Erskine deemed as simply Kenny's "bad luck".[1425] For example, after the Padova concert, the band had to rush to the station to catch an overnight train to Vienna. When they boarded the first-class sleeper car, they found that it was freezing cold and that some of their rooms were locked. The ones that were open were dirty, left unchanged after the departure of their previous occupants. The band soon deduced that some of the train cars – including the sleeper cabins they had booked – were "on strike", rendering their tickets invalid. The conductor of the train forced the band to pay cash for second-class tickets and threatened to throw them off the train unless they did so. John Abercrombie got into a loud argument with the conductor, calling him a "Mussolini-fascist-motherfucker".[1426] Meanwhile, Dave Holland figured out that the key that he used to open his bass case could also be used to break in to one of the locked cabins, so he managed to enter the room and sleep in his clothes beneath a large pile of blankets to stave off the freezing temperature. Given these conditions, it is no surprise that Peter came down with a terrible cold overnight on that cursed train trip.[1427]

Their streak of bad luck continued the next day in Vienna. The band headed to the club, Reigen Live, to get set up and do a soundcheck. J.T. started to play the bright white piano on the bandstand and found it to be unacceptable. Abercrombie laughed, remembering that the club owner was truly perplexed by this dissatisfaction, asking, "Why? We've just painted it!"[1428] Immovable, J.T. refused to play the instrument and demanded they replace it. Some of the other members of the band, including John Abercrombie and Peter Erskine, began to feel a little frustrated with J.T.'s lack of willingness to deal with the situation at hand. "We didn't really have a whole lot of time for all this to happen . . ." Peter wryly observed later.[1429] Abercrombie agreed, saying, "It was a disaster."[1430] The club finally complied and brought in a new piano that turned out to be no better. "So we wind up with this completely ridiculous-looking piano that sounds just as bad as the other one," Peter said, "and I was playing *drums du jour* – it wasn't a particularly a 'jazz' kit that they gave me – but you can hear [on a recording of the concert] the band sounds pretty good, despite the fact that I'm feeling sick as a dog!"[1431] The next night, back in Italy in Imola, Peter continued to fight his cold and was feeling out of sorts on the gig. "I took some cough syrup or something," Peter said, "and Dave Holland looked at me and said, 'Are you there, man?' I said, [*sounding dazed*] *Like . . . wow . . .*"[1432]

Just as much as the band could laugh off their misfortunes, they were very focused on the music. Kenny was "probably one of the most serious musicians," Peter said. "Nobody could bring it to the bandstand or to the recording studio like Kenny could." He continued:

> It wasn't easy, travelling to play this music. The booking agencies did the best they could, and you'd play a concert in a beautiful concert hall in Italy,

just stunning. And then the next night you're in some really disgusting place. But the fans, you know, they were true jazz fans that came out to hear it. And you're getting to play with Kenny Wheeler and Dave Holland and John Taylor and John Abercrombie.[1433]

Abercrombie remembered that Kenny did his best to keep things fresh, even though they were playing largely the same tunes night after night:

> He was very organized . . . When we would get ready to play the gig, he would actually sit down with a little pad and piece of paper and he would write the set list individually for every member of the band, and then bring it around to everybody . . . Every night the order would be different . . . Occasionally, he would throw in one we hadn't played in a while, but for the most part it was just the order [that] was always so completely different, you know . . . Because when you're on the road, you don't have a lot of time to learn a lot of new music because you're travelling too much and you can't always be adding new songs to your repertoire.[1434]

Abercrombie also enjoyed the role that he played in Kenny's quintet, more as a front-line instrument, rather than as simply an accompanist or soloist:

> It was very challenging, but also very, very rewarding, because . . . guitar players, we just don't get a chance to do that kind of a thing that much unless it's our own band. We're not usually used in that context . . . But he was using me like a real horn. And I was thrilled by that because I always wanted to be a horn player. I always listened more to trumpet players and saxophone players, probably as opposed to guitar players when I was growing up.[1435]

Even though the band was performing every night and he was as strong as ever, Kenny's nerves still managed to cause him difficulties. John Abercrombie said, "I think part of him was very uncomfortable with leading a band, standing in front of a band, and accepting accolades." (This is shown to great effect on a video from Reigen Live in Vienna, where Kenny retreats into the shadows behind J.T.'s substandard piano when he's not playing, personifying his old tune "Who's Standing in My Corner?") Abercrombie also remembered a nervous tick of Kenny's: "Just before he called the first tune," Abercrombie said, "one of the mutes would hit the floor, and he'd have to reach down and pick it up. I mean, he just dropped them. It was kind of funny . . . I remember then he would just calmly pick them up, and we'd start. Nothing was ever said about it."[1436]

As bumbling as he could be at times, Kenny would occasionally show the quintet another side of his personality. Abercrombie recalled the typically shy Kenny as leader hardly ever speaking on the microphone, but surprising them all once in France by "introducing the band and the first tune in perfect French . . . Every once in a while, this different Kenny would emerge," he said, "a little more forceful, and kind of 'take-charge'. But, generally, he just kind of let the music happen."[1437] A live recording of the quintet in Hamburg from 12 February 1990 – the last night of the tour – certainly shows Kenny taking charge musically. He sounds more powerful than ever, having played a long gig of his own music with an outstanding band of his own choosing every single night since the Queen Elizabeth Hall concert in London back on 18 January. The quintet is hard-hitting, playing with great vigour and excitement: not just on Kenny's tunes (including "Hotel Le Hot" and "Old Time"), but also Dave Holland's "Blues for CM" and "Jumpin' In". They also played the Dietz/Schwartz standard "By Myself", which Kenny introduced with a long unaccompanied solo, containing some of the most exciting and thematically interesting trumpet playing conceivable. These three minutes of virtuosity, using Kenny's unique melodic vocabulary, are simply astonishing. How was it that someone who was essentially self-taught could have figured the trumpet out for himself so well that he can still play like this after 25 gigs in a row, at the age of 60? The gruelling tour schedule had clearly not worn him down as it would many other trumpeters; instead, it seemed to energize him. This is a testament to his sheer will, intellect, intuition, and illustrates the lessons he must have learned from observing the master players he sat beside for decades in the studios.

To open their second set, the quintet played Kenny's "Everybody's Song But My Own". Afterwards, Kenny introduced the next song, saying of it "This is only the second performance. The first one was about seven years ago. We've only rehearsed it today. It's called 'Ma Belle Hélène'."[1438] This composition is unique in Kenny's output because of the harmony of the piece; nearly every chord in the song is a "slash chord", a term used by jazz musicians to describe chordal triads with a foreign note (usually outside the triad) in the bass. Kenny wrote this tune as an exercise, challenging himself to use that type of harmony exclusively. These chords could have been surprising – and potentially tricky – for the other players to sight-read and improvise over. Kenny might well have been thinking about the album they were about to make and wanted the band (and perhaps himself) to have a chance to work out the unique challenges of this tune before being confronted by them when the red light was on in the studio with Manfred Eicher listening from the booth.

The next day, the band departed for Oslo to record for ECM at Rainbow Studio. Once they were set up and got a good sound on everyone, the question came from J.T.: "Well, Ken, what do you think we ought to start with?" Without hesitation, Kenny said, "I think we should start with 'The Widow in the Window'."[1439] Abercrombie remembered the band's surprised reaction:

> We all looked at each other and realized that that song, "The Widow in the Window", we had rehearsed it one time, and never played it on a gig, to my knowledge, and J.T. said, "Are you sure, Ken, you want to start with

Photo 33: The all-star *The Widow in the Window* quintet at a signing at Tower Records London. Left to right: John Taylor, Dave Holland, Peter Erskine, John Abercrombie, Kenny.
Courtesy Peter Erskine

this tune?" He said, "Yeah, I want to start with 'Widow in the Window'." He was adamant about it, and we did it . . . That tune is really hard – and the fact that he called it to start with kind of amazed us all, because he knew that we hadn't been playing that tune live.[1440]

That John Abercrombie was still puzzled by Kenny's decision nearly 25 years later tells us that it was a significant departure from what they had expected. "That part of Kenny I never really understood," Abercrombie said, "if he was trying, in his own subtle way, to throw us off a bit, and make us all work a little harder, or have to think, you know . . . Or, it could have been that he just felt like doing that tune first. That part you never knew."[1441] Abercrombie admitted that for "The Widow in the Window" he had to go back and overdub some of the counterpoint lines Kenny had written for the guitar. "Thank God for modern technology," he laughed. "It was just a hard part for me to sight-read. Not to solo on it – we did that all in one take and most of the parts were played in one take, but . . . I blew [some of the written material] on the original take because I couldn't get to them in time." Once they finished that tune, they went on to record some tunes that they *had* been playing live – including "Aspire" and "Hotel Le Hot" – and some that were more recent additions, including the aforementioned "Ma Belle Hélène" (a take-off of Offenbach's opera *La belle Hélène*, altered to honour Kenny's sisters Mabel and Helen), which they'd just played two nights before in Hamburg. They also recorded Kenny's "Now, and Now Again" and the sombre "Ana", which had been recorded the previous year by the Berlin Contemporary Jazz Orchestra. Steve Lake's excellent liner notes for *The Widow in the Window* (again required reading for any Wheeler fan) say that "Ana" was dedicated to two of Kenny's loved ones, "One alive and one dead". Asked about the title several years later by Ian Carr, Kenny became quite uncomfortable with the question and just said, "I'd sooner leave that one, I think."[1442]

The overall mood of the resulting album, titled *The Widow in the Window*,[1443] is quite melancholy, even by Kenny's standards. Even the title, containing the usual Wheeler wordplay, is a bit gloomy. He said:

> I think I wrote the song first . . . I don't know where I got the title from but the vision of a sort of a middle-aged or older lady looking out of the window, a little bit sad . . . It came to me from that. And "widow" and "window" of course, are a bit tricky to say if you've had too much to drink. [*laughs*][1444]

This subdued feeling was present not only in the choices of repertoire (note that several of the livelier tunes the quintet had played on the tour were not written by Kenny), but also in the way they recorded them in the studio. Nick Purnell remembered walking into the studio and being taken aback by the change in energy in the room, especially when compared to how they had been playing for the past two weeks. "The quintet was much more hard-hitting in person than the resulting album," he said. "It was as if a calm had descended on the music."[1445]

However, while in the studio, the quintet also recorded a more uptempo standard that they had been playing on the road: "By Myself", the only non-Wheeler composition recorded that day. They also played several free improvisations in various trio and duet formats. Instead of being used for the album at hand (which would have given the album more contrast in mood and tempo), Manfred Eicher chose to include these free pieces (and "By Myself") as part of Kenny's big-band recording – now a double album – which had just been recorded as part of the previous month's birthday tour. Peter Erskine said:

> At the encouragement of Manfred, we strayed from the programme of the music that we'd been playing live and we did a number of improvisations . . . At the time, I don't think they were conceived as being part of that big-band recording. They were just two separate albums . . . I think it was Manfred's idea to kind of morph the big-band music into this larger work that included some of the small-group playing as well.[1446]

When *The Widow in the Window* was released, critics picked up on the fact that this album was singular among Kenny's catalogue thus far, having been recorded with a working band. They also did not fail to make mention of the subdued ambiance of the album. For example, in the *Sunday Times*, Richard Cook compliments the record's "luminous writing, reflective solos, [and] detailed interplay between an accomplished quintet" but added, "for once, though, Wheeler's music sounds too determinedly modest: it's so polite and well-spoken that the session grows lacklustre. One longs to hear somebody turn irritable or uncork some surprise."[1447] *Jazz Forum*'s review was similarly conflicted:

> If there is a criticism, it is that the palette of expression is limited. The album stays on a narrow track of sophisticated lyricism and rhythmic virtuosity. The risk is that of sounding too polite: the musicianship too effortless. But this record . . . is a necessary document of a dazzlingly successful set of recordings which mark a pinnacle of Wheeler's achievement on record to date.[1448]

*DownBeat*'s Kevin Whitehead felt similarly, saying:

> *Widow in the Window*, [Wheeler's] latest, succumbs to the old ECM stereotype – creative tension is restrained beneath a placid surface. According to Steve Lake's notes, this quintet had just come off the road, where the music got pretty hot; regrettably, they toned it down in the studio. There are some very pretty tunes, notably "Aspire", which leaps about without losing its poise, the way Kenny's solos do. But the band never quite ignites.

Whitehead ends on a hopeful note, though, perhaps capturing Kenny's feeling about what these tours and recordings with the quintet and big band might lead to: "Could this be Wheeler's year?" he asked. "A cynic might suggest the only thing this gifted trumpeter needs to make it big is a recent high-school diploma. Alas, he's a youthful 60. If you're tired of peachfuzz brass whizzes who sound a little unformed and unsure of a direction, check out a mature master with a distinctive voice of his own."[1449]

Kenny had high hopes that all this recent work might truly transform his fortunes. The incredible torrent of compositional productivity and improvisational creativity – performed throughout Europe in two exhausting tours, documented in a burst of two new outstanding ECM recordings – might just pay off.

———·———

In January 1991, Nick Purnell put together a short but successful American tour for Kenny's quintet with bassist Gary Peacock replacing Dave Holland, who was otherwise booked.[1450] This band played Blues Alley near Washington

Photo 34: The Kenny Wheeler Quintet outside Blues Alley, Washington DC. Left to right: John Taylor, Gary Peacock, Kenny, John Abercrombie, and Peter Erskine.

© Patrick Hinely, Work/Play®

DC, the Regattabar in Boston, and a week at the Blue Note in New York, where they shared a bill with members of the group Oregon.[1451] A piece in *JazzForum* written by the music writer and friend of Kenny, Patrick Hinely, detailed the night at Blues Alley and included several of the author's excellent photos of the band behind the scenes. In his article, Hinely was quick to point out the disparities between PolyGram's (ECM's American subsidiary at the time) promotion of Kenny's US appearances versus the (equally rare) appearances of his well-supported ECM label-mate Keith Jarrett. Highlighting many of the frustrations Kenny himself expressed over the years, Hinely called PolyGram's coverage "underwhelming, making his visit more of a musicians' event, a sort of inside job in more ways than someone of Wheeler's stature deserves".[1452]

The band met to rehearse for most of the afternoon before their gig at Blues Alley. In terms of repertoire, they played many of Kenny's tunes, including works from his recent *The Widow in the Window*, plus additional material from *Gnu High, Double, Double You* and *Flutter By, Butterfly*. They also played John Taylor's "Windfall" and Gary Peacock's, "Gardenia". Hinely said that, on "Foxy Trot", Kenny "caught his own thermal and commenced an ascent that never let up. Anything lost in precise navigation was more than made up for by the beauty of the view he described up there." After the tune, Kenny introduced each of his bandmates to the audience. "Everyone, that is," Hinely wrote, "except himself."[1453]

———·———

In April 1991, Kenny joined his Dave Holland Quintet bandmate, alto saxophonist and composer Steve Coleman, for a project called "Rhythm in Mind" in New York. The group was an all-star cast of musicians from several different generations of jazz artists. Coleman said he chose the musicians for both "the roles they have played in the past in the development of this music" as well as those who were associated with "recent developments of creative black music".[1454] In addition to Kenny, the players included tenor saxophonist Von Freeman, guitarist Kevin Eubanks, pianist Tommy Flanagan, Dave Holland on bass, and two drummers: Ed Blackwell and Marvin "Smitty" Smith.[1455] Ever since their days in Dave Holland's quintet, Steve had felt that Kenny was the "best orchestrator in the band". When *Rhythm in Mind* came about, he recalled: "I got Kenny on the recording . . . Tommy Flanagan was on the record date also, and Tommy's from Michigan like Thad, so he knew all these really obscure Thad Jones tunes. And so he brought them in and showed them to us, and then I asked Kenny to orchestrate them."[1456] (Kenny prepared the charts for "Slipped Again" and "Zec".)

The concert portion was the first to occur, on 27 April at Weill Recital Hall (located within New York's venerable Carnegie Hall) and was conceived as a part of Carnegie Hall's week-long Centennial Festival, which had featured visiting orchestras from around the United States and international soloists Placido Domingo, Yo-Yo Ma, and Jessye Norman, among many others.[1457] The *New York Times* reviewer Peter Watrous said that, despite all the jazz luminaries onstage, "tension and a clash of styles" were the real stars of the show, acknowledging the various generational and stylistic dialects represented.[1458] Steve Coleman agreed with this, fully aware that he was bringing together musicians from different eras with diverse approaches to the material. In his liner notes for the album (also called *Rhythm in Mind*), Coleman distinguishes Freeman, Flanagan, and Blackwell as being "veteran musicians", implying that he, Kenny, Dave, Eubanks, and Smith represented the new generation. This insinuation, of course, falls in line with other erroneous observations of Kenny appearing to be much younger – physically and musically – than he was; in fact, he was only a year younger than Blackwell and two months older than Flanagan, quite firmly in the "veteran" category.

The recording itself shows Kenny in a much more conventional setting than many recordings under his own name with this band of star soloists. Surprisingly, some of his best playing on the record is on the first tune, "Slipped Again" (one of the Thad Jones compositions he arranged), which is a blues in F, a form he had tried to avoid and, as he said himself, one he often found challenging to improvise on authentically.[1459] His solo, however, shows him in fantastic form, fitting his characteristic rhythmic quirks into this more straight-ahead context with apparent ease while still sounding as true to himself as ever, especially when he could have been intimidated by such an eminent group of mostly American musicians. But with Coleman not only including him as a player among all these stars but also praising him by featuring him as a writer, Kenny, still in his prime at 61, should have felt all the confidence in the world.

Kenny's relationship with the music of Mike Gibbs also continued throughout 1991. In February of that year, Gibbs performed two nights at the Jazz Cafe in Camden. This mini-residency evoked the spirit of Gil Evans's famous Monday nights at New York's Sweet Basil. As John Fordham noted in his *Guardian* review, "Such ruminations were intensified by the outfit Gibbs brought . . . because Evans's vigorous and vivid alto saxophonist Chris Hunter was in the ranks."[1460] Most of the music they performed was from Gibbs's album *Big Music*,[1461] recorded three years earlier in the US by a mostly American, and very impressive, band; the guitar chair alone was shared between heavyweights Bill Frisell, Kevin Eubanks, and John Scofield. On guitar for the Jazz Cafe gigs was Manchester-based Mike Walker, someone who was soon to become a regular collaborator with Kenny, particularly through his role in Nick Purnell's Creative Jazz Orchestra.

Later that year, a new Mike Gibbs Orchestra was formed for a substantial Contemporary Music Network tour with Scofield himself in the guitar chair. The tour featured an exceptional 14-piece group of American and English talent, including bassist Steve Swallow and drummer Bill Stewart in the rhythm section, with J.T. at the piano. Two French horns were complemented by the saxophones of Tony Coe and Julian Argüelles, with Chris Pyne, Dave Stewart and occasionally Mike Gibbs himself playing trombone, along with trumpeters John Barclay, Stuart Brooks and Kenny. Gibbs arranged all the music, the tunes themselves having been written by himself or Scofield. Thankfully, a beautifully recorded set from their tour performance at Birmingham Symphony Hall was eventually released commercially some 27 years later.[1462] The chemistry in this band was electrifying, and it is fascinating to hear Kenny's unmistakable sound within this reduced big-band setting.

There were exciting developments to come within the UK big-band scene, too. Back in 1989, his old friend Ian Carr had formed a new ensemble for a spring tour. At the time, Ian was doing research for his forthcoming book *Jazz: The Essential Companion*.[1463] He explained: "When I was collating all the information, I noticed that all the British musicians I most admired all seemed to be doing most of their work abroad. They simply weren't getting the offers here."[1464] In response, he established a mini-big band, replete with its knowingly ironic name, Orchestra UK, to feature some of the musicians he rightly felt were not getting the acknowledgement they deserved at home.[1465] The following year, Ian, Kenny, and J.T. were involved in the creation of another big band, the London Jazz Orchestra. This new ensemble was not related to the earlier band of the same name, other than their shared aesthetic: to create a platform for original big-band music. This LJO was formed by Scott Stroman and Noel Langley, a trumpeter who was just a few years out of the Guildhall School of Music and eager to establish a new creative outlet for the scene. Stroman and Langley put together a cross-generational wish-list of inaugural members, including established players like Kenny and Ian Carr in the trumpets and Stan Sulzmann in the saxophones, alongside some younger musicians like Noel and saxophonist/composer Tim Garland. From 1991 onwards, the LJO began a regular residency at the Vortex Jazz Club and Kenny would be part of it whenever he could. It is a testament to Kenny's commitment to new generations that he would agree to be part of such a big-band venture at the height of his career.[1466] His willingness to collaborate with the up-and-coming players of the day also led him to take part in a new project of Tim Garland's. As Tim was becoming known as a prolific young composer and bandleader, he formed the celebrated jazz/folk crossover ensemble Lammas, which recorded its debut album in 1990–91. Kenny was the invited guest soloist for the record, in an ensemble that also featured cameos from Norma Winstone and Irish-born London-based vocalist Christine Tobin.[1467]

Kenny played a long European tour in March and April 1992 with his quintet, this time Swedish bassist Palle Danielsson replacing Dave Holland. Like his new colleagues in Kenny's quintet, Danielsson had become an ECM regular, having played and recorded with Keith Jarrett's beloved 1970s trios and quartets. The three-week tour was made up of mostly one-nighters and just two travel-only days for the entire period, with the quintet playing Hungary, then Finland, Denmark, Italy, France, Switzerland, Austria, Germany, and Norway.[1468] Nick Purnell, who had once again put this tour together, travelled with the band at the beginning and said he was "keen to keep the group working to continue building Ken's name with audiences and promoters".[1469]

The first stop was the Tavaszi Festival in Budapest. Fortunately, this concert was documented on video, allowing us to see a strong, confident, and in-control Kenny playing trumpet on his composition "Mark Time" (dedicated to his son) and the wonderfully inventive rhythmic approach of the rhythm section, especially J.T.'s percussive piano playing alongside Peter Erskine. Palle fits in wonderfully with this new band, and Abercrombie and J.T. cover the tune's tricky countermelody with ease. Once again, this band is more energetic and dynamic than documented on *The Widow in the Window*. In addition to "Mark Time", they played Kenny's tunes "Hotel Le Hot" and "Everybody's Song But My Own", which he announced as having been "written by everybody but me".[1470] Kenny self-deprecation widened to include other members of the band, too. After introducing Peter Erskine's "Music of My People", he also set up the next tune they would play, John Abercrombie's song, "which he's not got a title for. For the moment, he's calling it 'JA-Bal' which means 'John Abercrombie Ballad'. Not very good, but it's all he could come up with!"[1471]

Peter Erskine remembers that, as the tour went on, the band became more active and progressively a bit louder, causing Kenny to need to hear himself more in his own monitor. So, to counter this (and very likely compensate for his diminished hearing as he grew older), he began to put his trumpet or flugelhorn bell directly over the microphone so that he could hear himself more clearly when the band got more intense on the gig. It probably didn't occur to him that this also meant that the other players in the band – who had calibrated their monitor levels to match what they needed of Kenny from his more politely distanced (softer) levels in the soundcheck – were getting aurally blasted by the suddenly louder trumpet. This situation reached a breaking point in Berlin at the Quasimodo club when, as Peter said, "Palle had to stop playing and he tore some sheets of paper – whatever chart we were playing – and made these impromptu ear plugs, because it was painfully loud."[1472] When they arrived the next day for soundcheck at the Fabrik in Hamburg, Peter politely asked Kenny to check his monitor more carefully: "Kenny, could you please just put the bell, over the microphone or whatever, kind of like you were doing last night, so we can get a maximum volume here?" Kenny replied, "Well, I won't do that." Peter responded:

> I said, "Yeah, you probably will. It's happened the last few nights. It's just so we can get a top level so we don't have a repeat of last night and hurt ourselves." He said, "Well, I don't do that." So he refused to – he's playing at this very respectable, proper distance and he won't go more on the mic during the soundcheck. And I keep asking him to, and he keeps declining. And I finally said, "OK, Kenny, then how about just for *my fucking sense of amusement...*" and he got so insulted he kicked his monitor off the stage and walked off.[1473]

Sound engineer Paul Sparrow was travelling with the band at the time, taking over after manager Nick Purnell went back to England halfway through the tour.[1474] His position was one of neutrality, feeling that Peter was "always terribly concerned about loud monitoring ... he hated anything too loud, anyway", but he also acknowledged:

> I think the problem with Ken was he wasn't a very good communicator, quite often. So, if there was a problem, he was just as likely to sort of go quiet and get angry, rather than talk about what is the problem, with the tone and so on ... Yeah, I think he did tend to have his monitor too loud, but I think as the years went on and I worked with him more, we got that problem sorted out to a happy medium in a way ... It was a perennial problem with Kenny and his monitor ... you did have to talk to him and get him to open up about the problems.[1475]

"That was the only time I'd ever seen him really get angry," Peter said, adding that "Kenny was such a mild-mannered man that it wouldn't surprise me if there were anger issues. Maybe that's why his playing was so impassioned."[1476] Even though Peter thought this was an "unfortunate incident", it didn't harm his friendship or working rapport with Kenny. "Kenny and I always enjoyed a very cordial relationship," he said. "I mean, I always remember Kenny as being very witty, very quiet, very hard-working, never complained."[1477]

In May of 1992, Kenny was finally able to record some of the music for jazz chamber ensemble that he had first written for and performed on his May 1984 and April 1985 BBC broadcasts as "The Kenny Wheeler Octet" and "Kenny Wheeler Tentette", respectively.[1478] Nick Purnell, who produced the new album, titled *Kayak*,[1479] said that the recording "stems from a time when Evan [Parker] and myself used to talk about recording Kenny projects, more for documentation purposes really . . . [*Kayak*] was based around two BBC sessions I had heard before I had met Ken and they were always favourites of mine. I still think it's some of his best writing . . ."[1480]

Kenny's success here may be due to the creativity he demonstrated in restricting himself to a more limited palette of instruments. *Kayak* is indeed unique in Kenny's recorded output because it features a medium-sized ensemble: smaller than a big band but larger than the typical small groups featured on most of his previous albums. For the first three tracks of the recording there is a slightly different band than the for rest of the album. Here, the ensemble is French horn (John Rook), trombone (Dave Horler), bass trombone or tuba (Dave Stewart), and Kenny on trumpet or flugelhorn, with two reed players (Stan Sulzmann and Julian Argüelles), piano (John Taylor), bass (Chris Laurence), and drums (Peter Erskine). For the final four tracks, another trombone (Chris Pyne) is added, and there is a second pianist (John Horler) as well. On this session, using two pianos proved to be problematic. Peter Erskine had a clear recollection of this reoccurrence of the "Wheeler bad luck":

> The two pianos were tuned differently – one was at A442 and the other was at A440 – and we had a heck of a time [*laughs*] getting one or the other of the pianos to stay in tune. It's interesting . . . there always seemed to be some amount of difficulty or obstacles in doing projects with Kenny. Maybe [it was] just part of the ambition that he had for his music . . . but there was always a fun but occasionally frustrating challenge to working with him.[1481]

According to Chris Laurence, everyone on the recording did the sessions for no remuneration: just to do it for Kenny. "We all did it for nothing," Chris said, adding, "nobody cared if there was any money involved, they just did it. Peter Erskine was one of those people as well. He didn't care either. He just came and did it." The fact some of England's most in-demand jazz artists and studio musicians would participate goes to show that people around Kenny loved him and his music enough to think it was important to document, regardless of compensation. To be sure, this labour of love was no small investment of time: the session lasted the entire day.[1482] Even though the session went late into the night, it may well have gone on without Peter Erskine's musical sensibilities. According to Chris Laurence, the drummer's sense of phrasing and form helped to organize the players and keep everyone grounded:

> Peter helped us get through it. He moved things on a bit. He had all the attributes, the professionalism, and he knew what to do, like a real top-class American drummer would. No disrespect for any British drummers, but there was just a way he could set things up. He knew what was going to happen . . . just to say, *here it comes* . . . and it would be on the button. He would just make it sound even more magnificent.[1483]

Wonderful (and helpful) as it was, Peter's contribution altered Kenny's original instrumentation, since he had not used a drummer on the BBC broadcasts of this material.

For the *Kayak* album, the group recorded Kenny's "Gentle Piece" (recorded on *Music for Large and Small Ensembles*) paired with "Old Ballad", "5 4 6" (listed as "5 Four Six" on Dave Holland's *The Razor's Edge*), and interestingly, a suite of tunes called the *C Suite* (all titles based on the word or sound of the letter C) which included the tunes "See Horse" (Kenny said this was "the idea of a child when it says, *Mummy, see, horse?*"), "Sea Lady", "C Man" (for Chris Laurence), and "C.C. Signor!" (for Chick Corea).[1484] The title tune "Kayak" had been written while Kenny was teaching at Banff. He said that he wanted to "call it something associated with Canada" since he composed it there, adding that he liked the title because it was a palindrome.[1485]

Nick Purnell's Ah Um label released the album, which had also put out Purnell's own debut record *Onetwothree* (also featuring Kenny and Peter Erskine) the previous year.[1486] Erskine considered Kenny's improvisation on Purnell's "Yes Or No" "one of the all-time great Kenny solos". Purnell said, "As the tune was somewhat Kenny-inspired, perhaps he felt at home."[1487] He likely did feel comfortable recording on Purnell's record, despite his complaints about playing other people's music more than his own. Many of Kenny's friends, including J.T., Julian Argüelles, and Mike Gibbs, recorded with him on Purnell's album, so he was in familiar and amicable company.

*Kayak* received mixed reviews, largely because of the sound quality and mixing of the record. For example, *The Penguin Guide to Jazz* called the record "marred by oddly balanced sound, but musically fascinating".[1488] Despite these criticisms, *Kayak* is a significant album in Kenny's output, truly the first one documenting this medium-sized ensemble. It is also important because it represents another temporary departure from ECM, a result of Kenny's inability to record for the label as often as he would have liked. Even though many ECM stalwarts including guitarist Ralph Towner experienced gaps in recording regularly for the label, Kenny seemed to take these breaks personally. Towner explained that, during this period "Manfred got so busy. There were so many records that were being recorded, and he produces every recording. If he's not there, it doesn't get recorded. So, there was basically quite a long line of waiting to get recorded . . . It could be frustrating; you could wait years . . ."[1489]

A month after recording *Kayak*, Kenny left on another tour, once again organized by Saudades and headed up by Nick Purnell. This instrumentation was different, however, in that it was with a trio comprising Ralph Towner and bassist Gary Peacock. (Towner also played piano in addition to guitar.) It was also shorter than the previous outing, with seven concerts in as many days, in Germany, England, France, and Poland.[1490] A bootleg recording shows the majority of the band's repertoire had been written by its members, including Kenny's "Smatter" and "The Mouse in the Dairy" and Towner's "Ballad for Janet", "The Glide", and "Beppo". They also played Miles Davis's "Nardis".[1491] "We played some really nice venues with that trio tour," Towner remembered, adding that he loved playing with Kenny. "[He had an] incredible combination of strengths. I always found it affecting to be around him," he said.[1492] "That might have been the last time that we played together as a group," Towner said, lamenting the fact that "[Kenny] wanted to do some more things and I remember I was kind of busy and I didn't do it . . . I think I was busy with Oregon or something and wasn't able . . . I regret not doing that. It was another formation . . . Kenny, Abercrombie, and I, as a trio, I think."[1493] Purnell remembered that he tried to get ECM to record this group, as all three players were mainstays of the label, but "Manfred Eicher turned it down as he didn't think it was a good idea," he said. Purnell pointed out that the label went on to put out two records of Towner and Peacock as a duo. "Make of that what you will," he said.[1494] Purnell must have been on to something, because it would be another four years after this tour before Kenny would record another album as a leader for ECM.

---

In autumn 1993, Kenny set off on a 16-stop concert tour of Europe with his quintet, now minus both Erskine and Dave Holland. American drummer Joe LaBarbera joined existing members J.T. and John Abercrombie, with Palle Danielsson once again on bass. They played together for nearly a month, from 22 October to 13 November, performing in Germany, Macedonia, Slovenia, Italy, France, and Austria.[1495]

As with previous tours, the quintet also travelled with Paul Sparrow, Kenny's trusted sound engineer, who had been on several of his previous tours going all the way back to the 1978 *Little Suite* tour.[1496] Sparrow recalled that, early in the tour, Kenny began to experience some health issues which affected his playing. He suspected that he'd had a minor stroke while they were in Ljubljana, the capital of Slovenia. "His lip felt a little bit numb and he was concerned about that," Sparrow said. "The rest of the tour went OK," he said, "but I think when he went back home he was diagnosed with high blood pressure."[1497]

Kenny's playing at the middle point of the tour (and less than a week after his scare in Slovenia) was recorded in Milan on 31 October and 1 November 1993, for an album that was released as *All the More*.[1498] It is significant because it documents several of his tunes rarely (if ever) recorded elsewhere and shows him at this stage with a notably different quintet than *The Widow in the Window*; however, it is not a recording that Kenny was particularly pleased with. His dissatisfaction was largely because of how his sound came through on the recording. Sparrow recalled a dispute he had with the record label's engineer at the beginning of the sessions:

> There was quite an elderly guy in the studio running [the session], and he had put an Electro-Voice [RE20] microphone on [Kenny's] flugelhorn and it ended up sounding just like a trumpet rather than a flugelhorn. And he had a big Neumann U87 condenser there, and I said, "Put that on" and he put that on him and then it was just like Ken. But then he said, "I'm going to use both mics." I think Ken, in the end, didn't want the album released.[1499]

Kenny's unhappiness with the album might also be attributed to the fact that he didn't have his entire touring quintet on the recording. Even though they played the tour that surrounded it, Palle Danielsson and John Abercrombie did not participate in the *All the More* recording sessions. Italian bassist Furio Di Castri played the session in Danielsson's place, but there was no guitarist hired. (Though not ideal, the music could be played without a guitarist, although not without a bassist.) Joe LaBarbera explained, saying that "both John Abercrombie and Palle Danielsson were concerned about upsetting Manfred Eicher if they recorded for a label other than ECM. That's why we used Furio and not John Abercrombie."[1500]

Abercrombie and Danielsson completed the gruelling tour with the rest of the band. Danielsson, no stranger to the difficulties of long concert tours, recalled the difficulty of the schedule more than nearly anything else about the tour. "It was a lot of travelling," he said.[1501] Palle also remembered all the travel getting to Kenny at one point, even though he tried not to show it. As the band got on the bus early one morning for a long day on the road, Palle asked, "Kenny, how are you today?" "Ah, not *too* bad" came the lethargic reply.[1502] Despite the schedule, Kenny's health worries and frustration with the recording, the tour was a generally joyous affair and provided LaBarbera and Danielsson many cherished memories. Joe LaBarbera said that he "loved

Kenny and his music so much", and was very happy to be playing with the quintet on this tour. "Kenny's music was so liberating for me because it was so original and personal . . ."[1503] Like LaBarbera, Palle Danielsson remained a fan of Kenny's music and musicianship. "He was a fantastic instrumentalist," Palle said, and was "producing many beautiful songs. His sense of harmony was extraordinary," calling his tunes "very special compositions – He was unique."[1504]

———·———

Back in 1990, Kevin Whitehead's *DownBeat* review of *The Widow in the Window* had implied that Kenny would likely have been a bigger star in the jazz world by then if only he had been younger.[1505] His reticent personality notwithstanding, there may be some truth to this. At this point in jazz history, there had been a recent boom owing a great deal to the revitalization of the music by mostly American "young lions" who dominated the attention of record labels and promoters. Already finding it difficult enough to get work in England under his own name and frustrated by lukewarm (or worse) reviews in the British press, Kenny's shyness began to fade away in interviews, casting him less as a quiet figure wanting to stay in the background and more of a complainer, dissatisfied with how his career had turned out. This is unfortunate, because it must have taken such courage for him to speak out on such matters when it was so difficult for him to say what was on his mind. Wanting more and more to be playing his own music, he had told Brian Priestley back in the mid-1980s that he would "really like to do more of my own. I now realize that I'm happiest when I'm playing my own music and I feel I play best when I play my music."[1506] That wish had largely been granted by Nick Purnell's vision and hard work on Kenny's behalf, which put him at the centre of big-name groups, helped him make two new ECM recordings, and expanded his reach with promoters and packed venues across Europe. Despite his discontent, there was every reason for Kenny to be optimistic about the future.

The good news around this time was that others were beginning to take note of his undeserved station in the jazz world. A 1990 profile in the *New Statesman and Society* called "Subtle Survivor" declared: "Unglamourous, shy, and introspective, [Wheeler] exemplifies what today's youthful club jazz mafia seem so relentlessly content to snipe at." The piece also recognized the trailblazing contributions of Kenny and his elder jazz cohorts in a profound way:

> As politics begin once more to surface in the UK tradition, these new players are hungrily turning to Joe Harriott in the past, and US contemporaries [Steve] Coleman and "Smitty" Smith in the present, for a sense of racial community and identity. And players like Wheeler, who worked directly with both Harriott and members of M-Base, who have a lifetime as daring innovators and subtle survivors, as well as an open respect for change

and challenge, seem to have been tricked into standing for the reaction-
aries they've never been. With the result that Wheeler's 60th birthday
gets celebrated by a jazz establishment that has consistently sidelined the
toughly unfashionable tradition of exploration and risk that he actually
represents.[1507]

The following year, perhaps feeling a bit more comfortable speaking his
mind while far away in his Canadian hometown, Kenny described how he felt
the media's selective coverage was distorting the scene: "It's got a bit like the
rock world, but not so big. A lot of the good players who have really got talent
don't get any prominence at all, but they decide to push somebody – whoever
'*they*' are – they will make them work and sell all kinds of records . . ."[1508] And
in a 1992 piece in the *Guardian* about the end of the "Jazz Boom", Kenny's
complaints about his fees and lack of work in England came filtered through
the numbers cited by Nick Purnell, which must have been shocking to see in
print:

> London-based Kenny Wheeler, reckoned to be one of the world's best
> trumpeters and a guru of modern jazz, made 49 appearances in the first
> three months of this year. Only two were in Britain. According to his man-
> ager Nick Purnell, his fees are about three times higher abroad – £4,500
> against £1,500 – and bookings are far more plentiful. As a result 95 per
> cent of his income comes from abroad.[1509]

This period marks a turning point in Kenny's attitudes and expectations
about his life. Although the *DownBeat* article about him might have helped
set up these expectations, after his 1990 tours, the ECM recordings, and
then the following quintet tours, Kenny, now well into his sixties, must also
have been thinking something akin to *If it's not going to happen now, when
is it going to happen?* At this point, it probably would have been impossible
for him to believe that his greatest sales and international fame would come
from an album he was yet to record. This peak of commercial success would
come just as he was starting to experience more signs of his age, with travel
becoming more difficult, and his previously explosive instrumental virtuosity
first showing signs of maturing into the refined artistry of his later years. "I
hope my teeth hold out for another ten years," he told an interviewer back in
late 1989, fully aware of the serious threat advancing age can pose for brass
players.[1510] Luckily for Kenny, however, his career – and his dental health –
had more time remaining than he might have expected.

---

Throughout the early 1990s, Kenny was involved in the resurrection of a project with South African drummer Louis Moholo, one in which he first participated back in 1978. Moholo had arrived in London as part of the South
African group the Blue Notes, in the mid-1960s. A mixed-race band, they left

South Africa to escape apartheid and decided to stay in Europe following an appearance in Antibes before eventually settling in London. The Blue Notes musicians had a huge impact on the creative happenings taking place around Ronnie Scott's Old Place. Pianist Chris McGregor and saxophonist Dudu Pukwana both led groups of their own, Brotherhood of Breath and Spear, respectively, which brought together leading improvisers on the London scene with their own South African colleagues. But it wasn't until 1978 that Louis Moholo made his own contribution as a leader to this stylistic partnership. The album *Spirits Rejoice!*[1511] included Kenny and Evan Parker with two bassists: another South African, Harry Miller, and another of the original Blue Notes, Johnny Dyani. Many of Moholo's original Blue Notes colleagues passed away far too young in the intervening years, and, in honour of their legacy, the Dedication Orchestra was formed. In 1992 they recorded their first album, which Moholo also titled *Spirits Rejoice*.[1512] A second release, *Ixesha*,[1513] followed in 1994. The Dedication Orchestra was a huge ensemble that featured some members of Moholo's original 1978 band, including Kenny and Evan, trombonist Radu Malfatti and pianist Keith Tippett, alongside some younger musicians from the next generation of creative improvisers such as Django Bates, Guy Barker, and Claude Deppa. Kenny would continue to participate in various reunion performances of the Dedication Orchestra in the coming years, and even contribute an arrangement of Dudu Pukwana's beautiful ballad, "B, My Dear".[1514]

During the same period, Kenny was involved in two acclaimed albums with the celebrated oud player Rabih Abou-Khalil. Both recordings appeared on the Enja label, *Blue Camel* (1992)[1515] and *The Sultan's Picnic* (1994),[1516] on which Kenny joined his old United Jazz+Rock Ensemble colleague Charlie Mariano in the front line. In 1993 he also recorded alongside Abou-Khalil for Mariano's own album, *Seventy*.[1517]

At the other end of the musical spectrum, in early 1995 Kenny played one of the last significant commercial recording sessions of his long career in the studios for the James Bond film *GoldenEye*. (The sequence they recorded in that session was for the movie's famous tank chase scene.[1518]) The music, composed by John Altman, features the powerful brass section prominently. "What a section!" Altman wrote. Trumpeter Guy Barker had fond memories of the recording as well. "I've gone to heaven," he said, "playing the James Bond theme sat between Derek [Watkins] and KW".[1519]

---

It had been nearly a decade since Azimuth had recorded for ECM. Although they all remained friends, John and Norma had each remarried by this point, their children were grown, and Kenny had become a grandfather. Gone was their old Volvo Estate named "SYD", and with it the sense of urgency from J.T. to book more gigs for them. When they entered Rainbow Studios in April 1994, there was an energy of frustration coupled with the knowledge that things would be changing soon for all of them. The album they recorded during these poignant sessions became known as *How It Was Then . . . Never Again*.[1520]

There was some tension in the air between the members of the trio during the recording and it emerged in different ways. At the end of the first day of recording, Manfred asked them, "For tomorrow, do you have anything with text?" Norma had begun working on lyrics for Kenny's tune "Old Time", although John had said the tune didn't need words. But she finished the lyric anyway ("We were just gonna have to put up with it if [Manfred] wanted text," Norma said) and the next morning, when they went into the studio, they began recording the tune, which became the title track for the album.

Kenny had been unhappy with his sound through his studio headphones and was already frustrated. "We'd never played it," Norma said, adding that John just started strumming the piano strings by hand and "we kept stopping and starting because I wasn't sure what I was supposed to be doing." After more discussion within the group (mostly between J.T. and Norma, since Kenny, of course, hardly spoke up), the frustration spread to the control booth, to the point that Manfred finally said, "*Stop!* Don't talk anymore about this piece – *just play it!* Whatever happens, happens." They began recording again. Norma said:

> I was singing, and I could see John. Kenny was behind this screen, and I had a screen in front of me. We were all in this room, not separated except for the screens. So I could see what John was doing. So that's how I knew he was ready for my pickups into the next key . . . I remember shrugging and thinking, "Well, I should carry on singing then."[1521]

During his second solo, Kenny's irritation with the sound – and possibly the entire situation – finally boiled over. He turned away from the microphone, blasting into the wall so loudly that it was still clearly audible over the microphone. (This moment is captured on the released track, at about 5:08.) Manfred said, "What's the matter with him?" Norma replied that she didn't know, but maybe his hearing was starting to trouble him. "Manfred was very nice, actually," she said. He said to her, "It's all very well, but he's not really thinking of you, is he, with your headphones on and *he's* busy blasting away."[1522]

It was during this difficult recording session that J.T. also found out some terrible news: his second wife, Di, was seriously ill with cancer. "In the breaks [John] had this newspaper about breast cancer," Norma remembered. "He was showing me that . . . it was all a bit strange and sad."[1523] It must have been difficult and somewhat awkward for them, once husband and wife, still friends and musical collaborators, to give and receive consolation for such an unfortunate situation.

There are two songs on this recording of most likely interest to Wheeler devotees. The first is undoubtedly his trumpet quartet arrangement of the

Irving Berlin standard "How Deep Is the Ocean". "He had originally sent me the music and wanted me to sing some of the other lines," Norma remembered, "but Manfred said, 'Why don't you do it with all trumpets, rather than trumpet and voice?'" So, Kenny recorded all four parts with no improvisation added, just the elegant counterpoint that had come to be at the heart of his compositional style.[1524] (Incidentally, this setting is a rare recorded example of the many multi-trumpet works he composed for trumpet ensemble for students at Banff and elsewhere.)

The second song of particular interest to Wheeler connoisseurs is his composition "Wintersweet". With lyrics by Norma, this version of the song – reminiscent of the gorgeous atmosphere of her 1987 ECM album *Somewhere Called Home* – is one of Azimuth's most superb recordings. Norma has named "Wintersweet" one of her most-loved tunes of Kenny's, and one of her favourite lyrics she ever composed for his music. "Extraordinary," she called it, explaining that J.T. had actually given Kenny (who was searching for a title for the song) the name for the tune, because his wife Di was an avid gardener, and there was this lovely flower they liked called a wintersweet. "I was thinking about that," she said, "the beauty of the winter flower, *such sweet surprise each time it's there*."[1525] When Azimuth was recording "Wintersweet" in the studio, however, there was an issue trying to figure out what to do with the key, since they usually played it in one key for Norma and then a perfect fourth higher for Kenny's solo. Norma explained: "[Kenny] always changed key after the chorus that I do. It was a key that he preferred to play in, I suppose." As would be customary, Norma wanted to sing the melody again after the solo to finish the tune, but it was a bit too high for her voice in Kenny's key. Here, as with the closing of *The Sweet Time Suite*, Manfred Eicher made a crucial musical suggestion in the studio:

> Manfred said, "Why doesn't the trumpet continue to play as you sing in the same key?" And that's what we did. It was doable, and it sounded much better. With the support of the flugel, the voice was much more a colour – still singing the words, but it was a really good suggestion. It sounded a bit thin and not the right key for me, but I could do it if I was singing along with Kenny. He filled it out.[1526]

After Kenny joins Norma near the end of the song, he plays an unbelievable leap covering two octaves effortlessly, seemingly responding to the lyric "magic" that she had just sung. Despite the difficulties experienced in the studio, this recording is, simply put, a masterpiece of late-period Azimuth, showing each musician in a beautiful and poignant light.

Around this time, Norma had the sense that Azimuth was nearing its end. "It didn't have its newness, and we weren't using synthesizer or organ anymore," she said. "It felt almost more 'normal,' but it wasn't like the unusual, original Azimuth . . . It felt like it was closing . . . I suppose everything has its time."[1527] Although they continued to do a few projects together over the next few years, the trio was rapidly winding down. It wouldn't be long before this captivating combination of musical personalities appeared together onstage for the last time, as Azimuth or otherwise.

# 7 Angel Song

... the guys were asking me, "What are you doing?" I would say, "I'm trying to sound like Kenny!"

*Vince Mendoza*

For a shy musician lacking a university degree of any kind, with a deep dislike of analysing his own processes, it is somewhat ironic that Kenny's life and music – especially his compositions – have become a frequent subject of literary interest and academic study. For decades, journalists and critics have been alert to the dichotomy between his humble personality and the strength of his playing and writing. And, as Kenny's career flourished, more and more biographical sketches and in-depth analyses appeared.

By the mid-1990s, Kenny's long-time friend from St. Catharines days Gene Lees had become a major figure in the jazz world. Appointed editor of *DownBeat* magazine in 1959, Lees was a lyricist for tunes by Bill Evans and Antonio Carlos Jobim, author of the monthly publication *JazzLetter*, and a well-respected, albeit controversial, presence in the jazz world. Many features from his *JazzLetter* became chapters in his acclaimed books, including *Meet Me at Jim & Andy's, Waiting for Dizzy, Cats of Any Color,* and *Friends Along the Way.*[1528] Another collection of his writings was published in the book *Arranging the Score,*[1529] which offered biographical sketches and anecdotes about great jazz composers and arrangers, including Gil Evans, Henry Mancini, and Kenny Wheeler. (His profile of Kenny in the book, titled "Come Back Last Summer" was first published in a two-volume set in the March and April 1993 issues of *JazzLetter.*) Lees's account of Kenny's early life is filtered through his own occasionally bitter interpretation of what growing up in St. Catharines had done to artistic and creative types perceived as "outsiders" by those the author viewed as "small-minded".[1530] It is hard to dispute the excellence of his storytelling, however, and he captures so many fundamental aspects of Kenny's life and personality that authors of previous profiles either missed or ignored: the importance of his Canadian family, his early gigs, the unsung hero that Doreen was, and especially Kenny's humour and sensitivity, reflected in the piece's title.[1531] His mischievous side is also depicted in this little story from their St. Catharines friend, drummer Rod North, with which Lees ends his profile:

During one of Kenny's periodic returns to St. Catharines, he went with [his sister] Helen and Bryon Ball, his nephew and son of his sister Mabel, to a jazz club. One of the musicians recognized him and started an effusive introduction from the bandstand . . .

"Ladies and gentlemen, we have with us tonight a real jazz celebrity"
Kenny sank lower in his chair.
"A man who left St. Catharines to become one of the great jazz musicians of our time!"
And Kenny sank lower still.
"Ladies and gentlemen, may I present . . . Mr. Kenny Wheeler!"
Kenny jabbed Bryon with an elbow and said, "Stand up!"[1532]

Another major piece of writing penned later about Kenny was by Canadian author Terrance Cox, who contributed a piece called "Kenny-ing: Kenny Wheeler and Local Jazz" to a larger volume titled *Covering Niagara: Studies in Local Popular Culture*.[1533] This outstanding work discussed Kenny's ties to the region, especially focusing on his early days and circle of friends in St. Catharines, his need to leave Canada to pursue an international career, and his return in later years as a hometown boy "done good", celebrated by young jazz musicians and even the local symphony orchestra. Cox spends several pages examining the roots of the jazz scene during Kenny's formative years there as a teenager, creating a sociologically grounded portrait of how it felt to be a shy kid interested in bebop in a small Canadian city in the late 1940s.

Kenny was also studied and written about by fellow musicians. In addition to the teaching work he did at Banff, universities were now more frequently hosting him as a featured guest soloist and dedicating entire concerts to his music. Bill Frisell remembered that, even as early as the late 1970s, students at the Berklee School in Boston were transcribing Kenny's tunes and trying to pick them apart, inevitably finding ways to absorb elements of his language into their own.[1534] Serious students of jazz began to write scholarly works investigating Kenny's writing. Several master's theses and doctoral dissertations have been written centred around his work. One major publication that brought his written music to a larger audience was a collection of Kenny's scores for big band and small group, assembled and edited by Fred Sturm and released by Universal Edition in 1997. Sturm was the chair of the Jazz and Contemporary Media department at the Eastman School of Music at the time, teaching there when Kenny visited in 1989 and 1999 as the guest soloist with the Eastman Jazz Ensemble. In addition to being a long-overdue resource for musicians worldwide who hungered to be able to study his music, the book also provided a candid interview in which Sturm asked Kenny several fairly analytical questions about his thoughts on his own writing – questions he normally could evade with tactics like his oft-repeated "I must have a system, but really don't want to know what it is" or using humour to deflect questions asked in person.[1535] One revealing response came from Sturm's question about Kenny's harmonic language. He replied: "As chords come into more general use in jazz and in the more commercial world, I tend to back away from them. For this reason, my harmonic language is getting smaller."[1536]

This points to a continuing trend within Kenny's music – one of distillation moving towards elegance and greater simplicity. His compositions early on, as evidenced in his annual BBC broadcasts from 1969 and into the '70s, use several techniques (abundant mixed meters, varying placement of free sections, extremely complex harmonic movement with disjunct root movement, complicated rhythmic and melodic/contrapuntal structures, and various takes on developing variation) and are generally more complex than the work of his middle (circa *Music for Large and Small Ensembles*) and later periods. As his writing matured, he continued to use these techniques, but with a more organic approach, saving them for when they could be most effective and not allowing them to interfere with the flow of the music. Composer, arranger, and pianist Bill Dobbins – once at the helm of the WDR Band in Cologne and Professor of Jazz and Contemporary Media at Eastman – noted that Kenny's avoidance of certain harmonic structures was what made his music "identifiable, because there are certain things that *aren't* there".[1537]

As attractive and natural as this gradual refinement may be, it might also have had the effect of making his music further stylized to the point that his playing and writing was eventually described by Dobbins as "a caricature of itself".[1538]

> When *Gnu High* first came out – there was a spirit in the playing that I really liked but what I was really drawn to was the compositions. It wasn't until several years later that I started to realize that if I was thinking of solos – trumpet or flugelhorn solos that I would maybe consider passing out to an improvisation class or a small group as models of improvised solos – they wouldn't be Kenny Wheeler solos. Because in just about every solo, there's a bunch of stuff that's just . . . [*sings garbled noise*], you know? It's almost the musical equivalent of Steve Martin's routine where he starts with about 45 seconds of nonsense syllables, and then just suddenly stops and says "But that was in *my own* words." [*laughs*] So one of the things that – I mean this is just my opinion and a lot of people think completely differently from me about it – but when I'm trying to help people learn to improvise, one of the things that I stress more than anything else is that you don't make up any words.[1539]

Certainly, Dobbins's is a point of contention, and for many improvisors (and even teachers of improvisation) those freer moments in Kenny's solos would be the exact reason they *did* include them as examples of something outside the conventional yet rooted in the jazz tradition. For them, they would be examples that encapsulate individuality and a personal quest to remain inventive and not get "comfortable".

It is arguable, however, that Kenny himself may even have felt the same predicament Dobbins described as he became more self-limiting, crystallizing his compositional and improvisational output into fewer types of harmonies and gestures and turning inward. This was all occurring at a time when he was becoming regarded as an elder statesman of jazz and more frequently asked to speak about his writing during guest artist residencies at universities. Also around this time, transcriptions of his solos were published in *Jazz Educator's Journal* and *DownBeat*, a book of his solo transcriptions was published by Universal Edition, he would get mentioned more often in the reviews of other young trumpeters as an audible influence on them, and colleges were using his music as course material in jazz arranging and composition classes. For someone so reluctant to understand and describe his musical processes, he must have felt as if he was being analysed from every direction.

An understanding of this increased scrutiny might help to shed light on Kenny's strong reaction to criticism, especially when added to the crippling self-doubt he had experienced since childhood. He was balancing the identifiable musical language that he had created – one that had now become widely emulated – with the need to distance himself from musical trends that developed from his influence, all while attempting to avoid becoming a cliché. It was a conundrum he would face for the rest of his life.

———·———

Kenny first played with saxophonist and composer Jane Ira Bloom at the Bermuda Onion nightclub as part of the Toronto Jazz Festival in 1991. In 1992, Bloom had just finished a composition project commissioned by the NASA Art Program (the first musician to receive that award), and the process of writing those works influenced the music she created for her upcoming album, *Art and Aviation*,[1540] which she described as "anti-gravity melodic writing".[1541] She and Kenny recorded the album in New York that July. Indeed, many of the melodies on this album are quite vertical with wide intervals over a formidable range, and the playing by both Jane and Kenny is extraordinary in its ability to escape terrestrial pull. In fact, the technical difficulty of this music on the trumpet approaches the level of challenge that Braxton's music had posed nearly two decades earlier. "Only Kenny Wheeler could do that," Jane said.[1542]

For her next album with Kenny, titled *The Nearness*,[1543] Jane said she had her "dream horn section, with Kenny on one side of me and Julian Priester on the other. There was something quite magical about that ensemble."[1544] That magic is quite understandable. Kenny and Priester already shared a connection from their time together in Dave Holland's quintet but, perhaps even more significantly, it is worth noting that Priester must hold the unique and extraordinary distinction of being the only musician to have spent substantial time playing with both Booker Little and Kenny Wheeler.[1545] It also couldn't have escaped Kenny that in playing alongside Julian he had a direct musical connection to one of his musical heroes, who had helped him crystallize his own voice perhaps more than any other. The rest of the band for Bloom's *The Nearness* recording included bassist Rufus Reid, pianist Fred Hersch, and Bobby Previte on drums. Jane had fond memories of recording with Kenny, saying how his mastery of the trumpet was similar to that of a "top fuel race car driver" in his ability to go from extremely soft to very loud and back. "Nobody else can do that," she said.[1546]

Another highlight of their association was a special concert at the Wigmore Hall in London, with Rufus Reid once again on bass. This time, however, John Taylor joined the trio for a drummerless quartet performance of her music in the revered classical music venue, renowned for its intimate acoustics. Nearly three decades later, Rufus Reid remembered the concert fondly, simply saying, "That was *special.*"[1547] Jane agreed. "His sound is like no other," she commented, adding:

> Playing melodic lines with him – there was something so lyrical and expressive, and explosive at the same time – that's all I can say about the dynamic of playing with Kenny. There was this sense of surprise in his melodic choices, and his dynamic range was unmatched . . . and it always kept me on my toes. I loved playing with him because he just filled me with so many ideas . . . The times that we played in unison together were so magical, and the times we were riffing off of one another were also equally as exciting . . . just to be in his universe! . . . To be honest, after I played with him . . . there's never been a sound to replace that feeling of playing with him . . . I've never found another trumpet player to play with who made me feel that way.[1548]

While Kenny was enjoying new-found recognition and increasing international demand as a guest soloist, his deep musical relationships with his long-standing UK colleagues continued. In 1995 and 1996 he began a series of occasional recording sessions at Gateway Studios with Stan Sulzmann and Ray Warleigh, alongside guitarist John Parricelli and the old J.T. rhythm section of Chris Laurence and Tony Levin. Instigated by Evan Parker, some of the music from these gatherings (compiled with two other sessions a few years later) eventually appeared as the album *Dream Sequence* in 2003 on Evan's psi label.[1549] There was some important work still to come for Azimuth, too, even though their activities had been winding down since the recording of their final ECM album in 1994. One of the trio's significant associations of this late period was with the Nova Scotia-based Maritime Jazz Orchestra (MJO). The group's leader, Greg Carter, had begun his association with Kenny in 1995 with a project leading to the ensemble recording the album *Who Are You* for the Canadian Broadcasting Corporation.[1550]

In July 1995, Kenny was back across the Atlantic again combining multiple bookings, which included: his yearly teaching at Banff, recording Bloom's

*The Nearness*, and an appearance at the Atlantic Jazz Festival in Halifax as the featured soloist with the MJO. The year ended with more recognition of his achievements at home and another guest invitation from a European big band. In November his music was featured alongside that of Duke Ellington and Gil Evans on BBC Radio 3's *Composer of the Week*. Presented by Ian Carr, the show included works from his *Music for Large and Small Ensembles* and from the smaller-ensemble recording *Kayak*. Later that month, Kenny recorded as a guest with the Upper Austrian Jazz Orchestra, resulting in the album *Plays the Music of Kenny Wheeler*.[1551,1552] Kenny was reunited with both Azimuth and the MJO in October 1996, returning to Canada for a two-week visit, this time joined by John and Norma. The Azimuth trio were guests of the Artist-in-Residency programme at St. Francis Xavier University, and, while there, they recorded the MJO album *Siren's Song*[1553] and performed concerts in the area.

The start of 1997 involved some gruelling international travel for Kenny, now 67 years old. In February he travelled all the way to the other side of the world at the invitation of pianist Mark Isaacs to perform in Australia at Sydney's jazz club "The Basement". The performances at the club resulted in a live album for Isaacs called *Elders Suite*,[1554] released on Grace Recordings. In addition to Isaacs's three-part suite, the album also includes a performance of Kenny's "Everybody's Song But My Own". The exhausting travel schedule took its toll. Mark Wheeler remembered:

> Until he got older he was never ill. I mean, he was quite [strong]; he never really missed a gig until he went to Australia for four days or something stupid, came back and went to Italy . . . and he was in bed for two weeks after that. And that was when he had his attack of the vertigo thing, with the inner-ear disease.[1555]

The "gig" he missed was actually a week-long residency at the Blue Note in New York, which had been scheduled for Azimuth to perform opposite the George Shearing Quintet, ostensibly in support of the US release of the trio's final ECM album.[1556] This was a huge blow for Azimuth and no doubt for ECM, who would have invested substantially in synchronizing the Blue Note appearance with the album release. Norma recalled the disappointment for her and John too:

> We were supposed to do the Blue Note. We were booked there for a week, and Kenny got ill and so they cancelled us. And John and I just said, "Can't we go with someone else?" or "Can't we just come as a duo?" but they wouldn't have it. They said, "No, if Kenny's not in the group you can't come." So that [gig] never happened . . . It was really annoying . . .[1557]

It must have weighed on Kenny that he had inadvertently let his trio colleagues down, and may have led to him to try to find some sort of representation that could guide his career and schedule in a manner more suited to his increasing status and his advancing years.

Following the let-down of their cancelled New York appearance, Azimuth did at least get to perform together in May of that year as part of the Bath Festival Jazz Weekend in the UK. The appearance received a positive review from Alyn Shipton in *The Times*. Shipton acknowledged the rarity of this gig at home, lamenting the fact that "such an accomplished British group should work so seldom in this country". He also highlighted the oft-neglected musical variety and momentum of their performances, saying that "their deft, fast-moving set, with dappled shading and chamber jazz effects, stilled the bustling Pavilion audience and created a nightclub atmosphere, especially as Winstone and Wheeler negotiated the rapids of Taylor's challenging *Whirlpool*." Norma sang her own clever lyrics on Steve Swallow's "Ladies in Mercedes", which remains one of the most brilliant examples of her evocative, poetic wit. Shipton called it "as urbane a piece of small-group jazz as one could hope for".[1558]

---

The next year, Azimuth was back in Nova Scotia with the MJO. They did a week-long tour of the Maritimes with the band and once again recorded an album with the ensemble, titled *Now and Now Again*.[1559] The most significant item on this recording is a new work of Kenny's listed as the *Sweet Ruby Suite*. The MJO recorded this in March of 1998, but the origin and development of this substantial work is less straightforward.

Sometime in the mid to late 1990s, Kenny wrote a suite for the WDR Big Band in Cologne.[1560] They recorded (but apparently never performed) the 600-bar 30-minute work in early 1998.[1561] When Greg Carter contacted Kenny for music for his upcoming project with the MJO that March, Kenny sent him this suite among the other music they planned for the visit. At this point, the score – still bearing the WDR stamp – was simply labelled *Untitled Suite*.[1562]

Saxophonist Tommy Smith, director of the Scottish National Jazz Orchestra (SNJO), had also commissioned Kenny to write a suite at around the same time, towards the end of 1995 or early 1996.[1563] Tommy asked Kenny, "'You wrote so much great big-band music,: have you got many commissions?' And he just said, 'No, I have none' . . . I remember saying, 'That's crazy: someone like you should be writing all the time' . . . I was just furious . . . I said, 'I'll commission you!'"[1564] The resulting suite that Kenny delivered to Tommy in the spring of 1998 for a May performance was a much longer 1,500 bars, nearly an hour long. Interestingly, the version of the suite Kenny sent to the SNJO used all of the WDR *Untitled Suite* (up to measure 645, just as had also been played and performed with the MJO), but then continues with another 863 measures of new material.[1565] Some of that "new material" is actually quite old; in a departure from Kenny's usual avoidance of jazz standards, he inserted a rubato vocal version of Cole Porter's "What Is This Thing Called

Love?" around three-quarters of the way through the suite. The music continues with an uptempo contrafact written on the tune's chord changes, with Kenny's reharmonization. That particular jazz standard must have held some fascination for Kenny. There are several examples of him experimenting with reharmonizations and altered time signatures in little arrangements he did of the piece. Kenny's tune "Foxy Trot" is also loosely modelled on its chord changes; on an unreleased sextet recording from around the time (and with the same band as *Dream Sequence*) he composes another variation which this time closes with a statement of Lee Konitz's famous contrafact on the tune, "Subconscious-Lee".

Tommy Smith remembered that Kenny wrote some of the new suite on the road while they were on tour in 1996 and requested the inclusion of voice in the band and that he might bring Norma with him. Smith also remembered Kenny being uncharacteristically involved and vocal in rehearsals as the big band was still relatively inexperienced and "raw" at that time.[1566] He interjected especially in the approach of the rhythm section and the phrasing, but also in the physical set-up. "Kenny had us set up in a kind of different way than we normally set up . . . in a big circle . . . and I remember there were a few errors in the typesetting of the music so he would stop and get them corrected . . . He knew how his music was supposed to sound . . . Kenny had to really lead it."[1567]

This finished version of the newly expanded work, titled on the score and parts as *The Sweet Sister Suite*, was premiered in Edinburgh and Glasgow in 1998 on 28 and 29 May respectively, with Kenny and Norma as the featured soloists.[1568] Kenny then took the suite to Banff, where he joined the student big band, along with Banff faculty Don Thompson (on vibes) and Hugh Fraser (playing trombone and conducting the ensemble) on 8 August of the same year. This performance listed the piece as the *The Sweet Sister Ruby Suite* in the programme, named for his granddaughter Ruby, who had just been born that February to Kenny's son Mark and his second wife, Tracy.[1569] When the MJO album *Now and Now Again* – which had been recorded back in March 1998 with Kenny, Norma, and J.T. – was released a few years later in 2002, the piece appeared under yet another title: simply *Sweet Ruby Suite*. When it was recorded 15 years later in 2017 and released – in its longer form – by the Scottish National Jazz Orchestra, it was listed once again under its printed title, *Sweet Sister Suite*.

Kenny's reasons for recycling the final, *full* suite for the WDR and MJO dates, ahead of delivering the finished *Sweet Sister Suite* commission for the SNJO, are not clear. It isn't likely that he had run out of ideas, because he composed nearly every day of his adult life; perhaps he simply ran out of time, or took the opportunity a few months ahead of the SNJO premiere to get a performance of the music he'd so far completed. Regardless, the words F---ING FINE scrawled across the right side of page 151 of the manuscript

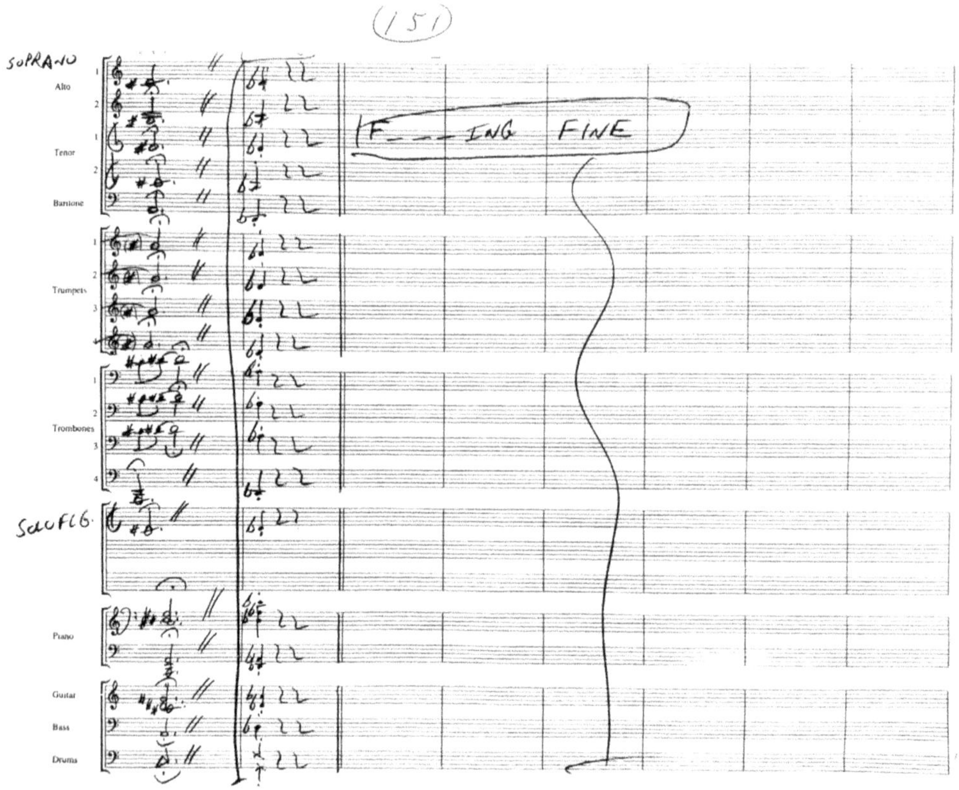

Photo 35: "F---ING FINE!" from the last page of Kenny's manuscript score of the *Sweet Sister Suite*.
Courtesy Wheeler Archive

score are a clue that he was relieved to have arrived at the final bar of this massive composition.[1570]

<hr/>

Throughout the late 1990s, the final seeds of the Azimuth story were being sown. John and Norma were happily settled with new partners but had still been performing together and maintaining a successful professional life well after their divorce in the early 1980s. Norma and John's new wife Diana were even friends early on. But following Diana's breast cancer diagnosis (around the time of the 1994 recording of *How It Was Then . . . Never Again*), she and John explored all treatment options with increasing urgency, including seeing a "healer". Norma said, "I'm sure [the healer] said, 'cut out anything negative in your life,' which was me . . . That's when he said he couldn't work with me anymore." She continued, "It was sort of prophetic, really. Because I called that tune, 'How it was then . . . never again.' It was the last one."[1571] Sure enough, *How It Was Then . . . Never Again* would be their final album as a trio.

John kept his promise to Diana to his dying day. According to Norma, from around 2002 he never played with her again: not even "big-band things", she said.[1572] It also caused considerable stress for Kenny. With all the pain he had endured in his own childhood, any disagreement between people he loved was both difficult and paralysing.[1573] Unable to choose between his two closest friends and collaborators, the rest of his career would be troubled by this conflict.

In 1998, the Maritime Jazz Orchestra commissioned Kenny's *One More Time Suite* and premiered it at the Halifax Jazz Festival the following summer. Greg Carter remembers a heatwave during the week of rehearsals leading up to the premiere, and Kenny had stripped down to his sleeveless T-shirt to stay cooler while playing.[1574] In their last appearance together, the MJO (with Kenny as their featured soloist) was one of the headlining groups at the International Association of Jazz Educators (IAJE) Convention in Toronto in January 2003. John Hollenbeck was once again with the ensemble, which performed the *Sweet Ruby Suite* at the featured concert.[1575] Paul Tynan, who was playing trumpet with the MJO that night, said that Kenny "sounded fantastic. He was really on his game; everything was crystal clear . . ." He continued:

> There were a lot of Canadians there, of course, who were familiar with his work – he's a national treasure to us – but a lot of the Americans, particularly those from the South or on the West Coast, weren't very familiar with [his music]. So the concert was *packed*. There was a huge standing ovation . . . And it was one of those moments where when you're done you can't remember exactly what happened, but you have this almost cathartic type of feeling . . .[1576]

Greg Carter also remembered that the large audience filled the room, and "people were lined up at the stage afterwards to shake hands with Kenny . . . He sounded incredible. When he was really on, it was just mesmerizing."[1577] What a feeling it must have been for Kenny to receive such a warm reception, fit for a triumphant hero, in the city of his birth.

One of the underappreciated gems of Kenny's discography in his later years is a collaboration with another Canadian, pianist Brian Dickinson, titled *Still Waters*.[1578] Before they recorded the album together, Kenny was playing with Dickinson on a tour of Ontario and upstate New York in the US led by vibraphonist Greg Runions during the early summer of 1998. Unable as always to say what he wanted, Kenny made his next album happen passively. Brian Dickinson explained:

> [On the tour], there were one or two pieces that had some duo playing between Kenny and myself . . . Kenny started suggesting things like, "Maybe when it comes to my solo, it could come down to trumpet and piano to start . . ." etc. There seemed to be more duo sections as it progressed! We were playing in Potsdam, New York, and after the concert there were a couple of people from *Cadence* magazine talking to Kenny. I ended up listening in to the conversation and when they asked him what he had coming up, he said, "Well, Brian and I are doing a duo album soon" . . . That was the first I'd heard of it!![1579]

The recording seemed cursed from the outset. Dickinson had booked a church on the west side of Toronto which possessed a good Steinway D piano and was apparently being used often for classical recordings. Finding the instrument terribly out of tune, Dickinson had it serviced and it sounded much better in a quick playing test. He continued: "We went to do the session and . . . within an hour or so after starting the session, the piano started going out [of tune]. Also, there were very audible bird sounds coming from outside of the church. It was a complete mess."[1580] Between the noisy birds and the increasingly ill-tempered piano, the recording was ruined. Dickinson was upset by all this and must have been worried that Kenny wouldn't want to repeat the recording process. Fortunately, Kenny was more than agreeable to starting over from scratch in a new venue. Dickinson booked the Glenn Gould Studio in Toronto and they remade the record in a single afternoon.[1581]

*Still Waters* turned out to be a beautiful recording, capturing Kenny's sound as it evolved in his late sixties. The album also documents several of Kenny's compositions presented in a well-matched duo format. One of the highlights of the recording is Dickinson's "Remembrance (For M.P.)", a tune clearly influenced by Kenny's writing, but with its own identity, and given a virtuosic performance by both musicians. Kenny was in especially jaw-dropping form here, in one phrase ascending through three octaves as if it were a single long note. "But even with that kind of virtuosity," Dickinson said, "he always had a warmth and vulnerability to his playing. And then there is his sound . . . No one can shape a note like that."[1582] Dickinson also remembered some touching anecdotes about being on the road with Kenny – his habits and his humour – including his legendary inability to keep any driver company on a road trip:

> For one of the gigs, I had to drive Kenny to Ottawa from Toronto. It's at least a four-and-a-half-hour drive. I was a little nervous, but I knew I'd have a chance to get Kenny to answer every possible musical question I had . . . Kenny did NOT stay awake in a moving car (probably a good thing he didn't drive!). I think he was "lights out" within about ten kilometers

outside of Toronto and woke up a block or two from our accommodations in Ottawa![1583]

Some years before, when Dickinson and Kenny were performing at the Toronto Jazz Festival with Norma, Jim Vivian, and Joe LaBarbera, the great Canadian trumpeter Guido Basso was listening to their rehearsal. "When we finished, Guido said, 'That's beautiful Kenny, how do you do that?', to which Kenny replied, 'I stole it all.' Guido came back with 'From where?' And Kenny immediately shot back, 'Maurice Ravel and Billy Strayhorn!' And it kind of made sense."[1584] Later, when Dickinson took his father out for dinner with Kenny at a local pub in Toronto, "the waitress read off the list of available beers on tap and the last was Kilkenny," Dickinson said. "Kenny immediately turned to me and said, 'Well I WON'T have one of those!'"[1585]

———·———

Dating back to his earliest coverage by Kitty Grime and others in the early 1960s, journalists often penned nearly the same piece about Kenny, commenting on his shy personality and near paralysing self-deprecation. This is not entirely the fault of these writers, as Kenny's anxiety about speaking to interviewers on the record led him to create "canned" quotes for convenient reuse when asked one of a handful of fairly predictable questions.[1586] Even the notebook he read from during lectures was likely created as an extension of this need to have his words planned in advance, so that, even when his nerves might have got the better of him, he still had thoughtful and informative things to say.

In addition to these unfortunately repetitive pieces on Kenny, some critics also levied unfair and short-sighted observations on his music. There were early jabs from the reviewer of the Tommy Whittle Band in the mid-'50s claiming that Kenny lacked "the confidence at present to express himself fully and pungently"; the sting of the *Times* preview of his 60th birthday tour which lamented that the "big band makes the best of some disappointing charts"; and finally there was the flat-out mean-spirited Azimuth review labelling the trio "wordless, doom-laden, and just plain dull" – the latter being a slight for which Kenny later attempted to block the reviewer from attending his gig at the Bass Clef.[1587] Hugh Fraser recalled a 1987 stay at the Wheelers' home during which he showed Kenny a negative review of Stan Sulzmann and John Taylor's duo album covering his tunes; he grabbed the magazine out of Hugh's hands and angrily tore it apart.[1588] As much as these negative reviews would understandably upset Kenny, sometimes the mixed reviews – with a compliment of this, a criticism of that – would almost bother him as much. His son Mark recalled, "He would read a review, and I'd read it and say, 'That's quite a good review' and he'd say, 'Yeah, but I don't know whether he *liked* it or not! Is he saying he likes it or isn't he?'"[1589] Kenny complained similarly to his friend Gene Lees, when he said that he felt like critics "still find little ways to put me down. As if I really don't know what I'm doing. In Canada and England, particularly . . . it's almost like, *Well, we've said enough good things, we'd better say something put-downish*."[1590] By the mid 1980s, he had reached the point where he didn't want critics to review his gigs at all.[1591]

Fortunately, some open-eared journalists managed to write supportive pieces about Kenny's music while not oversimplifying his personality into caricature. One such writer was Canadian jazz writer and historian Mark Miller. Miller, who worked for the *Toronto Globe & Mail* for over two decades, was an early champion of Kenny's music. He penned two features for *Down-Beat* magazine – the first published in March 1976 just after *Gnu High* was released in the US, and a second one in 1980, preceding *Around 6*. Miller's writing in both cases was very positive, and he did an admirable job of introducing Kenny to a predominantly American audience unfamiliar with his work, detailing the trumpeter and composer's wide-ranging musical interests.

Like nearly everyone who covered Kenny, however, Miller chose to highlight Kenny's reticent personality in many of his early pieces – but did so more deeply. The first *DownBeat* article begins with a quote from Kenny, saying he would ". . . like to think of myself as being a jazz musician. Or trying to be . . ."[1592] Another piece, one of Miller's earliest for the *Globe & Mail* from August 1978, lauded him as "arguably the most consistently creative jazzman (not to overlook Paul Bley) to come out of this country" but was titled "'If I ever got to like my own playing, I'd give up': Jazzman prefers anonymity", in which Miller described Kenny's "almost legendary aversion to recognition, and a sincere disbelief in himself".[1593] Another Miller review from a performance at Edmonton's Jazz City Festival in 1981 called Kenny "not a dominant figure – he's no Freddie Hubbard – he played some bristling solos and otherwise hid out in the stage's darkest corner."[1594] Miller goes on to imply that Kenny would be pressed into playing in a more conservative style than he'd like at Toronto's Bourbon Street jazz club the following week (due to the restrictions of either the Canadian jazz scene, the vibe of the club, or perhaps both) and would have another gig a few days later, by which Miller predicted Kenny would be "good and ready" to play his own music in his own way. This drew a written response from Art Ellefson, who called the review a "mass of contradictions" and went on to further defend his long-time friend:

> He and Freddie Hubbard are both brilliant players, but Mr. Wheeler has a quality that is rare these days – he's original. It wouldn't matter who he played with in Edmonton, he would be outstanding. So what if he doesn't prowl the stage and scream and dance. And since when has arrogance ever been an asset to a person's musical development? On the strength of reviews such as this, it's unlikely that Kenny Wheeler will ever be a star in his own country unless he hires a Las Vegas choreographer and takes screaming lessons. As for being "good and ready", I doubt if a week at Bourbon Street will make much difference. He's been good and ready for 30 years.[1595]

While Miller's observations about Kenny's personality were inarguably true and gave him, on balance, very positive press, the recurring focus on his self-doubt was probably a little unnerving. Context is relevant here: Kenny's return trips to play in Canada – especially near Toronto – brought him anxiety, with him putting pressure on himself to not disappoint audiences usually containing several old friends and members of his enormous extended family. So even though Miller felt that he was being supportive, this focus on his personality probably got under Kenny's skin. Unlike many artists, his sensitivity to criticism did not fade with age. By the early 1990s – after he had reached the age of 60 – Kenny had taken to telling Miller not to review him when he spotted the critic at his Toronto-based appearances. No doubt unaware of Kenny's similar attempts to boycott reviewers in the UK with whom he'd been upset, Miller said, "I thought he was joking – I thought he was sort of making fun of himself", with Kenny referencing his by-then famous shyness, somewhat propagated by Miller's own spotlight of this aspect of his personality. But a while later, in January 1993, when Kenny was about to embark on a Canadian tour with pianist Jeff Johnston's band to promote a recent recording, Miller penned a feature on the group, previewing the upcoming tour. Miller explained:

> Their last gig was in Toronto at the Top o' the Senator, and they were there for the week, and I went. I wasn't planning to review – it wasn't my intention, because I'd already done the advance piece . . . Kenny sees me, and he makes a beeline. He comes over and says, "Don't review this. I don't want you to review this." And I thought, *OK, this is different now, because this is getting into unprofessionalism – this is getting into real selfishness, because it's not his gig.* It was Jeff's gig, and Jeff may well have appreciated a review at that point beyond the initial advance piece, because that was a Canada Council tour. And when you make a report back to the Canada Council, it's really helpful to have all sorts of press, so it would have been to Jeff's advantage if I had, in fact, reviewed it. But there was Kenny saying, "No, you can't do this." And that's when I thought, there's something else going on here. This isn't just Kenny making fun of himself.[1596]

Unbeknownst to Miller, James Hale had already quite critically reviewed the group for the *Ottawa Citizen* not long before, saying that Kenny had "faltered with his opening flugelhorn solo" and that the "Jeff Johnston Quartet started its cross-Canada tour with a whimper, not a bang."[1597] It is possible that this review made Kenny, already wary of critics, especially defensive on seeing Mark Miller in person.

But, more than any of his fellow countrymen, Miller wrote about Kenny's importance as a Canadian-born artist of international stature, and often highlighted the fact that he should be more recognized and celebrated in his own country. In fact, the very next piece Miller wrote on Kenny, called "The Kenny Wheeler Orchestra: A Venture of Both Spirit and Symbolism" was practically glowing. The opening paragraph began:

The symbolism of Kenny Wheeler's appearance with a hand-picked Toronto orchestra at Nathan Phillips Square on Tuesday evening should not pass unremarked. At 63, Wheeler is, quite simply, this city's greatest gift to jazz . . . Wheeler's considerable achievements abroad as a trumpeter and composer at the leading edge of contemporary jazz have never been fully acknowledged at home, though, which makes a concert in front of City Hall seem like the next best thing to a key to the city.[1598]

Sadly, despite this most recent bit of positive coverage, the relationship only soured going forward. In 1994, Miller reviewed Kenny at the Montreal Bistro, with a quintet made up of saxophonist Phil Dwyer, pianist Don Thompson, bassist Jim Vivian, and drummer Joe LaBarbera. Miller remarked that Dwyer had taken over the band. "Somebody had to," Miller wrote, adding:

The notoriously reticent Wheeler, still nominally the quintet's leader, looked and sounded uncomfortable in the evening's opening set. His playing had all of its customary power – perhaps more – but was short its usual lilt, lyricism, and that curious acrobatic sense of balance that is Wheeler's and Wheeler's only. His phrasing was jerky, his ideas often elliptical; the hurting brilliance of his tone on both flugelhorn and trumpet seemed to make his solos sound even more awkward.[1599]

Onstage that night, Miller later observed:

it wasn't working and I wrote that . . . And the morning that the piece appeared in the paper, I got a phone call from him. I don't know where he got my number, but he had my number . . . and he was *mad*. He was like, *I told you, I don't want you to review me. Don't review me.* And there was probably more to it, but that was basically it. [In response,] I probably would have said, "Well, that's not a reasonable request."[1600]

Kenny returned to Toronto a year later for a residency playing his big-band music at the University of Toronto and stayed on for a week-long appearance at the Montreal Bistro,[1601] and Miller once again reviewed. "He was playing much better, he was more in command," Miller remembered, summarizing, "Positive review: no phone call."[1602]

But in 1997, Kenny appeared at the Montreal Bistro alongside guitarist Sonny Greenwich. Miller was there, of course, to cover what he described as this "pairing of the expatriate, London-based Wheeler and Montreal's Greenwich – two of Canada's true jazz originals" but didn't like what he heard and pulled no punches in his review: "Their second set the other night, however, was at best uneven and certainly not the proverbial sum of its considerable parts. Those parts also included pianist Don Thompson, bassist Jim Vivian and drummer Barry Elmes, who gave the performance its cohesion in the absence of any apparent initiative on the part of either of the two principals." He continued:

Their partnership seemed quite distant – little more than a match of two musicians who've by chance found themselves on the same bandstand for a week. They may simply be too deferential, one to the other. Or they may just be too different: Wheeler is an elusive, impulsive and surprising improviser, while Greenwich is invariably direct, methodical and arresting. Moreover, Wheeler's major solos, on "Hotel Le Hot" and "Past Present", were alarmingly inconsistent, the first (trumpet) a torture of sour notes and cracked notes, and the second (flugelhorn) strikingly elegant. Still, it was with "Past Present" that the quintet began to show some of its potential, as Wheeler finally made his presence felt, not by direct intervention – heaven forbid – but simply by example, which is the way he has always worked best.[1603]

Don Thompson was aware of Kenny's discomfort: "I know he was really disappointed with Sonny. Because, first of all, Sonny can't read. And he also sent him recordings of the tunes, and Sonny didn't learn them. Some of the tunes were hard, but some weren't *that* hard – but he didn't learn them, anyhow."[1604] When the review appeared in the next morning's *Globe & Mail*, Miller said the phone rang at his home. Expecting an angry trumpeter on the other end of the line, Miller let the call go to his answering machine. In the message Kenny left, he once again told Miller, "I don't want you to review me. Leave me alone", reserving some of his fury for the guitarist, saying, "Sonny can't even read my music." In case he hadn't made his point clearly, Kenny turned his sharpest words back on Miller at the end of the message with a caustic "*Fuck. You.*"[1605]

This whole episode stuck with both men for a long time. Over two decades later, Miller was still puzzled by it. "I was disappointed that all of the support I had offered Kenny over the years . . . seemed not to count for anything, evidently negated by some offence that he never discussed with me and that to this day I can't identify," he said.[1606] What Miller couldn't have possibly known was how deeply triggering any criticism could have been to Kenny, as explained by psychologist Dr. Arnon Bentovim:

> His own internal critic is so fierce that anybody who criticizes him is going to find a real friend in Kenny's *internal critic* and is going to absolutely destroy him. In other words, he has enough problems with managing his own personal internal critic that anybody external is just too much.[1607]

Both men clearly felt betrayed by the other, with Kenny reacting to a one-time supporter who he perceived was becoming increasingly critical of his playing, and Miller feeling that Kenny turned on him for merely doing his job honestly after having written positively about him for over 20 years. This sense of betrayal on both parts is quite possibly the unfortunate result of a confluence of events. Miller, by the nature of his position, was writing reviews at the outset of a tour or residency to create interest and inform a potential audience but heard the groups before they were fully functioning, often expounding on his perception that Kenny's playing was in decline. And Kenny, perennially critical of his own playing, was becoming even more aware of his approaching seventh decade; he was also on his home turf, where, despite the accolades showered on him by students and local jazz fans, he still felt the rejection of Toronto's jazz establishment from his teenaged years. All this, combined with the fact that Kenny was playing tunes that were not his own with a group of players with whom he didn't often play, it is no wonder that there would be some problems with the end product and its critical reception.

Even Kenny's family acknowledged the grudge against Miller. In a scrapbook of photos and newspaper clippings given to him years later as a gift by his granddaughters (containing a wealth of clips from his sister Helen, who would have been in the clubs for the Toronto concerts), one page with some of his Toronto-based reviews is sarcastically labelled "And There Was Mark Miller (Kenny's Favourite Music Critique)", noting on the bottom of the page that the critic "was told by Kenny not to come into any club he was playing in".[1608] Even Doreen took offence: "I used to get Christmas cards from the Wheelers – her doing, no doubt," Miller said. ". . . and then I didn't."[1609]

—·—

Kenny's performance anxieties continued well into his later life. Mark Wheeler remembered this paradoxical dimension of his father: "It was almost like he had the frustration and nervousness if work *didn't* come in, and then when he *did* get something and he knew that it was a big gig then he was VERY nervous . . ." Later in life, he took beta blockers before performances to help with his nervousness. "I don't know when he started to take the beta blockers," Mark said, "but he did used to take half a one . . . and I think that helped him." He recalled his father becoming a bit quieter and a bit more irritable before big concerts or recordings, acknowledging that "it just seemed to be a sort of process that he had to go through just to get that 'big-game-face' on."[1610] At home, Kenny could relax with his family, and his fascination with sport especially provided him with relief in these moments of stressful anticipation. He had embraced the UK football scene and once took Mark to a Tottenham versus Fulham game when he was young: "the match when Joe Kinnear broke his leg," Mark recalled.[1611] His Canadian roots led to a lifelong passion for ice hockey, too. One of Mark's lasting memories of Kenny at his most animated was the famous ice hockey final of the 2002 Winter Olympics. "When Canada beat America, he was literally jumping around the room!"[1612]

Regardless of Kenny's ongoing nerves about performing or the dissatisfaction with some of the reviews he would get, he was still very much in demand by eminent artists. American composer, arranger, and conductor Vince Mendoza became a fan of Kenny's as a young trumpet player, hearing him on Ralph Towner's *Old Friends, New Friends* album. "He was like no other trumpet player that I ever heard – his huge sound or his approach to improvisation, his phrasing and the way he approached the changes," Mendoza said.[1613] Like many aspiring trumpeters, Mendoza experienced Kenny's influence in a way that was all-consuming:

> Kenny is near the top of the list of music that made me want to create and made me want to play . . . As a trumpet player, hearing his sound, I wanted to sound like that. Even on my early college recordings when I was overdubbing solos, the guys were asking me, "What are you doing?" I would say, "I'm trying to sound like Kenny!" Of course, in those days, they were [asking], *Who?!*[1614]

Years later, when Mendoza had the opportunity to choose soloists for his album *Epiphany*,[1615] Kenny was one of the first he considered. "Kenny was instrumental in the development of my voice, so if I see that album as the ultimate goal of my dream project . . . then all the people involved represent that."[1616] To Mendoza, the album, rehearsed and recorded in July 1997 with the London Symphony Orchestra at Abbey Road Studios, "represented the ideal of what my music was supposed to be at that moment."[1617] The project contained Mendoza's originals exclusively, and many of the evocatively titled pieces including "Sanctus", "Wheaten Sky", "Esperança", and "Barcelona", cloak his soloists in rich and fresh orchestral colour. Mendoza featured Kenny, at this point a 67-year-old elder statesman of jazz, as a soloist on the record with long-time friends and bandmates including John Abercrombie, Peter Erskine, and John Taylor, as well as esteemed colleagues Michael Brecker, Joe Lovano, and Marc Johnson. *Times* reviewer Mike Bradley called Mendoza's *Epiphany* "quite simply one of the most moving albums ever made", praising the composer's gifts for bringing forth a "modern marriage of classical and jazz brokered by a man with a real understanding of how to write for an orchestra. It is no exaggeration to say that Mendoza has produced a classic which goes straight to the heart. Hear it once and there's no going back."[1618] Mendoza credits Kenny's profound influence on his music with no sense of hyperbole:

> In the formative years, his sound and lyricism made the biggest impact on me. And still, when I go back and listen to his music, there's something about the turns of the phrases and the harmony that he uses, and the melancholy and vulnerability of his music, even though it's presented in a very powerful manner, it's the most interesting dichotomy of artistry that I have ever experienced . . . As an improviser, that was very attractive to me . . . confident but vulnerable in his approach to improvisation and with the trumpet. Of course, years after that when I met him, it all made sense. He very much was expressing his personality through the instrument.[1619]

In 2002, Vince and Kenny collaborated again, this time on an album Mendoza arranged for legendary singer/songwriter Joni Mitchell with orchestra, titled *Travelogue*[1620] (a follow-up to their hugely successful collaboration on *Both Sides Now*). Bassist, music businessman and producer for the session, Larry Klein (who had been married to Mitchell for 12 years), was also a fan of Kenny's. Klein said, ". . . with *Gnu High*, I was just completely knocked out with the compositions and his playing . . . Years and years passed and I was working on *Travelogue* with Joni, we were thinking about trumpet voices, and I thought of Kenny."[1621] The album was organized into different configurations, including orchestral ensembles with strings and conventional big-band instrumentations. Mendoza noted that each track had a theme – a "stylistic reference" – and Kenny's selections were in the mode of Gil Evans instrumentation. Klein explained:

> that particular configuration is something that I love Vince writing for. I think he's one of the few people who really is able to do that kind of – not an imitation of Gil of course – but utilize that type of instrumentation in a really beautiful way, so we thought of [Kenny] kind of being a great trumpet voice in the context of that.[1622]

Mendoza confirmed Kenny as the obvious choice as trumpet soloist for the album.

> I don't think Joni knew who Kenny was; I think that Larry obviously did. But we were looking for musicians that were sympathetic to the poetry. That was the whole idea behind *Travelogue* really, since it was all Joni's music, the treatment of the songs one by one had to do with the poetry, and really zeroing in on word painting, and making the songs part of the drama as a whole. That's the way she constructed the recording, that there's narrative from the beginning to the end. So she wanted "actors" well picked for their sympathy to the songs.[1623]

Although she probably hadn't heard of Kenny before the sessions, Joni was won over quickly. Klein said, "she was thrilled with his playing. She really was."[1624] Not surprisingly, however, Kenny was a little nervous for the recording date. He was booked to play on the track "Trouble Child", and even though he was overdubbing without the rest of the orchestra present, it still took him some time to get comfortable. As would increasingly become the case in Kenny's old age, those around him were charged with making him feel at ease to get the best out of him. Larry Klein reminded Kenny that he was there because of his musical personality. Klein said, "I remember him coming in and initially, you know, sounding a little bit nervous, but gradually sort of synching into what he was doing and of course, you know, sounding great. The end product of what we did sounded amazing." Klein also suspected that Kenny might have been intimidated by Joni's presence. There is some logic to this assumption, with Mitchell being a Canadian musical star, but it's also possible that Kenny was just being his usual nervous self. Either way, Mendoza and Klein – and Joni Mitchell – were very pleased with their decision to involve

Kenny on *Travelogue*: "That record was a gargantuan undertaking," Klein said. "It ended up being, of course, a double CD, and just tons of music. And so, it was really quite a thrill for me to get him to come in and play on the things that he did."[1625]

Of course, Kenny was featured as a guest soloist in other pop settings. His individuality had long been embraced by David Sylvian, a singer and songwriter formerly with the group Japan. Kenny had originally first recorded with Sylvian nearly two decades before his work with Vince Mendoza, on the 1984 album *Brilliant Trees*,[1626] where he contributed to the tracks "The Ink in the Well" and "Nostalgia". He was invited back on the 1986 release *Gone to Earth*,[1627] this time also with John Taylor alongside him, accompanying Kenny's solo on the track "Laughter and Forgetting". In a UK *Independent* interview/feature in praise of Sylvian, the interviewer asks, ". . . who else knows how to use the jazz trumpeter Kenny Wheeler on a pop song?"[1628] Sylvian also compliments Kenny when asked about his penchant for collaborating with top jazz soloists: "I thought – why not go straight to the source? Nobody turned me down. Perhaps a certain naïveté worked to my advantage. Everybody was open and willing to give it a go, so that became a way of working."[1629] It is interesting how frequently David Sylvian's name would be mentioned as a notable part of Kenny's career. Even though playing with Sylvian was quite likely just another recording session for him, this association became a way for many people outside of the mainstream jazz idiom around the world to become familiar and even fall in love with Kenny's sound.

---

Interesting and flattering as it was that popular artists showed an interest in him, jazz musicians were, of course, the most deeply moved by their connection with Kenny. One who came into his life around this time was American jazz trumpeter and composer Dave Douglas, who first became a fan of his playing on Bill Frisell's *Rambler*. "It might have been the first time where I heard a record by a musician that I knew and idolized and heard the trumpet playing and said, 'Wow, that's something I really don't understand.'"[1630] Like Kenny, Douglas is a great admirer of the work of trumpeter and composer Booker Little. Just as hearing Little back in the mid-'60s had shown Kenny that there could be another way of playing, Dave said that hearing a cassette tape of Little's *Out Front* "opened me up to getting back into playing jazz. I had learned the standards and played a bunch of sideman gigs, and I sort of felt like there was no place to go. I was going to drop out and do something else in music."[1631] Interestingly, Booker Little affected Dave more as a composer than as a trumpet player, probably because, in addition to Kenny, he had already heard modernist trumpeters like Lester Bowie, Wadada Leo Smith, and Woody Shaw. Booker Little's music "had a very improvised and spontaneous feel and at the same time it had a very overarching compositional strategy going on," he said.

"That was really big for me. It inspired me back into having a sextet. So I transcribed a bunch of his works and made that record [*In Our Lifetime*] . . ."[1632]

Not content to merely play transcriptions of Booker Little's tunes, Douglas actually wrote new music inspired by Little's work for the recording of *In Our Lifetime*.[1633] "For me, the homage to Booker Little was more about *Let me think about – in the year 1994 – what's important about Booker Little that we should want to still present and make important.*" When it was released, the record received positive attention around the globe, including in the UK, where Kenny somehow managed to hear it. When Birmingham Jazz promoter Tony Dudley-Evans began to work on a tour of the UK for Douglas a couple of years later, he said, "Kenny Wheeler is a big Booker Little fan – would you mind if he sat in with your group?"[1634]

Kenny was soon on board with the project, so Douglas set about creating parts within his compositions for him to play. "I wanted him to come into the project as it was, which was a lot of original music. I didn't want to just make some Booker Little transcriptions and play them with Kenny," Douglas said.[1635] The two trumpeters came together for a single concert at the Custard Factory in Birmingham, the final stop of a UK tour, in late April 1997.[1636] Douglas had sent Kenny the music in advance, which the elder trumpeter had evidently practised diligently, with notes scrawled all over the parts. Despite his preparation, Kenny was still nervous about the gig. "I did everything I could to make him comfortable," Douglas said.[1637]

Douglas's group only had one rehearsal with Kenny, which doubled as the soundcheck in the venue. The other musicians, including Uri Caine, James Genus, and Chris Speed – jazz stars in their own right – were excited for Kenny to join their sextet. When they weren't rehearsing, Dave got the sense that Kenny was somewhat uncharacteristically enjoying the opportunity to "tell this young impressionable American trumpet player his stories".[1638] But when they started playing in the soundcheck/rehearsal, Kenny was showing alarming signs of difficulty on the trumpet. Dave said:

> He literally couldn't hit the notes. He didn't have a sound; it was *foof, foof* . . . It was like he wasn't getting a C in the middle of the treble clef. I was going, *Shit, what am I going to do!?* And I'm reconfiguring during the set in my mind as we go – I didn't want to make him uncomfortable, but he sounded *really* terrible. He sounded like a beginner. So I was just a little shaken up, and moved some of the solos around, and I set him up and made sure that it wasn't like I was playing right after him because I wanted to be really tasteful about it . . . [I thought,] *I have to not play too many high notes!* . . .[1639]

Kenny didn't say a word to Dave about the difficulty he seemed to be having, so Dave didn't say anything, either.

As had been planned, the sextet played the first set of the concert without Kenny. When it finally came time for Kenny to join them for the second set,

Dave was understandably beside himself. When they began the first tune of the set, Kenny had the first solo. His approach immediately changed. Dave said, "within the first bar, he's playing one of those incredible, like high B♭s! He played a higher note than I've ever played in my life! So I thought, *OK, back to plan A!*"[1640]

Looking back on this concert, Dave realized that Kenny probably hadn't had the chance – or had decided not to – warm up, and Kenny's lack of ego meant that he didn't really think it was important to tell Dave that he would be fine later. "He didn't say anything, and left me feeling like, 'Oy, OK, *former hero!*' [*laughs*] And then he just came out and was amazing." It was a lesson that Douglas continues to ponder. "I think about that all the time, especially when you're at a soundcheck – protect your chops. It's not the gig – don't get carried away. It was really valuable to me," he said.[1641] He also commented on the parallel way Booker Little's music had changed both of their lives:

> Years later, I talked to Kenny and he explained what happened to him – hearing Booker Little – and how it changed him and it led to *Windmill Tilter*. And the process as he described it was almost exactly how it happened to me. I was at a point where I didn't know what to write, and I heard that, and it inspired a whole legion of new sounds for me. So we were completely in the same boat . . . So for me, I felt like, "I don't have to write the way everyone else writes." But I do think the writing was [also] a big influence on Kenny . . . and the way that I see Kenny in the big picture is that the writing and the playing all goes together. I don't think you can separate the two.[1642]

Around this time, plans were in the works for Kenny to make a new recording for ECM. Perhaps more than any other in his extraordinary output for the label, Kenny's album *Angel Song*[1643] boosted his recognition and reputation. The beautifully austere quartet recording featured his flugelhorn and compositions with Dave Holland, Bill Frisell, and alto saxophonist Lee Konitz. It would be the greatest commercial success of his career.

Kenny's connection with Lee Konitz extended back further than one might expect. After he heard Lee play with Claude Thornhill's band in Niagara Falls as a high-school student in the late 1940s, they were reacquainted as members of George Gruntz's all-star Concert Jazz Orchestra in the late 1980s. By then, Konitz had become a legend of jazz and Kenny had achieved international recognition. A decade later, when it came time to make a new album, Kenny suggested Konitz to Manfred Eicher. "I've played odd gigs with Lee over the years, but *Angel Song* was probably the first time I really connected with him," Kenny said.[1644] "Lee was one of my childhood heroes . . . [He] really likes playing with no music there at all . . . He's been around for a long time, but he takes chances still. He'll say, 'You start this tune', and you'll say, 'What tune?' and he'll say, 'I don't care, just start.'"[1645]

Despite Kenny's reverence toward Lee, it was not easy to secure him for the record. In fact, his initial approach was rebutted, as Kenny admitted to Evan Parker in an interview a couple of years before *Angel Song*: "It did for a minute deflate me when [Lee] said [*puts on a voice*], *naaah, I don't wanna do that* when I'd said, 'I'd love to do a record with you'!"[1646] Seemingly resigned to the fact, he conceded, "I've asked and that's all I can do, I can't push it any more . . .". After a pause, Kenny couldn't help but continue: ". . . but he makes a lot of records, he never stops making records!"[1647] Lee eventually agreed to the project, after being asked officially by ECM.

Naturally, Kenny also wanted his old friend Dave Holland to play on the album. Kenny said that Dave was "kind of like an orchestra by himself in a way. And . . . I think anything I've ever done that's been sort of really important, he's been involved in."[1648] "So first Manfred suggested just doing it with the trio," Kenny said, "but I thought that might be too hard to sustain for the whole album without a harmony instrument." At this point Kenny assumed the project had been green-lighted. He said, "Apparently the fact that I got a quick fax back from [Manfred] was unheard of, so I thought, *Well, it's in the bag, you know.* But then I suggested using a harmonic person like Abercrombie . . . I've never heard from him again."[1649] These discussions with Manfred Eicher could be frustratingly erratic as he personally oversaw so many productions. But when momentum resumed in planning *Angel Song*, Eicher brought up the idea of adding guitarist Bill Frisell. "I couldn't argue with that," Kenny said.[1650]

A primary reason that *Angel Song* might be considered unique among Kenny's recorded output as a leader for ECM is that it is a "conventional" jazz album, but without drums. It was Eicher's idea to go with the quartet only, which Kenny thought was "a bit strange" at first, "but after I'd thought about it for a while it seemed like a good idea."[1651] Eicher explained:

> *Angel Song* was a record that I felt should go back to chamber music, like *Azimuth*. I felt it was a great idea to have Dave and Bill Frisell, you know, who was playing from such a rich harmonic concept. So, I thought let's have the architecture of sound that is very unusual; with Lee Konitz together [with Kenny], it was a different approach. And Lee Konitz and Kenny maybe understood intonation in a little different way, so it was fluctuating sometimes in the sense that Bill Frisell . . . could be the tuning element in this case, and Dave also doing his vertical kind of lines which were needed to keep the band rhythmically . . . So, that was enough – they didn't need any drummer. There could have been a drummer, but then the music would have been very different.[1652]

As the only two members of the rhythm section, Dave Holland and Bill Frisell chose to play differently on *Angel Song* than they might have with drums. Dave said:

> I remember Bill and I talking about, you know, how the guitar and bass worked; I won't say compensated for – but the way we worked together, how it gave a rhythmic basis for the band where you don't feel the drums are absent at all . . . I thought Bill and I hooked up in a way that made that really work on another level . . . Bill is extraordinary. He's . . . the *antithesis* of a guitarist.[1653]

Frisell commented that the nature of Kenny's compositional style – especially his sense of form – helped the group achieve a collective aesthetic: "He put this big frame around it that was so clearly his own . . . It's like the architecture was so strong, that you could go in it and you could push up against it and it didn't fall down."[1654]

In February 1996, Kenny flew 11 hours from his gig in Tel Aviv to New York for a brief rehearsal with the quartet at New York's Power Station on West 53rd Street. "We went into the studio at nine the next morning and didn't play any of the tunes we rehearsed. So, magic? Well, that was that!"

Photo 36: Kenny and Dave Holland at the recording session for the ECM album *Angel Song*.
© Patrick Hinely , Work/Play®

Kenny said.[1655] As with Kenny's other ECM projects, the quartet had never performed before as a unit before the recording.

Photographer, writer, and long-time Wheeler fan Patrick Hinely was present in the studio that day. (His photos were used in the CD booklet.) He recalled that during the session, Kenny was

> very deferential to Lee from the get-go, to the point of Lee reminding Kenny that it was *his* record. Kenny seemed most comfortable with Dave (not a surprise, given their extended shared history), whom I would unofficially credit as at least a co-producer in serving as Kenny's interlocutor/ translator/explainer not only with the other players but also with Manfred ... Bill mostly sat in his chair and was his usual quiet self ... Manfred was a master at steering the ship while his hand was seldom seen on the wheel. My impression was that he wanted to see what Kenny would do, and let him do it, especially in tandem with Lee, and must have been pleased with what evolved, for he subtly aided, abetted, encouraged and enabled, making sure the outside world stayed out, which is what all good producers do. Manfred was also the one who, at the end of an especially delicious playback, responded to Kenny, who expressed a preference for making another take since he thought his own solo wasn't very good, that he didn't think that was necessary, but if he really insisted, they could come back and revisit the tune tomorrow, if there was time. There was, but they didn't.[1656]

Eicher said, "It was like a string quartet – four independent roles coming together to serve Kenny's compositions ... And it was a very interesting juxtaposition of genres and generations of musicians among the four of them. It is not very often that you can get musicians like this together. These were very special sessions."[1657] Indeed, these sessions – and the players on them – were uniquely suited to the music Kenny had chosen for the recording. The counterpoint heard so clearly on this recording – although nothing new in his music – now was much more overtly stated, reminding observant listeners of polyphonic music from the Renaissance. Kenny said, "I love contrapuntal music, and I was listening to a lot of Byrd, Tallis, Gesualdo when I was composing the pieces on *Angel Song* ... I've been trying to capture the spirit of that era while still keeping it jazz."[1658]

The opening piece of the album, "Nicolette", is one of Kenny's most hauntingly beautiful compositions, its soaring melody gliding over the gently lolloping waltz time beneath. The tune was named for the granddaughter of one of Kenny and Doreen's nieces. Unfortunately, following a family rift some years later, he refused to play this particularly exquisite tune ever again. "Nicolette" opens with Frisell's resonant solo guitar, demonstrating what Kenny observed of his sound:

> You usually can tell within a few notes it's him. He has a special, well, that sort of generally country & western bit ... There's not too many I could

get to play that music and, he plays it with some kind of simplicity, I mean those quite complicated chords I wrote, he seems to be able to narrow them down to fewer notes but still get the sound of the chord.[1659]

Of course, Kenny's sound on *Angel Song* is just as instantly recognizable as that as any of his star colleagues. Despite the unique solo voices of each player, there is no doubt that there was a tangible simpatico and clarity of roles that brought a relaxed but chamber-like intensity to *Angel Song*. The open nature of the music also exposed some occasionally stark differences in concept between the players: especially, as Eicher mentioned, the intonation between Kenny and Lee. Kenny spent decades playing in studios with many classically trained brass players whose bread and butter is the ability to play in tune consistently. On the subject, Kenny once said:

> I never do have trouble with intonation unless somebody in a band starts to say, "Well we're not really in tune." Then I'm completely lost. Because once you decide prematurely to do this and say, "I'm flat", you have a problem. I never touch my tuning slide from one session to another. Something in the lip must adjust it. Especially when you're playing with a bass player like Dave Holland, who is very strong on pitch, and you've got that underneath you. It makes it a lot easier.[1660]

Conversely, Konitz openly acknowledged his tendency to play sharp, once saying that he feels that pitch is a personal matter that is "part of how that person hears a series of notes. Many of the modern players try to allow for flexible pitch. So they can justify playing on top of the pitch in that way, maybe" and that "since I can't always control it, I prefer to be sharp than underneath the pitch." (This statement is reminiscent of the old musician's quip *Better to be sharp than out of tune.*) Given the choice, though, Konitz would still like to have played in tune, saying:

> I've come to think of it as an antisocial musical disease, not fully identifying with your musical neighbour . . . I've worked a lot with Kenny Wheeler, and if anything he has a tendency to play at the bottom of the pitch. So I really have to be careful because we can sound pretty sour together. On the *Angel Song* record on ECM I was having that problem. My God, where were the angels![1661]

This is an interesting perception, considering Kenny's impeccable pitch. One would be hard pressed to find a musician who has played with Kenny and says that his pitch was anything other than flawless. One can't help but consider that, if Lee Konitz sensed that he was out of tune with him, the fault may not have been with Kenny.

Regardless of Kenny's impeccable pitch, *Angel Song* reveals a few signs of his advancing age. The sonic space in the orchestration and aesthetic of the

Photo 37: Kenny recording *Angel Song*, Lee Konitz in the background.
© Patrick Hinely, Work/Play®

quartet (not to mention the legendary ECM audio quality) allows the listener to hear even his breaths between phrases. This crystal-clear sound also allows the Wheeler devotee, long familiar with his formidable strength and endurance, to hear the hint of a decline in power just beginning to show in the 66-year-old's approach. Unfortunately, this element of his mature sound was picked up on by some reviewers, with Chris Parker identifying "slight hesitancies" in his playing, and Clive Davis referring to what he interpreted as Kenny's "limited stock of motifs".[1662] Piling on further, an unfortunate 2002 *DownBeat* magazine "Blindfold Test" gave Wallace Roney a vehicle with which to make some harsh observations about "Onmo" from *Angel Song*, saying that the trumpet player on the recording seemed "amateurish" and "sounds like he liked Freddie [Hubbard], but doesn't have the chops". He went on:

> He plays clichés. Some of this reminds me of Kenny Wheeler, but Kenny plays better than this. Don't tell me it's Kenny Wheeler. It is? I'm sorry . . . I respect him. He has a lot to offer, but I didn't like the piece. 5 stars for Lee Konitz. For the rest, please forgive me. I love you all, but I'm being honest. 1 star.

For all the criticisms of *Angel Song* – the reviewers noting his occasional frailty and especially those who found the album to be too gentle (one need only look briefly at online reviews to find cynical jazz trolls claiming it to be a cure for insomnia) – it was otherwise overwhelmingly lauded by critics and serious listeners. In 1997, *Angel Song* was named the *Guardian*'s "Jazz CD of the Year" and *Stereo Review*'s "Record of the Year", and was given very positive reviews in *DownBeat*, the London *Times* ("stirringly beautiful"), and *Jazz UK* ("masterful"). There are several possible reasons that *Angel Song* was the best-selling album of Kenny's career. The fact that it was a star-studded line-up of four jazz legends playing without drums certainly gave the record an angle that may have given it more attention than other recordings of Kenny's with more traditional instrumentation. This, combined with the notable lack of free playing perhaps gave the music an air of listenability that some of Kenny's previous recordings, however tuneful and harmonically attractive, did not as easily possess. It may also be that *Angel Song* was more highly anticipated than earlier releases, as it was his first ECM recording as a leader since his February 1990 release of *The Widow in the Window*. Furthermore, ECM seems to have promoted this record internationally in a way that it had not for his previous albums. In addition to the usual distribution and reviews a Kenny Wheeler album would have already warranted on its own, the album was given substantial pre-sale promotion, including a front-page story in the 8 February 1997 issue of *Billboard* titled "Wheeler's Luminous 'Angel' Set Features All-Star Quartet". It also received a three-minute feature on National Public Radio's *All Things Considered*, which aired during the late afternoon or early evening in America: prime time for their typical demographic of highly educated – and likely more jazz-friendly – American commuters.[1663]

Manfred Eicher was so thrilled with *Angel Song* that he would call Kenny up periodically to see if he had listened to it and ask, "Do you like it yet?"[1664] In another interview about the album Kenny explained, "sometimes I feel I could have done a little better in my playing, and this [record] was a little bit like that. But Manfred was so enthusiastic about it all that maybe I've talked myself into thinking that maybe I don't play too bad on it!"[1665] In the end, though, Kenny's perception of his own playing had not changed: "My jazz playing, I don't know, most of the solos I hear afterwards I'm not too happy with, still. I don't know what I'm looking for but whatever it is, maybe, the day I find it, that's when I have my heart attack and drop over, drop dead!"[1666]

Unlike Kenny's previous ECM albums from the early days, the *Angel Song* group did play two engagements together after the release of the recording. In February 1998, they performed a concert at London's Barbican, broadcast on BBC's *Jazz on 3*. It was the first time the quartet had performed together outside of the recording session, sharing the bill with the Paul Motian Trio, with saxophonist Joe Lovano and Bill Frisell. (The guitarist played with both groups.)[1667] According to *The Times*, this Barbican performance was "rapturously received", with the reviewer calling the quartet's members "peerless

Photo 38: The *Angel Song* quartet. Left to right: Bill Frisell, Lee Konitz, Kenny, and Dave Holland.
© Patrick Hinely, Work/Play®

soloists" and Kenny's compositions "intensely lyrical".[1668] The next morning, this short-lived *Angel Song* band travelled to Bergamo, Italy, where they performed at the Teatro Donizetti, paired once again in concert with Motian's trio.[1669]

Although Kenny played with Lee Konitz later, the quartet from *Angel Song* never performed together again. ECM's Paula Morris brushed off any regrets, saying "we can't sit around, lamenting the lack of a tour. If you have a great record, you don't need every part of the puzzle to have a success."[1670] But, at the time, Kenny expressed disappointment that there were no further opportunities for them to perform this music together and that this "particular quartet is almost impossible to get together, partly because Bill has decided to take most of this year completely off – he wants to stay at home and just do his own projects."[1671] It wasn't just Bill – Kenny added that Dave Holland had "moved up into the Herbie Hancock world and he's quite busy now, as he should have been years ago", and later said, "they're all leaders in their own right and to find a period when they're all free is very hard."[1672] Frisell agreed, saying, "everybody was so busy, it was just crazy".[1673]

Just a few months after recording *Angel Song* in New York, Kenny worked once again with Lee Konitz in London, playing a week-long residency at Ronnie Scott's with guitarist John Parricelli, bassist Mick Hutton, and drummer Stephen Keogh.[1674] Konitz remembered "the nice rhythm section", adding that he was "enjoying the situation".[1675] But Kenny's friend and jazz journalist Ted O'Reilly, visiting London from Toronto, remembered the evening with mixed feelings, saying:

> It's serious music. And yet – it seemed bland . . . so boring . . . And it just seemed to me was wonderful in a way, because Lee Konitz and Kenny both said, in their heads, it seemed to me, *Oh well, fuck it, I'm just going to go for myself* . . . He played like Kenny Wheeler, in a noisy room with people who weren't listening . . . And yet Kenny was like an angel, like a saint.[1676]

Ted should have stayed for the rest of the gig, however, because the night – if not the music – became much more exciting. A rowdier crowd of inebriated tourists came in for the second set. Lee said that "one guy shouted out some dumb thing and I shouted back, '*Shut up, you prick!*' You should have seen Kenny's face! That was a result of years of tolerating people, sitting directly in front, and talking loud."[1677] Kenny remembered Lee's reaction, saying, "he didn't like it much, but I did warn him that people do talk there!"[1678] A final Wheeler/Konitz collaboration for the decade came with a gig at the Neuberg (Germany) Birdland club in December 1999, in which the duo played with bassist Gunnar Plümer and pianist Frank Wunsch. The drummerless quartet played compositions by every person in the group, buttressed by Lee's classic tune "Thingin'" and Kenny's "Where Do We Go From Here", "Kind Folk", "Onmo" (from *Angel Song*), and "Olden Times", and was re-released nearly 20 years later on the Double Moon label.[1679]

---

Despite Kenny's complaints about a lack of commissions, they still came in occasionally due to his reputation on the Continent. In the early 1990s, Hamburg's NDR Big Band commissioned him to write a new suite for their brass players, featuring a trio of Kenny, John Taylor, and guitarist Mike Walker. After the music premiered in Hamburg in late April 1993, Nick Purnell wanted it to be heard in the UK, so he organized a tour coinciding with Kenny's 65th birthday. This tour featured members of the Creative Jazz Orchestra, a largely northwest-UK-based ensemble formed by Purnell. (The CJO collaborated on ambitious projects with many leading artists throughout this period, including Mike Gibbs, Mark Anthony-Turnage, Vince Mendoza, Peter Erskine, and others.) This tour included stops at Manchester's Royal Northern College of Music and Darlington,[1680] and the centrepiece of the programme was the half-hour *Jazzical Suite* (a portmanteau of *Jazz* and *Classical*). Other music included "Going for Baroque" (which Kenny described as "a gooey mess in the baroque style with a little bit of Hindemith thrown in") and an arrangement of part of Kenny's mid-1970s *Gnu Suite*.[1681]

After the tour, members of that original group and some new London-based players (including trumpet players Derek Watkins and John Barclay, who were brought in to substitute for two of the CJO trumpets) formed a new version of the all-brass ensemble for two further occasions in London. They were scheduled to perform live at the Purcell Room at London's Southbank Centre, just days before Kenny's birthday, and to go into Gateway Studios the day before to record the music.[1682] Unfortunately, there were some issues with the first day's recording. Because they were attempting to record the music the day *before* the Purcell Room gig, the new players were essentially sight-reading the parts. A whole album of brass music requires enormous – and not commonly required – levels of physical stamina, and with the recording session of already exhausting material now serving a double purpose as a rehearsal, there were considerable performance stresses added to the day.

Recollections vary as to what happened and how the various issues resulted in the recording being considered unusable, but one thing is certain: Kenny, the person best positioned to have sorted out any such conflicts between his colleagues – non-confrontational, non-self-promoting, indecisive, probably oblivious to any turmoil – was content to be absorbed in his inner musical world. His inability to simply intervene when needed left some relationships bruised and sour memories for some of those involved.

The next day, the group played at the Purcell Room. (Reviewer Chris Parker observed that the hall was "packed" and its audience showed "wild enthusiasm".)[1683] The concert opened with just Kenny and John Taylor, playing the trumpeter's "Everybody's Song But My Own" – after which he mumbled something unintelligible regarding his loss of rights to the tune, which he had re-dubbed "Everybody Owns My Song But Me".[1684] Kenny's mood brightened when the brass players arrived onstage to play the *Jazzical Suite* and "Going for Baroque". He was apparently in quite good playing form throughout the concert, with Parker observing that he "cut through the plush sonority of the brass arrangements with incisive solos packed with his trademark high-note flurries, tinged with gently buoyant melancholy, and capping a performance that richly merited the extended ovation it received."[1685]

Over two years after that Purcell Room performance, some of the players from the 1995 brass concert returned to Gateway Studios to re-record the music for the brass album, in what they hoped would be a more definitive outcome than the first attempt. Referring to one of the key instigators of this re-recording, Evan Parker made the point that "Derek Watkins's status is such that what he thinks should be done can be done."[1686] Indeed, some of Kenny's longest-standing brass colleagues felt very proud of – and became protective of – their relationship to his music. As Derek had once remarked to Henry, the UK players knew *how* his music should be played. This is a reasonable assertion, considering that they played with him from *Windmill*

*Tilter* onwards and the connection they forged together while creating the legendary UK brass sound. This proprietary feeling, however, was also prevalent among other people, like Nick Purnell, who had worked the hardest to promote Kenny and get his music played by some of the greatest jazz musicians in the world. For better or worse, those who were so invested in helping Kenny could sometimes also become defensive of him. So, occasionally, they would find themselves pitted against one another while Kenny sat silently in the middle, once again paralysed in the face of disagreement among his friends.

In September 1997 and October 1998, the second attempts at recording the brass album went ahead. Henry Lowther helped book the musicians and Evan Parker was chosen once more to produce. This time Evan asked Stan Sulzmann to join him for the producing and mixing duties, acknowledging that "there's a certain kind of harmonic sensibility that I need, and a little bit of help [with the score reading] . . ."[1687] Possibly because of the delicate matter of replacing some of the musicians from the previous recording effort with others, plans to re-record the album were kept "somewhat secret",[1688] which could understandably have been especially upsetting to Nick Purnell, who had organized the whole tour, birthday concerts, and initial recording session, not to mention, of course, several previous projects with Kenny.

One of the compositions newly arranged for brass ensemble for this album and not part of the original NDR concert or CJO tour is "Ballad for a Dead Child", one of the most strikingly beautiful pieces of melancholy that Kenny ever penned. Although we can only speculate as to the title's origin – perhaps a Wheelerian take on Maurice Ravel's "Pavane pour une infante défunte" – it could be a meditation on the profound feelings of loss he and Doreen experienced after the loss of their own third child, Alice, many years earlier. (Indeed, another of his compositions, "Alice My Dear", also appears on the album.) Another highlight of the recording is Kenny's "One Plus Three (version 1)", which begins with a rare chance to hear Kenny improvise unaccompanied before being joined by three overdubbed flugelhorns (hence the title). With the improvisation less overtly structured than that on "Solo One" from *Around Six*, "One Plus Three (version 1)" displays Kenny's more spontaneous approach and is at once satisfying musically and representative of his creative power at this late period. His extraordinary technical command still be drawn upon at nearly 70 years old.

Even though this new configuration included more of Kenny's usual colleagues, it did not completely solve the problems inherent in recording an album of such demanding, detailed brass music. Stan Sulzmann remembered listening from the booth to the challenges of these second sessions, saying "every time something was wrong . . . eight times, nine times out of ten, it was Ian Hamer! [*laughs*] . . . But of course, Ian, in his time, had been a great player. For Kenny, it was loyalty to people that had been important in his life."[1689] Stan continued: "You could have had a perfect band, and hired everybody who played perfect, but it wouldn't have had any character, so that's the payoff, isn't it?"[1690] adding that Kenny probably did this on purpose, mindful of the fact that he also just wanted to have his friends around. Although this recording must have been an improvement on the previous one, multiple people (who wish to remain anonymous) recall that there was at least one prominent musician on the sessions who felt that it still was not at a level that merited release.[1691] Some critics agreed; the ever-unimpressed Clive Davis, writing in the *Sunday Times*, called the "achingly slow layering of trumpets and trombones more repetitive than hypnotic".[1692] But there were more generous critical receptions, with Mike Bradley in *The Times* calling *A Long Time Ago* a "welcome opportunity to hear more of the expatriate Canadian trumpeter's large-scale writing for brass".[1693] The most effusive review of the album came from *DownBeat*'s Jon Andrews. Of Kenny, he said, "Few players can establish such a strong identity with just a few notes. He can break your heart with apparent ease, but his approach is consistently lyrical." Andrews gave the album 4½ stars, observing that "Wheeler uses the horns to create richly detailed harmonies and shimmering textures" and called the recording "gorgeous".[1694]

The album continues to be controversial, because of hard feelings among some of those involved at various points in its evolution, and because of disagreement about the quality of the final product. Considering the litany of challenges, the mere existence of *A Long Time Ago* is a miracle in itself. Although finally released on ECM in 1999, it was not initially commissioned by the label and is the only album in Kenny's ECM catalogue for which Manfred Eicher was absent from the recording and production. It would also be the last recording Kenny would release for ECM in his lifetime.

———·———

As Kenny approached 70, his period of teaching at the Banff Centre came to an end. Following a review of the programme, there was a change in the overall direction of the Jazz Workshop.[1695] After the summer of 1998, Banff removed Hugh Fraser as head of the jazz programme, and ended its relationship with two of Canada's leading musicians and educators: Kenny Wheeler and Don Thompson.

During that summer's jazz workshop, the centre threw an unceremonious farewell gathering: so low-key, in fact, that the students misinterpreted it as a celebration of the *achievements* of Kenny, Don, and Hugh, rather than the involuntary retirement party it actually was.[1696] A heartbreakingly unadorned sheet cake commemorated the bittersweet event, simply reading:

Thanks
Hugh, Don, Kenny
xoxox[1697]

Kenny later told his friend Bill Jelley that Banff "didn't want him anymore".[1698] He didn't mask his bitter feelings about the situation when he spoke to *Coda* magazine earlier that year:

> That is all the teaching I do. I'll be going this year and hopefully it will be the last. I've been saying that every year and now it's been twelve years. I think Kenny Werner is taking over the course next year and he'll want his own people. I don't mind. Anyway, I've been there too long.[1699]

The following year, Werner did indeed take over leadership of the Banff Summer Jazz Workshop, and with him came a new generation of faculty and students.

Kenny Wheeler's 17-year affiliation with the Banff Centre left an immeasurable legacy.[1700] Mark Miller surmised that it would be difficult to fathom the extent of "Kenny's impact on Canadian musicians of a certain generation (born early 1960s), generally through his ECM recordings but more specifically through his affiliation with the Banff Jazz Workshop, which drew players from across the country".[1701] Don Thompson once remarked that, at Banff, he and Kenny had helped to produce "about 75 percent of the finest younger jazz players in Canada".[1702] For many young Canadian musicians, who were proud to claim Kenny Wheeler as one of their own but found it difficult to meet him or hear him play live because he lived in London, Banff was *the* place to get to know Kenny and his music. Many of his students continued to correspond with Kenny after attending the workshop, keeping in touch via letters, fax, and the occasional transatlantic phone call; several even received Christmas cards from the Wheeler family. Many of these former Banff workshop participants subsequently exposed their students to Kenny's music and legacy once their careers as teachers or performers or composers bloomed. In fact, once they began to lead jazz programmes of their own throughout the world, many Banff alums brought Kenny himself in for residencies so that their students could experience the trumpeter's music with him in person.

Years after Kenny's passing, Banff remains a spiritual home for his legacy and memory. Some of the most innovative jazz musicians continue to teach and practise there each summer, and to be there – knowing all that it meant to Kenny despite the regrettable way he and the other faculty were dismissed at the end – is still special. Not only do many musicians across multiple generations treasure their encounters with him, but there is also a substantial archive of his manuscripts in the centre's library. It stands as a testament to the sheer volume of material he wrote or adapted for his residencies, including many premieres and one-offs for all kinds of ensembles. The archive of old concert programmes also reveals an array of faculty ensembles that would have headlined any major festival in the world.

Soon after his time at Banff ended, tensions once again crept into Kenny's long-standing association with the ECM label. Near the end of 1999, Michael Tucker at the University of Brighton was preparing to host a festival in celebration of the 30th anniversary of the ECM label. When Evan Parker was contacted with the invitation to bring his electro-acoustic ensemble to perform, he noticed a telling omission from the festival's roster. He recalled the incident with humorous affection for his long-time ECM producer:

> I couldn't see Ken's name here anywhere. I felt very weird about playing on an ECM festival without Ken. And the word got back to Manfred, and as usual, it was like, *When he wants your opinion he'll give it to you . . .* and he gave me the opinion that [*laughs*] I can keep my fucking opinions to myself![1703]

Evan remained defiant: "I thought, well yes, and no, . . . so I asked Ken if he wanted to play down there with me!"[1704] Accordingly, on 11 November, Kenny appeared in Evan's ensemble on a double bill with Barry Guy. ECM's Steve Lake was in attendance and was struck by Kenny's performance as part of Evan's ensemble: "Kenny was blazingly brilliant in this context, responding to the live sampling of his sound and interacting with it, soloing inside the reverberating electronic maze as if born to this radical idiom. It was one of those concerts you wished had been recorded . . ."[1705]

Just a year or so later, there was another episode of miscommunication between Kenny and the German label. ECM had begun the prestigious *:rarum* series, highlighting selected works of particular featured artists. Kenny was approached to compile one of these, which – contrary to his assumption – was an attempt to show in just what high regard he was held by the label. Steve Lake recalled the communications and Kenny's predictably slow response, being an artist more interested in looking forwards than backwards. They even approached him a second time. Steve said, "Invited to contribute his choice of favourite pieces, Kenny first of all demurred for all the usual self-critical reasons and didn't want to participate. We asked him again for the second group of *:rarum* discs in 2002 and he said OK. Evan offered to help Kenny get a liner note together."[1706] Kenny eventually compiled his list, but the task of revisiting his back catalogue for someone so self-critical and averse to listening to themselves led to substantial procrastination. Lake continued, "Deadlines came and went. Many months later we finally received a list of tracks and the notes from Kenny, but by then the *:rarum* series was behind us."[1707]

The letter (which Evan helped Kenny refine) provides an insight into his opinions about his own ECM output. As expected, it is full of deference to the other players. Choosing *Heyoke* from *Gnu High* for the opener, he wrote: ". . . is my favourite mostly for the beautiful interlude that Keith plays between parts one and two . . ." Kenny continued, " . . . although I can still hear the terrible moment when I got lost – around 15'02"!"[1708] He chose "3/4 in the Afternoon" from *Deer Wan* next, singling Ralph Towner out for praise. Two selections would come from *Around 6*: "Solo One" and "Follow Down", the latter described as having been "developed from a scale Evan Parker was working on". From *Double, Double You* he picked "Foxy Trot", which he rather touchingly described as "a tribute to my parents. I could imagine my father playing trombone at some dance in 1918 or 1919, while my mother danced the fox trot." Indecisive about *Music for Large and Small Ensembles*, he wrote, "I suppose I must make a choice so I would pick 'For PA (for Pepper Adams)."" Most self-deprecatingly of all, he described *Angel Song* as easy to choose from. "I would go for 'Kind of Gentle' even though I don't play on it. Lee's playing is beautifully mournful, and the three of them – Lee, Bill and Dave sound so great together that I think Manfred should record them!" To finish, he picked "Ballad for a Dead Child" from *A Long Time Ago* – but did not elaborate on its origin, simply saying it "has a feeling of baroque music which I love very much, and I like the way that the two different themes work together." It is a shame this *:rarum* collection never came to be; it would have been a wonderful "greatest hits" for listeners and a three-decade overview of his ECM output. And the liner notes would have added an intimate and honest insight into his choices – notes which he signed off with gratitude and perhaps with an attempt to repair relations: "Thank you Manfred and ECM – *Gnu High* established me on the international scene and made it possible to work with some of the best players in the world."

———·——

Despite recording for ECM less than he would have wished, Kenny found outlets beyond the label to record with some of the finest improvisers anywhere. One of the most significant of these encounters was a duo recording with pianist Paul Bley, a fellow Canadian regarded as one of the *other* true titans of contemporary jazz from that country. In mid-July 1996, after Kenny's residency at Banff and his three days at the Domaine Forget de Charlevoix International Festival in Quebec, he travelled to Montreal to record the album *Touché* with Bley.[1709] Despite the gravitas of these two giant improvisers recording for the first time, the one-day session presented some challenges. Paul Bley was of a similar generation and, like Kenny had a background playing tunes from the jazz tradition *and* was a great player of freely improvised music. *Unlike* Kenny, Bley wasn't afraid to speak his mind or ask for exactly what he wanted. So when Kenny brought some of his own tunes for them to record, Paul dismissed the idea and expressed his intention to play free; accordingly, the album comprised an entire set of free duos. Also difficult was Bley's insistence that they take a long break between recording each freely improvised piece in order to clear both of their heads and come up with a fresh approach for each. However, long breaks between takes can actually make recording more physically taxing for a trumpet player – repeatedly playing just long enough to get warmed up only to get cold again. But Kenny persevered, and participated in an album that is a fascinating testament to the artistry of both men and an important document of two of Canada's finest modern jazz musicians. Despite the challenges, the atmosphere must have been very friendly: both are pictured with beaming smiles on the cover; and, since all of the music was free, the two agreed to split the publishing for the album, by means of alternating the composition credit for each track.[1710]

Around this time, Kenny had begun to teach occasionally at other workshops during the summers. In addition to his work in Canada, he also began teaching more in Europe. For example, Italian jazz pianist and composer Glauco Venier asked him to join the faculty of a music workshop in Gorizia, a small city in northeast Italy at the foot of the Julian Alps. Kenny was involved in the week-long workshop each summer for four years, beginning in 1997. The faculty there represented expertise in both jazz and classical music; the great trumpet pedagogue Pierre Thibaud, professor emeritus of the Paris Conservatory, also taught there, although he and Kenny maintained a respectful distance from each other's classes.[1711]

Similar to his approach at Banff, Kenny would have the students warm up in the morning by playing his arrangements of early music like Byrd or Gabrieli. And, just like at Banff, Kenny quietly helped students whom he thought could benefit from his experience. One year, a trumpet student developed a nervous shake in his playing.[1712] During a class, Kenny told Glauco to continue to play with the students and give him some time with the student.[1713] When they came back to the class a couple of hours later, Kenny was happy to report that the student was doing much better.

One day, Glauco asked Kenny to go sailing, so they decided to go out on the water that evening after classes. Since Gorizia was very near the Gulf of Trieste, it was a beautiful sight to see the city in the distance, especially contrasted against the dark sky and the night-time sea. Glauco had also invited some of the other faculty to join them with their instruments for a jam session on the water. One student came along to listen: a female classical trumpet player who was in Pierre Thibaud's class. Glauco remembered, "I was swimming and they invented a kind of concert. They played for 45 minutes, free! It was so nice, in the middle of the sea in the dark." Glauco said that Kenny was playing very strong, full of ideas and not taking it easy, which he could have done in such a low-pressure situation. He continued, "At the end, I went to him and I said, 'Kenny, it's incredible what you did. What's going on? You put a lot of energy into this!' And he said, 'This lady is a classical trumpet player. I had to impress her, you know!'"[1714] When he got back to the hotel, Kenny called Doreen to tell her about the exciting evening he'd had on the boat.[1715] He had been so touched by his time with such a warm group of musicians in Gorizia that he composed a tune overnight for them, which he called "Phrase Three".[1716]

Kenny also became increasingly in demand as a guest artist and clinician in the United States, where his *Sweet Time Suite* was becoming a popular piece of repertoire for college big bands. Kenny's reluctance to speak in front of crowds and lack of interest in analysing his own work – or critiquing that of others – was apparently of little concern or interest to collegiate jazz faculty, who were likely so overwhelmed by the beauty of his compositions and his virtuosity (even at the age of 70) that such idiosyncrasies could be seen as part of his charm. Besides, as he aged, his demeanour became perceived as more endearing than evasive, taking on more of a grandfatherly role to a whole new generation of students of modern jazz: approachable, kind, warm, funny, and a little bumbling, all while carrying the mantle of a formidable trumpet master and genius-level composer.

In 1999, Kenny travelled to the United States to perform as a guest with jazz ensembles at prestigious conservatories. As well as a return visit to the Eastman School of Music, he was also invited to the University of Miami by pianist and composer Ron Miller. Kenny had clearly been an influence on Miller's own compositional approach, and they had similar ideas in their harmonic concepts; he was a champion of Kenny's in North America and brought him to the attention of many young musicians at Miami.

Possibly the most recognized American university in terms of big-band jazz education is the University of North Texas (UNT), where the big-band programme had flourished under the direction of Leon Breeden and Neil Slater, eventually growing to have nine such ensembles in the same department, each named after their rehearsal time. Thus, the top band is the famous One O'Clock Lab Band, from which jazz luminaries such as Maynard Ferguson and Stan Kenton chose rising stars for their own bands for decades. In 2000, Kenny was named the year's prestigious "Gomez Artist" at North Texas. As such, he was brought in to work with the students, lead masterclasses, and perform his music as a featured soloist with the faculty ensemble and the One O'Clock band.[1717] On campus, Kenny rehearsed *The Sweet Time Suite,* directed by Slater, and gave masterclasses on his compositions, even taking some time to look at music written by the student composers and arrangers. When looking at one of student Paul Tynan's scores (the young trumpeter who had been covering the solo flugel parts prior to Kenny's arrival), he said, "your handwriting is almost as bad as mine!" He also talked to some of the brass players about his daily routine, noting that maintaining his chops had gotten more difficult as he got older.[1718] He also went to a rehearsal with the UNT Jazz Singers. A member of that group, and the young woman who sang the suite with Kenny and the band, Rosana Calderon (now Rosana Eckert, UNT jazz voice faculty), had fond memories of singing next to him. "His music was very meaningful to me . . . I remember his gentle nature, his encouraging and kind spirit, and his masterful playing . . . and how hard I had to work on that music!"[1719] The jazz programme released a double CD on their in-house label documenting the concert later that year, titled *Kenny Wheeler at North Texas.*[1720]

As always, Kenny was generous with his resources at UNT, including scores of his tunes. He had brought along the spiral-bound notebook he used at Banff and other places where he was expected to talk; at this point, it was filled with over 60 pages of handwritten analysis and description (and somewhat funny rambling commentary). When Paul Tynan saw the notebook, he asked if he could copy it. Predictably, Kenny was amenable; when Paul later asked him if he could publish it, he also agreed, but with the condition that it only be available after his death.[1721]

Kenny was invited to perform at other universities around the same time. He was reunited with Canadian multi-instrumental virtuoso Don Thompson to play a rare piano and trumpet duo concert as part of a trip to Grand Valley State University (GVSU) in September 2000.[1722] Nearly missing their connecting flight and having to run to their gate in order to make it, the tall, gangly Thompson had no problem with the jaunt. But Kenny, who was around a foot shorter, a little rounder, and over a decade older, had some difficulty keeping up. Kenny had no problem maintaining pace with Don once it came time to play the concert, however. When asked if they wanted to play two sets or just one long one, Kenny surprisingly responded by saying he preferred to perform one long set. Accordingly, they played basically non-stop for an hour-and-a-half: a feat of endurance worthy of awe for any trumpet player, let alone one over 70. Don said Kenny "never cuffed a note the whole night".[1723] In fact, at the end of the concert, after they had played their encore of "Body and Soul", the classical trumpet teacher at GVSU, who was half Kenny's age at the time, came up to them and said, "Mr. Wheeler, I have to tell you, what you did, I could never do in a million years."[1724] It should be noted that Don Thompson – himself revered as much in Canada and beyond – admires Kenny without reservation:

> Once you've played with him, once you've experienced him, you can't get him out of your mind. It's like trying to get Bach out of your head. You can't do it. It's just there forever. And Kenny's the same thing . . . It was so personal . . . There's not a molecule of jive in anything he ever did![1725]

Early in the 2000s, Kenny was invited to be part of two ensembles led by close friends and colleagues from his own groups. First, Dave Holland formed a new all-star octet with Kenny, trombonist Robin Eubanks, vibraphonist Steve Nelson, drummer Billy Kilson, and Antonio Hart, Chris Potter, and Gary Smulyan on saxophones. Organized by Nick Purnell,[1726] their tour began on 1 March 2001 in Southampton and ran for eight dates in the UK and a final stop in Dublin on 11 March.[1727] Dave was inspired to form this unique line-up of instruments by an unlikely source:

> I had always loved the sound of the Duke Ellington small groups, often with a 5-horn front-line plus the rhythm section. The combination of 2 brass and 3 saxes gives access to a wide range of textures and colours and allows a composer to evoke the sound of a big band or create the more intimate sound of a small group.[1728]

Dave felt it was important to include Kenny in this group. "For this tour, I wanted to feature his very specific sound on flugelhorn, so I've written some ballad material that's unmistakably for him," Dave said.[1729] Reviewers certainly picked up on the special attention being paid to the elder master, with one calling him the "cornerstone of the ensemble sound . . . His unmistakable tone provides a wonderful romantic lilt to much of the performance."[1730] Another remarked on the loveliness of Holland's "Ballad for Kenny", observing that the composition "exploited the very personal lyricism of Kenny Wheeler (on flugelhorn) against nicely varied backgrounds from the rest of the octet . . . [Holland] also wrote an untitled piece, another beautiful ballad, which again showed Wheeler's gift for taking his lyricism in surprising directions."[1731]

Of course, Kenny's fellow musicians were moved by his presence. Saxophonist Chris Potter was by this time a close colleague of Dave's, but this was his first time playing with Kenny. As a young musician growing up in South Carolina, one of the first albums Potter owned was Dave's *Jumpin' In*, which was probably the first time he actually heard Kenny play.[1732] Chris recalled his anticipation about getting to tour with him:

> I'd been a fan of Kenny's music for a long time, so I was very excited that he was going to be on the tour, and I'd kind of heard a little bit from Dave that he was fairly shy and self-deprecating, you know, but I don't think I was prepared for the extent that . . . [*laughs*] he was *very, very* quiet and *very, very* self-deprecating! But also, just hearing him play every night was like, *Wow, there's the guy!*[1733]

In addition to Dave Holland's Octet, Kenny was also incorporated as a soloist into Peter Erskine's project *Music for Brass and Percussion* later that spring (May 2001). Peter had received the commission from BBC Radio 3's *Jazz On 3* in late 2000, which resulted in 11 pieces for a brass ensemble comprising three trumpets, three horns, trombone, and tuba, with rhythm section, percussion, and woodwind soloist. The work was premiered on 25 May and recorded live in Leeds at The Wardrobe. Since this was another Nick Purnell initiative centred around the Creative Jazz Orchestra, there was some personnel overlap from Kenny's first iteration of the *A Long Time Ago* project: notably, trumpeters John Barclay and Richard Iles. J.T. was also a soloist on the concert, which

Mike Gibbs conducted. A recording of the music was released nearly two decades later.[1734]

———·———

Like so many young Canadian jazz musicians, saxophonist Andrew Rathbun first met Kenny and Don Thompson at Banff. "He was one of the main reasons I wanted to go there," Rathbun said. "I'd never heard a sound that was so instantly penetrating emotionally, apart from Coltrane."[1735] In preparation for his second trip to the Banff Jazz Workshop, Andrew wrote a five-movement suite to feature Kenny, along with other Banff faculty including Hugh Fraser on trombone and Pat LaBarbera on tenor saxophone. "It was definitely a musical highlight at that point in my life," Andrew said.[1736]

A few years later, having settled in New York, Andrew brought Kenny to the city on three separate occasions. Most notably, he twice arranged opportunities for Kenny to perform his own music with an all-star big band at one of New York's most prestigious venues, Birdland. The first trip was in May 1999 and the band was due to perform his famous *Sweet Time Suite*, among other pieces, in a group including the original guitarist, John Abercrombie. Also in the ensemble was the Brazilian vocalist Luciana Souza. She remembered Kenny's *Music for Large and Small Ensembles* as being "life-changing" for her during college. As a vocalist, she was particularly struck by Norma Winstone and had begun to explore other music of Kenny's, including Azimuth. The use of the voice in this way struck a familiar note with one of the stars from her homeland, Hermeto Pascoal:

> I was coming from *that* background of also including voice . . . not necessarily with lyrics all the time. And of course, for me hearing Norma sing, and hearing the way that Kenny respected the voice and included the voice, and how vocal his lines were . . . that made *so much* sense to me. And then I became a fan . . . it just became sort of an intersection in my life where everybody seemed to be listening to him [Kenny] and loving him, and the musicians I love the most all love him![1737]

So, it was with some excitement that Luciana found herself sitting between Kenny and John Abercrombie to sing this iconic music at Birdland. She recalled the experience of singing alongside him:

> I have to say, sitting next to that sound was just glorious for me, you know. I found it extremely easy [blending with him] because I took the role of *following* . . . my idea was "this is not about the voice, the voice is an added colour in the ensemble" . . . and with him, his pitch was so beautiful [and] the *length* of his lines – I remember thinking about that . . .

The experience stuck with Luciana, even though she had sung a lot of great big-band music before: ". . . with *that* project, it was really a dream and I knew, 'that was it, nothing would ever top that'!"[1738] Bassist and composer Rufus Reid, who had played and recorded with Kenny in Jane Ira Bloom's band, was in the audience and found his own writing immediately influenced by hearing Luciana sing next to Kenny: "Hearing her sing those lines and just adding that texture in the voicings – that's where I got it. I just stole that! They say if you're going to steal something, get it from the best, you know!" Reid would go on to use wordless voice in his Grammy-nominated multi-movement opus for large ensemble, *Quiet Pride*.[1739,1740]

After the success of the first Birdland residency, Andrew Rathbun organized a recording session for his upcoming project titled *Sculptures*, a CD of original compositions for jazz quintet.[1741] Kenny accepted Andrew's invitation to play on the album, which was set to be recorded at The Studio in New York in late September, 2001. When terrorists attacked the United States on 11 September, air travel was so disrupted and the city was in such turmoil that Andrew was almost certain that Kenny would cancel. "We spoke a few times, and he eventually decided to give it a go. I suppose all those years in the UK created a 'stiff upper lip' in him," Andrew said, adding, "I think the events were on everyone's mind when we made the record."[1742] In addition to the obvious emotion of the occasion, part of what made *Sculptures* a successful project was the fact that Andrew wrote with Kenny in mind. His experiences writing

Photo 39: John Abercrombie warming up in the dressing room at Blues Alley while Kenny buzzes his mouthpiece.

© Patrick Hinely, Work/Play®

for Kenny at Banff informed this work, as he said: "I really tried to write as many things as possible that Kenny would feel comfortable with. I knew that having him play music that he wouldn't be comfortable with wouldn't produce the best results."[1743] Andrew loved playing next to the elder master. "He was so free in so many ways and played behind the beat, which I loved (especially when you got to play a melody with him) and his flights through the full range of the instrument were so exhilarating." When they went into the studio booth to listen to playbacks, Kenny was his usual self-deprecating self. "Kenny grunted something like, *Why do I keep doing those high whoops?!* I told him that he invented that gesture. It's what makes him Kenny Wheeler. He seemed to like that."[1744]

Not long after his trip to New York to play with Rathbun, Kenny returned to the US in December 2001 to play with John Abercrombie and Marc Copland. (The trio had released their first album together, *That's for Sure*, the previous December.[1745]) Jazz journalist and photographer Patrick Hinely was at their gig at Blues Alley in Washington DC to hear the ensemble and take photographs. Having known Kenny and Doreen for decades – and familiar with their uncanny ability to be the first Christmas card in his mailbox each year – he said:

> I thought I had finally got the jump on him when, rather than airmailing his card, I brought it with me to his early-December appearance, in Washington DC, and delivered it personally, for which he thanked me, his trademark poker face never flinching as he read the envelope and put it in his trumpet case, then went on about his tasks, preparing for the gig. Upon returning home the next day, I found in my mailbox the season's first card, from the Wheelers, postmarked in London a full week earlier . . .[1746]

The following year, Andrew Rathbun once again put together a big band and brought Kenny back to New York for another three-night engagement at Birdland in late August through early September 2002. There, they played music of Kenny's, including his *Sweet Ruby Suite*, "Gentle Piece", and "Kayak". The band included another all-star line-up with vocalist Luciana Souza, and this time a rhythm-section featuring guitar virtuoso Ben Monder, bassist John Hebert, and drummer Jeff Hirschfield.[1747] Alongside them completing the ensemble were some New York big-band veterans, such as lead alto/soprano player Dick Oatts, bass trombonist Dave Taylor, and legendary lead trumpeter and pedagogue Laurie Frink, from whom Kenny took a trumpet lesson while he was in the city.[1748]

In the rehearsals for Rathbun's *Atwood Suite* (also on the programme), Andrew noticed that even though the trumpet solo part had been professionally copied, Kenny was playing from some scraps of paper that he had written on; he had renamed some of the chords to match his own nomenclature, and apparently preferred to read his own handwriting when improvising.[1749] Kenny's usual nerves almost got the better of him on the first night of the residency. He was the first musician to arrive at the club, over an hour before the downbeat of the first set. He took the valves out of his flugelhorn to oil them and was so nervous that he hadn't put them out in order and sought help from a former Banff trumpet student he saw sitting in the club to get them back in correctly:

> Kenny came up behind me and said, "Hi Brian, could you come help me?" and then asked me to come up on stage with him, where he had his flugelhorn taken apart and parts spread out all over his chair. (In Kenny's defence, the valves weren't numbered like most, so this was not a straight-forward task; in my defence, I was completely intimidated by being on stage at Birdland with my hero, even though there was no one there but us.) Eventually, Laurie Frink arrived at the gig and saw Kenny and I fumbling with his flugelhorn. Amused, but feigning a slight disappointment and annoyance with both of us, she said, "Gimme that", and saved the day![1750]

Even though this points to nervousness on Kenny's part before the gig began, Andrew didn't sense that Kenny was too apprehensive about this New York performance. "This might have been because he was playing his music, or music of mine that was easily and quickly digestible by him," Andrew said. "I know that on other occasions when other people brought him and had him play their music, he felt a bit less comfortable . . . I think he was more nervous or agitated when he went into something where he felt less comfortable or out of his normal zone."[1751] Andrew remembered a final charming anecdote about Kenny and his formidable sweet tooth:

> We had him and Doreen to Brooklyn to dinner, and the last time we were in Canada, he ate about three or four butter-tarts, a Canadian delicacy (like a mini Pecan-pie). My wife made Kenny an honorary batch, and when dessert was served, after not really saying all that much during dinner, he boldly announced to the guests that they could have as much of whatever else they wanted, but please stay away from HIS butter-tarts. It got a big laugh.[1752]

Back in the 1990s, Kenny had the increasing sense that people were starting to take advantage of his generosity. This feeling of being used, combined with his desire to play his own music, was a frequent topic in interviews from the 1990s onward. He said,:

> Nowadays everybody is a composer and they all want to play their own music. Most of the time it is all right and I like it. But all of them are not great composers. Years ago when I went to play, they would say bring three

of four of your own songs and we'll play them. Now they all want to play their compositions and I'm not too happy with it.[1753]

Kenny also said that he "would like to have more control of my life so that in the future I might have more extended periods at home for writing, and during the time spent abroad playing I would like to play more of my own music."[1754]

His frustration was likely due to the dissonance between this desire to write and play more of his own music and his inability to say no. His shy and chronically polite Anglo-Canadian personality combined with his naturally kind and generous nature meant that he would almost always instinctively say yes but sometimes regret it later. He would often agree to play on aspiring professional or even student projects, basically playing with whomever called and asked him if he was available. Evan Parker said that

> Kenny was more and more being used by unscrupulous musicians, who would call him for what he thought was a sideman gig, and when he got there, he'd find that it was the *Mr. X/Kenny Wheeler Quintet featuring the compositions of . . .* They'd play some of his [Kenny's] tunes. Why not? They're great tunes. But they'd play some of "Mr. X's" tunes, which maybe weren't such good tunes. And the playing maybe wasn't up the [level] Kenny might expect . . .[1755]

Albums would come out that he had guested on or gigs with others would be publicized and inevitably be listed as something such as "The Kenny Wheeler Quartet" or "The _____ Trio featuring Kenny Wheeler", even though it was only something he'd done as a favour, not knowing his name would be attached to it. Mark Wheeler remembered: "He'd say, 'I know what they're doing. They'll stick my name on the cover, and everyone will think it's my record. I don't want them to think that. I want to play my tunes.' It genuinely irritated him . . . He was regularly saying that."[1756] In most cases, this was probably intended to increase sales or create publicity, and just give a fledgling project considerably more artistic heft. Evan Parker assessed the situation well, telling Kenny, "You're going to have to get someone to protect you . . . Somebody's going to have to say no for you because you're not very good at saying no."[1757]

In the past, Kenny had never had a formal manager. He had received huge assistance from Nick Purnell and others (with Purnell in particular doing everything a manager would do), but often on a per-project basis without the ongoing protection of long-term management. "The time was right for him to get an agent," Mark Wheeler said.[1758] Not knowing how to even start such a process, Kenny found Orpheus Management through his friend John Taylor, who was already represented by the agency.[1759] A company based in Italy and run by Andrea Marini, Orpheus managed (or collaborated frequently with) several close associates of Kenny's around that time, especially those based in the UK or Europe. This was an opportunity to finally get Kenny exactly what he needed: an intermediary who was not afraid of saying no on his behalf to projects that didn't fit his artistic vision, allowing him, now 70, to focus on his own projects. "I think there was a period of time when it was a good way of getting him to be able to play his own music with his own people," Mark said, adding that Kenny was now having to travel more to play. He was now "in Italy a lot, also Germany, France, Scandinavia. That seemed to be increasing. That all gradually grew when Andrea came on because, obviously, of his European contacts. [Dad] worked a lot away."[1760]

From now on, those who had booked Kenny directly for years – including some who considered him a friend and were used to him managing himself (with Doreen fielding calls to their home) – were being instructed to contact Marini at Orpheus Management. Inevitably, some had hard feelings about this change.

---

Around the time Kenny was talking about concentrating on playing his own music, he was actually beginning to do so with his new quartet, featuring long-standing friends John Taylor and Chris Laurence, joined by drummer Adam Nussbaum. This is the group he mentioned in his 1997 *DownBeat* interview and to *Coda* in 1998; as far back as his interview in 1990 with Chris Parker, he had described another iteration of this quartet: "I'd like to write and maybe take a quartet out in England, but there's a problem: unless you have a 'big name', people don't come out to see you. I like quartets – John Taylor's my favourite pianist, and Chris Laurence and John Marshall would suit me . . ."[1761] "It was a good little band," Laurence said.[1762] The addition of the American Adam Nussbaum, with whom he had played on John Abercrombie's *Open Land*[1763] in 1998, changed the playing and interpersonal dynamic a bit. "We had train journeys and mad things, getting Kenny across the track . . . There was a different sort of dynamic in the band; [Adam] wanted things to be more organized and stuff. Very different than Martin [France] or Tony Oxley – very different – but a lovely bloke."[1764] Adam's personality off the bandstand was also more outgoing than the eternally reticent Kenny and restrained J.T., which caused a change of energy in the band offstage, too. But Kenny, who was generally attracted to extroverts, enjoyed Adam, and especially liked him musically. "He's a fantastic player, and Kenny liked that strength – and he was great to play with," Chris said.[1765]

The quartet toured together intermittently, especially in France and Switzerland from the late 1990s into the early 2000s. On 3 February 2000, they did a live radio broadcast in Lugano (Switzerland) on RSI Radiotelevisione Svizzera. They did a set of mostly Kenny's tunes, several of which he rarely performed or recorded, including "Kind Folk", "Little Song", "3000", "Salina Street", "Springs Eternal", "Deer Wan", "Where Do We Go from Here?", and "Mark Time". The recording reveals a very rhythmically active ensemble, energized by Nussbaum's vitality and Laurence's free-floating bass, accentuated by J.T.'s elegantly percussive comping and imaginative improvising, all behind Kenny, who at this point is showing a few signs of his age. This manifested not in a loss of strength but some mild inaccuracy, often during the first note of a phrase or melody. Interestingly, trombonist Robin Eubanks had also recalled first hearing signs of this around the same time on the Dave Holland Octet tour, particularly evident to him being someone that didn't hear Kenny play regularly, and whose last memory of him was from the ferocious playing in the Holland quintet of the 1980s. Robin recalled: "It was hard for me to see him diminished like that . . . I guess it's hard to try to alter or compensate for your playing when you still hear the same ideas, I'm sure, and you try to execute the same stuff but it wasn't coming off as strong, obviously, as it was before."[1766] Despite these imperfections, the playing in this Lugano recording is fiery and perhaps more reminiscent of the energy heard in live performances by Kenny's *The Widow in the Window* quintet of the previous decade, with more risk-taking and liveliness in the ensemble evident than the more recent and reserved *Angel Song* quartet. The one standard on the programme was Billy Strayhorn's "A Flower Is a Lovesome Thing", presented by the quartet as a lush ballad feature for J.T., with one of Chris Laurence's most interesting and nimble bass solos and a presentation of the melody showcasing Kenny's still flawless intonation and his beautiful low register on the flugelhorn.[1767] Mark Wheeler remembered hearing this band live and thinking, *Wow, that was good!*[1768]

The quartet was set to record for ECM. Adam Nussbaum recalled they were actually booked to record twice but both times were cancelled; the second attempt had progressed to the point that even flights were booked when news of the cancellation came. This was a mystery to the band, but there are a few theories behind the cancellations. First, ECM was extremely busy during these years. The label recorded or released an average of 30 records annually between 1996 and 2001, with Manfred Eicher producing or overseeing *all of them*. It's possible that he was just too busy at the time, even though he was interested. Manfred himself remembered that group and the intention to record: "It fell through . . . it was something I really wanted to do. It was a very good band when I heard it live, *very* good."[1769] He also alluded to the fact that there were difficulties with Kenny's new-found management:

> In my opinion, the management (John Taylor was also with the same management) was probably not the most, let's say, *communicative*. It's probably difficult to handle these things, also for management, but it was not the most helpful situation for us . . . I had the feeling that maybe some vibes were not right here.[1770]

Mark Wheeler noticed a similar confluence between the end of a working relationship with Eicher and Kenny's getting management: ". . . that thing with ECM just kind of stopped," he said, before qualifying, "my dad *did* fall out with Manfred as well, so he's not entirely innocent in these proceedings!"[1771] We don't know the details of this, but do know that Kenny had a temper and could get very upset on the phone with Eicher occasionally. (Recall that he did this a couple of years before recording *Music for Small and Large Ensembles* during another long lull in recording as leader for ECM.)[1772] "I think we sometimes communicated on the telephone not in the best way," Eicher said, adding that Kenny's mild-mannered demeanour on the phone could also be coupled with a more forceful side: "Sometimes I felt Kenny could show a mixture of being shyly questioning . . . and demanding at the same time, and I thought I just cannot do everything that [he thought] would be a good idea."[1773] It is also important to remember that the sound of this group was a departure from groups that Kenny had led in the recent past – it was more intense and energetic especially in the rhythm section, and might have leaned a little too far into the more straight-ahead postmodern jazz style to fit in with the ECM aesthetic. (This echoes how the hard-hitting *The Widow in the Window* quintet had substantially toned down their approach in the studio with Eicher.)

Regardless of the reason, the group never recorded in the studio and fizzled out over time, except for a one-off gig in May 2002 at the Bath Festival, where American violinist Mark Feldman joined the quartet.[1774] Fortunately, this concert was broadcast the following month on BBC Radio 3. This must have been a difficult concert for Kenny, as he was dealing with an unusual case of gout in his thumb.[1775] He also suffered a couple of memory slips as he introduced the band members, which he handled with great humour and a sense of relaxation, seldom heard when he was on stage:

> You're listening to John Taylor on piano . . . [*applause, cheering*], Chris Laurence on the bass . . . [*applause, cheering*], Adam Nussbaum on drums . . . [*applause, cheering*], and our very special guest . . . [*pause*] . . . [*laughter from audience*] . . . I've gone blank! [*lots of laughter from audience*] . . . [*pause*] . . . [*Kenny chuckles*] . . . Mark Feldman!! [*big cheer from audience*]

Mark Wheeler remembers listening to this at home and being mortified by the long pause, yelling at the radio in vain: *Oh, God. Dad! Dad!* MARK FELDMAN!'[1776] The broadcast announcements continued, Kenny remaining in rare form:

> *Kenny:* Nobody should ever let me announce. I tried to get somebody else to do it, but nobody'll do it! The first piece we played was called "Kind Folk". It's written in 3/4 and 4/4. 3/4 it's "Kind Folk" and 4/4 it's called "For H." and it was written for Harry South. And the next piece we played was called . . . [*to himself*] aw, I've gone blank again . . . [*crowd laughs again*] [*helpful shout-outs from band members*] The third piece we played was called "3000", and it was a piece written for the new millennium. [*laughter from crowd*] I've told that about eight times – nobody laughed before! The

last piece we played was written by John Taylor. It was called "Ambleside". [*Kenny to John*] Is it "Ambleside Days" or "Ambleside"?

*J.T.:* Yep.

*Kenny:* Yes. [*big laugh from audience*] And I've made a very brave attempt to play it. And the next piece we're going to play starts off with the bow and the bass of Chris Laurence playing "Where Do We Go From Here?"[1777]

Rather than regret the lack of an ECM recording, Chris Laurence retained a positive attitude about the group's brief run. "With those sorts of disappointing things, you tend to just carry on and maybe they'll come back again," he said.[1778] But Kenny went public with his frustration in interviews, which couldn't have helped his relationship with Manfred Eicher. In one interview, Kenny said, "I offered things to Manfred and he didn't seem interested in any of them . . . We were supposed to do a quartet [recording] in 2000 and he cancelled it about two weeks before. That really was the end of my association with them. Now that I've recorded for CAM, I'm definitely in ECM's bad books," adding, "I don't know for sure but I think they've become enemies of ECM."[1779]

He wouldn't record another album for ECM for over a dozen years.

———·———

In 1999, concert promoter Olwen Richards contacted American pianist and composer Fred Hersch to organize a concert in Oxford with Kenny and Norma Winstone.[1780] Richards had booked Fred previously for solo piano tours of England and knew that he wanted to work with Kenny and Norma. Fred didn't want the band to appear to be another version of Azimuth, however, so he decided to add a fourth member to their line-up. Percussionist Paul Clarvis "is a party on wheels," Fred said, "and he's game for anything, so we did this concert." The quartet played the concert at St. Barnabas Church in Oxford, which was "absolutely packed", Olwen remembered, adding "the response was incredible".[1781] Andrew Hallifax recorded the concert, and Fred released it as an album titled *4 in Perspective*.[1782]

The album documents the quartet's performance of a few of Fred's tunes, some standards, and Kenny's "Wintersweet", featuring Norma's lyrics. An emotional highlight of the concert was Fred's "Out Some Place", written in memory of Matthew Shepard, a young American who had been targeted for his homosexuality and was brutally beaten and left to die in Wyoming just a year earlier. Called a "cinematic piece" by Fred, "Out Some Place" was very powerful to the audience in Oxford. "When it finished, I'd never quite experienced anything like it," Olwen said, recalling that she had tears running down her cheek. "It was so moving. Nobody clapped or did *anything* for a while," she said, adding, "That concert was magical."[1783] As an encore, Fred called the standard "Memories of You". "You don't hear Kenny with as much musical humour I think, ever, as there," Fred said.[1784]

The following year, Richards was able to get Arts Council funding for a tour of England, performing almost nightly from 6–15 October 2000. As they left the Wheeler's Leytonstone home, Kenny carried a brand-new Yamaha flugelhorn, still in the cardboard box it had arrived in, cellophane-wrapped and unopened. This was quite a remarkable thing for any instrumentalist to do. Kenny didn't concern himself much with the care of his instruments and was also seemingly unconcerned with the choice of instrument itself, not at all worried about taking an untested instrument on tour.[1785] Both Norma and Fred remembered that tour with fondness. Norma said that Fred "loved Ken". Fred recalled Kenny's sense of humour and general demeanour on tour, saying, "He didn't say much, but every once in a while he would come with some line that would just crack everybody up from left field in this little sweet voice that he had."[1786] Kenny's professionalism also clearly impressed him:

> He played his *heart* out when we played together . . . And we'd have rough tour days, not getting any rest and barely getting a shower and then getting to the gig . . . Soundchecking a piano/voice/trumpet/percussion gig is not easy. He was always really patient, and when the lights came up, no matter how it was, he played with the same level of care and . . . *immaculate-ness* every night. You know, there was a signature manoeuvre he would do, this kind of high squeal move. Very rarely did it sound like frustration. But, sometimes, it was really clear that it *was* frustration, like, *I'm just going to blow this out, and I can move on.* He managed all that really well.[1787]

Both also share an endearing little memory of Kenny, during an impromptu band meeting while on tour in Halifax. "We were all having a tough time . . ." Fred said. "We were all going to meet in Fred's room after the gig," Norma said, continuing:

> We had all had a few drinks. And suddenly, a knock at Fred's door, and it was Kenny in his pyjamas. Nothing on his feet, his little feet sticking out . . . And we started laughing, we couldn't stop laughing. I don't know what was funny, but it was just him standing there in his pyjamas all buttoned up, and no socks or anything . . .[1788]

Olwen remembered Kenny being very quiet on the road. "When we were in the van, he used to like to do that word game where you make as many words as you can out of so many letters," she said. "I remember once stopping at a service station on the motorway somewhere and I bought him a big slice of chocolate cake. He was so delighted – he just looked like a little boy when I gave it to him!"[1789]

The following November, the quartet had another English tour. Fred came to London early to rehearse and prepare for the tour and happened to be in the city for his birthday on 21 October. Paul Clarvis hosted a party for him. "I remember seeing Doreen there for sure," Fred said. "Norma and Kenny – we got him into playing all those old Dudley Moore comedy albums with Peter Cook . . . And Norma surprised me – she knew every line!" But this time the chemistry wasn't as strong as on the previous tour. The quartet, travelling together in close quarters with tour organizer Richards, had begun to get on each other's nerves a bit. One night, one of their friends, Father Colum Kelly – who happened to be a huge jazz fan as well as a priest – had been at that night's concert. After the gig, Colum offered the band his church's parish house as a place to hang out and relax. Fred declined and went back to the hotel with Olwen and Jim, their driver. Norma remembered: "Paul was driving, and took me and Kenny to come back to the house. They were drinking whisky . . . I don't remember what I was drinking – and Kenny was so drunk. Paul was drunk, he couldn't drive," so they stayed there.

> We were just talking and laughing. It sort of went on a bit. We had to help Kenny into bed – he could hardly walk. We had never told anyone where we were . . . so I think we tried to ring [Olwen]. I think she had a mobile, but they weren't so good then. The next morning we turned up, and I remember Olwen being very upset with us that we hadn't let anybody know where we were. We'd just disappeared for the night![1790]

Norma also recalls that, during this second tour, the band went into Maida Vale Studios in London in an attempt to make another recording . . .

> . . . but it didn't work somehow. I don't know what it was. And in the middle of this, we're all trying to improvise in this kind of free-ish section of the tune. And we were all at it – headphones on, couldn't really see each other. And then suddenly, Kenny's voice came into all of our headphones: "Olwen at night . . . is a beautiful sight . . ." And that was it.[1791]

The band all broke out in laughter. Kenny, usually reticent to take control, took it upon himself to sabotage the take the band was making and provide what was probably a welcome bit of good-natured comic relief, albeit at their dear tour promoter's expense.

Following this tour, the group didn't work together as a quartet again. "It was a great shame that it split up," Olwen Richards said. But Norma and Fred continued to have an association, and Kenny would perform with Fred again in New York just a year later.

---

Back in the busy summer of 1999, Kenny had found time to play on a big-band recording to mark the 50th birthday year of his close friend and colleague Stan Sulzmann. The resulting album, *Birthdays, Birthdays*,[1792] is an outstanding big-band record, showcasing Stan's substantial talents as a composer. The two days of sessions featured an all-star band that including long-time old friends Derek Watkins, Henry Lowther, and Ray Warleigh, alongside newer colleagues John Parricelli and Paul Clarvis. Recorded at Angel Studios in Islington, it was released on Clarvis's Village Life label.

But this period would have other memories for Kenny because of concerns about Doreen, who had gone back into hospital for another heart valve replacement. As worried as he was for her health, he also knew how reliant he was upon her. Friends used to affectionately joke (even in his presence) about the times he'd offered to make a cup of tea and, five minutes later, they'd find him still rifling through the cupboards searching for the required materials, before muttering an apologetic "Sorry, Doreen usually makes the tea."[1793] Chris Laurence recalled that " . . . he was not capable of making a cup of tea or even making a piece of toast, or doing anything in that respect, because Doreen did everything for him and he was quite helpless in that way . . . but then, he was a genius . . ."[1794] Kenny's sister Mabel shared the same observations and also gave Doreen the credit she deserved: "He just didn't do anything around the house . . . I don't think he'd have had the successful career if he hadn't had the wife that he had . . . Luckily, he had someone like Doreen, because she was the best thing that could've ever happened to him."[1795] Thankfully for everyone, Doreen's procedure was successful, and she was soon back to health and home with her Ken.

———

In January of 2000, Kenny led a short tour to mark his 70th birthday. It was just three dates: Manchester, Birmingham, and London, the last of which was at the Queen Elizabeth Hall on the 14th, which was his actual birthday. The band, listed as an iteration of "The Creative Jazz Orchestra", was made up of an unusual instrumentation. With Kenny on solo flugelhorn, the ensemble was absent other trumpeters, similar to the 1978 *Little Suite* instrumentation, and featured two pianists, John Taylor and Huw Warren. It was augmented by three trombones and a French horn, plus two saxophonists, Julian Argüelles and Stan Sulzmann. Completing the personnel was bassist Dave Holland and the great American drummer Billy Hart, whom Kenny had known since his tour with Stan Getz decades before.[1796]

Unlike his previous birthday tours on which he often premiered new works, Kenny chose music for this occasion that he had composed and arranged years earlier for two BBC broadcasts (1984 and 1985), featuring the drummerless ensembles listed as the "Kenny Wheeler Octet" and "Kenny Wheeler Tentette", respectively.[1797] The large ensemble material slated for the first half of the birthday tour concerts included "Kayak", "Old Ballad", "See Horse", "C Man", "Sea Lady", and "C.C. Signor", all of which had been recorded on 1992's *Kayak*. But the second half of the programme featured Kenny and the all-star rhythm section playing a mix of older repertoire ("Deer Wan", "Old Ballad", "Little Song"), and more recent tunes ("3000" and "Kind Folk"). In addition, at the Queen Elizabeth Hall concert, Norma Winstone joined the quintet for a performance of one of Kenny's newest compositions, "Where Do We Go from Here?"[1798]

Alyn Shipton noted in his review that, before taking the stage in Birmingham, Kenny said, "For God's sake, don't mention my bloody birthday." Shipton went on to call him, at age 70, "one of the most potent and influential trumpeters and composers in jazz", but labelled the first half of the concert "a dull blur". His review was much more complimentary of the second half of the concert, noting that the quintet had "found a perfect balance between composition and extended improvisation".[1799] Duncan Heining was similarly nonplussed by the opening music of the concert, saying that "it was all just a bit hesitant and never quite sparked, despite the quality of Wheeler's compositions." But, like Shipton, Heining was far more effusive in his praise of the second half of the concert, and especially its featured player:

> . . . the star of this show was Kenny Wheeler. He seems to be playing now with even greater confidence and sureness of touch. His tone on trumpet and flugelhorn is to die for. There's no drying up of ideas and no constriction of the imagination. At 70, Wheeler is at the top of his game . . . we, the audience, closed with a standing ovation for the performance, for the career and the man.[1800]

This reaction from the Queen Elizabeth Hall audience must certainly have echoed the reception he had witnessed there for the premiere of *The Sweet Time Suite* ten years prior. But Kenny, suspicious as ever of good publicity and his own ability to draw a crowd, told an interviewer before the concert when asked if it will be a sold-out affair: "I don't know, I'd like to think so . . .", adding with a chuckle, "you never know – there could be nobody there."[1801]

———·———

In Spring 2000, Kenny took part in another tour with drummer Billy Hart. Vocalist Christine Tobin had recorded a new album in New York with Hart and guest saxophonist Mark Turner. When it came time to launch the record around the Cheltenham Jazz Festival, Mark Turner was unavailable, so Christine asked Kenny to fulfil the role of guest front-line player. He joined Billy Hart in the group along with Austrian bassist Peter Herbert and guitarist Phil Robson.

When it came time for Christine's tour, they played four nights at London's Pizza Express before heading to Cheltenham. Phil remembered the warmth between Kenny and Billy on the road and the amiable vibe as they chatted about mutual friends and past experiences. When it came to the music itself, Kenny was on fire, not only blazing through an exceptionally uptempo version of "Just One of Those Things", but also weaving in and around the vocals with unparalleled grace and economy. Christine had some profound recollections of how Kenny approached playing with a singer:

I was in awe of him obviously, but he was just very gracious, and he really listened . . . everything just blossomed and opened up musically because of that, and because he's bringing so much to it . . . I think a great musician listens to the *spirit* of the thing, it's not necessarily the *notes* or the *intellectual*; they're picking up on whatever that person's spirit is in the music. That's the imaginative bit of the individual brain, and he's operating on that level in a very deep way . . . It was like he was totally himself, but also blended in as well. Just no ego, really.[1802]

Kenny's unintentionally comic nature showed in the pub after the Cheltenham gig. He shuffled over to the bar, already self-conscious of being in such a crowded space, particularly one crammed full of musicians and fans who recognized him. He insisted on buying a round for the band, but his demeanour made him so invisible that the bartender ignored him; Phil had to step in and help him get served. There was also a jazz photography exhibition adorning the walls of the pub, attracting more people. Eventually, Kenny parked himself at the end of the bar with his drink before looking up, only to discover he'd sat directly under an enormous photo of himself.[1803]

———·———

In 2002, the International Trumpet Guild (ITG) held its annual conference in Manchester, and chose to spotlight a number of artists from the UK; accordingly, they booked Kenny and John Taylor to offer a featured duo concert in one of the coveted evening spots. The typical ITG featured soloist is usually an extroverted type, generously displaying virtuosity of the "higher, faster, louder" category – in short, resembling a Derek Watkins far more than a Kenny Wheeler. Consequently, the audience was sparse, appreciative yet reserved, and certainly not as numerous nor demonstrative as it might have been for a Maynard Ferguson or Arturo Sandoval appearance.[1804] As with most featured events at ITG conferences, the programme began with a pre-concert fanfare. In this case, the "fanfare" was actually a ten-minute piece written for the occasion by Kenny himself for a quartet of American graduate student jazz trumpeters from the Eastman School of Music, including Eli Asher, Andrew Cheetham, Jason Price, and Brian Shaw.

Once the duo took the stage, they began with one of J.T.'s tunes, "Between Moons". Jason Price remembered that, not long after they began, "one trumpet jock started to sneak out until Kenny did one of those high squealy things and he turned around like, *Oh, he can play high and fast so it might get interesting . . .* But then it went to piano solo and he left!"[1805] The duo followed with several of Kenny's compositions, and then one of his favourite standards, "By Myself". By this point, the audience had warmed up considerably and gave Kenny and J.T. a standing ovation as they finished their programme. As an encore, they ended with a brilliant interpretation of another of Kenny's favourite tunes, Billy Strayhorn's "A Flower Is a Lovesome Thing". Although a few people approached Kenny to congratulate him after the concert, few lingered, so Kenny and J.T. joined the Eastman Quartet with their trumpet professor James Thompson and Canadian trumpet star Jens Lindemann for a pint of beer at the pub.[1806]

———··———

Although they had very different personalities, Kenny long enjoyed a mutual admiration with composer/valve trombonist Bob Brookmeyer. For at least a few years, they had exchanged letters, with Kenny interested in pursuing some sort of project together.[1807] Their chance to work together finally came in 2002 when the two agreed to record the album *Island* for Artists House records.[1808] Joining the brass soloist headliners were Frank Carlberg on piano, Jeremy Allen on bass, and John Hollenbeck on drums.[1809]

The Artists House production was not simply a recording project, but an interactive experience for fans and music students, including a DVD with the audio recording in surround sound and in 24-bit stereo. It also included video interviews with the quintet, video of the recording sessions, solo transcriptions, analyses of the tunes by Brookmeyer and Wheeler, and lead sheets of the compositions. For the purposes of this book, by far the most intriguing extra feature is the nearly 20-minute video interview with Kenny, filmed with him seated at his piano in his home music room in London. The format of this release, with all the accompanying resources, follows the trend of treating Kenny as a subject worthy of research, collecting and providing information for future study.

In one video, Brookmeyer takes apart the music, candidly discussing the composition of the title track. But Kenny is less comfortable discussing his tune "Before the First Time", spiralling into a rambling bit of self-analysis, never willing to expressly say *this is that* and shedding more light throughout the process on his self-doubting internal monologue than the theory behind his compositions:

> I guess I wrote "Before the First Time" six months to a year ago, I couldn't say exactly when. And it's a . . . simple 32-bar tune, which a lot of tunes are . . . Like most of my pieces, the second half is in a different pitch to the second half. [By "pitch" here he means "key."] I didn't really realize I was doing that for all of the years until maybe ten years ago, I thought, *oh, that's what I do.* And I was unhappy to know that because I don't like to know what I do. I like to think it's instinctive. I know I have a system, but I don't really want to know what the system is. Anyway, that's a typical example – the first half is in a different pitch . . . I never think about key signatures. I never put a key signature on any of my pieces. Sometimes I try to figure out what key they're in at the actual moment, but . . . there probably is, or maybe there is a key signature that goes through the whole thing, I don't know, but I could never say what it is. But I might look and say, the first three chords are C minor, and kind of a B7 going to E minor. So you could

say the first bar's in C minor but then it goes right away from there in the second bar towards E minor. And the whole piece is like that. You could sort of go through it and say *now we're here*, and *now we're there*, but not the whole piece. I couldn't say . . .[1810]

One gem of the bonus DVD is a video of the quintet listening to some play-backs of the recording. Kenny breaks the group up with laughter while punning on his title "Before the First Time". He said, "I've still got to write 'After the Last Time' and 'Halfway Between Midway'!" In another moment captured on the video, Hollenbeck addresses Kenny with great admiration and honesty, saying, "Sometimes it's hard for me when I'm playing with you. It's hard not to just go crazy, because there's something about your playing – all of a sudden you hit those high notes, I just get so excited, it's hard not to just, you know, let you have it." Always a fan of active drummers, Kenny replied, "I like that – the more the merrier!"[1811]

Reviews of the album were quite positive. In his review for *JazzTimes*, Thomas Conrad said the "music is first class", conceding that

> it would have been reasonable to wonder whether the former's linear, logical language would complement the latter's personal harmonic unpredictability and floating melodicism. No worries. Brookmeyer's valve trombone and Wheeler's flugelhorn irrefutably belong together, in a common zone of golden colour and rich timbre, whether flowing and commingling or arraying exactitudes of counterpoint or suggestively offsetting, in contrapuntal opposition.[1812]

---

During this time, Kenny appeared on a couple of other unlikely projects. One is the track "Punto a Capo", which was released in 2001 on an album called *Uno In Più* by the Italian pop rock group 883,[1813] which is about as much of a mismatch as one can imagine. It is especially head-scratching that there was someone associated with the band who obviously knew Kenny's playing well enough to have requested him as a special guest soloist; whoever it was, having made that decision, they then placed Kenny in an incredibly inappropriate musical context. Contrast this with a more successful pairing of Kenny at around the same time with a rock band that already had a leaning towards free improvisation and electronica: his 2003 collaboration with the group Spiritualized, on their album *Amazing Grace*,[1814] playing free with Evan Parker on the track "The Power and the Glory" and a short, understated solo on "Rated X". *Pitchfork* calls the former "the record's most forward-looking moment, as it builds to a massive, cacophonous swell, aided by a horn section that puts British improv legends Kenny Wheeler and Evan Parker in front of their largest audience yet."[1815]

Another unlikely context for Kenny is his appearance as soloist on composer Karl Jenkins's album *Adiemus V: Vocalise*,[1816] on the track "Berceuse pour un enfant solitaire". Jenkins, a successful composer blending world music with light classical sounds, goes all the way back to Kenny's days in the 1960s jazz scene, including when they briefly played together in Ronnie Scott's nine-piece group. Here Kenny is beautifully recorded; whatever he might have thought of the project, the auditory result presents his sound at age 73 with gorgeously stunning results.

———·———

Although he was recording more and more of his own music during this time, Kenny could still become frustrated when put in situations for which he felt ill-prepared. This occurred in an otherwise comfortable setting where he was recording *Brand New*, the second album he made as part of Marc Copland's trio with John Abercrombie.[1817] The record included two of his own compositions, including a new piece presumably dedicated to his Italian singer friend Tiziana, called "Watching Simona". Although the musical results don't seem to convey his uneasiness, Kenny was upset while attempting to record the Nat Adderley standard "Jive Samba". After several takes of the tune weren't quite working, producer Hein van de Geyn left the booth and came into the studio to suggest that perhaps they try recording a different tune. Van de Geyn remembered Kenny had teared up with emotion and said, "I just can't play that kind of stuff – I never could."[1818]

Van de Geyn made a couple of observations about this. The first, specific to the situation, was: "he was somehow so frustrated with that as well as apologetic – but he also knew that he was cornered in a musical expectation that he couldn't fight himself out of. And it was very interesting for me. That was a big lesson about, yes, we are stupid with our education [system] to try and make people do everything. There are people you just shouldn't put in a salsa band [for instance] – they just can't!"[1819] Van de Geyn also had a more general thought about Kenny's special way of playing: "I'm sure that Kenny cannot play bebop; but I'm so happy that because of that, he created something else that was his own."[1820]

A similarly uneasy episode was when Kenny teamed up again with pianist Fred Hersch at the Jazz Standard in New York from 19–22 November 2002. It was Hersch's first gig at the club, and getting Kenny on the engagement caused him to jump through a number of logistical hoops. Fred remembered:

> We had to go through a lot of Byzantine things to get him his work permit. Since he had his trumpet with him, he didn't want any problems with immigration, so I had to go through the Toronto musician's union . . . and they had to push some levers, and I had to write my congressman in New York to get [approval] . . .[1821]

All these hassles were worth it, since Fred was so eager to play with Kenny once again, and to get him on the bill with tenor saxophonist Mark Turner, bassist Ben Street, and drummer Nasheet Waits. "It was incredible to play with him, the way his sound would saturate the bandstand," Street remembered.[1822] However, despite the joy the musicians felt about playing with Kenny, Fred's choice of repertoire for these concerts proved to be problematic. "We played mostly my material including these two tunes that I wrote for him: 'A Lark' and 'Up in the Air', and he played them beautifully," Fred said. But even though the pianist was happy, Kenny was uncomfortable. Fred remembered that "One night we were just at the end of the set, and I called a blues of some sort, and I remember him getting off the stage saying, 'I haven't played a blues in 20 years . . .' because he doesn't really do that."[1823] Although he was aware of Kenny's preference for playing his own material, Fred pressed on, with the group playing the pianist's music and some tunes by Thelonious Monk. The younger musicians, especially Mark and Ben, were protective of Kenny, feeling that he had been inadvertently put on the spot his advanced age. This is yet another example of Kenny being so fluent in his own music but increasingly uncomfortable playing the music of others, especially something so inside the bebop tradition and away from his wheelhouse as "Rhythm-A-Ning". These musical circumstances at the Jazz Standard led to Kenny being despondent backstage. "It was Mark Turner and me consoling him in the dressing room about how great he sounded because he felt bad on the gig all week with Fred," Ben Street said. "We were really upset and didn't want him to be in that position, and of course, we loved him, you know." Kenny's diet at the club before the sets was not helping matters. Ben continued:

> He's not ordering any food, ever. He's just getting lemon meringue pie and a ginger ale, and I'm looking at him, and I'm like "Kenny, man, what are you doing!? That's the *last* thing you're going to want to eat." Even if you're 21 that might be a problem . . . Finally, on the fourth night of six nights, he concedes and has a little food, and it's macaroni and cheese! And *then* the pie and the ginger ale . . . Then of course the sugar crash, trying to play the [Monk] rhythm changes, and then [being] bummed out in the dressing room . . .[1824]

But Ben was sensitive to how the material was making Kenny feel, saying that "I liked what he was doing on the rhythm changes – it was just that he sounded uncomfortable . . . you know, like a genuine musician with taste *would* feel, like, *Am I getting the details of this?* and feeling bad that it was not his world. I would never say that he couldn't play rhythm changes – it's more like the feeling of a sensitive person knowing that he doesn't know the details . . ."[1825] And even though the music that Kenny wrote and played regularly on his own gigs is far more harmonically complex than the blues or rhythm changes, this was simply not where he spent his musical time or energy. All these issues would come to a more dramatic breaking point in the same city a few short years later, in a group led by a different pianist.

———·———

Thankfully, some of the other things Kenny was asked to do around this time were coming from a deeply familiar place. One notable project took him back to his beginnings as a bandleader: a UK tour of the music from his *Windmill Tilter* album. In the early 2000s, saxophonist and composer Tim Garland was working closely with John Dankworth, and a passing conversation between them about the fact that *Windmill Tilter* didn't get heard anymore led them to the library in Dankworth's Wavendon home. They dug out the original parts and remaining scores, finding some of the folders still held a pencil and eraser, seemingly untouched since the '60s.[1826] Tim secured funding to adapt the music for his new Underground Orchestra and take the project on the road in late 2002 into 2003, featuring Kenny as a soloist from within the trumpet section, alongside lead trumpeter and London Jazz Orchestra founder Noel Langley, plus Dankworth bandmate Henry Lowther. This band also included young trombonist Barnaby Dickinson, who would later become a regular part of Kenny's big bands.[1827]

The *Windmill Tilter* tour was a rewarding one for Kenny and was made even more enjoyable with his old friend Henry by his side. Whether Kenny's age affected his concentration or he simply got lost in the moment, on one occasion there was a silence between two of the movements. After a few too many seconds passed, Barnaby heard a soft voice mutter, "What happens now?" to which Henry calmly replied, "I think it's you, Ken . . ." Kenny immediately launched into an explosive solo cadenza.[1828]

As nice as it was for Kenny to revisit his old work and see it recognized, he was a musician that liked to move forward. Sometimes, when an established band or college would enquire about playing some of his past work, he would comment with his Eeyore-like persona, "Well, that's great, but what about the newer pieces?"[1829] As Kenny's 80th birthday approached, he still wanted to explore new projects, but to travel less and renew his focus on playing his own music. All this would bring about unexpected challenges and frustrations with the UK scene, and new personnel issues to overcome.

# 8  The Long Waiting

> Geniuses only come 'round once in a while. What's the point in waiting until he's dead?
>
> *Derek Watkins*

As the new millennium approached, Kenny found it harder than ever to get work in the UK. The fee his management was now asking for, though deserved, had made it nearly impossible for him to do regular club gigs in his home country. "Andrea insisted on Ken getting a huge fee, even for gigs in London," Stan Sulzmann said. This resulted in Marini booking Kenny most often in and around Italy, which meant the trumpeter always had to fly there for work. Stan also said that

> . . . it wasn't that Ken couldn't get any work, [but] there were lots of factors that made it impossible to get work: . . . the fact that in England – probably like most Americans or anyone else – if they do gigs in their own country, in their hometown, they're not going to get the same kind of money as when they go out touring around the world.[1830]

Knowing that Kenny was frustrated with the lack of local gigs and that travel was becoming more and more difficult for the nearly 70-year-old trumpeter, Evan Parker contacted Stan in an attempt to create more playing opportunities for Kenny near London. At the time, Stan and guitarist John Parricelli were playing with Kenny often, so they started a trio named Ordesa, which was their attempt to "keep something going with Ken", in an ensemble that was "workable", Stan said, adding "the smaller the group, the better it was" for Kenny.[1831]

The group often played at the Vortex in London, where Sulzmann had been running a regular night as a "house band" with John Parricelli and various special guests. The Vortex was near Kenny's home and was a place in which he was comfortable and with friends who knew his music. The trio played a BBC broadcast for Jez Nelson's *Jazz on 3* show and got some gigs in Germany from their self-titled album, released in 2002.[1832]

Through a connection with Evan Parker, they also secured a date at Amsterdam's Bimhuis, one of the premier jazz concert venues in Europe. Stan suggested that the particulars of booking the trio go through promoter and producer Christine Allen, who was doing a lot for Stan and other musicians at the time. But Stan claimed, "as soon as Andrea heard about it, he contacted the Bimhuis", and, in his view, "they cancelled the gig because [the promoter] didn't want to work with Andrea."[1833] All of this was further complicated by Kenny's non-confrontational nature: never taking charge or directly telling anyone what he wanted. "Ken just sits in the middle and doesn't do anything," Stan said: "He just sort of 'goes away', and I was trying to make things happen [for him]!"[1834] Thankfully, Kenny's loyal friends persisted and he continued to work in and around London. People like Stan and Evan would be increasingly leaned upon to create opportunities for him to play his music in later life with his fellow London musicians.

—————·—————

In 2003, Kenny composed a new suite for jazz ensemble. The yet-untitled work was over 40 minutes long and written for Kenny's standard instrumentation since *Music for Large and Small Ensembles*: a big band with added flugelhorn and voice. Soon after it was completed, Stan Sulzmann and Evan Parker once again stepped up to help realize the project. They contacted Christine Allen to see if she might be interested in organizing a new tour coinciding with his upcoming 75th birthday in January 2005, presenting Kenny's new suite as the centrepiece of the programme.[1835] Christine agreed, and began to raise the nearly £40,000 she estimated would be required to make the tour possible. She approached Andrew Kurowski of the BBC, who responded by supporting the new work as a commission and paying the substantial costs for a copyist to professionally prepare Kenny's score and create parts for the band. By pursuing additional funding sources, she secured the remaining amount, and the tour was on.[1836]

As soon as Kenny's manager Andrea Marini heard about Allen's plan to present the tour, he flew to London to discuss it with her. She met him in a café during the summer of 2003: "I walked in, and the first words he said to me were, 'I'm way ahead of you.' He didn't say *Hello* or anything . . . I just said, 'Oh, really? In what way?' He said, 'I've already got a performance of Kenny's [new] piece in Verona.'"[1837] This was problematic because the BBC required the first performance of the work in return for their support of the commission. "That's a shame," she said. "Well, that's how it's going to be," Marini replied. Allen asked him, "I guess if he's written that piece, he'll have to write another piece . . . Does he have time to write a whole new piece?" He told her that he had a tour of Italy planned with Kenny and the big band (which never materialized). Marini eventually relented, and Allen proceeded with planning the tour. She organized seven dates in all, with concerts in London, Manchester, Birmingham, Southampton, Basingstoke, Bristol, and Dublin.

The choice of personnel was also fraught with difficulties. At the outset, Kenny sent Christine Allen a list of potential players including Lee Konitz, for whom an additional solo role had been created. Kenny, of course, always wanted John Taylor to play, but since Norma was already on the tour, J.T. was not an option. After considering several other pianists, Stan Sulzmann got the idea to ask Gwilym Simcock, fast emerging as one of the major new stars in jazz. Kenny also contacted trombonist Hugh Fraser to conduct. When it came to the choice of trumpet section, Kenny was slightly more opinionated, writing that he wanted "Derek Watkins, Henry Lowther, John Barclay, and Ian Hamer" but remaining both characteristically non-committal and deferential to his long-standing lead player, adding " . . . if Derek agrees . . ."[1838]

The project was set to begin on 12 January with two days of rehearsals preceding the Queen Elizabeth Hall concert on the 14th, Kenny's birthday. When Hugh Fraser began to lead the rehearsals, he said, "My first job was to mediate between Lee Konitz and Kenny. I think Kenny wanted to sit, and Lee wanted to stand. We spent like half an hour trying to figure that out," he said. Kenny loved Konitz's playing, his admiration going all the way back to when he was a teenager in Canada. Some other members of the band weren't fans of Konitz's execution of the parts, however, complaining among themselves about his intonation in particular. (Lead trumpeter and self-appointed band prankster Derek Watkins would occasionally make jokes on the bus like "Watch out for that there, Lee, it's SHARP!" – once even going so far as adjusting the mouthpiece on Konitz's saxophone, which had been left alone onstage, to the amusement of a few bandmates looking on.[1839]) Konitz had been a hugely successful and effective small-group collaborator with Kenny on the recent *Angel Song*, but he was perhaps a more unorthodox choice for the shared solo spot at the front of the big band where other ensemble skills are needed. His inclusion was consistent with Kenny's original *Song for Someone* ethos of incorporating his favourite musicians regardless how unconventional their participation may appear. Fraser explained:

> I think Kenny was hoping he could have Lee on there to do his thing and it would fit into this greater good. In some places it did succeed, but there were some places where it definitely *did not* succeed . . . Kenny [would] rather have someone who was creative *do something* and have it not work than get some guys who could play through his music and just make it sound nice.[1840]

Other members of the band were less diplomatic about Konitz's involvement in the tour. One, who wishes to remain off the record, said:

> I didn't like what happened with Lee on that tour . . . I just felt Lee had his own agenda a little bit, and wasn't completely 100% there with Kenny being [the leader] . . . He loved the music, and he loved the thing, but he was, you know, being Lee . . . He brought his own stuff with him, and [said] how he thought things should go . . . And I don't know if Kenny wanted to say [something] – I had a feeling that he did.[1841]

In addition to negotiating between Kenny and Lee, Hugh also had to ease tensions with audio engineers during soundchecks and concerts. Despite

Photo 40: Kenny's big band in soundcheck for the 75th birthday tour, Bristol.
Courtesy Gwilym Simcock

having his regular sound engineer Paul Sparrow on the tour, Kenny's hearing was ailing and his impatience at soundchecks was only getting worse with age. "[Kenny] would get very upset and take it personally," Hugh said. "A lot of my job was trying to keep him calm . . . As he got deafer he needed a lot of [his sound] in the monitor, so it got overbearing sometimes for the rhythm section later on in his life."[1842]

The first concert of the tour in the Queen Elizabeth Hall began with three small-group tunes, including two Wheeler originals ("Kind Folk" and "Mark Time") and one tune by Konitz ("Subconscious Lee"). The big band came onstage for the final two numbers of this first half, playing Kenny's "Gentle Piece" and featuring Norma Winstone on Kenny's arrangement of the Irving Berlin standard "How Deep is the Ocean".

Unfortunately, the sound on the first half of the concert was marred by technical problems. Due to a fault with the mixing board, balances were off and the overall sound quality suffered greatly. The result must have been quite unpleasant: in his otherwise positive review for *The Times*, Alyn Shipton spent the first half of his write-up critiquing the "amateurism" of the audio crew, concluding "this painful first half is best forgotten".[1843] The *Guardian's* John Fordham ignored the sound issues and concentrated on the interaction between Kenny and his star soloist line-up, saving the most complimentary language for the youthful pianist:

> Konitz's filmy alto-sax lines complemented the typical Wheeler atmosphere of mournful ecstasy, before young piano recruit Gwilym Simcock delivered the first of a series of glittering solos. A startled turn of the head and appreciative smile from the old master Konitz confirmed what a class act Simcock has so quickly become.[1844]

The audio issue was fixed by the second half, which was an overall happier affair. Fordham noted that the band and sold-out Queen Elizabeth Hall audience startled Kenny by singing "a surprise rendition of 'Happy Birthday' created from what the startled Wheeler thought were the opening chords" before the band began to play his new suite.[1845] Alyn Shipton noted that the gesture was "a measure of the affection in which this Canadian expatriate trumpeter and composer is held in his adopted land . . ."[1846] Shipton was impressed: "At its best the new suite matched anything that Wheeler has created in his long career, and his elegantly wheezy solos proved that at 75 his own playing is still central to his tonal landscape." Considering the scope of Kenny's previous large-scale compositional output – including *Windmill Tilter*, *Song for Someone*, and *The Sweet Time Suite* – this is certainly high praise, and may be cause for fans of Kenny's music to reconsider and investigate this lesser-known work. The *2005 Suite*, as it became known, is indeed an exceptional piece of writing. It is a work of variety and development, full of Kenny's strong, memorable melodies, but also notable as one of his "true" suites. While some of his other larger works often consist of individual compositions that could stand alone, the *2005 Suite* has all the connecting material between "movements" written right into the music, creating a unified extended piece.

The day after the Queen Elizabeth Hall concert, the band set out for a concert at the Royal Northern College of Music in Manchester. Bus travel brought out all the musicians' personalities; the rambunctious brass players hung out in the back, with trumpeter John Barclay as the "life of the party", never letting anyone sleep.[1847] Dave Holland usually sat in the middle, surrounded by old friends from earlier tours and newer musicians to the band. Kenny and Doreen sat quietly in front. Although he was not frail at this point, Kenny still had to be careful when boarding and exiting the bus.[1848] Doreen remarked that Kenny's health declined a bit at some point preceding this tour after he suffered what she speculated had been a mini-stroke, noting that his speech had become a bit slurred.[1849] (Remarkably, his trumpet and flugelhorn playing seemed largely unaffected at the time.)

The review in the *Manchester Evening News* was less enthusiastic than its London counterparts, saying "the music didn't always match the grandeur of the occasion", adding that "Wheeler's orchestration of 'How Deep Is the Ocean' made rather a meal of a simple melody."[1850] Peter Bacon's review of the next night's concert in Birmingham reflected Kenny's love of wordplay in its clever title, "It's My Party, I'll Be Shy If I Want To", and was warmer to the band and seemed to embrace the music on a deeper level. "Rarely have we heard such consistently radiant music from this reticent man," wrote Bacon, adding "the rhythms were light, from bossa to waltz, the horns forceful and muscular, and the solo interludes full of fireworks." He also contrasted the audience's reaction to the concert with Kenny's onstage demeanour: "A full house had been buzzing with anticipation beforehand and was purring with contentment at the end. And Kenny? Well, as usual, once there was no more music to be made, he just looked anxious as anything to get away from all the adulation and out of the limelight."[1851]

The English portion of the tour ended with a concert at St. George's in Bristol on the 20th, with a two-day break before the final concert in Dublin on the 23rd. Due to prior commitments, Dave Holland and Lee Konitz were unable to play this final date. Chris Laurence as a replacement on bass was an easy choice for Kenny, but he could not decide how to handle Konitz's absence. He left this for others to figure out, ultimately leading to an argument between Ray Warleigh and Stan Sulzmann, which required their relationship to undergo some considerable repairing in the years that followed. Stan, logically wanted to preserve the same sax "section" so someone new wasn't coming in cold to the ensemble side of the music, and Ray, understandably, wanted to take up the chance of playing the soloist's role down front in Konitz's place. Kenny's fear of hurting either of his friends' feelings and his chronic inability to make a choice likely caused their regrettable falling out. Evan Parker said that Kenny had "what you would call a *negligent side* to him", even going so far as to say that he "was a dreadful coward of things like that". Although this sounds like a harsh assessment, Evan also profoundly understood and forgave the most frustrating elements of his friend's complex personality:

> . . . he was conveying about what was the best of him . . . through the music. All the other weaknesses and everything [else] became irrelevant, because you know it's only someone who's truly in touch with their own best self that can write melodies and harmonies like that.[1852]

Fortunately, the *Irish Times* reviewer Ray Comiskey was unaware of both the absence of two of the band's stars and of the interpersonal difficulties at the time; instead, he was simultaneously impressed with the band's performance and aware of the significance of Kenny's newest work:

> By some creative alchemy, Wheeler's compositions (and orchestrations) are often instantly identifiable as his. They have a very savoury melodic grace, a gentleness tinged with melancholy, sometimes with ominous undertones, but always with an underlying strength and, where necessary, enough grit to contrast with the beauty . . . Wheeler's lengthy suite,

*2005*, was remarkable not only for the quality of his writing again, and the superior solo work, but also for his ability to reconcile surprise with inevitability. It's an astonishing work . . . A night to remember.[1853]

With the music being so well received by listeners and musicians alike, Christine Allen had the idea of recording the music from the tour, especially the *2005 Suite* and releasing it as an album. An engineer recorded in multitrack the concerts in Birmingham, Southampton, and Basingstoke. He gave all the recorded data to her on 18 DVDs. Tragically, the DVDs were either damaged or formatted incorrectly, and despite significant data recovery efforts, at the time of this writing, they are unreadable.[1854]

Life at home on Wallwood Road continued to be Kenny's solace through this period. There, he made an unlikely domestic alliance late in his life: his granddaughter Sophie's dog, Alfie. According to the family, Kenny had always made friends around pets, theorizing that his quiet, gentle way probably made dogs and cats feel calm in his presence. Nick Smart remembers being at the Wheeler home on Wallwood Road one time and hearing Kenny in his music room, alone, talking to someone more than he usually ever did; that someone turned out to be Alfie the dog. On another occasion, Kenny decided to walk down to the corner store and buy a newspaper. Unable to find the leash, Kenny just let Alfie follow him to the store and back, the dog completely untethered. When they returned and Kenny told the family about their little excursion, the family was shocked that the dog would just follow him obediently, although some suspected that Alfie was keeping an eye on Kenny, and not the other way around.[1855]

Travelling long distances away from home was becoming more of an issue now that Kenny was well into his eighth decade, but he continued to take on guest residencies at universities around the world. But booking Kenny for such trips was beginning to bring its own new challenges. Several educational institutions in the US and Europe began to face unexpected difficulties once Kenny had accepted their invitation, including extra costs and a lack of flexibility with the management's demands.[1856] It was concerning that, on the one hand, these kinds of residencies were increasingly important for Kenny as both a source of employment and as an opportunity to teach now that his relationship with Banff was finished; also, the schools themselves were finding it harder to actually book him. These difficulties were beginning to be felt among concert promoters as well. Certain concert promoters at the time appear to have shared the opinion of John Cumming, director of Serious, a London production company (which, among other things, organized the

London Jazz Festival). Looking back, he expressed the view that, on balance, from a UK perspective, Kenny and J.T.'s management might inadvertently have reduced the opportunities they were both able to take.[1857]

Once any booking and logistical challenges had passed and Kenny arrived at an event in person, things would go much more smoothly and his presence became a thrill for those involved. During a 2004 visit to the University of Iowa campus, Kenny rehearsed and performed with the faculty and the student jazz ensemble. Professor John Rapson described the power of hearing Kenny play live for the first time: "I came back from first rehearsal and started to cry. To hear that sound I'd known so many years was tremendously moving. It was like a myth became physical right in your presence." During his residency, Kenny used Rapson's office to practise and write while the professor was teaching or in meetings. One day, as Rapson returned to his studio, Kenny asked him to play a newly minted tune for him at the piano. Rapson obliged. "I sat down and started to work out some things with the chords and so on. And [Kenny] said, 'No, no, no . . . Get up!' And he put the pedal all the way to the floor, and I couldn't believe it – just a *mash* of sound!" (Kenny's piano playing could be as powerful as his trumpet playing; his volume was surprising in person on either instrument.) A few months later, the tune, which he titled "Iowa City", would be the opening track on his next recording.

American pianist, composer, and teacher Kenny Werner first met Kenny Wheeler in the 1990s; they later worked together during the summer of 1998 as faculty at the Banff Centre in Canada. (It was Werner's first year, Wheeler's last.) The following year, they toured North America and Europe together as a duo. They played several of their own compositions and even covered music written by others, including Tom Harrell's "Sail Away". He played it "as if he'd written it himself," Werner said.[1858] The duo's plane was several hours delayed for their concert at The Outpost in Albuquerque. If this were not disastrous enough, the airline also lost their luggage, so they had to go for a quick shopping trip to purchase a new set of clothes. When they took the stage at 11 pm to start the concert four hours late, the trumpeter was wearing a new outfit with the tags still attached.[1859]

They began the concert with Wheeler's "Everybody's Song But My Own". "We played some of his tunes; I wrote a couple of tunes and brought some of my old tunes. They were beautiful concerts," Werner said. Despite their vastly different personalities, the duo had a deep level of musical interaction which Werner called "complete osmosis". "That was gold," he said. "We had a real thing. It's too bad we didn't record."[1860]

A few years after their initial work together as a duo, Kenny Werner conceived of an album's worth of material he had written with the trumpeter in mind. "I just never forgot his music," Werner said, continuing:

The tunes I wrote are not like any other tunes I've ever written, because I was thinking of Kenny's tunes – but it still had to be me. So if you hear those tunes, they have a harmonic basis that I didn't really indulge in that much anymore . . . I wrote them for him . . . Every tune on that record was conceived specifically for Kenny.[1861]

Werner's band was booked for a week in February 2006 at the Blue Note in New York, where they planned to record each night and create a live album. The group included saxophonist David Sanchez, bassist Scott Colley, and drummer Brian Blade. Early on, however, it was evident to Werner that there was something very wrong with the trumpeter:

He was sick or something – I don't know what was happening. All week – the one thing you wouldn't think would be a problem – he had no intonation . . . I was enjoying the funkiness of it, [but] I wasn't listening to the tapes . . . Somebody asked me if I'd listened to the tapes . . . [So] I listened to something, and I went, *Holy shit* . . .

Werner thought at first that maybe the problems were because the music he wrote was too challenging. "Sometimes I write something and I don't know that it's more difficult for other people than I thought," he said. But Kenny's issues were more fundamental and apparent not only to Werner but to the audience too. On hearing Kenny, Andrea Marini (who was travelling with him) panicked and called Norma Winstone for advice. "What do I do?" he asked. "Kenny can't play!"[1862]

To salvage the recording, Werner brought in another trumpeter (Matt Shulman, now known professionally as Matt Von Roderick) to play the soundcheck for the final day's gig, during which the band re-recorded the melodies to all the tunes while Kenny Wheeler sat in his dressing room. "Kenny still had a couple of solos, and we got away with it," Werner said. The resulting album from this week-long project was called *Democracy: Live at the Blue Note*.[1863] The only solo of Kenny Wheeler's that made the album was on a tune called "Hedwig's Theme" from the *Harry Potter* score by John Williams. It was "an open solo in E minor on the Harry Potter tune, and that was very profound," Werner said. Kenny Wheeler felt terrible about what had happened, and that the recording came so close to being ruined. Werner said, "I would get a call every once in a while, 'Hey Kenny, I'm so sorry I fucked up that record', and I would say, 'You didn't – we saved it.'" Werner noted that "a reviewer no less than [jazz historian and author] Dan Morgenstern wrote a review on how great Kenny sounded . . . He was really struggling, but in that context that struggle was real music . . . And I think that's what Dan was responding to."[1864]

On the surface, one might suspect the problems were related to Kenny's nerves, which had been an ongoing issue throughout his career. He fought valiantly – practising meditation and even taking beta blockers in his later years to ease his performance anxiety. But playing in New York brought out the worst of Kenny's nervousness. Dave Holland said that "New York was a challenge for him . . . It was the place that he always saw . . . all these great trumpet players lived, and when he would play with me in New York I know he was always a little anxious."[1865] But even when he had been nervous in the past, he could always pick up his horn to play and sound like *the* Kenny Wheeler, virtuoso trumpeter who could play things no one else could. His anxiety may have been exacerbated by some discomfort with this band; there is at least one report of Kenny saying that one of the musicians wasn't very friendly toward him.[1866] But this time it was different; the issues in Kenny's playing were more fundamental than those that might have been caused by any interpersonal discomfort or even by his chronic nervousness. It is not clear as to why his ability to play that week in particular was so beset with problems. Even with a little more erraticism creeping in due to his increasing age, he would still frequently play beautifully and with strength. But this near-disastrous episode in New York was certainly symptomatic of the frailty to come and it was something of a turning point that Kenny himself felt acutely. It is quite possible that it was somehow related to the mini-stroke Doreen suspected he had suffered shortly before the 75th birthday tour a year earlier. He also had other health problems. His hearing was damaged from years of loud gigs with a monitor turned up so he could hear himself over deafening big bands behind him. In addition, Kenny's eyesight was beginning to decline; he had to have his sheet music printed at a larger size just to read it, and, at one frightening point following that suspected stroke, his vision temporarily turned everything upside down.[1867]

The week at the Blue Note in New York was a decisive moment; going forward, Kenny and his management would need to be more mindful of and accommodating to his increasing age and health issues. After decades of work as a sideman, playing with everyone from Anthony Braxton, Bill Bruford, and Joni Mitchell – all the way down to selflessly lending his talents to make recordings with unknown college students and musician-composers – it was becoming obvious that he should avoid these sorts of situations. It is sad to think of someone so gifted – whose revered abilities and stamina on the trumpet were considered virtually endless by his colleagues – would ever lose those powers. And it is also heartbreaking that Kenny Werner – who loved Wheeler's music so much that he wanted to make an entire live album out of music he had written with the trumpeter in mind – had the unfortunate distinction of being the person with whom he was playing when this decline first became most evident. But, from this point on, Kenny Wheeler needed to be focused on playing his own music with his own people.

———·———

In February 2004, Kenny began his association with a new Italian label: CAM Jazz. (CAM stands for *Creazioni Artistiche Musicali*.) Part of the same parent company that owns Soul Note (on which Kenny had released *Flutter By,*

*Butterfly* and *All the More*), CAM Jazz became the label for which he recorded most often during the last decade of his life. This label produced eight albums with Kenny as a leader (only one less than ECM did in their 37-year relationship), beginning in 2004 and continuing until after his death. Although many fans would agree that Kenny's CAM Jazz catalogue does not represent the pinnacle of his playing career, its flurry of Wheeler-centred output contains many gems and illustrates an important point that ECM might well have missed: he remained an unbelievably prolific composer well into his eighth and ninth decades. His relationship with CAM gave him the chance he'd always craved but never been afforded with ECM: to record and release new projects on an almost annual basis. In addition to chronicling his fertile and productive later life, recording for CAM allowed Kenny the freedom to focus on recording with groups of his choice, usually made up of the long-time friends with whom he was most comfortable. In May 2004 Kenny was also commissioned to write an hour of new music, which sadly went unrecorded, for a single concert in Modena. Unique in his catalogue, the project comprised musical settings of religious psalms sung in Italian by a full choir, accompanied by a small chamber ensemble and Glauco Venier on the church organ

The eight CAM Jazz albums Kenny recorded document many Wheeler originals, several of which are presented in a duo setting (often with John Taylor), which became a sustaining outlet for his creativity later in life. In fact, Kenny's first record as leader for CAM is in this configuration. *Where Do We Go From Here?* from 2005, is a beautiful album that captures the unique connection between him and John that only time and experience can cultivate. There is also a certain poignancy, as this represents their first official studio session in this intimate setting without Norma Winstone. Ian Carr's liner notes call *Where Do We Go From Here?* "a triumph and a tour de force . . . The standard of playing and concentration borders on the superhuman."[1868]

Recording for CAM also gave Kenny the opportunity to record with people he might not otherwise have been associated with. For example, Kenny first played with bassist Charlie Haden as a sideman on Enrico Pieranunzi's star-filled *Fellini Jazz* on CAM in March 2003,[1869] on which Kenny, Chris Potter, and Haden joined pianist Pieranunzi and drummer Paul Motian.[1870] After this session, Chris played with Kenny again at the Montreal Jazz Festival (where Kenny was being awarded the *Prix Oscar Peterson*) in the summer of 2003, where the horn players formed a new quartet with J.T. and Dave Holland. (Significantly, the 73-year-old Kenny played another very long set – in a duo – with J.T. at the festival, a demonstration of his stamina still intact at this point.) Reviewer John Kelman said that, in Montreal, ". . . the empathy was so immediate that [the quartet] just begged to be recorded."[1871] This potential manifested itself in the next album Kenny would make for CAM.

Recorded with the same personnel from Montreal, *What Now?*[1872] is similar to *Angel Song*, in that it is another highly successful drummerless quartet record, but this time with J.T. and a younger, more virtuosic saxophonist.

Photo 41: Kenny and John Taylor.
Courtesy L. D'Agostino

Chris Potter remembered that, during the sessions, he "felt like a very fortunate observer", adding that he "got to be inside with these guys who had this history and this obvious kind of comfort being around each other". Chris also observed that when he played with Kenny, he "was conscious of trying to match his energy – which was definitely not macho trumpet playing – just the delicacy of the way he was phrasing, that the music demanded. You could focus on the subtleties and just be more breathy." [1873] Kenny was, as always, dissatisfied with his playing during the sessions but remained aware that they had limited time and needed to move on; J.T. and Dave encouraged him, often reassuring, *I think we got that one!* [1874] Their confidence was well founded: *What Now?* garnered a great deal of critical recognition. It even received a nomination for a Grammy for Best Jazz Instrumental Album in 2006 – the only nomination Kenny would ever receive as leader, and the first CAM Jazz album to be considered for the award. *What Now?* was also voted 2005's "Record of the Year" by BBC Radio's *Jazz on 3* programme. [1875]

2005 continued to be another busy year. That summer, he returned to the north of England, recording a free set with an all-star group of improvisers including Evan Parker at the Appleby Festival. (The recording, *Free Zone Appleby 2005*,[1876] was actually a follow-up to an album they'd made two years earlier at the same festival, titled *Free Zone Appleby 2003*.[1877]) In simpatico with Kenny's aesthetic, the Appleby Festival embraced straight-ahead, contemporary, and free jazz from composer/bandleaders like Kenny himself. They also invited him to put together one-off configurations of his own larger ensembles under his own name. These were much-needed opportunities for him to present groups of his own in the UK rather than appear as a guest, and these summer gigs also helped fill in the gaps between the "big birthday" tours every five years. For both of his Appleby appearances, though, Kenny presented more compact, chamber-type big bands rather than his full-sized ensemble, similar to his *Little Suite* tour of 1978, the *Kayak* tour, or other smaller-scale BBC broadcasts.

During this period, Kenny also made three new recordings for CAM. The first of these was another duo album with J.T. in March 2005, titled *On the Way to Two*.[1878] Although not released until ten years later, the recording is a wonderful companion to their earlier *Where Do We Go From Here?*[1879] For Kenny's second recording of 2005, he was reunited with guitarist John Abercrombie that July. *It Takes Two!*[1880] continued his trend of drummerless quartet recordings, this time with the empathetic second guitarist John Parricelli, sometimes utilizing the nylon-string guitar to provide more sonic variety and further contrast to Abercrombie. On bass is the Swedish bassist Anders Jormin, another ECM stalwart who had worked with Kenny before but never on one of his own recordings. John Kelman, in his *All About Jazz* review, pointed out that "Jormin – the perfect confluence of virtuosic technique, folkloric lyricism, European classicism and jazz tradition – is an ideal fit for Wheeler . . ."[1881] John Fordham also noted the evocative sound in his *Guardian* review, connecting it to Kenny's new-found home at CAM: "There's also a strongly southern European and Moorish feel about some of the music, as if Wheeler's sometimes remote persona has been warmed by the fruitful relationship with Italy's CAM Jazz label."[1882] Kenny would explore even further afield in the third and perhaps most significant recording of that year, *Other People*.[1883]

*Other People* features Kenny with the Vienna-based Hugo Wolf String Quartet and J.T. once again at the piano. The strings show a high level of devotion to and respect for Kenny's music and display a real sensitivity for his contrapuntal writing style. A highlight of this album is his 14-minute *String Quartet No. 1*. It is thrilling and ear-opening for even the most well-listened Wheeler fan to hear Kenny's voice thrive in a musical form that has challenged composers for centuries.[1884] One struggles to think of another primarily jazz-based composer who could show mastery of the integral elements of this genre and still retain their unique personality.

Kenny returned to the studio again the following year in July 2006 with J.T. on piano and the great bassist Steve Swallow, taking every advantage of this fruitful period being afforded him by CAM Jazz. The resulting album, *One of Many*,[1885] was the last in a steady line of drummerless outings for Kenny in these years before he would return to more conventional configurations. Although the trio album features only Kenny's compositions, Swallow himself is a composer with a melodic sensibility and harmonic mastery complementary to Kenny's. With a sound on his instrument as singular as the trumpeter's, Swallow's personality comes through in his uniquely tuneful, contrapuntal improvising and effortless time-keeping.

In 2006, Kenny was invited into a new educational role as Patron of the "Junior Jazz" course at London's Royal Academy of Music. These exceptionally talented students had been including Kenny's tunes in their studies and performances for years, and he proved to be a great role model for them. Kenny represented the very best of what was possible as instrumentalist, composer, improvisor: an overall *professional* musician. On taking up the position, Kenny played a Sunday afternoon concert with three groups of young players at the Pizza Express Jazz Club in Soho, performing his own music and some standards. He continued to visit his Junior Jazz students a couple of times a year on Saturday mornings, playing and talking with them. He occasionally brought Doreen with him, whose sweet and gregarious nature enhanced the storytelling and helped make Kenny more relaxed. He was astonishingly warm, funny company here, and was clearly touched to be sharing his wisdom with them.

Kenny also worked as a guest in 2006 with the senior Royal Academy jazz department, performing the *Long Time Ago* brass suite and the *2005 Suite* with the big band. This was a lot of music for Kenny to take on at this age in a single concert – two substantial suites plus some other individual pieces – but he played remarkably well on the programme considering his advanced years, especially after the soundcheck had been a bit shaky. Pianist Kit Downes, then an Academy student and later a rising star on ECM, was on the concert and recalled the experience: "Hearing that sound in person, playing his own originals (the same tunes that I tried to play with my friends), felt like being in touch with something really authentic," he said.[1886] For the concert, Kenny was joined by his friends John Barclay and Stan Sulzmann, who also played with the student groups.

Stan would continue to support Kenny musically and increasingly otherwise as the trumpeter's advancing age became more noticeable. Around the time of Kenny's second Appleby appearance in 2006, there were some signs that Kenny's suspected stroke might have affected his memory and mental faculties. The warm-up gigs for this Appleby concert were at the Bull's Head in London, and it was there that guitarist Phil Robson noticed Kenny seeming to be confused for the first time. They performed "Everybody's Song", which Norma always sang in a different key to the instrumental version. This time, however, this usual key change triggered a confusion that Kenny couldn't solve for a moment; he even seemed to forget it was even his composition, thinking it was Norma's.[1887] He found a way to get through the performance, but this episode was very troubling to those around him.

In 2007, Kenny would need assistance in another setting, cementing the point that he now needed to focus on playing his own music rather than anything too unfamiliar. This was a particularly stark transition for Kenny because he had always been a trumpeter who could play anything placed in front of him. At the 2007 Cheltenham Jazz Festival, pianist Hans Koller invited Kenny to be part of an ensemble that would also welcome Bob Brookmeyer as a special guest. Before that, there was a warm-up gig at The Vortex. Kenny was not in good shape; he was the only trumpeter and the parts often included long independent lines that were problematically difficult at this stage of his life. This also meant that his mental energy and confidence were taxed when it came time to play solos. Kenny could certainly still play brilliantly at this time, but the context and what was being asked of him needed to be tailored to ensure one got the best results out of him. Following the Vortex gig, Koller decided to call Nick Smart and ask him to join the ensemble for the Cheltenham gig so he could offer the elder trumpeter support on the written parts, which could free up his chops, and his mind, for the solos. Kenny was happy with this arrangement, too. Kenny had a warm reunion with Brookmeyer, and they both played brilliantly, with Nick next to Kenny giving him confidence, subtly cueing him and covering a few parts.

In another adjustment to old age, Kenny had to get used to being an audience member rather than a performer. In October 2007, Nick had taken Kenny and Doreen to London's Cadogan Hall to watch Mike Gibbs's 70th birthday gig. Seemingly unaware of the magnitude of his own reputation, Kenny lamented to Doreen and Nick, "I used to do Mike's band. I don't know why he doesn't ask me anymore . . ."[1888] When asked about this, Mike was exasperated:

> I never *stopped* using him . . . *oh, Kenny, Kenny*! The thing is, Kenny was too big, too famous, and I couldn't designate him to a sideman role . . . Had I known, I would have made sure that he was booked right away, but I felt that he was too big. It'd be like booking the Queen on fourth trumpet![1889]

The following year, in June 2008, John Dankworth decided he would dust off the original *Windmill Tilter* scores and perform the iconic work with his own band. They performed at lunchtime in the Wavendon gardens as part of the summer series "Music in the Garden", and then headed down to Ronnie Scott's for an evening performance at which Kenny and his son Mark were in the audience.[1890] Even though his mere presence in the crowd was certainly meaningful to the performers on stage, it was not easy for Kenny to accept this new figurehead position as a jazz statesman; he still wanted to be up there with them. Fortunately for both, in July 2009, Dankworth and Kenny did get one more chance to play together when they formed a sextet (featuring alto saxophonist Pete King) also in the Wavendon gardens.[1891] It was the last time they would play together before Dankworth died in February 2010.

---

Another gem in Kenny's CAM Jazz catalogue was the album *Six for Six*,[1892] which includes small-group versions of many of the tunes he would record later on his final big-band album. Recorded in April 2008, it features Kenny's old friends Chris Laurence, Stan Sulzmann, and John Taylor, with one of Kenny's favourite drummers, Martin France. As the title suggests, there was a sixth member: saxophonist Bobby Wellins. Kenny had not played with him regularly for some time, but they had remained close friends and shared a history playing together that went back to some of Kenny's earliest gigs in the UK. The recording has a warmth about it emanating from the friend-ships and musical history they shared, but the trip to the recording studio was beset with problems. Travelling was difficult for Kenny at this point, with the long walks between airport terminals becoming increasingly tiring. But Chris Laurence recalled happily that "the recordings we did there, the engineer was really good, it was a very nice studio, and then Kenny played some things that were just unbelievable."[1893] As he aged, Kenny preferred to record in total isolation so he could redo solos or make edits more easily, and despite the warmth of the friendship in the room, Stan remembered that there was "just a funny, uncomfortable vibe" about the session.[1894] In Bobby Wellins's opin-ion, Andrea's presence also made it a bit tense, with the manager becoming impatient when things were going roughly for Kenny early on in the process. Bobby described to a friend how when Kenny found his footing and things started to flow, Marini said, "*Finally*, we've got something." Bobby went on, "I was furious at [Andrea] . . . Who the *hell* do you think you're talking to?"[1895] Kenny also showed his frustrations. He was in the isolation booth, with only headphones to hear the other musicians. One of the tunes had a counterline that was difficult to get just right, especially for Bobby who was a tremendous jazz player but rarely did "reading" gigs anymore. Kenny, already on edge with his usual performance nerves and used to sight-readers getting things right quickly, muttered, "I don't understand, why can't they just play the fucking arrangement?!"[1896] Although he thought he was saying this to himself, his senti-ments were fed straight into the headphones of the entire band. Among these old friends, they could all just laugh about it.

Another CD from this period further illustrated Kenny's manager's con-nections, but for a different Italian label, Astarte Records. *Nineteen Plus One*[1897] was billed as "Kenny Wheeler with the Colours Jazz Orchestra" and recorded with the Italian big band in June 2007. It is unique in that it is almost entirely an album of Kenny's big-band arrangements of jazz standards, includ-ing such unlikely choices as the Sinatra staples "All Or Nothing At All" and "Only the Lonely", and tunes he had used frequently in his own concerts, including "How Deep Is the Ocean" and an old arrangement of "Stella By

Starlight". Reviewer John Kelman remarked that it is "no surprise that, despite an unfailing allegiance to the essence of these enduring songs, they sound as if Wheeler wrote them in the first place."[1898] The album closes with its sole Wheeler original, "W.W." – a version that first appeared in big-band form on the UMO Jazz Orchestra recording *One More Time* nearly a decade earlier.[1899] *Nineteen Plus One* also marks the first recording of Italian singer Diana Torto with Kenny. Kelman noted her "capably handling Wheeler's melody lines, originally written for Winstone . . ."[1900] (Although Marini had once also managed Norma, that relationship had soured and they had parted company.) Diana Torto would work more closely with Kenny and J.T. in the coming years. She and Marini were now romantically involved and, with Kenny and J.T. under Andrea's management, coupled with J.T.'s ongoing refusal to perform with Norma, she would sing more and more regularly alongside the previous Azimuth partners – inevitably sometimes singing Norma's lyrics, too.

There were some far-flung overseas trips for Kenny in the period after his 75th birthday. At a time when just getting to mainland Europe was proving stressful, one can only imagine how he must have felt jetting off to Azerbaijan and Syria. The Azerbaijan trip was part of a British Council-sponsored tour in a group that also included Paul Clarvis, and the Syria trip in 2008 was with pianist Frank Carlberg.

Mercifully, other trips would have him return to more familiar soil. In January 2008, Kenny was part of a contingent travelling from the UK to attend the International Association for Jazz Education (IAJE) conference in Toronto, the final event of its kind. For this trip, Kenny was to guest with the CUK Big Band, made up of students from various UK conservatoires, conducted by Mark Donlon from Leeds College of Music. Kenny was commissioned to write an arrangement of his tune "The Jigsaw" to feature himself and Norma.[1901] They flew out with Doreen, Norma, Nikki Iles, Pete Churchill, and Nick Smart, representing the Academy travelling with them. Kenny's sister Helen also came down to the city to stay with everyone, making it an even more joyous occasion. He even played a daytime session for Toronto's Jazz FM radio before heading up to his hometown of St. Catharines, where he played a concert in the auditorium of Laura Secord Secondary School a few days later. The evening in St. Catharines was particularly special – the audience, full of musicians, friends, and his large extended Canadian family, honoured Kenny with a huge standing ovation at the end of the concert.

As had been the case every five years since 1990, Kenny and his friends began to discuss a musical celebration of his upcoming 80th birthday. Around a year

Photo 42: Toronto Jazz FM studios for a live session. Left to right: Nikki Iles, Norma Winstone, Duncan Hopkins, Kenny, and Anthony Michelli.

Courtesy Nick Smart

in advance, Birmingham Jazz producer Tony Dudley-Evans started to assemble the dates, venues, and the actual musical programme. The difficulties began as soon as they tried to choose music in a way that Kenny could involve both John Taylor and Norma Winstone. This was a complex situation which was becoming ever more exasperating for Norma, never mind for Kenny, who loved them both and wanted them on the tour. But since J.T. was unwilling to share the stage with Norma, a separate vocalist (Diana Torto) would have to sing the first half with J.T., and a separate pianist (Gwilym Simcock) would play the big-band portion with Norma. It was also proposed that they try to include some of Kenny's recent string quartet music in the first half of the pro-gramme, which of course would have further increased costs. In the end, it was all unfortunately far too expensive, complicated, and unwieldy. Tony Dudley-Evans could not reconcile the musical goals of the tour with the expense of so many musicians. Although Marini was acting as manager for Kenny, J.T. and Diana, Tony felt he was not actually helping put the tour together for his art-ists: "There was no sort of *We'll make this work* or *We'll see how much we get*

... it was *This is the project – this is what we've got to do*. That was part of the process by which I said, 'I don't think I can do this.'" He added:

> If I commit to something I want to carry it through – and if we didn't get the funding, we'd have to do it anyway. The danger was that it would either bankrupt Birmingham Jazz, or I would feel the responsibility to step in and fund this myself. Everyone was saying, "Well, you shouldn't be doing that." I felt I'd got myself into something that is too big for me.[1902]

Although it is admirable that Andrea seemed to be acting as a fierce advocate for Kenny's musical vision, his efforts were unsuccessful. After exhausting all options and being unable to find a suitable compromise, Dudley-Evans felt he was left with no other option but to cancel the plans to tour.[1903]

Kenny was upset about the tour being cancelled. In fairness, it must be pointed out that he did not – or could not – bring himself to solve the problem on his own. Ultimately, it was *his* music, *his* band, *his* tour, *his* career – and he was heartbroken that two of his most essential collaborators could not appear on the same stage at the same time. Norma was aware of Kenny's frustration and sadness at the situation. Doreen once told her that "Kenny's greatest wish would be that you two would play together again with him. That's what he would love." Norma also explained that "It was difficult for [Kenny], because if John couldn't play with me, then I couldn't play in the big band with John. So if I was there, John wasn't there . . ." She tried to convince John otherwise, appealing to his reason: "This is ridiculous," she told him. "Kenny's asked me to do this big-band thing, but you're going to be in the first half with him and a string quartet and Diana, then you go off and you don't come on the stage because I'm on it with 18 or 19 other people? Come on." She continued:

> So, he said, "No, we're not working or playing together anymore. For God's sake, don't you want to be involved in Kenny's 80th birthday?" I said, "Of course I do! But I don't think I can stand to see you playing with him and another singer in the first half, and then you go off and I come on and another pianist comes on. No, I can't." He said, "Well, you have to decide, don't you?" . . . I just said, "I don't think I can do it."[1904]

In a way, though, all the problems that caused the tour to break up initially led to some happier outcomes. For one, there was a surge of goodwill among the musicians who wanted to see his 80th birthday celebrated with a concert, regardless of their own fees. The members of the band, including Kenny's long-time trumpet friends Derek Watkins and Henry Lowther, were upset at the collapse of the tour and offered to play for free, no doubt at a financial loss to themselves. Derek told Stan Sulzmann: "Why don't we just do a birthday gig and I'll play for nothing. Geniuses only come 'round once in a while. What's the point in waiting until he's dead?"[1905]

In search of a suitable venue, and with Kenny's connections with the Royal Academy of Music in mind, the idea arose of playing at the Academy in the prestigious Duke's Hall. The Royal Academy of Music didn't normally host 'non-student' concerts like this, so Nick Smart proposed the idea to their management, explaining about the cancelled tour and that all costs would be covered; in addition, all remaining revenue would be used to establish a (yet undefined) "Kenny Wheeler Prize" at the Academy.[1906] To help raise additional funds for the new award on top of the ticket income, a souvenir programme was created with photos and new tributes from the *Guardian's* John Fordham, and old friends Dave Holland, Henry Lowther, John Taylor, Evan Parker, and Norma Winstone, as well as from Mark and Louann, who wrote: "Our Dad would like to extend his thanks to the musicians he has worked with and the audiences who have supported him for the last fifty years."[1907] The Academy welcomed the proposal and the date was set for Kenny's 80th birthday: Thursday, 14 January 2010. All of Kenny's regular colleagues were booked to play in an ensemble as close to his 75th birthday big band as possible, plus a few extras, with the musicians unwilling to miss this for anything.

It was eventually settled that they would play small-group music in the first half with J.T. and Dave Holland, then have the big band on the second half with Norma singing, Chris Laurence playing bass, and John Horler and Nikki Iles sharing the piano bench (literally, on the encore). The main piece for this second half would be *The Sweet Time Suite,* since there was limited rehearsal time, and they already knew the music. They had one rehearsal at the Royal Academy the Sunday before the concert. Conductor Pete Churchill knew Kenny's *Sweet Time Suite* "back to front" so he was there to help the band – most of whom had played it many times before – get through a great deal of music quickly and efficiently. It was at this rehearsal that Pete recalled first getting "Derek-ed", his term for the hazing he received from the lead trumpet player:

> We all got set up, Ken was very comfortable, we were there in the Royal Academy in the Duke's Hall . . . people were smiling at me . . . but then, first thing, as I'm about to start, this voice from the back, Derek, said, "*Ken!*" and Ken looked around, and [Derek] said, "Remember 20 years ago when we didn't need a conductor? *Those* were the days!" That was the first thing. BAM! . . . I knew the power struggle had begun! But it's not a power struggle really. It's a certain kind of generational humour, hierarchy. I knew all the Derek Watkins stories, and I'd had lots of conversations with Nikki [Iles, Pete's wife] about lead trumpeters; and you cannot have any self-doubt if you're going to play that way . . . You have to live that kind of persona so you can stand up there and be consistent. And he was the best of the best. So it didn't actually bother me at all – I just said, "Thanks for that vote of confidence, Derek!"[1908]

Also at the rehearsal, Kenny was having trouble with his flugelhorn. John Barclay went to clean it for him, astonished that it had got into the state it was in. After removing a considerable amount of debris from the inside of the mouthpiece, he teased Kenny, telling him "I've saved some DNA from it, Kenny. We're going to clone you!"[1909]

As they rehearsed the rest of the suite, Pete Churchill made an observation about Kenny's music and the musicians he chose to play it: Kenny could have had almost any of the top jazz players in the UK – or even around the world – play with him, but he chose to surround himself with friends, some of whom were top studio players, and others who he had known for most of his life who were perhaps not the strongest "section" players but made him feel comfortable and had a personal and unique sound to which he was attracted. For example, Duncan Lamont's vision was so diminished by this point that Pete Churchill thought that he could not exactly tell what the right notes and rhythms were, so he was likely "in a very musical way approximating" what Kenny had written in his part.[1910] (Pete had once tried to get Duncan, whose eyes were straining to try and see the notes on the page, to try wearing glasses. "They ruin your eyes, you know" came the puzzling response.) Pete postulated that Kenny's loyalty to these individuals was beyond that of pure friendship; they were a crucial part of his overall aesthetic, and they were there for a very musical purpose:

> Ken doesn't really care . . . It's more important that Duncan's *there* than he play what's accurate . . . [Ken wrote] very exact music and got very inexact people to play it. And that's the balance between the kind of watchmaker precision of Ken's writing – which he probably mistrusted himself – and the necessary anarchists that gave him the balance he needed. That first became really clear to me on the [rehearsal for the 80th] birthday concert at the Academy with *The Sweet Time Suite* – when we got to that beautiful last chord on the end of "Consolation", it's ringing, and I was wanting to hold it because it's such a beautiful moment, and Ken – very rarely did he say anything – but he said, "Pete, when they hit that last chord, maybe bass trombone and baritone could suddenly play free, like, quite loudly" and basically fuck it all up . . . That was his thing. He thought, "No, I don't want it to sound that beautiful." He must have known that beauty thing that he was searching for wasn't always the best thing, and that the performers could make sure that it never came across as "too beautiful".

Many of Pete's musical observations were affirmed by Kenny himself, in a touching and beautifully produced piece for the *PM* programme aired the day of the concert on BBC Radio 4. It was testament to the attention this concert had attracted that it would be featured in this way on a prime, drive-time national station. "Everything I do has a touch of melancholy, and a touch of chaos, to it . . . yeah [*laughs*] . . . I write sad songs, and then I get the musicians to destroy them!" Kenny said.[1911] It is one of his most insightful quotes,

Photo 43: Kenny at his 80th birthday concert, Royal Academy of Music.
Courtesy Royal Academy of Music

Photo 44: Assembled performers at Kenny's 80th birthday concert, Royal Academy of Music. Left to right (back row): John Parricelli, Martin France, Andrew Bradley, Norma Winstone, Kenny, Derek Watkins, John Barclay, Julian Argüelles, Duncan Lamont, Martin Hathaway, Stan Sulzmann, Dave Holland, Dave Stewart, Mark Nightingale; (front row): Nick Smart, Pete Churchill, Nikki Iles, John Horler, Dave Horler, Chris Laurence, Evan Parker, John Taylor, Henry Lowther, Trevor Mires. Courtesy Royal Academy of Music

perhaps acknowledging how his sad and tumultuous early life found expression in his music.[1912]

The 80th birthday concert was a joyous affair. It was a sold-out event with many more musicians jammed into the audience than were on the stage. Derek Watkins, whose apparent bravado covered his own nerves at having to meet such astonishingly high expectations at all times, chose to offer words of comfort to Nick Smart before they went on stage, though they may have been a reminder to himself. "Don't be nervous, just enjoy it," Derek said, before adding: "*This* is the band everybody wants to be in."[1913] The evening earned a favourable review by the *Guardian's* John Fordham, calling Kenny "a unique improviser" and a "composer and arranger on a par with Gil Evans". Fordham also said that Kenny "put himself in the hot seat of a small band, unfolding his flugelhorn solos as lazily sketched shapes sporadically quickened by impulsive runs and soft squeals – before a storming rhythm section . . . pulled the music into freewheeling fast passages that found their way home by increasingly devious routes."[1914] The big band anchored the second half of the concert, with a few additional charts rounding out the set, including Kenny's arrangements of Dudu Pukwana's "B, My Dear" and Gordon Jenkins's "Goodbye", on which Andrew Bradley (partner of Kenny's daughter Louann) sang. "Wheeler's delectable 'Winter Sweet' let Winstone curl her voice plaintively over rich, Evans-like brass chords," Fordham wrote.[1915] On *The Sweet Time Suite*, Kenny was in top form, especially at the cadenza linking the final two sections of the eight-part work, his tritone-based gestures weaving a captivating melodic tapestry covering the entire range of the flugelhorn, leaving the band and audience astounded that the 80-year-old could have indeed rivalled his iconic recording from two decades earlier.[1916] Even the tension between Derek and Pete resolved. As if to apologize while simultaneously reasserting his dominance, the trumpeter said, "Well done, young Pete!" as they exited the stage.[1917]

———·———

The birthday concert at the Academy had been a huge success, but a feeling remained among the musicians that the original tour should still go forward if possible. Kenny had written a new collection of music for big band, and, with the goodwill that had been generated, there was a tangible momentum between all concerned to make a tour featuring this new music possible. Kenny's manager Andrea Marini set the schedule for late October, keeping most of the same venues the band had played on previous tours. The question of personnel was again an issue, with difficult discussion of whether either Norma Winstone or John Taylor would take part in the tour, and who would replace whichever of the two of them bowed out. Kenny also expressed his frustration at the old issue resurfacing once more between his two dearest friends. Norma spoke directly to Kenny about the tour: "When it came around again, I could've done it. He did ask me. But I said I couldn't." Since Andrea was booking the tour, Norma suspected that he would have wanted to book Diana Torto to sing anyway.[1918] Remembering the previous tour complications with J.T., Norma bowed out gracefully, "because otherwise it would've gotten ridiculous again . . . I just said to Kenny, 'No, I can't do it,' so he got Diana then."[1919] The tour went forward without her, with Diana Torto singing and J.T. playing piano. The rest of the band was almost the same as on his 2005 tour, apart from bass trombonist Dave Stewart and old colleague Dave Horler, newly retired from the WDR, also back in the trombone section. Nick Smart also joined in the trumpet section, replacing Ian Hamer, who had died in 2006.

The music for this tour was very difficult in some ways. Kenny's music, all new to the band, was more intense than ever. "It was relentless," Stan Sulzmann said. "Ken was writing in a strange way – no place to rest or take it off your chops." Regardless of its difficulty, the beautifully written music marked a real progression in Kenny's mature writing for big band, beyond even the mastery of *The Sweet Time Suite* or the *2005 Suite*. But in a departure from his late suites, he returned to the format of a collection of tunes, with no connecting material between the various pieces. Highlights of this programme are the gorgeously mournful "Comba No. 3" ("Comba" being Kenny's portmanteau of "Commercial Ballad") and "Enowena" ("A New One" spelled backwards). The recording also included a fresh take on Kenny's classic "Old Ballad", paired with his "Canter No. 1" (the latter title presumably a play on the gently lolloping underlying triplet groove, reminiscent of a horse's gait).

The band left on 21 October for their first gig in Basingstoke. *London Jazz News* called the opening night's concert "one of the most remarkable melodic outpourings in music: ten substantial, important and remarkable new pieces", adding that Kenny "looked less frail than he had done in January". The review closed simply, saying that "Wheeler demonstrates that he is indeed one of the great melodists of our time."[1920] Kenny was in good spirits on the tour. "He was so happy," Nick remembered, explaining that several times during a given concert, he saw Kenny revelling in the power of Derek Watkins and John Barclay's most explosive moments from his seat at the front of the band: "His neck was a bit stiff, but when there was some good trumpet playing in the band he would kind of look around . . . and you could see the side of his mouth smiling," he laughed.

After Basingstoke, the band played Southampton, Manchester, Leeds, then had two days off before playing Gateshead on the 27th. At the soundcheck in Gateshead, Andrea Marini reminded the band that there was a very early flight leaving the Newcastle airport for Belfast the next morning, apologizing for the fact that there was really no other way to get the band to their gig the following evening. Marini also let them know that they could not check in to the hotel in Belfast until the afternoon. At this, Derek – one of several players in the band doing this tour out of love and respect for Kenny but already losing money he could have been making in the studios – let his frustration get the better of him, roaring at Marini something to the effect of, *I'm 65 years old, I'm one of the greatest lead trumpet players in the world, and for you to treat me like this is unprofessional!* Watkins was indignant at the fact that he and his colleagues in the band – several of whom were even older than him – could not simply get some rest after their early flight and before the concert.[1921] Although Derek was sticking up for all of them, this scene made several members of the band "really, really uncomfortable".[1922] On arrival in Belfast, rooms were slowly allocated as they finally became available, and Kenny was given the first one. The rest of the band hung out and waited, getting coffee or going shopping. Pete Churchill, recognizing that Duncan Lamont was also over 80 years old at this point and needed to be looked after a bit, got a taxi and took him to an art gallery to pass the time.

The rest of the Belfast gig was happier and more celebratory. Since Kenny did not have a computer at home or any means to even email, the band decided to chip in and buy him an iPad as a late birthday gift. (They assumed that it might be easier for him to navigate the tablet than a computer, but the band failed to take fully into account Kenny's technical abilities!) Nick and Evan went to the Belfast Apple store, bought the iPad, and set Kenny up with an email account in the store. From there, Nick sent Kenny his first email, attaching a band photo from the previous day and welcoming him "to the technological age". The band presented the gift to Kenny at the soundcheck that afternoon in Belfast. During the dinner break before the concert, some of the band members were showing Kenny how to use the iPad and how to respond to his first email. Kenny wrote a sly reply to Nick, cracking some of his friends up while Nick, Derek, John Barclay, and Stan were at the pub enjoying a pre-concert Guinness. But since there was no internet connection in the concert venue, the message lay dormant in outgoing e-purgatory. Weeks later, when Mark Wheeler got his parents' house set up with wifi, the forgotten reply was finally sent. Nick, having forgotten about the original message, awoke to the following email, seemingly out of the blue:

> **From:** Ken Wheeler
> **Subject:** Re: Your 1st email!!!!
> **To:** Nick Smart
>
> Fuck you
> Love Kenny
>
> Sent from my iPad

Nick called Mark, leaving him a slightly panicked message, hoping there had been some sort of misunderstanding. Kenny returned the call right away saying, "I'm sorry, Nick – I thought you'd find it funny!" still not quite comprehending the nature of the time delay between the set-up and punchline of his joke. (He never really got the hang of email; Evan Parker remembered a message from Kenny, the entire contents of which had been typed into the subject line.) But, with Mark's help, he did send emails from time to time. One heartfelt message sent to the band after the tour simply read:

> Thanks for a great tour. No group of musicians could have played the music better.
> The iPad is great. Thank you all.
> Love, Ken

———·———

Throughout this period, organizations began to award Kenny with accolades. After the Grammy nominations and *DownBeat* poll honours marking singular achievements, he began to receive recognition for his life's work. The first of these came from his native Canada, where in 2003 he was awarded the Montreal Jazz Festival's *Prix Oscar Peterson*. Named for its original recipient, the award recognized "a performer's musicianship and exceptional contribution to the development of Canadian jazz". He also returned to his hometown of St. Catharines in 2005 for a concert of music featuring the work of outstanding musicians connected to the Niagara region. Having spoken with Kenny's sister and most outspoken champion Helen (Wheeler) Hill, Laura Thomas, conductor of the Niagara Symphony Orchestra, called Kenny for permission to arrange one of his compositions for the concert. As she spoke to him and mentioned his friends, local musicians Duncan Hopkins and Randy and Warren Stirtzinger, Thomas felt "a distinct warming in his reception. As discussion of the concert ensued, piqued by its focus on jazz's local roots and continuing presence, [Kenny] asked about the pieces already selected, the tempos, sequencing of the concert . . ."[1923] He suggested his tune "Sea Lady" in place of the piece she had originally chosen and offered to orchestrate it for her. When it came time for the concert, at Brock University's Sean O'Sullivan Theatre, Kenny and two of his sisters – Helen and Mabel – were in the audience for the premiere of his arrangement. Kenny characteristically dodged recognition at the end of the performance. As Terrance Cox reported, "when the conductor announced his presence for deserved acclaim, Kenny Wheeler stayed seated, 'invisible'".[1924]

In London in 2005, Kenny received the Parliamentary Jazz Award for "Jazz Musician of the Year"[1925] but sent Mark and Louann to receive the House of Commons Shield award on his behalf at the Westminster celebration.[1926] In 2007, he received a second Parliamentary Jazz Award, this time for "Services to Jazz". In December of that year, Kenny's homeland bestowed the prestigious Order of Canada on him, its "highest honour for lifetime achievement". The official press release for the award ceremony at the Canadian High Commission in London (which Kenny *did* attend) read:

> A trumpeter, composer and arranger, Kenny Wheeler is considered a giant of jazz who has helped put Canadians on the map internationally.

Admired by musicians and fans alike as an innovator whose work serves as a cornerstone, he has recorded more than 20 albums and played with the biggest names in the business. He has created new directions in both composition and arrangement, and his works are studied in music courses around the world. Humble yet generous, he is a beloved teacher and guide to younger musicians, who cite him as an example and inspiration.

In all Canadian publications from this point forward, he was referred to as "Kenny Wheeler, O.C."

Canadians were always proud to claim Kenny. Even from his earliest days, he would return home to newspaper and magazine features, even occasional interviews on radio and television, showcasing "their Ken" who had gone off to England to make a name for himself and become perhaps the most important jazz musician from their country, after pianist Oscar Peterson and trumpeter Maynard Ferguson. To this point, Mark Miller observed:

It seems to me, with all due respect, there are these four major figures [in Canadian jazz history] (and I'm not including Gil Evans because he was gone before he was playing) but you've got Oscar, you've got Maynard, you've got Kenny, and you've got Paul Bley. And Oscar and Maynard, in some sense, are aesthetically two of a kind. And Kenny and Paul are again, aesthetically two of a kind. And certainly, in Canada, Oscar and Maynard have a profile that Kenny and Paul never achieved. But I would think that in the longer scheme of jazz history, that Kenny and Paul have advanced the music in the ways that really matter in terms of personal voice, if only that . . . because that's what it's all about.[1927]

Duncan Hopkins explained the complicated nature of Kenny's relationship with his native country, and more specifically the city where he grew up:

He's sort of famous now, but St. Catharines had nothing to do with it . . . He had to leave, but he's the same guy, whether here or in London, but London recognized it and St. Catharines didn't. Maybe there's a bit of antagonism about that, I'm not sure . . . There's an underlying sense that he wants to have a belonging here [in Canada], but he never really belonged. He had to leave to find himself and his music.[1928]

That sentiment was expressed even more directly to Hopkins on one occasion by Kenny himself:

In fact, Ken said to me – we were having a beer somewhere I can't even remember where – and he said, "You have to leave Canada." And I said, "I have a wife now" – and I was only just married. But he said, "You have to leave Canada. Definitely St. Catharines. You have to leave St. Catharines. But if you can, you have to leave Canada." And that was over 20 – maybe 25 – years ago. I think some Canadians would be upset about that – but I think musicians would all know exactly where that comes from.[1929]

Gene Lees was even more vociferous in his assessment of the effect that St. Catharines had on Kenny and himself. In a letter to Kenny which referred to him as finally having the confidence to teach at Banff, Lees reflected on the environment in which they had both grown up:

> We were looked on as a little weird because we collected records. Our high school orchestra was rotten, and the principal was a rotten old drunk who mentally brutalized the kids. I always felt like a real loner, a real outsider . . . if you weren't brought up on Yates Street or in Glenn Ridge [the affluent parts of St. Catharines], you didn't grow up with confidence in that town. They really fucked us over.[1930]

Showing just how far Kenny's life had taken him since St. Catharines, prestigious honours continued to be bestowed upon him. After receiving Honorary Membership from the Guildhall School of Music in 2000, Kenny remarked: "I don't know what it means, but people are treating me with more respect!"[1931] Indeed they were: two more educational honours would follow before the decade's end. The first was from the Royal Academy of Music in 2009, where he was made an Honorary Member at that year's graduation ceremony, a recognition given to "distinguished musicians who did not attend the Academy". Later that summer, he was given an Honorary Doctorate by the University of York, where John Taylor had been teaching and PhD candidate Matt Postle had been focusing on Kenny's music. For the occasion, Kenny composed a new quartet with the punning title "For Trumpet Peace".[1932]

One of the greatest honours bestowed upon Kenny was by the Festival of New Trumpet Music (known as FONT) in New York. Founded by Dave Douglas, FONT is a non-profit organization whose mission is to support "new trumpet music in all forms, and provides a platform for emerging artists and creative pioneers".[1933] Early in its existence, FONT wanted to honour Kenny with their Award of Recognition. Dave Douglas contacted him to let him know that the organization wished to give him this award and to propose a four-day celebration of his career in New York at the Jazz Standard club, during which various ensembles would play his music with him. Kenny was touched by Douglas's offer and told him to get in touch with his manager Andrea Marini to work out the details. When Douglas contacted Andrea, he was told four nights wasn't enough, that Kenny would only do it if it were a week-long run with his "Italian quartet". This was a problem, since an important tenet of FONT is its collaborative nature. It wasn't intended to be just a club date: rather, a creatively and carefully curated festival with Kenny performing alongside New York musicians (especially trumpeters) who so admired him and his music. It would also reconnect him with his many New York-based friends. But these conditions were apparently a deal-breaker; Dave phoned Kenny to say it was not possible to proceed and it seemed that all hope was lost.[1934]

A couple of years later, in November 2010, Dave Douglas was in London, performing at the Queen Elizabeth Hall and giving a masterclass at the Royal Academy of Music. Before departing for the airport, Dave had lunch with Nick Smart. Dave casually asked Nick if he knew Kenny, explained the idea for the FONT celebration, and told him the story of their earlier failed attempt to honour him. To Nick, who had long since joined the likes of Evan and Stan and others who proactively sought to help Kenny secure opportunities and recognitions like this, it sounded like something Kenny would love to do. It was clear that he would relish the opportunity to get back to the US to connect with old friends such as Dave Holland, and more than likely combine it with visiting his family in Canada. And who *wouldn't* want to be celebrated in this way, by that calibre of artists, and in that city, at this stage of their life? It made no sense. This was all clearly upsetting and illustrated yet another example of the slow erosion of Kenny's relationship with his management. A week-long residency is not always possible in a busy city like New York, and an offer of four nights was hardly offensive anywhere for anyone. It could well have been difficult for charitable non-profit organizations like FONT to provide travel funding for a chaperone, and there was also confusion around the reference to an "Italian quartet". Of course, there were many wonderful Italian musicians Kenny was happy to play with – but there was no regular group of his own that he would have demanded over and above the offer that was being made by FONT.

Nick relayed Dave Douglas's story to Kenny and Mark Wheeler, who confirmed that they very much wanted to participate in FONT. After the previous exchange, Douglas was no longer interested in working with the management with whom it had fallen through the first time around, so Nick and Mark agreed – with Marini's knowledge and permission – to coordinate the trip and make it possible for Kenny to receive this honour.

With Kenny finally on board, the organizers of FONT began planning the details of each night of the festival, with Dave Douglas overseeing everything in consultation with the artists. He enlisted trumpeter Ingrid Jensen, who put together a brass ensemble and rhythm section for the first night; drummer and composer John Hollenbeck, whose Large Ensemble became the featured big band for the second and third nights of FONT; and Kenny's long-time friend and musical partner bassist Dave Holland, who formed a quintet to play the final night of the festival.

With Kenny's management no longer involved in FONT, there were delays in procuring his music as late as 5 September 2011, just over a month before the first night of the festival. Ultimately, it was Kenny's habitual generosity over decades of simply giving his music away to others that came back to benefit him when he needed it most. Hollenbeck contacted associates of Kenny's, from professional colleagues to university jazz ensemble directors, trying to piece together a programme of his big-band music. In turn, people around the world gladly emailed him scans of scores and lead sheets to Kenny's music which he had shared with them years earlier.[1935] As it would happen, necessity was again the mother of invention, as Hollenbeck used a lead sheet of the third part of the *Heyoke* suite to create a whole new, cleverly reimagined prologue which led into Kenny's original big-band score.

Looking forward eagerly to his upcoming trip to New York, Kenny wrote a note to the FONT organization expressing his excitement and appreciation at the opportunity that had so nearly been denied him. Published on the FONT website ahead of his appearance, it read:

> I first came to New York in the late 40s. I was with a big band attached to the American forces and I had joined with the sole purpose of getting to New York. I just wanted to find and maybe talk to Miles. I couldn't find him but in the process I had a really short (even for me) conversation with Charlie Parker. I was so disappointed I had missed Miles that it wasn't until hours later I realized I had actually spoken to Bird! By that time though New York had gone from being in my head to being in my blood, heart and soul. It's where most of the Jazz I listened to before and after that trip was born. Although I have played in New York a few times over the years, every time I come back I still feel the same excitement I felt that first time I visited all those years ago. For me New York is the place to play. The fact that I am being honored with a New York week and that so many fantastic trumpet players are involved is overwhelming. I am so proud and, before my nerves get the better of me, I would just like to say thank you to all of the people who have put this event together and thank you to New York for giving me the opportunity to come back and play here again.[1936]

At their own expense, Mark Wheeler and Nick travelled with Kenny to New York to help with Kenny's limited physical mobility and to assist in keeping Kenny's musical affairs in order. Nick said that "to be in New York and witness the emotional warmth and sheer joy that was expressed by audience upon audience at his presence in the city . . . was breathtaking."[1937] The first night, 20 October, featured Ingrid Jensen's brass quintet and rhythm section. She arranged Kenny's music and composed new works in tribute to him, and there was also a special guest appearance from her sister, saxophonist Christine Jensen, who wrote a new piece for the occasion. A trumpet quartet (made up of the same Eastman School of Music alumni that had opened the International Trumpet Guild duo concert nearly a decade earlier in Manchester) played Kenny's arrangement of his tune "Kind Folk" as a fanfare of sorts to accompany his slow, deliberate entry onto the crowded Jazz Standard stage.[1938] Trumpet quartets were a recurring theme for the night: a highlight of the evening was Kenny's arrangement for four trumpets of "How Deep Is the Ocean", played by Kenny and Ingrid, joined by Dave Douglas and Nick.[1939]

Friday and Saturday nights featured John Hollenbeck's Large Ensemble with notable guest soloists, including FONT trumpeters Shane Endsley and Nate Wooley. The band played some of Kenny's big-band music before he joined them on stage, including "Sea Lady", "Foxy Trot", "Kayak", and "Gentle Piece", plus Hollenbeck's arrangement of the *Heyoke* suite. The gig got off to an uncomfortable start: during the soundcheck, Hollenbeck found out that one of the members of the ensemble had been arrested that morning at the "Occupy Wall Street" protests and would have to spend that night in jail, necessitating an equally world-class substitute, fortunately found within 30 minutes. "That was a NYC moment!" Hollenbeck said. (For this, it was indeed fortunate that the concert was in a city crawling with excellent musicians.) Once Kenny took the stage, the band played Parts II and III of *The Sweet Time Suite* and some of the new pieces from the recent album *The Long Waiting*. Hollenbeck said:

> Everyone in the band was thrilled to play with and for Kenny and for most of the musicians in the band, his music was our music – the music that inspired us to play! It was definitely a magical few days . . . it was so satisfying and rewarding to play Kenny's music, especially his older music

Photo 45: Dave Douglas, Kenny, and Nick Smart at New York University.
Courtesy Nick Smart

that we knew so well from repeated listening on records. And the moment Kenny started playing, it was incredible, transporting himself and us in a way that only his playing could do. It was moving to see his family supporting him to continue to do what he loved. And while they were probably used to seeing many English musicians loving and appreciating his music, I can imagine and hope they were pleasantly surprised to see how many musicians revered Kenny as a living legend in the US as well.[1940]

On Saturday afternoon, Dave Douglas and Nick Smart led discussions and reading sessions on Kenny's compositions for students and anyone interested at New York University with the elder statesman in attendance. Kenny was in top form at FONT. The presence of so much of the New York trumpet community, either on the stage or in the audience, put an enormous amount of pressure on a man nearly 82 years old. If there was ever an occasion for him to deliver some of the most assured performances of the last ten years, both musically and technically, this was it. He did not disappoint. Night after night, Kenny demonstrated exactly how much he deserved this honour, playing captivating "free" introductions to tunes, floating beautifully over his harmonically adventurous compositions, his idiosyncratic soaring intervals as fluent and secure as ever. It was also a happy homecoming of sorts for him, with fans and friends coming not only from the city but from across North America. Members of his Canadian family, including his sister Helen and his old friend John Meloni, were also in attendance.[1941] Dave Douglas said, "to have that celebration with the man himself and hearing him play, seeing all the New York musicians checking him out and wanting to be around him, that was a good one."[1942]

Kenny was deeply moved by the event. Admirers of his approached the table where he was seated with family between sets, telling him how much they loved his music, prompting him to break out some new and artful deflections of compliments. One listener told him, "Kenny, I'm a big fan", to which he replied, "You're not *that* big!"[1943] Before the last tune of Saturday night, after letting John Hollenbeck announce all the tunes on both days of the big-band portion of the festival, once all the members of the band were introduced and thank-yous were distributed, Kenny asked for the microphone. The audience cheered, as he had said nothing for three days. When the room fell silent, Kenny said, "I just want to thank this wonderful group of musicians for playing my music so beautiful. I'll never forget it – not for a few days, anyway," he chuckled, the audience laughing. "The last piece we're going to play is called 'W.W.', which is for my father, Wilfred Wheeler . . . [long pause] . . . and that's all I've got to say."[1944]

FONT culminated Sunday evening with a quintet reuniting Kenny with his old friend Dave Holland. It was a touching reunion, and happened to be Dave's first gig back since his wife Clare had passed that summer. She had been at Dave's side throughout his career, managing and accompanying his travels, often alongside Kenny. The two friends were joined by a formidable trio of pianist Craig Taborn, drummer Rudy Royston, and rising star saxophonist Jon Irabagon, who had recently played in a quintet with Kenny, J.T., and bassist Michael Janisch. The *New York Times* review of the event observed:

> At 81, he shows some frailty: he sat throughout both sets, entrusting the announcements to Mr. Holland. His tone on the horn has lost some of its old luster, and his articulation has softened. But the center of his sound is still clear. And at times in the second set – notably on "Kind Folk," a rippling waltz – he soloed with striking self-assurance, forming a steady and unlabored flow of ideas. He was even more focused on "Old Ballad," a vintage reverie that he has recently refurbished.[1945]

After the final tune of the last quintet set, there was one final presentation by Douglas of the FONT Award of Recognition. The trophy itself, a plaque attached to an old trumpet bell, had been presented to Kenny after every set over the period of four days and was beginning to fall apart increasingly comically at each appearance. It read:

> On behalf of the community of
> creative trumpeters in New York
> The Festival of New Trumpet Music
> presents Kenny Wheeler this
> Award of Recognition,
> October 2011
> In recognition of a brilliant career on the forefront
> of jazz and creative music as a trumpeter, composer,
> arranger, and educator. You pursue your art with
> integrity, consistency, and depth.
> Through your hard work you have provided
> an example of international artistic citizenry
> from which we all draw inspiration.

During his announcements that night, Dave Holland had mentioned Kenny's old quote about himself: "I don't say much, but when I do, I don't say much." But like the previous night, Kenny once again reached for the microphone and thanked the band with some of his quirky comedy: "They're almost as good as I thought they were," he laughed, before adding, "I recently won a poll: *Old Players Deserving Less Recognition!*" parodying the *DownBeat* award category. Humour aside, he deserved this attention and to be honoured in this way. Dave Douglas said:

> I was very proud of that one – every night was so special and different. And to have Kenny there sounding so great and playing so well and interacting with everyone so vibrantly. I often feel like in this music people get their due when they're not really playing like themselves anymore – when it's too late, or posthumously.[1946]

The 2011 Festival of New Trumpet Music celebrating Kenny and his music would have been a significant event for him anywhere – but in New York, where he had faced perhaps the most devastating episode of his late career just five years earlier at the Blue Note, it was a monumental triumph. He had once again "faced the dragon" (as Dave Holland had so eloquently observed) and emerged victorious, lauded by the musical community of the city he had looked upon with such excited trepidation as a young man. Members of the bands Kenny played with that weekend at the Jazz Standard were sometimes moved to tears by the joy of playing their hero's music with him.[1947] Their energy had a profoundly positive effect on Kenny; Mark Wheeler went so far as to say that FONT had probably prolonged his dad's life, giving him another few years of strength and vitality in his old age.

After the successful (albeit delayed) 80th birthday tour of Kenny's new music for big band, the next step was to record it. The album, which would be titled *The Long Waiting*,[1948] is possibly the most significant of Kenny's association with the CAM Jazz record label – and even more so as his final big-band album.

Kenny's increasing age gave Mark Wheeler a sense of urgency in the period leading up to the recording. He had written to the band in April 2011: "My

Photo 46: The final night of FONT. Left to right: Craig Taborn, Kenny, and Dave Holland.
Courtesy Nick Smart

Dad is keeping well and practises every day but, as he is now 81, it would be great if we could do this sooner rather than later."[1949] The good feeling from the tour was still in place, and they felt as strongly as Mark did that this music – Kenny's first album truly under his own name with what he considered his *own* big band since *Music for Large and Small Ensembles* – needed to be recorded.[1950] The band readily agreed to play, but it took some time to work out the details. There was disagreement at the outset about where the album would be made, with Marini wanting to record in Italy with an Italian big band. Mark Wheeler recounted "having a very deep discussion with Andrea about recording *The Long Waiting* in London", conveying his dad's conviction about doing this with his own musicians:

> He said, "Your dad's music belongs to the world." I just said to him, "I know, Andrea, but let's be honest, it's probably going to be his last big-band CD, and this group of musicians, he's grown up with them. He met them all once he went to England – he's older than most of them but he grew up – in jazz terms – with most of the people in the *Long Waiting* band."[1951]

Eventually it was settled by Marini that CAM Records would record the album at London's Angel Studios, since all the musicians were based in the area.[1952] "I had to sort of get that through to him," Mark said. "I don't think he accepted it. He took it, but I don't think he liked it."[1953]

Once the location and studio were set, they planned the recording dates for 2–3 September 2011, just over a month before Kenny was headed to New York for FONT. There was one day of rehearsal on 1 September at the Royal Academy of Music to refresh the band, who had not really played the music since the previous October. Trumpeter John Barclay was unavailable, so Tony Fisher played for him, the first time Tony and Kenny had done anything together since their session days.[1954] Evan Parker was also unable to make the recording, so Julian Siegel played in his place. Evan's absence was especially disappointing for Kenny. Kenny told Evan's section-mate Duncan Lamont, "It's a real shame that we can't get everyone." Evan explained:

> . . . I seemed to have commitments at all the dates that came up, and said, "Look, you've got to go ahead and do it", but apparently he said to Duncan, "Yes. It's a shame that Evan's not here. He's part of the family!" So yeah, [Kenny] definitely had that kind of feeling, and loyalty, and all the rest of it. But it's one thing to be loyal and another to make it work.[1955]

Duncan was once again on the session, and Pete Churchill returned to conduct. Pete, remembering Duncan's problems seeing the music on the tour, and realizing that a recording required a more exact interpretation, came to the studio equipped with a pair of reading glasses to loan the saxophonist. Duncan tried them on and said, "Oh! You can see *everything*! Can I keep

Photo 47: Kenny recording in isolation for *The Long Waiting*.
Courtesy Nick Smart

these?" Duncan played the recording, armed with a new lease on life – or at least his vision.[1956]

Churchill planned the sessions carefully, consulting Derek Watkins about what order might be most advantageous in terms of the brass players' endurance. Pete described the first day, having been once again challenged by the dominant lead trumpet player from the start:

> So we got in there and it was all set up, sound guy got everyone set up in their tiers, rhythm section was in rooms on the side behind glass doors, and first thing Derek did – another kind of strategy, before anything started – was that he took off his headphones and said, "I can't wear these. You'll have to open the doors so we can hear the rhythm section." In one fell swoop, he turned that session into a live session, where the engineer had much less control . . . I mean, the *audacity* of that! I still think that was his master stroke in terms of putting his imprint on that. He said, "We'll be all right." What it meant is that people had to solo from their chairs . . . It made it difficult, and I had to pay the price for that in the mixing . . . but I think it was great for the vibe.[1957]

This change of set-up in the recording studio did make some things difficult afterwards in the mixing, which was done by Pete in Germany with CAM's recording engineer and producer. Solos couldn't be overdubbed, as rhythm-section parts now spilled over into the horn players' mics, so entire takes had to be repeated, and sometimes the editing of a missed note or bad entrance was made very difficult, if not virtually impossible. Churchill remembers also that Tony Fisher, substituting for John Barclay (who had played the tour), waited until everyone went to lunch and stayed behind to record the trumpet solo at the end of "Enowena"; but then Derek came back after lunch before everyone had returned to ask, "Ken, do you want me to put that down for you, just so you have a choice?" So Derek recorded it as well. Even though he'd been happy to give the solo to John Barclay on tour (which is why it was in his folder), "on the album, if it wasn't going to be John, [Derek] wanted to be the one to do it," Pete said. This is yet another example of Kenny's refusing to make a decision, forcing others, Pete in this case, to do the "dirty work" for him, having to choose one musician – and friend – over another.[1958]

Kenny's tracks were recorded in isolation during the full band sessions, but he was dissatisfied with some of his solos that day and wanted to re-record them. According to Mark Wheeler, Kenny – perhaps mistakenly – got the feeling that his manager wouldn't allow for a second session and maybe even didn't think he could do any better at a later date, something Andrea claimed was never his decision. Out of desperation, and possibly needlessly, he asked Mark and Nick to write to Andrea on his behalf, telling him how well he had just played in New York on the FONT trip and that he could do a good job if given the chance.[1959] Whatever the misunderstanding, it caused further friction between them all. Regardless, it is heartbreaking that an artist of Kenny's calibre would feel the need in old age to essentially beg permission to re-record and have others vouch for his performance in this way.[1960] When asked, CAM producer Ermanno Basso graciously said, "It's Ken! He can do what he likes. If he wants to re-record *all* his solos, that's fine!"[1961] With this, Kenny prevailed, and Nick took Kenny back to Angel Studios in November to re-record his solos, some two months after the original sessions. But the whole situation was another nail in the coffin for Kenny's relationship with his manager. According to Mark, this episode, combined with the exchanges and arguments over FONT, and general lack of trust stemming from how Kenny was being handled, ultimately led to Andrea ending his management relationship with Kenny. Andrea did not reply to the multiple invitations to contribute to this biography, but he did express his views to Mark that he felt he had done all he could for Kenny, and that it had not always been seen or appreciated by those on the periphery, and, if anything, his work may even have been made more difficult by other people's interference which he perceived as them acting in their own interest.[1962]

A notable difference between *The Long Waiting* and Kenny's earlier big-band albums is the absence of Norma Winstone, replaced on this album by vocalist Diana Torto. Norma's voice, possibly the single most distinctive element of Kenny's sound as an orchestrator of his own music, gave Kenny's melodic lines an ethereal, transparent, and floating quality that is as identifiable as his own flugelhorn sound. Trumpeter Henry Lowther called the effect of Kenny and Norma together being like "British music that I've always known – that sound . . . This is something unique, something very precious."[1963] Diana's voice is less transparent and brighter, and maybe more forthright than Norma's. "She's more accomplished in a way than I am with what she can do [technically]," Norma said, adding that Kenny had once told her that "[Diana] sings my music good."[1964] But some long-time members of the band begrudged the combination of factors that precluded Norma from being there, questioning whether on a big-band recording of Kenny's music the character of the voice was a more crucial element of the band's sound than the piano. Kenny once confided in a friend that it "really hurt him, this business with Diana", but that "he didn't have the energy to fight Andrea" about the matter.[1965] But the bottom line is that Diana had the skills to sing this music, by all accounts did an accomplished job with the difficult voice parts that Kenny had written, and cannot be blamed for the internal politics and behind-the-scenes complaints of some of the musicians who had worked together for many years, each with their own histories and prejudices.

After Kenny's solos were overdubbed, Pete Churchill went to Germany to edit and mix *The Long Waiting*. He remembered that the mixing engineer, Johannes Wohlleben, was stunned by how the British brass players could play "big chords so well in tune".[1966] Evan Parker, who had been unable to play on the sessions, contributed instead by writing liner notes for Kenny. "Somehow, he found a place for me," Evan said.[1967] In his notes, Evan remarked on the phenomenon of Kenny's recent massive output, quoting a critic who compared him to other great artists who experience a flurry of activity in their later years:

> It seems simple, listening to this work with particular attention to the melody, but in Wheeler's themes there is a compositional complexity that only a great craftsman of music is able to construct. "This torrent of beautiful melody, this acceleration in creativity reminded me of the surge in work-rate which Picasso went through, producing several works a day in 1968–1971", explains the critic Sebastian Scotney, "Or of the last four years (1893–7) and nine opus numbers (114–122) of Brahms, the period after he'd told his publisher he was packing it in. Who knows where these late flowerings in a creative life come from. They are miracles."[1968]

In his review for the *Guardian,* critic John Fordham said "the pieces here glow with his inimitably bittersweet harmonies and build melodic fragments that sound like snatches of wistful songs into richly layered, choirlike effects. They sound as fresh as if he'd just discovered his muse. Wheeler's flugelhorn-playing has its wobbly moments, but his upper-register sound still soars and glides." Fordham closed by calling the album "another essential item for followers of Britain's most reluctant jazz hero".[1969]

———

In December 2011, after recording *The Long Waiting,* Kenny was a guest on a revisit to some music he had recorded over 40 years earlier, written by his friend Duncan Lamont. Duncan rearranged music from the *Mr. Benn* series for a CD called *As If By Magic . . . ,*[1970] featuring a UK big band. In the liner notes, Duncan praises Kenny, saying he had "become a world-renowned figure in the world of jazz, so when the *Mr. Benn* project became a reality, it was wonderful to have him as a guest soloist on some of the tracks and playing so beautifully."[1971]

More significantly, in late January 2012 Kenny decided to give physical copies of all of the music in his possession to the library at the Royal Academy of Music in London. Nick Smart, by then Head of Jazz at the Academy, collected the countless boxes and old suitcases from Kenny's attic, filled with scores and parts written and collected over his five decades as a composer. (Fittingly, the acquisition was announced by trumpeter Dave Douglas, who happened to be onstage for a concert as a guest artist with the Royal Academy's jazz students on 26 January.) The Royal Academy's team of archivists began attempting to organize and collate the stacks of scores and parts, almost all of which were out of order, and many incomplete due to Kenny's non-existent "filing system". Nick and various fellow Wheeler researchers (including Paul Rushka and Brian Shaw) assisted in the slow process of identifying the many nonsequential parts and organizing the collection, spending

Photo 48: Kenny and Derek Watkins at Derek's party, May 2012.
Courtesy Chris Hughes

hours in the basement of the Academy library sorting the music from over 100 separate compositions – many times finding multiple arrangements of the same tune Kenny had written for various combinations of players over the years.[1972] To celebrate the arrival of the new archive, the Royal Academy Big Band played a concert of unknown or rarely heard Wheeler gems called "The Lost Scores" in the foyer of the Queen Elizabeth Hall as part of the London Jazz Festival on 18 November 2012, before Kenny's big band performed in the main hall that evening.

This Queen Elizabeth Hall concert would be the final time Kenny's band played together with him present. Nick had helped arrange this concert with John Cumming and set up a warm-up gig for them at Dorking Watermill Jazz Club ten days before. However, in addition to the inevitable celebratory atmosphere that occurred whenever the band reformed, there was a tinge of melancholy for these two final outings. John Taylor and Diana Torto were invited back for both gigs but they declined. Gwilym Simcock retook his place at the piano, and the band performed *The Long Waiting* music from the 80th birthday tour, with Norma Winstone poignantly at Kenny's side once again.

By this point, Derek Watkins's health was in decline. He had suffered from a few hernias, and the ongoing treatment for an earlier cancer diagnosis was taking its toll. He still played with all his exceptional vigour and intensity, but the trumpet appeared to take up more of his energy. By now, he probably knew his illness was serious; in May that year, he took the step to throw a big party, the stated purpose of which was to celebrate his 50 years as a professional musician. It was a huge gathering of trumpet royalty from across the generations, including Kenny, of course, as one of the VIPs. During the soundcheck for Kenny's Queen Elizabeth Hall appearance, Nick was busy conducting the Royal Academy band and put recent graduate Reuben Fowler in to deputize. The young trumpeter was thrilled to be sitting in that band surrounded by so many musical heroes. He recalled Derek's emotional response to this adulation: "I just wish you could have heard me when I could still play."[1973] Derek played brilliantly on the concert, as always, but became increasingly ill over the next few months. He passed away at home in March 2013, just 68 years old.

———·—·———

Modern folk singer and songwriter Sam Amidon had originally wanted the guitarist Bonnie Raitt to make a cameo appearance on his new album. She was unavailable, so Amidon's friend, drummer Chris Vatalaro, mentioned that Kenny Wheeler lived in London. They found the trumpeter's number and called him up:

> I was so nervous to call him. I got him on the phone, and I was kind of rambling on: "Hey, my name's Sam and I sing folk songs, but I kind of change them around, and I'm doing this album for Nonesuch, and I play

with Bill Frisell" – you know, just trying to make myself sound like some-body he wouldn't hang up on. And he just cut in eventually: "When's the date? When is it!?"[1974]

Amidon was excited that Kenny was on board, saying, "I was in search of a truly distinctive instrumental voice – not just a 'jazz' player, but somebody who sang through their instrument and whose appearance would feel like the presence of a personality and not just an instrumental part."[1975]

In February 2012, Kenny recorded solos on two tracks of what would be released as Amidon's *Bright Sunny South*.[1976,1977] There was concern about whether Kenny could play the session at all, given his frail shape. "He move[d] quite slowly, and I wasn't sure how it would go because trumpet is such a physical instrument," Amidon said.[1978] (The singer had underestimated Kenny's age in assuming that, since his ECM debut was in 1975, he must have been much younger than his actual 82 years.) When Kenny arrived by taxi, Amidon and the album's producer each took one of his arms to help him out of the taxi and into the studio, getting him into his chair near the microphone, where he slowly opened his case and retrieved his flugelhorn while chatting with them about Bill Frisell. In the studio, "he was his usual soft-spoken self . . . We got him a cup of coffee and set up his headphone mix; all he asked for was a bit of reverb on his trumpet in his 'cans,'" Amidon said.[1979] Kenny plays flugelhorn over "I Wish I Wish" and also plays a brief commentary on the lovely "He's Taken My Feet". Amidon remembered that as Kenny was overdubbing his part on the former, he and the others in the booth were sur-prised at how much he played. "If you heard the raw file of him playing, you might question whether he was listening, because he was playing right over the vocal. Yet his playing is so responsive to everything else that's going on around it – he was definitely listening," Amidon said.[1980] One can hear both Kenny's trademark sound and his age on this recording. Other than muting some bits of Kenny's playing where he was soloing over the top of Sam's voice, there was no processing or pitch correction used on his track, so what you hear on the final release is what he was playing in the moment. "Consider-ing how slowly he was moving and how fragile he seemed, I was amazed and moved by the power of his playing," Amidon said.[1981] Obviously affected by hearing this album, Kenny's long-time friend and producer Nick Purnell said that "Ken's playing on Sam Amidon's 'I Wish, I Wish' is a much better example of classic Kenny . . . Ken's playing transports me back to those incredible late '70s recordings."[1982] Purnell's nostalgia was indeed well timed, as Kenny would soon make a new recording for ECM – his first in nearly 15 years.

———·———

The most intimate and comprehensive celebration of Kenny's career came soon thereafter. To recognize the newly acquired Kenny Wheeler Archive and his connection with the Royal Academy of Music, the Academy's Museum

Photo 49: The opening reception of the Kenny Wheeler Exhibition. Left to right: John Taylor, Kenny, Chris Laurence, Martin France, Evan Parker, and Stan Sulzmann.

Courtesy Royal Academy of Music

and Collections team mounted a year-long exhibition of his life and work. It was to be on permanent display in the Academy's museum for a year, from Spring 2013 to 2014; referencing Kenny's quote about his own music, the exhibition was called *Kenny Wheeler: Master of Melancholy Chaos.* Nick Smart was charged with curating the presentation, drawing items collected from Kenny's archive and his family collection for display, with the assistance of Joanna Tapp from the Museums and Collections team, who had organized several such shows for the Academy in the past and helped Nick get a handle on the project's scope and potential contents. Tapp spent a great deal of time and energy investing in Kenny's life and music for the project – so much so that when Nick introduced her, he said, "Kenny, this is Joanna, who is helping put the exhibition together. She knows more about you than you do!" Kenny replied, "Oh, poor you!"[1983]

To open the exhibition, there was a reception introducing the highlights of the displayed items. Now well into his eighties, Kenny was getting a bit more used to being the centre of attention. Nevertheless, the attendees were surprised when he suddenly asked for the microphone at this opening event to pay tribute to his instrumental brother-in-arms. "I just want to say that Derek Watkins was one of the greatest trumpet players to ever live," he said.

It had been barely a month since Derek's death; his widow Wendy, sitting in the front row, was moved to tears.

Later, with Kenny playing his new Eclipse flugelhorn, his quintet (including Stan Sulzmann, John Taylor, Chris Laurence, and Martin France) performed a short set, joined by Evan Parker for the final tune. After the speeches and music, the attendees all went upstairs to tour the exhibition, but Kenny couldn't quite bring himself to look at his own life with everyone else present, saying "It's all a bit embarrassing." There are photos of the reception with Doreen – possibly also uncomfortable with all the fuss being made about "her Ken" – mugging in front of the six-foot-high photograph of Kenny welcoming visitors to the museum.

The exhibition was organized using the titles of Kenny's most important albums as chronological signposts for each stage of his career, including *Live at Newport*, *Windmill Tilter*, *Karyōbin*, *Gnu High*, *Music for Large and Small Ensembles*, *Angel Song*, and *The Long Waiting*. It included photos of him and his family from his childhood, letters written back home throughout his career, a battered flugelhorn (hilariously accompanied by a seemingly endless stack of instrument repair bills from Phil Parker, whose workshop had restored Kenny's ill-fated instruments after every mishap), album covers, a transcription of Kenny's "Solo One" with a recording on headphones available for listeners to follow along, and a specially commissioned video from his latest recording sessions for *The Long Waiting*, edited together with new interviews with Evan Parker and Norma Winstone, reflecting on their time working with him. Placards mounted throughout the display recounted Kenny's biography, leading the visitors' journey through a narrative account of his life. *Jazz UK* magazine called it "An intimate insight into the life and work of a true UK jazz institution".[1984] A bit after the exhibit opening, Kenny and Doreen returned with Mark to spend some time in the exhibition without the crowds and attention. Kenny was amused, but deeply moved, by this broad look back at his life and career.[1985] One wonders if he could finally grasp just how much he was admired, and feel some satisfaction with how much he had accomplished.

Over the year, there were several events tied to the exhibition, with concerts of Kenny's music and public lectures about his compositions and trumpet playing. In June 2013, Alyn Shipton led a panel discussion with Kenny's long-time collaborators Norma Winstone, Henry Lowther, and Chris Laurence. At the conclusion of the conversation, Shipton asked the panel to retell their favourite "Kenny-isms". Each person had their own recollection, eliciting laughter from the listeners. Norma told one that brings a laugh and, in equal measure, is telling about Kenny's personality:

> Kenny's notoriously sort of accident-prone – he says he has a bad relationship with mechanical things – but glasses don't count as mechanical. He's always dropping them, treading on them, and . . . he had this

Photo 50: Doreen Wheeler making friends laugh, feigning exasperation next to the giant photo of her husband.

Courtesy Nick Smart

collection of spectacles with arms missing, you know, screws missing, and lenses dropped out . . . So he decided he'd get them fixed, you see, so he collected them all together and took them to the local optician. And he went in, up to the young lady behind the counter and he said to her, "Can you do anything with these?" So she said, "Oh, thank you very much. We need them – we'll send them to Ethiopia!" And Ken didn't really want to disappoint her . . . He said, "Well, she was so grateful for them, so I just walked out!"[1986]

———·———

Back in 1993, Italian singers Tiziana Simona and Lorena Fontana commissioned Kenny to write settings of poetry by Lewis Carroll, William Butler Yeats, and Stevie Smith. The work was originally intended for five vocal soloists: two men and three women. Simona (with whom Kenny had recorded the album *Gigolo* in 1986), made no mistake about the personnel she wanted on the project. Norma Winstone said that the settings were "for [Tiziana] and three other singers. Ian Shaw and Cleveland Watkiss did it. But she didn't want me. Kenny said, 'Listen, I asked her about you being one of the singers and she said no.' She wanted to do it – I can't blame her, really; she wanted to sing the lead." One of the poems on the original iteration of this material was Stevie Smith's "The Hat". Norma still has sheet music from the original, labelled "Tiziana comes on wearing his hat . . ." written in Kenny's handwriting. "She was a bit of an actress," Norma said.[1987]

A few years later, in 1998, Pete Churchill resurrected Kenny's settings of poetry and organized performances at the Royal Northern College of Music in Manchester and the Berlin Jazz Festival. Norma instructed the singers, who were used to singing on top of the beat, to adjust their rhythmic interpretation once Kenny was performing with them. Pete, who sat right next to Kenny in the performances, said that he had never sat so far back on the beat in his life. Norma had warned them that they'd have to recalibrate how they were singing it once Kenny was with them, and emphasized to the group that it was for five individual voices, not a blended "Manhattan Transfer" sound.[1988]

Pete occasionally had to find diplomatic ways to discuss the settings with Kenny, who could sometimes be tone-deaf to subtleties in language due to context. "There was one for the male voices called 'I Hate This Girl', the Stevie Smith poem," Pete Churchill said, which was

> written by a woman about this girl – this is how Ken's naïveté is unbelievable – you want to say "Ken, she's a woman – she's *allowed* to write a poem called 'I Hate This Girl' because the girl has stolen her bloke, you know – but you can't then set it for two men!" It's a big 7/4, very muscular groove: *I hate this girl, She is so cold . . . I should like to kill her!* There's no other way of putting this across except like some sort of axe murderer – I

mean, it's very weird! And Ken would say, "You think that's weird?" I'd say, "Sorry Ken, it is a bit . . . !"[1989]

Despite Kenny's occasional semantic insensitivity, the performance in Berlin (including "I Hate This Girl") had gone over well. ("I don't know how much was lost in translation!" Churchill laughed.) He also remembered that, in Berlin, Kenny's mouthpiece had gotten stuck in his flugelhorn, causing him to be unable to close his case: another classic Wheeler mishap.

Several years later, Churchill expanded this music for his full Jazz Singers vocal ensemble at the Guildhall School of Music. When he founded the London Vocal Project ensemble, the group began to learn this music and several new settings Kenny had recently written. Kenny, who would have never been mistaken for a professional copyist even in his younger days, had begun to lose eyesight and acquire the uneven handwriting common to octogenarians. Accordingly, Pete had the task of deciphering the manuscript – and fixing any errors he found in the scores. Pete remembered that Kenny had "sent me vocal things where I'd say, 'Ken, you've shortened the blowing changes by eight bars – did you mean to?' Kenny would reply, 'Oh, no, can you put those back in?'"[1990]

It became obvious to Pete that this music should be recorded, and conversations began with Mark Wheeler and Nick Smart, who were by this point working as Kenny's de facto managers. They set about choosing the studio and coordinating dates for the sessions, which were set for June 2012.[1991] Around this time, Nick had been collaborating closely with Dave Stapleton (founder and boss of Edition Records) on the new Kenny Wheeler Prize, and Dave was also excited to do something with Kenny on his label. *Mirrors* seemed to be the perfect fit.[1992] Norma Winstone would be the featured soloist on the album, and Kenny would contribute flugelhorn solos. He and the vocal ensemble were joined by pianist Nikki Iles and the core of her own band, The Printmakers: saxophonist Mark Lockheart, bassist Steve Watts, and drummer James Maddren. Nikki was captivated by Kenny's writing in this genre:

> The astonishing thing is that it seemed like the music came first. That says so much about how strong his music is. And some of those poems, the scansion is not easy – they don't fit into neat boxes. But still, they were the kind of tunes that really get under your skin and become earworms. Even the one that's on one note [sings "Black March"] – because it's very wordy. What an amazing thing . . . You just realize what an astonishing composer he is.[1993]

In his lukewarm review, the *Guardian*'s John Fordham commented that "Wheeler's rare imagination often makes this unusual venture gleam, but the words do recede in the full-ensemble parts, and the most absorbing passages occur when Winstone, at her coolly ecstatic best, takes the spotlight." He called the album an ". . . uneven but intriguing addition to Wheeler's

Photo 51: Nikki Iles and Kenny laughing between takes at the *Mirrors* recording session.
Courtesy Nick Smart

remarkable canon".[1994] *JazzTimes*, more unabashedly positive, called the album "11 tracks of sheer beauty and perfection".[1995]

In October 2013, Kenny was asked to record on an album for the UK-based Sardinian singer Filomena Campus, titled *Scaramouche*.[1996] The recording was originally supposed to have taken place in a London studio, but when Kenny arrived in his wheelchair he discovered that the studio was on the floor above the ground floor, with no elevator to transport him. Instead, the producers decided to record Kenny's overdubs at his Wallwood Road home, a space where he would be more comfortable and could more easily navigate. The wisdom of this decision is evident in the results, which are stunning, especially given how weak he was at this point in his life. His musical fingerprint is evident from the opening seconds of the track "Momentum", on which he sounds strong, in control, and as much himself as ever. His pitch, which could be uneven in his later years, is dead on; his burnished lower notes are full and centred; and his trademark upper range, often missing from his last recordings, even makes a reappearance, manifest by a couple of high concert Gs. A listener might even find some poetry in the brief phrase Kenny played on the final chord of this, as the notes ascend and then suddenly disappear.

———··———

In November 2013, Kenny's quintet – with J.T. on piano – performed twice at the London Jazz Festival. The first was as part of a double bill in the Queen Elizabeth Hall with Lee Konitz's duo; the second was a few days later in the Royal Festival Hall Clore Ballroom as part of the "Jazz in the Round" recording for Jez Nelson's *Jazz on 3* show. They had shared a concert at the Queen Elizabeth Hall with Lee Konitz's duo as part of the London Jazz Festival, but Kenny found it increasingly difficult to play. "It was very shaky – it was not a good gig for Ken at all," Stan Sulzmann said. He continued:

> As long as you kept it sensible, he was kind of all right. The smaller the group, the better it was. Like in a trio, you could make changes quickly, so if he dropped a few bars, you could move. Because Ken couldn't hear, sometimes he would drop something and lose a bit halfway through a sequence and he'd never get back, which would *never* have happened ten years before – or even five years before – because he would hear it straight away and adjust. But he couldn't do it anymore . . .[1997]

But Manfred Eicher, the legendary producer who had worked with Kenny on so many of his classic ECM recordings, from *Gnu High* to *A Long Time Ago,* wanted to make another recording with him. Evan Parker, once again looking out for Kenny, had been talking with Manfred about the possibility of them recording together once more, reassuring him that Kenny was no longer with the management that Manfred had struggled to connect with in the past. "It was a very emotional feeling. We both felt we would really like to go into the studio again," Eicher said.[1998] Evan contacted Stan about the possibility of this happening. As Kenny's right-hand man in his quintet, Stan was concerned that Kenny might not be in good enough physical shape to record. Kenny "was slipping fast," he said, adding that he was worried that Eicher was unaware of Kenny's condition and that they needed to make a firm decision, believing that they needed to "do it soon . . . or don't do it". Knowing that time was of the essence, there was concern about when recording dates would get set; some members of the quintet had conflicting commercial sessions, which delayed things further. Finally, increasingly aware of Kenny's rapidly declining condition, Stan put his foot down, no longer willing to reschedule dates. "If we don't do this now, it's not going to get done," he said.[1999] It was the right decision.

Stan and John Parricelli went to Kenny's house to choose material. "I can remember sitting in his music room," Stan said, "and he was all over the place, and he could hardly play . . . nowhere near like someone who is about to make a record, or anything . . . He was having trouble reading . . ." Instead of the more comfortable and forgiving flugelhorn, he was playing trumpet that night, and having considerable problems producing a sound. They whittled down the list of material to what would eventually appear on the album and began to rehearse. Kenny had difficulty in the rehearsal, playing a few notes and stopping, getting lost and not being able to find his place again. Stan said, "I realized that the only stuff he's going to get through is the ones he knows well, that are comfortable, reasonable easy tempos, what Ken does beautifully, anyway, lovely melodies. *That's* the best choice." Stan and John Parricelli helped get Kenny through the choice of material, gently nudging him into a programme they thought would work well for him.[2000]

When the recording sessions for ECM finally came around that December, Stan was used to playing supportively for Kenny and adapting in the moment. Stan said he

> was watching and I could see if he was going to pick [the melody] up or not. If he doesn't, I'll play with him or we'll track it on later . . . It seemed to me the safest thing in the studio was to know exactly what you're doing, don't fuss around, and don't stop for mistakes, because you can repair it later.

Chris Laurence added, "You learned over many years to make sure he was sitting down, with the microphone in the right place . . . He liked to have the music bigger, plenty of light, plenty of reverb; he wanted to feel safe . . . We just sat him down and got him a cup of tea and we got the best out of him."[2001] Manfred Eicher had expected Kenny to be in a weakened condition at the studio, but was nonetheless surprised at the degree of his frailty.[2002] They recorded at London's famous Abbey Road Studios, in the iteration of Kenny's quintet which had become his final working group – with John Parricelli, Chris Laurence, and Martin France. Stan continued:

> [Studio 3 was] a beautiful room to play in live . . . but I could see it was going to be difficult, because Ken was in a booth, completely sound-proofed off in a booth with headphones, which is about as bad as it can be for Ken, because the headphones are never right, he can't hear anything, or he's not got it on properly, or there's not enough reverb, all the usual stuff that goes on . . . And these headphones were deafening, and still, [*Kenny said*] "I can't hear . . . !"

In the past, Kenny had always preferred to be in the room playing with the other musicians live in the studio rather than being isolated. Stan said, "he was old-school. He didn't like screens and headphones; he liked to be able to hear everything – he was not of that generation." Kenny chose to play flugelhorn, encouraged by the other guys in the band who told him how lovely he sounded on it, not mentioning the difficulties posed by the trumpet. There was also the question of who would lead the session and keep it moving to ensure they recorded everything they needed to make an album in two days. Kenny was in no shape to take charge, so Stan told Manfred Eicher that he would be helping run the recording session, for which the producer was grateful. By the time it got to 1 pm on the first day, Kenny was exhausted, telling Stan, "I think I'm going to have to go home and go to bed." The band had only got one take of everything once they got the soundcheck finished. Despite this early setback, Eicher was "very warm, very soft and gentle, absolutely lovely" with Kenny, Stan said. "Manfred is a very astute person . . . and he loved Ken . . . He was really nice and totally supportive."[2003] The appreciation was mutual. Eicher complimented Stan on how helpful he'd been and added, "Stan Sulzmann plays so beautifully."[2004]

That evening, Kenny had a difficult night; he was up several times and had a minor fall at one point. The next day, Manfred had to leave for another commitment, so ECM's Steve Lake produced the second session. The musicians continually checked on Kenny in his isolation booth, all concerned for him and aware of how significant this recording was. Understanding his lack of mobility, Manfred and Steve allowed Kenny to stay in the booth to listen to playbacks during the sessions. Despite all the difficulties, Manfred was pleased to hear Kenny's personality shine through his age. "It was Kenny Wheeler's tone, sound, and phrasing," he said. "I was also touched to see how the other musicians adjusted their own kind of musical lines to play with Kenny . . . Everybody played for Kenny. And we all felt happy to see Kenny happy."[2005] *Songs for Quintet*[2006] was the name of the resulting album, which ECM described as:

> an inspirational session featuring Wheeler compositions of recent vintage (plus a fresh approach to "Nonetheless", first heard on *Angel Song*), was recorded in London's Abbey Road Studio with four of Kenny's favourite players. Stan Sulzmann, John Parricelli, Chris Laurence and Martin France work together marvellously as an interactive unit, solo persuasively, and provide support for the tender and lyrical flugelhorn of the bandleader.[2007]

The label's description of the album continued, making reference to Kenny's audible frailty: "If age and illness temper the strength of his sound on *Songs for Quintet*, the melodic imagination and the improvisational courage remain; the flugelhorn soloist could not be anybody but Kenny Wheeler."[2008] "I was so happy and grateful to do this album," Eicher said.[2009]

Those two days recording at Abbey Road would be Kenny's last studio sessions.[2010] It is both poignant and fitting that ECM, the label that had launched him to international recognition and meant so much to him over the decades (and a label to which he had contributed in defining its iconic sound), would re-enter his life at the very end and give the world his final recording.

Throughout Kenny's life, Doreen had been his caretaker – not only raising their two children but doing basically everything else for him as well, allowing him to concentrate on trumpet playing and composing. "He had no idea of the problems that most of us have in our lives, because he had Doreen to do it all for him," Kenny's friend Henry Lowther said.

> He was a rather spoiled child at times. He really was. He couldn't do anything himself . . . There's an old saying about "There's a great woman behind a great man". She was definitely that. She allowed him to do his music . . . All he did was write music and practise! . . . Somebody once said, "We should all have a Doreen!"[2011]

At the end of March 2013, Kenny and Doreen were surrounded by friends, family and loved ones to celebrate their remarkable 60 years of marriage. It was a wonderful night of celebration, with many of his musical family there to share their joy.

There were challenging times ahead for the couple. As his health steadily worsened, Doreen also began to feel the effects of her own ageing, as his care became increasingly draining for her. As early as the early 2010s, Kenny had begun to show signs of decline. They were very slow in onset, but worrisome enough that he was taken to a doctor, who diagnosed him with frontal lobe dementia (which causes issues similar to those caused by Alzheimer's disease) in early 2011.[2012]

While Mark Wheeler was doing so much for his dad professionally in his older age, Kenny and Doreen's daughter Louann Newman was caring for them a great deal at home. Though Doreen's overall health was stable, her memory was starting to fade and she would forget if she had taken her medicine. While working her own full-time job, Louann would phone her parents multiple times a day to check on them, and bring them dinner on their way home, just to make sure they were looking after themselves. At the same time, Kenny's declining health (and his frustrations with the limitations it imposed) made life difficult for the entire family. His eyesight was rapidly diminishing, and walking – an important lifelong source of exercise and stress relief for him – was increasingly difficult. Mark and Louann decided it was time to have professionals come in to care for their parents while they were working. Leaning on Doreen throughout their marriage, Kenny's advancing lack of mobility put even more stress on his wife of over 60 years. "He couldn't do anything for himself," Louann said, adding that her mother "was literally exhausted. And [Dad] was getting up silly hours in the morning, just confused, trying to get dressed. She was just exhausted. Absolutely exhausted . . . It was just too much for her." Faced with an impossible situation, Mark and Louann decided they had no choice but to temporarily put their dad in a care home in May 2014, the only way Doreen could get enough of a break from caring for him and get much-needed rest herself.

Photo 52: Kenny and Doreen at their 60th anniversary party.
Courtesy Nick Smart

Almost immediately, however, Doreen's health took a turn for the worse. At one point, her condition was so concerning that the family worried that her decline might outpace Kenny's. In fact, she came perilously close to death when the heart valve she had replaced around 15 years earlier began to leak. Thankfully, she pulled through, stabilized, and was able to return home. During this time, Louann and Mark had a nightmarish schedule, constantly going from their jobs to the hospital to check on their mother, then to the care home to visit their father, every day. Kenny, meanwhile, was panicking, thinking he would never get out of the home because of her condition. Unfortunately, his health continued to worsen, and after a series of tests, it was determined that he had prostate cancer.

While Kenny was in the care home, friends and family came to visit. Louann and her long-time partner Andrew saw him often, as did Mark and his wife Tracy. He had a direct line to his room and Dave Holland talked to him on the phone a few times.[2013] Nick Smart paid Kenny several visits; during one, he brought Kenny his flugelhorn so he could practise in his room. Others tried to set him up with large-print manuscript paper and an electronic keyboard so he could compose and keep up some musical activity. As it happened, the facility was opening a newly constructed wing with a cafeteria in it, and on 24 July they held a launch party – centred around their jazz star resident. It was also on this day at the care home that Nick told Kenny about the plans to write this biography; he was pleased it was being done but, as always, surprised anyone would be interested in his story. They even clarified a few memories in his room before Nick wheeled Kenny into the lounge and the nurses tried to persuade him to play his flugelhorn for the ribbon-cutting ceremony. As the local paper's photographer and the town mayoress looked on, Kenny, oblivious to their wishes, absent-mindedly ran through a few scale patterns on his flugelhorn while looking bemused at the tragicomedy of the whole event. This was followed by a small party for the residents and their guests, J.T. and his wife Carol among them. Andrew organized a jazz trio to play for the event, with Norma Winstone joining them to sing a couple of tunes. Kenny was also going to play, but after a certain amount of time passed, he got too anxious and just sat slightly to the left of the stage listening, flugel-horn in his lap. This echoes the poignant story Gene Lees told of the two of them at a club in Montreal some 62 years earlier: an nervous young Kenny sitting at a table near the stage, waiting for an invitation from the bandstand that never came. But now, in this sad late portrait, Kenny is the star, very much welcomed by the musicians onstage to join in, this time prevented from taking part by his nerves, limited mobility, and his declining cognition.

Norma remembered another visit to Kenny in the care home, as his mental abilities continued to fade:

> . . . I met up with Hugh [Mitchell, Norma's husband] and we went up to see Ken. And because he didn't say much, you'd sometimes feel, *well, I'll keep talking* because it keeps the feeling that there's something happening. And I just said – "I don't know what's been the matter with me today." I said, "I just can't seem to remember anybody's name – I just can't remem-ber people's names today." And he just said, "Well, he's Hugh and I'm Ken!" and for a minute I thought, *That's the old Ken. He's still in there.*[2014]

Undoubtedly aware that his condition was rapidly worsening, Kenny became consumed with the idea of returning to Canada one last time. He called Mark often and asked him to take him. Mark would make excuses about why it wasn't possible and try to gently explain that he needed too much care. Kenny showed remarkable tenacity, calling Nick several times instead, practically begging him to make the journey with him. "I promise to do my best not to be a burden," Kenny would say. It was a heartbreaking situa-tion, full of unspoken finality. No one seems to know why Kenny wanted to return to his home country at this late stage in his life when the travel alone might have overcome him. Did he simply need to see his last remaining sib-ling, Mabel and his extended family? Did he want to die there?

During the first week of September 2014, Kenny was transferred from the care home into Whipps Cross University Hospital, Leytonstone with a uri-nary infection. He had not been eating or drinking and had to be given fluids intravenously. Mark played the latest mix of the recording he had made for ECM the previous December. "He thought it was OK," Mark said – Kenny being self-deprecating to the last.[2015] Norma also visited him in the hospital again, having just returned from a trip to Japan. Kenny asked her, "Did you do gigs?" She replied, "Yeah, and people came up with vinyls to sign – some of which you'd signed when you'd been there before because they love your music over there." He said, "Well, I'm glad somebody likes my music." "Ken! Stop it!" Norma said. "Don't just be glad *somebody* likes your music!" She sat down next to Kenny's bed. After a while, the conversation got quiet.

> And I thought, *I'd love to take his hand. I'd love to hold his hand*, but who-ever it is, you don't want to presume, even if it's your parent, you know, that they want you to hold their hand – maybe they don't. I just felt I really would like to take his hand. And he suddenly reached over with his hand and took hold of mine. I was resting it on the side rail that stops you from falling out . . . And he just reached over and put his hand . . . and took it over and put his other hand around it, and he just held it like that. And [*weeping*] . . . I just said, "I'd better go, I think." He said "OK. See you next year." I said, "I hope so, Ken . . ." It was like he read my mind somehow, or he wanted the same thing that I wanted.[2016]

The next week, Kenny's doctors ran tests and found that the disease had spread into his liver and lungs. Although he was in no apparent pain, he was still not eating.[2017] Kenny's condition worsened on the night of 17 September. Not totally certain if it was what he would have wanted, Mark erred on the side of caution and found a priest to administer Kenny's last rites, knowing it would at least bring comfort to Kenny's sister Mabel, who was a very faithful Catholic.

On the iPad that the big band had given Kenny back in Belfast, Mark had made a playlist of some things his dad loved that he thought would soothe him, including one of their old favourite comedy routines, Bob Newhart's *Sir Walter Raleigh Introduces Tobacco to Civilization*. With Miles Davis's *Milestones* album playing in his headphones, he quietly drifted out of consciousness. Kenny Wheeler died the next morning, at around 10:15 am, 18 September 2014, with Mark and Louann at his side. The cause of death was listed as metastatic cancer and advanced prostate cancer. He was 84 years old.[2018]

---

Word of Kenny's passing spread quickly through phone calls to the extended Wheeler family, emails between his close associates, and, inevitably, through social media, where tributes came flooding in. Nick released an official statement promptly through the Royal Academy confirming: "It was with great sadness that we learned today of the passing of Kenny Wheeler, the great jazz trumpet player and composer. It is hard to express just how large a contribution he made to the music in this country and around the world, and how deeply he touched the musicians that had the honour of working alongside him." It concluded:

> With Kenny's passing, we say goodbye to one of the great musical innovators of contemporary Jazz. His harmonic palette and singularly recognizable sound will live on in the memory of all who heard him and in the extraordinary legacy of recordings and compositions he leaves behind, inspiring generations to come. Famously self-deprecating, Kenny was always modest and humble about his own achievements. But the truth is, he was a genius walking amongst us, and it was the most tremendous privilege to have been able to consider him a dear colleague and friend.[2019]

Dave Holland was among the first of Kenny's close collaborators to mention Kenny's death, writing on Twitter, "Thinking about my dear friend Kenny Wheeler who passed away today. A beautiful spirit that lives on in his music & in our memory."[2020] Canadian-born trumpeter Ingrid Jensen wrote "Thank you Kenny Wheeler, for taking the bar and throwing it to the stars, and beyond."[2021] Jack DeJohnette said Kenny was "Not only a master musician but a truly humble and gentle soul. He touched many with his beautiful sound and compositions. May he rest in peace."[2022] In an eloquent post, composer Darcy James Argue observed that Kenny "genuinely did not want to think of himself as A Big Deal. But look, there is no getting around it: Kenny Wheeler was A Big Deal. I don't think there's any question that he belongs in the pantheon of greats, both as a player and as a composer." He continued:

> At a time when there was a fierce and highly partisan rift between the improv scene and the mainstream jazz world, Kenny showed everyone how to bridge the divide . . . His ability to draw from both is essential to his sound. If today that view seems to have acquired a bit more currency, it's in part because Kenny Wheeler, and musicians inspired by him, helped to make it so.[2023]

In a beautiful tribute penned for *JazzTimes* titled "Farewell Kenny Wheeler", Norma Winstone wrote:

> I feel very lucky to have stood next to him so often, trying to match my sound with his and hearing him create those lines in his improvisation that were so unpredictable and so recognizably his. His writing and playing were absolutely original – two notes and you knew it was him. He was a giant, and I'm sad that there will be no more music from him. How wonderful, though, that he has left us with so much.[2024]

And John Taylor, Kenny's musical partner throughout so much of his life, added this sentiment to his liner notes for the CAM Jazz release *On the Way To Two*: "It was a privilege and joy to play with you for most of my life, and I wish you were here now to listen to this music again with me."[2025] The outpouring of grief and remembrances of Kenny's career that came from his friends and musical colleagues, from his former students at Banff, and from fans, were indicative of the vast scope of his influence. Every major newspaper in his native Canada and his adopted UK published an obituary, as did leading publications around the world, including the *New York Times*, *Boston Globe*, Paris's *Le Monde*, and many others. Online music magazines posted tributes; print magazines *DownBeat*, *JazzWise*, and *JazzTimes* printed retrospectives of Kenny's career in their next issues. BBC's *Jazz on 3* broadcast a tribute on 29 September, presented by Jez Nelson and joined by John Fordham and Nick Smart, featuring brief interviews with some of Kenny's closest collaborators, including Norma Winstone, Stan Sulzmann, and Manfred Eicher. The programme also sampled the breadth of his career by playing selections from his BBC broadcasts, *The Sweet Time Suite*, Globe Unity Orchestra, *Angel Song*, *The Long Waiting*, and even an excerpt from his final ECM album *Songs for Quintet*, recorded less than a year earlier, slated to be released the following January.

At his funeral service on 11 October, Kenny's "Gentle Piece" played as mourners entered Manor Park Crematorium. Father Colum Kelly presided over the service, and Bobby Wellins, Henry Lowther, Norma Winstone, and Nick Smart spoke. Not surprisingly, music played a central role in the ceremony. Coleman Hawkins's "Body and Soul" – the recording that had moved Kenny to tears as a teenager – played over the loudspeaker, followed later in the service by Frank Sinatra's "For All We Know" and Miles Davis's "Milestones". The exit music was "On the Trail of the Lonesome Pine", performed by Laurel and Hardy. According to Mark, Kenny loved the comedy duo and "would watch Laurel and Hardy until the cows came home". Adding this song to the funeral, which had been a hit in the UK, was a way to "inject just a little bit of humour" into the end of the service. It was probably also served as the Wheeler family's little wink to each other, acknowledging Kenny's unintentional comic genius, sometimes embodying Oliver Hardy's catchphrase, "Well, here's another nice mess you've gotten me into!"[2026]

Twenty days after his funeral, Nick and Mark organized a memorial service to be held at St. James Church, Paddington, officiated by Fr. Paul Thomas. Kenny's music once again took centre stage at this event, with a trumpet quartet providing the entrance music, immediately followed by his big band playing the "Opening" of *The Sweet Time Suite*. They also played "Enowena" and "Canter No 1" from *The Long Waiting*, along with "Old Ballad". A brass ensemble performed part of the *Long Time Ago* suite, and Norma Winstone sang Kenny's "Comba No. 3" with her trio, with a touching lyric she had written about him, called "Vital Spark":[2027]

> The seasons come and the seasons go
> And everything lives again
> And every day is a miracle
> The sun, the moon, the rain;

All the lives you touched on the way
The links you held with the past.

But music lived in the heart of you
And passion's force held you true.
That vital spark that must drive us on
Will disappear from view.
I wanted you to know
You cast a fearless glow
May all the love you shared with us go with you.

Pete Churchill led the London Vocal Project, which sang "Breughel" from the *Mirrors* suite. Stan Sulzmann, Evan Parker, Dave Horler, and John Taylor spoke, with J.T. being so moved by sorrow he could barely make it through his remarks.

Fittingly, the service closed with a recording of Kenny himself – his unaccompanied "Solo One" from 1979's *Around Six*. As the sound of his lone flugelhorn filled every corner of the church's ambient acoustic, the afternoon sun appeared, gleaming through St. James's stained-glass windows. Even the musicians who knew Kenny and his career so well were overwhelmed, many of them hearing for the first time the only recording with which he was ever fully satisfied. They looked at each other with stunned glances, some afterwards exclaiming things like, *What was THAT?! That was unbelievable!*[2028]

Their friend had astonished them one last time.

# Epilogue
## Present Past, Past Present:
## The Musical Legacy of Kenny Wheeler

**How wonderful, though, that he has left us with so much.**

*Norma Winstone*

On 14 January 2015, which would have been Kenny's 85th birthday, ECM records released *Songs for Quintet*. "Following the widespread tributes to Wheeler's freethinking virtuosity, it would be all too easy to cheer his swan-song," reviewer John Fordham wrote for the *Guardian*, "but his sound does retain much of its old melancholy tenderness here, and in the context of this set's beautiful pieces and elegant improvisation, some hesitant flugelhorn moments mostly just reinforce the hypnotic humanity of the music." Praising the band, Fordham called it "an ideal ensemble to join one of jazz's most instantly recognizable voices on his last trip to a studio".[2029] *DownBeat's* Bill Milkowski said, "Wheeler's melodic imagination is fully intact in this emotive outing", dubbing the album a "poignant ending to a magnificent career".[2030] This posthumous ECM homecoming was cathartic for many of Kenny's fans, allowing them to enjoy one final new album and hear his trademark sound shining through the veneer of his frailty. In 2023, another ECM project, this time his classic album *Gnu High*, was re-released on vinyl as part of the label's new Luminessence series.

A week after the launching of *Songs for Quintet*, a blue plaque was unveiled on the Wheeler's Leytonstone home on Wallwood Road at a small ceremony commemorating his life and achievements, with Kenny's family and friends (including Dave Holland, Evan Parker, Norma Winstone, Chris Laurence, and Nick Smart) in attendance. These panels mark the birthplaces, residences, and workplaces of important UK residents. This recognition was in part brought about by the Borough of Waltham Forest, and trumpeter Digby Fairweather in his role at the National Jazz Archive. It reads simply:

KENNY WHEELER
Jazz trumpeter and composer,
lived here 1972–2014,
One of the most influential jazz musicians
of the late 20th century.

Beyond the new album and the blue plaque, other institutions took on the joyful work of keeping Kenny's memory alive. One of the most significant was the Kenny Wheeler Jazz Prize at the Royal Academy of Music in London, which was awarded each year to one graduating jazz musician at the Academy. The prize included the release of the winner's proposed recording on the Edition Records label, with support from founder Dave Stapleton. Other top universities and music conservatories around the world have continued to programme his music and introduce it to new generations of students and audiences. Indeed, compositions of Kenny's have found their way into the jazz canon in contemporary New York circles: pianists Fred Hersch and Sullivan Fortner were including "Everybody's Song But My Own" in their repertoire a decade after his passing.[2031]

In one of the most unlikely and far-reaching examples, Canadian rap artist Drake sampled a full minute of Azimuth's "The Tunnel" for his hit single "IDGAF" in October 2023. Although we suspect few Drake fans would recognize his name, this recording (which reached no. 1 on Billboard's Global 200 and Canada's Hot 100, and had nearly 400 million streams on Spotify in just the first eight months) improbably brought Kenny's sound to a younger and much wider audience than he ever reached during his lifetime. We can only hope that even a tiny percentage of those listeners will dig deeper and discover Kenny in a more substantial way.

Musicians who knew Kenny well – or at least were profoundly inspired by him – have also been busy tending the Wheeler flame since his death. Canadian trumpeter Ingrid Jensen and Seattle-based saxophonist Steve Treseler led two substantial projects – one at Seattle's landmark Royal Room club, broadcast on NPR for *Jazz Night in America* in 2015, and a subsequent recording of Kenny's tunes titled *Invisible Sounds: For Kenny Wheeler* in 2018. Another album, released in 2019 by a group called The North (David Braid, Mike Murley, Johnny Åman, and Anders Mogensen, featuring trumpeter Percy Pursglove), is titled *Plays the Music of Kenny Wheeler*[2032] and is centred around an account of Kenny's suite for small group, *Peace for Five*, originally recorded on *Deer Wan*. A follow-up album has also been recorded by the same group, this time including pianist Nikki Iles and featuring Norma Winstone, focusing on Norma's lyric settings of Kenny's tunes. Bassist Chris Laurence also released a homage to Kenny in 2021 – the album playfully entitled *Kenny Wheeler: Some Gnu Ones*. With his rhythm-section colleagues from Kenny's final quintet, John Parricelli and Martin France, this includes two previously unrecorded pieces that Kenny had written with Chris in mind: "Baroque Piece" and the mini-suite *Piece for Double Bass and Low Strings*. When Kenny gave the latter to Chris, it was still incomplete. So Chris enlisted the help of Pete Churchill, who skilfully filled in the missing elements.[2033]

Perhaps his long-time friend Dave Holland has done most to keep Kenny's music before a larger audience. In addition to introducing Kenny's work to wider exposure while he was living, Dave has subsequently worked passionately to keep his memory alive and his music performed by some of the world's greatest jazz players. For example, the tune he dedicated to Kenny, "Waltz for Wheeler", appears on *The Art of Conversation*,[2034] his duo album with pianist Kenny Barron. Dave also curated a tribute concert called "Kenny Wheeler: An Evocation" in Cadogan Hall at the London Jazz Festival in November 2015, celebrating Kenny's life and music and featuring Norma Winstone, Evan Parker, and Ralph Towner.[2035] And in November 2021 Dave Holland and John Scofield, as part of a duo tour, again played Cadogan Hall during the London Jazz Festival. On this concert, Dave introduced Kenny's "Old Ballad", calling him "one of my heroes". Afterwards, Scofield laughed, saying to the audience, "That's the first time we ever played that live. Turns out it's a hit!"[2036]

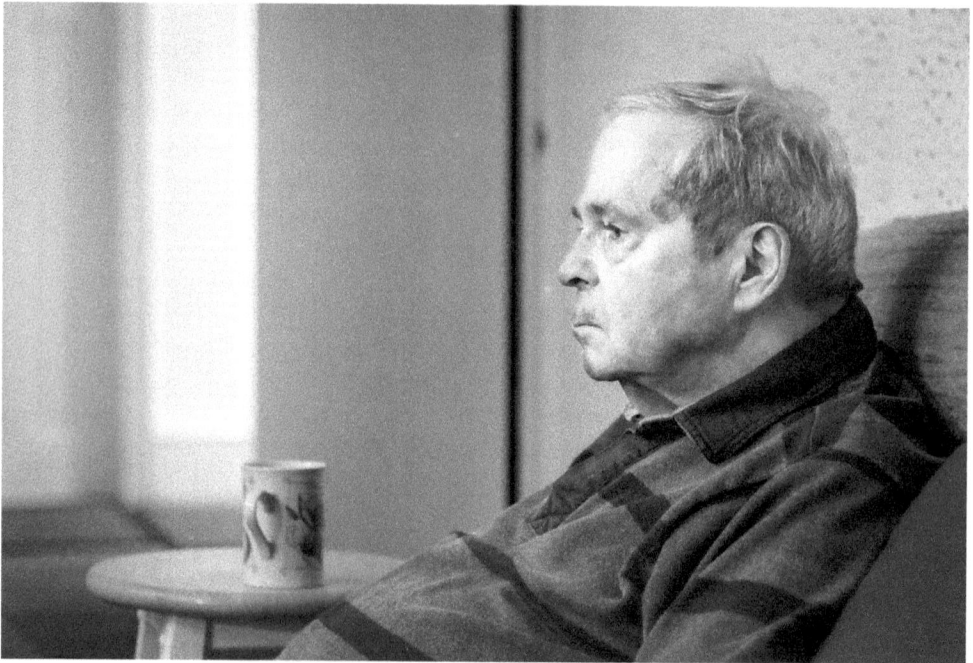

Photo 53: Kenny at his most pensive, at the *Mirrors* recording session.
Courtesy Nick Smart

Dave has championed Kenny's music in educational settings, too, leading week-long residencies and big-band performances with jazz programmes at the New England Conservatory, the University of Miami, and the Royal Academy of Music, among others. He also took over Kenny's position as patron of the Royal Academy of Music Junior Jazz course and has been every bit as generous with his time and encouragement in the role.

Kenny's final two projects as a composer were also fulfilled after his death. His final big-band composition, a five-movement suite he wrote in 2013 (commissioned by Vancouver's Hard Rubber Orchestra and led by trumpeter John Korsrud), was recorded and released in 2018. Rather than reflecting the writing style of Kenny's later large-ensemble works like the *2005 Suite* and the music from *The Long Waiting*, this seems to evoke Kenny's writing from the period around *The Sweet Time Suite*; fittingly, the recording prominently features the voice of Norma Winstone.[2037] A collaboration between the Royal Academy of Music and the Frost School of Music at the University of Miami used scores found in the Wheeler Archive and recorded some of Kenny's early big-band pieces at Abbey Road Studios in 2024. That same year, Pete Churchill and Dave Holland completed production on a follow-up to the vocal jazz album *Mirrors*, this time with Dave playing bass. The compositions for this album are very likely the last music that Kenny ever wrote.

———··———

Kenny Wheeler's life story shows what a powerful impact he had on the rest of his colleagues in the British and European jazz scenes. If one conceives of a "Kenny Wheeler network" within the context of British and European jazz, it is remarkable to note how comprehensively it covers all the major events of the period: the big bands, the giants of London bebop, the young innovators crafting a new British jazz sound, the emerging free scene, not to mention all his commercial work. Kenny was not only present, but frequently crucial, in so much of this. His musical "family tree" extends to practically every branch of jazz activity during his career.

His most formative period (spanning Chapters 3 and 4 of this book in particular) also coincides with the recognition elsewhere in Europe of the musical happenings within the UK, accompanied by frequent invitations for the leading British players – none more than Kenny – to feature with European jazz stars for festivals, broadcasts, recordings, and tours. This was made possible by the sheer breadth and range of his capability as an artist, as jazz trumpeter, free improviser, and composer/arranger. His story reveals that it was this unique group of skills, all at the highest levels of artistry and technique, that defined his musical evolution and set him apart from his peers. It is hard to imagine another musician around whom you could construct a network of similar musical and international range. To take it to the extreme, even figures as unquestionably significant as Miles Davis or Ornette Coleman had a different kind of breadth from that covered in Wheeler's network. For example, an iconic improvisor like Miles didn't *also* compose and arrange his classic jazz orchestra recordings as well as play on them, a free jazz pioneer like Ornette didn't *also* play commercial sessions and sideman work at the most complex technical level. Perhaps only the likes of Duke Ellington, Wayne Shorter, or Thelonious Monk could be considered on this extreme level of multi-genre versatile excellence in the history of jazz, being at once as uniquely identifiable as virtuoso instrumentalists, improvisors, and composers.

Kenny Wheeler's life is not only a prime demonstration of the creation of great beauty and profoundly emotional art from personal adversity: childhood trauma, shyness, chronic self-doubt and performance anxiety. His life also provides a timeless *musical* role model for musicians today, transcending any constraints of style or language. We emphasize "musical" here for a reason that should be acknowledged and then moved past: the one thing he most certainly did *not* possess is the business acumen (or even instinct) required in the current era, embracing social media and the tools of self-promotion. Although these are of unavoidable importance to contemporary musicians and any professional-in-training today, they could not be further from the core of his personality. His shyness and self-doubt would have made it very difficult for him to embrace any of the conventions with which current artists arguably need to be fluent. Nevertheless, it is no exaggeration to note the profound example he has left us as a professional musician, an artist, and as both composer and improviser.

Perhaps the most obviously apparent characteristic is that Kenny was undoubtedly a model of musical professionalism, being *eminently employable*. He was an impeccable instrumentalist, capable of working professionally in an exceptionally broad array of settings: commercial and studio sessions, pop recordings, contemporary improvisation, and a comprehensively wide spectrum of small-group and big-band jazz (all of this of course notwithstanding his singularity as a unique artist). Aside from his originality, what Kenny also epitomizes is pure instrumental "craft"; he had the ability to easily go to work as a professional musician in almost the complete range of employability as a trumpet player, save, perhaps, a chair in a major symphony orchestra.[2038]

Secondly, and still within the context of "skill", is his ability as a composer and arranger to generate income by providing scores for many varied musical contexts. (And he was an accomplished pianist with exceptional aural skills, able to transcribe and learn new music quickly.) Kenny's life story shows that his humility and reliability were also desirable, if not essential, attributes for a professional musician starting out. Admittedly, as has been mentioned, his self-doubt and nervousness were a constant struggle for him, even though it's likely that the facing of those fears played a vital role in his artistic development.

Another important reminder is that Kenny was an *exceptionally* hard worker in every sense. Early every morning at around 5 or 6 am, he started at the piano, waking up his mind by playing some Bach chorales, then setting pencil to paper for hours once something came to mind. (The massive volume of scores in the Kenny Wheeler Archive attest to the fact that he wrote *something* nearly every day of his life.) He would later spend substantial time keeping his chops up on the trumpet, even on gig days where physical endurance can be a concern. A charming story from his last years involves a new neighbour, who shared a wall with his music room at his London home, and slipped a kind but mildly exasperated note under his door:

> Hello!
>
> I am your neighbour who lives in the front room next door. I sometimes hear you playing jazz on the piano & the trumpet.
>
> I am sorry you couldn't sleep this morning – I heard the piano.
>
> Do you mind not playing the piano tomorrow morning if you can't sleep? I have a big work event tomorrow & and it is going to be a long day! Many thanks![2039]

In addition to his countless hours practising as an individual (albeit on his own schedule), it is also noteworthy and admirable that Kenny was constantly trying to improve himself as a lifelong learner, seeking out composition lessons well into his career as a writer and trumpet lessons even into his seventies and eighties.

From the story of Kenny's artistic development, we can draw what is perhaps the most valuable lesson for individuals. Many musicians battle with what they perceive as their shortcomings and weaknesses, but what his journey so powerfully demonstrates is that those things are also what uniquely made him sound like *him*. Another wonderfully relevant lesson is *to deliberately and consciously seek out new musical experiences to promote artistic growth*. In his case, this meant engaging with the improvised music scene, knowing somehow that it would indeed set him "free". But for contemporary musicians constantly exposed to new experiences, the opportunity for this kind of inspiration can strike at any time – so long as they are quite deeply attuned to their own processes, strengths, and weaknesses, ever aware of what new consideration might just provide the key to unlock a new part of their personal sound.

The last point, and perhaps the most profound because it extends beyond the individual, concerns Kenny's legacy as a composer. He engaged in one critical element of music that far exceeded the importance of his compositional content: more profound than harmonic language, form, or juxtaposition of melodic beauty with free improvisation. It is the essential component of his work from which we can take the biggest lesson without engaging in his stylistic language at all, purely "Ellingtonian" in spirit. It is ultimately Kenny's deep relationships with his musical community that led to his individual voice. It is by composing for specific people, creating work that can only exist because of the unique combination of voices – as a result of focusing on the people and not solely the notes – that the basis of a musical community can emerge, one that inspires growth and exploration. His example encourages musicians to create *for* their friends, rather than presuming their colleagues are there to create for them. In practice, that sort of transactional process is always flowing in both directions when it is working well: but having that mindset to begin with is key. It helps build a musical community that has the potential to be greater than the sum of its parts.

Setting out to compose something "original" brings untold pressure to the writer, and is a goal very few composers ever truly achieve: those that do become the once-in-a-generation leaders of their field. There is a finite number of notes, chords, and combinations. The element that is infinite, however, is the human component of the music. By this reckoning, no two parts are ever the same; there is no limit to the number of combinations; and a single indication can transform a section of the music when it is written with a specific person in mind: a *Song for Someone,* if you will. This is unquestionably what Kenny Wheeler did as a composer – and, even more poignantly – as a musician who brought people together. Of course, Kenny never deliberately set out to lay down an example for us to follow, but through sheer single-minded focus and artistry that is precisely what he did. For that, we can be eternally grateful.

# Sources

## Interviews and email exchanges with the authors

Abercrombie, John, interview with Brian Shaw, 16 July 2014.
Adams, Rob, email correspondence with Brian Shaw, 1 July 2014.
Allen, Christine to Nick Smart and Brian Shaw, 8 September 2015.
Amidon, Sam, email to Nick Smart and Brian Shaw, 19 July 2019.
Argüelles, Julian to Nick Smart, 13 September 2018.
Asher, Eli, email to Brian Shaw, 24 May 2019.
Ball, Mabel, interview with Brian Shaw, 12 May 2015
—— interview with Brian Shaw, 13 May 2015.
—— (with Bill Jelley and Jason Jelley), interview with Brian Shaw, 21 June 2015.
—— to Brian Shaw, 3 November 2015.
Beirach, Richie to Nick Smart, 2 October 2017.
—— to Nick Smart, 13 October 2017.
Bentovim, Dr. Arnon, interview with Nick Smart and Brian Shaw, 2 August 2021.
Bergeron, Wayne to Brian Shaw, 19 May 2024.
Bloom, Jane Ira to Brian Shaw, 21 July 2019.
Bowen, Greg, interview with Nick Smart, 4 June 2015
Bradley, Andrew, correspondence with Brian Shaw, 9 July 2014.
Brady, Tim to Brian Shaw, 10 August 2021.
Braxton, Anthony to Taylor Ho Bynum on behalf of Nick Smart and Brian Shaw, 9 July 2015.
Buffalo Colored Musicians' Union, email to Brian Shaw, 30 June 2015.
Carter, Greg, email to Nick Smart, 19 November 2016.
—— email to Brian Shaw, 29 July 2019.
Cheetham, Andrew to Brian Shaw at the FONT Festival, 22 October 2011.
—— email to Brian Shaw, 27 May 2019.
Chisholm, George, email to Nick Smart, 22 October 2019.
Churchill, Pete, interview with Nick Smart and Brian Shaw, 30 November 2015.
—— to Nick Smart and Brian Shaw, 1 August 2016.
—— to Brian Shaw, 7 August 2016.
—— to Nick Smart and Brian Shaw, 11 August 2016.
Coe, Tony, interview with Nick Smart, 20 August 2015.
Coleman, Steve, interview with Nick Smart, 4 April 2017.
Cumming, John to Nick Smart, 4 April 2017.
Danielsson, Palle, interview with Nick Smart, 6 August 2019.
DeJohnette, Jack to Brian Shaw, 25 May 2015.
Dickinson, Barnaby to Nick Smart, 3 September 2016.
Dickinson, Brian, email to Brian Shaw, 8 August 2018.
Dobbins, Bill, conversation with Brian Shaw, Rochester, NY, 2003.
—— interview with Brian Shaw, Rochester, NY, 16 November 2016.
Docherty, Jackie, interview with Nick Smart, 26 August 2015.
Donlon, Mark to Nick Smart, 16 February 2022.

Douglas, Dave, interview with Nick Smart, 16 December 2015.
Downes, Kit to Nick Smart, 12 August 2020.
Dudley-Evans, Tony, conversation with Nick Smart, 10 August 2016.
Eckert, Rosana, email to Brian Shaw, 17 July 2019.
Eicher, Manfred, interview with Nick Smart, 5 March 2017.
—— to Nick Smart, 12 February 2018.
Elgart, Bill, interview with Nick Smart, 6 August 2019.
Ellefson, Art, interview with Brian Shaw, 12 May 2015.
—— email correspondence, 18 May 2015.
Erskine, Peter to Brian Shaw, 23 May 2015.
—— conversation with Brian Shaw, 2018.
Eubanks, Robin, interview with Nick Smart, 25 October 2019.
Faddis, Jon, email to Brian Shaw and Nick Smart, 15 December 2015.
—— interview with Nick Smart and Brian Shaw, 13 August 2016.
Faulkner, Tony, interview with Nick Smart, 2 September 2015.
Fisher, Tony, interview with Nick Smart, 4 November 2015.
Fowler, Reuben, 9 August 2022.
Fraser, Hugh, interview with Brian Shaw, 25 May 2015.
Frisell, Bill, interview with Nick Smart, 30 November 2015.
Garbarek, Jan to Brian Shaw, 16 June 2015.
Garland, Tim to Nick Smart, 27 November 2015.
Gibbs, Mike, interview with Nick Smart, 24 August 2015.
Gill, Tania to Brian Shaw, 27 October 2015.
Guilfoyle, Ronan, interview with Nick Smart, 24 February 2015.
Hämmerli, Hämi (Lucerne School of Music), email to Nick Smart, 29 June 2015.
Hart, Billy to Nick Smart, 5 October 2015.
Hart, Jim to Nick Smart, 31 July 2022.
Hersch, Fred, interview with Nick Smart and Brian Shaw, 15 July 2018.
Hinely, Patrick, email to Brian Shaw, 1 August 2017.
Holland, Dave, interview with Nick Smart, 11 January 2015.
—— interview with Nick Smart, 20 January 2015.
—— interview with Nick Smart, 28 January 2015.
—— interview with Nick Smart, 8 August 2016.
—— interview with Nick Smart, 29 July 2019.
—— interview with Nick Smart, 26 July 2024.
Hollenbeck, John, email to Brian Shaw, 31 May 2017.
Hopkins, Duncan to Nick Smart, 27 August 2015.
Horler, Dave, interview with Nick Smart, 2 September 2015.
—— email exchange with Nick Smart, August 2017.
—— email to Nick Smart, 4 August 2019.
Iles, Nikki to Nick Smart, 14 January 2016.
—— to Nick Smart, 26 July 2019.
Jelley, Bill (with Mabel Ball and Jason Jelley), interview with Brian Shaw, 21 June 2015.
Jelley, Jayson (with Mabel Ball and Bill Jelley), interview with Brian Shaw, 21 June 2015.
Jensen, Ingrid to Nick Smart, 1 April 2015.
Klein, Larry, interview with Nick Smart, 31 August 2016.
LaBarbera, Joe to Brian Shaw, 31 July 2019.
Lake, Steve, email to Nick Smart, 24 March 2017.
—— email to Nick Smart, 16 February 2019.
Lamont, Duncan, interview with Nick Smart, 3 August 2014.
—— email exchange with Nick Smart, August 2017.
Lanese, Bob, email correspondence with Nick Smart, 5 May 2017.

Laurence, Chris, interview with Nick Smart and Brian Shaw, 8 September 2015.
—— email exchange with Nick Smart, August 2017.
Lee, Dave, interview with Nick Smart, 16 December 2015.
Liebman, Dave, interview with Nick Smart, 28 June 2015.
Lowther, Henry, interview with Nick Smart, 8 October 2014
—— email to Nick Smart, 18 January 2015.
—— email to Nick Smart, 18 June 2015.
—— email exchange with Nick Smart, August 2017.
—— interview with Nick Smart, 3 November 2021.
Marshall, John, interview with Nick Smart, 20 July 2018.
Mendoza, Vince, interview with Nick Smart, 17 November 2015.
Merz, Chris (University of Northern Iowa), email to Nick Smart, 15 September 2015.
Miller, Mark, email to Brian Shaw, 27 September 2014.
—— email to Brian Shaw, 29 September 2015.
—— to Brian Shaw, 7 October 2015.
—— (with Don Thompson and Ted O'Reilly), interview with Brian Shaw, 13 October 2015.
—— email to Brian Shaw, 20 January 2017.
Moore, Debby, interview and correspondence with Nick Smart, February 2016.
Morgan, Bob to Brian Shaw, 5 October 2020.
Newman, Louann (with Mark Wheeler), email to Nick Smart, 27 November 2015.
—— interview with Nick Smart, 21 June 2016.
—— interview with Nick Smart, 8 July 2016.
—— (with Doreen Wheeler, Mark Wheeler, and Sophie Wheeler), conversation at Wallwood Road, 16 July 2018.
North, Anne to Brian Shaw, 20 June 2015.
North, Rod, interview with Brian Shaw, 20 June 2015.
O'Reilly, Ted to Brian Shaw, 7 October 2015.
—— (with Don Thompson and Mark Miller), interview with Brian Shaw, 13 October 2015.
Parker, Evan (with Norma Winstone), interview with Nick Smart for Royal Academy of Music exhibition, November 2012.
—— interview with Nick Smart, 24 August 2015.
—— interview with Nick Smart, 25 August 2015.
—— interview with Nick Smart and Brian Shaw, 9 September 2015.
—— email to Nick Smart, 4 October 2015.
—— conversation following the Kenny Wheeler Prize Meeting at the Academy on 20 June 2016.
—— email to Nick Smart, 10 October 2016.
—— email exchange with Nick Smart, August 2017.
—— email, 4 August 2017.
—— email, 23 July 2018.
—— email to Nick Smart, 30 January 2019.
—— email, 29 April 2019.
—— interview with Nick Smart, 12 September 2019.
Parricelli, John to Nick Smart, 10 June 2024.
Potter, Chris, interview with Nick Smart, 3 October 2018.
Price, Jason, email to Brian Shaw, 26 May 2019.
Purcell, Simon to Nick Smart, 16 November 2015.
Purnell, Nick, email to Nick Smart, 19 October 2016.
—— email to Nick Smart, 31 October 2016.
—— email to Nick Smart, 3 November 2016.
—— email to Nick Smart, 28 July 2019.

—— email to Nick Smart, 31 July 2019.

Rapson, John (University of Iowa) email to Nick Smart, 29 June 2015.

Rathbun, Andrew, email to Brian Shaw, 9 August 2018.

Reid, Rufus to Brian Shaw, 24 July 2019.

Richards, Olwen to Nick Smart, 4 November 2015.

Robson, Phil to Nick Smart, 20 July 2018.

Rowe, Ellen, email to Brian Shaw, 17 July 2019.

Schaphorst, Ken, conversations with Nick Smart.

Schneider, Larry, email to Nick Smart, 21 May 2017.

Smith, Tommy, interview with Nick Smart, 10 October 2016.

—— email to Nick Smart, 11 October 2016.

Smith, Wadada Leo to Brian Shaw, 12 January 2016.

Souza, Luciana, interview with Nick Smart, 31 August 2016.

Sparrow, Paul, interview with Nick Smart, 3 April 2017.

Spillett, Simon, email, 17 October 2016.

Stamm, Marvin to Brian Shaw, 18 June 2020.

Stoneman, Noah, WhatsApp message to the authors, 5 March 2024.

Street, Ben to Nick Smart, 23 July 2017.

Stroman, Scott, interview with Nick Smart, 19 July 2018.

Sulzmann, Stan, email to Nick Smart, 21 June 2009.

—— interview with Nick Smart, 7 October 2014.

—— conversation with Nick Smart, 8 January 2016.

—— interview with Nick Smart and Brian Shaw, 4 August 2016.

—— email to Nick Smart, 10 April 2017.

—— interview with Nick Smart, 20 July 2018.

—— interviews with Nick Smart, 30 July 2019.

—— email to Nick Smart, 31 July 2019.

—— email exchange with Nick Smart, August 2017.

—— (with Mark Wheeler), conversation, 14 June 2016.

Surman, John, interview with Nick Smart, 15 September 2016.

—— story recounted during a rehearsal, Royal Academy of Music, 10 November 2017.

Taylor, John private conversation with Nick Smart in Café Rouge on Tottenham Court Road, 18 October 2012.

—— interview with Nick Smart, 2 April 2015.

Thiessen, John, email to Brian Shaw, 6 August 2020.

Thompson, Don to Brian Shaw, 7 October 2015.

—— to Brian Shaw, 13 October 2015.

—— (with Ted O'Reilly, and Mark Miller), interview with Brian Shaw, 13 October 2015.

Tobin, Christine to Nick Smart, 20 July 2018.

Towner, Ralph to Brian Shaw, 15 June 2015.

—— email correspondence with Brian Shaw, 28 June 2015.

Tynan, Paul to Brian Shaw, 13 June 2015.

van de Geyn, Hein to Nick Smart, 19 October 2016.

Venier, Glauco to Nick Smart, 4 November 2018.

Venier, Pete, interview with Nick Smart, 19 December 2018.

von Schlippenbach, Alexander, interview with Nick Smart, 15 June 2015

Watkins, Wendy to Nick Smart, 2017.

Wellins, Bobby, interview with Nick Smart, 26 September 2014.

—— interview with Nick Smart, 26 August 2015.

Werner, Kenny to Nick Smart, 28 June 2016.

Wheeler, Doreen, conversation with Brian Shaw, 15 January 2005.

—— interview with Nick Smart and Brian Shaw, 15 February 2015.

—— interview with Nick Smart, 17 August 2015.

—— interview, 21 June 2016.

—— (with Louann Newman, Mark Wheeler, and Sophie Wheeler), conversation at Wallwood Road, 16 July 2018.

Wheeler, Kenny, personal conversation with Brian Shaw, Banff, summer 1998.

—— interview with Nick Smart, 11 June 2010.

—— interview with Nick Smart, 23 April 2010

—— conversation with Brian Shaw, 13 May 2012.

—— correspondence with Brian Shaw through Andrew Bradley, 9 July 2014.

—— to Nick Smart in care home, 24 July 2014.

Wheeler, Mark, interview with Nick Smart, 24 July 2014.

—— email to Brian Shaw, 8 September 2014.

—— to Nick Smart, 3 February 2015.

—— email to Brian Shaw, 7 October 2015.

—— interview with Nick Smart and Brian Shaw, 27 November 2015.

—— (with Louann Newman), email to Nick Smart, 27 November 2015.

—— interview with Nick Smart and Brian Shaw, 22 January 2016.

—— (with Stan Sulzmann), conversation, 14 June 2016.

—— to Nick Smart and Brian Shaw, 11 August 2016.

—— interview with Nick Smart and Brian Shaw, 16 July 2018.

—— (with Doreen Wheeler, Louann Newman, and Sophie Wheeler), conversation at Wallwood Road, 16 July 2018.

—— text, 17 July 2018.

—— email to authors, 25 July 2018.

—— to Nick Smart, 31 July 2019.

Wheeler, Ruby, email to Brian Shaw, 7 July 2022.

Windsor Regiment members, email correspondence, July/August 2015.

Winstone, Norma (with Evan Parker), interview with Nick Smart for Royal Academy of Music exhibition, November 2012.

—— interview, 4 February 2015.

—— interview with Nick Smart, 31 March 2015.

—— interview with Nick Smart, 2 April 2015.

—— to Nick Smart, 16 August 2015.

—— interview with Nick Smart, 19 August 2015.

—— email to Nick Smart, 4/5 July 2017.

—— email exchange with Nick Smart, August 2017.

—— email to Nick Smart, 30 July 2019.

—— to Nick Smart, 9 November 2020.

# Archival resources

## Archives

*Banff Centre, Alberta, Canada*
  Archived programmes, collection of Kenny's music.

*BBC*
  BBC Archive (including "Programmes as Broadcast" [PasB] microfiches, BBC Written Archives Centre, Caversham
  BBC Genome website http://genome.ch.bbc.co.uk
  BBC Spreadsheet from 1982 EBU gig.
  *Broadcasts:*
    *Omnibus* (BBC 1, 27 October 1977).

University of Warwick concert, 28 January 1990 (BBC broadcast, 21 July 1990).
Kenny Wheeler interview with Peter Clayton (BBC Radio, 1990).
Kenny Wheeler, interview with Jez Nelson, *Jazz on 3* (BBC Radio 3, February 1998).
Live broadcast from Bath (BBC Radio, 26 May 2002).
*Jazz File* episode about the Dankworths (BBC Radio 3, 3 May 2003).
*Sir John Dankworth at the BBC* (BBC Four, 2010).
Compilation of *Jazz 625* performances (BBC Four, 2010).
Kenny Wheeler to Nigel Wrench, interview, 13 January 2010, *PM* (BBC Radio 4, 14 January 2010).
John Taylor, interview by Alyn Shipton, *Jazz Library* (podcast) (BBC Radio 3, 14 May 2011).

*Berlin Observer* newspaper archive, http://www.theberlinobserver.com/archive/1972V28/V28_N42_oct20.pdf

*British Library*
Kenny Wheeler, interview with Ian Carr, 7 September 1995 (Ian Carr tapes).
Oral History of Jazz in Britain; British Library: Duncan Lamont, interview with Andy Simons, 11 September 2002 (Collection, C122/429-430); Ian Carr interview with Alyn Shipton in June 2000. (ref. C122/450); John Stevens, interview with Victor Schonfield, December 1992; Paul Rutherford, interviews with Victor Schonfield (C122/298-302).

ECM, *:rarum* selection letters.

*Library of Congress*
Archive page (https://www.loc.gov/item/jots.200016721)
"Jazz on Screen" (https://www.loc.gov/item/jots.200014810)

*National Jazz Archive*
Chris Hayes, *Ken Wheeler biography*, February 1954.
Website (https://nationaljazzarchive.org.uk)

*National Sound Archive*
Brian Priestley's interview with Kenny Wheeler, 20 May 1986).

Newport Jazz Festival Programs Archive.

Royal Holloway Archives.

*Royal Academy of Music*
Wheeler Archive
Henry Lowther, Chris Laurence, and Norma Winstone, interview with Alyn Shipton, part of the Royal Academy of Music exhibition on Kenny Wheeler, 13 June 2013.

Saudades concert dates, provided 30 July 2019.

Wheeler family collection


## Public records

*Canada*
Archives of Ontario.
No. 1971, Toronto death registry, Adam Francis Reid, 1883.
1891 Canada Census, Ontario, district no. 119.
George Wheeler and Kathleen Ryan marriage certificate, record no. 014404, York County, Ontario, from 27 April 1892.
1901 Canada Census, Ontario, district no. 117.
1911 Canadian Census.
Wilf Wheeler and Mabel Reid marriage certificate.
1954 voting records for Robert Yeend.

Kenny Wheeler birth certificate.
Manifest, Detroit border crossing, 17 February 1944.

*UK*
Ancestry.com.
Birth records, England and Wales.
RMS *Scythia* ship's registry, arriving Southampton, 2 October 1952.
Kenny Wheeler's death certificate, filed 22 September 2014.


## Other

Hollenbeck, John: email to Dave Rivello, forwarded to Brian Shaw, 5 September 2011.
Lowther, Henry: diary.
McRae, Barry: review of the Camden Festival Jazz Week (screenshot from an unknown
    publication).
Smith, Tommy: private collection
Spillett, Simon: private collection.
Taylor, John: interview with Martin Speake, 11 February 2015.
Watts, Trevor: private collection.
Wheeler, Kenny: interview with Ted O'Reilly, 26 August 1980.
—— interview with Ted O'Reilly, 11 November 1985.
—— interviewed by Evan Parker, seemingly late 1994.
—— to Ian Carr, 9 July 1995.
—— interview for Artists House Music, 2002.
—— (and Doreen Wheeler): interview with Martin Speake, 4 April 2012.
Winstone, Norma: private collection; diary


## Books

Barber, Chris. *Jazz Me Blues: The Autobiography of Chris Barber* (Equinox Publishing,
    2014).
Borges, Jorge Luis .*The Book of Imaginary Beings* (E.P. Dutton, 1969).
Braxton, Anthony. *Tri-Axium Writings* Volumes 1–3 (Synthesis Music, 1985).
Carner, Gary. *Pepper Adams' Joy Road: An Annotated Discography* (Scarecrow Press, 2012).
Carr, Ian, Digby Fairweather, and Brian Priestley, *Jazz: The Essential Companion* (Simon &
    Schuster 1988)
Carr, Ian. *Keith Jarrett: The Man and His Music* (Da Capo Press, 1992).
Catalano, Nick. *Clifford Brown: The Life and Art of the Legendary Jazz Trumpeter* (Oxford
    University Press, 2002).
Cook, Richard, and Brian Morton, "Kenny Wheeler, 'Kayak'", *The Penguin Guide to Jazz on
    CD, LP, and Cassette* (Penguin, 1st edn, 1992), p. 1,140.
Cox, Terrance. "Kenny-ing: Kenny Wheeler and Local Jazz", in Joan Nicks and Barry Keith
    Grant (eds.), *Covering Niagara: Studies in Local Popular Culture* (Wilfrid Laurier
    University Press, 2010), p. 220.
Dankworth, John. *Jazz in Revolution* (Constable 1998).
Godbolt, Jim. *A History of Jazz in Britain: 1950–1970* (Quartet Books, 1989).
Grime, Kitty. *Jazz at Ronnie Scott's* (Robert Hale Ltd, 1979), p. 171.
Hamilton, Andy. *Lee Konitz: Conversations on the Improviser's Art* (University of Michigan
    Press, 2007).
Heile, Björn, Peter Elsdon, and Jenny Doctor (eds.), *Watching Jazz: Encounters with
    Performance on Screen* (Oxford University Press, 2016).
Hindemith, Paul. *A Concentrated Course in Traditional Harmony* (Schott, 1943).

Kriebel, Robert. *Blue Flame: Woody Herman's Life in Music* (Purdue University Press, 1995).

Laine, Cleo. *Cleo* (Simon & Schuster, 1994).

Lees, Gene. *Arranging the Score: Portraits of the Great Arrangers* (Continuum, 2000).

———. *Jazz Lives: 100 Portraits in Jazz* (Firefly Books, 1992).

———. *Leader of the Band; The Life of Woody Herman* (Oxford University Press, 1997).

Libbey, Ted. *The NPR Listener's Encyclopedia of Classical Music* (Workman Publishing Co., 2006).

Meeker, David. *Jazz on the Screen: A Jazz and Blues Filmography* (Library of Congress, 2009).

Radano, Ronald M. *New Cultural Figurations: Anthony Braxton's Cultural Critique* (University of Chicago Press, 1993).

Scott, Ronnie. *Some of My Best Friends Are Blues* (Northway Publications, 2013).

Shipton, Alyn. *Out of the Long Dark: The Life of Ian Carr* (Equinox Publishing, 2006).

Smith, Chris. *The View from the Back of the Band: The Life and Music of Mel Lewis* (UNT Press, 2016).

Spillett, Simon. *The Long Shadow of the Little Giant: The Life, Work and Legacy of Tubby Hayes* (Equinox Publishing, 2015).

Sturm, Fred. *Kenny Wheeler: Collected Works on ECM* (Universal Edition).

Teachout, Terry. *Pops: A Life of Louis Armstrong* (Mariner Books 2010).

Troupe, Quincy. *Miles: The Autobiography* (Picador 1990).

Wickes, John. *Innovations in British Jazz. Vol. 1: 1960–1980* (Soundworld 1999).

# Notes

## Introduction

1  Peter Von Bartkowski, *Highlights of the Jazz Story in USA: Musicians–Styles–Headlines–Bands*, 2007 (www.grandauctions.co.uk/auction/an-impressive-jazz-tree-poster-entitled-39-highlights-of-the-jazz-story-in-the-usa-39, accessed 22 July 2018).

2  Sean Condon, "Humble Legend", *St. Catharines Standard*, 28 June 1991, p. 17.

3  Anthony Braxton to Taylor Ho Bynum, on behalf of Nick Smart and Brian Shaw, 9 July 2015.

4  Manfred Eicher, interview with Nick Smart, 5 March 2017.

5  Don Thompson to Brian Shaw, 13 October 2015.

6  Ingrid Jensen to Nick Smart, 1 April 2015.

7  Dave Holland, interview with Nick Smart, 28 January 2015.

8  Chris Potter, interview with Nick Smart, 3 October 2018.

9  Norma Winstone, interview with Nick Smart, 19 August 2015.

10  Mark Miller, email to Brian Shaw, 27 September 2014. This comment came from Miller's pencil notes to the Wheeler interview from 2 November 1975. The first piece was published as: Mark Miller, "Profile: Kenny Wheeler", *DownBeat*, 11 March 1976, p. 32. That same quote was also used as the title of a second piece in Toronto: Mark Miller, "Kenny Wheeler says, 'If I ever got to like my own playing, I'd give up': Jazzman prefers anonymity", *Toronto Globe & Mail*, 12 August 1978, p. 33.

## Chapter 1: A Long Time Ago

11  Robert Wheeler entry in the 1891 Canada Census, Ontario, district no. 119.

12  George Wheeler and Kathleen Ryan marriage certificate, record no. 014404, York County, Ontario, from 27 April 1892.

13  George Wheeler entry in the 1901 Canada Census, Ontario, district no. 117. Also, see George Wheeler family photo in family scrapbook, Kenny Wheeler Archive.

14  Mabel Ball, interview with Brian Shaw, 12 May 2015.

15  No. 1971, Toronto death registry, Adam Francis Reid, 1883.

16  Ancestry.com marriage record: Ontario, Canada marriages, registration number 33351.

17  1911 Canadian Census: Reid, John.

18  Archives of Ontario; Series: MS932_94; Reel: 94. John Francis Reid and Mary Walsh were married on 14 September 1898.

19  1911 Canadian Census: Reid, John.

20  Mabel Ball, interview with Brian Shaw, 12 May 2015.

21  Ibid.

22  Family photo, Mabel Ball and Kenny Wheeler – the instrument, or part of an instrument, under his arm is thought to be either an Irish flute or the "chanter" of a set of Irish pipes (Wheeler Archive, Royal Academy of Music).

23  Mabel Ball, interview with Brian Shaw, 12 May 2015.

24  Wilf Wheeler and Mabel Reid marriage certificate.

25 Mabel Ball photo.

26 Kenny Wheeler, interview for Artists House Music, 2002. Kenny Wheeler on BBC *Omnibus*, 27 October 1977.

27 Mabel Ball, interview with Brian Shaw, 12 May 2015.

28 Kenny Wheeler birth certificate. Mabel said that there were so many children in the family that Mrs. Wheeler couldn't keep them all separated – therefore they mistakenly celebrated Kenny's birthday on 13 January for years.

29 Kenny Wheeler, interview with Nick Smart, 23 April 2010.

30 Kenny Wheeler, interview for Artists House Music, 2002.

31 Mabel Ball, interview with Brian Shaw, 12 May 2015.

32 BBC *Omnibus*, 27 October 1977.

33 Gene Lees, *Arranging the Score: Portraits of the Great Arrangers* (Continuum, 2000), p. 16.

34 *Toronto Daily Star*, 14 July 1942, p. 23.

35 Mabel Ball, interview with Brian Shaw, 12 May 2015.

36 Manifest, Detroit border crossing, 17 February 1944.

37 Kenny Wheeler, interview for Artists House Music, 2002.

38 Kenny Wheeler, interview with Nick Smart, 23 April 2010. Kenny had no clear recollection of exactly when he heard Ellington, but the band played the Motor City multiple times during this period, including week-long engagements in January and September 1944.

39 Kenny Wheeler, interview with Brian Priestley, 20 May 1986 (British Library, National Sound Archive).

40 Kenny Wheeler, interview with Nick Smart, 23 April 2010.

41 Kenny Wheeler, interview with Mark Miller, 3 January 1980, for the article "Kenny Wheeler's Many Vehicles", *DownBeat* 47(4) (April 1980), pp. 22–24.

42 Gene Lees, "Come Back Last Summer (Part 1)", *JazzLetter* 12(3) (March 1993).

43 Kenny Wheeler to Mark Miller, 3 January 1980.

44 Taken from Kenny's handwritten answers to Fred Sturm's October 1997 interview (Kenny Wheeler private collection). Later published in *Kenny Wheeler: Collected Works on ECM* (Universal Edition).

45 Ibid.

46 Kitty Grime, "Star Sideman: Kenny Wheeler," *Jazz News*, 18 October 1961.

47 Kenny Wheeler to Mark Miller, 3 January 1980.

48 Email correspondence with Windsor Regiment members, July/August 2015.

49 Lees, *Arranging the Score*, pp. 16–17.

50 Kenny Wheeler, interview with Nick Smart, 23 April 2010.

51 Kenny's early struggles with range on the trumpet are amusing considering his astounding three-and-a-half octave range during the mature period of his career.

52 Mabel Ball, interview with Brian Shaw, 12 May 2015.

53 Mabel Ball, interview with Brian Shaw, 13 May 2015. George and Wilf Jr. joined the Navy and the Air Force respectively. Even though he wasn't musical, George was very successful after the war, becoming the captain of the *Meisner*, which was, according to Kenny, "the biggest ship on the Great Lakes" (Kenny Wheeler to Gene Lees in Lees, "Come Back Last Summer [Part 1]", p. 3).

54 Kenny recounted this to a family friend later in life who wishes to remain anonymous.

55 Doreen Wheeler, interview with Nick Smart, 17 August 2015: "Kenny talked about it, about her getting drunk and disappearing. He talked about it, never kept anything back. I think that he felt lonely not having a mum. My parents made up for it; well, they couldn't make up for his parents, but they were very good to 'em."

56  Mabel Ball, interview with Brian Shaw, 13 May 2015. This sentiment must have been shared by most of the Wheeler siblings, most of whom remained in the area for the rest of their lives. Many of their descendants still live there as well.

57  Ibid.

58  Mabel Ball, interview with Brian Shaw, 12 May 2015.

59  Kitty Grime, *Jazz at Ronnie Scott's* (Robert Hale Ltd, 1979), p. 171.

60  Kenny Wheeler, interview with Brian Priestley, 20 May 1986 (National Sound Archive).

61  Grime, *Jazz at Ronnie Scott's*, p. 171.

62  Mabel Ball, interview with Brian Shaw, 13 May 2015.

63  Mabel Ball, interview with Brian Shaw, 12 May 2015.

64  Ibid. Kenny's oldest brother George was the only non-musical member of the family and excelled at hockey, even going so far as using his younger brother Wilf's birth certificate to qualify to play once he had aged out of the junior team.

65  Bill Jelley, interview with Brian Shaw, 21 June 2015.

66  Mabel Ball, interview with Brian Shaw, 12 May 2015.

67  Kenny Wheeler, interview with Nick Smart, 23 April 2010.

68  Bill Jelley, interview with Brian Shaw, 21 June 2015.

69  Grime, "Star Sideman: Kenny Wheeler".

70  Bill Jelley, interview with Brian Shaw, 21 June 2015.

71  Kenny Wheeler, interview with Nick Smart, 23 April 2010. Kenny's observation likely references the well-known dispute when bandleader Cab Calloway criticized Dizzy's trumpet solos with the same epithet, saying "I don't want you playing that Chinese music in my band."

72  Bill Jelley, interview with Brian Shaw, 21 June 2015.

73  Ibid. (The recordings Jelley mentions were actually released across 1945, 1946, and 1947 but we have no record of whether Kenny acquired these in one go at the end of that period or steadily over the years.)

74  Mabel Ball, interview with Brian Shaw, 12 May 2015. Mabel described the amount of walking they did as youngsters and how that led to his love of taking long walks in the places he'd visit; she also highlighted the sadness at his later loss of mobility when that was no longer possible for him.

75  Bill Jelley, interview with Brian Shaw, 21 June 2015.

76  From Mark Wheeler: "We celebrated it for years on the 13th! Then there was a change in the rules for Commonwealth people in the UK (think it was the Immigration Act of 1971) and they all had to get citizenship/passports. My Dad needed his birth certificate to do that. He was not happy as I am sure that he had a phobia related to admin and filling in forms. I remember him moaning lots" (Mark Wheeler, email to authors, 25 July 2018).

77  Bill Jelley, interview with Brian Shaw, 21 June 2015.

78  Ibid.

79  Dr. Arnon Bentovim, interview with Nick Smart and Brian Shaw, 2 August 2021. Dr. Bentovim has researched the impact of childhood adversity on the lives of adults, identifying harmful and protective influences. Nick Smart met Dr. Bentovim regularly over 20 years on a summer jazz course in Wales, and following a lecture about Kenny's life and musical development was interviewed by the authors in the likely impact his childhood had on his personality. Throughout this book, any observations made by the authors about the effect of Kenny's childhood upon his life have been discussed with Dr. Bentovim.

80  Kenny Wheeler, interview with Nick Smart, 23 April 2010.

81  Ibid.

82  Lees, *Arranging the Score*, p. 15.

83  Lees, "Come Back Last Summer (Part 1)", p. 4.

84 Ibid. This meeting probably occurred during Parker's residency at the Three Deuces between 7 and 20 August 1947 (www.plosin.com/milesahead/Bird/LBP_1947.htm, accessed December 2014).

85 Kenny Wheeler, interview with Nick Smart, 23 April 2010.

86 Kenny Wheeler, interview with Ted O'Reilly, 26 August 1980.

87 Ibid.

88 Ibid.

89 Ibid.

90 Email to Brian Shaw from Buffalo Colored Musicians' Union, 30 June 2015, matching information from Bill Jelley interview.

91 Kenny Wheeler, interview with Nick Smart, 23 April 2010.

92 Bill Jelley, interview with Brian Shaw, 21 June 2015. At the time of the interview, Art Talbot was still living in seclusion in a retirement community in St. Catharines.

93 Ibid.

94 Ibid.

95 Ibid. Gisele MacKenzie *New York Times* obituary, 9 September 2003.

96 Rod North, interview with Brian Shaw, 20 June 2015.

97 Ibid.

98 Ibid.

99 Rod North, interview with Brian Shaw, 20 June 2015.

100 Kenny Wheeler, interview with Nick Smart, 11 June 2010.

101 Bill Jelley, interview with Brian Shaw, 21 June 2015.

102 Terrance Cox, "Kenny-ing: Kenny Wheeler and Local Jazz", in Joan Nicks and Barry Keith Grant (eds.), *Covering Niagara: Studies in Local Popular Culture* (Wilfrid Laurier University Press, 2010), p. 220.

103 None of the family we have had contact with (including Bill and Jason Jelley) were able to find their copies, despite a few of them being sure they did have one at one time.

104 Gene Lees, *Jazz Lives: 100 Portraits in Jazz* (Firefly Books, 1992), p. 102.

105 St. Catharines Collegiate *Vox Collegiensis* 1947, p. 56.

106 Lees, "Come Back Last Summer (Part 1)", p. 4.

107 Kenny Wheeler, interview for Artists House Music, 2002.

108 Terry Teachout, *Pops: A Life of Louis Armstrong* (Mariner Books, 2010), pp. 190–191. The account of his rupturing his orbicularis oris onstage in 1933 is particularly gruesome.

109 Kenny Wheeler, interview with Nick Smart, 23 April 2010.

110 A letter by Kenny sent from Haliburton, 1949(?): "Please send up my alarm clock, metronome, and Araban's [sic] trumpet book".

111 Rod North, interview with Brian Shaw, 20 June 2015.

112 Kenny Wheeler, interview with Brian Priestley, 20 May 1986 (National Sound Archive).

113 St. Catharines Collegiate *Vox Collegiensis* 1948, p. 101.

114 In a letter to Canadian jazz historian and critic Mark Miller he said, "As far as studying music in Canada goes, I was mostly self taught but I did study harmony with John Weinzweig and trumpet with a teacher called (I think) Ross McClanathan" (Kenny Wheeler to Mark Miller, 2 November 1975). Gene Lees in his *JazzLetter* calls this person "Ross MacLathan". After speaking with several people familiar with the trumpet teaching and performance scene in Toronto in the 1950s, only one person present on the scene at that time, Canadian trumpeter Johnny Cowell (1926–2018), had a memory of a trumpet teacher with that last name, but they called him "Courson [spelling uncertain] MacLanathan," whom he called a "better than average" trumpet player, a "nice man", and recalled that he played with the Toronto Philharmonic.

115  Paul Hindemith, *A Concentrated Course in Traditional Harmony* (Schott, 1943).

116  Lees, "Come Back Last Summer (Part 1)", p. 5.

117  Kenny Wheeler, interview for Artists House Music, 2002.

118  Mabel Ball, interview with Brian Shaw, 13 May 2015.

119  Lees, *Arranging the Score*, p. 17.

120  Kenny Wheeler, interview with Nick Smart, 23 April 2010. Chris Hayes, *Ken Wheeler biography*, February 1954, National Jazz Archive collections.

121  Lees, "Come Back Last Summer (Part 1)", p. 4.

122  Kenny Wheeler, interview with Nick Smart, 23 April 2010.

123  Kenny Wheeler, interview for Artists House Music, 2002.

124  Kenny Wheeler, interview with Nick Smart, 23 April 2010.

125  Kenny Wheeler, interview with Brian Priestley, 20 May 1986 (National Sound Archive).

126  The pavilion no longer stands, but the beautiful 1905 carousel next door still entertains children for five cents a ride.

127  Cox, "Kenny-ing", p. 217.

128  Lees, "Come Back Last Summer (Part 1)", p. 5.

129  St. Catharines newspaper article on Bruce Anthony (scrapbook, Wheeler Archive, Royal Academy of Music).

130  Rod North, interview with Brian Shaw, 20 June 2015.

131  Bill Jelley, interview with Brian Shaw, 21 June 2015.

132  Kenny Wheeler, letter home to parents from Haliburton, summer 1948 or 1949.

133  Bill Jelley, interview with Brian Shaw, 21 June 2015.

134  Ibid.

135  Ibid.

136  Kenny Wheeler, interview for Artists House Music, 2002.

137  Anne North to Brian Shaw, 20 June 2015.

138  Mabel Ball to Brian Shaw, 21 June 2015.

139  Ibid.

140  Ibid.

141  Bill Jelley was sitting at Mabel's kitchen table at the same time I was, both of us hearing this story for the first time. Sharing Kenny's love of puns and slightly droll sense of humour, Bill titled the event "Fizz 'n' Chips". Bill Jelley, interview with Brian Shaw, 21 June 2015.

142  Mabel Ball, interview with Brian Shaw, 13 May 2015.

143  Ibid. Although this interview is the source of the story, other members of the Wheeler family remember this event and have told the interviewers the same story.

144  Ibid.

145  Kenny Wheeler, interview with Brian Priestley, 20 May 1986 (National Sound Archive).

146  Kenny Wheeler to Ian Carr, 9 July 1995.

147  Bill Jelley, interview with Brian Shaw, 21 June 2015.

148  Lees, "Come Back Last Summer (Part 1)", p. 5.

149  Kenny Wheeler, interview for Artists House Music, 2002.

150  *St. Catharines Standard* profile, 22 September 1962.

151  Kenny Wheeler to Mark Miller, 3 January 1980.

152  Kenny Wheeler, interview with Brian Priestley, 20 May 1986 (National Sound Archive).

153  Kenny Wheeler, interview for Artists House Music, 2002.

154  Lees, *Arranging the Score*, p. 21.

155  Gene Lees visa quote from "Come Back Last Summer (Part 1)", p. 6. Kenny's quote from interview for Artists House Music, 2002.

156  Bill Jelley, interview with Brian Shaw, 21 June 2015.

157 Kenny Wheeler, interview with Ted O'Reilly, 26 August 1980.

158 Kenny Wheeler, interview with Brian Priestley, 20 May 1986 (National Sound Archive).

159 Kenny Wheeler, letter home to parents from Haliburton, summer 1948 or 1949. It is notable that, although Kenny never attended London's Royal Academy of Music, he later had a significant relationship with the institution. He was Patron of the Junior Jazz course, awarded Honorary Membership of the RAM and had a career retrospective exhibition mounted in their Museum. Most significantly, the RAM now houses the Kenny Wheeler Archive, preserving his manuscript scores and other memorabilia.

160 Lees, "Come Back Last Summer (Part 1)", p. 5.

161 Ibid.

162 Ibid., p. 6.

163 Kenny Wheeler, interview with Nick Smart, 23 April 2010.

164 Kenny Wheeler, interview for Artists House Music, 2002.

165 RMS *Scythia* ship's registry, arriving Southampton, 2 October 1952. This entry – a paradigm shift from the immigration document listing his occupation as "bank clerk" just three years earlier – in correspondence with Brian Shaw through Andrew Bradley on 9 July 2014. Kenny said it was probably the first time he had referred to himself as a professional musician.

## Chapter 2: The Imminent Immigrant

166 Teachout, *Pops*, p. 59.

167 Howard Gillis, "Clifford Brown: A Short Life Well-Lived", *JazzTimes*, 20 September 2024, http://jazztimes.com/articles/26454-clifford-brown-a-short-life-well-lived.

168 Nick Catalano, *Clifford Brown: The Life and Art of the Legendary Jazz Trumpeter* (Oxford University Press, 2002), p. 45.

169 From Miles Davis's autobiography: "I even beat Clark Terry out of some money once in order to buy some drugs. I was down around the Hotel America, where Clark lived, too, sitting on the curb thinking about how and where I was going to get some money to get off when Clark walked up. My nose was runny and my eyes were all red. He bought me some breakfast and afterward he took me to his room at the hotel and told me to get some sleep. He was going out on the road with Count Basie and about to leave. He told me when I felt well enough to leave to just lock the door behind me, but I could stay as long as I wanted to. That's how tight we were. He knew what I was doing but he just figured I would never do nothing fucked up to him, right? Wrong. As soon as Clark left to catch his bus, I opened up his drawers and closets and took everything I could get my hands on to carry. Took a horn and a lot of clothes straight to the pawnshop and what I couldn't pawn, I sold for whatever little money I could get for the stuff . . . On top of everything, Clark forgave me for what I had done to him. But for a little while after that, I avoided being anyplace I thought Clark was going to be. When we did finally run into each other, I apologized and we went on like nothing had ever happened. Now, that's a good friend. A long time after that every time he caught me in a bar drinking with my change on the counter, he'd take it for payment on what I had stolen. Man, that was some funny shit" (Quincy Troupe, *Miles: The Autobiography* [Picador 1990], p. 136).

170 Kenny Wheeler, interview with Nick Smart, 23 April 2010.

171 Lees, "Come Back Last Summer (Part 1)", p. 8.

172 RMS *Scythia* ship's registry, arriving Southampton, 2 October 1952.

173 Kenny Wheeler, interview for Artists House Music, 2002.

174 Kenny Wheeler, interview with Nick Smart, 23 April 2010.

175 Grime, "Star Sideman: Kenny Wheeler".

176 Newspaper clipping from Wheeler family scrapbook, 24 October 1952 (Wheeler Archive, Royal Academy of Music).

177 Ronnie Scott, *Some of My Best Friends Are Blues* (Northway Publications, 2013), p. 51.

178 Ibid.

179 Art Ellefson, interview with Brian Shaw, 12 May 2015. The 100 Club is named for its address at 100 Oxford Street, between Oxford Circus and Tottenham Court Road.

180 Ibid.

181 Condon, "Humble Legend", p. 18.

182 Lees, "Come Back Last Summer (Part 1)", p. 7.

183 Mabel Ball, interview with Brian Shaw, 13 May 2015.

184 Lees, *Arranging the Score*, p. 21.

185 Ibid.

186 Mabel Ball, interview with Brian Shaw, 13 May 2015: "Kenny was living my Dad's dream – because he would have loved to have been a full-time musician."

187 Kenny Wheeler, interview with Martin Speake, 4 April 2012.

188 Condon, "Humble Legend".

189 Kenny Wheeler, interview for Artists House Music, 2002.

190 Kenny Wheeler, interview with Nick Smart, 23 April 2010.

191 Doreen Yeend, birth records, England and Wales, July–September 1933.

192 Doreen Wheeler, interview with Nick Smart and Brian Shaw, 15 February 2015.

193 Gene Lees, "Come Back Last Summer (Part 2)", *JazzLetter* 12(4) (April 1993), p. 1.

194 Kenny Wheeler, interview with Nick Smart, 23 April 2010.

195 Lees, *Arranging the Score*, p. 24.

196 Doreen Wheeler, interview with Nick Smart and Brian Shaw, 15 February 2015.

197 Kenny and Doreen Wheeler, interview with Martin Speake, 4 April 2012.

198 Lees, *Arranging the Score*, p. 24.

199 Condon, "Humble Legend".

200 Mabel Ball to Brian Shaw, 21 June 2015.

201 Doreen Wheeler, interview with Nick Smart and Brian Shaw, 15 February 2015.

202 Lees, *Arranging the Score*, p. 24.

203 Kenny Wheeler, correspondence with Brian Shaw through Andrew Bradley, 9 July 2014. He "had just been taken in as an innocent abroad and looked after while [I] concentrated on music. As it turned out, this was to set a pattern for the rest of [my] life."

204 Lees, "Come Back Last Summer (Part 2)", p. 1.

205 Michelle L. Bell, Devra L. Davis, and Tony Fletcher, "A Retrospective Assessment of Mortality from the London Smog Episode of 1952: The Role of Influenza and Pollution", *Environmental Health Perspectives* 112(1) (January 2004), https://www.ncbi.nlm.nih.gov/pmc/articles/PMC1241789/pdf/ehp0112-000006.pdf.

206 Greater London Authority, "50 Years On: The Struggle for Air Quality in London Since the Great Smog of December 1952", December 2002, https://cleanair.london/app/uploads/CAL-217-Great-Smog-by-GLA-20021.pdf.

207 Kenny Wheeler, interview with Nick Smart, 23 April 2010.

208 Gordon Thompson, "The Foundations of British Rock: Archer Street", OUP Blog, 20 May 2001, http://blog.oup.com/2011/05/archer-street, accessed 6 July 2014.

209 Ibid.

210 "Archer Street, London" from *The Musician Union: A Social History*, http://www.muhistory.com/?p=344, accessed 6 July 2014.

211 Dave Holland, interview with Nick Smart, 20 January 2015.

212 Art Ellefson, interview with Brian Shaw, 12 May 2015.

213 Kenny Wheeler, interview with Ted O'Reilly, 26 August 1980.

214 Henry Lowther, interview with Nick Smart, 8 October 2014.

215 Doreen's father was less hesitant about his daughter marrying a musician than he was about her marrying a Canadian, she recalled.
216 Kenny Wheeler, interview with Nick Smart, 23 April 2010.
217 Doreen Wheeler, interview with Nick Smart and Brian Shaw, 15 February 2015.
218 Art Ellefson, interview with Brian Shaw, 12 May 2015.
219 Mark Wheeler and Louann Newman, email to Nick Smart, 27 November 2015.
220 "Roy Fox", Apple Music, https://itunes.apple.com/us/artist/roy-fox/id82913798.
221 Kenny Wheeler, interview with Nick Smart, 23 April 2010.
222 Lees, *Arranging the Score*, p. 24.
223 "Roy Fox Launches His New Band", *New Musical Express*, April(?) 1953.
224 Doreen Wheeler, interview with Nick Smart and Brian Shaw, 15 February 2015.
225 Hayes, *Ken Wheeler*.
226 Kenny Wheeler, interview with Brian Priestley, 20 May 1986 (National Sound Archive).
227 Ibid.
228 "Feb. 1954", *Dance Band Diary* 16, p. 8. From the National Jazz Archive website, archive.nationaljazzarchive.co.uk/archive/journals/the-dance-band-diaries/volume-16-1953-1955/52091#prettyPhoto/0, accessed December 2014.
229 Kenny Wheeler, interview with Brian Priestley, 20 May 1986 (National Sound Archive).
230 Ibid.
231 Ibid.
232 Lees, *Arranging the Score*, p. 28.
233 Grime, "Star Sideman: Kenny Wheeler".
234 Mark Miller, *Boogie, Pete & the Senator. Canadian Musicians in Jazz: The Eighties* (Nightwood Editions, 1987), p. 293.
235 Lees, *Arranging the Score*, p. 25.
236 "Art Ellefson", *The Canadian Encyclopedia*. http://www.thecanadianencyclopedia.com/en/article/art-ellefson-emc, accessed 7 July 2014.
237 Lees, *Arranging the Score*, p. 24.
238 Art Ellefson, interview with Brian Shaw, 12 May 2015.
239 Kenny Wheeler, interview with Nick Smart, 23 April 2010.
240 Lees, *Arranging the Score*, p. 25.
241 Dr. Arnon Bentovim, interview with Nick Smart and Brian Shaw, 2 August 2021. When asked about Kenny's constant struggles with performance anxiety, Dr. Bentovim observed, "I would have thought that his crippling nerves would be to do with this internal critic. And so, if you like, the adversity elements which are to do with the [mother's] chaos, and also to do with his father's very strict, forceful, organizing [nature] . . . both have a very powerful positive organizing effect: he works hard, you know, nobody works harder, practises more and so on – but at the same time, it's there internally as a huge critic . . ."
242 Art Ellefson, interview with Brian Shaw, 12 May 2015.
243 Lees, *Arranging the Score*, p. 22.
244 Ibid., p. 23.
245 Doreen Wheeler, interview with Nick Smart, 17 August 2015.
246 Ibid.
247 Lees, *Arranging the Score*, p. 26.
248 Ibid., pp. 25, 26.
249 Mark Wheeler and Louann Newman, email to Nick Smart, 27 November 2015. Also found in 1954 voting records for Robert Yeend.
250 Ibid.
251 Mark Wheeler, interview with Nick Smart and Brian Shaw, 27 November 2015.
252 Mark Wheeler, email to Brian Shaw, 7 October 2015.

253 Mark Wheeler, interview with Nick Smart and Brian Shaw, 27 November 2015. Mark commented that his mother's aunt and uncle who shared the house with them "loved Lou and hated me!" – presumably because his eczema kept him – and in turn everyone else – awake.

254 Doreen Wheeler, interview with Nick Smart, 17 August 2015.

255 Mark Wheeler, email to Brian Shaw, 7 October 2015.

256 Mark Wheeler, interview with Nick Smart and Brian Shaw, 27 November 2015.

257 "Tommy Whittle Discography (Up to 1961)", *British Modern Jazz: From the 1940s Onwards . . .*, http://henrybebop.co.uk/whittle.htm.

258 Lees, *Arranging the Score*, p. 28.

259 Grime, "Star Sideman: Kenny Wheeler".

260 Kenny Wheeler, interview with Brian Priestley, 20 May 1986 (National Sound Archive).

261 Ibid.

262 Newspaper clipping from the Wheeler family scrapbook.

263 Rob Adams, "Tommy Whittle Obituary", *Herald Scotland*, 23 October 2013, and personal email correspondence with Brian Shaw, 1 July 2014.

264 Taken from Kenny's handwritten answers to Fred Sturm's October 1997 interview (Kenny Wheeler private collection). Later published in *Kenny Wheeler, Collected Works on ECM* (Universal Edition).

265 Benny Green's liner notes to Buddy Featherstonhaugh, *New Quintet Volume Two* (Pye Nixa NJE.1031, 1957).

266 Jim Godbolt, *A History of Jazz in Britain: 1950–1970* (Quartet Books, 1989), p. 42.

267 "Buddy Featherstonhaugh", *British Modern Jazz: From the 1940s Onwards . . .*, http://henrybebop.co.uk/feather.htm.

268 Bobby Wellins, interview with Nick Smart, 26 August 2015.

269 Kenny Wheeler, interview with Ian Carr, 7 September 1995 (Ian Carr tapes, British Library).

270 Kenny Wheeler, interview with Brian Priestley, 20 May 1986 (National Sound Archive).

271 Bobby Wellins, interview with Nick Smart, 26 August 2015.

272 Bobby Wellins, interview with Nick Smart, 26 September 2014.

273 Bobby Wellins, interview with Nick Smart, 26 August 2015.

274 Pye Nixa NJL 7.

275 "Kenny Wheeler", *British Modern Jazz: From the 1940s Onwards . . .*, http://henrybebop.co.uk/wheeler.htm. Discogs, "Don Rendell: Don Rendell Presents The Jazz Six & Tenorama Highlights", http://www.discogs.com/Don-Rendell-Don-Rendell-Presents-The-Jazz-Six-Tenorama-Highlights/release/1784774.

276 Duncan Lamont, interview with Andy Simons, 11 September 2002 (Oral History of Jazz in Britain; British Library Collection, C122/429-430).

277 Vic Lewis obituary, *The Independent*, 24 February 2009.

278 Mabel Ball to Brian Shaw, 3 November 2015.

279 Mark Wheeler, interview with Nick Smart and Brian Shaw, 27 November 2015.

280 Vic Lewis obituary.

281 Kenny Wheeler, interview with Brian Priestley, 20 May 1986 (National Sound Archive).

282 The principal UK band that went to the US so Herman could bring in his musicians was the Chris Barber Band plus Ottilie Patterson. That accounted for seven people, allowing Woody to bring in seven visiting US players plus himself.

283 Robert Kriebel, *Blue Flame: Woody Herman's Life in Music* (Purdue University Press, 1995), p. 170. Chris Barber, *Jazz Me Blues: The Autobiography of Chris Barber* (Equinox Publishing, 2014), p. 65.

284 Godbolt, *A History of Jazz in Britain*, p. 228.

285 Gene Lees, *Leader of the Band; The Life of Woody Herman* (Oxford University Press, 1997), p. 225.

## Chapter 3: Everybody's Song But My Own

286 Ken Wheeler and the John Dankworth Orchestra, *Windmill Tilter (The Story of Don Quixote)* (Fontana STL 5494, 1969).

287 Pam Bevin, "Canadians in London" (*Coda*, June 1962) mentions Kenny joining John Dankworth in May. Although a *St. Catharines Standard* feature in 1962 mentions Kenny joining Dankworth just two weeks before Newport, May seems most likely as the Dankworth band that recorded on May 12th, 13th and 19th still included Colin Wright – whom Kenny would replace. Dave Lee also recalled Kenny joining the band before Newport, which further corroborates the date in Pam Bevin's article.

288 In Brian Priestley's interview with Kenny Wheeler (National Sound Archive, 20 May 1986) Kenny confirms it was Colin Wright whom he replaced in the band.

289 Dave Lee, interview with Nick Smart, 16 December 2015.

290 Kenny Wheeler, interview for Artists House Music, 2002.

291 Kenny Wheeler, interview with Brian Priestley, 20 May 1986 (National Sound Archive).

292 Kenny Wheeler, interview with Nick Smart, 23 April 2010.

293 John Fordham, "Quiet Man on the Cutting Edge", interview with Kenny Wheeler, *The Guardian*, 14 October 2010.

294 Dave Lee, interview with Nick Smart, 16 December 2015.

295 A *St. Catharines Standard* feature on Kenny from 1978 ("Former City Trumpet Player One of World's Jazz Giants" [Wheeler family collection]) includes a quote from Dankworth saying he still feels Kenny is "the most brilliant, original and inventive jazz trumpet player in the world".

296 Kenny Wheeler, interview with Ian Carr, 7 September 1995 (Ian Carr tapes, British Library).

297 Lees, "Come Back Last Summer (Part 1)".

298 Dave Lee, interview with Nick Smart, 16 December 2015. It's a story he previously recounted on the BBC Radio 3 series *Jazz File* about the Dankworths – and heard by Nick Smart.

299 Ibid.

300 Top Rank International RS 614, 1959. The cover can be seen at https://www.discogs.com/release/7187349-John-Dankworth-And-His-Orchestra-Bundle-From-Britain.

301 John Dankworth autobiography, *Jazz in Revolution* (Constable 1998), p. 125.

302 Dave Lee, interview with Nick Smart, 16 December 2015.

303 Dankworth, *Jazz in Revolution*, p. 126.

304 Dave Lee, interview with Nick Smart, 16 December 2015.

305 *New Musical Express* 649 (19 June 1959) (www.skidmore.edu/~gthompso/britrock/NME/nme5906.html, accessed 26 October 2015). In Nat Hentoff's weekly US column "American Airmail" he reports "American Rank Records will release a record of Debbie Moore with Johnny Dankworth, as well as the Knightsbridge Strings in Britain." A website of Top Rank recordings (http://www.bsnpubs.com/nyc/toprank/toprank.html, accessed 16 February 2016) also lists Debby Moore and John Dankworth's *Bundle from Britain* on the same label, and shows that perhaps Nat Hentoff misspelled the name "Debby" in his own article.

306 Kenny Wheeler, interview with Nick Smart, 23 April 2010.

307 Kenny Wheeler, interview with Ian Carr, 7 September 1995 (Ian Carr tapes, British Library).

308 Lees, "Come Back Last Summer (Part 1)".

309 Ibid.
310 Dankworth, *Jazz in Revolution*, p. 127.
311 "Newport Jazz Festival: 1959", Rhode Island Rocks, http://www.rirocks.net/Band%20 Articles/Newport%20Jazz%20Festival%201959.htm, accessed 20 April 2016. This info was also listed on the website of Newport Jazz Festival under their Programs Archive section, but that is no longer active.
312 Ibid.
313 Dave Lee, interview with Nick Smart, 16 December 2015.
314 Ibid.
315 Debby Moore, interview and correspondence with Nick Smart, February 2016.
316 Dankworth, *Jazz in Revolution*, p. 128.
317 Dave Lee, interview with Nick Smart, 16 December 2015. Dave confirmed that whole extra solos were added as they would have been editable out, and that they took two whole sets' worth of time for their music so it must have been the case.
318 Dave Lee, interview with Nick Smart, 16 December 2015.
319 Ibid. Dave Lee takes solo duties on "Yesterday's Smiles" on the mellophonium, an instrument on which Kenny would often be called to double, although he later said he wished he had never let on that he could play it.
320 Colpix Records PXL 550.
321 Dankworth, *Jazz in Revolution*, p. 128. Dave Lee, interview with Nick Smart, 16 December 2015.
322 Cleo Laine, *Cleo* (Simon & Schuster, 1994).
323 Dave Lee, interview with Nick Smart, 16 December 2015.
324 Confirmed by Cleo in *Cleo*. There is some debate about whose trumpet was used. In the 1978 *St. Catharines Standard* feature on Kenny ("Former City Trumpet Player One of World's Jazz Giants"), it was suggested that Louis actually borrowed Kenny's trumpet to sit in that night. As much as this would be a great story, it does not seem to be true. Kenny never mentioned this to friends or family, which seems unlikely given the clarity with which he remembered starry encounters like the band bus collecting Dizzy Gillespie, for instance.
325 Dave Lee, interview with Nick Smart, 16 December 2015.
326 "The Duke: Where and When: Duke Ellington's Working Life and Travels", http:// ellingtonweb.ca/Hostedpages/TDWAW/removed20131124-nextTDWAWPartTwo. html, accessed 20 August 2015. This archive confirmed the 7–12 July dates and the presence of the Dankworth band.
327 Dave Lee, interview with Nick Smart, 16 December 2015. There is one curious anomaly here: Kenny never mentioned this experience of sharing a week opposite the Ellington band. Whenever asked about Ellington he would recite other, much less significant, chance encounters with him – such as being in the same coffee shop once in Toronto. So I checked with Dave Lee whether Kenny had definitely been in these concerts to which he responded yes, 100% sure, and he remembered seeing him talking to Hodges over a drink.
328 Bevin, "Canadians in London".
329 1959 Beaulieu Jazz Festival Programme (Royal Holloway Archives, ref. RW/3/19/9).
330 The 1959 Beaulieu Jazz Festival Programme lists Kenny as part of Dankworth's line-up whereas the Vic Lewis entry shows no mention of Kenny. Also, on "Vic Lewis (from 1949)" (*British Modern Jazz: From the 1940s Onwards . . .*, http://www. henrybebop.co.uk/lewis2.htm) it states the *At the Beaulieu Festival* recording (Ember Records CJS 807) was actually a studio session with applause dubbed on later.
331 Bevin, "Canadians in London".
332 Columbia SEG 8037 (7" EP).
333 Pete Churchill, interview with Nick Smart and Brian Shaw, 30 November 2015.

334 Doreen Wheeler, interview with Nick Smart, 17 August 2015. Exact dates confirmed in interview of 21 June 2016.
335 Mark Wheeler, interview with Nick Smart and Brian Shaw, 27 November 2015. Louann Newman, interview with Nick Smart, 21 June 2016.
336 Mark Wheeler, interview with Nick Smart and Brian Shaw, 27 November 2015.
337 Ibid.; Louann Newman, interview with Nick Smart, 21 June 2016.
338 Doreen Wheeler, interview with Nick Smart, 17 August 2015.
339 Kenny Wheeler, letter home to his parents dated August 1961 (Wheeler family collection).
340 Kenny Wheeler, letter home to his parents dated March 1963 (Wheeler family collection).
341 Kenny Wheeler, letter home to his parents dated August 1961 (Wheeler family collection).
342 ECM Records ECM 1691.
343 Kitty Grime, review of *The Criminal*, *Jazz News*, 26 November 1960.
344 Grime, "Star Sideman: Kenny Wheeler".
345 Kitty Grime, "Star Sideman: Dick Hawdon", *Jazz News*, 8 November 1961.
346 Grime, "Star Sideman: Kenny Wheeler".
347 In a *JazzWise* magazine feature ("Shy Guy", *JazzWise*, December 2004/January 2005), for example, he is very outspoken about being in ECM's "bad books". And there are countless interviews from the '80s and '90s where he is very vocal about his feelings regarding his lack of gigs in the UK.
348 Bevin, "Canadians in London".
349 Art Ellefson, interview with Brian Shaw, 12 May 2015. We are assuming it is Tony Russell to whom Art is referring as that is the only trombonist called Tony in the band throughout this period.
350 Mark Wheeler, interview with Nick Smart, 24 July 2014.
351 Chris Laurence, interview with Nick Smart and Brian Shaw, 8 September 2015.
352 Grime, "Star Sideman: Kenny Wheeler".
353 Bevin, "Canadians in London".
354 Ian Carr recalls this story both in his own interview with Kenny in 1995, and in an interview with Alyn Shipton in June 2000 (Oral History of Jazz in Britain; British Library, ref. C122/450).
355 Columbia SEG 8153 (June 1962).
356 Ian Carr, interview with Alyn Shipton, June 2000 (Oral History of Jazz in Britain).
357 Alyn Shipton, *Out of the Long Dark: The Life of Ian Carr* (Equinox Publishing, 2006), p. 73.
358 A BBC Four retrospective called *Sir John Dankworth at the BBC* (2010) included the film of this performance of "Just in Time" (available at the time of writing on YouTube, https://youtu.be/XN60oAji35M?si=8XYUyLnQ-T0ZO-SB) and the opening titles indicate the date and the name of the show, *Just Jazz*.
359 Fontana TL 5203 (1963).
360 Fontana TL 5229 (1965).
361 *St. Catharines Standard*, 22 September 1962.
362 He mentioned this often, just one example being the Ted O'Reilly interview, 26 August 1980.
363 Alyn Shipton's notes for the John Dankworth and Cleo Laine four-CD set *I Hear Music: A Celebration of Their Life and Work* (Salvo SALVOBX403, 2007).
364 Greg Bowen, interview with Nick Smart, 4 June 2015. Björn Heile, Peter Elsdon, and Jenny Doctor (eds.), *Watching Jazz: Encounters with Performance on Screen* (Oxford University Press, 2016), p. 139.
365 Fontana TL5209.

366 This confusion likely resulted from the fact it was an E♭ instrument, pitched the same as the tenor horn, most often found in brass bands.

367 Details of recording date and other tunes played are logged on the Library of Congress archive page (https://www.loc.gov/item/jots.200016721). Footage of "Mark 1" was included in a BBC Four compilation of *Jazz 625* performances (2010) (available at the time of writing on YouTube, https://youtu.be/tVxJoFjvDK4?si=3IA WrD4HqydEphIq).

368 Date confirmed in a letter from Wilf Wheeler Sr. in November 1964 in which he describes them having just returned home.

369 Kenny Wheeler, letter home to his parents dated March 1963 (Wheeler family collection).

370 Conversation with Doreen, Louann, and Mark at Wallwood Road, 16 July 2018.

371 Mark Wheeler, interview with Nick Smart and Brian Shaw, 22 January 2016.

372 Mark Wheeler had spoken about the tapes the families would send, and they are regularly mentioned in Kenny's letters home and the replies from his parents in letters given to us by Carri Driver.

373 Kenny Wheeler, interview with Brian Priestley, 20 May 1986 (National Sound Archive).

374 Grime, "Star Sideman: Kenny Wheeler".

375 Kenny Wheeler, letter home to his parents dated August 1961 (Wheeler family collection).

376 Kenny Wheeler letter home to his parents dated March 1963 (Wheeler family collection).

377 Kenny Wheeler, interview with Brian Priestley, 20 May 1986 (National Sound Archive).

378 Based on a variety of sources we can pin those dates down to around this period. In the March 1963 letter home he says he is now studying with Russo having studied first with Bennett. And in a number of interviews he says he only studied with Bennett for a few months (the Ian Carr interview [7 September 1995; Ian Carr tapes, British Library]) says six to eight months) so halfway into 1962 seems the likely starting period.

379 Lees, "Come Back Last Summer (Part 2)".

380 He mentions this both in a Martin Speake interview of 4 April 2012 and in Lees, "Come Back Last Summer (Part 2)".

381 Duncan Lamont, interview with Andy Simons, 11 September 2002 (Oral History of Jazz in Britain).

382 Kenny Wheeler, interview with Ian Carr, 7 September 1995 (Ian Carr tapes, British Library).

383 Kenny Wheeler, interview with Brian Priestley, 20 May 1986 (National Sound Archive).

384 *Jazz Session*, broadcast on 29 June 1964 on Network 3 ("Programme as Broadcast" [PasB] info from BBC Written Archives Centre).

385 Lees, "Come Back Last Summer (Part 2)".

386 Kenny Wheeler, letter home to his parents dated March 1963 (Wheeler family collection).

387 Lees, "Come Back Last Summer (Part 2)".

388 Mark Wheeler, interview with Nick Smart and Brian Shaw, 22 January 2016.

389 Louann Newman, interview with Nick Smart, 21 June 2016.

390 Doreen Wheeler, interview with Nick Smart, 17 August 2015.

391 Louann Newman, interview with Nick Smart, 21 June 2016.

392 Doreen Wheeler, interview with Nick Smart, 17 August 2015.

393 Mark Wheeler, interview with Nick Smart and Brian Shaw, 22 January 2016. Louann Newman, interview with Nick Smart, 8 July 2016.

394 Mark Wheeler, interview with Nick Smart and Brian Shaw, 22 January 2016. Confirmed in a letter from Wilf Sr.

395 Mark Wheeler, interview with Nick Smart and Brian Shaw, 27 November 2015.

396 Norma Winstone, interview with Nick Smart, 31 March 2015.

397 *Jazz Session*. BBC Programme Index, http://genome.ch.bbc.co.uk/8b1c88855b96465 29befdbb60db5f6b6.

398 Taken from an interview with Ronnie Scott on "Ronnie Scott's 47 Frith Street", *British Modern Jazz: From the 1940s Onwards . . .*, http://henrybebop.co.uk/frithst.htm.

399 Dave Holland, interview with Nick Smart, 20 January 2015.

400 "History of Ronnie Scott's Jazz Club", www.ronniescotts.co.uk/static/assets/ronnie_ scotts_history.pdf, accessed 6 August 2015.

401 Dave Holland, interview with Nick Smart, 26 July 2024.

402 All the Dave Holland biographical information from Dave Holland, interview with Nick Smart, 20 January 2015. Interestingly, two of his colleagues in the bass section of that orchestra were fellow students Chris Laurence and Barry Guy, both of whom would also go on to be significant jazz musicians and collaborators with Kenny.

403 John Taylor, interview with Nick Smart, 2 April 2015.

404 John Taylor, interview with Martin Speake, 11 February 2015.

405 Kenny Wheeler, interview with Nick Smart, 23 April 2010. Kenny also mentions this in a Martin Speake interview of 4 April 2012.

406 John Taylor, interview with Nick Smart, 2 April 2015.

407 Stan Sulzmann, interviews with Nick Smart, 7 October 2014 and 30 July 2019.

408 Columbia 33SX 1758, 1965.

409 Kenny's involvement with this is confirmed on Wikipedia, "The Animals", https:// en.wikipedia.org/wiki/The_Animals, accessed 6 August 2015, and www.slimsblues. com/early_animals.htm, accessed 6 August 2015, as well as the recollections of his nephew Jayson (Kenny's sister Helen's son) in an interview with Brian Shaw, 21 June 2015.

410 Shipton, *Out of the Long Dark*, p. 74.

411 Columbia SX 6051.

412 Columbia Studio 2 Stereo series TWO 146.

413 Fontana TL 5410.

414 Columbia SX 6076.

415 In his interview with Ian Carr (7 September 1995 [Ian Carr tapes, British Library]) Kenny reveals to whom each movement's title refers; "For H" was for Harry South. Norma Winstone and many of the musicians also recall that Harry was the dedicatee, but several people thought they remembered Kenny saying later that "For H" was for his sister Helen.

416 Polydor 582001.

417 Kenny's involvement in this 1962 NDR Jazz Workshop confirmed on both these Michael Frohne archives of NDR lists: www.plosin.com/frohne-ndr.html, accessed 29 December 2017 and http://jazzrealities.blogspot.com/2015/12/ndr-jazz-workshops-start-of-listing-i.html, accessed 29 December 2017.

418 SABA SB 15 097 ST.

419 Blue Note BLP 4175 1964.

420 Ken Schaphorst, conversations with Nick Smart, who recalled Kenny talking to him about this.

421 The Stan Tracey Quartet, *Jazz Suite (Inspired by Dylan Thomas's "Under Milk Wood")* (Columbia 33SX 1774, 1965).

422 Michael Frohne, "NDR Jazz Workshops", www.plosin.com/frohne-ndr.html, accessed 29 December 2017.

423 John Fordham, "The Windmill Tilter Dreams On", *Jazz UK* 61 (January/February 2005).

424 Fantasy F-9529, 1977.
425 Kenny Wheeler, interview with Ted O'Reilly, 26 August 1980. The group included Harold Land, Kenny Burrell, Ray Brown, and Philly Joe Jones. Jones was presumably aware of Kenny already, having hired him to record on his *Trailways Express* album in 1968 (released in 1971 on Black Lion Records BL-142).
426 Deram DML 1005, 1967.
427 Released in 2005 on a double CD on Cuneiform Records RUNE 213/214.
428 Henry Lowther to Nick Smart, 8 October 2014.
429 Fontana STL 5445.
430 Kenny would have known Derek by this point as they had worked together for Georgie Fame's *The Two Faces of Fame* album (CBS SBPG 63018) a few months previously.
431 Kenny Wheeler, interview with Nick Smart, 23 April 2010.
432 Bevin, "Canadians in London".
433 Kenny Wheeler, interview with Chris Parker, 1990 (londonjazznews. com/2014/09/19/interview-kenny-wheeler-in-1990, accessed 14 August 2015).
434 Miller, "Profile: Kenny Wheeler".
435 Kenny Wheeler, interviewed by Evan Parker, seemingly late 1994. Evan recalled the recording was to help him write the liner notes for Kenny's album *All the More* (Soul Note 121236-2, 1997).
436 Kenny Wheeler, interview with Brian Priestley, 20 May 1986 (National Sound Archive).
437 Kenny Wheeler, interview for Artists House Music, 2002.
438 Jerry D'Souza, interview with Kenny Wheeler, *Coda* 282 (November/December 1998).
439 Kenny Wheeler, interview with Brian Priestley, 20 May 1986 (National Sound Archive).
440 Recording of "Seven Steps to Heaven" from Simon Spillett collection.
441 James Hale, "Kenny Wheeler: In a Melancholy Tone", feature and interview, *DownBeat*, August 1997.
442 John Stevens, interview with Victor Schonfield, December 1992 (Oral History of Jazz in Britain, British Library Collection). Stevens confirmed it was the end of December 1965.
443 Kenny Wheeler, interview with Ted O'Reilly, 26 August 1980.
444 Martin Davidson, "John Stevens: An Appreciation", 1996 (www.efi.group.shef.ac.uk/mstevens.html, accessed 16 April 2018).
445 Paul Rutherford, interviews with Victor Schonfield (Oral History of Jazz in Britain, British Library Collection, C122/298-302).
446 John Stevens, interview with Victor Schonfield, December 1992 (Oral History of Jazz in Britain).
447 Evan Parker, interview with Nick Smart, 24 August 2015.
448 John Stevens, interview with Victor Schonfield, December 1992 (Oral History of Jazz in Britain).
449 Evan Parker, interview with Nick Smart, 24 August 2015.
450 This is the same consistent story he sticks to in interviews ranging from Mark Miller in 1976, Ted O'Reilly in 1980, Brian Priestley in 1986, Chris Parker in 1990, Ian Carr in 1995, *Coda* magazine in 1998, and up to Nick Smart and Martin Speake interviews in 2010 and 2012.
451 It is only in the Ted O'Reilly interview from 26 August 1980 that he explicitly says "I knew the guys already who were playing there."
452 Henry Lowther, interview with Nick Smart, 8 October 2014. And a recording of a 1965 John Stevens broadcast from the Simon Spillett collection.

453 Kenny Wheeler, interview with Ian Carr, 7 September 1995 (Ian Carr tapes, British Library).
454 Evan Parker, interview with Nick Smart, 25 August 2015.
455 Dave Holland, interview with Nick Smart, 20 January 2015.
456 Both quotes from Kenny Wheeler, interview with Nick Smart, 23 April 2010.
457 Kenny Wheeler, interview with Nick Smart, 23 April 2010.
458 Kenny Wheeler, interview with Brian Priestley, 20 May 1986 (National Sound Archive).
459 Kenny Wheeler, interview with Nick Smart, 23 April 2010.
460 Eyemark EMPL 1002.
461 John Stevens, interview with Victor Schonfield, December 1992 (Oral History of Jazz in Britain).
462 Evan Parker, interview with Nick Smart, 24 August 2015.
463 Ibid.
464 Martin Davidson, liner notes for Spontaneous Music Ensemble, *Withdrawal* (Emanem 4020, recorded in 1966–67, released in 1997); and email from Evan Parker, 30 January 2019, confirming he was also in Copenhagen with Stevens, after Armorel (Veryan Weston's sister) had told them that the people there were crazy about free jazz.
465 Dave Holland, interview with Nick Smart, 20 January 2015.
466 Paul Rutherford, interviews with Victor Schonfield (Oral History of Jazz in Britain).
467 Story recalled in both the Victor Schonfield–Paul Rutherford interview (ibid.) and in direct email correspondence with Art Ellefson on 18 May 2015.
468 Audio available at https://www.youtube.com/watch?v=LMZtNEeFcCs; proof of broadcast confirmed on BBC Programme Index: http://genome.ch.bbc.co.uk/schedules/light/1967-03-26.
469 Island Records ILPS 9079.
470 Evan Parker, interview with Nick Smart, 24 August 2015. Evan says, "But I know what I can say for sure, is the group that's on *Karyōbin* never did anything else except that record. That specific combination of players only ever got together in the studio to make that record."
471 Ibid.
472 John Stevens, interview with Victor Schonfield, December 1992 (Oral History of Jazz in Britain).
473 Ibid. Stevens says, "I heard this gagaku music and I managed to find a whole LP of this music, and one of the tracks on there is called 'Karyōbin' – that's where I got the title for that record."
474 "Chronoscope CPE 2001-2: Karyōbin Are the Imaginary Birds Said to Live in Paradise" (www.efi.group.shef.ac.uk/labels/chrono/cpe20012.html, accessed 28 August 2015).
475 John Stevens, interview with Victor Schonfield, December 1992 (Oral History of Jazz in Britain).
476 Evan Parker, interview with Nick Smart, 25 August 2015.
477 Ibid.
478 Dave Holland, interview with Nick Smart, 20 January 2015.
479 Kenny Wheeler, interview with Brian Priestley, 20 May 1986 (National Sound Archive).
480 Ibid.
481 Kenny Wheeler, interview with Ian Carr, 7 September 1995 (Ian Carr tapes, British Library).
482 Graham Lock, "Brass Menagerie" (Kenny Wheeler interview), *The Wire* 72 (February 1990).

483 Jackie had previously lived in a large place shared with many jazz musicians, including bassist Ron Mathewson's brother, pianist Matt Mathewson. That Northumberland Street flat was well known to visiting musicians who regularly attended parties hosted there after gigs in the city. Jackie remembered Tubby Hayes and Joe Harriott staying there, and Kenny had actually been there once before himself after Bobby Breen had taken them along following a Dankworth gig. But on this particular night, with Jackie now moved into his new flat in the Grassmarket, Kenny was the only one staying there; the other members of SME had somewhere else to go.

484 New Jazz 8236, 1960.

485 There is something different about it, perhaps something to do with Dolphy's music pushing him in a different direction.

486 Candid CJM 8027, 1961.

487 All this from Jackie Docherty, interview with Nick Smart, 26 August 2015. This event has taken some investigating as Kenny mistakenly recalls in some interviews that it was following a Globe Unity gig that someone played him Booker Little, although in other earlier (more reliable perhaps) interviews he remembers it was with John Stevens. Jackie himself is sure it was an SME gig at Edinburgh Art College; and indeed there is an article that confirms that such a gig did take place (www.variant. org.uk/11texts/Ramsay.html, accessed 28 August 2015). The year is not totally certain as that article blurs lines between 1966 and 1967, but Jackie remembered it being earlier rather than later so '66 seems likeliest. In Nick Smart's interview with John Cumming he also corroborated that Kenny came up to Edinburgh with members of SME at that time, and that Jackie worked in the record shop in the basement of the book store, so all in all it seems the most likely version of events.

488 Conversation with Evan Parker following the Kenny Wheeler Prize Meeting at the Academy on 20 June 2016. Nick Smart showed Evan his first draft of this topic and Evan offered that story in response to reading Jackie's account. He did not dispute it, however, so it is likely that both events happened, and the chronology will probably never be unpicked.

489 One author (Nick Smart)'s opinion is that, if it had been Evan who had first played Booker to Kenny, he would probably have remembered it – given how close they remained. Although when I raised this, Evan pointed out that it was very early in their friendship so that assumption might not necessarily obtain. Nevertheless, Nick is inclined toward Jackie's account as it seems to chime most with Kenny's own accounts of the story, as well as the chronology.

490 Kenny Wheeler, interview with Brian Priestley, 20 May 1986 (National Sound Archive). Jackie Docherty remembers clearly that it was only Kenny present as the other members of SME had somewhere else to stay, so John Stevens was not actually there.

491 Kenny Wheeler, interview with Ian Carr, 7 September 1995 (Ian Carr tapes, British Library).

492 Kenny Wheeler, interview with Nick Smart, 23 April 2010. Here he is misremembering it being with Globe Unity – which of course is much later.

493 Lees, "Come Back Last Summer (Part 2)".

494 Kenny Wheeler, interview with Ian Carr, 7 September 1995 (Ian Carr tapes, British Library).

495 Ibid.

496 Lees, "Come Back Last Summer (Part 2)".

497 See note 286.

498 Dates confirmed from Henry Lowther's 1968 diary; it was an all-day session on the 11th and a morning session on the 12th.

499 Dankworth, *Jazz in Revolution*, p. 145.

500 Henry Lowther, interview with Nick Smart, 8 October 2014.

501 Kenny Wheeler, interview with Nick Smart, 23 April 2010.

502 Fordham, "Quiet Man on the Cutting Edge".

503 Kenny Wheeler, interview with Nick Smart, 23 April 2010.

504 Fordham, "Quiet Man on the Cutting Edge".

505 Kenny Wheeler, interview with Ian Carr, 7 September 1995 (Ian Carr tapes, British Library).

506 Fordham, "Quiet Man on the Cutting Edge".

507 Kenny Wheeler, interview with Nick Smart, 23 April 2010.

508 Kenny Wheeler, interview with Ian Carr, 7 September 1995 (Ian Carr tapes, British Library).

509 Kenny Wheeler, interview with Nick Smart, 23 April 2010. In contrast to Kenny's own telling of the tale Evan Parker recalled, "Ken told me at the time that Dankworth thought the pieces overall had a Spanish feel and asked him to find a Spanish book that they could get titles from. Ken then asked the librarian for a famous Spanish book and she suggested Don Quixote (great suggestion!). I think the 'loser' theme may also have emerged post hoc" (email from Evan Parker to Nick Smart, 30 January 2019).

510 Parker, "Kenny Wheeler in 1990".

511 Kenny Wheeler, interview with Brian Priestley, 20 May 1986 (National Sound Archive).

512 Henry Lowther, email to Nick Smart, 18 January 2015.

513 Lees, "Come Back Last Summer (Part 2)".

514 Mark Wheeler, interview with Nick Smart and Brian Shaw, 22 January 2016.

515 Mark Wheeler, interview with Nick Smart and Brian Shaw, 27 November 2015.

516 Kenny Wheeler, interview with Ian Carr, 7 September 1995 (Ian Carr tapes, British Library).

517 Much research has gone into unpacking the order of events. Having established that at least two pieces had their origins earlier with Morley College and Graham Collier, Henry Lowther recalled that other of the pieces were performed at the May '67 residency at Ronnie Scott's. This means they must have been written before May '67, so the question arose as to when the wisdom tooth operation was. The only breaks in his recording/performing schedule long enough to have included this extended dental hiatus were in late '66 or mid–late '67. Give that the second option would have been after the Ronnie's gigs – and crediting Kenny with correct memory to the extent that he wrote at least *some* of the pieces during the wisdom tooth saga – then that places it at the end of 1966. It also makes sense of all the differing accounts of events; they now all have an answer. It wasn't written about Don Quixote – correct. The pieces existed under different titles and were all played on gigs before the recording – correct. Kenny wrote it after the dental operation – also basically correct.

518 BBC *Omnibus*, 27 October 1977.

519 Line-up compiled from Henry Lowther, interview with Nick Smart, 8 October 2014, and from Kenny's quote: "He had a weird band. He had three trumpets and he had a funny section of tenor, tuba and trombone, I think, and then he had the section that he always like to have, except it was augmented so he had five people, I think, in the front line which was including me and a trombone, I think. And the rhythm section, yeah. And that's more or less the band that I did the record for, wrote for the record" (Kenny Wheeler, interview with Brian Priestley, 20 May 1986 [National Sound Archive]).

520 Henry Lowther, email to Nick Smart, 18 January 2015.

521 *The $1,000,000 Collection* recording date is listed only as "May 67", but the Derek Jewell review in the *Sunday Times* of 21 May confirms "his recorded but as yet unreleased Million Dollar Collection".

522 Henry Lowther, interview with Nick Smart, 8 October 2014.

523 Ibid.

524 Ronald Atkins, "Dankworth Orchestra at the Ronnie Scott Club", *The Guardian*, 16 May 1967.

525 Conversations with Mark Wheeler and Stan Sulzmann, with Doreen Wheeler present, 14 June 2016. Shaw was a famous dabbler with electronics and was always offering to build high-end, bespoke sound systems for various friends and musicians. (Even Dankworth and Cleo were convinced to try his wares until the smell of a deceased rodent entombed in the speaker casing forced them to call him back.) He would turn up at Kenny's Ramsey Street house at 2:00 am with the newest innovation in custom-built speakers, spend hours soldering and tweaking it to perfection before finally declaring it ready and then . . . silence. Rarely did Shaw's systems work, so Mark Wheeler ended up with a bedroom full of hi-fi equipment that lay silently promising its unfulfilled sonic potential.

526 In the John Dankworth autobiography (*Jazz in Revolution*, p. 145), he recalls Kenny Napper cutting his finger on a bread knife, but incorrectly cites it as being on the morning of the session, whereas in our interview with Dave Holland on 20 January 2015 he remembers receiving the call the day before the session.

527 Dave Holland, interview with Nick Smart, 20 January 2015. Dave continued, discussing his feelings about how he'd played on the session: "When I listen now, sometimes I feel like I'm pushing the rhythm section too hard – I can feel myself kind of dragging it along, and I think I could have been more receptive to the feel that was actually there in the band, because everybody was great players. But I was trying to play like I was playing with Tony Williams, because I'd been playing with the records, so there are a couple of sections where I can feel myself pulling away. But generally, I came away feeling like I'd had a good go at it, you know. And I remember playing it for Chris McGregor, who was completely knocked out by it . . . and liked the way I'd approached the music, which made me feel a lot better because at times I felt I'd taken too many liberties; [like] maybe I should have been more supportive. You know, you kind of look at your playing those ways to see – maybe you could have done that a little better, or that a little better – that's how you learn – but Chris [McGregor] said, 'You've really taken care of that band, back there' and I said 'Thank you,' that made me feel OK about it."

528 Ibid.

529 Two reviews verified this: one from *The Guardian* (29 April 1968) of a Manchester gig they did where Ian Breach refers to the two months spent in London; the other a Derek Jewell review in the *Sunday Times* (10 March 1968) which refers to Johnny Griffin guesting – as well as confirming the residency must have run across 11–12 March when *Windmill Tilter* was recorded. In Sanford Josephson, *Jazz Notes: Interviews across Generations* (Praeger, 2009) Hendricks discusses living in London for about five years from this period onwards.

530 Henry Lowther, interview with Nick Smart, 8 October 2014.

531 All Mike Gibbs quotes are from Mike Gibbs, interview with Nick Smart, 24 August 2015.

532 The small-group interludes can't have been quite as much as a whole year later, as Dave Holland left London to join Miles Davis in August '68, so must have taken place before then.

533 Henry Lowther, email to Nick Smart, 18 January 2015.

534 John Dankworth, *Windmill Tilter*, original liner notes (Fontana STL 5494).

535 Bob Houston, review of *Windmill Tilter*, *Melody Maker*, 12 July 1969, p. 19.

536 Mark Wheeler, interview with Nick Smart and Brian Shaw, 27 November 2015, and further phone conversations, as well as a conversation with Doreen, Louann, and Mark at Wallwood Road, 16 July 2018.

## Chapter 4: Song for Someone

537 Details confirmed via BBC Archive research, PasB microfiche. Verified also as his first broadcast in Brian Priestley's 14 June 1969 *Melody Maker* interview with Kenny where he refers to it (Brian Priestley, "The Little Known Side of Kenny Wheeler", *Melody Maker*, 14 June 1969). The two sources correlate.
538 Kenny Wheeler, interview with Ted O'Reilly, 11 November 1985.
539 BBC *Omnibus*, 27 October 1977.
540 BBC Archive, PasB microfiche; as well as retrieved contracts from the session.
541 Priestley, "The Little Known Side of Kenny Wheeler".
542 In an email exchange in August 2017 between Nick Smart and a whole group of Kenny's colleagues – including Evan Parker, Stan Sulzmann, Henry Lowther, Dave Horler, Duncan Lamont, Norma Winstone, and Chris Laurence – the consensus was that the alto soloist was Ray Warleigh, and the bass clarinetist was Tony Roberts, with Duncan joking but meaning it when he said, "I don't remember playing bass clarinet with Kenny but I might have . . . The rule of thumb is, if it sounds really good it's Tony."
543 Dave Horler, interview with Nick Smart, 2 September 2015.
544 This SME session was only released many years later (in 2007) on the Emanem label, on an album they called *Frameworks* (Emanem 4134); this piece appeared under the title "Familie Sequence".
545 Norma Winstone, interview with Nick Smart, 31 March 2015.
546 Norma Winstone, interview with Nick Smart, 2 April 2015.
547 Kenny Wheeler, interview with Brian Priestley, 20 May 1986 (National Sound Archive).
548 There was some uncertainty from Norma as to which broadcast was her first. She remembered it being one shared with Bobby Breen singing "God Bless the Child", and she sang "I'll Never Be the Same". We found evidence of Breen being on a broadcast in 1971 that included "God Bless the Child" but there is no mention of Norma on that one; however, she is listed categorically on the 1970 one we have described here. In the end, we agreed it was probably just a case of her misremembering.
549 One studio session in July 1969 and one live from Ronnie Scott's in August 1969.
550 Conversation with Doreen, Louann, and Mark at Wallwood Road, 16 July 2018.
551 Ibid. The Nice recording was live in Croydon on 17 October.
552 Charles J. Gans, interview with Alan Skidmore, *Jazz Forum* 6 (March 1982).
553 John Taylor, interview with Nick Smart, 2 April 2015.
554 Brian Blevin's article about that summer's Montreux and Antibes festivals, *Coda*, December 1969.
555 Gans, interview with Alan Skidmore.
556 Deram SDN 11.
557 CBS 52664.
558 Charles Fox, "Contemporary British Jazz", reviewing various CBS releases, *Jazz Monthly*, October 1969.
559 We found various reviews of the band at Ronnie Scott's, and evidence of several broadcasts through BBC Archive research.
560 BBC Archive PasB microfiche; and retrieved contracts from the session; as well as from a recording of the show given to us by Simon Spillett.
561 Stan Sulzmann, interview with Nick Smart, 7 October 2014.

562 On his website (http://www.darylrunswick.net/earlyjazz.html) bassist Daryl Runswick posted a live recording of the group with Tubby, and refers to Pat Smythe as the bandleader. In Nick Smart's interview with Tony Coe (20 August 2015) Tony mentions the group being Pat's idea.

563 Tony Coe, interview with Nick Smart, 20 August 2015.

564 Mabel Ball, interview with Brian Shaw, 13 May 2015.

565 Priestley, "The Little Known Side of Kenny Wheeler".

566 Ember Records CJS 823.

567 Benny Green, review of Ken Moule's *Adam's Rib Suite*, *The Observer*, 8 February 1970.

568 This award is confirmed in a *Washington Post* feature from 1978 (Geoffrey Himes, "Trumpet Reemergent", *Washington Post*, 14 June 1978) as well as the Mark Miller *DownBeat* feature from 1980 (Miller, "Kenny Wheeler's Many Vehicles").

569 Himes, "Trumpet Reemergent".

570 A story told often by Kenny's friends. Evan Parker, Henry Lowther, and Norma Winstone have all recounted it before.

571 Ronnie Scott and the Band, *Live at Ronnie Scott's* (CBS 52661): recorded 25 and 26 October 1968.

572 Kenny refers to Ronnie's nickname for his band in the Chris Parker interview from 1990 (Parker, "Kenny Wheeler in 1990") and the 23 April 2010 interview with Nick Smart.

573 That is to say they played on this recording; on other occasions it was sometimes Tony Crombie instead of Kenny Clare.

574 Kenny mentioned Joe Henderson writing for the band in his interview with Chris Parker (Parker, "Kenny Wheeler in 1990"), and the "Joe Henderson Discography & Chronology", *JazzDiscography.com* (http://www.jazzdiscography.com/Artists/Henderson/JoeHenderson.php) also confirms that "Henderson appeared for a 3 to 4 week engagement with a quartet and provided arrangements for Ronnie Scott's octet."

575 John Surman, interview with Nick Smart, 15 September 2016.

576 Kenny Wheeler, interview with Nick Smart, 23 April 2010.

577 BBC 2's *Jazz at the Maltings* concert series was broadcast from the Britten-Pears concert hall in Snape, going out in late 1968 and early 1969.

578 National tours, the TV broadcast, Jon Hendricks's involvement and the Scott Walker tour are all listed on http://www.angelfire.com/planet/galatabridge/1960.htm, a page predominantly concerned with Surman's career.

579 John Surman, interview with Nick Smart, 15 September 2016.

580 Ibid. Dates confirmed on "Scott Walker: Timeline", http://www.anthonyreynolds.net/writing_walker_brothers/Scott_Walker-Timeline_2008-06-25.pdf.

581 John Surman, interview with Nick Smart, 15 September 2016.

582 Philips SBL.7881, 1969.

583 Rob Young, "British Visionary Jazz", *The Wire*, August 2009.

584 Kenny Wheeler, interview with Nick Smart, 23 April 2010.

585 John Surman, interview with Nick Smart, 15 September 2016. Following that quote Surman adds, "There you are, and I don't think I've told anybody that *ever* in my life. But I was definitely part of the reason that screwed up!" Curiously, John Taylor would face the same awkward decision 10 years later when quitting a new band of Ronnie's. He was tiring of the relentless drives up and down the country and the inability to do much other work, but it was difficult for J.T. to let Ronnie down, since they all recognized he had done so much for them and the jazz scene through his club and the Old Place.

586 Ibid.

587 Deram SML 1030.

588 John Surman, interview with Nick Smart, 15 September 2016.
589 A story Dave Holland has told many times, including in Phil Johnson, "Review: And All That Jazz", *Independent*, 5 April 1998, https://www.independent.co.uk/life-style/review-and-all-that-jazz-1154843.html.
590 Deram SML 1047 and Deram SML 1048.
591 RCA NE 10.
592 John Taylor, interview with Nick Smart, 2 April 2015.
593 Priestley, "The Little Known Side of Kenny Wheeler".
594 Mike Gibbs, interview with Nick Smart, 24 August 2015.
595 Ibid.
596 Tony Fisher, interview with Nick Smart, 4 November 2015.
597 Mike Gibbs, interview with Nick Smart, 24 August 2015.
598 *Michael Gibbs*; Deram SML 1063.
599 Derek Jewell in the *Sunday Times*, 23 May 1971.
600 Philips 6308 122.
601 A number of reviews at the time mentioned Henry in the soloist role and the fact that they played Kenny's music, e.g. Ronald Atkins in *The Guardian*, 18 March 1970, and Miles Kington in *The Times*, 13 March 1970.
602 Master Mix CHECD 00105, 1992.
603 Listed on "The Other Big Bands", *British Modern Jazz: From the 1940s Onwards . . .*, http://henrybebop.co.uk/bigbands.htm; confirmed in Simon Spillett, *The Long Shadow of the Little Giant: The Life, Work and Legacy of Tubby Hayes* (Equinox Publishing, 2015).
604 Deram SML 1064.
605 Dave Horler, interview with Nick Smart, 2 September 2015.
606 Tony Faulkner, interview with Nick Smart, 2 September 2015.
607 Dave Horler, interview with Nick Smart, 2 September 2015.
608 Pye Records NSPL 18349.
609 Henry Lowther, email to Nick Smart (18 June 2015) about Kenny's commercial work. Peck was actually American and had come over to the UK with the Glenn Miller Orchestra and stayed on after the war. Later, he would go into fixing a lot of studio work and regularly booked Kenny on commercial sessions.
610 Henry Lowther, interview with Nick Smart, 8 October 2014.
611 The Kenny Clarke Francy Boland Big Band, *At Her Majesty's Pleasure . . .* (Polydor 2460 131).
612 The concerts were: 7 September 1969 (WDR radio broadcast, Cologne), 9 September 1969 (TV broadcast, De Doelen Concert Hall, Rotterdam), 11 September 1969 (DRS-2 radio broadcast, Stadtcasino, Basel), 12 September 1969 (HR radio broadcast, Frankfurt) – as listed in Gary Carner, *Pepper Adams' Joy Road: An Annotated Discography* (Scarecrow Press, 2012).
613 Ronald Atkins, *The Guardian*, 23 February 1972.
614 Don Thompson, Ted O'Reilly, and Mark Miller, interview with Brian Shaw, 13 October 2015.
615 BBC Archive PasB microfiche; and retrieved contracts from the session.
616 The broadcast in question, from October 1973, was for the *Sounds of Jazz* show with his 17-piece band, again featuring Norma Winstone.
617 Incus INCUS 10, 1973.
618 John Taylor, interview with Nick Smart, 2 April 2015.
619 Norma Winstone, interview with Nick Smart, 2 April 2015.
620 BBC *Omnibus*, 27 October 1977.
621 John Taylor, interview with Nick Smart, 2 April 2015.
622 Kenny Wheeler, letter to sister Mary (Wheeler family collection); other details in the letter confirm the date as ~1970/71.

623 Mabel Ball, interview with Brian Shaw, 12 May 2015.
624 Blair had also been the other trumpet with Kenny on Dave Lee's . . . *Our Man Crichton* album.
625 Tony Fisher, interview with Nick Smart, 4 November 2015.
626 Ibid.
627 Henry Lowther, Chris Laurence, and Norma Winstone, interview with Alyn Shipton, part of the Royal Academy of Music exhibition on Kenny Wheeler, 13 June 2013.
628 Lees, "Come Back Last Summer (Part 2)".
629 Henry Lowther, Chris Laurence, and Norma Winstone, interview with Alyn Shipton, 13 June 2013.
630 Tony Fisher, interview with Nick Smart, 4 November 2015.
631 See note 622.
632 Mark Wheeler, interview with Nick Smart and Brian Shaw, 27 November 2015. Rent arrears letter from Wheeler family private collection.
633 Tony Fisher, interview with Nick Smart, 4 November 2015.
634 Pye Records NSPL 18339.
635 RAK SRKA 6751.
636 RAK SRAK 503.
637 Conversation with Doreen, Louann, and Mark at Wallwood Road, 16 July 2018. It is just possible that Kenny's occasional brushes with rock 'n' roll rubbed off on him. For all his famous mild-mannered-ness, the one situation in which he was frequently observed to lose his temper was soundcheck; several times when the circumstances were particularly bad, he displayed a talent for kicking his monitor off the stage in protest!
638 Gold Star 1500 009.
639 John Schroeder, *Latin Vibrations* (Polydor 2460 136).
640 EMI Columbia TWO 362.
641 Polydor 2310 285.
642 Fontana 6309 015.
643 Fontana 6309 013.
644 MCA Records MKPS 2011/2.
645 Barclay 920 214/Warner Bros. WS 1899.
646 Conversation with Doreen, Louann, and Mark at Wallwood Road, 16 July 2018. Mark Wheeler, interview with Nick Smart and Brian Shaw, 22 January 2016.
647 Greg Bowen, interview with Nick Smart, 4 June 2015; Heile, Elsdon, and Doctor, *Watching Jazz*. "Maynard Ferguson and the Top Brass" broadcast on 24 April 1968: recording shared by "Jazz in Britain" group from Ron Mathewson's private tapes. The broadcast featured a trumpet section of Maynard, Kenny, Greg Bowen and Derek Watkins.
648 Kenny Wheeler, letter to sister Mary (Wheeler family collection).
649 Columbia C 30466; released in the UK as *The World of Maynard Ferguson* (CBS 64101).
650 Kenny Wheeler, interview with Ted O'Reilly, 26 August 1980.
651 CBS S 64432.
652 Kenny Wheeler, interview with Ted O'Reilly, 26 August 1980.
653 Wayne Bergeron to Brian Shaw, 19 May 2024.
654 CBS S 65027.
655 KPM Music KPM 1061.
656 KPM Music KPM 1056.
657 KPM Music KPM 1065.
658 Liner notes to *As If By Magic . . . The Duncan Lamont Big Band featuring Kenny Wheeler plays Mr. Benn* (Jellymould Jazz, JM-JJ025, 2016).
659 Duncan Lamont, interview with Nick Smart, 3 August 2014.

660  Ibid.

661  Ibid.

662  Esquire ESQ 332 and ESQ 342.

663  Duncan Lamont, interview with Andy Simons, 11 September 2002 (Oral History of Jazz in Britain). Kenny is featured on another avant-garde Basil Kirchin soundtrack for the 1974 film *The Freakmaker* (also released under the name *The Mutations*) starring Donald Pleasence. Mark Wheeler recalled watching this film and recognizing his dad immediately from the solo he takes on the opening credits! (Mark Wheeler, interview with Nick Smart and Brian Shaw, 16 July 2018).

664  Duncan Lamont, interview with Andy Simons, 11 September 2002 (Oral History of Jazz in Britain). Liner notes from Alan Branscombe & Friends, *Swingin' on the Soundstage* Vol. 2 (Esquire ESQ 342).

665  Simon Spillett, email, 17 October 2016. Info on Annie Ross taken from "Straight on Till Morning (1972)", *KINDERTRAUMA*®, http://www.kindertrauma.com/?p=27444.

666  Sandy Brown and His Gentlemen Friends, *Hair at It's [sic] Hairiest* (Fontana SFJL 921).

667  Kenny Wheeler, interview with Ian Carr, 7 September 1995 (Ian Carr tapes, British Library).

668  Incidentally, Duff also happened to have come up in Edinburgh playing under Sandy Brown.

669  Mark Wheeler, interview with Nick Smart and Brian Shaw, 27 November 2015.

670  The Jack Duff Band, *The Enchanted Isle* (Avenue AVE 077, 1971).

671  Evan Parker, email to Nick Smart, 10 October 2016.

672  John Surman, interview with Nick Smart, 15 September 2016.

673  Music For Pleasure MFP 1307.

674  Vertigo 6360 091, 1973.

675  Ronald Atkins's review in *The Guardian*, 5 October 1974, confirms Kenny's presence in the Roundhouse performance of *Labyrinth*, along with Tony Coe and Norma Winstone.

676  Vertigo 6360 039.

677  Ian Carr, interview with Alyn Shipton, June 2000 (Oral History of Jazz in Britain; British Library, ref. C122/450).

678  In Mike Gibbs, interview with Nick Smart, 24 August 2015, Mike says the Rock label was something he was tagged with following his association with Gary Burton in the '70s, where he was only writing with that rhythm to satisfy Burton's requirements. But if one listens to a track from the 1970 release, such as "Some Echoes, Some Shadows", one can hear that influence is already in place.

679  Ibid.

680  Kenny Wheeler, interview with Brian Priestley, 20 May 1986 (National Sound Archive).

681  Mike Gibbs, interview with Nick Smart, 24 August 2015.

682  Deram SML 1087.

683  The Mike Gibbs Band, *Just Ahead* (double LP; Polydor 2683 011).

684  Polydor 2683 011.

685  Story told by Mark Wheeler while in conversation with Doreen, Louann, and Mark at Wallwood Road, 16 July 2018; details confirmed by text on 17 July 2018. The Rainbow Theatre date is confirmed on *A History of the Rainbow Theatre*, "1974", http://www.rainbowhistory.x10.mx/1974.htm.

686  Bronze BRON 353.

687  Mike Gibbs, interview with Nick Smart, 24 August 2015.

688  Mike Westbrook Orchestra, *Mike Westbrook's Metropolis* (RCA Neon NE 10).

689  Mike Westbrook Orchestra Featuring John Surman, *Citadel/Room 315* (RCA Victor SF 8433).

690 Deram SML 1094.

691 John Surman, interview with Nick Smart, 15 September 2016.

692 Ibid.

693 John Taylor, interview with Martin Speake, 11 February 2015.

694 Argo ZDA 164/5.

695 Jon Faddis, interview with Nick Smart and Brian Shaw, 13 August 2016. Chris Smith, *The View from the Back of the Band: The Life and Music of Mel Lewis* (UNT Press, 2016), p. 164.

696 Stan Sulzmann, conversation with Nick Smart, 8 January 2016, recalling the event.

697 Jon Faddis, email to Brian Shaw and Nick Smart, 15 December 2015.

698 Tony Faulkner, interview with Nick Smart, 2 September 2015.

699 Jon Faddis, interview with Nick Smart and Brian Shaw, 13 August 2016.

700 Mike Gibbs, interview with Nick Smart, 24 August 2015.

701 Listed in David Meeker, *Jazz on the Screen: A Jazz and Blues Filmography* (Library of Congress, 2009).

702 Deram SML-R 1045.

703 John Taylor, interview with Martin Speake, 11 February 2015.

704 Ibid.

705 John Surman, interview with Nick Smart, 15 September 2016.

706 Turtle Records TUR 302.

707 John Taylor, interview with Martin Speake, 11 February 2015.

708 Nick Smart witnessed a number of masterclasses with Kenny in which young musicians would ask, "Who's been your favourite musician you've ever worked with?" – or something similar – and time and again Kenny would answer that it was J.T.

709 Kenny Wheeler, interview with Nick Smart, 23 April 2010.

710 It may have been another Coe, Wheeler & Co. date on which Tony Coe was unavailable and it just became a generic quintet gig in Kenny's name.

711 John Taylor, interview with Martin Speake, 11 February 2015.

712 John Taylor Sextet Live on Capital Radio, *Fragment* (cassette; Jaguar JS4).

713 J.T. also recorded his *Decipher* album for the MPS label in 1973 (as John Taylor Trio; MPS Records 21 21290-4), between the two sextet records, but that was only a trio record featuring the sextet's rhythm section: J.T., Chris Laurence, and Tony Levin.

714 Chris Laurence, interview with Nick Smart and Brian Shaw, 8 September 2015.

715 Kenny Wheeler, interview with Nick Smart, 23 April 2010.

716 Stan Sulzmann, interview with Nick Smart, 7 October 2014.

717 Chris Laurence, interview with Nick Smart and Brian Shaw, 8 September 2015.

718 John Taylor, interview with Martin Speake, 11 February 2015.

719 Henry Lowther, interview with Nick Smart, 8 October 2014.

720 Ibid.

721 Stan Sulzmann, interview with Nick Smart, 7 October 2014.

722 Ibid. Henry Lowther, interview with Nick Smart, 8 October 2014.

723 Stan Sulzmann, interview with Nick Smart, 7 October 2014.

724 Stan Sulzmann, email to Nick Smart, 10 April 2017.

725 Argo ZDA 148.

726 The Michael Garrick Sextet with Norma Winstone (Argo ZDA 135).

727 Norma mentions the *Melody Maker* polls in her interview with Nick Smart, and the results are confirmed on "Melody Maker Readers Poll (1971)", *British Modern Jazz: From the 1940s Onwards . . .* , http://henrybebop.co.uk/mm1971.htm – she was actually placed third as early as 1965, and third again in 1966, before moving up to top the list in '70/'71.

728 Henry Lowther, Chris Laurence, and Norma Winstone, interview with Alyn Shipton, 13 June 2013.

729 Chris Laurence, interview with Nick Smart and Brian Shaw, 8 September 2015.

730 Although it was released in 1972, *Edge of Time* was recorded on 20 August and 4 September 1971; mixing was finished on 23 September, Norma's 30th birthday. Norma found these dates in her original 1971 diary and emailed Nick Smart on 4/5 July 2017; the diaries imply that they'd intended to record on consecutive days (20/21 August) but the second day was crossed out and rescheduled for 4 September.

731 Tony Oxley, *4 Compositions for Sextet* (CBS 64071).

732 Tony Oxley, Solo Percussion, Quarter and Sextet, *Ichnos* (RCA Victor SF 8215).

733 Tangent Records TNGS 107.

734 Spontaneous Music Ensemble, *Live Big Band and Quartet* (Vinyl Records VS 0015).

735 Tangent Records TGS 118.

736 Emanem 4018 (released in 1992).

737 Simon Spillett in *The Long Shadow of the Little Giant* (p. 267) confirms it was Stevens's idea.

738 Ibid.

739 The BBC Archive reveals on Kenny's contract a recording date of 8 May 1972 for the "wheeler & co" session when Tubby replaced Tony Coe. The Discogs website (https://www.discogs.com/Splinters-Split-The-Difference/release/3355488) – as well as much other writing about the album – confirms that Trevor Watts recorded the night: "Stereo recording on to Philips tape using two AKG D109 mics fed directly into a consumer Sony TC122 cassette machine. Microphones positioned and levels set by Trevor Watts." This gig was just two weeks after Tubby had covered for Tony Coe on that Wheeler & Co. broadcast.

740 Reel Recordings RR013.

741 Interestingly for Kenny, during the daytime on 22 May, warming himself up for that night's Splinters gig meant playing on the *Reebop* recording session for the Ghanian percussionist Anthony "Rebop" Kwaku Baah (Island Records SW-9304). It was Rebop's first solo record, and Kenny takes a quite free solo on the Afrobeat-inspired track "Zagapam".

742 John Stevens, interview with Victor Schonfield, December 1992 (Oral History of Jazz in Britain).

743 Spillett, *The Long Shadow of the Little Giant*, p. 267.

744 Kenny Wheeler to Mark Miller, 2 November 1975, although the subsequent 1976 *DownBeat* article did not include this quote about Splinters . . .

745 Henry Lowther, interview with Nick Smart, 3 November 2021.

746 Ibid. The actual effect of this technique on the instrument would be subtle at most. Locking down the first valve would mean you were playing marginally higher up the harmonic series so the intervals between notes would be closer. It's possible he was experimenting with trying to smooth out the "line" of this flurry of notes, which would be the most logical technical explanation for what is otherwise a slightly cumbersome move to have to make.

747 "Grass Roots" info from Spillett, *The Long Shadow of the Little Giant*, p. 267.

748 The 22 October Stockwell gig is listed in Spillett, *The Long Shadow of the Little Giant*, p. 272. The December BBC broadcast is listed on the BBC Genome website as having been broadcast on 28 December, although no recording date is given. The Notre Dame Hall date was confirmed by John Thurlow via the private recordings of Trevor Watts, which included a tape of that gig from 18 November 1972 (concert presented by Martin Davidson).

749 Quote from John Stevens, interview with Victor Schonfield, December 1992 (Oral History of Jazz in Britain). Pete King's involvement is mentioned in Spillett, *The Long Shadow of the Little Giant*, p. 290.

750 Mabel Ball, Bill Jelley, and Jason Jelley, interview with Brian Shaw, 21 June 2015.

751 There is documentation about this in the BBC Archive, including Kenny's contract and the PasB info. There is also a full record on the BBC Genome website.

752 The ensemble also included Robin Thompson on woodwinds and Peter Britton on percussion.

753 Kenny's BBC contract shows he was performing only on the Rzewski: "29-7-74 – 9.30pm at the Roundhouse, F. Rzewski: 'Les Moutons de Panurge' – to play trumpet as arranged – rhsls on 27th Maida Vale, 28th and 29th July Roundhouse, programme 'Proms 1974.'"

The PasB supplies this further information: "Proms 74 Direct from the Roundhouse, London. Part 1 – Intermodulation, Peter Britton, Roger Smalley, Tim Souster, Robin Thompson. Smalley, Monody for piano with live electronic modulation. Stockhausen, Across the Boundary (first broadcast in this country). Part 2 – Intermodulation with Alan Hacker (piccolo clt), Tony Coe (sop sax), Evan Parker (sop sax), Kenny Wheeler (tpt), Paul Rutherford (tbn), John White (euphonium), Barry Guy (dble bass), John Marshall (drums). Souster, Zorna, for soprano saxophone, live electronics and three drummers (world premier). Frederick Rzewski, Les Moutons de Panarge (first broadcast in this country)."

On the music reporting form, further information about the pieces are listed as: "Monody for piano with live electronic modulation" (comp. Smalley published by Faber) 'Across the Boundary' (comp. Stockhausen published Universal) 'Zorna, for soprano saxophone, live electronics and three drummers' (comp Souster published MSS) 'Les Moutons de Panurge' (comp Rzewski, published Scratch Orchestra [experimental music catalogue])."

Lastly, all pieces are listed as being performed by "ensemble" (i.e. Intermodulation), except for Rzewski, which is listed as "soloists and ensemble".

754 Evan Parker, email to Nick Smart, 4 October 2015, in which Evan misremembers it as a 64-note melody but which has been corrected for the sake of accuracy. Correct information is provided by the Rzewski score (aum.dartmouth.edu/~larry/ ucsc_classes/ucsc_classes_2013_14/spring_2014/music_203f/scores/process_music/ Rzewski2%20les%20moutons.pdf, accessed 5 October 2015).

755 Fordham, "Quiet Man on the Cutting Edge".

756 Evan Parker, email to Nick Smart, 4 October 2015.

757 Kenny Wheeler, interview with Brian Priestley, 20 May 1986 (National Sound Archive).

758 John Taylor talked about this in a private conversation with Nick Smart in Café Rouge on Tottenham Court Road on 18 October 2012. Nick remembers this because they had met to talk about some other issues regarding Kenny's management at the time, and then they walked to Ronnie Scott's together to see Dave Douglas and Joey Baron after they finished their soundcheck! They discussed Song for Someone along the way. The authors subsequently obtained approval for this quote (via email) for use as one of the display cards at the Academy exhibition.

759 Kenny's note on the back sleeve of the original Incus LP.

760 Kenny Wheeler, interview with Ian Carr, 7 September 1995 (Ian Carr tapes, British Library).

761 Ibid.

762 Ibid.

763 In an interview, Norma misremembered "Nothing Changes" from Song for Someone as her first, forgetting about this 1970 version of "Don No More" (Norma Winstone, interview, 4 February 2015). We are assuming that no other prior lyrics had slipped her mind – she firmly cited "Nothing Changes" as the first, so it seems unlikely – and we therefore feel confident in claiming that this "Don No More" is in fact her first lyric to one of Kenny's tunes.

764 Taken from Kenny's handwritten answers to Fred Sturm's October 1997 interview (Kenny Wheeler private collection). Later published in *Kenny Wheeler, Collected Works on ECM* (Universal Edition).

765 Details from master tapes; and Evan Parker, email, 4 August 2017. On 23 July 2018 Evan answered an email asking why the free links were dropped: "That will have been Ken's decision at the first edit and mix sessions at Olympic. By the time he had made it clear that he was not happy with that first mix those links had been left out of the sequence. Kenny never mentioned them again once they'd been done. Bob Cornford worked only on that sequence for his second mix which became the final mix." He ended the same email adding, "We considered using one or more of those links for the CD reissue but they didn't sound convincing."

766 Ronan Guilfoyle, interview with Nick Smart, 24 February 2015.

767 Strangely, the composition "Song for Someone" had an alternative title when it was recorded for the album – it is listed on the master tapes as "Eventually Yours" – despite having already appeared under its original name. It was common for him to change the name of a tune after writing it, but much less common to then change it back to the original. Evan Parker found the master tapes and emailed us the info in August 2017; all tunes are accounted for by title except for "Song for Someone", but there is one called "Eventually Yours", so that must be it.

768 On the BBC's PasB file the tune is listed as "Micka", but when Evan Parker found the original master tapes he discovered it listed as "Mickay"; either way, it's the same piece, which ended up on the album as "Toot Toot". On a 2023 EP called *Live '71: The Kenny Wheeler Big Band & Friends* (British Progressive Jazz BPJ018STC), the track is listed as "Mikei".

769 Incidentally, this was recorded on 7 May in the Camden Theatre, just one day before his *Wheeler & Co.* recording when Tubby Hayes deputized for Tony Coe. Details from BBC Archive, PasB microfiche; and retrieved contracts from the session.

770 Again, info taken from Evan Parker's discovery of the masters.

771 Norma Winstone, interview with Nick Smart, 2 April 2015. Norma thought she recalled that the change of title was down to the fact that Kenny had already published the tune "Eventually Yours" for another purpose so was giving it a new name to try to get it back. No record of a tune called "Eventually Yours" can be found in his catalogue or on anyone else's recording, but it makes sense.

772 Details of original title taken from Evan Parker's master tapes. See also note 763.

773 Taken from Kenny's handwritten answers to Fred Sturm's October 1997 interview (Kenny Wheeler private collection). Later published in *Kenny Wheeler, Collected Works on ECM* (Universal Edition).

774 Kenny only moved to a section of four trumpets in his October 1973 broadcast when Henry Lowther rejoined the ranks. Personnel info is from BBC Archives research and recordings we were given. We don't have the recording from February '71 so only know that there are three trumpets, but not who they were – although the broadcasts either side are Bowen, Hamer, and Hancock. And we don't have the recording from 1972 so again can only see it is three trumpets, not who it is – so it is possible Henry's first broadcast with Kenny was '72 and not '73, but the significance of '73 remains because of the use of four trumpets rather than the addition of Henry per se; besides, Henry himself has more significance than this minor detail due to his *Windmill Tilter* connection, albeit as part of the Dankworth band rather than Kenny's own booking.

775 Mark Wheeler, conversation about Alfie Reece over a curry in Marylebone! (Mark Wheeler, interview with Nick Smart and Brian Shaw, 27 November 2015). Kenny's quote is from the *Song for Someone* back cover. He later reiterated this sentiment even more plainly: "I wanted all my favourite people in the band no matter what area they came from."

776 In an email from Evan Parker to Nick Smart, 30 January 2019, Evan recalled that Ray Warleigh was away in Australia at the time of the *Song for Someone* recording, and he speculated that "I'm sure Ken would have wanted him to play lead on SfS" – adding, "Great as Ozzy was".

777 Kenny Wheeler, interview with Brian Priestley, 20 May 1986 (National Sound Archive).

778 Ibid.

779 BBC Archive; and a recording of "CPEP" on the May 1971 broadcast which we know Evan appears on as one of the three saxophonists listed in the line-up. We don't have a recording of the February 1971 broadcast, but it also lists three saxophones, so it's possible that the February recording was Evan's first. But it's definitely one of those two, because on the 1970 session, of which we do have a recording, Evan is not listed.

780 Musical information taken from both the recording and the score of "CPEP", which is in the Wheeler Archive, Royal Academy of Music.

781 1972 double LP; Incus INCUS 6/7.

782 Evan Parker, interview with Nick Smart, 24 August 2015. Evan Parker, email to Nick Smart, 30 January 2019, confirming that *Ode* was the only project to have received Arts Council funding prior to the *Song for Someone* application.

783 One early reference to this is in his BBC *Omnibus* interview, 27 October 1977. The transcript of the full interview, BBC Archive, has him describing his music as ". . . mixing a bit of chaos with a pretty tune". And much later, on his 80th birthday, in another BBC interview, this time for the *PM* radio programme, he delivered the now quite well-known quote: "Everything I do has a touch of melancholy and chaos."

784 Dave Horler, interview with Nick Smart, 2 September 2015.

785 Evan Parker, interview with Nick Smart, 24 August 2015.

786 Norma Winstone, interview with Nick Smart, 2 April 2015.

787 John Taylor, interview with Nick Smart, 2 April 2015.

788 Evan Parker, interview with Nick Smart, 24 August 2015.

789 Numerous people, including Dave Horler and Greg Bowen, have colloquially described Tony Oxley's set-up as including "pots and pans" – they meant it literally, too, as Oxley was famed for his unorthodox drum kit with all its eccentric extras!

790 Lees, "Come Back Last Summer (Part 2)".

791 Ibid.

792 This is a very well-remembered story told to us by Norma Winstone, Evan Parker, Dave Horler, Greg Bowen, and John Taylor – all of whom paraphrase the exact wording, some for more comic effect, but all of whom agree that the exchange was very close to how it is presented here.

793 Dave Horler, interview with Nick Smart, 2 September 2015.

794 Greg Bowen, interview with Nick Smart, 4 June 2015.

795 Dave Horler, interview with Nick Smart, 2 September 2015.

796 Kenny Wheeler, interview with Brian Priestley, 20 May 1986 (National Sound Archive).

797 Lees, "Come Back Last Summer (Part 2)".

798 Evan Parker, interview with Nick Smart, 24 August 2015.

799 Ibid.

800 Ibid.

801 "Ticketeeboo" remains less well known than the other music on the tour, since it didn't make it on to the accompanying recording: the double LP *Music for Large and Small Ensembles* (ECM Records ECM 1415/16).

802 BBC *Omnibus*, 27 October 1977. Kenny describes it as a "jazz centre society venue". Evan Parker confirmed (email to Nick Smart, 30 January 2019) that this organization was a promoter and "the only promoter in receipt of half decent funding at the time".

803 Ronald Atkins, *The Guardian*, 16 December 1974, p. 8.

804 Their partnership would last for the rest of Kenny's life and, thankfully, the height of their combined powers is documented on one of Kenny's finest recordings: 1987's *Flutter By, Butterfly* (Kenny Wheeler Quintet; Soul Note 121 146-1).

805 In a few interviews (such as with Brian Priestley, 4 April 1986, Ted O'Reilly, 26 August 1980, and BBC *Omnibus*, 27 October 1977) he refers to this mixed group of instruments as being a hangover from the Dankworth line-up. Sometimes he phrases it in a complimentary way (i.e. it was a good idea and he wanted to stick with it, as in the Brian Priestley interview); other times he refers to it less positively, as in the 1977 BBC interview in which he claims Dankworth only let him do *Windmill Tilter* on the condition that he used Dankworth's band ("which is natural", he acknowledged), and explains that it was then easier for him to carry on writing in that format. Information on personnel is taken from BBC Archive and reviews, plus the *Song for Someone* line-up.

806 Kenny Wheeler, interview with Ted O'Reilly, 11 November 1985.

807 Kenny Wheeler interviewed by Evan Parker, seemingly late 1994. Parker recalled that the recording was to help him write the liner notes for the album *All the More*.

808 Kenny mentions this on BBC *Omnibus*, 27 October 1977.

809 Atkins, *The Guardian*, 16 December 1974.

810 Kenny Wheeler, interview with Ian Carr, 7 September 1995 (Ian Carr tapes, British Library).

811 Taken from Kenny's handwritten answers to Fred Sturm's October 1997 interview (Kenny Wheeler private collection). Later published in *Kenny Wheeler, Collected Works on ECM* (Universal Edition).

812 Kenny Wheeler to Mark Miller, 2 November 1975.

813 Kenny Wheeler to Mark Miller, 3 January 1980.

814 The phrase "develop their art free of commercial pressure" appears on the NDR Jazz Workshop Wikipedia page, as well as within the text of numerous DVD releases from the time. It was clearly something of a mission statement for the organization.

815 "How It All Started . . .", *Hamburger Abendblatt*, 8 March 2018 – an article that marked the 60th anniversary of the NDR Jazz Workshops. This was the last year under Hans Gertberg's leadership before his death in 1970 when producer Michael Naura took over.

816 John Surman, interview with Nick Smart, 15 September 2016 . . . John was clear in his memory of Kenny's ballad so we knew they must have performed more music than made it onto the final Cuniform recording that was released many years later. In the Michael Frohne archive of NDR Workshops (see note 417) there is a full list of the pieces they played on the broadcast and that indeed confirms the presence of Kenny's "Dallab".

817 Michael Frohne, NDR archive (see note 417); also a recording online.

818 Evan Parker, email to Nick Smart, 30 January 2019. Parker adds further detail to this incident: "Alex [von Schlippenbach] asked for a bit more money to cover the extra work in Berlin or at least, as a minimum, that J-E Berendt would cover the extra day's hotel. Berendt refused saying he had already paid for rehearsals. Alex felt responsible for making sure the band were not out of pocket and there was a stalemate. Berendt then organized the performance next year with the whole GUO except Alex. I tried to talk everyone out of doing it but with no success. I turned the gigs down and Berendt wrote to me to try to get me to change my mind. I have the letter somewhere."

819 Kenny Wheeler, letter to sister Mary (Wheeler family collection), in which he describes having not visited the Continent since "last year" and how he is looking forward to the Don Cherry project. He also acknowledges Bill Jelley in saying Don Cherry was someone "Bill will have heard". Interestingly, despite Kenny's previously

busy periods in Europe throughout 1969 and 1970, the work was evidently not consistent; in 1971 he had not actually visited the Continent at all before this project.

820 The *London Music Now* showcase is documented in a live recording from the event; the details are additionally confirmed in the archive of the *Berlin Observer* newspaper which advertised the event (20 October 1972): http://www.theberlinobserver.com/archive/1972V28/V28_N42_oct20.pdf.

821 Barry Guy, private letter to Kenny at the end of his life (Wheeler family collection).

822 Alexander von Schlippenbach, interview with Nick Smart, 15 June 2015; www.efi.group.shef.ac.uk/mguo.html, accessed 9 June 2017.

823 Atavistic UMS/ALP223CD; released in 2001.

824 Alexander von Schlippenbach, interview with Nick Smart, 15 June 2015.

825 Lees, "Come Back Last Summer (Part 2)".

826 BBC *Omnibus*, 27 October 1977.

827 Kenny Wheeler, interview with Martin Speake, 4 April 2012.

828 FMP FMP 0160.

829 Released in the UK as The Rhythm Combination & Brass, *Live at Ronnie Scott's* (BASF BAP 5058).

830 On this, Kenny was part of a section that included the famed American trumpeter Art Farmer and the noted Danish trumpeter Palle Mikkelborg.

831 This version was performed here some three months before it appeared in his BBC broadcast of February 1971 and more than two years before *Song for Someone*.

832 Double LP; Freedom 28 459-6 Z/1-2. Released in the US and UK on Arista Records in 1977.

833 Kenny Wheeler, interview for Artists House Music, 2002.

834 Kenny Wheeler, interview with Nick Smart, 23 April 2010.

835 Dave Holland, interview with Nick Smart, 20 January 2015.

836 Anthony Braxton to Taylor Ho Bynum on behalf of Nick Smart and Brian Shaw, 9 July 2015.

837 Dave Liebman, interview with Nick Smart, 28 June 2015.

838 Anthony Braxton to Taylor Ho Bynum on behalf of Nick Smart and Brian Shaw, 9 July 2015.

839 Louann Newman, interview with Nick Smart, 21 June 2016. The Evan Parker story was recounted at an earlier date in conversation, and was confirmed on 15 July 2018.

840 Information about this concert in several Braxton archives, including *JazzDiscography.com*, "Anthony Braxton 1971–1979", https://jazzdiscography.com/Artists/Braxton/brax-1971-1979.php, which also has the review of the concert.

841 Anthony Braxton, *News from the 70s: Solos, Duo, Quartets* (Musica Jazz FY 7005), released in Italy in 1998.

842 Dave Holland, interview with Nick Smart, 20 January 2015. That album did happen: it ended up being the 11th release for ECM in 1971 – *Music from Two Basses* (ECM Records ECM 1011 ST).

843 Kenny Wheeler ECM bio on his *Songs for Quintet* album (ECM Records ECM 2388, 2015); Manfred Eicher, interview with Nick Smart, 5 March 2017.

## Chapter 5: Gnu High

844 Bill Smith, liner notes to *New York, Fall 1974* (Arista AL 4032).

845 Wadada Leo Smith to Brian Shaw, 12 January 2016.

846 Matthias Winckelmann on *JazzDiscography.com*, "Anthony Braxton 1971–1979".

847 This was broadcast on 1 June 1975, probably recorded in the last week of May. This was the version of Coe, Wheeler & Co. with Chris Pyne on trombone. The broadcast included Kenny's playfully titled composition "Shake a Spear". Incidentally, this

broadcast is the closest recording (date-wise) the authors are aware of to Kenny's recording of *Gnu High.*

848 *JazzDiscography.com*, "Anthony Braxton 1971–1979". Studio Rivbea was a performance space for new and improvised music set up in 1970 by Sam Rivers and his wife Bea. According to Alyn Shipton, it was probably as important in its era as the Five Spot in the late '50s and early '60s.

849 "Mercury hits 97 degrees here: Heat blankets North-East", *New York Times,* 3 August 1975.

850 Wadada Leo Smith to Brian Shaw, 12 January 2016.

851 Manfred Eicher to Nick Smart, 12 February 2018, when Eicher was at the Royal Academy of Music to receive an Honorary Fellowship.

852 ECM Records ECM 1069.

853 *JazzDiscography.com*, "Anthony Braxton 1971–1979". We are relying on a couple of other sources here as well. Manfred Eicher recalls how hot it was in New York on the day of the recording of *Gnu High.* 23 June 1975 was 32°C.

854 Manfred Eicher, interview with Nick Smart, 5 March 2017.

855 Ibid.

856 Ibid.

857 D'Souza, *Coda,* 1998.

858 Manfred Eicher, interview with Nick Smart, 5 March 2017.

859 D'Souza, *Coda,* 1998.

860 ECM Records ECM 1064/65 ST.

861 Observation made in conversation with Ronan Guilfoyle, 24 February 2019.

862 Although *Gnu High* is generally considered Jarrett's last album as a sideman – and it is his last significant recording in that role – he did make appearances on albums by Charlie Haden (one track) in 1976 and a trio record listed under Gary Peacock's name two years later, marking the first commercially recorded appearance of Jarrett's Standards Trio. There is one additional curious record in 1979, where Keith played on two tracks on his brother Scott's album, *Without Rhyme or Reason* (Arista GRP GRP 5007).

863 Dave Holland, interview with Nick Smart, 20 January 2015.

864 Ibid.

865 Ian Carr, *Keith Jarrett: The Man and His Music* (Da Capo Press, 1992), p. 91.

866 Jack DeJohnette to Brian Shaw, 25 May 2015.

867 A third possibility exists that allows for both Holland, Jarrett, and DeJohnette to be at least in partial agreement: there are memories from others who recall Kenny telling them that Jarrett arrived at the session with his charts in an unopened envelope. Since Keith Jarrett is the one member of the session who would not grant an interview for this book, we are unfortunately unable to ask him directly.

868 Kenny Wheeler, interview with Brian Priestley, 20 May 1986 (National Sound Archive).

869 Carr, *Keith Jarrett,* p. 91.

870 Kenny Wheeler, personal conversation with Brian Shaw, Banff, summer 1998.

871 Jack DeJohnette to Brian Shaw, 25 May 2015.

872 Dave Holland, interview with Nick Smart, 20 January 2015.

873 Manfred Eicher, interview with Nick Smart, 5 March 2017.

874 Fordham, "The Windmill Tilter Dreams On", p. 15.

875 Manfred Eicher, interview with Nick Smart, 5 March 2017.

876 Richie Beirach to Nick Smart, 2 October 2017.

877 Kenny Wheeler to Nick Smart in care home, 24 July 2014.

878 Ibid.

879 Kenny commented in 2012 that the piece not included on *Gnu High* was, in his words, an "Indian tune" which might be the tune "Indian PopPiece" ("Saso/Seso/

InPo"), both of which are currently housed in manuscript in the Wheeler Archives. (Kenny Wheeler, personal conversation with Brian Shaw, 13 May 2012).

880 Carr, *Keith Jarrett*, p. 91.
881 Jarrett to Carr in Carr, *Keith Jarrett*.
882 Manfred Eicher, interview with Nick Smart, 5 March 2017.
883 Jack DeJohnette to Brian Shaw, 25 May 2015.
884 Dave Holland, interview with Nick Smart, 20 January 2015.
885 Jarrett to Carr in Carr, *Keith Jarrett*.
886 Dave Holland, interview with Nick Smart, 20 January 2015.
887 Jarrett to Carr in Carr, *Keith Jarrett*.
888 Kenny Wheeler to Nick Smart in care home, 24 July 2014.
889 Dave Holland, interview with Nick Smart, 20 January 2015.
890 Jack DeJohnette to Brian Shaw, 25 May 2015.
891 Dave Holland, interview with Nick Smart, 20 January 2015.
892 Jorge Luis Borges, *The Book of Imaginary Beings* (E.P. Dutton, 1969).
893 Kenny Wheeler, personal conversation with Brian Shaw, Banff, summer 1998.
894 Kenny Wheeler, written lecture (date unknown) titled "Key Centres: Heyoke" (Wheeler Archive, Royal Academy of Music).
895 Scores found in the Wheeler Archive, Royal Academy of Music.
896 A story recounted by Kenny in conversation with Nick Smart and others.
897 BBC Archive research shows "S'matta" appearing on a big-band broadcast recorded in November 1974 with the same orchestration he had established on the *Song for Someone* album. *Heyoke* and "Slobal" appeared on a broadcast recorded in June 1974, with a sextet including Ray Warleigh and Evan Parker, which appears to be listed under the band name "Freedom for a Change".
898 Dave Holland, interview with Nick Smart, 20 January 2015.
899 There are many memories of students at Banff recalling Kenny playing *Gnu High* in public listening sessions and pointing out where he got lost in this tune. In a Facebook post about *Gnu High*, Canadian saxophonist Steve Kaldestad, who attended Banff in 1993, recalled Kenny telling this story: "Kenny Wheeler's 'Gnu High'. I must have listened to it about 300 times in 2nd year university and then it was pretty cool getting to discuss this recording the following year with Kenny Wheeler himself when I attended the Banff Workshop in summer 93. Ken had a great story about how Keith Jarrett said hardly anything to him at the recording session but after the take of *Heyoke* that made it onto the album, Keith walked over to him and explained where Ken had gotten lost in his own tune. Awkward . . ."
900 Steve Lake, "Marriage Made in Heaven", *Melody Maker*, 13 March 1976.
901 Mikal Gilmore, review of *Gnu High*, *DownBeat*, 21 October 1976, pp. 31–32.
902 Ibid. These oversights on Gilmore's part might appear more forgivable when considered within the context of his personal life. The review was published just 14 days after Gilmore's older brother, Gary, a convicted murderer, had been sentenced to the death penalty – the first person to be put to death after capital punishment was reinstated in the United States in 1976. Furthermore, David "Fathead" Newman's *Mr. Fathead*, reviewed by another critic in the column immediately preceding *Gnu High*, is alternately called "dull", "lifeless", and – startlingly – "crap", summarizing the album with a final single-word sentence: "Yawn". Considering the apparently harsh review climate at *DownBeat* at the time, perhaps Gilmore's appraisal was actually more glowing than it might seem to readers today.
903 Robert Palmer, "Records: Keith Jarrett's Jazz Piano", *New York Times*, 16 July 1976, p. 64.
904 Tom Moon, "Pioneering Record Label Celebrates Two Decades; Pride before Profits Has Made ECM Influential", *Philadelphia Inquirer*, 3 December 1989.
905 Bradley Bambarger, "ReDISCussion", *Billboard*, 8 February 1997.

906 "1000 Albums to Hear Before You Die", *The Guardian*, 22 November 2007.

907 Bill Frisell, interview with Nick Smart, 30 November 2015.

908 NPR interview with Steve Treseler: "A Tribute to Kenny Wheeler", *NPR Music*, 19 May 2015, http://www.npr.org/event/music/406618614/a-tribute-to-kenny-wheeler.

909 Tania Gill to Brian Shaw, 27 October 2015.

910 J.D. Considine, "Toronto-Born Kenny Wheeler Was a Fearless Jazz Improviser", *Toronto Globe & Mail*, 8 October 2014.

911 Kenny Wheeler to Mark Miller, 3 January 1980.

912 Ibid.

913 Dave Holland, interview with Nick Smart, 20 January 2015.

914 The BBC broadcast in September 1975 included scored-up versions of his recent *Gnu High* tunes: "S'matta" again and a new arrangement of *Heyoke*, plus the first appearance of a composition entitled "Half As Wear".

915 Arista AB 4064.

916 Anthony Braxton to Taylor Ho Bynum on behalf of Nick Smart and Brian Shaw, 9 July 2015.

917 Ibid.

918 Ronald M. Radano, *New Cultural Figurations: Anthony Braxton's Cultural Critique* (University of Chicago Press, 1993).

919 Michael Cuscana, liner notes for Anthony Braxton, *The Montreux/Berlin Concerts* (double LP; Arista AL 5002, 1977).

920 Kenny Wheeler to Mark Miller, 3 January 1980.

921 Kenny Wheeler, interview with Nick Smart, 23 April 2010.

922 Fordham, "The Windmill Tilter Dreams On".

923 Anthony Braxton to Taylor Ho Bynum on behalf of Nick Smart and Brian Shaw, 9 July 2015.

924 Kenny Wheeler, interview with Nick Smart, 23 April 2010.

925 Anthony Braxton to Taylor Ho Bynum on behalf of Nick Smart and Brian Shaw, 9 July 2015.

926 Ibid.

927 Kenny Wheeler to Mark Miller, 3 January 1980.

928 Anthony Braxton, *Creative Orchestra Music 1976* (Arista AL 4080, 1976).

929 Radano, *New Cultural Figurations*, p. 252.

930 Cuscana, notes for the *Montreux/Berlin Concerts*.

931 Kenny Wheeler to Mark Miller, 2 November 1975.

932 Anthony Braxton to Taylor Ho Bynum on behalf of Nick Smart and Brian Shaw, 9 July 2015. Those unfamiliar with Braxton's musical semantics are encouraged to consult Anthony Braxton, *Tri-Axium Writings* Volumes 1–3 (Synthesis Music, 1985).

933 Globe Unity Orchestra and Guests, *Pearls* (FMP FMP 0380, 1977).

934 Francy Boland & The Orchestra, *1. Blue Flame* (MPS Records 68.111, 1976); *2. Red Hot* (MPS Records 68.174, 1977); *3. White Heat* (MPS Records 0068.189, 1978), all released in Germany.

935 ECM Records ECM 1102.

936 Our research reveals no evidence of recordings or broadcasts with Kenny and any of the other members before this session, other than Danielsson's presence on the Lester Bowie 1969 Baden-Baden meeting.

937 *Kenny Wheeler Quintet* (Transcription series; Radio Canada International RCI 444, 1976).

938 Art Ellefson, interview with Brian Shaw, 12 May 2015.

939 Ibid. The comment about the Fender Rhodes is perhaps surprising, given how much of a feature Kenny had made in his own seminal big band of using both electric and acoustic pianos alongside one another.

940 Just A Memory JAS 9506-2, 1996.

941 Information on the August 1976 broadcast from the BBC Archive: contract and PasB.
942 Phil Woods with Chris Gunning and Orchestra, *Floresta Canto* (RCA PL 11800).
943 Gryphon G-907, released in 1979.
944 Tony Coe, *Zeitgeist (Based on Poems of Jill Robin)* (EMI EMC 3207).
945 *Clark After Dark: The Ballad Artistry of Clark Terry* (MPS Records 0068.194, Germany, 1978).
946 Dave Horler, interview with Nick Smart, 2 September 2015.
947 Kenny Wheeler to Mark Miller, 2 November 1975.
948 BBC *Omnibus*, 27 October 1977.
949 Ibid.
950 Ibid.
951 Bruford, *Feels Good to Me* (Polydor 2302 075).
952 Kenny Wheeler to Mark Miller, 3 January 1980.
953 Mabel Ball, Bill Jelley, and Jason Jelley, interview with Brian Shaw, 21 June 2015.
954 Kenny Wheeler, interview with Ted O'Reilly, 11 November 1985.
955 Mark Sinker, "Subtle Survivor", *New Statesman & Society*, 26 January 1990, p. 46.
956 Chris Laurence, conversation with Alyn Shipton, Royal Academy of Music, 13 June 2013.
957 Henry Lowther, Chris Laurence, and Norma Winstone, interview with Alyn Shipton, 13 June 2013.
958 Musicians' Union information, Wheeler Archive, 9 April 1975.
959 Robin Denselow, James Last obituary, *The Guardian*, 10 June 2015.
960 Various conversations with people connected to the band, including Wendy Watkins, Doreen Wheeler (16 July 2018), and Stan Sulzmann (30 July 2019).
961 Denselow, James Last obituary. *Gentleman of Music* refers to a 2001 Last album of that name.
962 Ibid.
963 Various conversations with the Wheeler family in which they recalled how it came about.
964 Documented in various James Last archives and YouTube videos.
965 Bob Lanese, email correspondence with Nick Smart, 5 May 2017.
966 Wendy Watkins to Nick Smart, 2017. She shared the photo from this jam session.
967 Conversation with Doreen, Louann, and Mark at Wallwood Road, 16 July 2018.
968 Kenny Wheeler, interview with Nick Smart, 23 April 2010.
969 John Surman, story recounted during a rehearsal, Royal Academy of Music, 10 November 2017.
970 Tony Fisher, interview with Nick Smart, 4 November 2015.
971 Mark Wheeler, interview with Nick Smart and Brian Shaw, 27 November 2015.
972 *Cadence*, May 1981 p. 15.
973 Shipton, *Out of the Long Dark*, p. 113.
974 Mood Records 22 666.
975 Ian Carr, interview with Alyn Shipton, June 2000 (Oral History of Jazz in Britain).
976 Shipton, *Out of the Long Dark*, p. 115.
977 Ibid., p. 113.
978 Ibid., p. 115.
979 PRS is the Performing Rights Society – for broadcasts on UK TV/radio/performances in public; MCPS is the Mechanical Copyright Protection Society – for recordings sold or used in UK TV/film/radio.
980 Kenny Wheeler accounts, Wheeler Archive, Royal Academy of Music.
981 Roger Cotterrell, "Kenny Wheeler Speaking Softly but Carrying a Big Horn", *Jazz Forum* 57, p. 41.
982 Ibid.

983  Priestley, "The Little Known Side of Kenny Wheeler".

984  Mood Records 23600, 1979.

985  Kenny Wheeler to Mark Miller, 3 January 1980.

986  Parker, "Kenny Wheeler in 1990".

987  "South Bank Shuffle", *Jazz Journal International*, November 1977.

988  John Abercrombie, Dave Holland, and Jack DeJohnette, *Gateway* (ECM Records ECM 1061 ST, 1975).

989  John Abercrombie, interview with Brian Shaw, 16 July 2014, in which Abercrombie recalled it being Manfred who recommended him. Interestingly, none of the musicians involved (nor Manfred) suggested the obvious economic rationale stemming from the fact that the *Gateway* trio were recording that same week, so that is merely the authors' own conjecture.

990  John Abercrombie, Dave Holland, and Jack DeJohnette, *Gateway 2* (ECM Records ECM 1105 ST, 1978).

991  ECM Records ECM 1109.

992  Dave Holland, interview with Nick Smart, 20 January 2015.

993  Manfred Eicher, interview with Nick Smart, 5 March 2017.

994  Jan Garbarek and the Bobo Stenson Quartet with Palle Danielsson and Jon Christensen, *Witchi-Tai-To* (ECM Records ECM 1041 ST, 1974).

995  Keith Jarrett, Jan Garbarek, Palle Danielsson, and Jon Christensen, *Belonging* (ECM Records ECM 1050 ST, 1974).

996  Keith Jarrett and Jan Garbarek, *Luminessence* (ECM Records ECM 1049 ST, 1975).

997  Jan Garbarek to Brian Shaw, 16 June 2015. (Jan had obviously forgotten the exact chronology, in that he and Kenny had actually done the live NDR radio broadcast in Germany the year before in January 1976.)

998  Garbarek and DeJohnette have no recollection of being at the hotel room for this "rehearsal"; perhaps they were not.

999  John Abercrombie, interview with Brian Shaw, 16 July 2014. (Interestingly, there is no record of a BBC broadcast with the *Deer Wan* tunes prior to the recording date and the hotel room rehearsal! Nor did searches of NDR broadcasts yield anything; perhaps the performance Abercrombie alludes to happened elsewhere, or perhaps it was a bootleg of a gig?)

1000  Ibid.

1001  Ralph Towner to Brian Shaw, 15 June 2015.

1002  Jan Garbarek to Brian Shaw, 16 June 2015.

1003  Ibid.

1004  Ralph Towner to Brian Shaw, 15 June 2015.

1005  John Abercrombie, interview with Brian Shaw, 16 July 2014.

1006  This is the title that appears on Kenny's manuscripts (found in the Wheeler Archive, Royal Academy of Music) for the first part of what became "Peace for Five" on the *Deer Wan* album.

1007  Kenny Wheeler to Ian Carr, 9 July 1995.

1008  Lees, *Arranging the Score*, p. 31.

1009  ECM Records ECM 1080, 1976.

1010  Ralph Towner, email correspondence with Brian Shaw, 28 June 2015.

1011  Barry Long, "Transcribed Solo: An Artist's Signature – Kenny Wheeler's Improvised Solo on '3/4 in the Afternoon'", *Jazz Educators Journal* 30(5) (March 1998): 54-56.

1012  Kenny Wheeler notebook, entry on "Sumother Song".

1013  Ibid.

1014  Jan Garbarek to Brian Shaw, 16 June 2015.

1015  Chuck Berg, *Deer Wan* review, *DownBeat*, June 1978, p. 29.

1016  Kenny Wheeler notebook, entry on "Sumother Song".

1017  Manfred Eicher, interview with Nick Smart, 5 March 2017.

1018 Evan Parker, interview with Nick Smart and Brian Shaw, 9 September 2015.

1019 The programme included "'Smatta" and *Heyoke* from *Gnu High*, "Peace for Five"; "3/4 in the Afternoon", and the title track from *Deer Wan*; and "The Good Doctor" and the title track from *Song for Someone*.

1020 The contract for his 1976 broadcast (recorded 11 August and broadcast 20 September) show the personnel listed as "KW + 13 musicians, 5 saxes, tuba, fr hn, 2 tbns, tpt, pno, bass, drums" (BBC Archive). All the earlier big-band sessions have trumpet sections.

1021 Chris Laurence, interview with Nick Smart and Brian Shaw, 8 September 2015.

1022 Norma Winstone and Evan Parker, interview with Nick Smart for Royal Academy of Music exhibition, November 2012.

1023 Richard Williams, "Ken Wheeler Orchestra, Nottingham", *The Times*, 17 January 1978, p. 9.

1024 Ronald Atkins, "Manchester: Ken Wheeler," *The Guardian*, 23 January 1978, p. 8.

1025 Henry Lowther, Chris Laurence, and Norma Winstone, interview with Alyn Shipton, 13 June 2013.

1026 John Surman, interview with Nick Smart, 15 September 2016.

1027 Manfred Eicher, interview with Nick Smart, 5 March 2017.

1028 Norma Winstone, interview with Nick Smart, 19 August 2015.

1029 Manfred Eicher, interview with Nick Smart, 5 March 2017.

1030 Norma Winstone, interview with Nick Smart, 19 August 2015.

1031 Kenny Wheeler, interview with Nick Smart, 23 April 2010.

1032 Kenny Wheeler, interview with Ted O'Reilly, 11 November 1985.

1033 Norma Winstone, interview with Nick Smart, 19 August 2015.

1034 Ibid.

1035 BBC *Omnibus*, 27 October 1977.

1036 Ibid.

1037 Norma Winstone, interview with Nick Smart, 19 August 2015.

1038 BBC *Omnibus*, 27 October 1977.

1039 Norma Winstone, interview with Nick Smart, 19 August 2015.

1040 John Wickes, *Innovations in British Jazz. Vol. 1: 1960–1980* (Soundworld, 1999), p. 139.

1041 John Taylor, Norma Winstone, and Kenny Wheeler/Azimuth, *Azimuth* (ECM Records ECM 1099, 1977).

1042 Manfred Eicher, interview with Nick Smart, 5 March 2017.

1043 Mark Wheeler later recalled that they hadn't actually used Leytonstone station as it wasn't deemed photogenic enough, so another nearby alternative was found instead!

1044 Norma Winstone, interview with Nick Smart, 19 August 2015.

1045 BBC *Omnibus*, 27 October 1977. According to Alyn Shipton (email to Nick Smart, 28 October 2022): "Just as the BBC Omnibus document suggests Kenny was living on the breadline in Kilburn, it is inaccurate about Nat Gonella. 1977 was the year he moved from his bungalow in Leyland (to which he had only moved in 1973) to Gosport . . . During his time in his 'miserable retirement bungalow' Nat was actually working regularly in Holland with Ted Easton, toured there with Bud Freeman, Wild Bill Davison and other old chums, and was crowned Dutch King of Jazz. He also got into the Dutch hit parade in 1976–7 with the re-release of his old hit 'Oh Monah'."

1046 Chris Sheridan, "Caught! Norma Winstone/John Taylor/Kenny Wheeler at Band on the Wall, Manchester, England", *DownBeat*, December 1978, p. 36.

1047 Norma Winstone's diary of this event confirms the date, coinciding with Chris Sheridan's review ("Caught!") of the Manchester gig in *DownBeat*.

1048 Sheridan, "Caught!" ("John" is a North American colloquialism for "toilet".)

1049 Wickes, *Innovations in British Jazz Vol. 1*, p. 138.

1050 Kenny Wheeler, interview with Ted O'Reilly, 11 November 1985.

1051 *Cadence*, May 1981, p. 18. (Interview conducted in 1979.)

1052 Kenny Wheeler to Mark Miller, 3 January 1980.

1053 "Former City Trumpet Player One of World's Jazz Giants", *St. Catharines Standard*, 1978.

1054 "Trumpet Reemergent", *Washington Post*, 14 June 1978, p. B7.

1055 Fantasy F-9529.

1056 John Fordham, review of Stan Getz *Moments in Time* [Resonance Records HCD-2020, 2016], *The Guardian*, 7 April 2016.

1057 Kenny Wheeler, interview with Nick Smart, 23 April 2010.

1058 Ibid.

1059 BBC *Omnibus*, 27 October 1977.

1060 *Seven Steps to Evans: A Tribute to the Compositions of Bill Evans* (MPS Records 0068.248).

1061 Larry Schneider, email to Nick Smart, 21 May 2017.

1062 Richard Williams, review of Horace Silver, *The Times*, 20 July 1977.

1063 The trumpeter Kenny was subbing for was Lew Soloff. Stephanie Stein Crease, *Out of the Cool* (Chicago Review Press, 2002).

1064 Kenny Wheeler to Ian Carr, 9 July 1995.

1065 Details for both these recordings are found on Jazz Live Trio with Kenny Wheeler and Alan Skidmore, *Jazz Live Trio with Guests* (TCB Records TCB 02282, 2012), a recording spanning three years of the *Jazz Live Trio* series (1978–80). No earlier performance – recorded or otherwise – of "A Simple Toon" has come to light.

1066 As simply "Azimuth" (ECM Records ECM-1-1130).

1067 Norma Winstone to Nick Smart, 19 August 2015.

1068 Ibid.

1069 Norma Winstone, interview with Nick Smart, 19 August 2015.

1070 "Uncle Bert"(!) tape, Norma Winstone private collection.

1071 Don Thompson to Brian Shaw, 13 October 2015.

1072 Henry Lowther, Chris Laurence, and Norma Winstone, interview with Alyn Shipton, 13 June 2013.

1073 Ibid.

1074 Billed as Azimuth with Ralph Towner (ECM Records ECM 1163).

1075 Norma Winstone, interview with Nick Smart, 19 August 2015.

1076 Ralph Towner to Brian Shaw, 15 June 2015.

1077 Kenny Wheeler to Mark Miller, 3 January 1980.

1078 Manfred Eicher, interview with Nick Smart, 5 March 2017.

1079 Originally on ECM sister label JAPO Records (JAPO 60021, 1978).

1080 ECM Records ECM-1-1143.

1081 "The closing act on Sunday night was a stellar quartet of Kenny Wheeler, Evan Parker, Barry Guy, and Paul Lytton, who put on an incredible display of collective and spontaneous improvising" (Frank Rubolino, "FLASHBACK #02: Moers International New Jazz Festival: 12–15 May 1978", June 2000, http://www.onefinalnote.com/features/2000/moers). Interestingly, this quartet played a few times that year as there are two concerts recorded (bootlegs) in Italy in the same year, in Lovere and Rome. (All the above confirmed via email with Evan Parker, 29 April 2019.)

1082 Wadada Leo Smith to Brian Shaw, 12 January 2016.

1083 A recording of the Baden-Baden and Mainz concerts, plus the accompanying information, was posted at "Baden Baden New Jazz Meeting 1978", *Inconstant Sol*, 23 September 2014, http://inconstantsol.blogspot.com/2014/09/baden-baden-new-jazz-meeting-1978.html.

1084 Manfred Schoof broadcast information in Naoyuki Kamiko discography, of which Kamiko has a copy.

1085 ECM Records ECM 1141.

1086 Richie Beirach to Nick Smart, 13 October 2017.

1087 Ibid.

1088 BBC broadcast information from BBC Archive. This March 1979 septet broadcast was also for two tenors and Kenny, so the same front-line arrangement as *Sound Suggestions*, but with Evan Parker and Alan Skidmore on the BBC date, joined in the rhythm section by John Taylor, Bill Le Sage on vibes, Chris Laurence, and Tony Oxley. They also played "Piece for Five (Part 3)" from *Deer Wan*, and two other compositions: "Try and Fly" and "Count Every Point". This broadcast was in fact just three days before his 1979 trip to Zurich for the Swiss Radio Days Jazz Series.

1089 Kenny Wheeler to Ian Carr, 9 July 1995.

1090 Kenny Wheeler, personal conversation with Brian Shaw, Banff, summer 1998. John Abercrombie said the same in his interview with Brian Shaw, 16 July 2014.

1091 Richie Beirach to Nick Smart, 13 October 2017.

1092 ECM Records ECM 1153.

1093 Ralph Towner to Brian Shaw, 15 June 2015.

1094 Ibid.

1095 Simon Purcell to Nick Smart, 16 November 2015.

1096 ECM Records ECM 1187.

1097 Manfred Eicher, interview with Nick Smart, 5 March 2017.

1098 Mark Miller, "Return to Toronto Has Wheeler Worried", *Toronto Globe & Mail*, 25 August 1980.

1099 Ibid.

1100 Kenny Wheeler, interview with Ted O'Reilly, 26 August 1980.

1101 Information from BBC Archive research: his contract included a letter from the BBC acknowledging they would pay his airfare. Interestingly, the BBC was involved in another European collaboration earlier that year with the Dutch Broadcasting Foundation, NOS. In March 1979 Kenny was contracted for a full day's recording in Hilversum, Netherlands with the Metropole Orchestra, broadcast in May that year.

1102 Again under its sister label, JAPO Records (JAPO 60027, 1980).

1103 Evan Parker, interview with Nick Smart, 25 August 2015.

1104 Kenny Wheeler to Mark Miller, 3 January 1980.

1105 Alexander von Schlippenbach, interview with Nick Smart, 15 June 2015.

1106 Kenny and Doreen Wheeler, interview with Martin Speake, 4 April 2012.

1107 Gilles Laheurte, "Steve Lacy's Japan Tours: 1975–2004", *All About Jazz*, 15 February 2006, https://www.allaboutjazz.com/index_new.php?url=steve-lacys-japan-tours-1975-2004-steve-lacy-by-gilles-laheurte.php&page=1&width=1600#4.

1108 Kenny and Doreen Wheeler, interview with Martin Speake, 4 April 2012.

1109 Evan Parker, interview with Nick Smart, 25 August 2015.

1110 Kenny and Doreen Wheeler, interview with Martin Speake, 4 April 2012.

1111 Evan Parker, interview with Nick Smart, 25 August 2015.

1112 Alexander von Schlippenbach, interview with Nick Smart, 15 June 2015. If it was indeed the Chinese New Year, then this concert must have happened on 16 February 1980.

1113 Ibid.

1114 Ibid. Kenny and Stan Getz already knew each other, of course – Getz having tried to persuade him to join his group after Kenny did the short tour with him in the mid-1970s. Evan Parker even recalls seeing Kenny and Doreen hanging out at the hotel with Getz and his wife.

1115 Ibid.

1116 Ibid.

1117 Kenny Wheeler, interview for Artists House Music, 2002.

1118 Kenny Wheeler, interview with Nick Smart, 23 April 2010.

1119 Advertisement for the tour found on the "British Jazz 1945–80" Facebook page and saved by the authors.

1120 "Bracknell Jazz Festivals 1980–1984", *Jazz in Britain*, https://jazzinbritain.wordpress.com/bracknell-jazz-festivals-1980-1984.

1121 ECM Records ECM 1156.

1122 Evan Parker, interview with Nick Smart and Brian Shaw, 9 September 2015.

1123 Kenny Wheeler, interview with Ted O'Reilly, 26 August 1980.

1124 Ibid.

1125 Kenny Wheeler to Mark Miller, 3 January 1980.

1126 One might speculate that the lines that Kenny overdubbed for the final recording might well have been inner parts originally intended for Thelin.

1127 Evan Parker, interview with Nick Smart and Brian Shaw, 9 September 2015.

1128 Jan Garbarek to Brian Shaw, 16 June 2015.

1129 Kenny Wheeler to Peter Clayton, BBC radio interview, 1990.

1130 In fact, when Brian Shaw began a project of transcribing some of Kenny's solos for publication in 1999, he asked Wheeler if there were any solos he'd like to be included. The only one he mentioned was "Solo One".

1131 Kenny Wheeler to Mark Miller, 3 January 1980.

1132 John Diliberto, *DownBeat* 47(11) (1980), p. 32.

1133 Peter Goddard, *Toronto Star*, 23 August 1980, p. F5.

1134 Kenny Wheeler, interview with Nick Smart, 23 April 2010.

1135 Lees, "Come Back Last Summer (Part 2)", p. 8.

1136 "A Brief History of Jazz and Creative Music", Banff Centre for Arts and Creativity, https://www.banffcentre.ca/history-jazz-banff-centre.

1137 Dave Holland, interview with Nick Smart, 28 January 2015.

1138 Hugh Fraser, interview with Brian Shaw, 25 May 2015.

1139 Brian Shaw's memory of Banff, summer 1998.

1140 Don Thompson to Brian Shaw, 13 October 2015.

1141 Ingrid Jensen to Nick Smart, 1 April 2015.

1142 Dave Holland, interview with Nick Smart, 28 January 2015.

1143 Every student from Banff that we spoke to still has copies of tunes Kenny gave them, precious mementos reminding them of their time with him. In April 2011 saxophonist Rob Schepps recounted – in conversation with Nick Smart in Denver's Dazzle Jazz Club – his memory of Kenny at Banff, who basically announced "help yourself to anything" to all the students while leaving a pile of his manuscripts for them!

1144 Ronan Guilfoyle, interview with Nick Smart, 24 February 2015.

1145 Hugh Fraser, interview with Brian Shaw, 25 May 2015. "Dave [Holland], Julian Priester, Kenny, and others had brand new charts that they'd bring to Banff to try out," Hugh said.

1146 Tania Gill to Brian Shaw, 27 October 2015.

1147 "Everybody's Song But His Own (by Darcy James Argue)", Ethan Iverson's blog, posted in Kenny's memory in 2014: https://ethaniverson.com/guest-posts/everybodys-song-but-his-own-by-darcy-james-argue.

1148 Ronan Guilfoyle, interview with Nick Smart, 24 February 2015.

1149 Richie Beirach to Nick Smart, 13 October 2017.

1150 Dave Holland, interview with Nick Smart, 28 January 2015.

1151 Kenny Wheeler notebook, entry on "Kayak".

1152 Kenny Wheeler, interview with Brian Priestley, 20 May 1986 (National Sound Archive).

1153 Ellen Rowe, email to Brian Shaw, 17 July 2019. Duncan Hopkins was also in that combo, and remembers Kenny saying he was "*Mr.* Banff".

1154 Duncan Hopkins to Nick Smart, 27 August 2015.

1155 Ingrid Jensen, "Time, Marked", Ethan Iverson's blog, https://ethaniverson.com/guest-posts/time-marked-by-ingrid-jensen.

1156 Ingrid Jensen to Nick Smart, 1 April 2015.

1157 Don Thompson to Brian Shaw, 13 October 2015.

1158 Ellen Rowe, email to Brian Shaw, 17 July 2019.

1159 Evan Parker, interview with Nick Smart and Brian Shaw, 9 September 2015.

1160 London *Times* listing, 19 March 1982.

1161 Ibid.

1162 London *Times* listing, 2 April 1982.

1163 Evan Parker, interview with Nick Smart and Brian Shaw, 9 September 2015.

1164 Bobby Wellins, interview with Nick Smart, 26 August 2015. The Stan Tracey album is listed under the band name Spectrum (*Tribute to Monk*, Switch SWLP 001, April 1982), but Bobby recalled that being very much Stan's recording. And Bobby's record was made in two sessions – one in 1980 and one in 1982 (George W. Harris, "Bobby Wellins Quartet: Birds of Brazil", *Jazz Weekly*, October 18, 2012, http://www.jazzweekly.com/2012/10/bobby-wellins-quartet-birds-of-brazil). It was not released until 1989 (Sungai BW11).

1165 Mabel Ball to Brian Shaw, 3 November 2015.

1166 Cox, "Kenny-ing", p. 223.

1167 Mabel Ball to Brian Shaw, 3 November 2015.

1168 Ibid.

1169 Ibid.

1170 John Fordham, "Roundhouse; Gordon Beck", *The Guardian*, 18 January 1983, p. 11.

1171 Mabel Ball to Brian Shaw, 3 November 2015.

1172 Helen Hill to Gene Lees (Lees, "Come Back Last Summer [Part 2]").

1173 Mabel Ball to Brian Shaw, 3 November 2015.

1174 Lees, "Come Back Last Summer (Part 2)", p. 7.

1175 Mabel Ball to Brian Shaw, 3 November 2015.

1176 Norma Winstone, interview with Nick Smart, 19 August 2015.

1177 Richard Williams, "Gary Burton", *The Times*, 25 April 1978, p. 19.

1178 Derek Jewell, "Vibrating with Emperor Burton", *Sunday Times*, 30 April 1978, p. 35.

1179 Despite this review being crystal clear in Norma's mind, especially as it had been immortalized in John Surman's joke with them, we were not able to find any primary record of where it came from. Kenny said it was Ray Coleman writing for the *Melody Maker*, but the review doesn't show up in the *Melody Maker* archives from the period. It may be found in the *Daily Mail*, but we have yet to locate it.

1180 Kenny Wheeler, interview with Brian Priestley, 20 May 1986 (National Sound Archive).

1181 Norma Winstone, interview with Nick Smart, 19 August 2015. Norma said the card was from Bob Cornford at the Jazzhus Montmartre in Copenhagen, where he lived at the time.

1182 Ibid.

1183 ECM Records ECM 1262.

1184 The telephone company in the US and Canada in those days was sometimes referred to by the matriarchal title "Ma Bell".

1185 Kenny Wheeler notebook, entry on "Sophie".

1186 Dave Holland, interview with Nick Smart, 20 January 2015.

1187 Ibid.

1188 Kevin Whitehead, *DownBeat* review, October 1990, pp. 41–43.

1189 Geoffrey Himes, "Dave Holland Is Back", *Washington Post*, 11 May 1984, p. 58.

1190 Mark Miller, review of *Double, Double You*, Toronto Globe & Mail, 19 April 1984, p. E3.

1191 Kenny Wheeler to Eric Nemeyer, *Jazz Inside* magazine, October 2011. This statement is further backed up in the liner notes for the 2004 *What Now?* album: jazz writer Ira Gitler write how he ". . . first became aware of Wheeler when Pepper Adams pointedly lent me his LP of 'Windmill Tilter' that Kenny wrote for John Dankworth's band . . ."

1192 *Jazz Inside*, October 2011.

1193 Ibid.

1194 Uptown Records UP 27.16, 1984.

1195 Mark Miller, *Toronto Globe & Mail*, 18 October 1984.

1196 "Talking Jazz with Ben Sidran", interview with Phil Woods, 5 February 1985, Ben Sidran website, https://bensidran.com/conversation/talking-jazz-phil-woods.

1197 Letter from Grammy Committee to Kenny Wheeler, January 1985. This was Adams's fourth nomination. It seems unusual that the two of them were nominated jointly in the category of "soloist" but that's how it was – all the others were single musicians with Ira Sullivan, Zoot Sims, and Tommy Flanagan listed alongside that year's winner, Wynton Marsalis.

1198 Brian Shaw, memory of Banff, summer 1998.

1199 "Talking Jazz with Ben Sidran".

1200 *Jazz Inside*, October 2011.


## Chapter 6: Music for Large and Small Ensembles

1201 Dave Holland, interview with Nick Smart, 11 January 2015.

1202 Jon Pareles, "Healthy New Start for David Holland", *New York Times*, 8 April 1983.

1203 Dave Holland, interview with Nick Smart, 11 January 2015.

1204 Ibid.

1205 This story comes from pianist Pax Wallace, who claimed to have asked Wynton this question at a workshop in the late '80s.

1206 Dave Holland, interview with Nick Smart, 11 January 2015.

1207 Ibid.

1208 Ibid.

1209 Ibid.

1210 The cornet and flugelhorn are conical bore instruments, unlike the cylindrical bore trumpet and trombone.

1211 Steve Coleman, interview with Nick Smart, 4 April 2017.

1212 *Jazz Inside*, October 2011.

1213 Ibid.

1214 Ibid.

1215 Ronan Guilfoyle, interview with Nick Smart, 24 February 2015.

1216 Dave Holland, interview with Nick Smart, 11 January 2015.

1217 Steve Coleman, interview with Nick Smart, 4 April 2017.

1218 Ibid.

1219 Ibid.

1220 Ronan Guilfoyle, interview with Nick Smart, 24 February 2015.

1221 Dave Holland, interview with Nick Smart, 11 January 2015.

1222 It is for Trutt that Kenny named his "5 Four Six", a composition in 5/4 time.

1223 Dave Holland Quintet, *Jumpin' In* (ECM Records ECM 1269, 1984).

1224 Dave Holland, interview with Nick Smart, 11 January 2015.

1225 John Fordham, "Back to Bop", *The Guardian*, 6 September 1984, p. 10.

1226 John Fordham, "Dave Holland", *The Guardian*, 8 November 1984, p. 20.

1227 Taken from Kenny's handwritten answers to Fred Sturm's October 1997 interview (Kenny Wheeler private collection). Later published in *Kenny Wheeler, Collected Works on ECM* (Universal Edition).

1228 Dave Holland, interview with Nick Smart, 11 January 2015.

1229 Ibid.

1230 South Tyrol performance confirmed in "Jazz Festival 25 Anniversary", *Südtirol Jazz Festival*, https://www.suedtiroljazzfestival.com/media/pdf/Jazz%20Festival_25%20 anniversary_low.pdf.

1231 ECM Records ECM 1292.

1232 Bill Frisell, *Rambler* (ECM Records ECM 1287, 1985).

1233 Bill Frisell, interview with Nick Smart, 30 November 2015.

1234 Ibid.

1235 Ibid.

1236 Ibid.

1237 Ibid.

1238 ECM Records ECM 1241, 1983.

1239 ECM Records ECM 1287.

1240 Bill Frisell, interview with Nick Smart, 30 November 2015.

1241 Letter from Bill Frisell to Kenny Wheeler, 17 February 1984, Wheeler family archive.

1242 Bill Frisell, interview with Nick Smart, 30 November 2015.

1243 Ibid.

1244 Ibid.

1245 Globe Unity Orchestra, *20th Anniversary* (FMP FMP CD 45), recorded live, 4 November 1986; released in 1993.

1246 Larry Kart, *Chicago Tribune,* 7 September 1987.

1247 Notable in the UK were two nights of improvised music March 1984 at The Place, the first night in a quartet with Paul Lytton and Evan Parker, and the second as part of the London Jazz Composers Orchestra.

1248 The Ronnie Scott's programme confirmed in Richard Williams's review in *The Times*, 30 May 1984.

1249 Norma Winstone, Kenny Wheeler, Paolo Fresu, John Taylor, Paolo Damiani, and Tony Oxley, *Live at Roccella Jonica* (Ismez/Polis Music I.P. 26003, Italy, 1985).

1250 Tiziana Simona and Kenny Wheeler, *Gigolo* (ITM Records ITM 0014, Germany, 1986).

1251 ECM Records ECM 1298.

1252 Norma Winstone, interview with Nick Smart, 19 August 2015.

1253 Kenny Wheeler, interview with Brian Priestley, 20 May 1986 (National Sound Archive).

1254 John Fordham, *The Guardian*, 29 March 1985.

1255 Derek Jewell, *Sunday Times*, 31 March 1985.

1256 Ibid.

1257 Kenny Wheeler, interview with Brian Priestley, 20 May 1986 (National Sound Archive).

1258 Kenny Wheeler, interview with Ted O'Reilly, 26 August 1980.

1259 Richard Williams, *The Times*, 30 May 1984.

1260 Kenny Wheeler, interview with Brian Priestley, 20 May 1986 (National Sound Archive).

1261 Norma Winstone, interview with Nick Smart, 19 August 2015.

1262 Ibid.

1263 The Guildhall Jazz Band Featuring Kenny Wheeler, *Walk Softly* (Wave WAVE CD 32), recorded March 1987, released July 1998. It features some of Kenny's best pieces from the preceding period, including *The Little Suite* and more recent compositions "Kayak", "The Widow in the Window", and "Who Are You?"

1264 Scott Stroman, interview with Nick Smart, 19 July 2018.

1265 Patrick Hinely, "A Remembrance of Kenny Wheeler", *Cadence*, April 2015, pp. 43–51.

1266 Norma Winstone, email to Nick Smart, 30 July 2019.

1267 The debut of the Brass Project is confirmed in the brochure for Surman's March 1984 quintet concert as part of the Camden Jazz Festival. This music had premiered (without Kenny) during the Camden Jazz Week of 1981.

1268 John Fordham, *The Guardian*, 28 January 1984.

1269 Their last release together was as part of Graham Collier's *Hoarded Dreams* in 1983 (Cuneiform Records, Rune 252, 2007).

1270 John Surman, interview with Nick Smart, 15 September 2016.

1271 Screenshot of the Barry McRae review of the Camden Festival Jazz Week from an unknown publication.

1272 Original tour poster of 1985 tour shared on "British Jazz 1945–80" Facebook page. Curiously, the band didn't play in London.

1273 John Surman, interview with Nick Smart, 15 September 2016.

1274 ECM Records ECM 1353.

1275 These faculty ensembles comprised Dave's quintet plus one or two extra staff: in the case of 1985 and 1987, Don Thompson (playing piano) and guitarist John Abercrombie joined them. It was nearly the same line-up in 1986, too, but with trombone faculty member George Lewis playing that year (in place of Priester) and vocalist Jay Clayton. Info about faculty and performances taken from archived programmes at the Banff Centre.

1276 Robin Eubanks, interview with Nick Smart, 25 October 2019.

1277 Date of 31 May 1986 confirmed on "Jazz on Screen", *Library of Congress*, www.loc.gov/item/jots.200014810, accessed 21 July 2018.

1278 Kenny Wheeler, interview with Ted O'Reilly, 26 August 1980.

1279 Kevin Whitehead, review of *The Razor's Edge*, NPR Fresh Air, 30 November 1987, transcribed from https://freshairarchive.org/segments/dave-hollands-exciting-quintet.

1280 Dave Holland, interview with Nick Smart, 29 July 2019.

1281 Kenny Wheeler, interview with Ted O'Reilly, 11 November 1985.

1282 George Chisholm, email to Nick Smart, 22 October 2019.

1283 Information about these two tunes is confirmed via the private recording of Naoyuki Kamiko, whose notes show the inclusion of vibes; verified by our BBC research, which includes a contract for Kenny that lists vibes. The broadcast date from the contract also confirmed on the BBC Genome. For what it's worth, Stan Sulzmann had forgotten this broadcast; his recollection of the *Jazz at the Gateway* television show was because he'd had to memorize the tune for that one.

1284 Stan Sulzmann, interview with Nick Smart, 20 July 2018. *Jazz at the Gateway* information: "Jazz on Screen", *Library of Congress*, www.loc.gov/item/jots.200014810, accessed 21 July 2018.

1285 Ibid.

1286 John Marshall, interview with Nick Smart, 20 July 2018.

1287 This ensemble was closer to a regular personnel (notably with no vocalist), but with six saxophones and only three trumpets. They performed a full set of Kenny's music, including "Toot Toot", "The Widow in the Window", and "The Mouse in the Dairy". They also played something he called *Foxy Trot Suite*, which lasted over 30 minutes and lists within it "3/4am", "Sly Eyes", "Foxin' the Chase", "Foxly Lady: A Gentle Piece", and "The Little Fella".

1288 Incidentally, this was one of the last big-band appearances in which Bobby Wellins appeared as a member of the saxophone section, although he remained close with his old friend. Wellins and Kenny would occasionally reunite for small groups and, notably, on one of Kenny's late albums (*Six for Six* [see note 1885]).

1289 Soul Note 121 146-1.

1290 Bill Elgart, interview with Nick Smart, 6 August 2019. Pete O'Mara interview with Nick Smart, 19 December 2018.

1291 Bill Elgart, interview with Nick Smart, 6 August 2019.

1292 Stan Sulzmann, interviews with Nick Smart, 7 October 2014 and 30 July 2019.

1293 This memory chimes with a recollection of Nick Purnell's that they had pitched an album to ECM that included Elvin Jones but it had been turned down. We haven't gone into this here because Nick Purnell hasn't been introduced to the story yet, but the memory does suggest there is something in Stan's recollection about a "big name" drummer being accurate . . . (Nick Purnell, email to Nick Smart, 31 July 2019).

1294 Bill Elgart, interview with Nick Smart, 6 August 2019.

1295 Stan Sulzmann, interviews with Nick Smart, 7 October 2014 and 30 July 2019.

1296 Ibid.

1297 Ibid.

1298 Ibid.

1299 Stan Sulzmann, interview with Nick Smart, 7 October 2014. Stan thought it may have been in a single day but the record lists two days.

1300 Mike Hennessey, liner notes, *Flutter By, Butterfly*. He had resisted the temptation to call it "The *Reel* McCoy".

1301 Ibid.

1302 Amigo AMCD 883 1998.

1303 Mike Hennessey, liner notes, *Flutter By, Butterfly*.

1304 Loose Tubes Limited ltlp 004, 1987.

1305 Mark Wheeler, conversation with Nick Smart, 22 January 2016. Mark noted that, notwithstanding J.T. and Stan being his friends, his dad was so pleased and flattered that two musicians of this stature had recorded an album of all his compositions.

1306 Mike Hennessey, liner notes, *Flutter By, Butterfly*.

1307 Ibid.

1308 Stan Sulzmann, email to Nick Smart, 31 July 2019.

1309 Mike Hennessey, liner notes, *Flutter By, Butterfly*.

1310 Mark Wheeler, interview with Nick Smart and Brian Shaw, 22 January 2016.

1311 Louann Newman, interview with Nick Smart, 21 June 2016.

1312 "Illness Postpones Kenny Wheeler Concert", *Toronto Star*, 17 January 1988.

1313 Mabel Ball, interview with Brian Shaw, 13 May 2015.

1314 "Meniere's disease", Mayo Clinic, http://www.mayoclinic.org/diseases-conditions/ menieres-disease/basics/definition/con-20028251. Mabel Ball said he had Ménière's disease, whereas Mark Miller's *Globe & Mail* article, 20 January 1988, called the condition simply an "ear infection".

1315 "Illness Postpones Kenny Wheeler Concert", *Toronto Star*, 17 January 1988; Mark Miller, *Toronto Globe & Mail*, 20 January 1988; Arthur Kaptainis, "Wheeler Concert Off as Trumpeter Enters Hospital in Toronto", *Montreal Gazette*, 19 January 1988.

1316 Mabel Ball, interview with Brian Shaw, 13 May 2015.

1317 Nick Purnell, email to Nick Smart, 19 October 2016.

1318 Nick Purnell, email to Nick Smart, 31 October 2016.

1319 Ibid.

1320 Ibid.

1321 Ibid.

1322 Ibid.

1323 Nick Purnell, email to Nick Smart, 3 November 2016.

1324 John Taylor, interview by Alyn Shipton, BBC Radio 3 *Jazz Library* (podcast), 14 May 2011.

1325 Richard Cook, "Gracenotes with a Steel Lining", *Sunday Times*, 14 February 1988.

1326 Clive Davis, "Perfect Partners", *The Times*, 22 February 1988.

1327 Nick Purnell, email to Nick Smart, 3 November 2016.

1328 Ibid.

1329 Ibid.

1330 Dave Holland, interview with Nick Smart, 28 January 2015.

1331 Nick Purnell, email to Nick Smart, 3 November 2016.

1332 Helen Wheeler Jelley to Kenny Wheeler, June 1984.

1333 Mabel Ball, Bill Jelley, and Jason Jelley, interview with Brian Shaw, 21 June 2015.

1334 Mabel Ball to Brian Shaw, 21 June 2015.

1335 Louann Newman to Nick Smart and Brian Shaw, 16 July 2018.

1336 Mark Wheeler, interview with Nick Smart and Brian Shaw, 27 November 2015.

1337 Louann Newman, interview with Nick Smart, 21 June 2016.

1338 Mark Wheeler to Nick Smart and Brian Shaw, 11 August 2016.

1339 Ruby Wheeler, email to Brian Shaw, 7 July 2022.

1340 Louann Newman, interview with Nick Smart, 21 June 2016.

1341 Ibid.

1342 Marvin Stamm to Brian Shaw, 18 June 2020.

1343 Personnel listed by Tom Varner, who played horn on the tour, in the comments section of "Joe Henderson & Kenny Wheeler 'Inner Urge'", YouTube, https://www.youtube.com/watch?v=Lp6nDX5Cz3o.

1344 Marvin Stamm to Brian Shaw, 18 June 2020.

1345 Ibid.

1346 Bob Morgan to Brian Shaw, 5 October 2020.

1347 Marvin Stamm to Brian Shaw, 18 June 2020.

1348 Tour stops and personnel listed by Tom Varner in the comments section of "Kenny Wheeler: 'Everybody's Song But My Own' – George Gruntz Big Band", YouTube, https://www.youtube.com/watch?v=2PuxE2GsB0M.

1349 Marvin Stamm to Brian Shaw, 18 June 2020.

1350 Contract between EuroMusic and Kenny Wheeler, 1988.

1351 Dave Holland, interview with Nick Smart, 20 January 2015.

1352 Gruntz later arranged three of Marvin Stamm's tunes and, according to Stamm, the contract he signed was basically identical to the one Kenny had signed.

1353 Marvin Stamm to Brian Shaw, 18 June 2020.

1354 Ibid. "I'm not a composer; I've written *tunes*," Stamm said.

1355 Chris Parker, "Adulation beyond Our Ken", *The Times*, 10 January 1995.

1356 Fred Hersch, interview with Nick Smart and Brian Shaw, 15 July 2018.

1357 Mark Miller, "Wheeler's Too Good to Hide under a Bushel", *Toronto Globe & Mail*, 2 December 1985.

1358 Ibid.

1359 Tim Brady to Brian Shaw, 10 August 2021. Brady recalled that they had found large propane heaters as a makeshift solution that probably made it less uncomfortable.

1360 Miller, "Wheeler's Too Good to Hide under a Bushel".

1361 Tim Brady to Brian Shaw, 10 August 2021.

1362 Ibid.

1363 Ronald Atkins, "High Notes – Trad, Thrash, Modern, Smooth: The Outside In Jazz Festival Had a Virtuoso for Everyone", *The Guardian*, 5 September 1989.

1364 www.loc.gov/item/jots.200159634, accessed 5 August 2019.

1365 Henry Lowther to Nick Smart, 8 October 2014.

1366 Kenny Wheeler, interview with Brian Priestley, 20 May 1986 (National Sound Archive).

1367 Henry Lowther to Nick Smart, 8 October 2014.

1368 Ibid.

1369 Ibid.

1370 Ibid.

1371 Ibid.

1372 Manfred Eicher, interview with Nick Smart, 5 March 2017.

1373 Henry Lowther to Nick Smart, 8 October 2014.

1374 Ibid.

1375 Ibid.

1376 Ibid.

1377 Ibid.

1378 Nick Purnell, email to Nick Smart, 3 November 2016.

1379 The date of 13 January is shown on photo of Helen and Mabel with Kenny at this party (Wheeler Archive, Royal Academy of Music). We believe that, at this point, Kenny still thought his birthday was 13 January. It is thought that he didn't find out he was born on the 14th until 1992 when he applied to be naturalized as a British citizen (photo of naturalization certificate, Royal Academy of Music Exhibition documents).

1380 Evan Parker, interview with Nick Smart and Brian Shaw, 9 September 2015.

1381 Julian Argüelles to Nick Smart, 13 September 2018.

1382 Peter Erskine to Brian Shaw, 23 May 2015.

1383 Hugh Fraser, interview with Brian Shaw, 25 May 2015.

1384 Record found in the BBC Archive, recorded 15 April 1981.

1385 Kenny Wheeler to Ian Carr, 9 July 1995. Many Wheeler fans have believed that "For H" was written for his sister Helen, but Kenny categorically said in this interview that the piece was dedicated to South:

> Kenny Wheeler: H is Harry South.
>
> Ian Carr: Oh, was it?
>
> KW: Yeah.
>
> IC: Oh, well that . . .
>
> KW: I don't know if his wife ever realized that or not, but . . . I should have rang her up I suppose.
>
> IC: Yes, they're all . . .
>
> KW: Just, I liked him a lot.
>
> IC: I did too.
>
> KW: I never saw much of him, I never had much social contact but I just liked him, you know. He was a nice, easy-going person.
>
> IC: Yeah.
>
> KW: Good to play with.

1386 Scores found in the Banff Archives show a version of "Pt. 1, Opening" of the *Sweet Time Suite* for saxophone quartet – followed by an arrangement of "Kind Folk" in 3/4 which goes into 4/4 (the suite version does the opposite). Banff score has "Le Grand Bill Evans" scratched out, renamed "B Minor Get Out". "Gentle Piece" from *Music for Large and Small Ensembles* is probably around this vintage (from the early 1980s), as well, since a score for it is also found in the Banff Archives, listed alongside "Foxly Lady – A Gentle Piece", which was probably part of the *Foxy Trot Suite*, listed on BBC Spreadsheet from 1982 EBU gig.

1387 Kenny Wheeler to Ian Carr, 9 July 1995.

1388 Kenny's letter, worth reproducing here, reads: "Dear Norma, Here's a tune that I might use in January. I wondered if you felt like trying to write some words for it. If you don't fancy it – just say so, but if you do like it please have a try. The only thing is I promised Jan I would write a tune for her. If you don't feel you could use the word "Jan" in the lyrics, maybe you could just write about some objective young woman who could have any name, and I can simply title it "JAN". If I'm an effing nuisance, just say so. All the best, Ken" (Kenny Wheeler, letter to Norma Winstone, c. 1989).

1389 Norma Winstone, interview with Nick Smart, 19 August 2015.

1390 Hugh Fraser, interview with Brian Shaw, 25 May 2015.

1391 John Thiessen, email to Brian Shaw, 6 August 2020.

1392 Peter Erskine to Brian Shaw, 23 May 2015.

1393 Charles Fox, introduction, University of Warwick concert, 28 January 1990, BBC broadcast aired 21 July 1990.

1394 Clive Davis, "Sated on the First Date: Kenny Wheeler, Queen Elizabeth Hall", *The Times*, 19 January 1990.

1395 Norma Winstone, interview with Nick Smart, 19 August 2015.

1396 Argue, "Everybody's Song But His Own", Ethan Iverson's blog.

1397 Kenny Wheeler told this story to Brian Shaw at Banff, summer 1998.

1398 Dave Holland, interview with Nick Smart, 28 January 2015.

1399 John Abercrombie, interview with Brian Shaw, 16 July 2014.

1400 Dave Holland, interview with Nick Smart, 28 January 2015.

1401 Norma Winstone, interview with Nick Smart, 19 August 2015.

1402 Peter Erskine to Brian Shaw, 23 May 2015.

1403 On the way to the recording session, Peter Erskine had been telling the band – many of whom had never recorded for ECM – how wonderful the mix that head ECM engineer Jan Erik Kongshaug would create for them would be in their headphones, making it so easy to play on the recording. ("It'll sound just like a record," Peter had said, "It's going to be so great!") But, once the band sat down in their places, arranged in a big circle in this large room, with very low screens (leading to lots of microphone bleed), they put their headphones on – and what they heard sounded awful. Peter explained: "What had happened was that Jan Erik was busy at the board and had left the mixing of the headsets to the guy that was the regular assistant at the studio, and this guy was used to dialling up headphone mixes for film cues, which normally was just to turn on the click [track] and make sure everybody can hear that . . . So, we were going by the seat of our pants for much of that recording." Peter Erskine to Brian Shaw, 23 May 2015.

1404 Stan Sulzmann, interview with Nick Smart and Brian Shaw, 4 August 2016.

1405 It's difficult to say with certainty which lead parts in particular Kenny overdubbed, but the high concert F and G in Part 5, "Know Where You Are" (incidentally the highest written trumpet notes of the entire suite) are likely candidates. Several members of the band, including Dave Horler and Stan Sulzmann, remember that Kenny indeed recorded some of the lead parts for the session.

1406 Jazz theory aficionados will enjoy knowing that in this improvised fill over the final Dbmaj7 harmony, Kenny imposes all 12 chromatic pitches, organized into major triads on C, Bb, and B, before landing on a low G, the ♯11 of the harmony, which transforms the last chord into what is probably his most often-used sonority, a maj7♯11.

1407 Actually, although Manfred's genius idea to add the chorale at the end of the suite was made at the recording on 26/27 January, they did not immediately adopt that idea "live". The Coventry date on 29 January was recorded by the BBC and showed they were still not including the chorale as a "closing" at that point.

1408 Evan Parker, interview with Nick Smart and Brian Shaw, 9 September 2015.

1409 Manfred Eicher, interview with Nick Smart, 5 March 2017.

1410 Norma Winstone, interview with Nick Smart, 19 August 2015.

1411 Hugh Fraser, interview with Brian Shaw, 25 May 2015.

1412 Dave Holland, interview with Nick Smart, 28 January 2015.

1413 Peter Erskine to Brian Shaw, 23 May 2015.

1414 Manfred Eicher, interview with Nick Smart, 5 March 2017.

1415 Kenny Wheeler, *Music For Large and Small Ensembles* (ECM Records ECM 1415/16, 1990).

1416 Nick Purnell, email to Nick Smart, 3 November 2016.

1417 Peter Erskine to Brian Shaw, 23 May 2015.
1418 Duncan Lamont, interview with Nick Smart, 3 August 2014.
1419 Duncan Lamont, interview with Nick Smart, 3 August 2014.
1420 Jonathan Coe, review of *Music for Large and Small Ensembles*, *The Wire*, December 1990–January 1991.
1421 Ronald Atkins, review of *Music for Large and Small Ensembles*, *The Guardian*, 14 March 1991.
1422 Kenny Wheeler to Ian Carr, 9 July 1995.
1423 Peter Erskine to Brian Shaw, 23 May 2015.
1424 Tour schedule from Saudades.
1425 Peter Erskine to Brian Shaw, 23 May 2015.
1426 Ibid.
1427 Ibid.
1428 John Abercrombie, interview with Brian Shaw, 16 July 2014.
1429 Peter Erskine to Brian Shaw, 23 May 2015. Peter pointed out that he himself had been regularly playing on substandard equipment throughout the tour.
1430 John Abercrombie, interview with Brian Shaw, 16 July 2014.
1431 Peter Erskine to Brian Shaw, 23 May 2015.
1432 Peter Erskine to Brian Shaw, 23 May 2015.
1433 Ibid.
1434 John Abercrombie, interview with Brian Shaw, 16 July 2014.
1435 Ibid.
1436 Ibid.
1437 Ibid.
1438 Recording of Kenny Wheeler Quintet live in Hamburg, 12 February 1990.
1439 John Abercrombie, interview with Brian Shaw, 16 July 2014.
1440 Ibid.
1441 Ibid.
1442 Kenny Wheeler to Ian Carr, 9 July 1995.
1443 ECM Records ECM 1417.
1444 Kenny Wheeler to Ian Carr, 9 July 1995.
1445 Nick Purnell, email to Nick Smart, 19 October 2016.
1446 Peter Erskine to Brian Shaw, 23 May 2015.
1447 Richard Cook, "Revitalising the True Tango Spirit", review of *The Widow in the Window*, *Sunday Times*, 19 August 1990.
1448 Review of *The Widow in the Window*, *Jazz Forum*, 1991.
1449 Kevin Whitehead, review of *The Widow in the Window*, *DownBeat*, 1990.
1450 Nick Purnell, email to Nick Smart, 28 July 2019.
1451 Patrick Hinely, "This Wheeler's on Fire", *JazzForum* 128 (1991).
1452 Ibid.
1453 Ibid.
1454 Liner notes by Steve Coleman on his album *Rhythm in Mind* (Novus 01241 63125 2, 1992).
1455 Ibid. Blackwell played the Carnegie Hall concert; Smith played the recording session only.
1456 Steve Coleman, interview with Nick Smart, 4 April 2017.
1457 "Carnegie Hall at 100: The Centennial Hits a Crescendo", *New York Times*, 28 April 1991, https://www.nytimes.com/1991/04/28/arts/carnegie-hall-at-100-the-centennial-hits-a-crescendo.html.
1458 Peter Watrous, "'Rhythm in Mind' Spans the Generations", *New York Times*, 29 April 1991, https://www.nytimes.com/1991/04/29/arts/review-jazz-rhythm-in-mind-spans-the-generations.html.

1459 Kenny Wheeler, interview with Ian Carr, 7 September 1995 (Ian Carr tapes, British Library).

1460 John Fordham, review of Jazz Cafe: Michael Gibbs, *The Guardian*, 28 February 1991, p. 30.

1461 The Mike Gibbs Orchestra, *Big Music* (Venture CDVE 27, 1988).

1462 Mike Gibbs Band, *Symphony Hall, Birmingham 1991* (2CD, Dusk Fire Records, DUSKCD116, 2018).

1463 Ian Carr, Digby Fairweather, and Brian Priestley, *Jazz: The Essential Companion* (Simon & Schuster, 1988)

1464 Clive Davis, "Riding an Old Wave", *The Times*, 5 May 1989.

1465 Shipton, *Out of the Long Dark*, p. 153.

1466 Scott Stroman, interview with Nick Smart, 19 July 2018.

1467 *Lammas with Guest Kenny Wheeler* (FMR Records FMR CD04-0791, 1991).

1468 Saudades tour listing, sent 30 July 2019.

1469 Nick Purnell, email to Nick Smart, 28 July 2019.

1470 Video of Tavaszi Festival, Budapest, 27 March 1992, YouTube, https://www.youtube.com/watch?v=bRoX0VFoEZg&list=PLIB_kyBSn-Orndzcs9Hfu3owjWxPMZIGO&index=3.

1471 Ibid.

1472 Peter Erskine to Brian Shaw, 23 May 2015. A note is necessary here to explain the importance for brass players of hearing themselves play. Brass players rely on feedback they get from the room in which they're playing to make subtle adjustments in how they physically approach their instrument. If they are playing in a large, acoustically "dead" space, the instinct is usually to play louder to hear oneself, which can quickly destroy a player's endurance, because they will have to over-play for long periods of time. A monitor allows players to hear themselves and keep their playing dynamic in check, freeing them to play less forcefully and therefore longer without tiring.

1473 Ibid.

1474 Nick Purnell, email to Nick Smart, 28 July 2019.

1475 Paul Sparrow, interview with Nick Smart, 3 April 2017.

1476 Peter Erskine to Brian Shaw, 23 May 2015. In Dr. Arnon Bentovim's interview with Nick Smart and Brian Shaw (2 August 2021), he speculated along similar lines: "I mean, the amount of anger he *must* have had at some level . . . because it's interesting that when you talk to young people who have been exposed to a great deal of adversity, what they describe in spades is *yes* they're anxious, and they often get dissociated . . . they often have this moving from state to state, but then they also have a huge amount of anger. Well, I think one of the issues is whether there's an element of suppressed, or expressed, anger around in some way in Kenny's work and so on . . . I would have thought he must have grown up with an enormous amount of frustration and anger, I'm sure that must have been an important theme. And that anger gives a terrific drive doesn't it?"

1477 Peter Erskine to Brian Shaw, 23 May 2015.

1478 BBC Archive.

1479 Ah Um ah um 012.

1480 Nick Purnell, email to Nick Smart, 19 October 2016.

1481 Peter Erskine to Brian Shaw, 23 May 2015.

1482 Chris Laurence, interview with Nick Smart and Brian Shaw, 8 September 2015.

1483 Ibid.

1484 Kenny Wheeler to Ian Carr, 9 July 1995. Although the album introduced several new tunes to Kenny's recorded output, "Sea Lady" had already been recorded on Norma Winstone's album *Somewhere Called Home* (ECM Records ECM 1337) and Kenny's *Music for Large and Small Ensembles*, both of which featured her lyrics.

1485 Kenny Wheeler notebook, entry on "Kayak".
1486 Ah Um ah um 006, 1991.
1487 Nick Purnell, email to Nick Smart, 19 October 2016. (Peter Erskine also said the same to Brian Shaw in conversation in 2018.)
1488 Richard Cook and Brian Morton, "Kenny Wheeler, 'Kayak'", *The Penguin Guide to Jazz on CD, LP, and Cassette* (Penguin, 1st edn, 1992), p. 1,140.
1489 Ralph Towner to Brian Shaw, 15 June 2015.
1490 Saudades tour listing, sent 30 July 2019.
1491 This recording titles itself as *Live from Holland*, claiming it was recorded in Enschede, Netherlands, although the Saudades-provided tour sheet says the stop on that date was "Eschede, Germany".
1492 Ralph Towner to Brian Shaw, 15 June 2015.
1493 Ibid.
1494 Nick Purnell, email to Nick Smart, 28 July 2019.
1495 Saudades concert dates, provided 30 July 2019.
1496 Paul Sparrow, interview with Nick Smart, 3 April 2017.
1497 Ibid.
1498 Soul Note 121236-2, 1997.
1499 Paul Sparrow, interview with Nick Smart, 3 April 2017.
1500 Joe LaBarbera to Brian Shaw, 31 July 2019.
1501 Palle Danielsson, interview with Nick Smart, 6 August 2019.
1502 Ibid.
1503 Joe LaBarbera to Brian Shaw, 31 July 2019.
1504 Palle Danielsson, interview with Nick Smart, 6 August 2019.
1505 Whitehead, *DownBeat* magazine, 1990. "A cynic might suggest the only thing this gifted trumpeter needs to make it big is a recent high-school diploma," it read, "Alas, he's a youthful 60."
1506 Kenny Wheeler, interview with Brian Priestley, 20 May 1986 (National Sound Archive).
1507 Sinker, "Subtle Survivor".
1508 Condon, "Humble Legend".
1509 Martin Linton, "Jazz Pulls in its Horns", *The Guardian,* 2 January 1992.
1510 Lock, "Brass Menagerie".
1511 Louis Moholo Octet, *Spirits Rejoice!* (Ogun OG 520, 1978).
1512 Ogun OGCD101.
1513 *Ixesha (Time)* (2CD, Ogun OGCD 102/103).
1514 Evan Parker, interview with Nick Smart and Brian Shaw, 9 September 2015. Evan described how Kenny did the arrangement of "B, My Dear" in record time! "Well, I said, 'Ken. I've got this fantastic ballad of Dudu's, could you do an arrangement?' And he said, 'OK'. So I put it in the post. I sent him this cassette and he phones me up and said, 'I can't tell whether it's in . . . the cassette is somewhere between (the keys . . . let's say between) D and E♭'. And I said, 'Which is more likely?' And he said '*The key*'. And I said 'Well, write it in that then'. And I think that was Thursday, and on the next Tuesday, the 26-page arrangement arrived in the post. So I know it was fast. And it's a lovely arrangement."
1515 Enja Records ENJ-7053 2.
1516 Enja Records ENJ-8078 2.
1517 Mariano & Friends, *Seventy* (veraBra Records vBr 2149 2, Germany, 1993).
1518 "John Altman: Putting Some Big Band Brass into 'No Time to Die'", *UK Jazz News*, 2 October 2021, https://londonjazznews.com/2021/10/02/john-altman-putting-some-big-band-brass-into-no-time-to-die.
1519 Ibid.
1520 ECM Records ECM 1538.

1521 Norma Winstone, interview with Nick Smart, 19 August 2015.

1522 Ibid.

1523 Ibid.

1524 Kenny wrote several trumpet quartets for his trumpet students at Banff, and continued to compose such pieces after his time there. There is a small trove of this repertoire which has still, at this writing, not been recorded.

1525 Norma Winstone, interview with Nick Smart, 19 August 2015.

1526 Ibid.

1527 Ibid.


## Chapter 7: Angel Song

1528 "The Origins of Gene Lees' *The JazzLetter*: The First Jazz Blog?", *JazzProfiles*, 24 September 2012, http://jazzprofiles.blogspot.co.uk/2012/09/the-origins-of-gene-lees-jazzletter.html.

1529 Lees, *Arranging the Score*.

1530 Anne North, a childhood friend of both Kenny and Gene Lees, remembers a return visit Lees made to St. Catharines later in his life, during which she drove him around to see his old neighbourhood: "We hit this house on Albert St. And he said 'Come with me' and we went up and I thought he was going to knock on the door. He opens the door and goes flying up the stairs – these people [in the house] have got people in playing cards! The guy stood up and said 'Where the hell do you think you're going?!' Gene said, 'Well, my father built these stairs.' And the guy said, 'I don't give a G[od] D[amn]! Who do you think you are?!' And I said, 'Look, sir, I'm very sorry. He's here visiting and he hasn't been back in a long time.' [Gene] comes down the steps and says '. . . small-minded people.' I said 'No, Gene, you can't go busting into people's houses like that!'" (Anne North to Brian Shaw, 20 June 2015).

1531 Gene was complaining about how rainy that summer in Canada was, comparing it to how beautiful and warm it had been the previous year. Kenny's reply was: "I guess I should go back to England and come back last summer."

1532 Lees, "Come Back Last Summer (Part 2)", p. 28.

1533 Cox, "Kenny-ing".

1534 Bill Frisell, interview with Nick Smart, 30 November 2015.

1535 Taken from Kenny's handwritten answers to Fred Sturm's October 1997 interview (Kenny Wheeler private collection). Later published in *Kenny Wheeler, Collected Works on ECM* (Universal Edition).

1536 Ibid.

1537 Bill Dobbins, interview with Brian Shaw, Rochester, NY, 16 November 2016.

1538 Bill Dobbins, conversation with Brian Shaw, Rochester, NY, 2003.

1539 Bill Dobbins, interview with Brian Shaw, Rochester, NY, 16 November 2016.

1540 Arabesque Jazz AJ0107, 1992.

1541 Jane Ira Bloom to Brian Shaw, 21 July 2019.

1542 Ibid.

1543 Arabesque Jazz AJ0120, 1996.

1544 Jane Ira Bloom to Brian Shaw, 21 July 2019.

1545 Although Kenny had passing interactions with other musicians who played and recorded with Booker Little, including Ron Carter on a few early Friedrich Gulda projects, or Tommy Flanagan on Steve Coleman's *Rhythm in Mind* project, trombonist Julian Priester was unique in having spent a significant amount of time playing alongside both Booker and Kenny – and especially as a fellow brass player.

1546 Jane Ira Bloom to Brian Shaw, 21 July 2019.

1547 Rufus Reid to Brian Shaw, 24 July 2019.

1548 Jane Ira Bloom to Brian Shaw, 21 July 2019.

1549  psi 03.04.
1550  Greg Carter, email to Brian Shaw, 29 July 2019. (Greg also noted that Kenny played lead trumpet on the recording of "Song for Someone" on *Who Are You*, a rare published example of him displaying this specialized skill.) Greg said that he would never forget this date for a very personal reason: his wife had gone into labour that evening, giving birth to their daughter just after midnight. "I was up all night with our new baby and then drove two and a half hours in winter weather to get to a first rehearsal with Kenny and a bunch of musicians who had never played together, let alone played Kenny's music. *What the hell was I thinking?*" he joked.
1551  West Wind WW 2097.
1552  These invitations represented an increasing trend for Kenny: it was his second successive invitation to a European big band after the previous year's recording with the Italian-based European Music Orchestra for their album *Guest* (Soul Note 121299-2), which featured Kenny's compositions "W.W." and "The Sweet Yakity Waltz".
1553  Justin Time JTR 8465-2.
1554  Grace Recordings GR001.
1555  Mark Wheeler, interview with Nick Smart and Brian Shaw, 27 November 2015. This was actually Ménière's disease – the same condition that had first afflicted him in Canada in 1988.
1556  Jim Macnie, "Jazz Blue Notes", *Billboard*, 11 January 1997. It is strange that the US release of the album apparently occurred so far after its European release, but this is the only explanation we can find.
1557  Norma Winstone to Nick Smart, 9 November 2020.
1558  Alyn Shipton, "A Bigger Splash on Bath Nights", *The Times*, 28 May 1997.
1559  The Maritime Jazz Orchestra Featuring Kenny Wheeler, John Taylor, Norma Winstone, *Now And Now Again* (Justin Time JTR 8491-2, 2002).
1560  Trombonist and long-time Kenny friend Dave Horler said that he remembered recording the piece with the WDR at the same session as his piece "Chrissie" – his score of which is dated as being finished on 25 January 1998 – and he recalled the recording not being long after. Dave Horler, email to Nick Smart, 4 August 2019.
1561  Interestingly, Bill Dobbins, who would have been the head of the WDR Big Band at the time, has no memory of commissioning such a piece from Kenny, nor performing it with him – but the fact remains that the original (shorter) version of this *Untitled Suite* retains the WDR stamp.
1562  First page of WDR solo flugelhorn part, emailed from Greg Carter to Nick Smart, 19 November 2016. Dave Horler remembered it from that '98 WDR recording as well.
1563  "Kenny Wheeler's Sweet Sister Suite", Scottish National Jazz Orchestra, https://snjo.co.uk/discography/sweet-sister-suite-2. Also Tommy Smith, interview with Nick Smart, 10 October 2016.
1564  Tommy Smith, interview with Nick Smart, 10 October 2016.
1565  The suite as recorded by Greg Carter and the MJO includes an ending that is basically a reprise of the slow tempo, introductory first 13 measures of the suite, but up a whole step. This music is deleted from the SNJO versions as performed in 1998 and as recorded in 2012.
1566  Tommy Smith, interview with Nick Smart, 10 October 2016.
1567  Ibid.
1568  Ibid. Confirmed by Smith's private minidisc collection; email from Tommy Smith to Nick Smart, 11 October 2016.
1569  Dates of granddaughters' births found in family scrapbook (Wheeler Archive, Royal Academy of Music). Co-author of this book Brian Shaw played lead trumpet in the student big band in this performance at Banff.
1570  Final page of manuscript score of *Sweet Sister Ruby Suite* (Wheeler Archive, Royal Academy of Music).

1571 Norma Winstone, interview with Nick Smart, 19 August 2015.

1572 Ibid.

1573 Dr. Arnon Bentovim, interview with Nick Smart and Brian Shaw, 2 August 2021. When asked about the likely impact of Kenny's childhood on his lifelong avoidance of conflict, Dr. Bentovim said ". . . when you're faced with your parents squabbling, fighting, arguing – who knows what was going on between them – you keep your head down. . . . So, I think conflict avoidance is a very common theme . . . I'm sure that being faced with conflict between [those close to him] would be just overwhelming. I think that he emotionally couldn't cope with it. It's not because he sort of cynically stood on the sidelines saying, *well, I can't help* . . . I think the impact to him of having couples in conflict would be emotionally overwhelming for him . . ."

1574 Greg Carter, email to Brian Shaw, 29 July 2019.

1575 Paul Tynan to Brian Shaw, 13 June 2015.

1576 Ibid.

1577 Greg Carter, email to Brian Shaw, 29 July 2019.

1578 Hornblower Recordings HR99105, 1999.

1579 Brian Dickinson, email to Brian Shaw, 8 August 2018.

1580 Ibid.

1581 Ibid.

1582 "Brian Dickinson Explains Why he's Paying Tribute to Kenny Wheeler in Toronto", *Ottawa Citizen*, 30 January 2015, https://ottawacitizen.com/entertainment/jazzblog/bryan-dickinson-explains-why-hes-paying-tribute-to-kenny-wheeler-in-toronto.

1583 Brian Dickinson, email to Brian Shaw, 8 August 2018.

1584 Ibid.

1585 Ibid.

1586 Some examples of these quotes are as follows. On bebop: "It's my roots but I could never do it . . ."; playing free music: "very therapeutic. I feel much better afterward, although I would find it hard to say whether what we played was good or bad. I just knew I'd gotten something out of my system"; his preference for his writing over his playing: "I seldom like what I play but often like the tunes I write"; and his predilection for sad music: "I suppose I'm twisted because sad music makes me feel happy".

1587 Mark Wheeler, interview with Nick Smart and Brian Shaw, 27 November 2015.

1588 Hugh Fraser, interview with Brian Shaw, 25 May 2015. Fraser: "The critic, from a magazine in London . . . a really pretentious magazine . . . And at that point John Taylor and Stan Sulzmann had just released an album of Kenny duos . . . and he didn't pan it but he wasn't very happy . . . I was talking up a storm and Kenny was just quietly having a cigarette, and I showed him this magazine and said, 'What do you think of that?' He grabbed this magazine – a pretty robust magazine – and just tore it to shreds and threw it on the floor!"

1589 Mark Wheeler, interview with Nick Smart and Brian Shaw, 27 November 2015.

1590 Lees, "Come Back Last Summer (Part 2)".

1591 Kenny Wheeler, interview with Brian Priestley, 20 May 1986 (National Sound Archive).

1592 Miller, "Profile: Kenny Wheeler".

1593 Mark Miller, "Kenny Wheeler Says, 'If I ever got to like my own playing, I'd give up': Jazzman Prefers Anonymity", *Toronto Globe & Mail*, 12 August 1978. It is worth noting that the quote that forms this piece's title was from the interview for the 1976 *DownBeat* piece (Miller, "Profile: Kenny Wheeler").

1594 Mark Miller, "A Spectacular Return by Hubbard", *Toronto Globe & Mail*, 22 August 1981.

1595 Art Ellefson, letter to the *Toronto Globe & Mail*, 18 September 1981.

1596 Mark Miller, email to Brian Shaw, 20 January 2017.

1597  James Hale, "Shaky Start Blown Away as Quartet Finds Road Legs", *Ottawa Citizen*, 19 January 1993.
1598  Mark Miller, "The Kenny Wheeler Orchestra: A Venture of Both Spirit and Symbolism", *Toronto Globe & Mail*, 1 July 1993.
1599  Mark Miller, "The Kenny Wheeler Quintet: Band's Feet Solidly on the Ground", *Toronto Globe & Mail*, 24 February 1994.
1600  Mark Miller to Brian Shaw, 7 October 2015.
1601  "Jazz Trumpeter Displays Composing Skills", *Toronto Star*, 10 March 1995.
1602  Mark Miller to Brian Shaw, 7 October 2015.
1603  Mark Miller, "Jazz Rooms Compete with Noted Players", *Toronto Globe & Mail*, 18 April 1997.
1604  Don Thompson to Brian Shaw, 7 October 2015.
1605  Mark Miller to Brian Shaw, 7 October 2015.
1606  Mark Miller, email to Brian Shaw, 20 January 2017.
1607  Dr. Arnon Bentovim, interview with Nick Smart and Brian Shaw, 2 August 2021.
1608  Wheeler family scrapbook, p. 18 (Wheeler Archive, Royal Academy of Music).
1609  Mark Miller, email to Brian Shaw, 20 January 2017.
1610  Mark Wheeler, interview with Nick Smart and Brian Shaw, 22 January 2016.
1611  Ibid. That said, Kenny was a dedicated Manchester United supporter.
1612  Ibid.
1613  Vince Mendoza, interview with Nick Smart, 17 November 2015.
1614  Ibid.
1615  Vince Mendoza and the London Symphony Orchestra, *Epiphany* (VIA Jazz 9920822, 1997).
1616  Vince Mendoza, interview with Nick Smart, 17 November 2015.
1617  Ibid.
1618  Mike Bradley, review of *Epiphany*, *The Times*, 18 February 2000.
1619  Vince Mendoza, interview with Nick Smart, 17 November 2015.
1620  Joni Mitchell, *Travelogue* (2CD, Nonesuch 79817-2).
1621  Larry Klein, interview with Nick Smart, 31 August 2016.
1622  Ibid.
1623  Vince Mendoza, interview with Nick Smart, 17 November 2015.
1624  Larry Klein, interview with Nick Smart, 31 August 2016.
1625  Ibid.
1626  Virgin V2290.
1627  Double LP; Virgin VDL1.
1628  John L. Walters, "Music: Notes from a Quiet Life", *The Independent*, 26 March 1999.
1629  Ibid.
1630  Dave Douglas, interview with Nick Smart, 16 December 2015.
1631  Ibid.
1632  Ibid.
1633  New World Records 80471-2.
1634  Dave Douglas, interview with Nick Smart, 16 December 2015.
1635  Ibid.
1636  "Jazz: Dave Douglas Quartet – Custard Factory, Birmingham," *The Independent*, 29 April 1997.
1637  Dave Douglas, interview with Nick Smart, 16 December 2015.
1638  Ibid.
1639  Ibid.
1640  Ibid. Reviewer Phil Johnson, writing for *The Independent*, said: "It was a glorious performance, both with Wheeler and without", continuing that adding Kenny "provided an extra edge for the programme of Booker Little themes and variations. Wheeler's tone on flugelhorn manages to create a signature-sound of almost

unbearable poignancy. It was a stormer of a gig, validating equally the great tradition and the continued shock of the new" (Phil Johnson "Jazz: Dave Douglas Quartet – Custard Factory, Birmingham," *The Independent*, 29 April 1997).

1641 Dave Douglas, interview with Nick Smart, 16 December 2015.
1642 Ibid.
1643 Kenny Wheeler, Lee Konitz, Dave Holland, and Bill Frisell, *Angel Song* (ECM Records ECM 1607).
1644 Andy Hamilton, *Lee Konitz: Conversations on the Improviser's Art* (University of Michigan Press, 2007), p. 48.
1645 John Fordham, "Trumpet Voluntary", *The Guardian*, 11 April 1997.
1646 Kenny Wheeler interviewed by Evan Parker, seemingly late 1994. See note 807.
1647 Ibid.
1648 Kenny Wheeler, interview with Jez Nelson, *Jazz on 3*, February 1998.
1649 Kenny Wheeler interviewed by Evan Parker, seemingly late 1994. See note 807.
1650 Pete Martin, "Kenny Wheeler: Playing with Angels", *Jazz UK*, March/April 1997. The two had more recently played a jazz festival together in France along bassist Steve Swallow and drummer Paul Motian.
1651 Ibid.
1652 Manfred Eicher, interview with Nick Smart, 5 March 2017.
1653 Dave Holland, interview with Nick Smart, 28 January 2015.
1654 Bill Frisell, interview with Nick Smart, 30 November 2015.
1655 Juan Rodriguez, "Humblest of Heroes", *Montreal Gazette*, 28 June 2003. This clipping is in the family scrapbook, p. 33.
1656 Patrick Hinely, email to Brian Shaw, 1 August 2017.
1657 Bradley Bambarger, "Wheeler's Luminous 'Angel'": review of *Angel Song*, *Billboard*, 8 February 1997.
1658 Ibid.
1659 Kenny Wheeler, interview with Jez Nelson, *Jazz on 3*, February 1998.
1660 Lees, "Come Back Last Summer (Part 2)".
1661 Hamilton, *Lee Konitz*, p. 179.
1662 Chris Parker, *The Times*, 29 March 1997, p. 20; Clive Davis, *Sunday Times*, 30 March 1997, p. 26.
1663 Bambarger, "Wheeler's Luminous 'Angel'". At the time, ECM's label director Paula Morris explained to *Billboard* magazine (ibid.) that a similarly poised review for another album on the label had recently quadrupled sales "not only the week of the broadcast but for weeks after the piece's airing". The article also pointed out that ECM planned to promote *Angel Song* "into the summer and into the label's *Jazz Cafe* retail campaign, with listening posts, endcap positioning, and sale pricing part of the program".
1664 John Fordham, "Those Classic Wheeler Recordings", *The Guardian*, 11 April 1997, p. A19.
1665 Martin, "Kenny Wheeler: Playing with Angels".
1666 Kenny Wheeler, interview with Jez Nelson, *Jazz on 3*, February 1998.
1667 Chris Parker, "Brilliance Before, After and During the Break. Kenny Wheeler/Paul Motian", *The Times*, 25 February 1998, p. 32.
1668 Ibid.
1669 www.ecodibergamo.it/planner/dettaglio/bill-frisell-kenny-wollesen-duo-regina-carter_1072126_832, accessed 31 July 2019.
1670 Bambarger, "Wheeler's Luminous 'Angel'".
1671 Kenny Wheeler, interview with Jez Nelson, *Jazz on 3*, February 1998.
1672 Martin, "Kenny Wheeler: Playing with Angels".
1673 Bill Frisell, interview with Nick Smart, 30 November 2015.
1674 Chris Parker, "Subtle Lee: It's Heads he Wins", *The Times*, 9 May 1996, p. 39.

1675 Hamilton, *Lee Konitz*, p. 234.
1676 Ted O'Reilly to Brian Shaw, 7 October 2015.
1677 Hamilton, *Lee Konitz*, p. 234.
1678 Ibid, p. 48.
1679 Lee Konitz/Kenny Wheeler Quartet, *Olden Times: Live at Birdland Neuburg* (Double Moon Records DMCHR 71014, 2016).
1680 Tony Faulkner, interview with Nick Smart, 2 September 2015.
1681 Parker, "Adulation beyond Our Ken".
1682 Memories differ as to whether this was just for documentation or for future commercial release.
1683 Parker, "Adulation beyond Our Ken".
1684 Ibid.
1685 Ibid.
1686 Liner notes for Kenny Wheeler, *A Long Time Ago* (ECM Records ECM 1691, 1999).
1687 Evan Parker, interview with Nick Smart and Brian Shaw, 9 September 2015. Parker hastened to explain that ECM didn't "do co-productions", so they were listed as "Evan Parker, producer, with Stan Sulzmann" on the ECM release.
1688 Nick Purnell, email to Nick Smart, 31 October 2016.
1689 Stan Sulzmann, interview with Nick Smart and Brian Shaw, 4 August 2016.
1690 Ibid.
1691 Anonymous email to Nick Smart.
1692 Clive Davis, review of *A Long Time Ago*, *Sunday Times*, 27 June 1999, p. 19.
1693 Mike Bradley, "Nothing beyond These Kennys", *The Times*, 2 July 1999, p. 39.
1694 Jon Andrews, review of *A Long Time Ago*, *DownBeat*, February 2000, p. 68.
1695 Edmonton Jazz Festival Society's Mark Vasey had led a review of the programme in order to "learn from the members what they considered to be strong points of the Banff Jazz Workshop, where each thought jazz was headed in the world of music – especially in Canada, what kind of jazz programming Banff should offer to be relevant to the needs of jazz musicians, and how the programme could best continue to act as a leader in the field." www.banffcentre.ca/history-jazz-banff-centre, accessed August 2016.
1696 Brian Shaw, memory of Banff, summer 1998; and a photo of Kenny, Hugh, and Don with the cake.
1697 Brian Shaw was at the party and took a photo of the sad cake.
1698 Bill Jelley, interview with Brian Shaw, 21 June 2015.
1699 D'Souza, *Coda*, 1998, p. 11.
1700 Kenny did return in 2005, as the featured guest of the Banff Jazz Orchestra Workshop. Fraser continued to lead this workshop after he was no longer head of the Banff Summer Workshop.
1701 Mark Miller, email to Brian Shaw, 29 September 2015.
1702 Lees, "Come Back Last Summer (Part 1)".
1703 Evan Parker, interview with Nick Smart, 12 September 2019.
1704 Ibid.
1705 Steve Lake, email to Nick Smart, 16 February 2019. Whether or not there had been subsequent changes to the programme Evan had first seen, Kenny was also featured on the first half of the 7 November concert with Azimuth, in what must have been among their final live performances together.
1706 Steve Lake, email to Nick Smart, 24 March 2017.
1707 Ibid.
1708 A scan of these *:rarum* selection letters from Kenny, edited by Evan Parker, was sent to Nick Smart by Evan on 12 September 2019.
1709 Justin Time JUST 97-2, 1999.

1710 Kenny told this story to Pete Churchill on a bus in Finland. Nikki Iles to Nick Smart, 26 July 2019.

1711 Glauco Venier to Nick Smart, 4 November 2018. Glauco joked that they were "scared of each other, so they didn't want to meet!"

1712 This could, of course, be nerves, but it could also be a physical condition, such as a tremor in the embouchure or simply the common issue of using a constant vibrato, which is an undesirable habit for jazz players.

1713 Glauco Venier to Nick Smart, 4 November 2018.

1714 Ibid.

1715 Louann Newman, interview with Nick Smart, 21 June 2016.

1716 Glauco Venier to Nick Smart, 4 November 2018.

1717 Paul Tynan to Brian Shaw, 13 June 2015.

1718 Ibid.

1719 Rosana Eckert, email to Brian Shaw, 17 July 2019.

1720 North Texas Jazz LI0002-NS.

1721 Kenny's notebook was loaned to the authors by the Wheeler family. This biography represents the first time that excerpts of it have been reproduced in print.

1722 Don Thompson to Brian Shaw, 7 October 2015. According to Don, this was the only concert they ever did in a duo format.

1723 Ibid.

1724 Ibid. Interestingly, in an example of "small world/full circle", at this writing, the teacher, Rich Stoezel, teaches trumpet at McGill University, the institution Kenny turned down almost three decades earlier when he decided not to become a music teacher.

1725 Don Thompson to Brian Shaw, 7 October 2015.

1726 Dave Holland, interview with Nick Smart, 28 January 2015 and 29 July 2019.

1727 Personnel and tour date information found in contemporary previews and reviews in *The Guardian*, *BBC Online*, and the *Irish Times*.

1728 "Dave Holland Octet: Pathways", *100 Greatest Jazz Albums*, https://100greatestjazzalbums.blogspot.com/2010/02/dave-holland-octet-pathways_21.html.

1729 Alyn Shipton, "The Bassman Cometh", *The Times*, 27 February 2001, p. 15. Dave almost always found a way to include Kenny in his projects. When he formed a big band around the same time, Dave asked Kenny to pen a couple charts for the band, even though distances and schedules prevented him from actually playing with the group.

1730 "Dave Holland Octet at St George's, Bristol, Brandon Hill, Saturday 3rd March 2001", *BBC "Bristol Music"*, http://www.bbc.co.uk/bristol/content/music/2001/03/05/holland_octet.shtml.

1731 Ray Comiskey, "Dave Holland Octet", *Irish Times*, 13 March 2001, https://www.irishtimes.com/culture/dave-holland-octet-1.290042. One of the ballads written for Kenny to play here became "A Time Remembered" from Dave's *The Monterey Suite*, released on his big-band album *Overtime* (Dare2 Records 982 714 2).

1732 Chris Potter, interview with Nick Smart, 3 October 2018.

1733 Ibid.

1734 Peter Erskine, *Brass and Percussion* (download only; https://petererskine.com/store/products/bundled-entire-concert-music-for-brass-percussion).

1735 Andrew Rathbun, email to Brian Shaw, 9 August 2018.

1736 Ibid.

1737 Luciana Souza, interview with Nick Smart, 31 August 2016.

1738 Ibid.

1739 *Quiet Pride: The Elizabeth Catlett Project* (Motéma MTM-114, 2014).

1740 Rufus Reid to Brian Shaw, 24 July 2019.

1741 Fresh Sound New Talent FSNT 135.

1742 Andrew Rathbun, email to Brian Shaw, 9 August 2018.

1743 Ibid.

1744 Ibid.

1745 Marc Copland, John Abercrombie, and Kenny Wheeler, *That's for Sure* (Challenge Records CHR 70098).

1746 Hinely, "A Remembrance of Kenny Wheeler".

1747 Bill Milkowski, "Duos at Vancouver International Jazz Festival", *JazzTimes*, 2 September 2002, updated 25 April 2019, https://jazztimes.com/archives/duos-at-vancouver-international-jazz-festival-4.

1748 Kenny's notes from his lesson with Laurie are in the Wheeler Archive, Royal Academy of Music. The exercises she gave him dealt with pedal tones – from pedal C to double high C. A final note at the bottom of the page says "do pedals as a 'warm down' & then put the horn away and have a drink"!

1749 Andrew Rathbun, email to Brian Shaw, 9 August 2018.

1750 Brian Shaw to Nick Smart, recollection of the concert at Birdland.

1751 Andrew Rathbun, email to Brian Shaw, 9 August 2018.

1752 Ibid.

1753 D'Souza, *Coda*, 1998.

1754 Taken from Kenny's handwritten answers to Fred Sturm's October 1997 interview (Kenny Wheeler private collection). Later published in *Kenny Wheeler, Collected Works on ECM* (Universal Edition).

1755 Evan Parker, interview with Nick Smart and Brian Shaw, 9 September 2015.

1756 Mark Wheeler, interview with Nick Smart and Brian Shaw, 22 January 2016.

1757 Evan Parker, interview with Nick Smart and Brian Shaw, 9 September 2015.

1758 Mark Wheeler, interview with Nick Smart and Brian Shaw, 22 January 2016.

1759 Ibid.

1760 Mark Wheeler to Nick Smart and Brian Shaw, 11 August 2016.

1761 Parker, "Kenny Wheeler in 1990".

1762 Chris Laurence, interview with Nick Smart and Brian Shaw, 8 September 2015.

1763 ECM Records ECM 168.

1764 Chris Laurence, interview with Nick Smart and Brian Shaw, 8 September 2015.

1765 Ibid.

1766 Robin Eubanks, interview with Nick Smart, 25 October 2019.

1767 Kenny Wheeler Quartet, off-air recording of Lugano Broadcast, 3 February 2000.

1768 Mark Wheeler to Nick Smart, 3 February 2015.

1769 Manfred Eicher, interview with Nick Smart, 5 March 2017.

1770 Ibid.

1771 Mark Wheeler to Nick Smart and Brian Shaw, 11 August 2016.

1772 Henry Lowther to Nick Smart, 8 October 2014.

1773 Manfred Eicher, interview with Nick Smart, 5 March 2017.

1774 "Bootlist", *Yours & Oblig*, 16 August 2011, http://yoursoblig.blogspot.com/2011/08/bootlist-john-abercrombie-sendehalle.html. (Feldman and Kenny had already met for projects with Klaus Koenig's Orchestra and on John Abercrombie's *Open Land* recording.)

1775 Mark Wheeler to Nick Smart, 31 July 2019.

1776 Ibid.

1777 Transcription of BBC Radio broadcast from Bath, recorded live, 26 May 2002.

1778 Chris Laurence, interview with Nick Smart and Brian Shaw, 8 September 2015.

1779 "Shy Guy", *JazzWise*, December 2004/January 2005.

1780 A long-time fan of Kenny's music, Fred was especially fond of his 1976 album *Gnu High*: "I remember buying *Gnu High* because I had Keith Jarrett's Bremen and Lausanne concerts . . . Keith might argue but I think it's some of his best playing on record – probably because he wasn't able to totally run the show . . . I just remember loving Kenny's sound" (Fred Hersch, interview with Nick Smart and Brian Shaw, 15 July 2018).

1781 Olwen Richards to Nick Smart, 4 November 2015.
1782 Fred Hersch, Norma Winstone, Kenny Wheeler, and Paul Clarvis, *4 in Perspective* (Village Life 00909VL, 2000).
1783 Olwen Richards to Nick Smart, 4 November 2015.
1784 Fred Hersch, interview with Nick Smart and Brian Shaw, 15 July 2018.
1785 Brian Shaw had been visiting the day before and had stayed the night. He had just finished a book of transcriptions of Kenny's solos (Brian Shaw, *Kenny Wheeler Solo Transcriptions* [Universal Edition, 2000]). At the breakfast table that morning, Brian asked Norma, with whom he was starstruck, if she had perfect pitch. Norma, not hearing Brian's question, asked him to repeat himself. Before he had the chance, Kenny interrupted with "Brian wants to know if you're the perfect bitch!"
1786 Fred Hersch, interview with Nick Smart and Brian Shaw, 15 July 2018.
1787 Ibid.
1788 Norma Winstone, interview with Nick Smart, 19 August 2015.
1789 Olwen Richards to Nick Smart, 4 November 2015.
1790 Norma Winstone, interview with Nick Smart, 19 August 2015.
1791 Ibid.
1792 The Stan Sulzmann Big Band, *Birthdays, Birthdays* (Village Life 99108VL, 1999).
1793 This was a story often shared among their friends, often with Kenny and Doreen present and laughing along, so it was never framed in a critical sort of way. Doreen would just knowingly roll her eyes.
1794 Chris Laurence, interview with Nick Smart and Brian Shaw, 8 September 2015.
1795 Mabel Ball, interview with Brian Shaw, 13 May 2015.
1796 Billy Hart to Nick Smart, 5 October 2015. Although the time with Getz had drifted from Billy's memory, he did say, "I was already a fan, because I had known Dave Holland", and he had checked out *Gnu High* as had so many other musicians. "That's the one that sticks in my mind," he said.
1797 BBC Archive.
1798 Duncan Heining, "Kenny Wheeler, Queen Elizabeth Hall", *The Independent*, 17 January 2000.
1799 Alyn Shipton, "Kenny Wheeler, Adrian Boult Hall, Birmingham", *The Times*, 17 January 2000.
1800 Heining, "Kenny Wheeler, Queen Elizabeth Hall".
1801 Oliver Jones, "Brassed Off", *What's On*, 12 January 2000.
1802 Christine Tobin to Nick Smart, 20 July 2018.
1803 Phil Robson to Nick Smart, 20 July 2018.
1804 Eli Asher, email to Brian Shaw, 24 May 2019.
1805 Jason Price, email to Brian Shaw, 26 May 2019.
1806 Andrew Cheetham, email to Brian Shaw, 27 May 2019.
1807 These letters are in the Wheeler Archive, Royal Academy of Music. Brookmeyer replied to one of Kenny's letters in 2000 saying, "Would love to do anything with you, anytime! 2001 looking flexible – this year is gone already. Would you like to record something? Do a writing project together? Let me know – Warm regards, Bob." In a reply to another letter, apparently quite complimentary of Brookmeyer, the trombonist invited Kenny to visit him at his home in New Hampshire, near Boston: "Glad to hear from you and you say such nice things! From you, a compliment is high praise . . . I would like very much to do some things with you. Recording? Touring? What sounds good? I like documentation so recording appeals to me . . . maybe try and come down for a couple days. It's pretty here – mountains, woods and nice house – AND warm welcome. All best, BB."

1808 Kenny Wheeler, interview for Artists House Music, 2002.

1809 Record of a 17 February 1989 concert with Kenny and the Eastman Jazz Ensemble, Ray Wright (director), Sibley Archive, University of Rochester, accessed 15 July 2019. Hollenbeck, like many of Kenny's younger generation of musical collaborators, had first played with Kenny in February 1989 while a student at the Eastman School of Music, before seeing him again at Banff later that summer.

1810 "Bob Brookmeyer and Kenny Wheeler recording 'Before the First Time' for Album 'Island'", YouTube, https://www.youtube.com/watch?v=LDuZONsyz6w.

1811 Ibid.

1812 Thomas Conrad, review of *Island*, *JazzTimes*, 1 December 2003.

1813 883, *Uno In Più* (aka *1 In +*) (CGD East West 857389582, 2001).

1814 Spaceman Records OPM015CD.

1815 Andy Beta, "Amazing Grace, Spiritualized, 2003", *Pitchfork*, https://pitchfork.com/reviews/albums/7422-amazing-grace.

1816 Decca 00028948178100.

1817 Copland, Abercrombie, Wheeler, *Brand New* (Challenge Jazz CHR 70122, 2004).

1818 Hein van de Geyn to Nick Smart, 19 October 2016.

1819 Ibid.

1820 Ibid.

1821 Fred Hersch, interview with Nick Smart and Brian Shaw, 15 July 2018.

1822 Ben Street to Nick Smart, 23 July 2017.

1823 Fred Hersch, interview with Nick Smart and Brian Shaw, 15 July 2018.

1824 Ben Street to Nick Smart, 23 July 2017.

1825 Ibid.

1826 Tim Garland to Nick Smart, 27 November 2015.

1827 Barnaby Dickinson to Nick Smart, 3 September 2016. They first met while Barnaby was a student at the Guildhall. While listening to the students rehearse some improvised interludes between pieces, Kenny addressed the students, urging them all to work more on their free playing. This unusually direct comment from Kenny shows what high value he placed on having those skills in their overall musical development.

1828 Ibid.

1829 A comment Nick Smart heard Kenny allude to on a number of occasions when he was acting as go-between for some enquiry or other to play one of the classic pieces – usually *The Sweet Time Suite*, it must be said.

## Chapter 8: The Long Waiting

1830 Stan Sulzmann, interview with Nick Smart and Brian Shaw, 4 August 2016.

1831 Ibid.

1832 Symbol Records SR20011001.

1833 Stan Sulzmann, interview with Nick Smart and Brian Shaw, 4 August 2016.

1834 Ibid.

1835 www.londonjazznews.com/2011/03/women-behind-music-christine-allen.html, accessed 25 March 2021.

1836 Christine Allen to Nick Smart and Brian Shaw, 8 September 2015.

1837 Ibid.

1838 Kenny Wheeler, fax to Evan Parker, 17 September 2003.

1839 Stan Sulzmann, interview with Nick Smart and Brian Shaw, 4 August 2016.

1840 Hugh Fraser, interview with Brian Shaw, 25 May 2015.

1841 Anonymous member of the band to Nick Smart, 2014.

1842 Hugh Fraser, interview with Brian Shaw, 25 May 2015.

1843 Alyn Shipton in *The Times*, 18 January 2005, p. T2.

1844 John Fordham in *The Guardian*, 18 January 2005.
1845 Ibid.
1846 Shipton, *The Times*.
1847 Christine Allen to Nick Smart and Brian Shaw, 8 September 2015.
1848 Ibid.
1849 Doreen Wheeler, conversation with Brian Shaw following the Manchester concert, 15 January 2005.
1850 *Manchester Evening News*, 15 January 2005.
1851 Peter Bacon, "It's My Party, I'll Be Shy If I Want To; Kenny Wheeler 75th Birthday Orchestra Adrian Boult Hall", *Birmingham Post*, 18 January 2005.
1852 Evan Parker, interview with Nick Smart and Brian Shaw, 9 September 2015.
1853 Ray Comiskey, "Kenny Wheeler Big Band: Vicar Street", *Irish Times*, 23 January 2005.
1854 Christine Allen to Nick Smart and Brian Shaw, 8 September 2015.
1855 This section from a chat with Doreen, Louann, Mark, and Sophie at Wallwood Road, 16 July 2018.
1856 Emails and interviews from three jazz institution leaders outlined difficulties when booking Kenny residencies at their schools: John Rapson (University of Iowa) to Nick Smart, 29 June 2015; Chris Merz (University of Northern Iowa) to Nick Smart, 15 September 2015; and Hämi Hämmerli (Lucerne School of Music) to Nick Smart, 29 June 2015.
1857 John Cumming to Nick Smart, 4 April 2017.
1858 Kenny Werner to Nick Smart, 28 June 2016.
1859 Paul Tynan to Brian Shaw, 13 June 2015.
1860 Kenny Werner to Nick Smart, 28 June 2016.
1861 Ibid.
1862 Norma Winstone to Nick Smart, 4 August 2016.
1863 Half Note 4528, 2006.
1864 Kenny Werner to Nick Smart, 28 June 2016.
1865 Dave Holland, interview with Nick Smart, 11 January 2015.
1866 Among other friends, Chris Laurence mentioned this to Nick Smart and Brian Shaw (interview, 8 September 2015).
1867 Mark Wheeler to Nick Smart and Brian Shaw, 11 August 2016.
1868 Ian Carr, liner notes to *Where Do We Go From Here?* (CAM Jazz CAM 5004, 2005).
1869 Wheeler, Potter, Pieranunzi, Haden, Motian, *Fellini Jazz* (CAM Jazz CAMJ 7761-2).
1870 Notes for *Fellini Jazz* written by Enrico Pieranunzi. Kenny recorded once more with Pieranunzi the following year, in November 2004, as the guest with Pieranunzi's trio featuring Marc Johnson and Joey Baron for the album *As Never Before* (CAM Jazz CAMJ 7807-2).
1871 John Kelman, "Kenny Wheeler: What Now?", *All About Jazz*, 12 May 2005, https://www.allaboutjazz.com/what-now-kenny-wheeler-cam-jazz-review-by-john-kelman.php.
1872 Kenny Wheeler, Chris Potter, John Taylor, and Dave Holland, *What Now?* (CAM Jazz CAM 5005, 2005).
1873 Chris Potter, interview with Nick Smart, 3 October 2018.
1874 Ibid.
1875 Kenny, along with John Taylor, had the opportunity to perform much of the music from this album at a Jazz festival in Clusone, Italy, in July 2004. With the two US members of the band otherwise engaged, Stan Sulzmann played in place of Chris Potter and Chris Laurence stepped in for Dave Holland. It is a wonderful performance that was thankfully recorded and broadcast on Rai 3.
1876 Kenny Wheeler, Philipp Wachsmann, Evan Parker, Gerd Dudek, Paul Dunmall, Paul Rogers, John Edwards, Tony Marsh, and Tony Levin, *Free Zone Appleby 2005* (psi psi 06.06, 2006).

1877 Tony Coe, John Edwards, Alan Hacker, Sylvia Hallett, Marcio Mattos, Evan Parker, Philipp Wachsmann, and Kenny Wheeler, *Free Zone Appleby 2003* (psi psi 04.05, 2004).
1878 CAM Jazz CAMJ 7892-2, 2015.
1879 This recording is even more poignant because, with such a backlog of CAM recordings to release, the ten-year delay of *On the Way to Two* made it tragically posthumous for both musicians.
1880 CAM Jazz CAMJ 7786-2.
1881 John Kelman, "Kenny Wheeler: It Takes Two!", *All About Jazz*, 29 July 2006, https://www.allaboutjazz.com/ it-takes-two-kenny-wheeler-cam-jazz-review-by-john-kelman.
1882 John Fordham in *The Guardian,* 11 August 2006.
1883 CAM Jazz CAMJ 7801-2, 2005.
1884 Ted Libbey, *The NPR Listener's Encyclopedia of Classical Music* (Workman Publishing Co., 2006), p. 823. See also an interview with cellist Christopher Costanza of the St. Lawrence String Quartet: Charles Donelan, "St. Lawrence String Quartet Preview", *Santa Barbara Independent*, 19 April 2011, https://www.independent. com/2011/04/19/st-lawrence-string-quartet-preview.
1885 CAM Jazz CAMJ 7835-2, 2011.
1886 Kit Downes to Nick Smart, 12 August 2020.
1887 Phil Robson to Nick Smart, 20 July 2018.
1888 Nick Smart memory of driving Kenny and Doreen to Cadogan Hall, 5 October 2007, for Mike Gibbs's 70th birthday tour (London gig).
1889 Mike Gibbs, interview with Nick Smart, 24 August 2015.
1890 Jim Hart to Nick Smart, 31 July 2022.
1891 John Parricelli to Nick Smart, 10 June 2024.
1892 CAM Jazz CAMJ 7866-2, 2013.
1893 Chris Laurence, interview with Nick Smart and Brian Shaw, 8 September 2015.
1894 Stan Sulzmann, interview with Nick Smart and Brian Shaw, 4 August 2016.
1895 Pete Churchill to Nick Smart and Brian Shaw, 11 August 2016.
1896 Stan Sulzmann, interview with Nick Smart and Brian Shaw, 4 August 2016.
1897 Astarte NC/1838, 2009.
1898 John Kelman, "Kenny Wheeler/Colours Jazz Orchestra: Nineteen Plus One", *All About Jazz*, 7 May 2010, https://www.allaboutjazz.com/nineteen-plus-one-kenny-wheeler-astarte-records-review-by-john-kelman.php.
1899 UMO Jazz Orchestra with Kenny Wheeler and Norma Winstone, *One More Time* (A-Records AL 73202, 2000).
1900 Kelman, "Kenny Wheeler/Colours Jazz Orchestra: Nineteen Plus One".
1901 Mark Donlon to Nick Smart, 16 February 2022.
1902 Tony Dudley-Evans, conversation with Nick Smart, 10 August 2016.
1903 Ibid.
1904 Norma Winstone, interview with Nick Smart, 19 August 2015.
1905 Stan Sulzmann, email to Nick Smart, 21 June 2009.
1906 Nick Smart, email to Royal Academy Deputy Principal, 7 July 2009.
1907 Mark Wheeler and Louann Newman in the Kenny Wheeler 80th birthday souvenir programme.
1908 Pete Churchill to Nick Smart and Brian Shaw, 11 August 2016.
1909 Nick Smart to Brian Shaw, 9 August 2010.
1910 Pete Churchill to Nick Smart and Brian Shaw, 11 August 2016.
1911 Kenny Wheeler to Nigel Wrench, interview on 13 January 2010 for the BBC Radio 4 *PM* programme, broadcast on 14 January 2010.
1912 Dr. Arnon Bentovim, interview with Nick Smart and Brian Shaw, 2 August 2021. When asked about this repeated theme of melancholy and chaos, Dr. Bentovim

observed "I think the duality in his personality – enormous strength and at the same time tremendous anxiety, trepidation, the fear of chaos – and one feels that he's always on the boundary between coping and chaos. . . . his love of melancholy, and his identification with sad and beautiful themes which also comes through . . ."

1913 Nick Smart, recollections to Brian Shaw, August 2020.

1914 John Fordham, "Kenny Wheeler's 80th Birthday", *The Guardian*, 15 January 2010, https://www.theguardian.com/music/2010/jan/15/kenny-wheeler-80th-birthday-review.

1915 Ibid.

1916 Observations made from an archival recording of the concert, recorded 14 January 2010.

1917 Pete Churchill to Nick Smart and Brian Shaw, 11 August 2016.

1918 Norma Winstone, interview with Nick Smart, 19 August 2015.

1919 Ibid.

1920 www.londonjazznews.com/2010/10/review-kenny-wheeler-80th-birthday-uk.html, accessed 2 July 2020.

1921 Pete Churchill to Nick Smart and Brian Shaw, 11 August 2016. Nick Smart also remembers a similar quote, told to Brian Shaw, 7 August 2016. Several other members of the band also recall this scene.

1922 Pete Churchill to Nick Smart and Brian Shaw, 11 August 2016.

1923 Cox, "Kenny-ing", p. 230.

1924 Ibid.

1925 These awards were organized and presented by the All Party Parliamentary Jazz Appreciation Group (APPJAG), in association with the collections agency PPL.

1926 Cox, "Kenny-ing", p. 216.

1927 Mark Miller in conversation with Brian Shaw, Don Thompson, and Ted O'Reilly, 7 October 2015.

1928 Duncan Hopkins to Terrance Cox, in Cox, Kenny-ing", p. 231.

1929 Duncan Hopkins to Nick Smart, 27 August 2015.

1930 Gene Lees, letter to Kenny Wheeler, 7 September 1986.

1931 Quote from a family scrapbook made for Kenny by his granddaughters, celebrating many of his life's achievements. The quote is actually written in Kenny's own handwriting and stuck into the book! (Wheeler Archive, Royal Academy of Music).

1932 "Kenny Wheeler receives honorary doctorate from University of York", *All About Jazz*, 18 July 2009, https://news.allaboutjazz.com/kenny-wheeler-receives-honorary-doctorate-from-university-of-york.php.

1933 https://fontmusic.org.

1934 Dave Douglas, interview with Nick Smart, 16 December 2015.

1935 John Hollenbeck, email to Dave Rivello, forwarded to Brian Shaw, 5 September 2011. Hollenbeck made it clear that he had not been able to get music for FONT through Kenny's management.

1936 Kenny Wheeler, on FONT website, https://fontmusic.org, accessed 4 August 2016.

1937 Nick Smart on FONT for London Jazz News.com, www.londonjazznews.com/2011/10/round-up-kenny-wheeler-in-new-york.html, accessed 19 July 2020.

1938 This was a short excerpt from the 10-minute "Eastman Trumpet Quartet" piece Kenny had written for these same players that was used to open for his duo concert with J.T. at the International Trumpet Guild conference in Manchester on 5 July 2002.

1939 It was the four-trumpet arrangement of "How Deep Is the Ocean" that had appeared originally on the Azimuth album *How it Was Then . . . Never Again*, on which Kenny overdubbed all four parts.

1940 John Hollenbeck, email to Brian Shaw, 31 May 2017.

1941 This would be one of the last times Kenny saw his sister Helen, who followed his career the most closely of any of his family. She died in May 2012.

1942 Dave Douglas, interview with Nick Smart, 16 December 2015.

1943 Andrew Cheetham to Brian Shaw at the FONT Festival, 22 October 2011.

1944 Archival recording of Kenny Wheeler at the FONT Festival, the Jazz Standard, New York, 22 October 2011.

1945 Nate Chinen, "An Influence and Songs that Grow on You", *New York Times*, 25 October 2011.

1946 Dave Douglas, interview with Nick Smart, 16 December 2015.

1947 Brian Shaw observed this on several occasions at FONT, 20–22 October 2011.

1948 Kenny Wheeler Big Band, *The Long Waiting* (CAM Jazz CAMJ 7848-2, 2012).

1949 Mark Wheeler, email to *The Long Waiting* band, 13 April 2011.

1950 While Kenny did big-band projects with other groups – notably the albums with the UMO Jazz Orchestra and the Maritime Jazz Orchestra, these were not *his* bands. It should also be noted that the music for the 2005 tour was recorded multitrack live in concert, but the DVDs on which the files were kept were damaged and are, at this writing, unable to be salvaged.

1951 Mark Wheeler to Nick Smart and Brian Shaw, 22 January 2016.

1952 Nick Smart to Brian Shaw, 9 August 2016.

1953 Mark Wheeler to Nick Smart and Brian Shaw, 11 August 2016.

1954 Interestingly, and frustratingly enough, John Barclay was committed to a film recording session which took place downstairs in the same building.

1955 Evan Parker, interview with Nick Smart and Brian Shaw, 9 September 2015. It was actually a conversation Evan remembered having with Duncan at Ray Warleigh's funeral.

1956 Pete Churchill to Nick Smart and Brian Shaw, 11 August 2016.

1957 Ibid.

1958 Ibid.

1959 Nick Smart (on 27 October 2011) and Mark Wheeler (on 2 November 2011) emailed Andrea Marini to make the request on Kenny's behalf that he be allowed to have a go at re-recording his solos. Kenny felt reinforcement from them was needed about how well he had played in New York at FONT and how he should also be invited to the mixing of the album.

1960 Mark Wheeler to Nick Smart and Brian Shaw, 11 August 2016.

1961 Pete Churchill to Nick Smart and Brian Shaw, 11 August 2016.

1962 Email from Mark Wheeler to Nick Smart, 6 November 2011, sharing Andrea Marini's email to Mark resigning his position as manager on 5 November 2011.

1963 Henry Lowther to Nick Smart, 8 October 2014.

1964 Norma Winstone to Nick Smart, 16 August 2015.

1965 Ibid., relaying a conversation between herself and Andrew Bradley.

1966 Pete Churchill to Nick Smart and Brian Shaw, 11 August 2016.

1967 Evan Parker, interview with Nick Smart and Brian Shaw, 9 September 2015.

1968 Evan Parker, liner notes to *The Long Waiting*, http://www.camjazz. com/8052405140555-the-long-waiting-cd.html.

1969 John Fordham, review of *The Long Waiting*, *The Guardian*, 26 January 2012.

1970 The Duncan Lamont Big Band Featuring Kenny Wheeler, *As If By Magic . . .* (Jellymould Jazz JM-JJ025, 2016).

1971 Duncan Lamont, liner notes to *As If By Magic . . .*

1972 At this writing, the process of sorting and adding to the archive continues, with Smart and Shaw locating an enormous collection of Kenny's music – refreshingly, lovingly preserved – at the Banff Centre in Alberta, Canada, where he had spent so many years teaching and donating his music to their students. The Banff Centre's library and archive generously agreed to share copies of its Wheeler holdings with the Wheeler Archive, Royal Academy of Music.

1973  Nick Smart memory from the day. Confirmed by Reuben Fowler, 9 August 2022.
1974  Stephen Weil, "Sam Amidon", *Tiny Mixtapes*, 24 May 2013, https://www.tinymixtapes.com/features/sam-amidon.
1975  Sam Amidon, email to Nick Smart and Brian Shaw, 19 July 2019.
1976  Ibid.
1977  Nonesuch 7559-79619-4.
1978  Weil, "Sam Amidon".
1979  Sam Amidon, email to Nick Smart and Brian Shaw, 19 July 2019.
1980  Weil, "Sam Amidon".
1981  Sam Amidon, email to Nick Smart and Brian Shaw, 19 July 2019.
1982  Nick Purnell, email to Nick Smart, 19 October 2016.
1983  Nick Smart to Brian Shaw, 7 August 2016.
1984  *Jazz UK*, April 2013.
1985  Nick Smart to Brian Shaw, 7 August 2016.
1986  Henry Lowther, Chris Laurence, and Norma Winstone, interview with Alyn Shipton, 13 June 2013.
1987  Norma Winstone to Nick Smart, 16 August 2015.
1988  Pete Churchill to Nick Smart and Brian Shaw, 11 August 2016.
1989  Ibid.
1990  Ibid.
1991  Nick Smart to Brian Shaw, 9 April 2017.
1992  Kenny Wheeler, Norma Winstone and London Vocal Project, *Mirrors* (Edition Records Edition EDN1038V, 2013).
1993  Nikki Iles to Nick Smart, 14 January 2016.
1994  John Fordham, "Kenny Wheeler/Norma Winstone/London Vocal Project: Mirrors – Review", *The Guardian*, 7 March 2013, https://www.theguardian.com/music/2013/mar/07/kenny-wheeler-norma-winstone-mirrors-review.
1995  Edition Records website, https://editionrecords.com/releases/kenny-wheeler-norma-winstone-london-vocal-project-mirrors.
1996  Filomena Campus and Giorgio Serci, *Scaramouche* (Incipit Records INC 189, 2015).
1997  Stan Sulzmann, interview with Nick Smart and Brian Shaw, 4 August 2016.
1998  Manfred Eicher, interview with Nick Smart, 5 March 2017.
1999  Stan Sulzmann, interview with Nick Smart and Brian Shaw, 4 August 2016.
2000  Ibid.
2001  Chris Laurence, interview with Nick Smart and Brian Shaw, 8 September 2015.
2002  Manfred Eicher, interview with Nick Smart, 5 March 2017.
2003  Stan Sulzmann, interview with Nick Smart and Brian Shaw, 4 August 2016.
2004  Manfred Eicher, interview with Nick Smart, 5 March 2017.
2005  Ibid.
2006  ECM Records ECM 2388.
2007  ECM website, "Songs for Quintet", https://ecmrecords.com/product/songs-for-quintet-kenny-wheeler-stan-sulzmann-john-parricelli-chris-laurence-martin-france.
2008  Ibid.
2009  Manfred Eicher, interview with Nick Smart, 5 March 2017.
2010  We believe this to be the case. Nick was closely involved with much of what Kenny was doing at that stage and has no record of any other sessions, nor does Mark Wheeler. All the other late recordings were little cameos and we've been able to confirm they preceded the *Songs for Quintet* sessions.
2011  Henry Lowther to Nick Smart, 8 October 2014.
2012  Mark Wheeler to Nick Smart and Brian Shaw, 11 August 2016.
2013  Dave Holland, interview with Nick Smart, 8 August 2016.

2014  Norma Winstone to Nick Smart, 19 August 2015.

2015  Mark Wheeler, email to Brian Shaw, 8 September 2014.

2016  Norma Winstone to Nick Smart, 16 August 2015.

2017  Nick Smart, email to Brian Shaw, 13 September 2014.

2018  Kenny Wheeler's death certificate, filed 22 September 2014.

2019  Nick Smart, "Kenny Wheeler, 1930–2014", news article, Royal Academy of Music website, 18 September 2014.

2020  @TheDaveHolland, Twitter, 18 September 2014, 12:58 pm.

2021  Jensen, "Time, Marked".

2022  Jack DeJohnette, Facebook, 20 September 2014, https://www.facebook.com/ jackdejohnette/posts/10152631945271878#.

2023  Argue, "Everybody's Song But His Own", Ethan Iverson's blog.

2024  Norma Winstone, "Farewell: Kenny Wheeler", *JazzTimes*, 25 March 2015 (updated 19 July 2024), https://jazztimes.com/features/tributes-and-obituaries/ farewell-kenny-wheeler.

2025  John Taylor, liner notes to Kenny Wheeler and John Taylor, *On the Way to Two* (CAM Jazz CAMJ 7892-2, 2015). Sadly, John Taylor passed away suddenly in France on 17 July 2015, only a few months after Kenny, and didn't live to see the release of this album.

2026  Mark Wheeler to Nick Smart and Brian Shaw, 11 August 2016.

2027  These lyrics were written by Norma for Kenny's "Comba No. 3" from *The Long Waiting* album, originally intended for the memorial service of friend and fan Reg Simmonds, whose family asked Kenny to play the tune (one of his favourites) at his funeral. Kenny asked Norma to sing with him, and then Kenny's lack of mobility at the time – combined with the lack of a suitable pianist at the venue – led to the family simply to choose to play the recording instead. So, since Norma had written the lyrics about Kenny anyway, she chose to sing it as his memorial service.

2028  Nick Smart to Brian Shaw, 8 August 2016.

## Epilogue

2029  John Fordham, "Kenny Wheeler: Songs for Quintet review – Final Set from Jazz's Modest Maestro", *The Guardian*, 8 January 2015, https://www.theguardian.com/ music/2015/jan/08/kenny-wheeler-songs-for-quintet-review.

2030  "Kenny Wheeler: Songs for Quintet", *DownBeat*, March 2015, http://www.downbeat. com/digitaledition/2015/DB1503/single_page_view/64.html.

2031  Noah Stoneman, WhatsApp message to the authors, 5 March 2024, referring to both Fred Hersch and Sullivan Fortner playing "Everybody's Song But My Own" at Mezzro in New York, including a performance of Fortner's from December 2022 (available on YouTube at time of writing, www.youtube.com/live/8vYTLgG3F-A?si=vItnk_3XqRokf3-x, accessed 5 March 2024).

2032  https://open.spotify.com/album/1XznKANeyAhmdDyB4KSJ3r?si=v6Oci3fFSdWHIv 1UzVWEAg.

2033  "Chris Laurence – 'Kenny Wheeler: Some Gnu Ones'", *UK Jazz News*, 11 December 2021, https://londonjazznews.com/2021/12/11/ chris-laurence-kenny-wheeler-some-gnu-ones.

2034  Kenny Barron and Dave Holland, *The Art of Conversation* (Impulse! 379 466-1, 2914).

2035  Stewart Smith, "Preview: London Jazz Festival", *The Quietus*, 9 November 2015, https://thequietus.com/articles/19186-preview-london-jazz-festival.

2036  Nick Smart memory, who was present in the audience.

2037  Hard Rubber Orchestra Featuring Norma Winstone, *Kenny Wheeler: Suite for Hard Rubber Orchestra* (Justin Time JTR 8614-2 2018).

2038 Even so, the authors, who knew him personally (and one of whom, Brian Shaw, plays regularly with some of the top symphony orchestras in the United States), contend that he would have figured that role out in no time, given the chance. The evidence of his recording of "Solo One" alone shows he could have been an exceptional modern classical trumpet soloist, had he chosen to be.

2039 Note to Kenny from 2012 (undated), found in the Wheeler Archive, Royal Academy of Music.

# Index

Page numbers in *italics* refer to photos.

883 (band) 351

## A

Abbot, Derrick 60
Abercrombie, John 185, 186, 188–190, 203, 238, *240*, 249, 263, 265, 269, *271*, 272, 274–278, *278*, *281*, 284, 288–289, 313, 318, 336–338, *337*, 367, 472
Abou-Khalil, Rabih 292
Abrams, Muhal Richard 173
Adams, George 204, 205
Adams, Pepper 131, 132, 215, 224–265
Adderley, Nat 54, 55
Adzenyah, Abraham 214
Alan Branscombe & Friends 125
Alan Skidmore Quintet 103, 104, 128, 132
Alexander, Monty. *See* Monty Alexander Trio
Allen, Christine 355–356
Allen, Jeremy 350
Altena, Maarten 234
Altman, John 292
Altschul, Barry 157–159, 162, 172
Åman, Johnny 415
Ambrosetti, Franco 253
Amidon, Sam 396
Andersen, Arild 207, 221, 243
Andrews, Jon 328
Animals, The (band) 77
Anthony, Bruce *27*, 35
Anthony-Turnage, Mark 325
Arban, Jean-Baptiste 25
Ardley, Neil 130, 136
Argue, Darcy James 216, 268, 411
Argüelles, Julian 135, 263, 265, *271*, 283, 286–287, 347, *377*
Argüelles, Steve 234
Armstrong, Louis 1, 25, 35, 50, 56, 58, 62. *See also* Louis Armstrong All Stars

Art Blakey's Jazz Messengers 210
Art Ensemble of Chicago 154, 213
Asher, Eli 349
Atkins, Ronald 96, 115, 150, 191, 274
Auld, Georgie 22
Ayler, Albert 137
Azimuth 111, 194–197, 199, 201, 203, 207, 222, 234–238, *237*, 250, 259, 292, 294, 300–302, 304, 307, 336

## B

Bacon, Peter 359
Bailey, Benny 114, 261
Bailey, Derek 86–88, *87*, 104, 125, 137, 141, 146, 154–156, 191
Baker, Ronnie 47–48, *49*
Ball, Bryon (nephew) 31, 297
Ball, Mabel (sister) 9, *11*, 14–16, 30, *32*, 36, 38, 53, 105, 139, 221–222, 248, 251, *264*, 279, 297, 347, 381, 409–410, 435
Bambarger, Bradley 170
Banff Big Band 218–219, *219*
Barber, Chris. *See also* Chris Barber Band
Barclay, John 283, 326, 335, 357, 359, 368, 375, *377*, 379–380, 390, 392
Barker, Guy 292
Baron, Joey 490
Barriteau, Carl 44–45, 47
Barron, Kenny 416
Basie, Count 174, 434
Basso, Ermanno 393
Basso, Guido 307
Bates, Django 292
Beckett, Harry 79, 155
Beck, Gordon 107, 130, 134, 199, 243
Beirach, Richie 165, 205, 206, 215–216
Bell, Johnny (aka Thick Wilson) 35
Bell, Kitty 46
Bellson, Louie 114

Bennett, Richard Rodney 72
Bennink, Han 155
Bentovim, Arnon 18, 436
Berendt, Joachim-Ernst 197, 208, 458
Berger, Karl 213–214
Bergeron, Wayne 122
Berlin Contemporary Jazz Orchestra 260, 261
Berne, Tim 244
Bevin, Pam 67
Bigger, Stan 17
Blackwell, Ed 214, 282
Blade, Brian 363
Blair, Eddie 114, 118, 125, 451
Blair, Tony 118
Bley, Carla 260
Bley, Paul 331
Bloom, Jane Ira 299
Blue Notes, the (band) 291
Bobby Wellins 370
Bob Leaper Big Band 120
Bob Wybrow 29
Boland, Francy 114. *See also* Francy Boland Orchestra; Kenny Clarke/Francy Boland Big Band
Bolden, Buddy 1
Boulanger, Nadia 33, 71
Boulez, Pierre 72
Bowen, Greg 69, 78, 144, 148, 451
Bowie, Lester 122, 154, 204, 315, 462
Bradley, Andrew (son-in-law) *377*, 378, 408–409
Bradley, Bill 22–23, 28
Bradley, Howard 22–23, 28
Bradley, Mike 313, 328
Brady, Tim 115, 257–259
Braid, David 415
Branscombe, Alan *63*, 79, 95, 125, 145
Brass Fantasy 122
Brass Project 238, 239
Braxton, Anthony xv, 4, 157–163, *158*, 171–174, *171*, 178, 204, 219, 232. *See also* Creative Music Orchestra/Creative Jazz Orchestra
Brecker, Michael 224, 243, 247, 313
Brecker, Randy 224, 230
Breeden, Leon 333
Breen, Bobby 143, 445, 448
Bridgewater, Cecil 131
Britton, Peter 455
Brookmeyer, Bob 69, 350, 369
Brooks, Stuart 283
Brotherhood of Breath 89, 292

Brötzmann, Peter 155–156
Brown, Clifford 35, 66
Brown, Lawrence 12
Brown, Ray 443
Brown, Sandy 98, 126
Brown, Tony 48
Bruce, Jack 102, 128
Bruford, Bill 177
Brüninghaus, Rainer 207
Bucovitz, Larry 97
Buddy Featherstonhaugh New Quintet 50
Burdon, Eric 77
Burrell, Kenny 443
Burton, Gary 129, 232, 452. *See also* Gary Burton Quartet
Bush, Lennie 126
Butterfield, Billy 23
Byrd, William 332

**C**

Caine, Uri 316
Calarco, Joe 26
Calderon, Rosana 333
Cale, Bruce 85
Calloway, Cab 431
Calvert, Leon 36, *63*, 69
Campus, Filomena 403
Carlberg, Frank 350, 371
Carr, Ian 67, 77, 128, 130, 141, 165–166, 182–184, 188, 238, 283–284, 301, 365, 475
Carr, Mike 67
Carson, Bob 58, 60
Carter, Greg 300, 302, 305
Carter, Ron 78, 480
Catherine, Philip 232, 243
Cavalli, Pierre 153
CCS 120
Chaikin, Carol 218
Cheetham, Andrew 349
Cherry, Don 155, 458
Chisholm, George 126, 242
Chris Barber Band 437
Christensen, Jon 174, 207, 243
Christie, Keith 47–48, *49*, 141, 144
Churchill, Pete 371, 374–375, *377*, 378, 380, 390, 392–393, 401, 413, 415, 417
Chycoski, Arnie 115, 258
Circle (band) 157, 159
Clare, Kenny 60, 78, 107
Clarke, Kenny 114. *See also* Kenny Clarke/Francy Boland Big Band

Clarvis, Paul 344, 346–347, 371
Clayton, Buck 12, 23
Clayton, Freddy 266
Clayton, Jay 472
Cliff Hardie Big Band 72
Clyne, Jeff 79, 85, 104, 137–138, 154
Coe, Tony 78–79, 95–96, 104–105, 107, 114, 128, 130, 139, 175, 191, 199, 221, 283, 449, 453–454. *See also* Coe, Wheeler & Co.
Coe, Wheeler & Co. 104–105, 121, 163, 453. *See also* Wheeler & Co.
Cohen, Alan 77, 97
Coleman, Ornette 213, 417
Coleman, Steve 214–215, 228–230, *240*, 282, 290, 480
Colley, Scott 363
Collier, Graham 79, 93, 110, 132, 146, 446
Colours Jazz Orchestra 370
Comiskey, Ray 360
Composers' Cooperative Jazz Orchestra 257
Concert Jazz Band (George Gruntz) 253–254, 317
Condon, Les 78, 95, 97
Conflagration (band) 157
Conrad, Thomas 351
Convolution (band) 154, 156
Cook, Richard 249, 280
Copland, Marc 338
Corea, Chick 157, 161, 164
Cornford, Bob 96, 107, 116, 149, 223, 243, 456
Costanza, Christopher 491
Cotterrell, Roger 183
Courtenay, Freddie 42
Cowell, Johnny 432
Cox, Terrance 23, 297, 381
Creative Music Orchestra/Creative Jazz Orchestra 174, 204, 283, 325, 335, 347
Crombie, Tony 107, 449
CUK Big Band 371
Cumming, John 259, 361, 396
Cuscana, Michael 172

**D**

Damiani, Paolo 234
Danielsson, Palle 154, 174, 284–285, 288, 289
Dankworth, John xv, 55–61, *63*, 64, 67, 69, 70, 73, 77, 92, 94–95, 98, 123, 132, 134, 141, 150, 354, 369, 446. *See also* John Dankworth Orchestra

Darling, Wayne 243
Dauner, Wolfgang 182
Dave Holland Octet 334–335, 342
Dave Holland Quintet 227–232, 240–242, *240*, 282, 299, 342
Davis, Art 23
Davis, Clive 249, 267, 322, 328
Davis, Miles 17, 21, 35, 55, 66, 89, 110, 164, 167, 227, 410, 417, 434, 447
Davison, Harold 61
Davison, Wild Bill 62
Davis, Richard 97, 131
Dawson, Eric 60
Dedication Orchestra 292
DeJohnette, Jack 164–165, 167–168, 185, 187–188, 205–206, 211, 213, 223–224, 249, 411
Del Fra, Riccardo 221
Delmar, Elaine 110
Deppa, Claude 292
Deuchar, Jimmy 69, 80, 82, 85
Di Castri, Furio 289
Dickinson, Barnaby 354
Dickinson, Brian 305–306
Diliberto, John 212
Dizzy Gillespie Quintet 60
Dobbins, Bill 298
Dobrogosz, Steve 207
Docherty, Jackie 90, 445
Dolphy, Eric 90
Domingo, Placido 282
Donlon, Mark 371
Don Rendell's Jazz Six 51
Doonican, Val 176
Dorham, Kenny 22
Dougan, Jackie 50, 79
Douglas, Dave 315–317, 383–388, *386*, 394
Downes, Kit 368
Downey, Alan 263, 270, *271*
Dudek, Gerd 154
Dudley-Evans, Tony 316, 372
Duff, Jack 126
Duhamel, Antoine 160
Duke Ellington Band 63, 439
Dwyer, Phil 310
Dyani, Johnny 292

**E**

Eastman Jazz Ensemble 259, 297
Eastman Quartet 350
East, Roy *63*
Eckert, Rosana. *See* Calderon, Rosana

Edelhagen, Kurt 157. *See also* Kurt Edelhagen Orchestra
Eden, Peter 133
Edison, Harry 65
Eero Koivistoinen Quartet 104
Eicher, Manfred 5, 160–166, 169, 185, 187, 190, 192, 193–195, 197, 203–207, 211–212, 232, 235, 260–263, 270, 272, 279, 288–289, 293–294, 317–318, 320, 323, 328, 330–331, 342, 344, 404–406, 412
Eldridge, Roy 25, 60, 205
Elgart, Bill 243–244, *245*
Ellefson, Art 36, 40, 44, 46, 55, *63*, 64, 66–67, 69, 70, 73, 78, 86, 175, 308
Ellington, Duke 1, 12, 17, 32, 56, 58, 62, 141, 147, 152, 174, 229, 417. *See also* Duke Ellington Band
Ellington, Steve 228, 230
Elmes, Barry 310
Emcee Five 67, 77
Emerson, Keith 103
Endsley, Shane 385
Erskine, Peter 238, 249, 263, 265–266, 269, *271*, 272, 274–275, *278*, 279, *281*, 284–287, 313, 325, 335, 476
Eubanks, Dwayne 241
Eubanks, Kevin 241, 282–283
Eubanks, Robin 241, 334, 342
European Broadcasting Union (EBU) Big Band 243, 246
Evans, Bill 79, 198, 265
Evans, Gil 199, 257, 283, 314

**F**

Faddis, Jon 131–132, 230
Fairweather, Digby 414
Fame, Georgie 78
Fancy, Tommy 19
Farmer, Art 66, 459
Fasoli, Claudio 235
Faulkner, Tony 113, 131
Favre, Pierre 199
Featherstonhaugh, Buddy 49, 50, *52*. *See also* Buddy Featherstonhaugh New Quintet
Feldman, Mark 343
Feldman, Victor 247
Ferguson, Maynard 34, 60, 66, 121–122, 184, 451. *See also* Maynard Ferguson Orchestra

Fisher, Tony 78, 111, 118–120, 182, 390, 392
Fitzgerald, Ella 17
Flanagan, Tommy 282, 480
Fontana, Lorena 401
Fordham, Jack 36
Fordham, John 230, 235–236, 283, 367, 374, 378, 394, 402, 412, 414
Fortner, Sullivan 415
Fowler, Reuben 396
Fox, Charles 104, 264, 267
Fox, Roy 41
France, Martin 341, 370, *377*, *398*, 399, 405–406, 415
Francy Boland Orchestra 174
Fraser, Hugh 214, 263, 265, *271*, 272, 303, 307, 328, 336, 357–358
Freeman, Von 282
Frei, Peter 199
Fresu, Paolo 234
Frink, Laurie 338–339
Frisell, Bill 170, 232–233, 283, 297, 317–320, 323–324, *324*, 331, 397
Fry, Tristan 95

**G**

Gabrieli, Giovanni 332
Galbraith, Gus *63*, 64, 69, 80
Ganley, Alan 78
Garbarek, Jan 174, 185, 188, 190, 249, 252, 265
Garland, Tim 284, 354
Garrick, Michael 102, 136
Garriock, Gus 22–23
Gary Burton Quartet 223
Genus, James 316
George Shearing Quintet 301
Gerry Mulligan Tentet 49
Gertberg, Hans 152–153, 458
Getz, Stan 173, 198, 210, 347
Getz, Steve 238
Gibbs, Mike 79, 89, 95, 98, 102–103, 111–112, 128–130, 132, 138, 184, 232, 283, 287, 325, 336, 369. *See also* Mike Gibbs Orchestra
Gillespie, Dizzy 17, 21, 23, 25, 35, 59, 60, 66, 431, 439. *See also* Dizzy Gillespie Quintet
Gill, Tania 215
Gilmore, Mikal 169
Glaser, Joe 58, 62, 63
Glenn Miller Orchestra 450

Globe Unity Orchestra 91, 155–156, 174, 183, 203, 208, 210, 234, 445, 458
Godbolt, Jim 55
Goddard, Peter 213
Golson, Benny 75
Gomez, Eddie 211
Gonella, Nat 196
Gonsalves, Paul 113–114
Goodman, Benny (drummer) 62, 113
Gordon, Dexter 84
Gould, Glenn 5
Graham, Victor 128
Grant, Keith 146
Green, Benny (writer) 106
Greene, Jackie 60–61
Greenwich, Sonny 310
Griffin, Johnny 59, 97, 114, 447
Griffiths, Malcolm 137, 144, 150, 191
Grime, Kitty 48, 65–66
Gruntz, George 253–254, 256, 317. *See also* Concert Jazz Band
Guaraldi, Vince 55
Guildhall Jazz Orchestra 238
Guilfoyle, Ronan 143, 215, 229
Gulda, Friedrich 78, 131, 153, 480
Guy, Barry 86, 140, 146, 151, 154–155, 210, 330, 442, 466

**H**
Hacker, Alan 139
Haden, Charlie 365
Haig, Al 22
Hale, James 309
Hallifax, Andrew 344
Hamer, Ian 78, 106, 128, 138, 144, 150, 263–264, 266, *271*, 327, 357, 379
Hampel, Gunter 156
Hampton, Lionel 21–22, 29
Hancock, Dave 144
Hancock, Herbie 78, 164
Hanna, Roland 132
Hardie, Cliff. *See* Cliff Hardie Big Band
Harrell, Tom 199
Harriott, Joe 40, 79, 85, 128, 290, 445. *See also* Joe Harriott Double Quintet
Harrison, George 122
Harry South Big Band 78
Hart, Antonio 334
Hart, Billy 198, 347, 348
Hart, Dick 79, 95–96
Harvey, Eddie 55, *63*, 64
Hatch, Tony 120

Hathaway, Martin *377*
Hattey, Edward 33
Hawdon, Dickie 64–65
Hawkins, Coleman 12, 60
Hayes, Louis 225
Hayes, Tubby 40, 78, 80, 82, 85–86, 105, 112, 137, 139, 445, 449, 454. *See also* Tubby Hayes Orchestra/Big Band
Hazlehurst, Ronnie 118
Healey, Derek 129
Heath, Ted. *See* Ted Heath Band
Heatley, Spike *63*
Hebert, John 338
Heining, Duncan 348
Henderson, Joe 97, 107, 138, 449
Henderson, Russ 110
Hendricks, Jon 97, 107, *108*, 447
Hendrix, Jimi 88
Hennessey, Mike 247
Herbert, Peter 348
Herbolzheimer, Peter 157
Herman, Woody 55. *See also* Woody Herman Orchestra; Woody Herman's Anglo-American Herd
Hersch, Fred 257, 300, 344–346, 352, 415
Hewson, Rick 98
Hill, Helen (sister). *See* Wheeler, Helen
Hindemith, Paul 26, 326
Hinely, Patrick 238, 281, 320, 338
Hirschfield, Jeff 338
Hodges, Johnny 63, 439
Hoff, Brynjar 207
Holdsworth, Allan 177
Holiday, Billie 12
Holland, Clare 224, 387
Holland, Dave xv, 1, 5–6, 39, 75, 77, 84–87, *87*, 89, 96, 110, 137, 157–165, 167, 169–170, 172, 185, 205–206, 210, 213–216, 219, *220*, 223–224, 227–228, 231, 234, 239–243, *240*, *245*, 249–250, 256, 263, 265, 267, 269, *271*, 272, 274–275, *278*, 280, 282, 284, 317–321, *319*, 324, *324*, 331, 334–335, 347, 359–360, 364–365, 374, *377*, 384, 387–389, *389*, 408, 411, 414–417, 447, 468, 486. *See also* Dave Holland Octet; Dave Holland Quintet
Holland, Louise 256
Hollenbeck, John 305, 350–351, 384, 386–387. *See also* John Hollenbeck's Large Ensemble
Holloway, Laurie 96
Hopkins, Duncan 218, *372*, 381–382
Horace Silver Quintet 60

Horler, Dave 114, 145–146, 148, 150, 176, 191, 263, *271*, 272, 286, *377*, 379, 413, 448
Horler, John 286, 374, *377*
Houmark, Karsten 234
Houston, Clint 225
Howard Riley Trio 155
Hubbard, Freddie 78, 90, 308
Hughes, Spike 50
Hugo Wolf String Quartet 367
Humair, Daniel 235
Humble, Derek 114
Hunter, Chris 283
Husby, Per 225
Hutton, Mick 325

**I**

Iles, Nikki 371, *372*, 374, *377*, 402, *403*, 415
Iles, Richard 335
Indo-British Ensemble 128
Ingman, Nick 120
Intermodulation (band) 139
Irabagon, Jon 388
Isaacs, Mark 301
Iskra (bands) 137, 155

**J**

Jackson, Alan 110
Jacquet, Illinois 23
James, Harry 25, 66
James Last Orchestra 180–181, *181*
Janisch, Michael 388
Jarman, Joseph 154
Jarrett, Keith 163–169, 186, 224, 281, 284, 330
Jeff Johnston Quartet 309
Jeffreys, Mike 77
Jelley, Bill 16–18, 21–24, *24*, 26, 29–30, 32–33, 105, 329, 433, 458
Jelley, Jayson (nephew) 177, 251
Jenkins, Karl 79, 109, 115, 352
Jenny-Clark, J.-F. 160, 211, 221, 235
Jensen, Christine 385
Jensen, Ingrid 5, 214, 219, *219*, 384–385, 411, 415
Jewell, Derek 223, 235–236
Joe Harriott Double Quintet 79
John Dankworth Orchestra 55–56, 58–60, 62–64, *63*, 67–71, 79, 92–96, 111–112, 121, 141, 145, 178
John, Elton 122, 178

John Hollenbeck's Large Ensemble 385
Johnson, J.J. 21, 78
Johnson, Marc 238, 313, 490
Johnston, Jeff 309. *See also* Jeff Johnston Quartet
John Surman Octet 103
John Taylor Sextet 150
Jones, Elvin 473
Jones, Hank 225
Jones, Philly Joe 113, 443
Jones, Quincy 59, 60–61
Jones, Thad 78, 97, 132. *See also* Thad Jones/Mel Lewis Orchestra
Jones, Tom 118
Joplin, Scott 1
Jordan, Sheila 253–254
Jormin, Anders 367

**K**

Kaldestad, Steve 461
Katz, David 178
Kelehan, Noel 143
Kelly, Colum 346, 412
Kelman, John 365, 367, 371
Kenny Clarke/Francy Boland Big Band 114, 262
Kenny Wheeler Big Band/Orchestra 150–151, 185, 190, *358*
Kenny Wheeler Octet 243, 286, 347
Kenny Wheeler Quintet 244–245, 249–250, 259, 268, 274, 276–281, *281*, 284, 288–290, 310–311, 343, 348, 399, 404–405, 415
Kenny Wheeler Tentette 286, 347
Kenton, Stan 21
Keogh, Stephen 325
Kilson, Billy 334
King, Pete 36, 64, 75, 107, 113, 139, 370
Kirchin, Basil 125, 452
Kirk, Rahsaan Roland 206
Klein, Larry 314
Kleinschuster, Erich 153
Koenig, Klaus 199
Koivistoinen, Eero. *See* Eero Koivistoinen Quartet
Koller, Hans 369
Kongshaug, Jan Erik 187, 194, 476
Konitz, Lee 21, 214, 253, 303, 317–318, 320–325, *322*, *324*, 331, 356–360, 404
Korsrud, John 417
Krahmer, Carlo 125
Kramer, Eddie 88

Kriegel, Volker 182
Kurowski, Andrew 356
Kurt Edelhagen Orchestra 114

**L**

LaBarbera, Joe 288–289, 307, 310
LaBarbera, Pat 336
Lacy, Steve 191
Laine, Cleo 59–62, 69, 130, 134
Lake, Steve 169, 273, 279, 330, 406
Lamb, Bobby 112, 144
Lammas (band) 284
Lamont, Duncan 1, 52, 72, 100, 106, 123–125, 145, 150, 243, 263, *271*, 272–273, 375, *377*, 380, 390, 394, 448
Land, Harold 443
Lanese, Bob 181
Langley, Noel 284, 354
Last, James 180. *See also* James Last Orchestra
Laurence, Chris 66, 133–134, 136, 178, 191, 213, 234–235, 239, 243, 259, 286–287, 300, 341–344, 347, 360, 370, 374, *377*, *398*, 399, 405–406, 414–415, 442, 448, 453, 467, 490
Lawson, Don 51
Leaper, Bob. *See* Bob Leaper Big Band
Lee, Dave 56, 58–63, 438, 451
Lees, Gene 19, 25, 34, 37, 44–45, 59, 296, 307, 383, 409
Legrand, Michel 122, 265
Leighton, David 213
Lemer, Pepi 130
Le Sage, Bill 467
Levin, Tony 130, 133–134, 269, 300, 453
Lewis, George 173–174, 234, 472
Lewis, Jerry Lee 78
Lewis, Mel 78, 131–132. *See also* Thad Jones/Mel Lewis Orchestra
Lewis, Vic 44, 51, 64
Liebermann, Rolf 152
Liebman, Dave 159
Lifetime (band) 126
Lindemann, Jens 350
Lindo, Paul 17, 21, 23, *24*, 26, 29, 32, 35
Lindup, David 123
Little, Booker 90–92, 110, 127, 140, 190, 299, 315–317, 445
Lockheart, Mark 402
Logan, Freddy 47, *49*
London Jazz Composers Orchestra 146, 155, 210, 471

London Jazz Orchestra (1) 72, 77
London Jazz Orchestra (2) 284
London Vocal Project 402, 413
Louis Armstrong All Stars 62
Lovano, Joe 313, 323
Lowther, Henry 79–80, 83, 95, 97, 98, 112, 119, 128–129, 135–136, 138, 178, 242, 260–263, 267, *271*, 327, 347, 354, 357, 373–374, *377*, 393, 399, 407, 412, 446, 448
Lusher, Don 72
Lyttelton, Humphrey 86, 121
Lytton, Paul 145, 155, 466, 471

**M**

MacKenzie, Gisele 22
MacLeod, John 258
Maddren, James 402
Malfatti, Radu 292
Mangelsdorff, Albert 110, 154, 157, 182
Mansfield, Keith 123
Mariano, Charlie 129, 182, 184, 232, 292
Marini, Andrea 340, 355–356, 363, 370–372, 378–379, 383–384, 390, 392, 393
Maritime Jazz Orchestra (MJO) 300–303, 305
Mark Wheeler 392
Marsalis, Wynton 225, 227
Marshall, John 76, 96, 140, 232, 235, 239, 243, 259, 341
Martin, Stu 157
Mathewson, Matt 445
Mathewson, Ron 104, 107, 113, 130, 142, 145–146, 199, 264, 445
Mathis, Johnny 176
Mayer, John 79, 128
Maynard Ferguson Orchestra 60
Ma, Yo-Yo 282
M-Base (band) 290
McCall, Steve 154
McDougall, Ian 64, 67, 258
McGregor, Chris 96, 292, 447
McKee, David 123
McKinley, Ray 52
McLanathan, Ross 26
McLaughlin, John 98, 126
McNair, Harold 67, 113
McRae, Barry 239
Mechali, François 160
Meloni, John 387
Mendoza, Vince 296, 312–313, 325
Mengelberg, Misha 260

Michelli, Anthony *372*
Mike Gibbs Orchestra 102, 283
Mike Westbrook's Concert Band 111, 132
Mikkelborg, Palle 204, 459
Milkowski, Bill 414
Miller, Glenn 52. *See also* Glenn Miller
    Orchestra
Miller, Harry 83, 103–104, 292
Miller, Hazel 139
Miller, Mark 6, 152, 176, 184, 197, 203, 207,
    212, 224–225, 257–258, 308–311, 329,
    382
Miller, Ron 333
Mires, Trevor *377*
Mitchell, Hugh 409
Mitchell, Joni 313–314
Mitchell, Roscoe 154, 162, 174, 204
Mogensen, Anders 415
Moholo, Louis 291
Monder, Ben 338
Monk, Thelonious 60, 417. *See*
    *also* Thelonious Monk Quartet
Montgomery, Marion 130
Monty Alexander Trio 234
Moore, Colin 42
Moore, Debby 59–61
Moore, Dudley 52, 64, 101
Moore, Pete 120
Morell, Marty 175
Morgan, Bob 254
Morgan, Lee 207
Morgenstern, Dan 363
Morris, Paula 324
Morton, Jelly Roll 1
Moses, Bob 129
Moss, Danny 60, *63*, 69
Motian, Paul 207, 210–211, 221, 249, 323,
    365, 484. *See also* Paul Motian Trio
Moule, Ken 51, 106
Mraz, George 131
Mulligan, Gerry 49. *See also* Gerry
    Mulligan Tentet
Murley, Mike 258, 415
Murphy, Phil 12
Music Improvisation Company 163
Mussorgsky, Modest 94

**N**
Napper, Kenny 79, 95, 96, 447
Nascimento, Milton 183
Naura, Michael 458
Navarro, Fats 23

NDR Big Band 325
Nelson, Jez 355, 404, 412
Nelson, Steve 334
Newbrook, Peter 125
New, Derek 42
New Jazz Orchestra 68, 130, 136
Newman, Louann (daughter) 54, *54*, 62,
    65, 73, 120–121, 160, 223, 247, 248,
    251–253, 374, 381, 407–408, 410
Newman, Mark (son-in-law) 247, 251–252
Newman, Phoebe (granddaughter) 252
Newman, Sophie (granddaughter) 251, 265
Niagara Symphony Orchestra 381
Nightingale, Mark *377*
Niles, Richard 129
Nimmons, Phil 213
Norman, Jessye 282
North, Rod 22–23, 25, 296
North, The (band) 415
Nucleus (band) 128
Nucleus Plus (band) 128
Nussbaum, Adam 341–343

**O**
Oatts, Dick 338
Oliver, Joe "King" 35
O'Mara, Pete 243
One O'Clock Lab Band 333
Ono, Yoko 88
Orchestra UK 283
Ordesa (band) 355
Oregon (band) 281, 288
O'Reilly, Ted 193, 236, 241, 325
Orr, Bobby 126
Osborne, Mike 134, 136, 142, 145, 150,
    153, 157
Oscar Peterson Trio 60
Oxley, Tony 97, 103–104, 107, 137–138,
    145–148, 154, 191, 199, 210, 213, 234,
    239–240, 244, 341, 467. *See also* Tony
    Oxley Sextet

**P**
Palmer, Stan 60, 62
Parker, Charlie 1, 17, 21–22
Parker, Chris 184, 257, 322, 326
Parker, Evan 81, 84–90, *87*, *89*, 104, 125,
    127, 135, 137, 139–140, 145–148, 150,
    154, 155–156, 159–160, 163, 184,
    190–191, 209–211, 213, 221, 234, 239,
    263–264, 270, *271*, 286, 292, 300, 318,

326–327, 330–331, 340, 351, 355–356, 360, 367, 374, *377*, 380, 390, 393, *398*, 399, 404, 413–414, 416, 445–446, 448, 456–457, 461, 466–467, 471
Parker, Phil 399
Parricelli, John 300, 325, 347, 355, 367, *377*, 404–406, 415
Pascoal, Hermeto 336
Patterson, Ottilie 437
Pauer, Fritz 153
Paul Motian Trio 323
Peacock, Gary 280, *281*, 288
Pearson, Johnny 123
Peck, Nat 114, 450
Pedersen, Niels-Henning Ørsted 243
Penderecki, Krzysztof 155
Peterson, Oscar 22, 34, 60, 208, 213. *See also* Oscar Peterson Trio
Phillips, Barre 86, 153, 154, 157, 160, 163
Pieranunzi, Enrico 365
Pilz, Michel 204
Plümer, Gunnar 325
Postle, Matt 383
Potter, Chris 5, 334–335, 365–366
Potter, Tommy 22
Premru, Ray 78, 112
Previte, Bobby 300
Price, Jason 349
Priester, Julian 228–229, 231, *240*, 241, 299, 468, 480
Priestley, Brian 184, 235–237, 290
Printmakers, The (band) 402
Proctor, Jud 118
Pukwana, Dudu 96, 292
Purcell, Simon 207
Purim, Flora 183
Purnell, Nick 248–251, 263, 272, 279, 280, 284–286, 288, 290–291, 325, 327, 334–335, 340, 397
Pursglove, Percy 415
Pyne, Chris 79–80, 95–96, 98, 104–105, 107, 113, 13–135, 144–146, 191, 263–264, 267, *271*, 283, 286, 459
Pyne, Mick 113

**R**
Raitt, Bonnie 396
Rand, Ronnie 42. *See also* Ronnie Rand's Blue Rockets
Ranger, Claude 258
Rapson, John 362
Rathbun, Andrew 336–338

Rauschenberg, Robert 127
Rava, Enrico 204, 253
Ravel, Maurice 307
Ray, Johnnie 76
Rebop (Anthony "Rebop" Kwaku Baah) 454
Reece, Alfie 78, 95, 144–145, 148
Reece, Dizzy 36, 82, 85
Reid, Francis 8
Reid, Jack 8–10, *9*
Reid, John Francis 8
Reid, Rufus 300, 337
Rena Rama (band) 246
Rendell, Don 51, 55. *See also* Don Rendell's Jazz Six
Reynolds, Stan 114
Rhythm Combination & Brass 157
Richards, Olwen 344–346
Ricotti, Frank 242
Riddell, Don 47, *49*
Riley, Howard 154–155. *See also* Howard Riley Trio
Rimsky-Korsakov, Nikolai 180
Rivers, Sam 227–228, 460
Roach, Max 22
Roberts, Tony 95, 100, 142, 448
Robson, Phil 348, 368
Roderick, Stan 78, 114
Roney, Wallace 322
Ronnie Rand's Blue Rockets 42
Ronnie Scott Quintet 108
Rook, John 286
Ross, Annie 126
Ross, Ronnie 51, 78
Rowe, Ellen 218, 220
Royal Academy Big Band 396
Royston, Rudy 388
Runions, Greg 305
Runswick, Daryl 105, 449
Rushing, Jimmy 61
Rushka, Paul 394
Russell, Tony *63*, 66
Russo, William 72, 77, 93
Rutherford, Paul 83–86, 102, 110, 135, 137, 140, 155, 156, 191, 210, 263, *271*. *See also* Iskra
Ryan, Kathleen 7
Rzewski, Frederic 139, 168

**S**
Sanchez, David 363
Sandoval, Arturo 254
Sauer, Heinz 204

Sayer, Leo 178
Schepps, Rob 468
Schneider, Larry 199
Schneider, Maria 268
Schoof, Manfred 154–156, 204, 253–254
Schretzmeier, Werner 182
Schroeder, John 451
Scofield, John 283, 416
Scottish National Jazz Orchestra (SNJO) 302
Scott, Mike 98
Scott, Ronnie 36, 40, 69, 75, 97, 100, 106–107, 109, 114, 125, 132, 153, 233, 449. *See also* Ronnie Scott Quintet
Seamen, Phil 137–139
Seven Souls, The (band) 75
Sharpe, Jack 113
Shaw, Artie 23
Shaw, Brian 349, 394
Shaw, Charles "Bobo" 160
Shaw, Hank 85, 96–97, 447
Shaw, Ian 401
Shaw, Woody 106, 198, 315
Shearing, George 62. *See also* George Shearing Quintet
Sheridan, Chris 196
Shihab, Sahib 114
Shipton, Alyn 302, 348, 359, 399
Shorter, Wayne 97, 417
Shulman, Matt 363
Sidran, Ben 225
Siegel, Julian 390
Silver, Horace 55, 60, 199. *See also* Horace Silver Quintet
Simcock, Gwilym 357, 359, 372, 396
Simmonds, Ron *63*
Simona, Tiziana 234, 352, 401
Sims, Zoot 55, 69
Sinatra, Frank 21
Skidmore, Alan 103–104, *103*, 128, 132, 136, 153–154, 157, 213, 467. *See also* Alan Skidmore Quintet
Slater, Neil 333
Smalley, Roger 139
Smart, Nick 361, 369, 371, 374, *377*, 378–380, 384–387, *386*, 393–394, 396, 398, 402, 408–409, 412, 414
Smith, Bill 162
Smith, Leo 162–163, 174, 203, 315
Smith, Marvin "Smitty" 230, *240*, 241, 282, 290
Smith, Tommy 302
Smith, Wadada Leo. *See* Smith, Leo

Smulyan, Gary 334
Smythe, Pat 79, 104–105, 191, 247, 449
Snyder, Ron *63*
Soloff, Lew 466
Souster, Tim 139
South, Harry 78, 265. *See also* Harry South Big Band
Souza, Luciana 336, 338
Sparrow, Paul 285, 288–289, 358
Spear (band) 292
Speed, Chris 316
Spiritualized (band) 351
Splinters (band) 137, 138
Spontaneous Music Ensemble (SME) 83, 85–88, 90, 102, 137, 210, 445
Spooner, John 79, 95
Stamm, Marvin 253–254, 257
Stańko, Tomasz 155–156, 204
Stanwyk, Al 115
Stapleton, Dave 402, 415
Stark, Bill 50
Stenson, Bobo 174
Stephenson, Ronnie *63*, 78
Stevens, John 81, 83–88, 90–91, 137–139, 159, 163, 210, 445
Stewart, Bill 283
Stewart, Dave 283, 286, *377*, 379
Stirtzinger, Randy 381
Stirtzinger, Warren 221, 381
Stockhausen, Karlheinz 139
Stoezel, Rich 486
Stöwsand, Thomas 221, 243
Strayhorn, Billy 307
Street, Ben 353
Stroman, Scott 238–284
Sturm, Fred 297
Sulzmann, Stan 77, 79, 105, 131, 133–135, 150, 199, 243,–247, *245*, 259, 263, 270, *271*, 284, 286, 300, 307, 327, 346–347, 355–356, 360, 368, 370, 373, *377*, 379–380, *398*, 399, 404–406, 412–413, 448, 472, 490
Surman, John 79, 89, 100, 107, 109–110, 127, 129, 133, 135–136, 142, 152–154, 157, 182, 184, 192, 210–211, 222, 238–239, 449. *See also* John Surman Octet
Sutton, Mynie 22
Swallow, Steve 129, 283, 367, 484
Swinfield, Ray 95
Sylvian, David 315
Symphony Sid. *See* Torin, "Symphony Sid"

**T**

Taborn, Craig 388, *389*
Takase, Aki 262
Talbot, Art 17, 21–23, *24*, 26, 29, 32, 35, 432
Tapp, Joanna 398
Taylor, Alex *200*
Taylor, Carol 409
Taylor, Dave 253, 338
Taylor, Diana 267, 293, 294, 304
Taylor, Eddie 47, *49*
Taylor, James 122
Taylor, John ("J.T.") 2, 76–77, 102–103, 111, 116–117, 130, 132, 133–136, 141, 145, 147, 164, 166, 191–196, 199, 201–203, 207–208, 213, 221–224, 234–240, *237*, 243, *245*, 246, 249, 257, 259–260, 263, 267, 269, *271*, 274–275, 277, *278*, *281*, 283–284, 286–288, 292–293, 300–301, 304, 307, 313, 315, 325–326, 335, 340–344, 347, 349–350, 356, 365–367, *366*, 370–374, *377*, 378–379, 388, 396, *398*, 399, 404, 409, 411, 413, 449, 455, 467, 490. *See also* Azimuth; John Taylor Sextet
Taylor, Leo *200*
Taylor, Mike 136
Teachout, Terry 35
Ted Heath Band 175
Temperley, Joe 47–48, *49*
Terry, Clark 35, 69, 176, 434
Thad Jones/Mel Lewis Orchestra 78, 114–115, 131, 224, 265
Thelin, Eje 157, 211
Thelonious Monk Quartet 60
Themen, Art 136
Thibaud, Pierre 332
Thiessen, John 266
Thigpen, Ed 262
Thomas, Laura 381
Thompson, Barbara 184
Thompson, Charles 23
Thompson, Don 5, 115, 214, 217–219, *220*, *240*, 258, 303, 310–311, 328–329, 334, 336, 472
Thompson, James 350
Thompson, Kenny 17
Thompson, Robin 455
Thornhill, Claude 21, 317
Tippett, Keith 292
Tobin, Christine 284, 348
Tomkins, Trevor 130
Tommy Whittle Orchestra 47–48, *49*, 307

Tony Oxley Sextet 155
Torin, "Symphony Sid" 17
Torto, Diana 371–372, 379, 393, 396
Towner, Ralph 187, 189, 203, 206, 208, 288, 331, 416
Tracey, Jackie 139
Tracey, Stan 78–79, 82, 123, 130, 135, 137–138, 185, 221
Trent, Jackie 120
Treseler, Steve 170, 415
Tristano, Lennie 17
Trutt, Renate 230
Trutt, Six 230
Tubby Hayes Orchestra/Big Band 78, 82, 102, 106, 112
Tucker, Michael 330
Turner, Mark 348, 353
Tynan, Paul 305, 334

**U**

Underground Orchestra 354
United Jazz+Rock Ensemble (UJRE) 121, 182–184, 234, 250
UNT Jazz Singers 333
Upper Austrian Jazz Orchestra 301

**V**

van de Geyn, Hein 352
van der Geld, Tom 204, 211
Van Rooyen, Ack 184, 204
Varner, Tom 253
Vatalaro, Chris 396
Venier, Glauco 332, 365
Very Original Brasso Band 120
Vesala, Edward 211
Vic Lewis's Orchestra 51–52, 54
Vitet, Bernard 156
Vitous, Miroslav 78
Vivian, Jim 258, 307, 310
Von Roderick, Matt. *See* Shulman, Matt
von Schlippenbach, Alexander 155–156, 209, 260, 262, 458

**W**

Waits, Nasheet 353
Walker, Mike 283, 325
Walker, Scott 107
Wallace, Pax 470
Wantanabe, Butch 34

Warleigh, Ray 1, 78, 100, 107, 109, 137, 150, 191, 263, *271*, 300, 347, 360, 448, 457, 461
Warren, Huw 347
Warren, John 129, 136, 238
Watkins, Derek 80, 95–96, 98, 112, 114, 128, 135, 180–181, *181*, 243, 261, 263, 267, 269, *271*, 326, 347, 349, 355, 357, 373–374, *377*, 378–380, 392, *395*, 396, 398, 451
Watkins, Wendy 181, 399
Watkiss, Cleveland 401
Watrous, Peter 282
Watson, Gilbert 8, *10*
Watts, Arthur 51
Watts, Steve 402
Watts, Trevor 83, 85–86, 102, 137, 138, 155, 210, 454
WDR Big Band 302
Weber, Eberhard 182, 232
Wein, George 60
Weinzweig, John 26, 140, 432
Weiss, Klaus 153
Wellins, Bobby 35, 40, 50–51, 75–76, 79, 221, 370, 412, 469, 472
Wells, Spike 104–105, 145
Welte, Arthur F. 19–20
Werner, Kenny 329, 362
Westbrook, Mike 89, 102, 110–111, 129, 178. *See also* Mike Westbrook's Concert Band
Weston, Armorel 83, 444
Weston, Veryan 83
Wheeler, Alice (daughter) 64–65, 327
Wheeler, Bethan (granddaughter) 252
Wheeler & Co. 104, 105, 121. *See also* Coe, Wheeler & Co.
Wheeler, Doreen (wife) 37–38, 40, *41*, 43, 45–46, 50, 53–54, *53*, 62, 64, 73, 118–119, 139, 145, 182, 201, 208–209, 214, 221, 223, 239, 248, 252, 263, 296, 312, 332, 339, 341, 346–347, 359, 364, 368, 369, 371, 373, 399, *400*, 407, *408*, 430
Wheeler, George (brother) 8, *11*, 13, *32*, 431
Wheeler, Helen (sister) 9, *11*, 14, 16, 23–24, 30, *32*, 33, 37, 222, 251, *264*, 279, 312, 371, 381, 387, 493
Wheeler, Jan (daughter-in-law) 252
Wheeler, Louise (daughter). *See* Newman, Louann

Wheeler, Mabel (mother) 7, 8, 9, 12–13, *15*, 31, *32*, 70, 221, 223, 251
Wheeler, Mabel (sister). *See* Ball, Mabel
Wheeler, Mark (son) 46, 50, 53, *53*, *54*, 62, 64, 66, 70, 73–74, 93–94, 99, 102–103, 119, 121, 127, 129, 145, 159, 181–182, 207, 223, 247, 252, 301, 307, 312, 340, 342, 369, 374, 380–381, 384–385, 389–390, 393, 402, 407–410, 412, 431, 447, 452
Wheeler, Mary (sister) 8, *11*, 12, *32*, 118–119, 121, 139
Wheeler, Paul (brother) 9, *11*, 14, 16, *32*, 70, 221
Wheeler, Rachel (granddaughter) 252
Wheeler, Ruby (granddaughter) 252, 303
Wheeler, Tracy (daughter-in-law) 252, 408
Wheeler, Wilf Jr. (brother) 8, *11*, 13, 16, 105, 221, 222, 251
Wheeler, Wilfred Sr. (father) 7–13, *10*, *11*, *15*, 19–20, 26, 30–31, *32*, 36–37, 46, 70, 221–223, 387
Whitehead, Kevin 224, 241, 280, 290
White, Jane 235
White, John 140
Whiteman, Paul 8
Whittle, Tommy 47, 49, *49*, 77. *See also* Tommy Whittle Orchestra
Williamson, Gary 175
Williams, Richard 191, 199, 223
Williams, Tony 97, 126, 447
Williams, Wilf 28
Wilson, Jim 144
Wilson, John S. 61
Wilson, Thick. *See* Bell, Johnny
Winstone, Norma 6, 75, 101–102, 111, 116–117, 128, 130, 132–133, 135–137, 142, 144–145, 147–148, 150, 191–196, 201–203, 208, 212, 217, 222–223, 234–238, *237*, 243, 263, 266–267, 269–270, *271*, *273*, 284, 292–294, 301–304, 307, 336, 344–346, 348, 356, 358, 363, 365, 368, 371–374, *372*, *377*, 378, 393, 396, 399, 401–402, 409–412, 414–417, 448, 450, 455–456, 488. *See also* Azimuth
Wohlleben, Johannes 393
Wolf, Hugo. *See* Hugo Wolf String Quartet
Wonder, Stevie 183
Woode, Jimmy 114
Wood, Ken 42
Woods, Phil 69, 175, 225–226
Woody Herman Orchestra 199

Woody Herman's Anglo-American Herd 55
Wooley, Nate 385
Wright, Colin 42, 56, 438
Wright, Rayburn 259
Wunsch, Frank 325

## Y

Yeend, Bobby 71
Yeend, Doreen (wife). *See* Wheeler, Doreen
Young, Dave 175

## Z

Zawinul, Joe 78
Zenchuck, Boris 22, *24*